50 in 50

50 in 50

A Collection of Short Stories
One for Each of Fifty Years

Harry Harrison

 A Tom Doherty Associates Book
New York

50 IN 50

Copyright © 2001 by Harry Harrison

Design by Jane Adele Regina

Edited by Patrick Nielsen Hayden

A Tor Book
Published by Tom Doherty Associates, LLC
175 Fifth Avenue
New York, NY 10010

www.tor.com

Tor® is a registered trademark of Tom Doherty Associates, LLC.

ISBN 0-312-87789-7

First Edition: June 2001

Printed in the United States of America

0 9 8 7 6 5 4 3 2 1

This book is for

Paul Tomlinson,

with thanks for his endless kindnesses

and selfless dedication

Contents

ALIEN SHORES

Aliens are the stock-in-trade of science fiction. *Alien*, the film, used the alien cliché as horror, always good for a chill thrill. But the theme of the alien as other, perhaps a warped image of mankind, provides a theme of much greater interest.

MAKE ROOM! MAKE ROOM!

This was the title of my novel that was deeply concerned with the looming dangers of overpopulation. Long after I had finished writing the book, I was still concerned with these dangers. Through the years that followed I was pressed more than once to return to this theme as the world continues to stagger steadily towards the brink.

MIRACULOUS INVENTIONS

Well, yes, that is what it is all about, isn't it? The invention that keeps science fiction chuntering along for a great deal of the time. After all, SF is the only form of fiction where the

idea—or the machine—can be the hero. And here
are some rather unlikely heroes . . .

LAUGH—I THOUGHT I WOULD CRY

Humor is rare in the world—and even rarer in
science fiction. But it belongs there—and I just
wish that there was more of it.

OTHER WORLDS

Alien landscapes and distant planets—all are part
and parcel of the SF package. They are there to
be explored.

R.U.R.

Rossum's Universal Robots. No matter that
Čapek's robots were really humanoid and not
metallic life forms. The name stuck and robots
have been clanking and rattling through SF ever
since.

ONE FOR THE SHRINKS

Psychology, the use and the misuse thereof, is a
topic that has always fascinated me. How the
brain works, what it can and cannot do—this is
the stuff of inquiry—and of story.

THE LIGHT FANTASTIC

I have never been much of a fan of fantasy. I find
it too loose, too able to fly off in any direction
without notice. But this does not mean that I
shrink away from writing it when the Great Idea
strikes.

SQUARE PEGS IN ROUND HOLES

And then there are the head-scratchers, the
undefinable, the stories that just do not fit into
any category. They are the one-offs—and this
difference makes them, many times, the best of
the lot.

The First Fifty Years

INTRODUCTION

They say that the first fifty years are the hardest, that it gets easier after that. I am about to find out if that is true.

In the autumn of the year 1950 I sold my first science fiction story, "Rock Diver," to the magazine *Worlds Beyond*. After that I never looked back—until now. Looking forward was enough. I had a career to build and many, many ideas to write about. It has been a busy fifty years. In that time I published forty-four novels, and the forty-fifth is now in production for publication. My books have been translated into thirty-three languages.

It is now the new century, the new millennium, the year 2000. It is time to look back at the years when I started writing SF, to search for some understanding of what has shaped my life and my work.

Like all of the writers of my generation I did everything except academically study writing. Military service, then strange jobs like hydraulic press operator, commercial artist, art director, editor, publisher. But I was one of the second-generation SF writers who got started after the Second World War. It was the older writers who were the product of the pulps and who managed to stay in there, still writing, when the pulp category of science fiction mutated into the SF of today. The postwar writers, myself included, had grown up reading these pulps; had made them a part of their lives. That world is gone and will never return. But it was a warm and friendly world to live in.

We writers-to-be read everything we could lay our hands on: books, textbooks, library books, even the newly published comic books. But mostly we read the pulp magazines. Before TV this was where the entertainment arts were best displayed to the youngsters who grew up during the Depression years. Depression kids were born into the period and knew no better. Like children of Stone Age rain-forest Indians, we only knew that one slightly miserable, impoverished world. It was a time of poverty and grayness; only the pulps burned brightly in that particular social night: the garish covers promising much; the contents occasionally supplying some of the promise. There were rocket ships inside those untrimmed pages, and aliens, girls and adventure and more and more. For a nickel, secondhand, you could escape into paradise.

Sure *Doc Savage* was OK, as were *Operator No. 5, G-8 and His Flying Aces*, and *The Shadow*. But none of them could match *Amazing*

Stories—until along came the incomparable *Astounding Science Fiction*. Before the Second World War we readers wrote letters to the SF magazines and to each other. Then we met and formed clubs, even managed a science fiction fan conference or two.

At that point the war intervened and we were all drafted. We did our time, survived for the most part, and returned to civilian life—and science fiction.

The army prepared me to face the adult world as a gunnery instructor and an analog computer engineer. After the war, courtesy of the GI Bill, I extended my education. While attending Hunter College, during the day, I studied easel painting under the gifted artist John Blomshield. In the evening I learned comic illustration from the gifted artist Burne Hogarth. Thus equipped I began a career as an illustrator, comic book artist, art director, editor and publisher. I am sure that my years of rendering visual art had a profound effect upon my writing.

In the beginning I did not make any sharp differentiation between the two. Because I was writing—and selling my writing—at the same time that I was drawing. In fact my first ever sale of my writing was to *Writer's Digest*: an article titled "How to Write for the Comics." The scripts that I was illustrating were so bad that I worked out some simple instructions that, if applied, would greatly enhance the final product. After this, hand in hand with my illustrating career, I wrote and sold many articles and stories. This appeared to be a simple progression for me. Since as a commercial artist I was told what I was to draw, how to render the art, the size and other limitations—I quite naturally applied the restrictions of commercial art to commercial writing. The conventions of the western story are quickly learned: I soon had six-guns blazing and horses bucking wildly. I branched out into true confessions, a very well-paid market, with some very strict rules. (A happy ending was not needed each time—but a moral lesson *must* be taught.) Men's adventures were much easier and shorter: open with the cliffhanger, flash back to the "How did I get in this jam?," close with a justifier and a resolution. I wrote an awful lot of these, because they are easy to do once the idea or the device is clear in mind. They were always submitted first to the top markets like *Argosy*, which paid up to $500 if the idea was a really good one. More important were the salvage markets, grotty little magazines that paid around $75. It may have taken time for a men's adventure to make the rounds of all the magazines, but in the end every one I wrote sold. Although some of the editors were, shall we say, slightly eccentric. I remember one returned manuscript had a very crumpled look to it. When I turned it over I realized that every page had a big dirty footprint on it. The editor had carefully spread my article on the floor—then walked over it. Criticism takes many forms.

I liked to add documentation to these "true" articles that would lend to their apparent verity. I recall one entitled "I Cut Off My Own Arm," by "Augie Ulmer." Poor Augie was prospecting for uranium when a boulder fell on his arm and trapped it. (Broke it too, of course. There is no way you can cut through your humerus with a pocket knife.) Ever-resourceful Augie tied a tourniquet around his trapped arm—then cut it off with his knife. As proof that this arrant nonsense had happened I pinned up one arm of my field jacket. My artist friend Roy Krenkel put his arm behind his back, pulled on the jacket, looked suitably glum when I took his picture. Photo and article sold.

I found that "real" photos helped sell these articles and brought in a higher price. And the more outrageous the better. I had read that some centuries ago the decadent ruling Chinese had a taste for live monkey brains. The monkey would have the top of its skull cut off and would be secured under a table with its brain through a hole in the table and another hole in the golden plate. Take your spoon and tuck in. I modernized the tale and brought it to French Equatorial Africa where the colonials ruled with a savage and sadistic hand. (Their favorite toast, in French of course, was "Here is to our horses and our women—and those who ride them." Charming.) I couldn't get the brain to work in a photograph, so I substituted simple cannibalism. My friend Hubert Pritchard, then an art student, sculpted a small fist in clay—theoretically that of a pygmy. We put the hand on a plate then, for realism, and to disguise the clay, poured a ten-cent can of stew over it. We had planned to eat the stew afterward. But there was instant revulsion; it looked too realistic. I took the photo and we threw the whole thing out. The article—and pic—sold well. So with men's adventure, western, detective, confessions, I was well trained in the craft of writing well before I attempted my first science fiction story.

By hindsight, writing—and selling—various kinds of fiction and pseudo-fact was the best possible way of honing my authorial skills. I had room to be bad. These markets were not known for their literary attributes, so I could serve my apprenticeship—learn to write, as well as sell what I did produce. I was a conscious artist and knew what I was doing. I did not look down nor sneer at these pulp products; you cannot write hypocritically and sell. The reader, if not the editor, can sniff out the difference. My writing improved, as did my sales and markets. It was now time to think about science fiction which was still my biggest enthusiasm and interest.

It was not a requirement, but it surely helped a science fiction writer to be in New York after the war. The magazines were there—as well as most of the editors. And, even more important, there were the writers themselves. Everyone knew everyone else and at the core of these relationships was the Hydra Club.

By this time I was well-known in the field, since I had created SF book jackets and had done illustrations for many SF magazines. It must be understood that I had been a science fiction fan ever since I had been hooked by my first SF mag at the age of five. To work in science fiction was my goal and my greatest pleasure. At that time I was doing most of the illustrations for editor Damon Knight's magazine *Worlds Beyond*. So when I wrote my first SF story, clunkily titled "I Walk Through Rocks," I asked Damon what I should do with it. He bought it, paid me a hundred dollars for it, and instantly changed the title to "Rock Diver." Which indicated to me that I could write and sell science fiction—but I had to work harder on my titles.

There were a great many SF magazines around in those days; thirty of them at least. A few of them I edited, such as *Rocket Stories* and *Science Fiction Adventures*. I have the May 1954 edition of the latter before me now. What talent was around in those days! There is a short novel, *Rule Golden*, by Damon Knight, along with stories by Katherine MacLean and Judy Merrill. Damon Knight also wrote the book reviews in his column "The Dissecting Table." Here is the heading for his column—that is Damon looking a good deal younger. I'm happy to say that I drew this art.

BOOK REVIEWS:

BY DAMON KNIGHT

Since my budget was so tiny, I illustrated most of the magazine myself, wrote the blurbs between stories, even ghosted some of the stories. In order to stretch the budget I inaugurated a column called

"Fanmag," which was an issue of a fanzine. I paid a half-cent a word for this and the fans were queueing up. I was paying two cents a word for stories; every bit helped.

Particularly the letter column which costs nothing a word. Here is the artwork that headed the letter section and, yes, I drew this as well.

But I was still writing as well as editing. With all these magazines around there were plenty of markets for the beginning writer to learn his trade. With no book markets, neither paperback nor hardback, the magazines were the name of the game. Stories were read, judged, quoted, discussed. *Astounding*, later *Analog*, was tops: the best editor, John W. Campbell, who paid the top rate—three cents a word—and his readers voted each month for the best story. Which would then be awarded a penny a word as a prize. Every issue contained part of a serial, a book-length manuscript serialized in three or four parts. To be later sold as a novel when the book market opened up.

And the editors knew exactly what they wanted. Horace Gold of *Galaxy* told his writers to deal with the softer sciences, such as psychiatry and ecology, rather than with the physics and mechanical engineering of *Astounding*. Tony Boucher of *Fantasy & Science Fiction* had a keen eye for quality of writing and encouraged it. The writers rose to the challenge and the magazines were vibrant with talent; a pleasure to read and behold. And the writers who lived in New York seemed to be producing almost all of the SF that was then published. They met at the Hydra Club, talked, argued, knocked sparks from one another; it was a good time to work and a good time to be a science fiction author. Science fiction was alive and well and entertaining to a degree never obtained since.

That was a long time ago. Over fifty years, in fact. I feel a bit sorry for the SF writers who are breaking in today. Yes, there are still magazines to write for. But they do not have the importance and relevancy of those magazines that were published when the SF world was young. Today the novel is the thing and the writer lives or dies at novel length. There is no place to serve an apprenticeship. All writing is hard; novel length the most difficult of all. The writer needs more time to master his craft before being tossed off the novel-writing cliff.

But it is in the short stories that a writer learns his trade. Sparse, lean, hard, taut. Not one word extra and no self-indulgence. Get it right. Make your point. Surprise the reader and entertain him at the same time. We learned a lot in the long-defunct Hydra Club.

It was Martin R. Greenberg who first brought me there. Marty was the publisher of Gnome Press and I had done some covers for him. It was at Fletcher Pratt's flat on Fifty-seventh Street that the club usually met. Pratt, a tiny man who always wore tailor-made plaid shirts, greatly resembled one of his pet marmosets. I had read his SF and fantasy collaborations with L. Sprague de Camp for many years. Sprague was at the meetings as well. The eagles were gathering and it was my proud pleasure to be there among them. These were the people I had been reading down through the years; now I was rubbing shoulders with them.

Memories. Frederick Brown, a talented and witty short-story writer and novelist was also a small man; I remember he had the same shoe size as his wife. But he had the mind of a giant. We played an informal championship of chess at the club. I was good then, and managed to beat Fletcher, the ex-champion. But I lost to Fred, the new and reigning champion, possibly because he got me drunk; but that's gamesmanship. I met briefly his many-times collaborator, Mack Reynolds, when he came through town. Mack and I became great friends after that, meeting in Spain, Denmark, England—and finally Mexico where Mack finally settled down.

Mexico. A fan sent me a copy of one of my books, translated and published in Mexico. Only I had never sold the Spanish rights. Piracy. I wrote to Mack and asked him, the next time he was in Mexico City, to call on this crook publisher and get some of my money out of him. Sure, Mack wrote. But added later, "Went to see him and asked for the money. He smiled and opened a drawer. He took out a gun. I smiled and went away. After this collect your own money, Harrison."

They were all there. Household names now, blossoming writers then. Cyril Kornbluth. One of the best, with the promise of a golden career. With a dry wit none surpassed. Returning from the war in the East he had a suit made for him in Hong Kong. As he stood before us he described, the tailoring, fitting and such, and as he spoke he turned back the cuff of the jacket: MADE IN ENGLAND it said. As he went on talking he turned back the collar, the trouser cuff, the lapel; all had the same brand. It was perfectly delivered, hysterical. Cyril died, untimely, a few years later.

His many-times collaborator, Frederik Pohl, was also an agent. My first agent. And he bought the anthology rights to my first story thereby setting my feet on the road to posterity. Later Fred also edited *Galaxy*. Years later, when I was living overseas, I would make an annual visit to New York and would always visit Fred at his office. His publisher was a sucker for buying art cheap—and giving the paintings to Fred to use as covers. Many they were, and exceedingly exotic. If you wrote a story to fit the cover Fred used the story with a cover credit. A big thing. I wrote many a story to fit these confused masterpieces; Fred published them all.

We were young and the world was young—and we inspired each other. Philip Klass was there, one of the finest short-story writers under his SF pen name of William Tenn. He had a critic's eye—as well as having a font of stories and limericks that seemed bottomless. I remember one, with feeling:

There was an old Jew from Salonika
Who for Christmas wanted an harmonica.
His wife, to annoy him, said, "Christmas's for goyim—
But I'll give you a Jew's harp for Hanukkah."

It was Phil who also pointed out an inconsistency in space opera, with a particular example of the works of E. E. Smith, Ph.D. (A wonderful and unassuming man, a midwesterner and lifetime cereal chemist, who would bring his entire family to conventions.) Phil observed that while thousands of spaceships were destroyed every second in these books—we only heard about the battle from the point of view of the commander-in-chief. What about tail-end Charlie? The rear gunner on one of these mile-long ships? A sobering thought. Years later when I was writing *Bill, the Galactic Hero*, my military-SF novel, I remembered this and I believe that my hero owes a lot to Phil's observation.

Katherine McLean was also there. At the time one of the two or three woman SF authors. We argued ideas. So much so that we actually collaborated on a fantasy story, "The Web of the Norns." It was Kay who observed that some things never change. Mankind has always has its parasites and commensal life forms. Now we live in wooden houses and they are occupied by flesh-and-blood rats. In the future, when our dwellings will be concrete and steel—will there be stainless steel rats? The term stuck, the idea expanded. You know the results.

There were always visiting firemen. Any SF author who passed through New York attended a meeting. Anthony Boucher was mobbed when he came through the door; he had just been appointed editor of *F&SF*. Even Olaf Stapleton put in an appearance from England; a living icon; some of the writers literally sat at his knee.

These were very good times. And an unexpected blessing for me when the comic industry died. Well, not all of the comic books perished—but enough of them did to almost sink the industry. Horror comics were big sellers and for some reason Congress decided to investigate them. (These were the days of the McCarthy witch hunts in Congress. Perhaps, since McCarthy tied up the Commy menace, they had to go after other targets.) I remember the beginning of the end. A publisher whom I had worked for and knew well was on the stand. Defending his horror comics on television. One of his covers was shown: a bloody headsman's axe next to a hand holding a decapitated head by the hair. The publisher defended the art, said it wasn't horrible. It could be worse. When a Congressman asked how—he pointed out that the severed end of the neck could be shown. The end of the windpipe, the severed bones, the cut and dripping blood vessels . . .

Distributors began returning bundles of comics—unopened. The smaller firms went to the wall; the bigger ones mended their ways. But from over six hundred titles being published every month the number was down to a little over two hundred. Comic artists and editors were walking the streets.

It was the best thing that ever happened to me. I took one step to the right, one forward, and began editing pulps instead of comics. *Science Fiction Adventures, Rocket Stories, Fantasy Magazine, Sea Stories*. I did them all—and I was still selling freelance. Men's adventures, the occasional true confession when money was running out—and science fiction short stories. And an SF novel was beginning to cook in the back of my head.

By this time Joan and I were happily married; our son Todd was one year old. But New York City was beginning to be a drag. Joan had given up her most successful dress designing career when he had been born. Our little apartment in the Village—which had been liberation when we both had been working, partying, dancing all night, entertaining friends—had suddenly changed. The walls were closing in and we did not like it. It was time for a change, a major change.

We decided that we would go to Mexico.

The decision was not that abrupt, but grew and strengthened over a span of time. I had spent most of the war stationed on the Texas-Mexican border. I had taken all my leave in Mexico and was charmed and excited by that country. It was unbelievably cheap—and connected to the U.S. by road. We had a little Anglia English car that would take us there. Why not? Save up some money, give it a try. If it didn't work out we could crawl back with our tails between our legs, get new jobs in New York, be no worse off then we were at that time.

Our parents hated us for taking away their grandson. Our friends thought that we were mad. We were firm. Bust out of the publishing cycle and the editorial world and make a break. For what? Independence, freedom, distant horizons, adventure? All of that I suppose. Motives were clear and jumbled both. When friends asked us why we were doing it—the best we could answer was that it seemed like a good idea at the time.

And it worked out. After a year in Mexico we were well bitten by the travel bug. There really was a world beyond the last stop on the IRT. From Mexico we went on to England and settled in London. But this was before the Clean Air Act and the fog and the damp cold were life-destroying. Packing up our bags, I wrote one last true confession for travel money, and we went on to sunny Italy and the simple joys of Capri in the Bay of Naples.

I was working on my first novel, which was coming very slowly indeed. I was writing some short SF, but living mostly on the proceeds of scripts for English comics, as well as writing daily and Sunday scripts for the *Flash Gordon* comic script. I loathed comics—but they kept us alive. The world became a better place when I finished my first novel, *Deathworld*, and sold it to *Astounding* as a serial. Bantam Books bought the paperback rights so that, for the first time in our lives, we had money in the bank.

We found safe harbor in Denmark. (Why? you might ask. Well it seemed like a good idea at the time . . .) Todd, and his new sister Moira, grew up there, spoke the Danish language and thrived in that Scandinavian country at the northern edge of Europe. We made it our home for many years and were incredibly happy. With the dollar strong and the taxes low we thrived. Skiing in the winter in Norway. Summer in Italy. It was the closest thing to an earthly paradise that a writer could imagine. I was writing a novel a year and they were all being published. Not only in Britain and America—but right around the world. (Literally—Japan published every one of them.) We traveled and became friends with our Swedish, Italian, French, German publishers.

But I never forgot the short story. One year I actually wrote and sold seven of them. This was between novels. The succinct length of the short story is the place to express short but important ideas. In between my novels, which I see as the towers of my career, are the short stories. Bricks to build the wall that connects the towers, to construct the city of my writing life.

As I shuffle through these pages now I feel a certain pleasure. I meet a younger self, enthusiastic and filled with the fire of creativity. What energy! I would not begin to do this again. But I do not have to. I have done it all already.

Here are fifty of my stories—one for every year that I have been writing science fiction. I look at the records and realize that some of the stories here have been anthologized up to twenty times. They have been translated into over thirty languages. As I run my finger down the table of contents I smile at memories.

"The Streets of Ashkelon" was rejected by all the American magazines because the lead character was an atheist; the story was later published in a Jesuit monthly as the world matured.

I sent a copy of "Captain Honario Harpplayer, R.N." to C. S. Forester since it was both a parody and a tribute to his wonderful fictions. No answer. I later discovered that the great man was quite recently dead. Did I kill him? Did he read my story and die of apoplexy?

"I Always Do What Teddy Says." A fiction at the time. You can now buy my robot Teddies. Should I sue for royalties?

"Roommates." Amplified into a novel then made into a film *Soylent Green*. It took me a while to find out how the cannibalism got into the film—it was certainly not in the novel. Finally I discovered what had happened. The producer was trying to sell the film to MGM as an overpopulation film. MGM didn't think that theme was important enough to do a film about. So back to the drawing board. The captive screenwriter added the cannibalism theme—and they bought it for that . . . We will recall the last scene in the film where a bloodied Charlton Heston is carried out shouting, "Soylent Green . . . is people!" (In reality the Soylent Green biscuits in the film were cut from plywood and dyed green. I still have a few; I take them out and look at them whenever I want to consider the mystery of the film business.) But I do remember, with great pleasure, the opening night of the film. The theatre manager was selling orange and lime slushies to the audience. He enthusiastically labeled the lime "Soylent Green-ade." He had of course never seen the film. Going in the audience enthusiastically noshed down the slushies. Exiting later they turned soylent green when they saw the slushy machine.

But I digress. Do read these stories and enjoy them. That is what this book is about.

Fifty years . . .

My, oh my.

Harry Harrison
Dublin, Ireland
A.D. 2000

ALIEN SHORES

I am one of those doubters who believe that UFOs and alien contacts are just mere figments of imagination, part of mankind's demented search for help from supernatural powers. Big daddy in the sky defying all logic—as in *Close Encounters of the Third Kind*—drops down to save mankind. Not only don't I believe in salvation by aliens, but I also doubt quite strongly that there is anyone out there to send us SETI signals. It would sure be nice to chat with neighbors from the stars; I doubt if we ever will.

That doesn't mean, though, that I can't write about aliens. I don't believe in time machines either—or faster-than-light travel. This does not stop me from writing stories using these themes. They are important SF hardware, and are there to be utilized. The alien-as-other is too rich a seam not to be mined.

And distant planets are there to be mined as well. We visited the moon in fiction long before the astronauts walked on it. Exploring other planets is just another step in the same direction. So these stories of alien shires divide neatly between tales of physical adventure on distant planets—and close encounters of a fictional kind.

The Streets of Ashkelon

Somewhere above, hidden by the eternal clouds of Wesker's World, a thunder rumbled and grew. Trader Garth stopped suddenly when he heard it, his boots sinking slowly into the muck, and cupped his good ear to catch the sound. It swelled and waned in the thick atmosphere, growing louder.

"That noise is the same as the noise of your sky-ship," Itin said, with stolid Wesker logicality, slowly pulverizing the idea in his mind and turning over the bits one by one for closer examination. "But your ship is still sitting where you landed it. It must be, even though we cannot see it, because you are the only one who can operate it. And even if anyone else could operate it we would have heard it rising into the sky. Since we did not, and if this sound is a sky-ship sound, then it must mean—"

"Yes, another ship," Garth said, too absorbed in his own thoughts to wait for the laborious Weskerian chains of logic to clank their way through to the end. Of course it was another spacer, it had been only a matter of time before one appeared, and undoubtedly this one was homing on the S.S radar reflector as he had done. His own ship would show up clearly on the newcomer's screen and they would probably set down as close to it as they could.

"You better go ahead, Itin," he said. "Use the water so you can get to the village quickly. Tell everyone to get back into the swamps, well clear of the hard ground. That ship is landing on instruments and anyone underneath at touchdown is going to be cooked."

This immediate threat was clear enough to the little Wesker amphibian. Before Garth had finished speaking Itin's ribbed ears had folded like a bat's wings and he slipped silently into the nearby canal. Garth squelched on through the mud, making as good time as he could over the clinging surface. He had just reached the fringes of the village clearing when the rumbling grew to a head-splitting roar and the spacer broke through the low-hanging layer of clouds above. Garth shielded his eyes from the down-reaching tongue of flame and examined the growing form of the gray-black ship with mixed feelings.

After almost a standard year on Wesker's World he had to fight down a longing for human companionship of any kind. While this buried fragment of herd-spirit chattered for the rest of the monkey tribe, his trader's mind was busily drawing a line under a column of figures and adding up the total. This could very well be another trader's ship, and if it was his monopoly of the Wesker's trade was at an end. Then again, this might not be a trader at all, which was the reason he stayed in the shelter of the giant fern and loosened his gun in its holster. The ship baked dry a hundred square meters of mud, the roaring blast died, and the landing feet crunched down through the crackling crust. Metal creaked and settled into place while the cloud of smoke and steam slowly drifted lower in the humid air.

"Garth—you native-cheating extortionist—where are you?" the ship's speaker boomed. The lines of the spacer had looked only slightly familiar, but there was no mistaking the rasping tones of that voice. Garth had a twisted smile when he stepped out into the open and whistled shrilly through two fingers. A directional microphone ground out of its casing on the ship's fin and turned in his direction.

"What are you doing here, Singh?" he shouted towards the mike. "Too crooked to find a planet of your own and have to come here to steal an honest trader's profits?"

"Honest!" the amplified voice roared. "This from the man who has been in more jails than cathouses—and that a goodly number in itself, I do declare. Sorry, friend of my youth, but I cannot join you in exploiting this aboriginal pesthole. I am on course to a more fairly atmosphered world where a fortune is waiting to be made. I only stopped here since an opportunity presented, to turn an honest credit by running a taxi service. I bring you friendship, the perfect companionship, a man in a different line of business who might help you in yours. I'd come out and say hello myself, except I would have to decon for biologicals. I'm cycling the passenger through the lock so I hope you won't mind helping with his luggage."

At least there would be no other trader on the planet now, that worry was gone. But Garth still wondered what sort of passenger would be taking one-way passage to an undeveloped world. And what was behind that concealed hint of merriment in Singh's voice? He walked around to the far side of the spacer where the ramp had dropped, and looked up at the man in the cargo lock who was wrestling ineffectually with a large crate. The man turned towards him and Garth saw the clerical dog-collar and knew just what it was Singh had been chuckling about.

"What are you doing here?" Garth asked, and in spite of his attempt at self-control he snapped the words. If the man noticed this he ignored it, because he was still smiling and putting out his hand as he came down the ramp.

"Father Mark," he said, "of the Missionary Society of Brothers. I'm very pleased to meet—"

"I said what are you doing here." Garth's voice was under control now, quiet and cold. He knew what had to be done, and it must be done quickly or not at all.

"That should be obvious," Father Mark said, his good nature still unruffled. "Our missionary society has raised funds to send spiritual emissaries to alien worlds for the first time. I was lucky enough—"

"Take your luggage and get back into the ship. You're not wanted here—and have no permission to land. You'll be a liability and there is no one on Wesker's World to take care of you. Get back into the ship."

"I don't know who you are sir, or why you are lying to me," the priest said. He was still calm but the smile was gone. "But I have studied galactic law and the history of this planet very well. There are no diseases or beasts here that I should have any particular fear of. It is also an open planet, and until the Space Survey changes that status I have as much right to be here as you do."

The man was of course right, but Garth couldn't let him know that. He had been bluffing, hoping the priest didn't know his rights. But he did. There was only one distasteful course left for him, and he had better do it while there was still time.

"Get back in that ship," he shouted, not hiding his anger now. With a smooth motion his gun was out of the holster and the pitted black muzzle only inches from the priest's stomach. The man's face turned white, but he did not move.

"What the hell are you doing, Garth?!" Singh's shocked voice grated from the speaker. "The guy paid his fare and you have no rights at all to throw him off the planet."

"I have this right," Garth said, raising his gun and sighting between the priest's eyes. "I give him thirty seconds to get back aboard the ship or I pull the trigger."

"Well, I think you are either off your head or playing a joke," Singh's exasperated voice rasped down at them. "If it is a joke, it is in bad taste. But either way you're not getting away with it. Two can play at that game—only I can play it better."

There was the rumble of heavy bearings and the remote-controlled four-gun turret on the ship's side rotated and pointed at Garth. "Now—down gun and give Father Mark a hand with the luggage," the speaker commanded, a trace of humor back in the voice now. "As much as I would like to help, Old Friend, I cannot. I feel it is time you had a chance to talk to the father; after all, I have had the opportunity of speaking with him all the way from Earth."

Garth jammed the gun back into the holster with an acute feeling of loss. Father Mark stepped forward, the winning smile back now and a Bible, taken from a pocket of his robe, in his raised hand. "My son—" he said.

"I'm not your son," was all Garth could choke out as the bitterness and defeat welled up within him. His fist drew back as the anger rose, and the best he could do was open the fist so he struck only with the flat of his hand. Still the blow sent the priest crashing to the ground and hurled the white pages of the book splattering into the thick mud.

Itin and the other Weskers had watched everything with seemingly emotionless interest. Garth made no attempt to answer their unspoken questions. He started towards his house, but turned back when he saw they were still unmoving.

"A new man has come," he told them. "He will need help with the things he has brought. If he doesn't have any place for them, you can put them in the big warehouse until he has a place of his own."

He watched them waddle across the clearing towards the ship, then went inside and gained a certain satisfaction from slamming the door hard enough to crack one of the panes. There was an equal amount of painful pleasure in breaking out one of the remaining bottles of Irish whiskey that he had been saving for a special occasion. Well this was special enough, though not really what he had had in mind. The whiskey was good and burned away some of the bad taste in his mouth, but not all of it. If his tactics had worked, success would have justified everything. But he had failed and in addition to the pain of failure there was the acute feeling that he had made a horse's ass out of himself. Singh had blasted off without any goodbyes. There was no telling what sense he had made of the whole matter, though he would surely carry some strange stories back to the trader's lodge. Well, that could be worried about the next time Garth signed in. Right now he had to go about setting things right with the missionary. Squinting out through the rain he saw the man struggling to erect a collapsible tent while the entire population of the village stood in ordered ranks and watched. Naturally none of them offered to help.

By the time the tent was up and the crates and boxes stowed inside it the rain had stopped. The level of fluid in the bottle was a good bit lower and Garth felt more like facing up to the unavoidable meeting. In truth, he was looking forward to talking to the man. This whole nasty business aside, after an entire solitary year any human companionship looked good. *Will you join me now for dinner? John Garth*, he wrote on the back of an old invoice. But maybe the guy was too frightened to come? Which was no way to start any kind of relationship. Rummaging under the bunk, he found a box that was big enough and put his pistol inside. Itin was of course waiting outside the door when he opened it, since this was his tour as Knowledge Collector. He handed him the note and box.

"Would you take these to the new man," he said.

"Is the new man's name New Man?" Itin asked.

"No, it's not!" Garth snapped. "His name is Mark. But I'm only asking you to deliver this, not get involved in conversation."

As always when he lost his temper, the literal-minded Weskers won the round. "You are not asking for conversation," Itin said slowly, "but Mark may ask for conversation. And others will ask me his name; if I do not know his na—"

The voice cut off as Garth slammed the door. This didn't work in the long run either because next time he saw Itin—a day, a week, or even a month later—the monologue would be picked up on the very word it had ended and the thought rambled out to its last frayed end. Garth cursed under his breath and poured water over a pair of the tastier concentrates that he had left.

"Come in," he said when there was a quiet knock on the door. The priest entered and held out the box with the gun.

"Thank you for the loan, Mr. Garth, I appreciate the spirit that made you send it. I have no idea of what caused the unhappy affair when I landed, but I think it would be best forgotten if we are going to be on this planet together for any length of time."

"Drink?" Garth asked, taking the box and pointing to the bottle on the table. He poured two glasses full and handed one to the priest. "That's about what I had in mind, but I still owe you an explanation of what happened out there." He scowled into his glass for a second, then raised it to the other man. "It's a big universe and I guess we have to make out as best we can. Here's to Sanity."

"God be with you," Father Mark said, and raised his glass as well.

"Not with me or with this planet," Garth said firmly. "And that's the crux of the matter." He half-drained the glass and sighed.

"Do you say that to shock me?" the priest asked with a smile. "I assure you that it doesn't."

"Not intended to shock. I meant it quite literally. I suppose I'm what you would call an atheist, so revealed religion is no concern of mine. While these natives, simple and unlettered Stone Age types that they are, have managed to come this far with no superstitions or traces of deism whatsoever. I had hoped that they might continue that way."

"What are you saying?" The priest frowned. "Do you mean they have no gods, no belief in the hereafter? They must die . . . ?"

"Die they do, and to dust returneth. Like the rest of the animals. They have thunder, trees and water without having thunder-gods, tree sprites, or water nymphs. They have no ugly little gods, taboos, or spells to hag-ride and limit their lives. They are the only primitive people I have ever encountered that are completely free of superstition and appear to be much happier and sane because of it. I just wanted to keep them that way."

"You wanted to keep them from God—from salvation?" The priest's eyes widened and he recoiled slightly.

"No," Garth said. "I wanted to keep them from superstition until they knew more and could think about it realistically without being absorbed and perhaps destroyed by it."

"You're being insulting to the Church, sir, to equate it with superstition . . ."

"Please," Garth said, raising his hand. "No theological arguments. I don't think your society footed the bill for this trip just to attempt to convert me. Just accept the fact that my beliefs have been arrived at through careful thought over a period of years, and no amount of undergraduate metaphysics will change them. I'll promise not to try and convert you—if you will do the same for me."

"Agreed, Mr. Garth. As you have reminded me, my mission here is to save these souls, and that is what I must do. But why should my work disturb you so much that you try and keep me from landing? Even threaten me with your gun, and—" The priest broke off and looked into his glass.

"And even slug you?" Garth asked, suddenly frowning. "There was no excuse for that, and I would like to say that I'm sorry. Plain bad manners and an even worse temper. Live alone long enough and you find yourself doing that kind of thing." He brooded down at his big hands where they lay on the table, reading memories into the scars and calluses patterned there. "Let's just call it frustration, for lack of a better word. In your business you must have had a lot of chance to peep into the darker places in men's minds and you should know a bit about motives and happiness. I have had too busy a life to ever consider settling down and raising a family, and right up until recently I never missed it. Maybe leakage radiation is softening up my brain, but I had begun to think of these furry and fishy Weskers as being a little like my own children, that I was somehow responsible to them."

"We are all His children," Father Mark said quietly.

"Well, here are some of His children that can't even imagine His existence," Garth said, suddenly angry at himself for allowing gentler emotions to show through. Yet he forgot himself at once, leaning forward with the intensity of his feelings. "Can't you realize the importance of this? Live with these Weskers a while and you will discover a simple and happy life that matches the state of grace you people are always talking about. They get pleasure from their lives—and cause no one pain. By circumstances they have evolved on an almost barren world, so have never had a chance to grow out of a physical Stone Age culture. But mentally they are our match—or perhaps better. They have all learned my language so I can easily explain the many things they want to know. Knowledge and the gaining of knowledge gives them real satisfaction. They tend to be exasperating at times because every new fact must be related to the structure of all other things, but the more they learn the faster this process becomes. Someday they are going to be man's equal in every way, perhaps surpass us. If—would you do me a favor?"

"Whatever I can."

"Leave them alone. Or teach them if you must—history and science, philosophy, law, anything that will help them face the realities of the greater universe they never even knew existed before. But don't confuse them with your hatreds and pain, guilt, sin, and punishment. Who knows the harm—"

"You are being insulting, sir!" the priest said, jumping to his feet. The top of his grey head barely came to the massive spaceman's chin, yet he showed no fear in defending what he believed. Garth, standing now himself, was no longer the penitent. They faced each other in anger, as men have always stood, unbending in the defense of that which they think right.

"Yours is the insult," Garth shouted. "The incredible egotism to feel that your derivative little mythology, differing only slightly from the thousands of others that still burden men, can do anything but confuse their still fresh minds. Don't you realize that they believe in truth—and have never heard of such a thing as a lie? They have not been trained yet to understand that other kinds of minds can think differently from theirs. Will you spare them this . . . ?"

"I will do my duty which is His will, Mr. Garth. These are God's creatures here, and they have souls. I cannot shirk my duty, which is to bring them His word so that they may be saved and enter into the Kingdom of Heaven."

When the priest opened the door the wind caught it and blew it wide. He vanished into the storm-swept darkness and the door swung back and forth and a splatter of raindrops blew in. Garth's boots left muddy footprints when he closed the door, shutting out the sight of Itin sitting patiently and uncomplaining in the storm, hoping only that Garth might stop for a moment and leave with him some of the wonderful knowledge of which he had so much.

By unspoken consent that first night was never mentioned again. After a few days of loneliness, made worse because each knew of the other's proximity, they found themselves talking on carefully neutral grounds. Garth slowly packed and stowed away his stock and never admitted that his work was finished and he could leave at any time. He had a fair amount of interesting drugs and botanicals that would fetch a good price. And the Wesker artifacts were sure to create a sensation in the sophisticated galactic market. Crafts on the planet here had been limited before his arrival, mostly pieces of carving pain-fully chipped into the hard wood with fragments of stone. He had supplied tools and a stock of raw metal from his own supplies, noth-ing more than that. In a few months the Weskers had not only learned to work with the new materials, but had translated their own designs and forms into the most alien—but most beautiful—artifacts that he had ever seen. All he had to do was release these on the market to create a primary demand, then return for a new supply. The Weskers wanted only books and tools and knowledge in return, and through their own efforts he knew they would pull themselves into the ga-lactic union.

This is what Garth had hoped. But a wind of change was blowing through the settlement that had grown up around his ship. No longer was he the center of attention and focal point of the village life. He had to grin when he thought of his fall from power; yet there was very little humor in the smile. Serious and attentive Weskers still took turns of duty as Knowledge Collectors, but their recording of dry facts was in sharp contrast to the intellectual hurricane that sur-rounded the priest.

Where Garth had made them work for each book and machine, the priest gave freely. Garth had tried to be progressive in his supply of knowledge, treating them as bright but unlettered children. He had wanted them to walk before they could run, to master one step before going on to the next.

Father Mark simply brought them the benefits of Christianity. The only physical work he required was the construction of a church, a place of worship and learning. More Weskers had appeared out of the limitless planetary swamps and within days the roof was up, sup-ported on a framework of poles. Each morning the congregation worked a little while on the walls, then hurried inside to learn the all-promising, all-encompassing, all-important facts about the uni-verse.

Garth never told the Weskers what he thought about their new interest, and this was mainly because they had never asked him. Pride or honor stood in the way of his grabbing a willing listener and pour-ing out his grievances. Perhaps it would have been different if Itin was on Collecting duty, he was the brightest of the lot, but Itin had been rotated the day after the priest had arrived and Garth had not talked to him since.

It was a surprise then when after seventeen of the trebly-long Wes-ker days, he found a delegation at his doorstep when he emerged after breakfast. Itin was their spokesman, and his mouth was open slightly. Many of the other Weskers had their mouths open as well, one even appearing to be yawning, clearly revealing the double row of sharp teeth and the purple-black throat. The mouths impressed Garth as to the seriousness of the meeting: this was the one Wesker expression he had learned to recognize. An open mouth indicated some strong emotion: happiness, sadness, anger, he could never be really sure which. The Weskers were normally placid and he had never seen enough open mouths to tell what was causing them. But he was surrounded by them now.

"Will you help us, Garth?" Itin said. "We have a question."

"I'll answer any questions you ask," Garth said, with more than a hint of misgiving. "What is it?"

"Is there a God?"

"What do you mean by 'God'?" Garth asked in turn. What should he tell them? What had been going on in their minds that they should come to him with this question?

"God is our Father in Heaven, who made us all and protects us. Whom we pray to for aid, and if we are Saved will find a place—"

"That's enough," Garth said. "There is no God."

All of them had their mouths open now, even Itin, as they looked at Garth and thought about his answer. The rows of pink teeth would have been frightening if he hadn't known these creatures so well. For one instant he wondered if perhaps they had been already indoctrinated and looked upon him as a heretic, but he brushed the thought away.

"Thank you," Itin said, and they turned and left.

Though the morning was still cool, Garth noticed that he was sweating and wondered why.

The reaction was not long in coming. Itin returned that same afternoon. "Will you come to the church?" he asked. "Many of the things that we study are difficult to learn, but none as difficult as this. We need your help because we must hear you and Father Mark talk together. This is because he says one thing is true and you say another is true and both cannot be true at the same time. We must find out what is true."

"I'll come, of course," Garth said, trying to hide the sudden feeling of elation. He had done nothing, but the Weskers had come to him anyway. There could still be grounds for hope that they might yet be free.

It was hot inside the church, and Garth was surprised at the number of Weskers who were there, more than he had seen gathered at any one time before. There were many open mouths. Father Mark sat at a table covered with books. He looked unhappy but didn't say anything when Garth came in. Garth spoke first.

"I hope you realize this is their idea—that they came to me of their own free will and asked me to come here?"

"I know that," the priest said resignedly. "At times they can be very difficult. But they are learning and want to believe, and that is what is important."

"Father Mark, Trader Garth, we need your help," Itin said. "You both know many things that we do not know. You must help us come to religion, which is not an easy thing to do." Garth started to say something, then changed his mind. Itin went on. "We have read the bibles and all the books that Father Mark gave us, and one thing is clear. We have discussed this and we are all agreed. These books are very different from the ones that Trader Garth gave us. In Trader Garth's books there is the universe which we have not seen, and it goes on without God, for He is mentioned nowhere, we have searched very carefully. In Father Mark's books He is everywhere and nothing can go without Him. One of these must be right and the other must be wrong. We do not know how this can be, but after we find out which is right then perhaps we will know. If God does not exist . . ."

"Of course He exists, my children," Father Mark said in a voice of heartfelt intensity. "He is our Father in Heaven who has created us all . . ."

"Who created God?" Itin asked and the murmur ceased and every one of the Weskers watched Father Mark intensely. He recoiled a bit under the impact of their eyes, then smiled.

"Nothing created God, since He is the Creator. He always was—"

"If He always was in existence—why cannot the universe have always been in existence? Without having had a creator?" Itin broke in with a rush of words. The importance of the question was obvious.

The priest answered slowly, with infinite patience.

"Would that the answers were that simple, my children. But even the scientists do not agree about the creation of the universe. While they doubt—we who have seen the light *know*. We can see the miracle of creation all about us. And how can there be a creation without a Creator? That is He, our Father, our God in Heaven. I know you have doubts and that is because you have souls and free will. Still the answer is simple. Have faith, that is all you need. Just believe."

"How can we believe without proof?"

"If you cannot see that this world itself is proof of His existence, then I say to you that belief needs no proof—if you have faith!"

A babble of voices arose in the room and more of the Wesker mouths were open now as they tried to force their thoughts through the tangled skein of words and separate the thread of truth.

"Can you tell us, Garth?" Itin asked, and the sound of his voice quieted the hubbub.

"I can tell you to use the scientific method which can examine all things—including itself—and give you answers that can prove the truth or falsity of any statement."

"That is what we must do," Itin said. "We had reached the same conclusion." He held a thick book before him and a ripple of nods ran across the watchers. "We have been studying the Bible as Father Mark told us to do, and we have found the answer. God will make a miracle for us, thereby proving that He is watching us. And by this sign we will know Him and go to Him."

"This is a sign of false pride," Father Mark said. "God needs no miracles to prove His existence."

"But *we* need a miracle!" Itin shouted, and though he wasn't human there was still the cry of need in his voice. "We have read here of many smaller miracles, loaves, fishes, wine, snakes—many of them, for much smaller reasons. Now all He need do is make a miracle and He will bring us all to Him—the wonder of an entire new world worshiping at His throne, as you have told us, Father Mark. And you have told us how important this is. We have discussed this and find that there is only one miracle that is best for this kind of thing."

His boredom and amused interest in the incessant theological wrangling drained from Garth in an instant. He had not been really thinking or he would have realized where all this was leading. By turning slightly he could see the illustration in the Bible where Itin held it open, and knew in advance what picture it was. He rose slowly from his chair, as if stretching, and turned to the priest behind him.

"Get ready!" he whispered. "Get out the back and get to the ship, I'll keep them busy here. I don't think they'll harm—"

"What do you mean . . . ?" Father Mark asked, blinking in surprise.

"Get out, you fool!" Garth hissed. "What miracle do you think they mean? What miracle is supposed to have converted the world to Christianity?"

"No!" Father Mark said. "It cannot be. It just cannot—"

"GET MOVING!" Garth shouted, dragging the priest from the chair and hurling him towards the rear wall. Father Mark stumbled to a halt, turned back. Garth leaped for him, but it was already too late. The amphibians were small, but there were so many of them. Garth lashed out and his fist struck Itin, hurling him back into the crowd. The others came on as he fought his way towards the priest. He beat at them but it was like struggling against the waves. The furry, musky bodies washed over and engulfed him. He struggled until they tied him, and he still struggled until they beat on his head until he stopped. Then they pulled him outside, where he could only lie in the rain and curse and watch.

Of course the Weskers were marvelous craftsmen, and everything had been constructed down to the last detail, following the illustration in the Bible. There was the cross, planted firmly on the top of a small hill, the gleaming metal spikes, the hammer. Father Mark was stripped and draped in a carefully pleated loincloth. They led him out of the church and at the sight of the cross he almost fainted. After that he held his head high and determined to die as he had lived, with faith.

Yet this was hard. It was unbearable even for Garth, who only watched. It is one thing to talk of crucifixion and look at the gentle carved bodies in the dim light of prayer. It is another to see a man naked, ropes cutting into his skin where he hangs from a bar of wood. And to see the needle-tipped spike raised and placed against the soft flesh of his palm, to see the hammer come back with the calm deliberation of an artisan's measured stroke. To hear the thick sound of metal penetrating flesh.

Then to hear the screams.

Few are born to be martyrs and Father Mark was not one of them. With the first blows, the blood ran from his lips where his clenched teeth met. Then his mouth was wide and his head strained back and the awful guttural horror of his screams sliced through the susurration of the falling rain. It resounded as a silent echo from the masses of watching Weskers, for whatever emotion opened their mouths was now tearing at their bodies with all its force, and row after row of gaping jaws reflected the crucified priest's agony.

Mercifully he fainted as the last nail was driven home. Blood ran from the raw wounds, mixing with the rain to drip faintly pink from his feet as the life ran out of him. At this time, somewhere at this time, sobbing and tearing at his own bonds, numbed from the blows on the head, Garth lost consciousness.

He awoke in his own warehouse and it was dark. Someone was cutting away the woven ropes they had bound him with. The rain still dripped and splashed outside.

"Itin," he said. It could be no one else.

"Yes," the alien voice whispered back. "The others are all talking in the church. Lin died after you struck his head, and Inon is very sick. There are some that say you should be crucified too, and I think that is what will happen. Or perhaps killed by stoning on the head. They have found in the Bible where it says—"

"I know." With infinite weariness. "An eye for an eye. You'll find lots of things like that once you start looking."

"You must go, you can get to your ship without anyone seeing you. There has been enough killing." Itin as well spoke with a new-found weariness.

Garth experimented, pulling himself to his feet. He pressed his head to the rough wall until the nausea stopped.

"He's dead." He said it as a statement, not a question.

"Yes, some time ago. Or I could not have come away to see you."

"And buried of course, or they wouldn't be thinking about starting on me next."

"And buried!" There was almost a ring of emotion in the alien's voice, an echo of the dead priest's. "He is buried and he will rise on High. It is written and that is the way it will happen. Father Mark will be so happy that it has happened like this." The voice ended in a sound like a human sob, but of course it couldn't have been that since Itin was alien, and not human at all. Garth painfully worked his way towards the door, leaning against the wall so he wouldn't fall.

"We did the right thing, didn't we?" Itin asked. There was no answer. "He will rise up, Garth, won't he rise?"

Garth was at the door and enough light came from the brightly lit church to show his torn and bloody hands clutching at the frame. Itin's face swam into sight close to his, and Garth felt the delicate, many-fingered hands with the sharp nails catch at his clothes.

"He will rise, won't he, Garth?"

"No," Garth said, "he is going to stay buried right where you put him. Nothing is going to happen, because he is dead and he is going to stay dead."

The rain runneled through Itin's fur and his mouth was opened so wide that he seemed to be screaming into the night. Only with effort could he talk, squeezing out the alien thoughts in an alien language.

"Then we will not be saved? We will not become pure?"

"You were pure," Garth said, in a voice somewhere between a sob and a laugh. "That's the horrible ugly dirty part of it. You were pure. Now you are—"

"Murderers," Itin said, and the water ran down from his lowered head and streamed away into the darkness.

Rescue Operation

"Pull! Pull steadily . . . !" Dragomir shouted, clutching at the tarry cords of the net. Beside him in the hot darkness Pribislav Polasek grunted as he heaved on the wet strands. The net was invisible in the black water, but the blue light trapped in it rose closer and closer to the surface.

"It's slipping . . ." Pribislav groaned and clutched the rough gunwale of the little boat. For a single instant he could see the blue light on the helmet, a faceplate and the suited body that faded into blackness, then it slipped free of the net. He had just a glimpse of a dark shape before it was gone. "Did you see it?" he asked. "Just before he fell he waved his hand."

"How can I know? The hand moved, it could have been the net, or he might still be alive." Dragomir had his face bent almost to the glassy surface of the water, but there was nothing more to be seen. "He might be alive."

The two fishermen sat back in the boat and stared at each other in the harsh light of the hissing acetylene lamp in the bow. They were very different men, yet greatly alike in their stained, baggy trousers and faded cotton shirts. Their hands were deeply wrinkled and callused from a lifetime of hard labor, their thoughts slowed by the rhythm of work and years.

"We cannot get him up with the net," Dragomir finally said, speaking first as always.

"Then we will need help," Pribislav added. "We have anchored the buoy here, we can find the spot again."

"Yes, we need help." Dragomir opened and closed his large hands, then leaned over to bring the rest of the net into the boat. "The diver, the one who stays with the widow Korenc, he will know what to do. His name is Kukovic and Petar said he is a doctor of science from the university in Ljubljana."

They bent to their oars and sent the heavy boat steadily over the glasslike water of the Adriatic. Before they had reached shore, the sky was light and when they tied to the sea wall in Brbinj the sun was above the horizon.

Joze Kukovic looked at the rising ball of the sun, already hot on his skin, yawned and stretched. The widow shuffled out with his coffee, mumbled good morning and put it on the stone rail of the porch. Ho pushed the tray aside and sat down next to it, then emptied the coffee from the small, long-handled pot into his cup. The thick Turkish coffee would wake him up, in spite of the impossible hour. From the rail he had a view down the unpaved and dusty street to the port, already stirring to life. Two women, with the morning's water in brass pots balanced on their heads, stopped to talk. The peasants were bringing in their produce for the morning market, baskets of cabbages and potatoes and trays of tomatoes, strapped onto tiny donkeys. One of them brayed, a harsh noise that sawed through the stillness of the morning, bouncing echoes from the yellowed buildings. It was hot already. Brbinj was a town at the edge of nowhere, located between empty ocean and barren hills, asleep for centuries and dying by degrees. There were no attractions here, if you did not count the sea. But under the flat, blue calm of the water was another world that Joze loved.

Cool shadows, deep valleys, more alive than all the sun-blasted shores that surrounded it. Excitement, too: just the day before, too late in the afternoon to really explore it, he had found a Roman galley half-buried in the sand. He would get into it today, the first human in two thousand years, and heaven alone knew what he would find there. In the sand about it had been shards of broken amphorae; there might be whole ones inside the hull.

Sipping happily at his coffee he watched the small boat tying up in the harbor, and wondered why the two fishermen were in such a hurry. They were almost running, and no one ran here in the summer. Stopping below his porch the bigger one called up to him.

"Doctor, may we come up? There is something urgent."

"Yes, of course." He was surprised and wondered if they took him for a physician.

Dragomir shuffled forward and did not know where to begin. He pointed out over the ocean.

"It fell, out there last night, we saw it, a sputnik without a doubt?"

"A traveler?" Joze Kukovic wrinkled his forehead, not quite sure that he heard right. When the locals were excited it was hard to follow their dialect. For such a small country Yugoslavia was cursed with a multitude of tongues.

"No, it was not a *putnik*, but a sputnik, one of the Russian spaceships."

"Or an American one." Pribislav spoke for the first time, but he was ignored.

Joze smiled and sipped his coffee. "Are you sure it wasn't a meteorite you saw? There is always a heavy meteor shower this time of the year."

"A sputnik." Dragomir insisted stolidly. "The ship fell far out in the Jadransko Mor and vanished, we saw that. But the space pilot came down almost on top of us, into the water . . ."

"The WHAT?" Joze gasped, jumping to his feet and knocking the coffee tray to the floor. The brass tray clanged and rattled in circles unnoticed. "There was a man in this thing—and he got clear?"

Both fishermen nodded at the same time and Dragomir continued. "We saw this light fall from the sputnik when it went overhead and drop into the water. He couldn't see what it was, just a light, and we rowed there as fast as we could. It was still sinking and we dropped a net and managed to catch him . . ."

"You have the pilot?"

"No, but once we pulled him close enough to the surface to see he was in a heavy suit, with a window like a diving suit, and there was something on the back that might have been like your tanks there."

"He waved his hand," Pribislav insisted.

"He might have waved a hand, we could not be sure. We came back for help."

The silence lengthened and Joze realized that he was the help that they needed, and that they had turned the responsibility over to him. What should he do first? The astronaut might have his own oxygen tanks, Joze had no real idea what provisions were made for water landings, but if there were oxygen the man might still be alive.

Joze paced the floor while he thought, a short, square figure in khaki shorts and sandals. He was not handsome, his nose was too big and his teeth were too obvious for that, but he generated a certainty of power. He stopped and pointed to Pribislav.

"We're going to have to get him out. You can find the spot again?"

"A buoy."

"Good. And we may need a doctor. You have none here, but is there one in Osor?"

"Dr. Bratos, but he is very old . . ."

"As long as he is still alive, we'll have to get him. Can anyone in this town drive an automobile?"

The fishermen looked towards the roof and concentrated, while Joze controlled his impatience.

"Yes, I think so," Dragomir finally said. "Petar was a partisan."

"That's right," the other fisherman finished the thought. "He has told many times how they stole German trucks and how he drove . . ."

"Well, then one of you get this Petar and give him the keys to my car, it's a German car so he should be able to manage. Tell him to bring the doctor back at once."

Dragomir took the keys, but handed them to Pribislav who ran out.

"Now let's see if we can get the man up," Joze said, grabbing his scuba gear and leading the way towards the boat.

They rowed, side by side though Dragomir's powerful stroke did most of the work.

"How deep is the water out here?" Joze asked. He was already dripping with sweat as the sun burned on him.

"The Kvarneric is deeper up by Rab, but we were fishing off Trstenilc and the bottom is only about four fathoms there. We're coming to the buoy."

"Seven meters, it shouldn't be too hard to find him." Joze kneeled in the bottom of the boat and slipped into the straps of the scuba. He buckled it tight, checked the valves, then turned to the fisherman before he bit into the mouthpiece. "Keep the boat near this buoy and I'll use it for a guide while I search. If I need a line or any help, I'll surface over the astronaut, then you can bring the boat to me."

He turned on the oxygen and slipped over the side, the cool water rising up his body as he sank below the surface. With a powerful kick he started towards the bottom, following the dropping line of the buoy rope. Almost at once he saw the man, spread-eagled on white sand below.

Joze swam down, making himself stroke smoothly in spite of his growing excitement. Details were clearer as he dropped lower. There were no identifying marks on the pressure suit, it might be either American or Russian. It was a hard suit, metal or reinforced plastic, and painted green, with a single, flat faceplate in the helmet.

Because distance and size are so deceptive under water, Joze was on the sand next to the figure before he realized it was less than four feet long. Ho gasped and almost lost his mouthpiece.

Then he looked at the faceplate and saw that the creature inside was not human.

Joze coughed a bit and blew out a stream of bubbles: he had been holding his breath without realizing it. He just floated there, paddling slowly with his hands to stay in a position, looking at the face within the helmet.

It was still as a waxen cast, green wax with roughened surface, slit nostrils, slit mouth and large eyeballs unseen but prominent as they pushed up against the closed lids. The arrangement of features was roughly human, but no human being had skin this color or had a pulpy crest, partially visible through the faceplate, growing up from above the closed eyes. Joze stared down at the suit made up of some unknown material, and at the compact atmosphere-regeneration apparatus on the alien's back. What kind of atmosphere? He looked back at the creature and saw that the eyes were open and the thing was watching him.

Fear was his first reaction, he shot back in the water like a startled fish then, angry at himself, came forward again. The alien slowly raised one arm, then dropped it limply. Joze looked through the faceplate and saw that the eyes were closed again. The alien was alive, but unable to move, perhaps it was injured and in pain. The wreck of the creature's ship showed that something had been wrong with the landing. Reaching under as gently as he could he cradled the tiny body in his arms, trying to ignore a feeling of revulsion when the cold fabric of the thing's suit touched his bare arms. It was only metal or plastic; he had to be a scientist about this. When he lifted it up the eyes still did not open as he bore the limp and almost weightless form to the surface.

"You great stupid clumsy clod of peasant, help me," he shouted, spitting out his mouthpiece and treading water on the surface, but Dragomir only shook his head in horror and retreated to the point of the bow when he saw what the physicist had borne up from below.

"It is a creature from another world and cannot harm you!" Joze insisted but the fisherman would not approach.

Joze cursed aloud and only managed with great difficulty to get the alien into the boat, then climbed in after him. Though he was twice Joze's size, threats of violence drove Dragomir to the oars. But he used the farthest set of tholepins, even though it made rowing much more difficult. Joze dropped his scuba gear into the bottom of the boat and looked more closely at the drying fabric of the alien spacesuit. His fear of the unknown was forgotten in his growing enthusiasm. He was a nuclear physicist, but he remembered enough of his chemistry and mechanics to know that this material was completely impossible by Earth's standards.

Light green, it was as hard as steel over the creature's limbs and torso, yet was soft and bent easily at the joints as he proved by lifting and dropping the limp arm. His eyes went down the alien's tiny figure. There was a thick harness about the middle, roughly where a human waist would be, and hanging from this was a bulky container, like an oversize sporran. The suiting continued without an apparent seam—but the right leg! It was squeezed in and crushed as though it had been grabbed by a giant pliers. Perhaps this explained the creature's lack of motion. Could it be hurt? In pain?

Its eyes were open again and Joze realized in sudden horror that the helmet was filled with water. It must have leaked in, the thing was drowning. He grabbed at the helmet, seeing if it would screw off, tugging at it in panic as the eyes rolled up towards him.

Then he forced himself to think, and shakingly let go. The alien was still quiet, eyes open, no bubbles apparently coming from lips or nose. Did it breathe? Had the water leaked in—or was it possible that it had always been there? Was it water? Who knew what alien atmosphere it might breathe: methane, chlorine, sulfur dioxide. Why not water? The liquid was inside, surely enough, the suit wasn't leaking and the creature seemed unchanged.

Joze looked up and saw that Dragomir's panicked strokes had brought them into the harbor. There was a crowd already waiting on the shore.

The boat almost overturned as Dragomir leaped up onto the harbor wall, kicking backward in his panic. They drifted away and Joze picked the mooring line up from the floorboards and coiled it in his hands. "Here," he shouted, "catch this. Tie it onto the ring there."

No one heard him, or if they heard, did not want to admit it. They stared down at the green-cased figure lying in the stern sheets and a rustle of whispering blew across them like wind among pine boughs. The women clutched their hands to their breasts, crossing themselves.

"Catch this!" Joze said through clenched teeth, forcing himself to keep his temper.

He hurled the rope onto the stones and they shied away from it. A youth grabbed it and slowly threaded it through the rusty ring, hands shaking and head tilted to one side, his mouth dropped in a permanent gape. He was feebleminded, too simple to understand what was going on: he simply obeyed the shouted order.

"Help me get this thing ashore," Joze called out, and even before the words were out of his mouth he realized the futility of the request.

The peasants shuffled backwards, a blank-faced mob sharing the same fear of the unknown, the women like giant, staring dolls in their knee-length flaring skirts, black stockings and high felt shoes. He would have to do it himself. Balancing in the rocking boat he cradled the alien in his arms and lifted it carefully up onto the rough stone of the harbor wall. The circle of watchers pushed back even farther, some of the women choking off screams and running back to their houses, while the men muttered louder: Joze ignored them.

These people were going to be no help to him—and they might cause trouble. His own room would be safest, he doubted if they would bother him there. He had just picked up the alien when a newcomer pushed through the watchers.

"There—what is that? A *vrag!*" The old priest pointed in horror at the alien in Joze's arms and backed away, fumbling for his crucifix.

"Enough of your superstition!" Joze snapped. "This is no devil but a sentient creature, a traveler. Now get out of my way."

He pushed forward and they fled before him. Joze moved as quickly as he could without appearing to hurry, leaving the crowd behind. There was a slapping of quick footsteps and he looked over his shoulder; it was the priest, Father Perc. His stained cassock flapped and his breath whistled in his throat with the unaccustomed exertion.

"Tell me, what are you doing . . . Dr. Kukovic? What is that . . . thing? Tell me . . ."

"I told you. A traveler. Two of the local fishermen saw something come from the sky and crash. This . . . alien came from it." Joze spoke as calmly as possible. There might be trouble with the people, but not if the priest were on his side. "It is a creature from another world, a water-breathing animal, and it's hurt. We must help it."

Father Perc scrambled along sideways as he looked with obvious distaste at the motionless alien. "It is wrong," he mumbled, "this is something unclean, *Sao duh* . . ."

"Neither demon nor devil, can't you get that through your mind? The Church recognizes the possibility of creatures from other planets—the Jesuits even argue about it—so why can't you? Even the Pope believes there is life on other worlds."

"Does he? Does he?" the old man asked, blinking with red-rimmed eyes.

Joze brushed by him and up the steps to the window Korenc's house. She was nowhere in sight as he went into his room and gently lowered the still-unconscious form of the alien onto his bed. The priest stopped in the doorway, quivering fingers on his rosary, uncertain. Joze stood over the bed, opening and closing his hands, just as unsure. What could he do? The creature was wounded, perhaps dying, something must be done. But what?

The distant droning whine of a car's engine pushed into the hot room and he almost sighed with relief. It was his car, he recognized the sound, and it would be bringing the doctor. The car stopped outside and the doors slammed, but no one appeared.

Joze waited tensely, realizing that the townspeople must be talking to the doctor, telling him what had happened. A slow minute passed and Joze started from the room, but stopped before he passed the priest, still standing just inside the door. What was keeping them? His window faced on an alleyway and he could not see the street in front of the building. Then the outside door opened and he could hear the widow's whispered voice, "In there, straight through."

There were two men, both dusty from the road. One was obviously the doctor, a short and dumpy man clutching a worn black bag, his bald head beaded with sweat. Next to him was a young man, tanned and windburned, dressed like the other fishermen: this must be Petar the ex-partisan.

It was Petar who went to the bed first, the doctor just stood clutching his bag and blinking about the room.

"What is this thing?" Petar asked, then bent over, hands on his knees, to stare in through the faceplate. "Whatever it is, it sure is ugly."

"I don't know. It's from another planet, that's the only thing I know. Now move aside so the doctor can look." Joze waved and the doctor moved reluctantly forward. "You must be Dr. Bratos. I'm Kukovic, professor of nuclear physics at the university in Ljubljana." Perhaps waving around a little prestige might get this man's reluctant cooperation.

"Yes, how do you do. Very pleased to meet you, Professor, an honor I assure you. But what it is you wish me to do, I do not understand?" He shook ever so lightly as he spoke and Joze realized that the man was very old, well into his eighties or more. He would have to be patient.

"This alien . . . whatever it is . . . is injured and unconscious. We must do what we can to save its life."

"But what can we do? The thing is sealed in a metal garment—look, it is filled with water. I am a doctor, a medical man, but not for animals, creatures like that."

"Neither am I, Doctor. No one on earth is. But we must do our best. We must get the suit off the alien and then discover what we can do to help."

"It is impossible! The fluid inside of it, it will run out."

"Obviously, so we will have to take precautions. We will have to determine what the liquid is, then get more of it and fill the bathtub in the next room. I have been looking at the suit and the helmet seems to be a separate piece, clamped into position. If we loosen the clamps we should be able to get a sample."

For precious seconds Dr. Bratos stood there, nibbling at his lip, before he spoke. "Yes, I suppose we could, but what could we catch the sample in? This is most difficult and irregular."

"It doesn't make any difference what we catch the sample in," Joze snapped, frustration pushing at his carefully held control. He turned to Petar who was standing silently by, smoking a cigarette in his cupped hand. "Will you help? Get a soup plate, anything from the kitchen."

Petar simply nodded and left. There were muffled complaints from the widow, but he was back quickly with her best pot.

"That's good," Joze said, lifting the alien's head, "now slide it under here." With the pot in position he twisted one of the clamps; it snapped open but nothing else happened. A hairline opening was visible at the junction, but it stayed dry. But when Joze opened the second clamp there was a sudden gush of clear liquid under pressure, and before he fumbled the clamp shut again the pot was half full. He lifted the alien again and, without being told, Petar pulled the pot free and put it on the table by the window. "It's hot," he said.

Joze touched the outside of the container. "Warm not hot, about one hundred twenty degrees I would guess. A hot ocean on a hot planet."

"But . . . is it water?" Dr. Bratos asked haltingly.

"I suppose it is—but aren't you the one to find out? Is it fresh water or sea water?"

"I'm no chemist . . . how can I tell? . . . It is very complicated."

Petar laughed and took Joze's water glass from the nightstand. "That's not so hard to find out," he said, and dipped it into the pot. He raised the half-filled glass, sniffed at it, then took a sip and puckered his lips. "Tastes like ordinary sea water to me, but there's another taste, sort of bitter."

Joze took the glass from him. "This could be dangerous," the doctor protested, but they ignored him. Yes, salt water, hot salt water with a sharpness to it. "It tastes like more than a trace of iodine. Can you test for the presence of iodine, Doctor?"

"Here . . . no, it is quite complicated. In the laboratory with the correct equipment—" his voice trailed off as he opened his bag on the table and groped through it. He brought his hand out empty. "In the laboratory."

"We have no laboratory or any other assistance, Doctor. We will have to be satisfied with what we have here, ordinary sea water will have to do."

"I'll get a bucket and fill the tub," Petar said.

"Good. But don't fill the bathtub yet. Bring the water into the kitchen and we'll heat it, then pour it in."

"Right." Petar brushed past the silent and staring priest and was gone. Joze looked at Father Perc and thought of the people of the village.

"Stay here, Doctor," he said. "This alien is your patient and I don't think anyone other than you should come near. Just sit by him."

"Yes, of course, that is correct," Dr. Bratos said relievedly, pulling the chair over and sitting down.

The breakfast fire was still burning in the big stove and flamed up when Joze slid in more sticks. On the wall hung the big copper washtub and he dropped it onto the stove with a clang. Behind him the widow's bedroom door opened, but slammed shut again when he turned. Petar came in with a bucket of water and poured it into the tub.

"What are the people doing?" Joze asked.

"Just milling about and bothering each other. They won't be any trouble. If you're worried about them, I can drive back to Osor and bring the police, or telephone someone."

"No, I should have thought of that earlier. Right now I need you here. You're the only one who isn't either senile or ignorant."

Peter smiled. "I'll get some more water."

The bathtub was small and the washtub big. When the heated water was dumped in it filled it more than halfway, enough to cover the small alien. There was a drain from the bathtub but no faucets: it was usually filled with a hose from the sink. Joze picked up the alien, cradling it like a child in his arms, and carried it into the bath. The eyes were open again, following his every movement, but making no protest. He lowered the creature gently into the water, then straightened a moment and took a deep breath. "Helmet first, then we'll try to figure out how the suit opens." He bent and slowly twisted the clamps.

With all four clamps open the helmet moved freely. He opened it a wide crack, ready to close it quickly if there were any signs of trouble. The ocean water would be flowing in now, mixing with the alien water, yet the creature made no complaint. After a minute Joze slowly pulled the helmet off, cradling the alien's head with one hand so that it would not bump to the bottom of the tub.

Once the helmet was clear the pulpy crest above the eyes sprang up like a coxcomb, reaching up over the top of the green head. A wire ran from the helmet to a shiny bit of metal on one side of the creature's skull. There was an indentation there and Joze slowly pulled a metal plug out, perhaps an earphone of some kind. The alien was opening and closing its mouth, giving a glimpse of bony yellow ridges inside, and a very low humming could be heard.

Petar pressed his ear against the outside of the metal tube. "The thing is talking or something, I can hear it."

"Let me have your stethoscope, Doctor," Joze said, but when the doctor did not move he dug it from the bag himself. Yes—when he pressed it to the metal he could hear a rising and falling whine, speech of a kind.

"We can't possibly understand him—not yet," he said, handing the stethoscope back to the doctor who took it automatically. "We had better try to get the suit off."

There were no seams or fastenings visible, nor could Joze find anything when he ran his fingers over the smooth surface. The alien must have understood what they were doing because it jerkingly raised one hand and fumbled at the metal sealing ring about the collar. With a liquid motion the suit split open down the front, the opening bifurcated and ran down each leg. There was a sudden welling of blue liquid from the injured leg. Joze had a quick glimpse of green flesh, strange organs, then he spun about. "Quick, Doctor—your bag. The creature is hurt, that fluid might be blood, we have to help it."

"What can I do?" Dr. Bratos said, unmoving. "Drugs, antiseptics—I might kill it—we know nothing of its body chemistry."

"Then don't use any of those. This is a traumatic injury, you can bind it up, stop the bleeding, can't you?"

"Of course, of course," the old man said and at last his hands had familiar things to do, extracting bandages and sterile gauze from his bag, tape and scissors.

Joze reached into the warm and now murky water and forced himself to reach under the green leg and grasp the hot, green flesh. It was strange—but not terrible. He lifted the limb free of the water and they saw a crushed gap oozing a thick blue fluid. Petar turned away, but the doctor put on a pad of gauze and tightened the bandages about it. The alien was fumbling at the discarded suit beside it in the tub, twisting its leg in Joze's grip. He looked down and saw it take something from the sporran container. Its mouth was moving again, he could hear the dim buzz of its voice.

"What is it? What do you want?" Joze asked.

It was holding the object across its chest now with both hands: it appeared to be a book of some kind. It might be a book, it might be anything.

Yet it was covered in a shiny substance with dark markings on it, and at the edge seemed to be made of many sheets bound together. It could be a book. The leg was twisting now in Joze's grasp and the alien's mouth was open wider, as if it were shouting.

"The bandage will get wet if we put it back into the water," the doctor said.

"Can't you wrap adhesive tape over it, seal it in?"

"In my bag—I'll need some more."

While they talked the alien began to rock back and forth, splashing water from the tub, pulling its leg from Joze's grasp. It still held the book in one thin, multifingered hand, but with the other one it began to tear at the bandages on its leg.

"It's hurting itself, stop it. This is terrible," the doctor said, recoiling from the tub.

Joze snatched a piece of wrapping paper from the floor.

"You fool! You incredible fool!" he shouted. "These compresses you used—they're impregnated with sulfanilamide."

"I always use them, they're the best, American, they prevent wound infection."

Joze pushed him aside and plunged his arms into the tub to tear the bandages free, but the alien reared up out of his grasp, sitting up above the water, its mouth gaping wide. Its eyes were open and staring and Joze recoiled as a stream of water shot from its mouth. There was a gargling sound as the water died to a trickle, and then, as the first air touched the vocal cords, a rising howling scream of pain. It echoed from the plaster ceiling in inhuman agony as the creature threw its arms wide, then fell face forward into the water. It did not move again and, without examining it, Joze knew it was dead.

One arm was twisted back, out of the tub, still grasping the book. Slowly the fingers loosened, and while Joze looked on numbly, unable to move, the book thudded to the floor.

"Help me," Petar said, and Joze turned to see that the doctor had fallen and Petar was kneeling over him. "He fainted, or a heart attack. What can we do?"

His anger was forgotten as Joze kneeled. The doctor seemed to be breathing regularly and his face wasn't flushed, so perhaps it was only a fainting spell. The eyelids fluttered. The priest brushed by and looked down over Joze's shoulder.

Dr. Bratos opened his eyes, looking back and forth at the faces bent over him. "I'm sorry," he said thickly, then the eyes closed again as if to escape the sight of them.

Joze stood and found that he was trembling. The priest was gone. Was it all over? Perhaps they might never have saved the alien, but they should have done better than this. Then he saw the wet spot on the floor and realized the book was gone.

"Father Perc!" he shouted, crying it out like an insult. The man had taken the book, the priceless book!

Joze ran out into the hall and saw the priest coming from the kitchen. His hands were empty. With sudden fear Joze knew what the old man had done and brushed past him into the kitchen and ran to the stove, hurling open the door.

There, among the burning wood, lay the book. It was steaming, almost smoking as it dried, lying open. It was obviously a book, there were marks on the pages of some kind. He turned to grab up the shovel and behind him the fire exploded, sending a white flame across the room. It had almost caught him in the face, but he did not think of that. Pieces of burning wood lay on the floor, and inside the stove there was only the remains of the original fire. Whatever substance the book had been made of was highly inflammable once it had dried out.

"It was evil," the priest said from the doorway. "A *Sao duh*, an abomination with a book of evil. We have been warned, such things have happened before on Earth, and always the faithful must fight back—"

Petar pushed in roughly past him and helped Joze to a chair, brushing the hot embers from his bare skin. Joze had not felt their burn, all he was aware of was an immense weariness.

"Why here?" he asked. "Of all places in the world why here? A few more degrees to the west and the creature would have come down near Trieste with surgeons, hospitals, men, facilities. Or, if it had just stayed on its course a little longer, it could have seen the lights, and would have landed at Rijeka. Something could have been done. But why here?" He surged to his feet, shaking his fist at nothing—and at everything.

"Here, in this superstition-ridden, simple-minded backwater of the country! What kind of world do we live in where there is a five-million-volt electron accelerator not a hundred miles from primitive stupidity? That this creature should come so far, come so close . . . why, why?"

Why?

He dumped back into the chair again feeling older than he had ever felt before and tired beyond measure. What could they have learned from this book?

He sighed, and the sigh came from so deep within him that his whole body trembled as though shaken by awful fever.

The Repairman

The Old Man had that look of intense glee on his face that meant someone was in for a very rough time. Since we were alone, it took no great feat of intelligence to figure it would be me. I talked first, bold attack being the best defense and so forth.

"I quit. Don't bother telling me what dirty job you have cooked up, because I have already quit and you do not want to reveal company secrets to me."

The grin was even wider now and he actually chortled as he thumbed a button on his console. A thick legal document slid out of the delivery slot onto his desk.

"This is your contract," he said. "It tells how and when you will work. A steel-and-vanadium-bound contract that you couldn't crack with a molecular disrupter."

I leaned out quickly, grabbed it and threw it into the air with a single motion. Before it could fall, I had my Solar out and, with a wide-angle shot, burned the contract to ashes.

The Old Man pressed the button again and another contract slid out on his desk. If possible, the smile was still wider now.

"I should have said a duplicate of your contract—like this one here." He made a quick note on his secretary plate. "I have deducted thirteen credits from your salary for the cost of the duplicate—as well as a hundred-credit fine for firing a Solar inside a building."

I slumped, defeated, waiting for the blow to land. The Old Man fondled my contract.

"According to this document, you can't quit. Ever. I therefore I have a little job I know you'll enjoy. Repair job. The Centauri beacon has shut down. It's a Mark III beacon. . . ."

"What kind of beacon?" I asked him. I have repaired hyperspace beacons from one arm of the galaxy to the other and was sure I had worked on every type or model made. But I had never heard of this kind.

"Mark III," the Old Man repeated with sly humor. "I never heard of it either until Records dug up the specs. They found them buried in the back of their oldest warehouse. This was the earliest type of beacon ever built—by Earth, no less. Considering its location on one of the Proxima Centauri planets, it might very well be the first beacon."

I looked at the blueprints he handed me and felt my eyes glaze with horror. "It's a monstrosity! It looks more like a distillery than a beacon—it must be at least a few hundred meters high. I'm a repairman, not an archaeologist. This pile of junk is over two thousand years old. Just forget about it and build a new one."

The Old Man leaned over his desk, breathing into my face. "It would take a year to install a new beacon—besides being too expensive—and this relic is one of the main routes. We have ships making fifteen-light-year detours now."

He leaned back, wiped his hands on his handkerchief and gave me Lecture Forty-four on Company Duty and My Troubles.

"This department is officially called Maintenance and Repair, when it really should be called Troubleshooting. Hyperspace beacons are made to last forever—or damn close to it. When one of them breaks down, it is never an accident, and repairing the thing is never a matter of just plugging in a new part."

He was telling me—the guy who did the job while he sat back on his fat paycheck in an air-conditioned office.

He rambled on. "How I wish that were all it took! I would have a fleet of parts ships and junior mechanics to install them. But it's not like that at all. I have a fleet of expensive ships that are equipped to do almost anything—manned by a bunch of irresponsibles like you."

I nodded moodily at his pointing finger.

"How I wish I could fire you all! Combination space jockeys, mechanics, engineers, soldiers, con men and anything else it takes to do the repairs. I have to browbeat, bribe, blackmail and bulldoze you thugs into doing a simple job. If you think you're fed up, just think how I feel. But the ships must go through! The beacons must operate!"

I recognized this deathless line as the curtain speech and crawled to my feet. He threw the Mark III file at me and went back to scratching in his papers. Just as I reached the door, he looked up and impaled me on his finger again.

"And don't get any fancy ideas about jumping your contract. We can attach that bank account of yours on Algol II long before you could draw the money out."

I smiled, a little weakly, I'm afraid, as if I had never meant to keep that account a secret. His spies were getting more efficient every day. Walking down the hall, I tried to figure a way to transfer the money without his catching on—and knew at the same time he was figuring a way to outfigure me.

It was all very depressing so I stopped for a drink, then went on to the spaceport.

By the time the ship was serviced, I had a course charted. The nearest beacon to the broken-down Proxima Centauri beacon was on one of the planets of Beta Circinus and I headed there first, a short trip of only about nine days in hyperspace.

To understand the importance of the beacons, you have to understand hyperspace. Not that many people do, but it is easy enough to understand that in this nonspace the regular rules don't apply. Speed and measurements are a matter of relationship, not constant facts like the fixed universe.

The first ships to enter hyperspace had no place to go—and no way to even tell if they had moved. The beacons solved that problem and opened the entire universe. They're built on planets and generate tremendous amounts of power. This power is turned into radiation that is punched through into hyperspace. Every beacon has a code signal as part of its radiation and represents a measurable point in hyperspace. Triangulation and quadrature of the beacons works for navigation—only it follows its own rules. The rules are complex and variable, but they are still rules that a navigator can follow.

For a hyperspace jump, you need at least four beacons for an accurate fix. For long jumps, navigators use as many as seven or eight. So every beacon is important and every one has to keep operating. That is where I and the other troubleshooters came in.

We travel in well-stocked ships that carry a little bit of everything; only one man to a ship because that is all it takes to operate the overly efficient repair machinery. Due to the very nature of our job, we spend most of our time just rocketing through normal space. After all when a beacon breaks down, how do you find it?

Not through hyperspace. All you can do is approach as close as you can by using other beacons, then finish the trip in normal space. This can take months, and often does.

This job didn't turn out to be quite that bad. I zeroed the Beta Circinus beacon and ran a complicated eight-point problem through the navigator, using every beacon I could get an accurate fix on. The computer gave me a course with an estimated point of arrival as well as a built-in safety factor I never could eliminate from the machine.

I would much rather take a chance of breaking through near some star than spend time just barreling through normal space, but apparently Tech knows this, too. They had a safety factor built into the computer so you couldn't end up inside a sun no matter how hard you tried. I'm sure there was no humaneness in this decision. They just didn't want lose the ship.

It was a twenty-hour jump, ship's time, and I came through in the middle of nowhere. The robot analyzer chuckled to itself and scanned all the stars, comparing them to the spectra of Proxima Centauri. It finally rang a bell and blinked a light. I peeped through the eyepiece.

A last reading with the photocell gave me the apparent magnitude and a comparison with its absolute magnitude showed its distance. Not as bad as I had thought—a six-week run, give or take a few days. After feeding a course tape into the robot pilot, I strapped into the acceleration tank and went to sleep.

The time went fast. I rebuilt my camera for about the twentieth time and just about finished a correspondence course in nucleonics. Most repairmen take these courses. They have a value in themselves, because you never know what bit of odd information will come in handy. Not only that, the company grades your pay by the number of specialties you can handle. All this, with some oil painting and free-fall workouts in the gym, passed the time. I was asleep when the alarm went off that announced planetary distance.

Planet Two, where the beacon was situated according to the old charts, was a mushy-looking, wet kind of globe. I worked hard to make sense out of the ancient directions and finally located the right area. Staying outside the atmosphere, I sent a Flying Eye down to look things over. In this business, you learn early when and where to risk your own skin. The Eye would be good enough for the preliminary survey.

The old boys had enough brains to choose a traceable site for the beacon, equidistant on a line between two of the most prominent mountain peaks. I located the peaks easily enough and started the Eye out from the first peak and kept on a course directly toward the second. There was a nose and a tail radar in the Eye and I fed their signals into a scope as an amplitude curve. When the two peaks coincided, I spun the Eye controls and dived the thing down.

I cut out the radar and cut in the nose orthicon and sat back to watch the beacon appear on the screen.

The image blinked, focused—and a great damn pyramid swam into view. I cursed and wheeled the Eye in circles, scanning the surrounding country. It was flat, marshy bottomland without a bump. The only thing within a ten-mile circle was this pyramid—and that definitely wasn't my beacon.

Or was it?

I dived the Eye lower. The pyramid was a crude-looking thing of undressed stone, without carvings or decorations. There was a shimmer of light from the top and I took a closer look at it. On the peak of the pyramid was a hollow basin filled with water. When I saw that, something clicked in my mind.

Locking the Eye in a circular course, I dug through the Mark III plans—and there it was. The beacon had a precipitating field and a basin on top of it for water; this was used to cool the reactor that powered the monstrosity. If the water was still there, the beacon was still there—inside the pyramid. The natives, who, of course, weren't even mentioned by the idiots who constructed the thing, had built a nice heavy, thick stone pyramid under the beacon.

I took another look at the screen and realized that I had locked the Eye into a circular orbit about twenty feet above the pyramid. The summit of the stone pile was now covered with lizards of some type, apparently the local life form. They had what looked like throwing stones and arbalests and were trying to shoot down the Eye; a cloud of rocks and arrows was flying in every direction.

I pulled the Eye straight up and away and threw it in the control circuit that would return it automatically to the ship.

Then I went to the galley for a long strong drink. My beacon was not only locked inside a mountain of handmade stone, but I managed to irritate the things who had built the pyramid. This was clearly designed to drive a stronger man than me to the bottle.

Normally, a repairman stays away from native cultures. They are poison. Anthropologists may not mind being dissected for their science, but a repairman wants to make no sacrifices of any kind for his job. For this reason, most beacons are built on uninhabited planets. If a beacon has to go on a planet with a culture, it is usually built in some inaccessible place.

Why this beacon had been built within reach of the local claws, I had yet to find out. But that would come in time. The first thing to do was to make contact. To make contact, you have to know the local language.

And for that, I had long before worked out a system that was foolproof.

I had a Pryeye of my own construction. It looked like a piece of rock about a foot long. Once on the ground, it would never be noticed, though it was a little disconcerting to see it float by. I located a lizard town about a thousand kilometers from the pyramid and dropped the Eye. It swished down and landed at night in the bank of the local mud wallow. This was favorite spot that drew a good crowd during the day. In the morning, when the first wallowers arrived, I flipped on the recorder.

After about five of the local days, I had a sea of native conversation in my memory bank of the machine translator and had tagged a few expressions. This is fairly easy to do when you have a machine memory to work with. One of the lizards gargled at another one and the second one turned around. I tagged the expression with the phrase "Hey, George!" and waited my chance to use it. Later the same day, I caught one of them alone and shouted "Hey, George!" at him. It gurgled out through the speaker in the local tongue and he turned around.

When you get enough reference phrases in the memory bank, the

MT brain takes over and starts filling in the missing pieces. As soon as the MT could give a running translation of any conversation it heard, I figured it was time to make contact.

I found him easily enough. He was the Centurian version of a goat boy and he herded a particularly loathsome form of local life, in the swamps outside the town. I had one of the working Eyes dig a cave in an outcropping of rock and wait for him.

When he passed next day, I whispered into the mike: "Welcome, O Goat Boy Grandson! This your grandfather's spirit speaking from paradise." This fitted in with what I could make out of the local religion.

Goat Boy stopped as if he'd been shot. Before he could move, I pushed a switch and a handful of the local currency, wampum-type shells, rolled out of the cave and landed at his feet.

"Here is some money from paradise, because you have been a good boy." Not really from paradise—I had lifted it from the treasury the night before. "Come back tomorrow and we'll talk some more," I called after the fleeing figure. I was pleased to notice that he took the cash before taking off.

After that, Grandpa in paradise had many heart-to-heart talks with Grandson, who found the heavenly loot more than he could resist. Grandpa had been out of touch with things since his death and Goat Boy happily filled him in.

I learned all I needed to know of the history, past and recent, and it wasn't nice.

In addition to the pyramid being around the beacon, there was a nice little religious war going on around the pyramid.

It all began with the land bridge. Apparently the local lizards had been living in the distant swamps when the beacon had been built, but the builders hadn't thought much of them. They were a low type and confined to a distant continent. The idea that the race would develop and might reach this continent never occurred to the beacon mechanics. Which is, of course, what happened.

A little geological turnover, a swampy land bridge formed in the right spot, and the lizards began to wander up Beacon Valley. And found religion. A shiny metal temple out of which poured a constant stream of magic water—the reactor-cooling water pumped down from the atmosphere condenser on the roof. The radioactivity in the water didn't hurt the natives. It caused mutations that bred in time.

A city was built around the temple and, through the centuries, the pyramid was put up around the beacon. A special branch of the priesthood served the temple. All went well until one of the priests violated the temple and destroyed the holy waters. There had been revolt, strife, murder and destruction since then. But still the holy waters would not flow. Now armed mobs fought around the temple each day and a new band of priests guarded the sacred fount.

And I had to walk into the middle of that mess and repair the thing.

It would have been easy enough if we were allowed a little mayhem. I could have had a lizard fry, fixed the beacon and taken off. Only "native life forms" were quite well protected. There were spy cells on my ship, all of which I hadn't found, that would cheerfully rat on me when I got back.

Diplomacy was called for. I sighed and dragged out the plastifresh equipment.

Working from 3-D snaps of Grandson, I modeled a passable reptile head over my own features. It was a little short in the jaw, me not having one of their toothy mandibles, but that was all right. I didn't have to look exactly like them, just something close, to soothe the native mind. It's logical. If I were an ignorant aborigine of Earth and I ran into a Spican, who looks like a two-foot gob of dried shellac, I would immediately leave the scene. However, if the Spican was wearing a suit of plastifresh that looked remotely humanoid, I would at least stay and talk to him. This was what I was aiming to do with the Centaurians.

When the head was done, I peeled it off and attached it to an attractive suit of green plastic, complete with tail. I was really glad they had tails. The lizards didn't wear clothes and I wanted to take along a lot of electronic equipment. I built the tail over a metal frame that anchored around my waist. Then I filled the frame with all the equipment I would need and began to wire the suit.

When it was done, I tried it on in front of a full-length mirror. It was horrible but effective. The tail dragged me down in the rear and gave me a duck waddle, but that only helped the resemblance.

That night I took the ship down into the hills nearest the pyramid, an out-of-the-way dry spot where the amphibious natives would never go. A little before dawn, the Eye hooked onto my shoulders and we sailed straight up. We hovered above the temple at about two thousand meters, until it was light, then dropped down. It must have been a grand sight. The Eye was camouflaged to look like a flying lizard, sort of a cardboard pterodactyl. The slowly flapping wings obviously had nothing to do with our flight. But it was impressive enough for the natives. The first one that spotted me screamed and dropped over on his back. The others came running. They milled about and piled on top of one another, and by the time I had landed in the plaza fronting the temple the priesthood arrived.

I folded my arms in a regal stance. "Greetings, O noble servers of the Great God," I said. Of course I didn't say it out loud, just whispered softly enough for the throat mike to catch. This was radioed back to the MT and the translation shot back to a speaker in my jaws.

The natives chomped and rattled and the translation rolled out almost instantly. I had the volume turned up and the whole square echoed.

Some of the more credulous natives prostrated themselves and others fled screaming. One doubtful type raised a spear, but no one else tried that after the pterodactyl eye picked him up and dropped him in the swamp. The priests were a hard-headed lot and weren't buying any lizards in a poke; they just stood and muttered. I had to take the offensive again.

"Begone, O faithful steed," I said to the Eye, and pressed the control in my palm at the same time.

It took off straight up a bit faster than I wanted; little pieces of wind-torn plastic rained down. While the crowd was ogling this ascent, I walked through the temple doors.

"I would talk with you, O noble priests," I said.

Before they could think up a good answer, I was inside.

The temple was a small one built against the base of the pyramid. I hoped I wasn't breaking too many taboos by going in; I wasn't stopped, so it looked all right. The temple was a single room with a murky-looking pool at one end. Sloshing in the pool was an ancient reptile who clearly was one of the leaders. I waddled toward him and he gave me a cold and fishy eye, then growled something.

The MT whispered into my ear, "Just what in the name of the thirteenth sin are you and what are you doing here?"

I drew up my scaly figure in a noble gesture and pointed toward the ceiling. "I come from your ancestors to help you. I am here to restore the Holy Waters."

This raised a buzz of conversation behind me, but got no rise out of the chief. He sank slowly into the water until only his eyes were showing. I could almost hear the wheel turning behind that moss-covered forehead. Then he lunged up and pointed a dripping finger at me.

"You are a liar! You are no ancestor of ours! We will—"

"Stop!" I thundered before he got so far in that he couldn't back out. "I said your ancestors sent me as emissary—I am not one of your ancestors. Do not try to harm me or the wrath of those who have Passed On will turn against you."

When I said this, I turned to jab a claw at the other priests using the motion to cover my flicking a coin grenade toward them. It blew a nice hole in the door with a great show of noise and smoke.

The First Lizard knew I was talking sense then and immediately called a meeting of the shamans. It, of course, took place in the public bathtub and I had to join them there. We jawed and gurgled for about an hour and settled all the major points. I found out that they were new priests; the previous ones had all been boiled for letting the Holy Waters cease.

I explained that I was there only to help them restore the flow of the waters. They bought this, tentatively, and we all heaved out of the tub and trickled muddy paths across the floor. There was a bolted and guarded door that led into the pyramid proper. While it was being opened, the First Lizard turned to me.

"Undoubtedly you know of the rule," he said. "Because the old priests did pry and peer, it was ordered henceforth that only the blind could enter the Holy of Holies." I'd swear he was smiling, if thirty teeth peeking out of what looked like a crack in an old suitcase can be called smiling.

He was also signaling to him an underpriest who carried a brazier of charcoal complete with red-hot irons. All I could do was stand and watch as he stirred up the coals, pulled out the ruddiest iron and turned toward me. He was just drawing a bead on my right eyeball when my brain got back in gear.

"Of course," I said, "blinding is only right. But in my case you will have to blind me before I leave the Holy of Holies, not now. I need my eyes to see and mend the Fount of Holy Waters. Once the waters flow again, I will laugh as I hurl myself on the burning iron."

He took a good thirty seconds to think it over and had to agree with me. The local torturer sniffled a bit and threw a little more charcoal on the fire. The gate crashed open and I stalked through; then it banged to behind me and I was alone in the dark.

But not for long—there was a shuffling nearby and I took a chance and turned on my flash. Three priests were groping toward me, their eye sockets red pits of burned flesh. They knew what I wanted and led the way without a word.

A crumbling and cracked stone stairway brought us up to a solid metal doorway labeled in archaic script MARK III BEACON AUTHORIZED PERSONNEL ONLY. The overly trusting builders counted on the sign to do the whole job, for there wasn't a trace of a lock on the door. One lizard merely turned the handle and we were inside the beacon.

I unzipped the front of my camouflage suit and pulled out the blueprints. With the faithful priests stumbling after me I found that there was a residue of charge in the emergency batteries, just enough to give a dim light. The meters and indicators looked to be in good shape; if anything, unexpectedly bright from constant polishing. I checked the readings carefully and found just what I had suspected.

One of the eager lizards had managed to open the circuit box and had polished the switches inside. While doing this, he had thrown one of the switches and that had caused the trouble.

Rather, that had started the trouble. It wasn't going to be ended by just reversing the water-valve switch. This valve was supposed to be used only for repairs, after the pile had been damped. When the water was cut off with the pile in operation, it had started to overheat and the automatic safeties had dumped the charge down the pit.

I could start the water again easily enough, but there was no fuel left in the reactor.

I wasn't going to play with the fuel problem at all. It would be far easier to install a new power plant. I had one in the ship that was about a tenth of the size of the ancient bucket of bolts. Before I sent for it, I checked over the rest of the beacon. In two thousand years there should be some sort of wear.

The old boys had built well, I'll give them credit for that. Ninety percent of the machinery had no moving parts and had suffered no wear whatever. Other parts they beefed up figuring they would wear, but slowly. The water-feed pipe from the roof for example. The pipe walls were at least three meters thick—and the pipe opening itself no bigger than my head. There were some things I could do, though, and I made a list of parts.

The parts, the new power plant and a few other odds and ends were chuted into a neat pile on the ship. I checked all the parts by screen before they were loaded into a small metal crate. In the darkest hour before dawn, the heavy-duty Eye dropped the crate outside the temple and darted away without being seen.

I watched the priests thorough the Pryeye while they tried to open it. When they had given up, I boomed orders at them through a speaker in the crate. They spent most of the day sweating the heavy box up through the narrow temple stairs and I enjoyed a good sleep. It was resting inside the beacon door when I woke up.

The repair didn't take long, though there was plenty of groaning from the blind lizards when they heard me ripping the wall open to get to the power leads. I even hooked a gadget to the water pipe so their Holy Waters would have the usual refreshing radioactivity when they started flowing again. The moment this was all finished, I did the job they waited for.

I threw the switch that started the water flowing again.

There were a few minutes while the water began to gurgle down through the dry pipe. Then a roar came from outside the pyramid that must have shaken its stone walls. Shaking my hands once over my head, I went down for the eye-burning ceremony.

The blind lizards were waiting for me by the door and looked even unhappier than usual. When I tried the door, I found out why—it was bolted and barred from the other side.

"It has been decided," a lizard said, "that you shall remain here forever and tend to the Holy Waters. We will stay with you and serve your every need."

A delightful prospect, eternity spent in a locked beacon with three blind lizards. In spite of their hospitality, I couldn't accept.

"What! You dare interfere with the messenger of your ancestors!" I had the speaker on full volume and the vibration almost shook my head off.

The lizards cringed and I set my Solar for a narrow beam and ran it around the doorjamb. There was a great crunching and banging from the junk piled against it, and then the door swung free. I threw it open. Before they could protest, I had pushed the priests out through it.

The rest of their clan showed up at the foot of the stairs and made a great ruckus while I finished welding the door shut. Running through the crowd, I faced up to the First Lizard in his tub. He sank slowly beneath the surface.

"What lack of courtesy!" I shouted. He made little bubbles in the water. "The ancestors are annoyed and have decided to forbid entrance to the Inner Temple forever; though, out of kindness, they will let the waters flow. Now I must return—on with the blinding ceremony!"

The torture-master was too frightened to move, so I grabbed out his hot iron. A touch on the side of my face dropped a steel plate over my eyes, under the plastiskin. Then I jammed the iron hard into my phony eye sockets and the plastic gave off an authentic odor. A cry went up from the crowd as I dropped the iron and staggered in blind circles. I must admit it went off pretty well.

Before they could get any more bright ideas, I threw the switch and my plastic pterodactyl sailed in through the door.

I couldn't see it, of course, but I knew it had arrived when the grapples in the claws latched onto the steel plates on my shoulders. I had got turned around after the eye burning and my flying beast hooked onto me backward. I had meant to sail out bravely, blind eyes facing into the sunset. Instead, I faced the crowd as I soared away, so I made the most of a bad situation and threw them a snappy military salute. Then I was out in the fresh air and away.

When I lifted the plate and poked holes in the seared plastic, I could see the pyramid growing smaller behind me, water gushing out of the base and a happy crowd of reptiles sporting in its radioactive rush. I counted off on my talons to see if I had forgotten anything.

One: The beacon was repaired.

Two: The door was sealed, so there should be no more sabotage, accidental or deliberate.

Three: The priest should be satisfied. The water was running again, my eyes had been duly burned out, and they were back in business. Which added up to—

Four: The fact that they would probably let another repairman in, under the same conditions, if the beacon conked out again. At least I had done nothing, like butchering a few of them, that would make them antagonistic toward future ancestral messengers.

I stripped off my tattered lizard suit back in the ship, very glad it would be some other repairman who would get the job.

Pressure

The tension inside the ship rose as the pressure outside increased—
and at the same rate. Perhaps it was because Nissim and Aldo had
nothing at all to do. They had time to think too much. They would
glance at the pressure gauges and then quickly away, reluctantly repeating this action over and over. Aldo knotted his fingers and was
uncomfortably aware of the cold dampness of his skin, while Nissim
chain-smoked cigarette after cigarette. Only Stan Brandon—the man
with the responsibility—stayed calm and alert. While he studied his
instruments he appeared completely relaxed, and when he made an
adjustment on the controls there was a certain dash to his actions.
For some reason this infuriated the other men, though neither would
admit it.

"The pressure gauge has failed!" Nissim gasped, leaning forward
against the restraint of his safety harness. "It reads zero."

"It's supposed to, Doc, built that way," Stan said, smiling. He
reached over and flicked a switch. The needle jumped while the
scale reading changed. "Only way to measure these kind of pressures. Chunks of metal and crystal in the outer hull, different com-
pressibilities, and they compress to destruction. So we switch to the
next one—"

"Yes, yes, I know all that."

Nissim contained his temper and dragged heavily on his cigarette.
Of course he had been told about the gauges during the briefings. For
an instant there it had just slipped his mind. The needle once more
moved in steady pace up the scale. Nissim looked at it, looked away,
thought about what was outside this seamless, windowless metal
sphere, then, in spite of himself, glanced back at the dial again and
felt the dampness on the palms of his hands. Nissim Ben-Haim, leading physicist at the University of Tel Aviv, had too much imagination.

So did Aldo Gabrielli and he knew it; he wished that he had something to do besides watch and wait. Dark-haired, swarthy, with a
magnificent nose, he looked typically Italian and was an eleventh-
generation American. His position in electronic engineering was a
secure as Nissim's in physics—if not better. He was considered a
genius whose work with the scantron amplifier had revolutionized
matter transmitter mechanics. He was scared.

The *C. Huygens* fell down through the thickening atmosphere of

Saturn. That was the ship's official name, but the men who had assembled her at Saturn One called the vehicle simply "the Ball." Essentially that is just what it was, a solid metal sphere with walls ten meters thick, enclosing the relatively minuscule space in its center. The immense, wedge-shaped sections had been cast in the asteroid belt and sent to the Saturn One satellite station for assembly. There, in high orbit, with the unbelievable beauty of the rings and the great bulk of the planet hanging above them, the Ball had taken shape. Molecular welding had joined the sections into a seamless whole, and, just before the final wedge had been slid into place, the MT screen had been carefully placed inside. When the last piece had been joined to the others the only access to the center of the Ball was through the matter transmitter. Once the welders, with their destroying radiation, were through, the final construction could begin. The specially constructed large MT screen had been built under the floor, on which was soon mounted the supplies, atmosphere equipment, and apparatus that made the Ball livable for men. Then the controls were installed, as well as the external tanks and jets that transformed it into an atomic-engined space vessel. This was the ship that would drop down to the surface of Saturn.

Eighty years previously the *C. Huygens* could not have been built since the pressure-compacted alloys had not yet been developed. Forty-two years earlier it could not have been assembled because molecular welding had not been invented. Ten years ago the unpierced hull could not have been used since that was when atomic differentiation had first been made practical. No wires or wave guides weakened the solidity of the metal hull of the Ball. Instead, areas of differentiation passed through the alloy, chemically and physically the same as the metal around them, yet capable of carrying separate electric impulses. Taken in its entirety, the Ball was a tribute to the expanding knowledge of mankind. Taking the three men to the bottom of Saturn's twenty-thousand-mile-deep atmosphere, it was a sealed prison cell.

All of them had been conditioned against claustrophobia, yet still they felt it.

"Come in control, how do you read me?" Stan said into his microphone, then switched to receive with a quick movement of his jaw against the switch. There was a few seconds' delay as the recording tape clicked out through the MT screen and the return tape rolled into his receiver.

"One and three," the speaker hissed, a sibilant edge to all the sounds.

"That's the beginning of the sigma effect," Aldo said, his hands still for the first time. He looked deliberately at the pressure gauge.

"A hundred thirty-five thousand atmospheres, that's the usual depth where it begins."

"I want to look at the tape that came through," Nissim said, grinding out his cigarette. He reached for his harness release.

"Don't do that, Doc," Stan said, raising a warning hand. "This has been a smooth drop so far but it's sure to get bumpy soon. You know what the winds in this atmosphere must be like. So far we've been in some kind of jet stream and moving laterally with it. That's not going to last forever. I'll have them send another tape through your repeater."

"It will take only a moment," Nissim said, but his hand hesitated on the release.

"You can break your skull quicker than that," Stan said and, as if to verify his words, the immense bulk of the Ball surged violently sideways, tipping as it did so. The two scientists clung to their couches while the pilot rightened the ship.

"You're an accurate prophet of doom," Aldo said. "Do you dispense good omens as well?"

"Only on Tuesdays, Doc," Stan answered imperturbably as the pressure gauge died again and he switched to the next transmitter. "Rate of fall steady."

"This is taking an infernally long time," Nissim complained, lighting a cigarette.

"Twenty thousand miles to the bottom, Doc, and we don't want to hit too hard."

"I am well acquainted with the thickness of Saturn's atmosphere," Nissim said angrily. "And could you refrain from calling me Doc? If for no other reason than that you address Doctor Gabrielli in the same way, and a certain confusion results."

"Right you are, Doc." The pilot turned and winked as he heard the physicist's angry gasp. "That was just a joke. We're all in the same boat so we can all be cobbers just like at home. Call me Stan and I'll call you Nissim. And what about you, Doc, going to be Aldo?"

Aldo Gabrielli pretended that he did not hear. The pilot was an infuriating man. "What is that?" he asked as a continuous, faint vibration began to shake the Ball.

"Hard to tell," the pilot answered, throwing switches rapidly, then examining the results on his screens. "Something out there, clouds maybe, that we're moving through. Varying impacts on the hull."

"Crystallization," Nissim said, looking at the pressure gauge. "The top of the atmosphere is two hundred and ten degrees below zero Fahrenheit, but up there the low vapor pressure prevents freezing. The pressure is much higher now. We must be falling through clouds of methane and ammonia crystals—"

"I've just lost my last radar," Stan said. "Carried away."

"We should have had television pickups; we could see what is out there," Nissim said.

"See what?" Aldo asked. "Hydrogen clouds with frozen crystals in them? They would have been destroyed like the other instruments. The radio altimeter is the only instrument that's essential."

"And it's working fine," Stan announced happily.

"Still too high for a reading, but it's in the green. Should be; it's an integral part of the hull."

Nissim sipped from the water tube on the side of his couch. Aldo's mouth was suddenly dry as he saw this and he drank, too. The endless fall continued.

"How long have I been asleep?" Nissim asked, surprised that he had actually dropped off despite the tension.

"Just a few hours," Stan told him. "You seemed to enjoy it. Snored like a water buffalo."

"My wife always says a camel." He looked at his watch. "You've been awake for over seventy-two hours. Don't you feel it?"

"No. I'll catch up later. I've got pills here, and it's not the first time that I've pulled a long watch."

Nissim settled back on the couch and saw that Aldo was muttering figures to himself while he worked out a problem on his hand calculator. No sensation can be experienced indefinitely, he thought, even fear. We were both bloody frightened up there, but it can't go on forever.

He felt a slight tremble of emotion as he looked at the pressure gauge, but it passed quickly.

"It reads solid," Stan said, "but the height keeps shifting." There were dark smears, like arcs of soot, under his eyes, and he had been on drugs for the last thirty hours.

"It must be liquid ammonia and methane," Nissim said. "Or semi-liquid, changing back and forth from gas to liquid. God knows, anything is possible with those pressures outside. Just under a million atmospheres. Unbelievable."

"I believe it," Aldo told him. "Can we move laterally and perhaps find something solid underneath us?"

"I've been doing that for the last hour. We either have to sink into that soup, or hop up again for another drop. I'm not going to try and balance her on her jets, not with the G's we have waiting for us out there."

"Do we have fuel for a hop?"

"Yes, but I want to hold it for a reserve. We're down close to thirty percent."

"I vote to take the plunge," Nissim said. "If there is liquid down there it probably covers the entire surface. With these pressures and the wind I'm sure that any irregularities would be scoured flat in a relatively short geological time."

"I don't agree," Aldo said. "But someone else can investigate that. I vote to drop on the fuel situation alone."

"Three to nothing then, gents. Down we go."

The steady descent continued. The pilot slowed the immense weight of the Ball as they approached the shifting interface, but there was no unusual buffeting when they entered the liquid because the change was so gradual.

"I have a reading now," Stan said, excited for the first time. "It's holding steady at fifteen kilometers. There may be a bottom to all this after all."

The other two men did not talk as the drop continued, fearful of distracting the pilot. Yet this was the easiest part of the voyage. The lower they sank the less the disturbance around them. At one kilometer there was no buffeting or sideways motion in the slightest. They fell slowly as the bottom approached. At five hundred meters Stan turned over the landing to the computer and, hand poised, stood ready to take command should there be difficulties. The engines blasted lightly, cut off, and, with a single grinding thud, they were down. Stan flipped the override and killed the engines.

"That's it," he said, stretching hugely. "We've landed on Saturn. And that calls for a drink." He mumbled a complaint when he discovered that it took most of his strength to push up from the chair.

"Two point six-four gravities," Nissim said, looking at the reading on the delicate quartz spring balance on his board. "It's not going to be easy to work under all these G's."

"What we have to do shouldn't take long," Aldo said. "Let's have that drink. Then Stan can get some sleep while we start on the MT."

"I'll buy that. My job is done and I'm just a spectator until you boys get me home. Here's to us." They raised their glasses with difficulty and drank.

The burden of the more-than-doubled gravity had been anticipated. Aldo and the pilot changed acceleration couches so that the engineer could face the instrument panels and the MT screen. When the restraining catches were released, Nissim's couch also swung about so that he could reach the screen. Before these preparations were finished Stan had flattened his couch and was soundly asleep. The other two men did not notice: they were now able to start on their part of the mission. Aldo, as the MT specialist, made the preparatory tests while Nissim watched closely.

"All the remotes we sent down developed sigma effect before they had penetrated a fifth of the atmosphere," Aldo said, plugging in the test instruments. "Once the effect was strong enough we lost all control and we have never had an accurate track past the halfway mark. We've just lost contact with them." He checked all the readings twice and left the wave form on the scope when he sank back to rest his tired back and arms.

"The wave looks right," Nissim said.

"It is. So is everything else. Which means that one half of your theory, at least, is correct."

"Wonderful!" Nissim said, smiling for the first time since they had begun the flight. His fists clenched as he thought of the verbal drubbings he would administer to the other physicists who had been rash enough to disagree with him. "Then the error is not in the transmitter?"

"Absolutely."

"Then let's transmit and see if the signal gets through. The receiver is tuned and waiting."

"*C. Huygens* calling Saturn One, come in. How do you read me?"

They both watched as the transcribed tape clicked into the face of the screen and vanished; then Aldo switched the MT to receive. Nothing happened. He waited sixty seconds and sent the message again—with the same results.

"And there is the proof," Nissim said happily. "Transmitter, perfect. Receiver, perfect—we can count on that. But no signal getting through. Therefore my spatial distortion factor must be present. Once we correct for that, contact will be reestablished."

"Soon, I hope," Aldo said, slightly depressed, looking up at the curved walls of their cell. "Because until the correction is made we are staying right here, sealed into the heart of this king-sized ball bearing. And even if there were an exit we have no place to go."

Stan was still exhausted when he woke up; sleep under this heavy gravity was less than satisfactory. He yawned and shifted position, but stretching proved more debilitating than satisfying. When he turned to the others he saw Nissim working concentratedly with his computer while Aldo held a bloodstained handkerchief to his nose.

"Gravity bleeding?" Stan asked. "I better paint it with some adrenaline."

"Not gravity." Aldo's voice was muffled by the cloth. "That bastard hit me."

"Right on that big beak," Nissim said, not looking up from his computer. "It was too good a target to miss."

"What seems to be the trouble?" Stan asked, glancing quickly from one to the other. "Isn't the MT working?"

"No it's not," Aldo said warmly. "And our friend here blames me for that and—"

"The theory is correct, the mechanics of application are wrong."

"—when I suggested that there might be an error or two in his equations he swung on me in a fit of infantile anger."

Stan moved in quickly to stop the developing squabble, his drill-field voice drowning out the others.

"Hold on now. Don't both talk at once because I can't understand a thing. Won't someone please put me into the picture and let me know exactly what's happening?"

"Of course," Nissim said, then waited impatiently until Aldo's complaints had died down. "How much do you know about MT theory?"

"The answer is simple—nothing. I'm a torch jockey and I stick to my trade. Someone builds them, someone fixes them, I fly them. Would you kindly simplify?"

"I'll attempt to." Nissim pursed his lips in thought. "The first thing you must realize is that an MT does not scan and transmit like, say, a television transmitter does. No signal, as we commonly think of signals, is sent. What is done is that the plane of the screen of the transmitter is placed into a state of matter that is not a part of space as we normally know it. The receiving screen is placed in the same condition and tuning is accomplished once they are locked onto the same frequency. In a sense they become part of one another and the distance of the intervening space does not matter. If you step into one you will step out of the other without any awareness of either time or spatial separation. I am explaining very badly."

"You're doing fine, Nissim. What comes next?"

"The fact that spatial distance between transmitter and receiver does not matter, but the condition of that space does—"

"You're beginning to lose me."

"I'll give you a not unrelated example. Light rays travel in a straight line through space, unless interfered with in some physical manner—refraction, reflection, so forth. But—these rays can also be bent when they pass through an intense gravitational field such as that of the sun. We have noticed the same kind of effect in MT, and corrections are always made for the bulk of the Earth or other planetary bodies. Another condition affecting space appears deep in the frigid soup this planet calls an atmosphere. The incredible pressures affect the very binding energy of the atoms and stresses are produced. These interfere with the MT relationships. Before we can move an object from one MT screen to another down here we must make allowances and corrections for these new interferences. I have worked out the corrections, we must now apply them."

"Very simple the way he explains it," Aldo said distastefully, dabbing at his nose and examining the results on his handkerchief. "But it doesn't work out that way in practice. No signals are getting through. And our friend will not agree with me that we'll have to step up the strength of our output if we're ever going to punch through all that pressurized gunk out there."

"It's quality not quantity!" Nissim shouted, and Stan stepped in once again.

"By that do you mean that we're going to have to unlimber the MT monster down under the floor?"

"I damned well do. That's why it was built in the first place, with adjustable components rather than sealed block units."

"It will take us a month to move everything and we'll probably kill ourselves trying," Nissim shouted.

"Not that long, I hope," Stan said, sitting up and trying not to groan with the effort. "And the exercise will be good for our muscles."

It took them almost four days to clear away and get up the flooring, and they were over the edge of exhaustion before they had finished. Mechanical preparations had been made with this eventuality in mind; there were ringbolts to suspend the equipment from, and power hoists to lift it, but a certain amount of physical effort was still needed. In the end almost the entire floor area had been cleared and raised, leaving a ledge around the wall, on which their test equipment and couches alone remained. The rest of the floor consisted of MT screen. From the hard comfort of their couches they looked at it.

"A monster," Stan said. "You could drop a landing barge through it."

"It has more than size," Aldo told him, gasping for air. He could hear the hammer of blood in his ears and was sure that his heart had suffered from the strain. "All the circuitry is beefed up, with spare circuits and a hundred times the power-handling capacity it would need anywhere else."

"How do you dig into its guts for adjustments? I can't see anything except the screen?"

"That's deliberate." He pointed into the threaded hole in the armor, from which they had unscrewed a foot-thick plug. "Our operating controls are in there. Before we leave we put the plug back and it seals itself into place. To make adjustments we have to lift up sections of the screen."

"Am I being dense or is it the gravity? I don't understand."

Aldo was patient. "This MT screen is the whole reason for this expedition. Getting the MT to work down here is vital to us—but only secondary to the original research. When we get out the technicians will come through and replace all the circuitry with solid-state, block-sealed units—then evacuate. The upper section of the interior of the hull will be progressively weakened by automatic drills. This screen will be tuned to another MT in space above the ecliptic. Eventually the weakened Ball will collapse, implode, push right down on top of the screen. The screen will not be harmed because it will transmit all the debris through into space. Then the phasing will be adjusted slowly until transmission stops. At which point we will have access to the bottom of Saturn's sea. The cryogenicists and high-pressure boys are looking forward to that."

Stan nodded but Nissim was looking up at the cluttered dome above, almost openmouthed, thinking of that imploding mass of metal, the pressure of the poison sea behind it . . .

"Let's get started," he said quickly, struggling to rise. "Get the screens up and the changes made. It's time we were getting back."

The other men helped with the labor of lifting the screen segments, but only Aldo could make the needed adjustments. He worked intensely, cursing feebly, on the units that the remote handler placed before him. When he was too tired he stopped and closed his eyes so he would not see Nissim's worried glances at him, up at the dome above, and back to him again. Stan served them food and doled out the G drugs and stimulants with a cheerful air. He talked about the varied experiences of space flight, which monologue he enjoyed even if they did not.

Then the job was done, the tests completed and the last segment of screen slid back into place. Aldo reached into the control pit and pressed a switch: the dark surface changed to the familiar shimmer of MT operation.

"Transmitting," he said. "Here, send this," Stan said, scribbling *How do you read us?* on a piece of paper. He threw it far out into the center of the screen and it sank from sight. "Now receive."

Aldo flipped the switch and the surface of the screen changed. Nothing else happened. For a heartbeat of time they watched, unmoving, not breathing, staring at that barren surface.

Then, with smooth sinuousness, a length of recording tape sprang into existence and, bent by its own weight, curved and began to pile up. Nissim was the nearest and he reached out and grabbed it, reeling it in until the cut end appeared.

"It works!" Stan shouted.

"Partially," Nissim said coldly. "The quality of transmission is sure to be off and finer adjustments will have to be made. But they can analyze at the receiving end and send us specific instructions."

He fed the tape into the player and switched it on. A booming squawking echoed from the metal walls. It could be perceived as the sound of a human voice only with a great effort.

"Finer adjustments," Nissim said with a small smile. The smile vanished instantly as the Ball rocked to one side, then slowly returned to vertical. "Something has pushed us," he gasped.

"Currents perhaps," Aldo said, clutching to his couch as the motion slowly damped, "or maybe solid floes; there's no way to tell. It's past time we got out of here."

They were fighting against the unending fatigue now, but they tried to ignore it. The end was so close and the security of Saturn One station just a step away. Nissim computed the needed adjustments while the other two lifted up the screen sections again and reset the components. It was the worst kind of work to do in the more-than-doubled gravity. Yet, within a solar day they were getting sound-perfect tapes and the samples of materials they sent back tested out correct to five decimal places. The occasional jarring of the Ball continued and they did their best not to think about it.

"We're ready to begin live testing now," Nissim said into the microphone. Aldo watched the tape with these recorded words vanish into the screen and resisted a strong impulse to hurl himself after it. Wait. Soon now. He switched to receive.

"I do not think I have ever been in one place for so long before in my entire life," Nissim said, staring, like the others, at the screen. "Even in college in Iceland I went home to Israel every night."

"We take the MT screens for granted," Aldo said. "All the time we were working at Satellite One on this project I commuted to New York City after work. We take it for granted until something like this happens. It's easier for you, Stan."

"Me?" the pilot looked up, raising his eyebrows. "I'm no different. I get to New Zealand every chance I have." His gaze went back instantly to the empty screen.

"I don't mean that. It's just that you are used to being alone in a ship, piloting, for longer times. Maybe that's good training. You don't seem as . . . well, as bothered by all this as we do."

Nissim nodded silent agreement and Stan barked a short, hard laugh.

"Don't kid yourself. When you sweat, I sweat. I've just been trained different. Panic in my work and you're dead. Panic in your work and it just means taking a few extra drinks before dinner to cool down.

You've never had the need to exercise control so you've never bothered to learn."

"That's just not true," Nissim said. "We're civilized men, not animals, with willpower—"

"Where was it when you popped Aldo on the beak?"

Nissim grinned wryly. "Score one for your side. I admit that I can be emotional—but that's an essential part of the human existence. Yet you personally have—what should I say—perhaps the kind of personality that is not as easily disturbed."

"Cut me, I bleed. It's training that keeps one from pressing the panic button. Pilots have been like that right back to the year one. I suppose they have personalities that lean that way to begin with, but it's only constant practice that makes the control automatic. Did you ever hear the recordings in the Voices of Space series?"

The other two shook their heads, looking at the still-empty screen.

"You should. You can't guess the date that any recording was made to within fifty years. Training for control and clarity is always the same. The best example is the first, the first man in space, Yuri Gagarin. There are plenty of examples of his voice, including the very last. He was flying an atmosphere craft of some sort, and he had trouble. He could have ejected and escaped safely—but he was over a populated area. So he rode the craft in and killed himself. His voice, right up to the very end, sounded just like all of his other recordings."

"That's unnatural," Nissim said. "He must have been a very different kind of man from the rest of us."

"You've missed my point completely."

"Look!" Aldo said. They all stopped talking as a guinea pig came up through the screen and dropped back to its surface. Stan picked it up.

"Looks great," he said. "Good fur, fine whiskers, warm. And dead." He glanced back and forth at their fatigue-drawn, panicked faces and smiled. "No need to worry. We don't have to go through this instant corpse-maker yet. More adjustments? Do you want to look at the body or should I send it back for analysis?"

Nissim turned away. "Get rid of it and get a report. One more time should do it."

The physiologists were fast: cause of death functional disability in the neural axon synapses. A common mishap in the first MTs, for which there was a known correction. The correction was made, although Aldo passed out during it and they had to revive him with drugs. The constant physical drain was telling on them all.

"I don't know if I could face lifting those segments again," Aldo said, almost in a whisper, and switched to receive.

A guinea pig appeared on the screen, motionless. Then it twitched its nose and turned and wriggled about painfully, looking for some refuge. The cheer was hoarse, weak, but still a cheer.

"Goodbye, Saturn," Nissim said. "I have had it."

"Agreed," Aldo said, and switched to send.

"Let's first see what the docs say about the beast," Stan said as he dropped the guinea pig back into the screen. They all watched it as it vanished.

"Yes, of course." Nissim spoke the words reluctantly. "A final test."

It was a long time coming and was highly unsatisfactory. They played the tape a second time.

". . . And those are the clinical reports, gentlemen. What it seems to boil down to is that there is a very microscopic slowing of some of the animal's reflexes and nerve transmission speeds. In all truth we cannot be sure that there has been an alteration until more tests are made with controls. We have no recommendations. Whatever actions you take are up to you. There seems to be general agreement that some evidence of disability is present, which appears to have had no overt effect on the animal, but no one here will attempt to guess at its nature until the more detailed tests have been made. These will require a minimum of forty-five hours . . ."

"I don't think I can live forty-five hours," Nissim said. "My heart . . ."

Aldo stared at the screen. "I can live that long, but what good will it do? I know I can't lift those segments again. This is the end. There's only one way out."

"Through the screen?" Stan asked. "Not yet. We should wait out the tests. As long as we can."

"If we wait them out we're dead," Nissim insisted. "Aldo is right, even if corrections are given to us we can't go through all that again. This is it."

"No, I don't think so," Stan said, but he shut up when he realized that they were not listening. He was as close to total collapse as they were. "Let's take a vote then, majority decides."

It was a quick two to one.

"Which leaves only one remaining question," Stan said, looking into their exhausted, parchment faces, the mirror images of his own. "Who bells the cat? Goes first?" There was an extended silence.

Nissim coughed. "There is one thing clear. Aldo has to stay because he is the only one who can make adjustments if more are needed. Not that he physically could, but he still should be the last to leave."

Stan nodded agreement, then let his chin drop back onto his chest. "I'll go along with that; he's out as the guinea pig. You're out, too,

Dr. Ben-Haim, because from what I hear you are the bright hope of physics today. They need you. But there are a lot of jet jockeys around. Whenever we go through, I go first."

Nissim opened his mouth to protest, but could think of nothing to say.

"Right then. Me first as guinea pig. But when? Now? Have we done the best we can with this rig? Are you sure that you can't hold out in case further correction is needed?"

"It's a fact," Aldo said hoarsely. "I'm done for right now."

"A few hours, a day perhaps. But how could we work at the end of it? This is our last chance."

"We must be absolutely sure," Stan said, looking from one to the other. "I'm no scientist, and I'm not qualified to judge the engineering involved. So when you say that you have done the absolute best possible with the MT I have to take your word for it. But I know something about fatigue. We can go on a lot longer than you think—"

"No!" Nissim said.

"Hear me out. We can get more lifting equipment sent through. We can rest for a couple of days before going back on drugs. We can have rewired units sent through so that Aldo won't have to do the work. There are a lot of things that might be done to help."

"None of those things can help corpses," Aldo said, looking at the bulging arteries in his wrist, throbbing with the pressure needed to force the blood through his body under the multiplied gravity. "The human heart can't work forever under these kind of conditions. There is strain, damage—and then the end."

"You would be surprised just how strong the heart and the entire human organism can be."

"Yours, perhaps," Nissim said. "You're trained and fit and we, let's face it, are overweight and underexercised. And closer to death than we have ever been before. I know that I can't hold on any longer, and if you're not going through—then I'm going myself."

"And how about you, Aldo?" Stan said.

"Nissim is speaking for me, too. If it comes to a choice I'll take my chances with the screen rather than face the impossibility of surviving here. I think the odds on the screen are much better."

"Well then," Stan said, struggling his legs off the couch. "There doesn't seem to be very much more to say. I'll see you boys back in the station. It's been good working with you both and we'll all sure have some stories to tell our kids."

Aldo switched to transmit. Stan crawled to the edge of the screen. Smiling, he waved goodbye and fell, rather than stepped out onto its surface, and vanished.

The tape emerged instants later and Aldo's hands shook as he fed it to the player.

"... Yes, there he is, you two help him! Hello, *C. Huygens*, Major Brandon has come through and he looks awful, but I guess you know that, I mean he really looks all right. The doctors are with him now, talking to him ... just a moment ..."

The voice faded to a distant mumble as the speaker put his hand over the microphone, and there was a long wait before he spoke again. When he did his voice was changed.

"I want to tell you ... it's a little difficult. Perhaps I had better put on Dr. Kreer." There was a clatter and a different voice spoke. "Dr. Kreer. We have been examining your pilot. He seems unable to talk, to recognize anyone, although he appears uninjured, no signs of physical trauma. I don't know quite how to say this—but it looks very bad for him. If this is related to the delayed responses in the guinea pig there may be some connection with higher brain function. The major's reflexes test out A1 when allowance is made for fatigue. But the higher capacities—speech, intelligence—they seem to be, well, missing. I therefore order you both not to use the screen until complete tests have been made. And I am afraid I must advise you that there is a good chance that you will have to remain a longer period and make further adjustments ..."

The end of the tape clicked through and the player turned itself off. The two men looked at each other, horrified, then turned away when their eyes met.

"He's dead," Nissim said. "Worse than dead. What a terrible accident. Yet he seemed so calm and sure of himself ..."

"Gagarin flying his craft into the ground to save some others. What else could he have done? Could we have expected him to panic—like us? We as much as told him to commit suicide."

"You can't accuse us of that, Aldo!"

"Yes I can. We agreed that he had to go first. And we assured him that we were incapable of improving the operation of the machine in our present physical condition."

"Well ... that's true."

"Is it?" Nissim looked Aldo squarely in the eyes for the first time. "We are going back to work now, aren't we? We won't go through the MT as it is. So we will work on it until we have a good chance of making it—alive."

Aldo returned his gaze, steadily. "I imagine we can do that. And if it is true now—were we really speaking the truth when we said we would have gone through the screen first?"

"That is a very hard question to answer."

"Isn't it, though. And the correct answer is going to be very hard to live with. I think that we can truthfully say that we killed Stan Brandon."

"Not deliberately!"

"No. Which is probably worse. We killed him through our inability to cope with the kind of situation that we had never faced before. He was right. He was the professional and we should have listened to him."

"Hindsight is wonderful stuff. But we could have used a little more foresight."

Aldo shook his head. "I can't bear the thought that he died for absolutely no reason."

"There was a reason, and perhaps he knew it at the time. To bring us back safely. He did everything he could to get us all returned without harm. But we couldn't be convinced by words. Even if he had stayed we would have done nothing except resent him. I don't think either of us would have had the guts to go through first. We would have just lain here and given up and died."

"Not now we won't," Aldo said, struggling to his feet. "We are going to stick with it until the MT is perfect and we both can get out of this. We owe him at least that much. If his death is going to have any meaning we are both going to have to return safely."

"Yes, we can do it," Nissim agreed, forcing the words through his taut, closed lips. "Now we can."

The work began.

Welcoming Committee

It was a lousy landing. The tall spaceship tilted, wobbled, and finally jarred into the sand with a fin-rending crunch. Captain Moran looked at the back of Pilot Sinkley's sweating neck and resisted the impulse to close his hands around it.

"That was the worst landing I have seen since I have been in the service," he said. "*This* is a rescue mission—so who is going to rescue us?"

"I'm sorry . . . Captain . . ." Sinkley's voice shook as badly as his hands. "It was the glare . . . first from the sand . . . then the canal . . ." His voice died away like a run-down record.

There was a grinding crunch from somewhere below and emergency lights began to dance across the board. Captain Moran cursed and thumbed the telltales. Trouble. Engine room. Aft quadrant. The intercom suddenly belched out the gravel voice of Chief Engineer Beckett.

"Some gear carried away when we landed, nothing serious. Two ratings injured. Out."

The pilot sat with his back hunched, in either prayer or fear. He had goofed and goofed badly and he knew it. Captain Moran shot one tension-loaded glare at the back of the lowered head, then stamped out towards the lock. Too much was going wrong and the responsibility was all his.

Dr. Kranolsky, the medical officer, was already at the lock, taking samples through the bleeder tube. Captain Moran chewed his lip and waited while the fat little doctor fussed with his instruments. The vision plate next to the port was on and he looked at it, at the dusty red landscape that stretched away outside. Like a questioning metal finger, the tall bulk of the other ship stood silhouetted against the sky.

That was the reason they had come. One year since the first ship had left; one year without a report or a signal. The first ship, *Argus*, had carried at least a ton of signaling equipment. None of it had been used. A puzzled world had built a second interplanet ship—the *Argus II*. Moran had brought her this far—now he had to finish the job. Find out what had happened to the crew of the *Argus*. And get a report back to earth.

"More air pressure than had expected, Captain." Dr. Kranolsky's voice knifed through his thoughts. "And oxygen as well. About equal to the top of a high mountain on Earth. Also, the culture plates remain clear. Most interesting, because—"

"Doctor. Make it short and make it clear. Can I take my men out there?"

Kranolsky stopped in mid-phrase, deflated. He had no defenses against a man like the captain.

"Yes . . . yes. You could go outside. Just be sure that certain precautions are followed—"

"Tell me what they are. Want to get over to the *Argus* while it's still light."

Back on the bridge the captain started to growl through the door of the radio room, but the operator beat him to the punch.

"I've tried to contact the *Argus* on all frequencies, Captain, right down to the infrared. Nothing. Either that ship is empty or the crew is—" He left the sentence unfinished, but the captain's thundercloud scowl finished it for him.

"What about search radar?" Captain Moran asked. "They might still be in the vicinity."

Sparks shook his head in a slow negative. "I've been looking at the slow sweep detail screen until I have pips on my eyeballs. There ain't *nothing* out there—Earthman or Martian. And at the distance I was using it that screen would show anything bigger than a baseball."

Captain Moran had a decision to make and it was a rough one. Almost every man aboard was essential to the operation of the ship. If he sent a small party to examine the other ship they might run into trouble that they couldn't handle. If they didn't come back, none of them would get back to Earth. But the only alternative to a small party was taking the entire ship's complement. That would leave the ship empty—looking just like the *Argus*.

Moran chewed the problem for a minute and a half, then banged the intercom board with decision.

"Attention, ship's crew, all ratings attention. We are going out of here in fifteen minutes—*all* of us. Draw Marsuits and the weapons you can carry. Now *jump*."

When they were all out on the red sand, Moran shut the massive lock door behind them and spun the combination lock. Then, dispersed like an infantry squad, they slowly circled towards the *Argus*.

In alternate rushes they approached the lock of the other ship. It was wide open and there was no resistance or sign of life. In a matter of minutes the captain was standing under the gaping mouth of the lock. There was complete silence except for the rustling of wind-churned sand granules. Redfaced and panting hard, Pilot Sinkley raced up and slammed down next to the captain.

"Concussion grenade," Moran whispered.

Sinkley fumbled one out of his chest pack and handed it to the captain. He pulled the pin, counted slowly, then flipped it through the open port. There was a blasting roar and Moran was through the port before the echoes died away.

Nothing. No one in sight and no one in the carefully searched ship. The captain went to the empty bridge and tried to understand what had happened.

Moran was reading the log when he heard a hoarse shout from the guard he had left at the lock. He made it on a dead run, almost slamming into the men crowded there. Pushing them roughly aside he looked out.

There were four of them. Four girls. Lovely as any he had ever seen if you didn't take offense at their pale green skin.

"A welcoming committee. Boyoboy!" one of the crewmen said before Moran growled him into silence.

Yet that was all they seemed to be. They weren't armed and seemed incapable of any offense. The captain insisted on their being searched, to everyone's enjoyment. Including the girls. They answered questions in clear and incomprehensible voices. The only information they conveyed was that they wanted the spacemen to go with them. In unmistakable gestures they waved towards the canal and beckoned the men to follow them. Captain Moran was the only one who showed any hesitation about accepting. He finally posted a guard over the girls and called his officers aside for a conference.

There was only one course, and they finally took it. They had to find out about the men of the other ship, and the green girls were the only sign of a possible solution. There was no sign of any other kind of life on the red planet.

Well-armed, they went in force. The girls were bubbling with happiness at the move and the whole thing had more of the air of a picnic than an expedition. Particularly when they found the boats moored at the canal's edge with two or three more girls in each boat. After a careful search that disclosed nothing, Moran allowed his men to embark, one man to a boat.

A barely perceptible current moved them along and the whole expedition took on the air of a punting trip in paradise. Captain Moran ordered and roared but it did little good. The sudden change after the long trip was dismembering what few shards of military morale the men had left.

Only one incident marred the even placidity of the trip. Dr. Kranolsky—whose scientific interest seemed to rise above his libido—was making a detailed examination of the boats. He called to the captain, who guided his craft over until they touched.

"Something here, Captain. I have no idea what it might mean."

Following the doctor's pointing finger, Captain Moran saw faintly discernible scratches on one of the seats. Twisting and turning until the light hit them right he realised suddenly they were letters.

"SPII . . . that's what it looks like. Could one of the men from the *Argus* have written it?"

"They had to," the doctor said excitedly. "It is beyond reason that these Martians have an alphabet so similar to ours. But what can it mean?"

"It means," Captain Moran said grimly, "that they came this way and we had better keep our eyes open. I don't feel safe in these damn boats. At least we have the girls. Whoever or whatever is behind this won't start anything while we have them as hostages."

As the hours went by the current increased; they were soon moving at a deceptively rapid speed between the wide banks. Moran was worried and had his gun out instantly when he heard the doctor's shout.

"Captain, I have been thinking about those letters. They could mean only one word. If the man who scratched them here hadn't finished the last letter, only made the vertical mark, the word could be SPIDER."

The captain put his gun down and scowled at the doctor. "And do *you* see any spiders, Doctor? There are none in these boats and these women are the only life we have found so far. Perhaps he meant water spiders. And if so—so what?"

Following this possibility, Dr. Kranolsky took closer notice of the water. Captain Moran shouted orders to his men, but the boats were drifting further apart and some of them didn't hear him, or pretended they didn't. He couldn't be sure, but he thought things were going on in some of the furthest boats that were definitely against orders. Also, the current was much faster. Only the presence of the green girls gave him any feeling of security.

There seemed to be a dark spot on the horizon, dead ahead. He tried vainly to make it out. Dr. Kranolsky's voice knifed irritatingly across his concentration.

"Being logical, Captain, whoever scratched this word here thought it was important. Perhaps he never had time to finish it."

"Don't be fantastic, Doctor. There are more important things to concern ourselves with."

For the first time since he had served under the captain, Dr. Kranolsky disagreed.

"No, I think this is the most important thing we have to concern ourselves with. If the man meant 'spider'—where is the beast? Certainly these girls are harmless enough. Or the spider web—where is that?" He mused for a second, his brow tight, then laughed. "It makes me think of a fantasy I had when we approached Mars. The canals looked like a giant spider web scratched on the surface of the planet."

Moran snorted with disgust. "And I suppose if this canal is a strand of the web, these girls are the 'bait.' And this building we are coming to is the spider's lair. Really, Doctor!"

The canal swept towards the giant black structure and seemingly vanished though an opening in its side. They couldn't control their small craft and within minutes were passing under a giant archway. Moran was frightened and to conceal his fear he poked fun at the doctor.

"And now we are in the lair, Doctor, what do you think a planet-wide spider should look like? How would you describe a beast that lives on a world as an earth spider lives on an apple?"

A scream was his only answer, a good enough answer.

Words were inadequate to describe the *thing* that completely filled the building.

Waiting.

Reaching for them . . .

Heavy Duty

"But why you?" she asked.

"Because it happens to be my job." He clicked the last belt loop into place on his pack and shifted weight comfortably on his shoulders.

"I don't understand why those men, the ones flying the delivery ship, why they couldn't have looked around first. To help you out a little bit, perhaps let you know what you were getting into. I don't think it's fair."

"It's very fair," he told her, tightening up one notch on the left shoulder strap and trying to keep his temper. He did not like her to come here when he was leaving, but there was no easy way to stop her. Once again he explained.

"The men who fly the contact ships have a difficult time of it just staying alive and sane, trapped in their ships while they go out to the stars. Theirs is a specialized job, only certain men with particular dispositions can survive the long flight. These same characteristics are outstandingly unsuited to planetary contact and exploration. It is work enough for them to do a high-level instrument and photographic sweep, and then to drop a transmatter screen on retrojets at a suitable spot. By the time the transmatter touches down and sends back their report they are well on their way to the next system. They've done their job. Now I'll do mine."

"Ready for me yet, Specialist Langli?" a man asked, looking in through the ready-room door.

"Just about," Langli said, disliking himself for the relief he felt at the other's intrusion.

"Artificer Meer, this is my wife, Keriza."

"A great honor, Wife Keriza. You must be proud of your husband."

Meer was young and smiled when he talked, so it could be assumed that he was sincere about what he said. He wore a throat mike and earphones and was in constant contact with the computer.

"It is an honor," Keriza said, but could not prevent herself from adding, "but not an eternal one. This is a first betrothal and it expires in a few days, while my husband is away."

"Fine," Artificer Meer said, not hearing the bitterness behind her words. "You can look forward to a second or final when he returns. A good excuse for a celebration. Shall I begin, Specialist?"

"Please do," Langli said, lifting his canteen with his fingertips to see if it was full.

Keriza retreated against the wall of the drab room while the checklist began; she was already left out. The computer murmured its questions into the artificer's ear and he spoke them aloud in the same machine-made tones. Both men attended to the computer, not to her, alike in their dark-green uniforms, almost the same color as the green-painted walls. The orange and silver of her costume was out of place here and she unconsciously stepped backward toward the entrance.

The checklist was run through quickly and met the computer's approval. Far more time was then taken up making the needed adjustments on Langli's manpower gear. This was a powered metal harness that supported his body, conforming to it like a flexible exoskeleton. It was jointed at his joints and could swivel and turn to follow any motion. Since the supporting pads were an integral part of his uniform, and the rods were thin and colored to match the cloth, it was not too obvious. An atomic energy supply in his pack would furnish power for at least a year.

"Why are you wearing that metal cage?" Keriza asked. "You have never done that before." She had to repeat her question, louder, before either man noticed her.

"It's for the gravity," her husband finally told her. "There's a two-point-one-five-three-plus G on this planet. The manpower can't cancel that, but it can support me and keep me from tiring too quickly."

"You didn't tell me that about this planet. In fact you have told me nothing . . ."

"There's little enough. High gravity, cold and windy where I'm going. The air is good; it's been tested, but oxygen is a little high. I can use it."

"But animals, wild animals, are there any of them? Can it be dangerous?"

"We don't know yet, but it appears peaceable enough. Don't worry about it." This was a lie, but one officially forced upon him. There were human settlers on this new planet, and this was classified information. A public announcement would be made only after official appraisal of his report.

"Ready," Langli said, pulling on his gloves. "I want to go before I start sweating inside this suit."

"Suit temperature is thermostatically controlled, Specialist Langli. You should not be uncomfortable."

He knew that: he just wanted to leave. Keriza should not have come here.

"Restricted country from here in," he told her, taking her arms and kissing her quickly. "I'll send you a letter as soon as I have time."

He loved her well enough, but not here, not when he was going on a mission. The heavy door closed behind them, shutting her out, and he felt relieved at once. Now he could concentrate on the job.

"Message from control," the artificer said when they entered the armored transmatter room through the thick triple doors. "They want some more vegetation and soil samples. Life forms and water, though these last can wait."

"Will comply," Langli said, and the artificer passed on the answer through his microphone.

"They wish you quick success, Specialist," the artificer said in his neutral voice; then, more warmly, "I do, too. It is a privilege to have assisted you." He covered the microphone with his hand. "I'm studying, a specialist course, and I've read your reports. I think that you . . . I mean what you have done . . ." His words died and his face reddened. This was a breach of rules and he could be disciplined.

"I know what you mean, Artificer Meer, and I wish you all the best of luck." Langli extended his hand and, after a moment's reluctance, the other man took it. Though he would not admit it aloud, Langli was warmed by this irregular action. The coldness of the transmatter chamber, with its gun snouts and television cameras, had always depressed him. Not that he wanted bands or flags when he left, but a touch of human contact made up for a lot.

"Goodbye, then," he said, and turned and activated the switch on the preset transmatter control. The wire lattice of the screen vanished and was replaced by the watery blankness of the operating Bhattacharya field. Without hesitating Langli stepped into it.

An unseen force seized him, dragging him forward, hurling him face-first to the ground. He threw his arms out to break his fall and the safety rods on his wrists shot out ahead of his hands, telescoping slowly to soften the shock of impact; if they had not he would surely have broken both his wrists. Even with this aid the breath was knocked from him by the impact of the manpower pads. He gasped for air, resting on all fours. His mouth burned with the coldness of it and his eyes watered. The uniform warmed as the icy atmosphere hit the thermocouples. He looked up.

A man was watching him. A broad, solidly built man with an immense flowing black beard. He was dressed in red-marked leather and furs and carried a short stabbing spear no longer than his forearm. It was not until he moved that Langli realized he was standing up—not sitting down. He was so squat and wide that he appeared to be truncated.

First things came first: control had to have its samples. He kept a wary eye on the bearded man as he slipped a sample container from the dispenser on the side of his pack and put it flat on the ground. The ground was hard but ridged like dried mud, so he broke off a chunk and dropped it into the middle of the red plastic disc. Ten seconds later, as the chemicals in the disc reacted with the air, the disc curled up on the edges and wrapped the soil in a tight embrace. The other man shifted his spear from hand to hand and watched this process with widening eyes. Langli filled two more containers with soil, then three others with grass and leafy twigs from a bush a few feet away. This was enough. Then he backed slowly around the scarred bulk of the retrorockets until he stood next to the transmatter screen. It was operating but unfocused: anything entering it now would be broken down into Y-radiation and simply sprayed out into Bhattacharya space. Only when he pressed his hand to the plate on the frame would it be keyed to the receiver; it would operate for no one else. He touched the plate and threw the samples through. Now he could turn to the more important business.

"Peace," he said, facing the other man with his hands open and extended at his sides. "Peace."

The man did nothing in response, though he raised the spear when Langli took a step toward him. When Langli returned to his original position he dropped the spear again. Langli stood still and smiled.

"It's a waiting game, is it? You want to talk while we're waiting?" There was no answer, nor did he really expect one. "Right then, what is it we're waiting for? Your friends, I imagine. All of this shows organization, which is very hopeful. Your people have a settlement nearby, that's why the transmatter was dropped here. You investigated it, found no answers, then put a guard on it. You must have signaled them when I arrived, though I was flat on my face and didn't see it."

There was a shrill squealing behind a nearby slope that slowly grew louder. Langli looked on with interest as a knot of bearded men, at this distance looking identical with his guard, struggled into sight. They were all pulling a strange conveyance which had three pairs of wooden wheels: the apparently unoiled axles were making the squealing. It was no more than a padded platform on which rested a man dressed in bright-red leather. The upper part of his face was hidden by a metal casque pierced with eyeslits, but from below the rim a great white beard flowed across his chest. In his right hand the man held a long, thin-bladed carving knife which he pointed at Langli as he slowly stepped down from the conveyance. He said something incomprehensible in a sharp hoarse voice at the same time.

"I'm sorry, but I cannot understand you," Langli said.

At the sound of his words the old man started back and nearly dropped the weapon. At this sudden action the other men crouched and raised their spears toward Langli. The leader disapproved of this and shouted what could only have been commands. The spears were lowered at once. When he was satisfied with the reaction the man turned back to Langli and spoke slowly, choosing his words with care.

"I did not know . . . think . . . I would these words hear spoken by another. I know it only to read." The accent was strange but the meaning was perfectly clear.

"Wonderful. I will learn your language, but for now we can speak mine . . ."

"Who are you? What is it . . . the thing there? It fell at night with a loud noise. How come you here?"

Langli spoke slowly and clearly, what was obviously a prepared speech.

"I come with greetings from my people. We travel great distances with this machine you see before you. We are not from this world. We will help you in many ways which I will tell you. We can help the sick and make them well. We can bring food if you are hungry. I am here alone and no more of us will come unless you permit it. In return for these things we ask only that you answer my questions. When the questions are answered we will answer any questions that you may have."

The old man stood with his legs widespread and braced, unconsciously whetting the blade on his leg. "What do you want here? What are your real needs . . . desires?"

"I have medicine and can help the sick. I can get food. I ask only that you answer my questions, nothing more."

Under the flowing moustache the old man's lips lifted in a cold grin. "I understand. Do as you say—or do nothing. Come with me, then." He stepped backward and settled slowly onto the cart, which creaked with his weight. "I am Bekrnatus. You have a name?"

"Langli. I will be happy to accompany you."

They went in a slow procession over the crest of the rise and down into the shallow valley beyond. Langli was already tired, his heart and lungs working doubly hard to combat the increased gravity, and was exhausted before they had gone a quarter of a mile.

"Just a moment," he said. "Can we stop for a short while?"

Bekrnatus raised his hand and spoke a quick command. The procession stopped and the men immediately sat, most of them sprawling out horizontally in the heavy grass. Langli unclipped his canteen and drank deeply. Bekrnatus watched every move closely.

"Would you like some water?" Langli asked, extending the canteen.

"Very much," the old man said, taking the canteen and examining it closely before drinking from it. "The water has a taste of very difference. Of what metal is this . . . container made?"

"Aluminum I imagine, or one of its alloys." Should he have answered that question? It certainly seemed harmless enough. But you never could tell. Probably he shouldn't have, but he was too tired to really care. The bearded men were watching intently and the nearest one stood up, staring at the canteen.

"Sorry," Langli said, blinking a redness of fatigue from his eyes and extending the canteen to the man. "Would you like a drink as well?"

Bekrnatus screamed something hoarsely as the man hesitated a moment—then reached out and clutched the canteen. Instead of drinking from it he turned and started to run away. He was not fast enough. Langli looked on, befuddled, as the old man rushed by him and buried his long knife to the hilt in the fleeing man's back.

None of the others moved as the man swayed, then dropped swiftly and heavily to the ground. He lay on his side, eyes open and blood gushing from his mouth, the canteen loose in his fingers. Bekrnatus kneeled and took away the canteen, then jerked the knife out with a single powerful motion. The staring dead eyes were still.

"Take this water thing and do not come . . . go near other people or give them anythings."

"It was just water—"

"It was not the water. You killed this man."

Langli, befuddled, started to tell him that it was perfectly clear who had killed him, then wisely decided to keep his mouth shut. He knew nothing about this society and had made a mistake. That was obvious. In a sense the old man was right and he had killed the man. He fumbled out a stimulant tablet and washed it down with water from the offending canteen. The march resumed.

The settlement was in the valley, huddled against the base of a limestone cliff, and Langli was exhausted when they reached it. Without the manpower he could not have gone a quarter of this distance. He was in among the houses before he realized they were there, so well did they blend into the landscape. They were dugouts, nine-tenths below the ground, covered with flat sod roofs; thin spirals of smoke came from chimney openings in most of them. The procession did not stop, but threaded its way through the dug-in houses and approached the cliff. This had a number of ground-level openings cut into it, the larger ones sealed with log doors. When they were closer Langli saw that two window-like openings were covered with glass or some other transparent substance. He wanted to investigate this— but it would have to wait. Everything would have to wait until he regained a measure of strength. He stood, swaying, while Bekrnatus climbed slowly down from the wheeled litter and approached a log door which opened as he came near. Langli started after him—then found himself failing, unable to stand. He had a brief moment of surprise, before the ground came up and hit him, when he realized that for the first time in his life he was fainting.

The air was warm on his face and he was lying down. It took him some moments, even after he had opened his eyes, to realize where he was. An immense fatigue gripped him and every movement was an effort; even his thoughts felt drugged. He looked about the darkened room several times before the details made any meaning. A window that was set deep into the stone wall. The dim bulk of furniture and unknown objects. A weaker, yellow light from the fire on the grate. A stone fireplace and stone walls. Memory returned and he realized that he must be in one of the rooms he had noticed, hollowed out of the face of the cliff. The fire crackled; there was the not-unpleasant odor of pungent smoke in the air; soft, slapping footsteps came up behind him. He felt too tired to turn his head, but he banished this unworkmanlike thought and turned in that direction.

A girl's face, long blond hair, deep blue eyes.

"Hello. I don't believe we have met," he said.

The eyes widened, shocked, and the face vanished. Langli sighed wearily and closed his own eyes. This was a very trying mission. Perhaps he should take a stimulant. In his pack—

His pack! He was wide awake at the thought, struggling to sit up. They had taken his pack from him! At the same instant of fear he saw it lying next to the cot where it had been dropped. And the girl returned, pressing him back to a lying position. She was very strong.

"I'm Langli. What's your name?"

She was attractive enough, if you liked your girls squarefaced. Good bust, filled the soft leather dress nicely. But that was about all. Too broad-shouldered, too hippy, too much muscle. Very little different really from the other natives of this heavy planet. He realized that her eyes had never left his while he had been looking her up and down. He smiled.

"Langli is my name, but I suppose I shall never learn yours. The leader—what did he call himself—Bekrnatus, seems to be the only one who speaks a civilized tongue. I suppose I shall have to learn the local grunts and gurgles before I will be able to talk to you?"

"Not necessarily," she said, and burst out laughing at the surprised look on his face. Her teeth were even, white, and strong. "My name is Patna. Bekrnatus is my father."

"Well, that's nice." He still felt dazed. "Sorry if I sounded rude. The gravity is a little strong for me."

"What is gravity?"

"I'll tell you later, but I must talk to your father first. Is he here?"

"No. But he will be soon back. Today he killed a man. He must now the man's wife and family look after. They will go to another. Can I not answer your questions?"

"Perhaps." He touched the button on his waist that switched on the recorder. "How many of your people speak my language?"

"Just me. And Father, of course. Because we are The Family and the others are The People." She stood very straight when she said it.

"How many are there, of The People I mean?"

"Almost six hundred. It was a better winter than most. The air was warmer than in other years. Of course there was more—what is the word?—more rot in the stored food. But people lived."

"Is winter over yet?"

She laughed. "Of course. It is almost the warmest time now."

And they believed that this is warm, he thought. What can the winters possibly be like? He shivered at the thought.

"Please tell me more about The Family and The People. How are they different?"

"They just are, that is all," she said and stopped, as though she had never considered the question before. "We live here and they live there. They work and they do what we tell them to do. We have the metal and the fire and the books. That is how we talk your language, because we read what is written in the books."

"Could I see the books?"

"No!" She was shocked at the thought. "Only The Family can see them."

"Well—wouldn't you say that I qualify as a member of The Family? I can read, I carry many things made of metal." At that moment he realized what the trouble had been with his canteen. It was made of metal, for some reason taboo among most of these people. "And I can make fire." He took out his lighter and thumbed it so that a jet of flame licked out.

Patna looked at this, wide-eyed. "Our fires are harder to make. But, still, I am not sure. Father will know if you should look at the books." She saw his expression and groped around for some compromise. "But there is one book, a little book, that Father lets me have for my own. It is not an important book, though."

"Any book is important. May I see it?"

She rose hesitantly and went to the rear of the room, to a log door let into the stone, and tugged at the thick bars. When it was open she groped into the darkness of another room, a deeper cavern cut into the soft stone of the cliff. She returned quickly and resealed the door.

"Here," she said, holding it out to him, "you may read my book."

Langli struggled to a sitting position and took it from her. It was crudely bound in leather—the original cover must have worn out countless years earlier—and it crackled when he opened it. The pages were yellowed, frayed, and loose from the backbone. He poked through them, squinting at the archaic typeface in the dim light from the window, then turned back to the title page.

"*Selected Poems,*" he read aloud. "Published at, I've never heard of the place, in—this is more important—785 P.V. I think I've heard of that calendar, just a moment."

He put the book down carefully and bent to his pack, almost losing his balance as the more-than-doubled gravity pulled at him. His ex-oskeleton hummed and gave him support. The handbook was right on top and he flipped through it.

"Yes, here it is. Only went to 913 in their reckoning. Now to convert to Galactic Standard . . ." He did some silent figuring and put the handbook away, taking up the other book again. "Do you like poetry?" he asked.

"More than anything. Though I only have these. There are no other poems in the books. Though of course there are some others . . ."

She lowered her eyes and, after a moment's thought, Langli realized why.

"These others, you wrote them yourself, didn't you? You must tell me one sometime—"

There was a sudden rattling at the bolts that sealed the front door and Patna tore the book from his hands and ran with it to the dark end of the room.

Bekrnatus pushed open the door and came in wearily. "Close it," he ordered as he threw aside his helmet and dropped into a padded lounge, half bed, half chair. Patna moved quickly to do his bidding.

"I am tired, Langli," he said, "and I must sleep. So tell me what you are doing here, what this all means."

"Of course. But a question or two first. There are things I must know. What do your people do here, other than sleep and eat and gather food?"

"The question makes no sense."

"I mean anything. Do they mine and smelt metal? Do they carve, make things from clay, paint pictures, wear jewelry—"

"Enough. I understand your meaning. I have read of these things, seen pictures of them. Very nice. In answer to your question—we do nothing. I could never understand how these things were done and perhaps you will tell me when it suits you to answer questions rather than ask them. We live, that is hard enough. When we have planted our food and picked our food we are through. This is a hard world and the act of living takes all of our time."

He barked a harsh command in the local language, and his daughter shuffled to the fireplace. She returned with a crude clay bowl which she handed to him. He raised it to his lips and drank deeply, making smacking noises with his lips.

"Would you care for some?" he asked. "It is a drink we make; I do not know if there is a word for it in the book language. Our women chew roots and spit them into a bowl."

"No, none thank you." Langli fought to keep his voice even, to control his disgust. "Just one last question. What do you know of your people coming to this world? You do know that you came here?"

"Yes, that I know, though little more. The story is told, though nothing is written, that we came from another world to this world, from the sky, though how it was done I know not. But it was done, for the books are not of this world and they have pictures of scenes not of this world. And there is the metal, and the windows. Yes, we came here."

"Have others come? Like myself? Are there records?"

"None! That would have been written. Now you tell me, stranger from the metal box. What do you do here?"

Langli lay down, carefully, before he spoke. He saw that Patna was sitting as well. The gravity must be fought, constantly, unceasingly.

"First you must understand that I came from inside the metal box, then again I didn't. At night you see the stars and they are suns like the one that shines here, yet very distant. They have worlds near them, like this world here. Do you know what I am talking about?"

"Of course. I am not of The People. I have read of astronomy in the books."

"Good. Then you should know that the metal box contains a transmatter which you must think of as a kind of door. One door that is at the same time two doors. I stepped through a door on my planet, very far away, and stepped out of your door here. All in an eye-blink of time. Do you understand?"

"Perhaps." Bekrnatus dabbed at his lips with the back of his hand. "Can you return the same way? Step into the box and come out on a planet, up there in the sky?"

"Yes, I can do that."

"Is that how we came to this world?"

"No. You came by a ship of space, a large metal box built to move between the stars, in the years before the transmatter could be used at stellar distances. I know this because your window there is the window from a spacer, and I imagine your metal was salvaged from the ship as well. And I also know how long you have been here, since there was a date in the front of that poetry book your daughter showed me."

Patna gasped, a sharp intake of air, and Bekrnatus pulled himself to a sitting position. The clay bowl fell, unheeded, and shattered on the floor.

"You showed him a book," Bekrnatus hissed, and struggled to his feet.

"No, wait!" Langli said, realizing he had precipitated another crisis through ignorance. Would the man try to kill his daughter? He tore at his pack. "It was my fault, I asked for the book. But I have many books; here, I'll show you. I'll give you some books. This . . . and this."

Bekrnatus did not heed the words, if he even heard them, but he stopped as the books were pushed before him. He reached for them hesitantly.

"Books," he said, dazedly. "Books, new books, books I have never seen before. It is beyond wonder." He clutched the books to his chest and half fell back into his chair. A good investment, Langli thought. Never were a first reader and a basic dictionary more highly prized.

"You can have all the books you want now. You can discover your history, all of it. I can tell you that your people have been here, roughly, about three thousand years. Your coming here may have been an accident; two things lead me to believe that. This is a very grim world with little to offer. I can't picture it being selected for colonization. Then there is the complete break with technology and culture. You have a few books; they could have been salvaged. And metal, perhaps from the wreck of the ship. That you have survived is little short of miraculous. You have this social or class distinction that has also passed down. Your ancestors were perhaps scientists, ship's officers, something that set them apart from ordinary men. And you have kept the distinction."

"I am tired," Bekrnatus said, turning the books over and over in his hands, "and there are many new things to think about all at once. We will talk tomorrow."

He dropped back, eyes closed, books still in his grasp. Langli was ready to sleep himself, exhausted by the efforts he had forced himself to. The light seemed to be fading; he wondered how long the local day was, and did not really care. He took an eight-hour sleeping pill from his medical kit and washed it down with water from his canteen. A night's sleep would make things look a good deal different.

During the night he was aware of someone moving about, going to the fire. At one time he thought he felt the soft touch of hair across his face and lips upon his forehead. But he could not be sure and thought it was probably a dream.

It was bright morning when he awoke, with the sun striking directly through the window, the shaft of light adding unexpected color to the gray stone of the back wall. Bekrnatus' couch was empty and Patna was working at the fireplace, humming quietly to herself. When he shifted position his bed squeaked and she turned to look at him.

"You are awake. I hope that you slept well. My father has gone out with the axe so wood can be chopped."

"You mean that he chops the wood?" Langli yawned, his head still thick with sleep.

"No, never. But the axe head is metal so he carries it and must be there when it is used. Your morning food is ready." She ladled one of the clay bowls full of gruel and brought it to him. He smiled and shook his head no.

"Thank you, that is very hospitable. But I cannot eat any of your food until laboratory analysis has been made—"

"You think I am trying to poison you?"

"Not at all. But you must realize that major metabolic changes take place in human beings cut off from the mainstream. There may be chemicals in the soil here, in the plants, that you can ingest but that would be sure death for me. It smells wonderful, but it could hurt me. You wouldn't want that to happen?"

"No! Of course not." She almost hurled the bowl from her. "What will you eat?"

"I have my own food here, see." He opened his pack and took out a mealcel, pulling the tab so the heating began. He was hungry, he realized, hungrier than he had ever felt before, and began spooning down the concentrate before the heat cycle was finished. His body needed nourishment, fighting constantly against the drag of gravity.

"Do you know what this is?" Patna asked, and he looked up to see her holding a brownish, ragged-edged fragment of some kind.

"No, I don't. It looks like wood or bark."

"It is the inner bark of a tree, we use it to write on, but that is not what I meant. I meant there is something on it. That is what I meant . . ."

Even in the dim light Langli could realize that she was blushing. Poor girl, a literate among savages, trapped on this dismal and isolated world.

"I might guess," he said carefully. "Could it be one of the poems you wrote? If it is—I would like to hear it."

She shielded her eyes with her hand and turned away for a moment, a caricature of a shy maiden in a squat wrestler's body. Then she struggled with herself and started the poem in a weak voice, but continued, louder and louder.

"I dare not ask a kiss,
I dare not beg a smile,
Lest having that, or this,
I might grow proud the while.
No, no, the utmost share
Of my desire shall be
Only to kiss the air
That lately did kiss thee."

She almost cried the last words aloud, then turned and fled to the far side of the room and stood with her face against the wall. Langli groped for the right words. The poem was good; whether she had written it herself or copied it he did not know—nor did it matter. It said what she wanted to say.

"That's beautiful," he told her. "A really beautiful poem—"

Before he could finish she ran, feet slapping hard against the floor, across the room and knelt beside his bed. Her solid, powerful arms were about him and her face against his, buried in the pillow. He could feel the tear-wetness of her cheeks against his own and her muffled voice in his ear.

"I knew you would come, I know who you are, because you had to come from far away like a knight in the poems riding a horse to save me. You knew I needed you. My father, I, the only Family left, I must marry one of The People. It has been done before. Ugly, stupid, I hate them, the brightest, we tried to teach him to read, he couldn't, stupid. But you came in time. You are The Family, you will take me . . ."

The words died away and her lips found his, urgent and strong with desire, and when he held her shoulders and tried to push her away his exoskeleton whined with the effort but she did not move. Finally, exhausted, she released him and pushed her face deep into the pillow again. He stood, swaying, bracing himself on the back of a chair. When he spoke it was with sincerity as he tried to make the truth less harsh than it really was.

"Patna, listen, you must believe me. I like you, you're a wonderful, brave girl. But this just can't be. Not because I am already married, that marriage will be terminated before I return, but because of this world. You can't leave it, and I would die if I stayed here. The adaptations your people have been forced to make to survive must be incredible. Your circulatory system alone must be completely different—your blood pressure much more than normal to get blood to your brain, with more muscles in the walls of the arteries to help pump it. Perhaps major valve changes and distribution. You can't possibly have children with anyone from off this planet. Your children would be stillborn, or die soon after birth, unfit. That is the truth, you must believe—"

"Ugly, skinny, too tall, too weak, shut up!" she screeched and lashed out at him, her head still turned away.

He tried to move aside, he could not, not fast enough. Her hand slapped against his arm with a sudden explosion of pain. A sharp cracking sound.

The bitch has broken my arm, he screamed to himself, staggering, sitting down slowly. His forearm hung crookedly in the brace of the exoskeleton and how it hurt! He cradled it on his knees and fumbled through his medical supplies with his good hand. She tried to help him and he snarled at her and she went away.

Bekrnatus came in, an axe over his shoulder, while the emergency cast was hardening and Langli was giving himself a shot of painkiller, with a tranquilizer for his nerves.

"What is wrong with your arm?" Bekrnatus asked, dropping the axe and falling into his couch.

"I had an accident. I will have to go get medical help from my people soon so I must talk to you now. Tell you what you need to know—"

"Do that. I have questions—"

"There is no time for questions." The pain was still there and he snapped the words out. "If I had the time I would explain everything slowly and in great detail so you would understand and agree. Now I will just tell you. If you want help you must pay for it. It costs a great deal to plant an MT screen on a planet as distant as this one. Medical supplies, food, energy sources, anything that we supply you will also cost a good deal. You will have to repay us."

"You have our thanks, of course."

"Not negotiable!" The pain was almost gone but he could feel the broken ends of the bones grate together when he moved. His nerves felt the same way despite the tranquilizer.

"Listen carefully and try to remember what I say. There is no pie in the sky. What you get for nothing is worth it. Out there are more planets than you could possibly count—and more people on them than I could count. And the transmatter makes them all next-door neighbors. Can you imagine what hell that has wreaked with culture, government, finances, down through the millennia? No, I can see by your face that you can't. Then just think about this one bit of it. To further certain ends individuals form a cooperation, a sort of cross between a cooperative and a corporation, if those words are in any of your books. I belong to one of these called World Openers. We explore unsettled planets and occasionally contact worlds like yours that aren't on the MT net. For services rendered we demand payment in full."

Patna had come to stand by her father, silently, her arm about his thick knobbed shoulders. Her face, as she looked at Langli, was a study in hatred, contempt. Bekrnatus, a lord on his own world, would still not comprehend the realities of the galaxy outside.

"We will pay what you ask, gladly, but pay with what? We have no money, none of the resources you were asking about last night."

"You have yourselves," Langli said, emotionlessly, as the drugs took hold. "Because that is all you have, it will take generations to repay your debt. You will breed faster and better, and we will help you with that. For a price, of course. We have operations on heavy-gravity worlds that must be supervised. Automatic machinery can't do everything. And there are others who can use workers of your type as well—"

"You come to enslave us, imprison us!" Bekrnatus roared. "To make free men into beasts of burden. Never!"

He grabbed up the axe from the floor and climbed to his feet, swinging it high. Langli was ready. His gun snapped just once and the explosion shook the room as a great pit was blown from the stone wall behind Bekrnatus.

"Just imagine what that would have done to you. Now sit down and don't be foolish. I will kill you to save my own life, be sure of that. We can't imprison you—because you are in prison already on this high-G world. The force that pulls you down, that makes things fall when dropped. This force is weaker on other worlds. I can leave and seal the transmatter and that will be the end of it. If that is what you really wish. The choice is yours to make." He waved the gun at Patna. "Now open that door."

Bekrnatus stood, the axe dangling forgotten from his hand; the world he knew had changed, everything changed. Langli struggled his pack to one shoulder and waved Patna aside. He moved slowly toward the door.

"I will return and you can tell me your decision then."

Patna called to him as he went out, fighting down her loathing.

"The transmatter, when will we get to use it? To see the wonders of other worlds?"

"Never in your lifetime. Use of the MT is granted only when all the debts are paid." He had to say it because the sooner she faced the truth the better she would adjust. "And you will be occupied else-wise. Intelligent operators will be needed, not strong backs. Yours is the only womb from which intelligence may spring on this world. Keep it busy."

He hobbled away until he was clear of the buildings, then gratefully set the pack down. It was too much of a burden to take back to the transmatter. He triggered the destruct and went on while it burned fiercely behind him. Expensive equipment, but it would go on the bill. They would choose to accept and pay; they really did not have much of a choice. It would be for their benefit. Not so much now, but in the long run. The two squat figures were still in the doorway looking after him and he turned quickly away.

What did they expect, charity? The universe was uncharitable. You had to pay for what you took from it. That was a natural law that could not be broken.

And he was doing his job, that was all.

It was just a job.

He was helping them.

Wasn't he?

Stumbling, sweating, and gasping, he hurried to be away from this place.

MAKE ROOM! MAKE ROOM!

When I wrote my novel *Make Room! Make Room!* I was greatly concerned about the threat presented by uncontrolled population growth and environmental destruction. (After all, one causes the other.) Some thirty-five years later my worst predictions seem to be coming true. The developing nations—which truthfully should be called the never-to-be-developed nations—are already on the slippery slope to destruction. Too many people competing for too few resources, and the scourge of AIDS decimating them as well—as if they did not have enough trouble already.

The developed world apparently cannot care less. Many countries are approaching ZPG, zero population growth. Apparently preferring the better life—and a better TV set—to a third child. While at the same time refusing to do anything about planetary warming. There is cause for despair.

So what will happen to our overpopulated globe? In the stories here I have explored some possible futures.

A Criminal Act

The first blow of the hammer shook the door in its frame, and the second blow made the thin wood boom like a drum. Benedict Vernall threw the door open before a third stroke could fall and pushed his gun into the stomach of the man with the hammer.

"Get going. Get out of here," Benedict said, in a much shriller voice than he had planned to use.

"Don't be foolish," the bailiff said quietly, stepping aside so that the two guards behind him in the hall were clearly visible. "I am the bailiff and I am doing my duty. If I am attacked these men have orders to shoot you and everyone else in your apartment. Be intelligent. Yours is not the first case like this. Such things are planned for."

One of the guards clicked off the safety catch on his submachine gun, smirking at Benedict as he did it. Benedict let the pistol fall slowly to his side.

"Much better," the bailiff told him and struck the nail once more with the hammer so that the notice was fixed firmly to the door.

"Take that filthy thing down," Benedict said, choking over the words.

" 'Benedict Vernall,' " the bailiff said, adjusting his glasses on his nose as he read from the proclamation he had just posted. " 'This is to inform you that pursuant to the Criminal Birth Act of 2053 you are guilty of the act of criminal birth and are hereby proscribed and no longer protected from bodily injury by the forces of this sovereign state . . . ' "

"You're going to let some madman kill me—what kind of a dirty law is that?"

The bailiff removed his glasses and gazed coldly along his nose at Benedict. "Mr. Vernall," he said, "have the decency to accept the results of your own actions. Did you or did you not have an illegal baby?"

"Illegal? Never! A harmless infant . . ."

"Do you or do you not already have the legal maximum of two children?"

"We have two, but . . ."

"You refused advice or aid from your local birth control clinic. You expelled, with force, the birth guidance officer who called upon you. You rejected the offer of the abortion clinic—"

"Murderers!"

"—and the advice of the Family-Planning Board. The statutory six months have elapsed without any action on your part. You have had the three advance warnings and have ignored them. Your family still contains one consumer more than is prescribed by law, therefore the proclamation has been posted. You alone are responsible, Mr. Vernall, you can blame no one else."

"I can blame this foul law."

"It is the law of the land," the bailiff said, drawing himself up sternly. "It is not for you or me to question." He took a whistle from his pocket and raised it to his mouth. "It is my legal duty to remind you that you still have one course open, even at this last moment, and may still avail yourself of the services of the Euthanasia Clinic."

"Go straight to hell."

"Indeed. I've been told that before." The bailiff snapped the whistle to his lips and blew a shrill blast. He almost smiled as Benedict slammed shut the apartment door.

There was an animal-throated roar from the stairwell as the policemen who were blocking it stepped aside. A knot of fiercely tangled men burst out, running and fighting at the same time. One of them surged ahead of the pack but fell as a fist caught him on the side of the head; the others trampled him underfoot. Shouting and cursing, the mob came on and it looked as though it would be a draw, but a few yards short of the door one of the leaders tripped and brought two others down. A short fat man in the second rank leaped their bodies and crashed headlong into Vernall's door, with such force that the ballpoint pen he extended pierced the paper of the notice and sank into the wood beneath.

"A volunteer has been selected," the bailiff shouted and the waiting police and guards closed in on the wailing men and began to force them back toward the stairs. One of the men remained behind on the floor, saliva running down his cheeks as he chewed hysterically at a strip of the threadbare carpet. Two white-garbed hospital attendants were looking out for this sort of thing and one of them jabbed the man expertly in the neck with a hypodermic needle while the other unrolled the stretcher.

Under the bailiff's watchful eye the volunteer painstakingly wrote his name in the correct space on the proclamation, then carefully put the pen back in his vest pocket.

"Very glad to accept you as a volunteer for this important public duty, Mr.—" The bailiff leaned forward to peer at the paper—"Mr. Mortimer," he said.

"Mortimer is my first name," the man said in a crisply dry voice as he dabbed lightly at his forehead with his breast-pocket handkerchief.

"Understandable, sir. Your anonymity will be respected as is the right of all volunteers. Might I presume that you are acquainted with the rest of the regulations?"

"You may. Paragraph 46 of the Criminal Birth Act of 2053, subsection 14, governing the selection of volunteers. Firstly, I have volunteered for the maximum period of twenty-four hours. Secondly, I will neither attempt nor commit violence of any form upon any other members of the public during this time, and if I do so I will be held responsible by law for all of my acts."

"Very good. But isn't there more?"

Mortimer folded the handkerchief precisely and tucked it back into his pocket. "Thirdly," he said, and patted it smooth, "I shall not be liable to prosecution by law if I take the life of the proscribed individual, one Benedict Vernall."

"Perfectly correct." The bailiff nodded and pointed to a large suitcase that a policeman had set down on the floor and was opening. The hall had been cleared. "If you would step over here and take your choice." They both gazed down into the suitcase that was filled to overflowing with instruments of death. "I hope you also understand that your own life will be in jeopardy during this period and if you are injured or killed you will not be protected by law?"

"Don't take me for a fool," Mortimer said curtly, then pointed into the suitcase. "I want one of those concussion grenades."

"You cannot have it," the bailiff told him in a cutting voice, injured by the other's manner. There was a correct way to do these things. "Those are only for use in open districts where the innocent cannot be injured. Not in an apartment building. You have your choice of all the short-range weapons, however."

Mortimer laced his fingers together and stood with his head bowed, almost in an attitude of prayer, as he examined the contents. Machine pistols, grenades, automatics, knives, knuckle dusters, vials of acid, whips, straight razors, broken glass, poison darts, morning stars, maces, gas bombs, and tear-gas pens.

"Is there any limit?" he asked.

"Take what you feel you will need. Just remember that it must all be accounted for and returned."

"I want the Reisling machine pistol with five of the twenty-cartridge magazines and the commando knife with the spikes on the handguard and fountain-pen tear-gas gun."

The bailiff was making quick check marks on a mimeographed from attached to his clipboard while Mortimer spoke. "Is that all?" he asked.

Mortimer nodded and took the extended board and scrawled his name on the bottom of the sheet without examining it, then began at once to fill his pockets with the weapons and ammunition.

"Twenty-four hours," the bailiff said, looking at his watch and filling in one more space in the form. "You have until 1745 hours tomorrow."

"Get away from the door, please, Ben," Maria begged.

"Quiet," Benedict whispered, his ear pressed to the panel. "I want to hear what they are saying." His face screwed up as he struggled to understand the muffled voices. "It's no good," he said, turning away. "I can't make it out. Not that it makes any difference. I know what's happening . . ."

"There's a man coming to kill you," Maria said in her delicate, little girl's voice. The baby started to whimper and she hugged him to her.

"Please, Maria, go back into the bathroom like we agreed. You have the bed in there, and the food, and there aren't any windows. As long as you stay along the wall away from the door nothing can possibly happen to you. Do that for me, darling. So I won't have to worry about either of you."

"Then you will be out here alone."

Benedict squared his narrow shoulders and clutched the pistol firmly. "That is where I belong, out in front, defending my family. That is as old as the history of man."

"Family," she said and looked around worriedly "What about Matthew and Agnes?"

"They'll be all right with your mother. She promised to look after them until we got in touch with her again. You can still be there with them; I wish you would."

"No, I couldn't. I couldn't bear being anywhere else now. And I couldn't leave the baby there; he would be so hungry." She looked down at the infant, who was still whimpering, then began to unbutton the top of her dress.

"Please, darling," Benedict said, edging back from the door. "I want you to go into the bathroom with baby and stay there. You must. He could be coming at any time now."

She reluctantly obeyed him, and he waited until the door had closed and he heard the lock being turned. Then he tried to force their presence from his mind because they were only a distraction that could interfere with what must be done. He had worked out the details of his plan of defense long before and he went slowly around the apartment making sure that everything was as it should be. First the front door, the only door into the apartment. It was locked and bolted and the night chain was attached. All that remained was to push the big wardrobe up against it. The killer could not enter now without a noisy struggle and if he tried Benedict would be there waiting with his gun. That took care of the door. There were no windows in either the kitchen or the bathroom, so he could forget about these rooms. The bedroom was a possibility since its window looked out onto the fire escape, but he had a plan for this too. The window was locked and the only way it could be opened from the outside was by breaking the glass. He would hear that and would have time to push the couch in the hall up against the bedroom door. He didn't want to block it now in case he had to retreat into the bedroom himself.

Only one room remained, the living room, and this was where he was going to make his stand. There were two windows in the living room and the far one could be entered from the fire escape, as could the bedroom window. The killer might come this way. The other window could not be reached from the fire escape, though shots could still be fired through it from the windows across the court. But the corner was out of the line of fire, and this was where he would be. He had pushed the big armchair right up against the wall and, after checking once more that both windows were locked, he dropped into it.

His gun rested on his lap and pointed at the far window by the fire escape. He would shoot if anyone tried to come through it. The other window was close by, but no harm could come that way unless he stood in front of it. The thin fabric curtains were drawn and once it was dark he could see through them without being seen himself. By shifting the gun barrel a few degrees he could cover the door into the hall. If there were any disturbance at the front door he could be there in a few steps. He had done everything he could. He settled back into the chair.

Once the daylight faded the room was quite dark, yet he could see well enough by the light of the city sky, which filtered in through the drawn curtains. It was very quiet and whenever he shifted position he could hear the new chair springs twang beneath him. After only a few hours he realized one slight flaw in his plan. He was thirsty.

At first he could ignore it, but by nine o'clock his mouth was as dry as cotton wool. He knew he couldn't last the night like this; it was too distracting. He should have brought a tug of water in with him. The wisest thing would be to go and get it as soon as possible, yet he did not want to leave the protection of the corner. He had heard nothing of the killer and this only made him more concerned about his unseen presence.

Then he heard Maria calling to him. Very softly at first, then louder and louder. She was worried. Was he all right? He dared not answer her, not from here. The only thing to do was to go to her, whisper through the door that everything was fine and that she should be quiet. Perhaps then she would go to sleep. And he could get some water in the kitchen and bring it back.

As quietly as he could he rose and stretched his stiff legs, keeping his eyes on the gray square of the second window. Putting the toe of one foot against the heel of the other he pulled his shoes off, then went on silent tiptoe across the room. Maria was calling louder now, rattling at the bathroom door, and he had to silence her. Why couldn't she realize the danger she was putting him in?

As he passed through the door the hall light above him came on.

"What are you doing?" he screamed at Maria who stood by the switch, blinking in the sudden glare.

"I was so worried—"

The crash of breaking glass from the living room was punctuated by the hammering boom of the machine pistol. Arrows of pain tore at Benedict and he hurled himself sprawling into the hall

"Into the bathroom!" he screamed and fired his own revolver back through the dark doorway.

He was only half aware of Maria's muffled squeal as she slammed the door and, for the moment, he forgot the pain of the wounds. There was the metallic smell of burnt gunpowder and a blue haze hung in the air. Something scraped in the living room and he fired again into the darkness. He winced as the answering fire crashed thunder and flame toward him and the bullets tore holes in the plaster of the hall opposite the door.

The firing stopped but he kept his gun pointed as he realized that the killer's fire couldn't reach him where he lay, against the wall away from the open doorway. The man would have to come into the hall to shoot him, and if he did that Benedict would fire first and kill him. More shots slammed into the wall but he did not bother to answer them. When the silence stretched out for more than a minute he took a chance and silently broke the revolver and pulled out the empty shells, putting live cartridges in their place. There was a pool of blood under his leg.

Keeping the gun pointed at the doorway he clumsily rolled up his pants leg with his left hand, then took a quick glimpse. There was more blood running down his ankle and sopping his sock. A bullet had torn through his calf muscle and made two round, dark holes from which the thick blood pumped. It made him dizzy to look at; then he remembered and pointed the wavering pistol back at the doorway. The living room was silent. His side hurt too, but when he pulled his shirt out of his trousers and looked he realized that although this wound was painful, it was not as bad as the one in his leg. A second bullet had burned along his side, glancing off the ribs and leaving a shallow wound. It wasn't bleeding badly. But something would have to be done about his leg.

"You moved fast, Benedict, I must congratulate you."

Benedict's finger contracted with shock and he pumped two bullets into the room, toward the sound of the man's voice. The man laughed.

"Nerves, Benedict, nerves. Just because I am here to kill you doesn't mean that we can't talk."

"You're a filthy beast, a foul, filthy beast!" Benedict splattered the words from his lips and followed them with a string of obscenities, expressions he hadn't used or even heard since his school days. He stopped suddenly as he realized that Maria could hear him. She had never heard him curse before.

"Nerves, Benedict?" The dry laugh sounded again. "Calling me insulting names won't alter this situation."

"Why don't you leave? I won't try to stop you," Benedict said as he slowly pulled his left arm out of his shirt. "I don't want to see you or know you. Why don't you go away?"

"I'm afraid that it is not that easy, Ben. You have created this situation; in one sense you have called me here. Like a sorcerer summoning some evil genie. That's a pleasant simile, isn't it? May I introduce myself. My name is Mortimer."

"I don't want to know your name, you . . . piece of filth." Benedict half mumbled, his attention concentrated on the silent removal of his shirt. It hung from his right wrist and he shifted the gun to his left hand for a moment while he slipped it off. His leg throbbed with pain when he draped the shirt over the wound in his calf and he gasped, then spoke quickly to disguise the sound. "You came here because you wanted to—and I'm going to kill you for that."

"Very good, Benedict, that is much more the type of spirit I expected from you. After all, you are the closest that we can come to a dedicated lawbreaker these days. The antisocial individualist who stands alone, who will carry on the traditions of the Dillingers and the James brothers. Though they brought death and you brought life, and your weapon is far humbler than their guns . . ." The words ended with a dry chuckle.

"You have a warped mind, Mortimer, just what I would suspect of a man who accepts a free license to kill. You're sick."

Benedict wanted to keep the other man talking, at least for a few minutes more until he could bandage his leg. The shirt was sticky with blood and he couldn't knot it in place with his left hand. "You must be sick to come here," he said. "What other reason could you possibly have?" laid the gun down silently, then fumbled with haste to bandage the wound.

"Sickness is relative," the voice in the darkness said, "as is crime. Man invents societies and the rules of his invented societies determine the crimes. *O tempora! O mores!* Homosexuals in Periclean Greece were honored men, and respected for their love. Homosexuals in industrial England were shunned and prosecuted for the criminal act. Who commits the crime—society or the man? Which of them is the criminal? You may attempt to argue a higher authority than man, but that would be on an abstract predication and what we are discussing here are realities. The law states that you are a criminal. I am here to enforce that law." The thunder of his gun added punctuation to his words and long splinters of wood flew from the doorframe. Benedict jerked the knot tight and grabbed up his pistol again.

"I do invoke a higher authority," he said. "Natural law, the sanctity of life, the inviolability of marriage. Under this authority I wed and I love, and my children are the blessings of this union."

"Your blessings—the blessings of the rest of mankind—are consuming this world like locusts," Mortimer said. "But that is an observation. First I must deal with your arguments.

"Primus. The only natural law is written in the sedimentary rocks and the spectra of suns. What you call natural law is man-made law and varies with the varieties of religion. Argument invalid.

"Secundus. Life is prolific and today's generations must die so that tomorrow's may live. All religions have the faces of Janus. They frown at killing and at the same time smile at war and capital punishment. Argument invalid.

"Ultimus. The forms of male and female union are as varied as the societies that harbor them. Argument invalid. Your higher authority does not apply to the world of facts and law. Believe in it if you wish, if it gives you satisfaction, but do not invoke it to condone your criminal acts."

"Criminal!" Benedict shouted, and fired two shots through the doorway, then cringed as an answering storm of bullets crackled by. Dimly, through the bathroom door, he heard the baby crying, awakened by the noise. He dropped out the empty shells and angrily pulled live cartridges from his pocket and jammed them into the cylinder. "You're the criminal, who is trying to murder me," he said. "You are the tool of the criminals who invade my house with their unholy laws and tell me I can have no more children. You cannot give me orders about this."

"What a fool you are," Mortimer sighed. "You are a social animal and do not hesitate to accept the benefits of your society. You accept medicine, so your children live now as they would have died in the past. And you accept a ration of food to feed them, food you do not even work for. This suits you, so you accept. But you do not accept planning for your family and you attempt to reject it. It is impossible. You must accept all or reject all. You must leave your society or abide by its rules. You eat the food, you must pay the price."

"I don't ask for more food. The baby has its mother's milk; we will share our food ration . . ."

"Don't be fatuous. You and your irresponsible kind have filled this world to bursting with your get, and still you will not stop. You have been reasoned with, railed against, cajoled, bribed and threatened, all to no avail. Now you must be stopped. You have refused all aid to prevent your bringing one more mouth into this hungry world, and since you have done so anyway, you are to be held responsible for closing another mouth and removing it from this same world. The law is a humane one, rising out of our history of individualism and the frontier spirit, and gives you a chance to defend your ideals with a gun. And your life."

"The law is not humane," Benedict said. "How can you possibly suggest that? It is harsh, cruel, and pointless."

"Quite the contrary, the system makes very good sense. Try to step outside yourself for a moment, forget your prejudices and look at the problem that faces our race. The universe is cruel but it's not ruthless. The conservation of mass is one of the universe's most ruthlessly enforced laws. We have been insane to ignore it so long, and it is sanity that now forces us to limit the sheer mass of human flesh on this globe. Appeals to reason have never succeeded in slowing the population growth, so, with great reluctance, laws have been passed. Love, marriage, and the family are not affected up to a reasonable maximum of children. After that a man voluntarily forsakes the protection of society, and must take the consequences of his own acts. If he is insanely selfish, his death will benefit society by ridding it of his presence. If he is not insane and has determination and enough guts to win—well then, he is the sort of man that society needs and he represents a noble contribution to the gene pool. Good and law-abiding citizens are not menaced by these laws."

"How dare you!" Benedict shouted. "Is a poor, helpless mother of an illegitimate baby a criminal?"

"No, only if she refuses all aid. She is even allowed a single child without endangering herself. If she persists in her folly, she must pay for her acts. There are countless frustrated women willing to volunteer for battle to even the score. They, like myself, are on the side of the law and eager to enforce it. So close my mouth, if you can, Benedict, because I look forward with pleasure to closing your incredibly selfish one."

"Madman!" Benedict hissed and felt his teeth grate together with the intensity of his passion. "Scum of society. This obscene law brings forth the insane dregs of humanity and arms them and gives them license to kill.

"It does that, and a useful device it is, too. The maladjusted expose themselves and can be watched. Better the insane killer coming publicly and boldly than trapping and butchering your child in the park. Now he risks his life and whoever is killed serves humanity with his death."

"You admit you are a madman—a licensed killer?' Benedict started to stand but the hall began to spin dizzily and grow dark: he dropped back heavily.

"Not I," Mortimer said tonelessly. "I am a man who wishes to aid the law and wipe out your vile, proliferating kind."

"You're an invert then, hating the love of man and woman."

The only answer was a cold laugh that infuriated Benedict.

"Sick!" he screamed. "Or mad. Or sterile, incapable of fathering children of your own and hating those who can—"

"That's enough! I've talked enough to you, Benedict. Now I shall kill you."

Benedict could hear anger for the first time in the other's voice and knew that he had goaded the man with the prod of truth. He was silent, sick and weak, the blood still seeping through his rough bandage and widening in a pool on the floor. He had to save what little strength he had to aim and fire when the killer came through the doorway. Behind him he heard the almost silent opening of the bathroom door and the rustle of footsteps. He looked helplessly into Maria's tear-stained face.

"Who's there with you?" Mortimer shouted from where he crouched behind the armchair. "I hear you whispering. If your wife is there with you, Benedict, send her away. I won't be responsible for the cow's safety. You've brought this upon yourself, Benedict, and the time has now come to pay the price of your errors, and I shall be the instrumentality of that payment."

He stood and emptied the remainder of the magazine bullets through the doorway, then pressed the button releasing the magazine and hurled it after the bullets, clicking a new one instantly into place. With a quick pull he worked the slide to shove a live cartridge into the chamber and crouched, ready to attack.

This was it. He wouldn't need the knife. Walk a few feet forward. Fire through the doorway, then throw in the tear-gas pen. It would either blind the man or spoil his aim. Then walk through firing with the trigger jammed down and the bullets spraying like water and the man would be dead. Mortimer took a deep, shuddering breath then stopped and gasped as Benedict's hand snaked through the doorway and felt its way up the wall.

It was so unexpected that for a moment he didn't fire and when he did fire he missed. A hand is a difficult target for an automatic weapon. The hand jerked down over the light switch and vanished as the ceiling lights came on.

Mortimer cursed and fired after the hand and fired into the wall and through the doorway, hitting nothing except insensate plaster and feeling terribly exposed beneath the glare of light.

The first shot from the pistol went unheard in the roar of his gun and he did not realize that he was under fire until the second bullet ripped into the floor close to his foot. He stopped shooting, spun around, and gaped.

On the fire escape outside the broken window stood a woman. Slight and wide-eyed and swaying as though strong wind tore at her, she pointed the gun at him with both hands and jerked the trigger spasmodically. The bullets came close but did not hit him, and in panic he pulled the machine pistol up, spraying bullets towards the window. "Don't! I don't want to hurt you!" he shouted even as he did it.

The last of his bullets hit the wall and his gun clicked and locked out of battery as the magazine emptied. He hurled the barren metal magazine away and tried to jam a full one in and the pistol banged again and the bullet caught him in the side and spun him about. When he fell the pistol fell from his hand. Benedict, who had been crawling slowly and painfully across the floor, reached him at the same moment and clutched his throat with hungry fingers.

"Don't . . ." Mortimer croaked and thrashed about. He had never learned to fight and did not know what else to do.

"Please Benedict, don't," Maria said, climbing through the window and running to them. "You're killing him."

"No, I'm not," Benedict gasped. "No strength. My hands are too weak."

Looking up he saw the pistol near his head and he reached and tore it from her.

"One less mouth now!" he shouted and pressed the hot muzzle against Mortimer's chest and the muffled shot tore into the man, who kicked violently once and died.

"Darling, you're all right?" Maria wailed, kneeling and clutching him to her.

"Yes . . . all right. Weak, but that's from losing the blood, I imagine, but the bleeding has stopped now. It's all over. We've won. We'll have the food ration, and they won't bother us anymore and everyone will be satisfied."

"I'm so glad," she said, and actually managed to smile through her tears. "I really didn't want to tell you before, not bother you with all this other trouble going on. But there's going to be . . ." She dropped her eyes.

"What?" he asked incredulously. "You can't possibly mean . . ."

"But I do." She patted the rounded mound of her midriff. "Aren't we lucky?"

All he could do was look up at her, his mouth wide and gaping like some helpless fish cast up on the shore.

Roommates

The August sun struck in through the open window and burned on Andrew Rusch's bare legs until discomfort dragged him awake from the depths of heavy sleep. Only slowly did he become aware of the heat and the damp and gritty sheet beneath his body. He rubbed at his gummed-shut eyelids, then lay there, staring up at the cracked and stained plaster of the ceiling, only half awake and experiencing a feeling of dislocation, not knowing in those first waking moments just where he was, although he had lived in this room for over seven years. He yawned and the odd sensation slipped away while he groped for the watch that he always put on the chair next to the bed. Then he yawned again as he blinked at the hands mistily seen behind the scratched crystal. Seven . . . seven o'clock in the morning, and there was a little number 9 in the middle of the square window. Monday the ninth of August, 1999—and hot as a furnace already, with the city still embedded in the heat wave that had baked and suffocated New York for the past ten days. Andy scratched at a trickle of perspiration on his side, then moved his legs out of the patch of sunlight and bunched the pillow up under his neck. From the other side of the thin partition that divided the room in half there came a clanking whir that quickly rose to a high-pitched drone.

"Morning . . ." he shouted over the sound, then began coughing. Still coughing he reluctantly stood and crossed the room to draw a glass of water from the wall tank; it came out in a thin, brownish trickle. He swallowed it, then rapped the dial on the tank with his knuckles and the needle bobbed up and down close to the Empty mark. It needed filling; he would have to see to that before he signed in at four o'clock at the precinct. The day had begun.

A full-length mirror with a crack running down it was fixed to the front of the hulking wardrobe and he poked his face close to it, rubbing at his bristly jaw. He would have to shave before he went in. No one should ever look at himself in the morning, naked and revealed, he decided with distaste, frowning at the dead white of his skin and the slight bow to his legs that was usually concealed by his pants. And how did he manage to have ribs that stuck out like those of a starved horse, as well as a growing potbelly—both at the same time? He kneaded the soft flesh and thought that it must be the starchy diet, that and sitting around on his chunk most of the time. But at least the fat wasn't showing on his face. His forehead was a little higher each year, but wasn't too obvious as long as his hair was cropped short. You have just turned thirty, he thought to himself, and the wrinkles are already starting around your eyes. And your nose is too big—wasn't it Uncle Brian who always said that was because there was Welsh blood in the family? And your canine teeth are a little too obvious so when you smile you look a bit like a hyena. You're a handsome devil, Andy Rusch, and it's a wonder a girl like Shirl will even look at you, much less kiss you. He scowled at himself, then went to look for a handkerchief to blow his impressive Welsh nose.

There was just a single pair of clean undershorts in the drawer and he pulled them on; that was another thing he had to remember today, to get some washing done. The squealing whine was still coming from the other side of the partition as he pushed through the connecting door.

"You're going to give yourself a coronary, Sol," he told the gray-bearded man who was perched on the wheelless bicycle, pedaling so industriously that perspiration ran down his chest and soaked into the bath towel that he wore tied around his waist.

"Never a coronary," Solomon Kahn gasped out, pumping steadily. "I been doing this every day for so long that my ticker would miss it if I stopped. And no cholesterol in my arteries either since regular flushing with alcohol takes care of that. And no lung cancer since I couldn't afford to smoke even if I wanted to, which I don't. And at the age of seventy-five no prostatitis because—"

"Sol, please—spare me the horrible details on an empty stomach. Do you have an ice cube to spare?"

"Take two—it's a hot day. And don't leave the door open too long."

Andy opened the small refrigerator that squatted against the wall and quickly took out the plastic container of margarine, then squeezed two ice cubes from the tray into a glass and slammed the door. He filled the glass with water from the wall tank and put it on the table next to the margarine.

"Have you eaten yet?" he asked.

"I'll join you, these things should be charged by now."

Sol stopped pedaling and the whine died away to a moan, then vanished. He disconnected the wires from the electrical generator that was geared to the rear axle of the bike, and carefully coiled them up next to the four black automobile storage batteries that were racked on top of the refrigerator. Then, after wiping his hands on his soiled towel sarong, he pulled out one of the bucket seats, salvaged from an ancient 1975 Ford, and sat down across the table from Andy.

"I heard the six o'clock news," he said. "The Eldsters are organizing another protest march today on relief headquarters. That's where you'll see coronaries!"

"I won't, thank God, I'm not on until four and Union Square isn't in our precinct." He opened the breadbox and took out one of the six-inch-square red crackers, then pushed the box over to Sol. He spread margarine thinly on it and took a bite, wrinkling his nose as he chewed. "I think this margarine has turned."

"How can you tell?" Sol grunted, biting into one of the dry crackers. "Anything made from motor oil and whale blubber is turned to begin with."

"Now you begin to sound like a naturist," Andy said, washing his cracker down with cold water. "There's hardly any flavor at all to the fats made from petrochemicals, and you know there aren't any whales left so they can't use blubber—it's just good chlorella oil."

"Whales, plankton, herring oil, it's all the same. Tastes fishy. I'll take mine dry so I don't grow no fins." There was a sudden staccato rapping on the door and he groaned. "Not yet eight o'clock and already they are after you."

"It could be anything," Andy said, starting for the door.

"It could be but it's not, that's the callboy's knock and you know it as well as I do and I bet you dollars to doughnuts that's just who it is. See?" He nodded with gloomy satisfaction when Andy unlocked the door and they saw the skinny, bare-legged messenger standing in the dark hall.

"What do you want, Woody?" Andy asked.

"I don' wan' no-fin," Woody lisped over his bare gums. Though he was in his early twenties he didn't have a tooth in his head. "Lieutenan' says bring, I bring." He handed Andy the message board with his name written on the outside.

Andy turned toward the light and opened it, reading the lieutenant's spiky scrawl on the slate, then took the chalk and scribbled his initials after it and returned it to the messenger. He closed the door behind him and went back to finish his breakfast, frowning in thought.

"Don't look at me that way," Sol said, "I didn't send the message. Am I wrong in guessing it's not the most pleasant of news?"

"It's the Eldsters, they're jamming the Square already and the precinct needs reinforcements."

"But why you? This sounds like a job for the harness bulls."

"Harness bulls! Where do you get that medieval slang? Of course they need patrolmen for the crowd, but there have to be detectives there to spot known agitators, pickpockets, purse grabbers and the rest. It'll be murder in that park today. I have to check in by nine, so I have enough time to bring up some water first."

Andy dressed slowly in slacks and a loose sport shirt, then put a pan of water on the windowsill to warm in the sun. He took the two five-gallon plastic jerry cans, and when he went out Sol looked up from the TV set, glancing over the top of his old-fashioned glasses.

"When you bring back the water I'll fix you a drink—or do you think it is too early?"

"Not the way I feel today, it's not."

The hall was ink black once the door had closed behind him and he felt his way carefully along the wall to the stairs, cursing and almost falling when he stumbled over a heap of refuse someone had thrown there. Two flights down a window had been knocked through the wall and enough light came in to show him the way down the last two flights to the street. After the damp hallway the heat of Twenty-fifth Street hit him in a musty wave, a stifling miasma compounded of decay, dirt and unwashed humanity. He had to make his way through the women who already filled the steps of the building, walking carefully so that he didn't step on the children who were playing below. The sidewalk was still in shadow but so jammed with people that he walked in the street, well away from the curb to avoid the rubbish and litter banked high there. Days of heat had softened the tar so that it gave underfoot then clutched at the soles of his shoes. There was the usual line leading to the columnar red water point on the corner of Seventh Avenue, but it broke up with angry shouts and some waved fists just as he reached it. Still muttering, the crowd dispersed and Andy saw that the duty patrolman was locking the steel door.

"What's going on?" Andy asked. "I thought this point was open until noon."

The policeman turned, his hand automatically staying close to his gun until he recognized the detective from his own precinct. He tilted back his uniform cap and wiped the sweat from his forehead with the back of his hand.

"Just had the orders from the sergeant, all points closed for twenty-four hours. The reservoir level is low because of the drought, they gotta save water."

"That's a hell of a note," Andy said, looking at the key still in the lock. "I'm going on duty now and this means I'm not going to be drinking for a couple of days . . ."

After a careful look around, the policeman unlocked the door and took one of the jerry cans from Andy. "One of these ought to hold you." He held it under the faucet while it filled, then lowered his voice. "Don't let it out, but word is that there was another dynamiting job on the aqueduct upstate."

"Those farmers again?"

"It must be. I was on guard duty up there before I came to this precinct and it's rough, they just as soon blow you up with the aqueduct at the same time. Claim the city's stealing their water."

"They've got enough," Andy said, taking the full container. "More than they need. And there are 35 million people here in the city who get damn thirsty."

"Who's arguing?" the cop asked, slamming the door shut again and locking it tight.

Andy pushed his way back through the crowd around the steps and went through to the backyard first. All of the toilets were in use and he had to wait, and when he finally got into one of the cubicles he took the jerry cans with him; one of the kids playing in the pile of rubbish against the fence would be sure to steal them if he left them unguarded.

When he had climbed the dark flights once more and opened the door to the room he heard the clear sound of ice cubes rattling against glass.

"That's Beethoven's Fifth Symphony that you're playing," he said, dropping the containers and falling into a chair. "It's my favorite tune," Sol said, taking two chilled glasses from the refrigerator and, with the solemnity of religious ritual, dropped a tiny pearl onion into each of them and passed one to Andy, who sipped carefully at the chilled liquid.

"It's when I taste one of these, Sol, that I almost believe you're not crazy after all. Why do they call them Gibsons?"

"A secret lost behind the mists of time. Why is a Stinger a Stinger or a Pink Lady a Pink Lady?"

"I don't know—why? I never tasted any of them."

"I don't know either, but that's the name. Like those green things they serve in the knockjoints, Panamas. Doesn't mean anything, just a name."

"Thanks," Andy said, draining his glass. "The day looks better already."

He went into his room and took his gun and holster from the drawer and clipped it inside the waistband of his pants. His shield was on his key ring where he always kept it and he slipped his notepad in on top of it, then hesitated a moment. It was going to be a long and rough day and anything might happen. He dug his nippers out from under his shirts, then the soft plastic tube filled with shot. It might be needed in the crowd, safer than a gun with all those old people milling about. Not only that, but with the new austerity regulations you had to have a damn good reason for using up any ammunition. He washed as well as he could with the pint of water that had been warming in the sun on the windowsill, then scrubbed his face with the small shard of gray and gritty soap until his whiskers softened a bit. His razor blade was beginning to show obvious nicks along both edges and, as he honed it against the inside of his drinking glass, he thought that it was time to think about getting a new one. Maybe in the fall.

Sol was watering his window box when Andy came out, carefully irrigating the rows of herbs and tiny onions. "Don't take any wooden nickels," he said without looking up from his work. Sol had a million of them, all old. What in the world was a wooden nickel?

The sun was higher now and the heat was mounting in the sealed tar and concrete valley of the street. The band of shade was smaller and the steps were so packed with humanity that he couldn't leave the doorway. He carefully pushed by a tiny, runny-nosed girl dressed only in ragged gray underwear and descended a step. The gaunt women moved aside reluctantly, ignoring him, but the men stared at him with a cold look of hatred stamped across their features that gave them a strangely alike appearance, as though they were all members of the same angry family.

Andy threaded his way through the last of them and when he reached the sidewalk he had to step over the outstretched leg of an old man who sprawled there. He looked dead, not asleep, and he might be for all that anyone cared. His foot was bare and filthy and a string tied about his ankle led to a naked baby that was sitting vacantly on the sidewalk chewing on a bent plastic dish. The baby was as dirty as the man and the string was tied about its chest under the pipestem arms because its stomach was swollen and heavy. Was the old man dead? Not that it mattered, the only work he had to do in the world was to act as an anchor for the baby and he could do that job just as well alive or dead.

Out of the room now, well away and unable to talk to Sol until he returned, he realized that once again he had not managed to mention Shirl. It would have been a simple enough thing to do, but he kept forgetting it, avoiding it. Sol was always talking about how horny he always was and how often he used to get laid when he was in the army. He would understand.

They were roommates, that was all. There was nothing else between them. Friends, sure. But bringing a girl in to live wouldn't change that.

So why hadn't he told him?

FALL

"Everybody says this is the coldest October ever, I never seen a colder one. And the rain too, never hard enough to fill the reservoir or anything, but just enough to make you wet so you feel colder. Ain't that right?"

Shirl nodded, hardly listening to the words, but aware by the rising intonation of the woman's voice that a question had been asked. The line moved forward and she shuffled a few steps behind the woman who had been speaking—a shapeless bundle of heavy clothing covered with a torn plastic raincoat, with a cord tied about her middle so that she resembled a lumpy sack. Not that I look much better, Shirl thought, tugging the fold of blanket farther over her head to keep out the persistent drizzle. It wouldn't be much longer now, there were only a few dozen people ahead, but it had taken a lot more time than she thought it would; it was almost dark. A light came on over the tank car, glinting off its black sides and lighting up the slowly falling curtain of rain. The line moved again and the woman ahead of Shirl waddled forward, pulling the child after her, a bundle as wrapped and shapeless as its mother, its face hidden by a knotted scarf, that produced an almost constant whimpering.

"Stop that," the woman said. She turned to Shirl, her puffy face a red lumpiness around the dark opening of her almost toothless mouth. "He's crying because he's been to see the doc, thinks he's sick but it's only the kwash." She held up the child's swollen, ballooning hand. "You can tell when they swell up and get the black spots on the knees. Had to sit two weeks in the Bellevue clinic to see a doc who told me what I knew already. But that's the only way you get him to sign the slip. Got a peanut-butter ration that way. My old man loves the stuff. You live on my block, don't you? I think I seen you there?"

"Twenty-sixth Street," Shirl said, taking the cap off the jerry can and putting it into her coat pocket. She felt chilled through and was sure she was catching a cold.

"That's right, I knew it was you. Stick around and wait for me, we'll walk back together. It's getting late and plenty of punks would like to grab the water, they can always sell it. Mrs. Ramirez in my building, she's a spic but she's all right, you know, her family been in the building since the World War Two, she got a black eye so swole up she can't see through it and two teeth knocked out. Some punk got her with a club and took her water away."

"Yes, I'll wait for you, that's a good idea," Shirl said, suddenly feeling very alone.

"Cards," the patrolman said and she handed him the three Welfare cards, hers, Andy's and Sol's. He held them to the light, then handed them back to her. "Six quarts," he called out to the valve man.

"That's not right," Shirl said.

"Reduced ration today, lady, keep moving, there's a lot of people waiting."

She held out the jerry can and the valve man slipped the end of a large funnel into it and ran in the water. "Next," he called out.

The jerry can gurgled when she walked and was tragically light. She went and stood near the policeman until the woman came up, pulling the child with one hand and in the other carrying a five-gallon kerosene can that seemed almost full. She must have a big family.

"Let's go," the woman said and the child trailed, mewling faintly, at the end of her arm.

As they left the Twelfth Avenue railroad siding it grew darker, the rain soaking up all the failing light. The buildings here were mostly old warehouses and factories with blank solid walls concealing the tenants hidden away inside, the sidewalks wet and empty. The nearest streetlight was a block away. "My husband will give me hell coming home this late," the woman said as they turned the corner. Two figures blocked the sidewalk in front of them.

"Let's have the water," the nearest one said, and the distant light reflected from the knife he held before him.

"No, don't! Please don't!" the woman begged and swung her can of water out behind her, away from them. Shirl huddled against the wall and saw, when they walked forward, that they were just young boys, teenagers. But they still had a knife.

"The water!" the first one said, jabbing his knife at the woman.

"Take it," she screeched, swinging the can like a weight on the end of her arm. Before the boy could dodge it caught him full in the side of the head, knocking him howling to the ground, the knife flying from his fingers. "You want some too?" she shouted, advancing on the second boy. He was unarmed.

"No, I don't want no trouble," he begged, pulling at the first one's arm, then retreating when she approached. When she bent to pick up the fallen knife, he managed to drag the other boy to his feet and half carry him around the corner. It had only taken a few seconds and all the time Shirl had stood with her back to the wall, trembling with fear.

"They got some surprise," the woman crowed, holding the worn carving knife up to admire it. "I can use this better than they can. Just punks, kids." She was excited and happy. During the entire time she had never released her grip on the child's hand; it was sobbing louder.

There was no more trouble and the woman went with Shirl as far as her door. "Thank you very much," Shirl said. "I don't know what I would have done . . ."

"That's no trouble," the woman beamed. "You saw what I did to him—and who got the knife now!" She stamped away, hauling the heavy can in one hand, the child in the other. Shirl went in.

"Where have you been?" Andy asked when she pushed open the door. "I was beginning to wonder what had happened to you." It was warm in the room, with a faint odor of fishy smoke, and he and Sol were sitting at the table with drinks in their hands.

"It was the water, the line must have been a block long. They only gave me six quarts, the ration has been cut again." She saw his black look and decided not to tell him about the trouble on the way back. He would be twice as angry then and she didn't want this meal to be spoiled.

"That's really wonderful," Andy said sarcastically. "The ration was already too small—so now they lower it even more. Better get out of those wet things, Shirl, and Sol will pour you a Gibson. His home-made vermouth has ripened and I bought some vodka."

"Drink up," Sol said, handing her the chilled glass. "I made some soup with that Ener-G junk, it's the only way it's edible, and it should be just about ready. We'll have that for the first course, before—" He finished the sentence by jerking his head in the direction of the refrigerator.

"What's up?" Andy asked. "A secret?"

"No secret," Shirl said, opening the refrigerator, "just a surprise. I got these today in the market, one for each of us." She took out a plate with three small soylent burgers on it. "They're the new ones, they had them on TV, with the smoky-barbecue flavor."

"They must have cost a fortune," Andy said. "We won't eat for the rest of the month."

"They're not as expensive as all that. Anyway, it was my own money, not the budget money, I used."

"It doesn't make any difference, money is money. We could probably live for a week on what these things cost."

"Soup's on," Sol said, sliding the plates onto the table. Shirl had a lump in her throat so she couldn't say anything; she sat and looked at her plate and tried not to cry.

"I'm sorry," Andy said. "But you know how prices are going up—we have to look ahead. City income tax is higher, eighty percent now, because of the raised Welfare payment, so it's going to be rough going this winter. Don't think I don't appreciate it . . ."

"If you do, so why don't you shut up right there and eat your soup?" Sol said.

"Keep out of this, Sol," Andy said.

"I'll keep out of it when you keep the fight out of my room. Now come on, a nice meal like this, it shouldn't be spoiled."

Andy started to answer him, then changed his mind. He reached over and took Shirl's hand. "It is going to be a good dinner," he said. "Let's all enjoy it."

"Not that good," Sol said, puckering his mouth over a spoonful of soup. "Wait until you try this stuff. But the burgers will take the taste out of our mouths."

There was silence after that while they spooned up the soup, until Sol started on one of his army stories about New Orleans and it was so impossible they had to laugh, and after that things were better. Sol shared out the rest of the Gibsons while Shirl served the burgers.

"If I was drunk enough this would almost taste like meat," Sol announced, chewing happily.

"They are good," Shirl said. Andy nodded agreement. She finished the burger quickly and soaked up the juice with a scrap of weedcracker, then sipped at her drink. The trouble on the way home with the water already seemed far distant. What was it the woman had said was wrong with the child?

"Do you know what 'kwash' is?" she asked.

Andy shrugged. "Some kind of disease, that's all I know. Why do you ask?"

"There was a woman next to me in line for the water, I was talking to her. She had a little boy with her who was sick with this kwash. I don't think she should have had him out in the rain, sick like that. And I was wondering if it was catching."

"That you can forget about," Sol said. "Kwash is short for kwashiorkor. If, in the interest of good health, you watched the medical programs like I do, or opened a book, you would know all about it. You can't catch it because it's a deficiency disease like beriberi."

"I never heard of that either," Shirl said.

"There's not so much of that, but there's plenty of kwash. It comes from not eating enough protein. They used to have it only in Africa but now they got it right across the whole U.S. Isn't that great? There's no meat around, lentils and soybeans cost too much, so the mamas stuff the kids with weedcrackers and candy whatever is cheap . . ."

The lightbulb flickered, then went out. Sol felt his way across the room and found a switch in the maze of wiring on top of the refrigerator. A dim bulb lit up, connected to his batteries. "Needs a charge," he said, "but it can wait until morning. You shouldn't exercise after eating, bad for the circulation and digestion."

"I'm sure glad you're here, Doctor," Andy said. "I need some medical advice. I've got this trouble. You see—everything I eat goes to my stomach . . ."

"Very funny, Mr. Wiseguy. Shirl, I don't see how you put up with this joker."

They all felt better after the meal and they talked for a while, until Sol announced he was turning off the light to save the juice in the batteries. The small bricks of sea coal had burned to ash and the room was growing cold. They said good night and Andy went in first to get his flashlight; their room was even colder than the other.

"I'm going to bed," Shirl said. "I'm not really tired, but it's the only way to keep warm."

Andy flicked the overhead light switch uselessly. "The current is still off and there are some things I have to do. What is it—a week now since we had any electricity in the evening?"

"Let me get into bed and I'll work the flash for you—will that be all right?"

"It'll have to do."

He opened his notepad on top of the dresser, lay one of the reusable forms next to it, then began copying information into the report. With his left hand he kept a slow and regular squeezing on the flashlight that produced steady illumination. The city was quiet tonight with the people driven from the streets by the cold and the rain; the whir of the tiny generator and the occasional squeak of the stylo on plastic sounded unnaturally loud. There was enough light from the flash for Shirl to get undressed by. She shivered when she took off her outer clothes and quickly pulled on heavy winter pajamas, a much-darned pair of socks she used for sleeping in, then put her heavy sweater on top. The sheets were cold and damp, they hadn't been changed since the water shortage, though she did try to air them out as often as she could. Her cheeks were damp, as damp as the sheets were when she put her fingertips up to touch them, and she realized that she was crying. She tried not to sniffle and bother Andy. He was doing his best, wasn't he? Everything that it was possible to do. Yes, it had been a lot different before she came here, an easy life, good food and a warm room, and her own bodyguard, Tab, when she went out. And all she had to do was sleep with him a couple of times a week. She had hated it, even the touch of his hands, but at least it had been quick. Having Andy in bed was different and good and she wished that he were there right now. She shivered again and wished she could stop crying.

WINTER

New York City trembled on the brink of disaster. Every locked warehouse was a nucleus of dissent, surrounded by crowds who were hungry and afraid and searching for someone to blame. Their anger incited them to riot, and the food riots turned to water riots and then to looting wherever this was possible. The police fought back, only the thinnest of barriers between angry protest and bloody chaos.

At first nightsticks and weighted clubs stopped the trouble, and when this failed gas dispersed the crowd. The tension grew, since the people who fled only reassembled again in a different place. The solid jets of water from the riot trucks stopped them easily when they tried to break into the welfare stations, but there were not enough trucks, nor was there more water to be had once they had pumped dry their tanks. The Health Department had forbidden the use of river water: it would have been like spraying poison. The little water that was available was badly needed for the fires that were springing up throughout the city. With the streets blocked in many places the firefighting equipment could not get through and the trucks were forced to make long detours. Some of the fires were spreading and by noon all of the equipment had been committed and was in use.

The first gun was fired a few minutes past twelve on the morning of December twenty-first, by a Welfare Department guard who killed a man who had broken open a window of the Tompkins Square food depot and had tried to climb in. This was the first but not the last shot fired—nor was it the last person to be killed.

Flying wire sealed off some of the trouble areas, but there was only a limited supply of it. When it ran out the copters fluttered helplessly over the surging streets and acted as aerial observation posts for the police, finding the places where reserves were sorely needed. It was a fruitless labor because there were no reserves, everyone was in the front line.

After the first conflict nothing else made a strong impression on Andy. For the rest of the day and most of the night, he along with every other policeman in the city was braving violence and giving violence to restore law and order to a city torn by battle. The only rest he had was after he had fallen victim to his own gas and had managed to make his way to the Department of Hospitals ambulance for treatment. An orderly washed out his eyes and gave him a tablet to counteract the gut-tearing nausea. He lay on one of the stretchers inside, clutching his helmet, bombs and club to his chest, while he recovered. The ambulance driver sat on another stretcher by the door, armed with a .30 caliber carbine, to discourage anyone from too great an interest in the ambulance or its valuable surgical contents. Andy would like to have lain there longer, but the cold mist was rolling out through the open doorway, and he began to shiver so hard that his teeth shook together. It was difficult to drag to his feet and climb to the ground, yet once he was moving he felt a little better—and warmer. The attack had been broken up and he moved slowly to join the nearest cluster of blue-coated figures, wrinkling his nose at the foul odor of his clothes.

From this point on, the fatigue never left him and he had memories only of shouting faces, running feet, the sound of shots, screams, the thud of gas grenades, of something unseen that had been thrown at him and hit the back of his hand and raised an immense bruise.

By nightfall it was raining, a cold downpour mixed with sleet, and it was this and exhaustion that drove the people from the streets, not the police. Yet when the crowds were gone the police found that their work was just beginning. Gaping windows and broken doorways had to be guarded until they could be repaired, the injured had to be found and brought in for treatment, while the Fire Department needed aid in halting the countless fires. This went on through the night and at dawn Andy found himself slumped on a bench in the precinct, hearing his name being called off from a list by Lieutenant Grassioli.

"And that's all that can be spared," the lieutenant added. "You men draw rations before you leave and turn in your riot equipment. I want you all back here at 1800 and I don't want excuses. Our troubles aren't over yet."

Sometime during the night the rain had stopped. The rising sun cast long shadows down the crosstown streets, putting a golden sheen on the wet, black pavement. A burned-out brownstone was still smoking and Andy picked his way through the charred wreckage that littered the street in front of it. On the corner of Seventh Avenue were the crushed wreckage of two pedicabs, already stripped of any usable parts, and a few feet farther on, the huddled body of a man. He might be asleep, but when Andy passed, the upturned face gave violent evidence that the man was dead. He walked on, ignoring it. The Department of Sanitation would be collecting only corpses today.

The first cavemen were coming out of the subway entrance, blinking at the light. During the summer everyone laughed at the cavemen—the people whom Welfare had assigned to living quarters in the stations of the now-silent subways—but as the cold weather approached, the laughter was replaced by envy. Perhaps it was filthy down there, dusty, dark, but there were always a few electric heaters turned on. They weren't living in luxury, but at least Welfare didn't let them freeze. Andy turned into his own block.

Going up the stairs in his building, he trod heavily on some of the sleepers but was too fatigued to care—or even notice. He had trouble fumbling his key into the lock and Sol heard him and came to open it.

"I just made some soup," Sol said. "You timed it perfectly."

Andy pulled the broken remains of some weedcrackers from his coat pocket and spilled them onto the table.

"Been stealing food?" Sol asked, picking up a piece and nibbling on it. "I thought no grub was being given out for two more days?"

"Police ration."

"Only fair. You can't beat up the citizenry on an empty stomach. I'll throw some of these into the soup, give it some body. I guess you didn't see TV yesterday so you wouldn't know about all the fun and games in Congress. Things are really jumping . . ."

"Is Shirl awake yet?" Andy asked, shucking out of his coat and dropping heavily into a chair.

Sol was silent a moment, then he said slowly, "She's not here."

Andy yawned. "It's plenty early to go out. Why?"

"Not today, Andy." Sol stirred the soup with his back turned. "She went out yesterday, a couple of hours after you did. She's not back ye—"

"You mean she went out all the time during the riots—and last night too? What did you do?" He sat upright, his bone-weariness forgotten.

"What could I do? Go out and get myself trampled to death like the rest of the old fogies? I bet she's all right, she probably saw all the trouble and decided to stay with a friend instead of coming back here."

"What friends? What are you talking about? I have to go find her."

"Sit!" Sol ordered. "What can you do out there? Have some soup and get some sleep, that's the best thing you can do. She'll be okay. I know it," he added reluctantly.

"What do you know, Sol?" Andy took him by the shoulders, half turning him from the stove.

"Don't handle the merchandise!" Sol shouted, pushing the hand away. Then, in a quieter voice: "All I know is she just didn't go out of here for nothing, she had a reason. She had her old coat on, but I could see what looked like a real nifty dress underneath. And nylon stockings. A fortune on her legs. And when she said so long I saw she had lots of makeup on."

"Sol—what are you trying to say?"

"I'm not trying—I'm saying. She was dressed for visiting, not for shopping, like she was on the way out to see someone. Her old man, maybe, she could be visiting him."

"Why should she want to see him?"

"You tell me? You two had a fight, didn't you? Maybe she went away for a while to cool off."

"A fight . . . I guess so." Andy dropped back into the chair, squeezing his forehead with his palms. Had it only been last night? No, the night before last. It seemed one hundred years since they had had that stupid argument. But they were bickering so much these days.

One more fight shouldn't make any difference. He looked up with sudden fear. "She didn't take her things—anything with her?" he asked.

"Just a little bag," Sol said, and put a steaming bowl on the table in front of Andy. "Eat up. I'll pour one for myself." Then, "She'll be back."

Andy was almost too tired to argue—and what could be said? He spooned the soup automatically, then realized as he tasted it that he was very hungry. He ate with his elbow on the table, his free hand supporting his head.

"You should have heard the speeches in the Senate yesterday," Sol said. "Funniest show on earth. They're trying to push this Emergency Bill through—some emergency, it's only been one hundred years in the making—and you should hear them talking all around the little points and not mentioning the big ones." His voice settled into a rich southern accent. "Faced by dire straits, we propose a survey of all the ee-mense riches of this the greatest eeluvial basin, the delta, suh, of the mightiest of rivers, the Mississippi. Dikes and drains, suh, science, suh, and you will have here the richest farmlands in the Western World!" Sol blew on his soup angrily. " 'Dikes' is right—another finger in the dike. They've been over this ground a thousand times before. But does anyone mention out loud the sole and only reason for the Emergency Bill? They do not. After all these years they're too chicken to come right out and tell the truth, so they got it hidden away in one of the little riders tacked onto the bottom."

"What are you talking about?" Andy asked, only half listening, still worrying about Shirl.

"Birth control, that's what. They are finally getting around to legalizing clinics that will be open to anyone—married or not—and making it a law that all mothers must be supplied with birth-control information. Boy, are we going to hear some howling when the bluenoses find out about that—and the Pope will really plotz!"

"Not now, Sol, I'm tired. Did Shirl say anything about when she would be back?"

"Just what I told you . . ." He stopped and listened to the sound of footsteps coming down the hall. They stopped and there was a light knocking on the door.

Andy was there first, twisting at the knob, tearing the door open.

"Shirl!" he said. "Are you all right?"

"Yes, sure—I'm fine."

He held her to him, tightly, almost cutting off her breath. "With the riots—I didn't know what to think," he said. "I just came in a little while ago myself. Where have you been? What happened?"

"I just wanted to get out for a while, that's all." She wrinkled her nose. "What's that funny smell?"

He stepped away from her, anger welling up through the fatigue. "I caught some of my own puke gas and heaved it up. It's hard to get off. What do you mean that you wanted to get out for a while?"

"Let me get my coat off."

Andy followed her into the other room and closed the door behind them. She was taking a pair of high-heeled shoes out of the bag she carried and putting them in the closet. "Well?" he said.

"Just that, it's not complicated. I was feeling trapped in here, with the shortages and the cold and everything, and never seeing you, and I felt bad about the fight we had. Nothing seemed to be going right. So I thought if I dressed up and went to one of the restaurants where I used to go just to have a cup of coffee or something, I might feel better. A morale booster, you know." She looked up at his cold face, then glanced quickly away.

"Then what happened?" he asked.

"I'm not in the witness box, Andy. Why the accusing tone?"

He turned his back and looked out the window. "I'm not accusing you of anything, but you were out all night. How do you expect me to feel?"

"Well, you know how bad it was yesterday, I was afraid to come back. I was up at Curley's—"

"The meateasy?"

"Yes, but if you don't eat anything it's not expensive. It's just the food that costs. I met some people I knew and we talked, they were going to a party and invited me and I went along. We were watching news about the riots on TV and no one wanted to go out, so the party just went on and on." She paused. "That's all."

"All?" An angry question, a dark suspicion.

"That's all," she said, and her voice was now as cold as his.

She turned her back to him and began to pull off her dress, and their words lay like a cold barrier between them. Andy dropped onto the bed and turned his back on her as well so that they were like strangers, even in the tiny room.

SPRING

The funeral drew them together as nothing else had during the cold depths of the winter. It was a raw day, gusting wind and rain, but there was still a feeling that winter was on the way out. But it had been too long a winter for Sol and his cough had turned into a cold, the cold into pneumonia, and what can an old man do in a cold room without drugs in a winter that does not seem to end? Die, that was all. So he had died. They had forgotten their differences during his illness and Shirl had nursed him as best she could, but careful nursing does not cure pneumonia. The funeral had been as brief and cold as the day and in the early darkness they went back to the room. They had not been back half an hour before there was a quick rapping on the door. Shirl gasped.

"The callboy. They can't. You don't have to work today."

"Don't worry. Even Grassy wouldn't go back on his word about a thing like this. And besides, that's not the callboy's knock."

"Maybe a friend of Sol's who couldn't get to the funeral."

She went to unlock the door and had to blink into the darkness of the hall for a moment before she recognized the man standing there.

"Tab! It is you, isn't it? Come in, don't stand there. Andy, I told you about Tab my bodyguard . . ."

"Afternoon, Miss Shirl," Tab said stolidly, staying in the hall. "I'm sorry, but this is no social call. I'm on the job now."

"What is it?" Andy asked, walking over next to Shirl.

"You have to realize I take the work that is offered to me," Tab said. He was unsmiling and gloomy. "I've been in the bodyguard pool since September, just the odd jobs, no regular assignments, we take whatever work we can get. A man turns down a job, he goes right back to the end of the list. I have a family to feed . . ."

"What are you trying to say?" Andy asked. He was aware that someone was standing in the darkness behind Tab and could tell by the shuffle of feet that there were others out of sight down the hall.

"Don't take no guff," the man in back of Tab said in an unpleasant nasal voice. He stayed behind the bodyguard where he could not be seen. "I got the law on my side. I paid you. Show him the order!"

"I think I understand now," Andy said. "Get away from the door, Shirl. Come inside so we can talk to you."

Tab started forward and the man in the hall tried to follow him. "You don't go in there without me—" he shrilled. His voice was cut off as Andy slammed the door in his face.

"I wish you hadn't done that," Tab said. He was wearing his spike-studded iron knuckles, his fist clenched tight around them.

"Relax," Andy said. "I just wanted to talk to you alone first, find out was going on. He has a squat-order, doesn't he?"

Tab nodded, looking unhappily down at the floor.

"What on earth are you two talking about?" Shirl asked, worriedly glancing back and forth at their set expressions.

Andy didn't answer and Tab turned to her. "A squat-order is issued by the court to anyone who can prove they are really in need of a place to live. They only give so many out, and usually just to people with big families that have had to get out of some other place. With a squat-order you can look around and find a vacant apartment or room or anything like that, and the order is sort of a search warrant. There can be trouble, people don't want to have strangers walking in on them, that kind of thing, so anyone with a squat-order takes along a bodyguard. That's where I come in, the party out there in the hall, name of Belicher, hired me."

"But what are you doing here?" Shirl asked, still not understanding.

"Because Belicher is a ghoul, that's why," Andy said bitterly. "He hangs around the morgue looking for bodies."

"That's one way of saying it," Tab answered, holding on to his temper. "He's also a guy with a wife and kids and no place to live, that's another way of looking at it."

There was a sudden hammering on the door and Belicher's complaining voice could be heard outside. Shirl finally realized the significance of Tab's presence, and she gasped. "You're here because you're helping them," she said. "They found out that Sol is dead and they want this room."

Tab could only nod mutely.

"There's still a way out," Andy said. "If we had one of the men here from my precinct living in here, then those people couldn't get in."

The knocking was louder and Tab took a half-step backwards toward the door. "If there was somebody here now, that would be okay, but Belicher could probably take the thing to squat court and get occupancy anyway because he has a family. I'll do whatever I can to help you—but Belicher, he's still my employer."

"Don't open that door," Andy said sharply. "Not until we have this straightened out."

"I have to—what else can I do?" He straightened up and closed his fist with hard knuckles on it. "Don't try to stop me, Andy. You're a policeman, you know the law about this."

"Tab, must you?" Shirl asked in a low voice.

He turned to her, eyes filled with unhappiness. "We were good friends once, Shirl, and that's the way I'm going to remember it. But you're not going to think much of me after this because I have to do my job. I have to let them in."

"Go ahead, open the damn door," Andy said bitterly, turning his back and walking over to the window.

The Belichers swarmed in. Mr. Belicher was thin, with a strangely shaped head, almost no chin and just enough intelligence to sign his name to a Welfare application. Mrs. Belicher was the support of the family; from the flabby fat of her body came the children, all seven of them, to swell the Relief allotment on which they survived. Number 8 was pushing an extra bulge out of the dough of her flesh; it was really number 11 since three of the younger Belichers had perished through indifference or accident. The largest girl, she must have been all of twelve, was carrying the sore-covered infant which stank abominably and cried continuously. The other children shouted at each other now, released from the silence and tension of the dark hall.

"Oh looka the nice fridge," Mrs. Belicher said, waddling over and opening the door.

"Don't touch that," Andy said, and Belicher pulled him by the arm.

"I like this room—it's not big you know, but nice. What's in here?" He started toward the door in the partition.

"That's my room," Andy said, slamming it shut in his face. "Just keep out of there."

"No need to act like that," Belicher said, sidling away quickly like a dog that has been kicked too often. "I got my rights. The law says I can look wherever I want with a squat-order." He moved farther away as Andy took a step toward him. "Not that I'm doubting your word, mister, I believe you. This room here is fine, got a good table, chairs, bed . . ."

"Those things belong to me. This is an empty room, and a small one at that. It's not big enough for you and all your family."

"It's big enough. We lived in smaller—"

"Andy—stop them! Look—" Shirl's unhappy cry spun Andy around and he saw that two of the boys had found the packets of herbs that Sol had grown so carefully in his window box, and were tearing them open, thinking that it was food of some kind.

"Put those things down," he shouted, but before he could reach them they had tasted the herbs, then spat them out.

"Burn my mouth!" the bigger boy screamed and sprayed the contents of the packet on the floor. The other boy bounced up and down with excitement and began to do the same thing with the rest of the herbs. They twisted away from Andy and before he could stop them the packets were empty.

As soon as Andy turned away, the younger boy, still excited, climbed on the table—his mud-stained foot wrappings leaving filthy smears—and turned up the TV. Blaring music crashed over the screams of the children and the ineffectual calls of their mother. Tab pulled Belicher away as he opened the wardrobe to see what was inside.

"Get these kids out of here," Andy said, white-faced with rage.

"I got a squat-order, I got rights," Belicher shouted, backing away and waving an imprinted square of plastic.

"I don't care what rights you have," Andy told him, opening the hall door. "We'll talk about that when these brats are outside."

Tab settled it by grabbing the nearest child by the scruff of the neck and pushing it out through the door. "Mr. Rusch is right," he said. "The kids can wait outside while we settle this."

Mrs. Belicher sat down heavily on the bed and closed her eyes, as though all this had nothing to do with her. Mr. Belicher retreated against the wall saying something that no one heard or bothered to listen to. There were some shrill cries and angry sobbing from the hall and the last child was expelled.

Andy looked around and realized that Shirl had gone into their room; he heard the key turn in the lock. "I suppose this is it?" he said, looking steadily at Tab.

The bodyguard shrugged helplessly. "I'm sorry, Andy, honest to God I am. What else can I do? It's the law, and if they want to stay here you can't get them out."

"It's the law, it's the law," Belicher echoed tonelessly.

There was nothing Andy could do with his clenched fists and he had to force himself to open them. "Help me carry these things into the other room, will you, Tab?"

"Sure," Tab said, and took the other end of the table. "Try and explain to Shirl about my part in this, will you? I don't think she understands that it's just a job I have to do."

Their footsteps crackled on the dried herbs and seeds that littered the floor and Andy did not answer him.

The Pliable Animal

Man is a pliable animal,
a being who gets accustomed to everything.
—*Feodor Dostoyevsky*

Commander Rissby was squat and square, planted solidly behind the desk as if he had been grown there. He gave an impression of strength and determination—which was true—and of slowness and stupidity—which was completely false. He looked particularly bovine at this moment, scratching his close-cropped gray hair with one thick finger and blinking slowly while he talked.

"If I knew what you were looking for, Honorable Sir Petion, maybe then I could be of more help . . . ?"

The thin albino sitting opposite snapped his answer, cutting through the tentative advance of the Commander's words. "What I'm doing here is my business—not yours. You will help me and you won't ask questions. At the proper time you will be informed. Not before. In the meantime you will be able to assist me. First thing—can you get me into the palace without arousing any suspicion as to why I am here?"

The Honorable Sir Jorge Suvarov Petion didn't really enjoy throwing his weight around. But it had to be done. It was one of the uncomfortable things that occurred in his line of duty—like looking at violently battered corpses. With other men he acted differently. He spoke to Commander Rissby in this manner not from malice but from previous knowledge. It was the only way one could get along with the stolid, unimaginative men of Tacora. They made the most loyal soldiers the Empire had—if you took into consideration their grim fixation with status. Speaking as he had, Petion established his superiority of person as well as of rank. His relationship with the Commander and his soldiers would now be a good one.

Truthfully, Commander Rissby was not insulted by the reprimand. He had questioned the other's authority and now knew where they both stood. The white-haired man across from him was one of those who held the Empire together. It would be a pleasure to take orders from him. He wasn't one of those pink-eyed social parasites who grew fat off the work of others. At the appropriate moment Sir Jorge would tell his reasons for being here. Meanwhile, the Commander could be patient.

Commander Rissby wasn't mentioning it aloud, but he could make a good guess as to what Sir Petion was really after. The palace, that was the key. Turning his chair slightly, he could see it, just above the barracks roof, perched on top of the hill. An unusual structure completely covered with overlapping ceramic plates, all of them in soft pastel colors. Like a candy castle. As if one good kick would send it smashing into a thousand pieces.

"You will have no trouble getting into the palace, Honorable Sir," the Commander said. "Not after your name and rank are known to the royal family. Very few of the nobility ever visit an off-the-track planet like this, and there is always an official invitation. Would you like me to . . . ?" He added the question carefully, more of a suggestion than an interrogation.

Sir Petion proved he was not vindictive by nodding at the idea. "Later. Not right now. I want to do a little looking around first. I'll need your help, but we can't be too obvious about it. Until the proper time you are the only person who is to know that I am an investigator."

"As you say, so shall I act." The Commander repeated the ritual words with sincerity, standing first and clashing the heels of his boots together as Sir Petion left.

Kai was waiting halfway across the barracks square, short and ugly as a tree stump. Even the squat Tacora soldiers towered over him, the one-and-a-half Earth gravities of their home world having had only a slight effect on their height. Kai thought that four gravities were normal, and ruthless genetic selection had compacted his people into almost solid lumps of bone and muscle. His strength was beyond imagining.

There was no hurry in Petion's step, and apparently no direction. The boredom and dilettantism of the nobility was well known, and made a perfect cover for an investigator's operation. As he strolled near Kai he snapped his fingers loudly. The short man trundled over with deceptive speed.

"What did you find out?" Sir Petion asked without bothering to look down.

"Everything, but everything, Georgie," Kai rumbled. "I copied the entire file while the clerk was out." Kai had worked with the Honorable Sir long before he had been called by that title. He enjoyed a friendship shared by very few others.

"You mean you know who did it?" Petion yawned as he said it. Their conversation couldn't be overheard, and they kept up the appearance of master and servant to anyone watching from a distance. Kai gave a quick bow that seemed to break him in half and growled his answer.

"I'm good, old buddy, but I'm not that good. We've only been on this lightweight planet a couple of hours. But I have a complete transcript of the file, notes, observations—the works. It's a first step."

"Well let's take a second one," Petion said, starting off. "The palace gate will probably be as good a place to start as any." Kai scuttled after him as he left.

A brief walk took them to the palace. The streets weren't crowded, and the native Andriadans had a very low curiosity quotient. They made way for the white-haired Earthman, but did it in an automatic manner, their long legs working like stilts.

"Beanpoles!" Kai muttered, offended by the exaggerated length of their legs and thin forms. Any one of them could have stepped over him without breaking stride.

Kai had his notes concealed in an Andriadan guidebook. He apparently read from the book, nodding at the pink, scale-covered wall in front of them. "This is the main gate, the one the car came out of. At exactly 2135 hours according to the guard's log. It turned down the street behind us."

"And Prince Mello was alone in it?" Petion asked.

"The driver said he was, and so did the gate guard. One driver, one passenger."

"All right. How far did they go?" He led the way down the street.

"Just as far as this corner here," Kai said, seemingly pointing at a mobile of ceramic bells that hung from the building, tinkling in the wind. "The Prince shouted 'Stop' and the driver hit the brakes. Before the car had completely stopped moving the prince opened the right-hand door and jumped out, running down this passage." They followed the route the unlucky Prince had taken a year earlier, Kai tracing the course with his notes.

"The Prince left no orders, nor did he return. After a few minutes the driver began to be worried. He followed the same way—as far as this little intersection—and found the Prince lying on the ground."

"Dead from a stab wound in the heart, lying alone, soaked with his own blood," Petion added. "And no one saw him, or heard him or had the slightest idea what had happened."

He turned in a slow circle, looking at the intersection. Mostly blank walls broken by a few doors. There was no one in sight. Two other streets led away from the small square.

There was a thin creak of unoiled ceramic and Petion turned quickly. One of the doors had opened and a tall Andriadan stood looking at them, blinking. His eyes met the Earthman's for a single instant. Then he stepped back and closed the door.

"I wonder if that door is locked?" Petion asked. Kai had missed none of the interchange. He moved swiftly up the two steps and leaned against the door. It groaned but did not move.

"A good lock," Kai said. "You want I should push against it a little?"

"Not now. It'll keep. The chances are it means nothing."

They took a different route back to the Imperial compound, enjoying the warmth of the golden afternoon. Andriad's primary glowed with a yellow brilliancy in the sky, coaxing pastel reflections from the sheen of the ceramic buildings. The air, the background murmur of the city, everything combined to produce a feeling of peace that the two men found alien after the mechanized roar of the central worlds.

"Last place you would expect to find bloody murder," Kai said.

"My very thought. But are these people as relaxed as they look? They're supposed to be, I know. Peaceful, law-abiding agrarians, leading lives of unparalleled sweetness and domesticity. All the time—or is there a hidden tendency towards violence?"

"Just like that nice little lady boardinghouse keeper on Westerix IV," Kai reminisced. "The one who killed seventy-four lodgers before we caught up with her. What a collection of luggage she had in that storeroom . . . !"

"Don't make the mistake of assuming similarity just because of superficial resemblance. Many planets—like Andriad here—were cut off from mainstream galactic culture for centuries. They developed trends, characteristics, personality quirks that we know nothing about. That we *have* to know about if we are working on a case."

"How about some original research?" Kai asked. "In here." He jerked his thumb at an outdoor restaurant, with shaded tables around a gently splashing fountain. "I'm dehydrated."

The Andriad beer was chilled and excellent, served in cold ceramic mugs. Kai sat opposite Petion at the table—no need to keep up the master-and-servant pretense here where they were unknown—and drained his beer almost at a swallow. He banged for more and rumbled deep in his chest as the waiter shambled slowly to fetch it. Sipping slowly at the beer he looked around the garden.

"Have the place practically to ourselves," he said. "The kitchen must be open, I can smell it. Let's try the local food. That army chow we had for breakfast is still sitting in my stomach, unchanged and undigested."

"Order if you like," Petion said, looking through the carved wood screen at the slow traffic of the street outside. "I doubt if you will like it, though. In case you didn't read all of the guidebook, the Andriadans are strict vegetarians."

"No steaks!" Kai groaned. "If I wasn't starving I wouldn't consider touching their slop. Order up—I'm game if you are."

Petion left the choice of food to the waiter, who brought them a large compartmented tray filled with oddly shaped bowls. Their contents differed in flavor and texture, but had an overall sameness.

"Tasteless," Kai snorted and shook a coating of dried herbs over everything. He ate quickly, cleaning a number of bowls, hoping that quantity might make up for quality. Petion ate slowly, savoring the variety of flavours.

"The different dishes have their own charm," he said. "But the flavors are very subtle never anything strong or overpowering like onion or garlic. If you make an effort to appreciate it, it's not too bad."

"It's terrible!" Kai said, pushing away the empty plates and belching. A plate of exotic fruits occupied his attention next.

It wasn't that the scream was particularly loud or terrifying. It was just unexpected and completely out of place. The peaceful murmur from the streets and the delicate music of the wind-stirred ceramic bells was rudely sliced into by the suddenness of the cry. Kai choked on a mouthful of fruit, his glass knife falling and shattering on the stone floor; an ugly little gun appeared in his hand. Petion did nothing, just sat absolutely still and observed.

Waiters and customers, moving with haste unusual for Andriadans, crowded to the screen facing the street. Outside there were suddenly more people, pressing back against the walls on both sides of the street. They were all looking expectantly, and a little fearfully, in the same direction.

"What's the occasion?" Kai asked. The gun was gone now but he was still alert. The scream sounded again, closer and louder, and it was obvious now that it had been made by an animal of some kind.

"We'll know in a moment," Petion said. "Here they come."

Men pulled on ropes attached to the large wooden cage, others pushed on bars fixed to the sides. The cage moved slowly, lurching and scratching along on wooden runners—even though wheels were used on all of the other Andriadan vehicles. This was something special. Everything about the cage and the fixed, half-horrified attention of the crowd spelled out the importance of the event. It was only the animal in the cage that seemed very unimpressive for the stir it caused. A mottle-furred, long-toothed and clawed carnivore, about the size of a terrestrial lion. It paced the cage, looking in bewilderment at the crowd. Again it opened its mouth and roared piercingly. A ripple of motion passed across the tall Andriadans.

"What is that beast?" Petion asked the customer nearest to him.

"Sinnd . . ." the man said and shuddered. "What are they going to do with it?"

This question was obviously the wrong one, because the man

turned shocked eyes on the Earthman. When Petion returned his gaze the Andriadan blushed and murmured something and turned quickly away.

"Pay the bill," Petion told Kai, "and let's follow that cage. This is something that is definitely not mentioned in the guidebooks." The Sinnd's cry, muffled now by distance, echoed in the empty street.

By the time they had caught up with it the cage had almost reached its destination, an open field just below the palace. The cage had been pulled onto a raised platform and men with ropes gathered around it. Getting close enough to watch was no problem, since the native Andriadans seemed torn between horrified attraction and repugnance. There were large gaps in the crowd that stirred and shifted in an unceasing Brownian movement. An empty space surrounded the platform. Petion and Kai stood in the first rank and watched the strange ceremony approach its climax.

A webwork of ropes now held the Sinnd immobile. It mewled in terror as a noose pulled its head up, stretching its neck to the utmost. Thin white cloth was now wrapped firmly round and round its neck. The entire affair seemed meaningless.

"Look!" Kai hissed. "The man in the white nightshirt. Recognize him from the photographs?"

"The King," Petion said. "This is getting more interesting all the time."

Nothing was said from the platform and the affair proceeded at breakneck speed. It was over in less than thirty seconds. The King looked only once at the crowd and lowered his chin. A rustle swept the field as the gathered thousands bowed in answer. The King turned and took the sword from an attendant. With a single quick thrust he plunged it into the white wrappings, severing the bound beast's throat.

A voiceless gasp swept the audience as they drew in their breaths, almost in unison. Struggling against its bindings, the Sinnd burbled a last horrible cry, then slumped down. The King withdrew the sword and the white bindings turned a brilliant scarlet. Next to Petion a man bent over and vomited on the ground.

He wasn't the only one; the repugnance seemed universal. There were only a few women in the crowd, and all had apparently fainted at the moment of execution, as had a number of the men. Their friends were quickly carrying them off. The field cleared with suspicious speed; even the King and officials from the platform joined the exodus. Within a minute the two offworlders and the dead beast were alone.

"Well I'll be damned!" Kai exploded. "It wasn't that bad. Why, I've seen infinitely worse things than that. I can recall—"

"Save your sordid reminiscences," Petion told him. "I've heard them all. In addition to which—you are correct. It *wasn't* that bad, particularly with the bandage to cover the wound." He walked over and looked pensively at the slain Sinnd, freed of life and bondage at last.

"What does it all mean?" Kai asked.

"We're going to have to find out. The whole thing seems meaningless now, but it was obviously of great importance to the locals. Let's get back to the base and talk to Rissby. He's been stationed here nine years, and should know what it's about."

"So you've uncovered the local secret," Commander Rissby said. "It's hard to tell if they are ashamed or proud of it. Anyway they make no attempt to stop people from watching, though they do fight strongly against any kind of publicity or official attention. Our policy during ninety-six years of occupation has been simply hands off."

"Is it a religious ceremony?" Petion asked.

"Might be, Honorable Sir. We had an anthropology team through here once, and they were getting interested until they were officially requested to leave. One of them told me that the ceremony has an historical necessity that developed into a public ritual of exorcism."

"How?"

"I don't know how much you know of this planet's history, Honorable Petion . . . ?" He hesitated, afraid to presume too much.

"For Empress's sake, tell us man!" Kai snapped. "If you think Sir Petion has the time to bone up on the history of every off-trail planet—you're completely wrong. He knows what I tell him because I handle the mechanics of these investigations and keep the records. All he has to do is solve the problem. We know next to nothing about this rock; we came here direct from the last job and never got back to the archives."

"Then you'll forgive a short lecture," Commander Rissby said placidly, still not knowing where he stood in the chain of command. "Early history is obscure, but it is obvious this planet passed through a simple agrarian economy after being settled. Almost Stone Age, at least as far as artifacts go, since Andriad has no heavy metals. If the Honorable Sir has deemed it necessary to make a study of anthropology he will know that one of the theories of the development of mankind on Earth concerned man's using his long legs for running, to escape predators. This happened, in actuality, right here. With no real mountains or forests, Andriad is a perfect habitat for herbivores. You've seen the gigantic herds that still roam the grasslands. Of course, as part of the ecology, there were the carnivores. One species dominated almost completely, the Sinnd that you saw today."

"Men are better carnivores," Kai said. "So they knocked the Sinnd over the head and ate the ruminants themselves?"

"Quite the contrary. They ran away along with the other animals." Kai snorted in contempt, but the other two ignored him. "They became pure vegetarians—as they still are today. This period of food gathering and flight must have lasted quite a number of years."

"But not forever," Petion said, "or this city wouldn't be here. Sooner or later they had to stop running and find another way to deal with the carnivores."

"Of course. They found that the Sinnd could be trapped in pits, captured alive. By this time they had developed such an aversion to taking life that they found it hard to kill. Rather they found it impossible. Yet a crime even worse than killing would be to let the animals starve to death. That was when Grom—ancestor of the present King—started the royal family. He killed a trapped Sinnd. That's the way the myths have it and for a change they're probably true. Of course the rest of the Andriadans were horrified that a man could do this—yet at the same time strangely attracted. Grom was obviously the strongest man and quickly gained the power passed on to the present King Grom. They have all had the same name."

"And the same job," Petion said. "Killing Sinnd. Does it happen often now?"

"Only a few times a year when a Sinnd will raid one of the towns. Most of them stay away, following the herds. Then the captured Sinnd is sent here to be dispatched in the proper manner. The professor who told me all this also claimed it was a ritual murder of evil. The king-protector destroys the symbolic and the real devil at the same time."

"Probably true," Petion considered. "It certainly explains what we saw today. Don't think these questions foolish, Commander. Everything on this planet is relevant to the case under investigation. I imagine you know why I'm here?"

"One can only guess . . ." Commander Rissby murmured politely.

"The murder of Prince Mello."

"The murder of course," Rissby agreed with no surprise.

"Tell me about Prince Mello. What kind of reception did he have here?"

Commander Rissby was no longer at ease. He mumbled something and suddenly his collar was tight enough to need easing with his forefinger.

"Louder please, Commander," Petion asked.

"Prince Mello . . . Why the Prince was of course a nobleman, a gentleman. All admired him and praised him . . ."

"Rubbish and nonsense!" Petion exploded, angry for the first time.

"This is an investigation, not an attempt to whitewash the already tarnished name of a wastrel and a dolt! Why do you think a prince of the House, eighty-second cousin of the Empress, should be pleasure-jaunting in an out-of-the-way spot like this? Because the departed Prince's intelligence just cleared the moron borderline and he had trouble signing his own name. Through stupidity compounded by arrogance he caused more trouble for the Empire than an army of liberationists."

Rissby's face and neck were flushed bright red. He looked like a bomb ready to explode and Petion took pity on him. "You know all this—or suspected it," he said gently. "You must realize if the Empire is to prosper—as we both want it to prosper—some of the evils of generations of inbreeding must be eliminated. Mello's death was more of a blessing than a tragedy. Just the manner of his going reflects ill on the Empire and must be investigated. You are too long in the service not to know these things. Now tell me about the Prince's activities here."

Commander Rissby opened his mouth, but no words came out. Loyalty fought with honesty. Petion respected the combination—knowing how rare it was—and treated the old soldier gently.

"It is no crime to discuss the faults of members of the royal family, since there is no doubt of your loyalty. You may talk safely to me." Petion put his hand to one eye and when he removed it the iris was brown, in striking contrast to the pink albinism of the other eye. Rissby gasped.

"It is an open secret," Petion said, "that a reward of great service merits admission to the royal family. The Empress was good enough to reward my police work with a knighthood. With it goes the honor of royal albinism. I have had the operations to change my coloring; the manipulating techniques even changed my genes so the trait is hereditary in me now. I have not had the time for the eye operation— it means months in bed—so wear these contact lenses instead. So you see I am half of one world, half of the other. You can talk to me, Commander. You can tell me about Prince Mello."

Rissby recovered quickly, with a trained soldier's resiliency. "I thank you for taking me into your confidence, Sir Petion. You will understand then that I attempt no rumor or slander when I tell you that Prince Mello was—unpopular here . . ."

"That's the strongest term you can use?"

"Perhaps—'detested' might be a better one. It hurts me to say it, but it was the truth. My own soldiers felt it and only strong discipline kept them in line. The Prince laughed at the native customs, paid no attention to the people's sensitivities, blundered in where he had no business, in general he, you might say—"

"Made an ass of himself."

"Precisely. He was tolerated by the Andriadans because of his nobility and his relationships with the royal family here. He was with them quite often. He favored King Grom's daughter, Princess Melina, and I understand the attraction was mutual. She was so upset by his death that she was confined to her bed for weeks. I visited her myself, in the name of the Empress. Shock. Crying. Very unhappy case."

"Then everything was peaceful inside the castle?" Petion asked.

"I would say so. King Grom is very reserved, so there is no way of telling his feelings at any time. But if he did not encourage, he certainly did nothing to hinder the romance of the royal youths."

"What about in the city?" Kai broke in. "Mello make enemies there? Go to gambling joints? Have girls? Associate with toughs?"

"Never!" Rissby gasped, shocked in spite of himself. "The Prince may have had his failings, but he was still nobility! He rarely ventured into the city, and certainly had no acquaintances there."

"Yet he did see someone in the city," Petion said. "Someone he knew well enough to recognize from a moving car at night. Someone he rushed to meet, never considering it a risk. Someone who may have killed him. I'll need more information on the Prince's activities outside of the palace. He may have been visiting the city unknown to you. Have you any spies or paid informers? Reliable ones I can contact?"

"Intelligence Section can give you more detailed information on that, though I don't think you will need it. We have one operative who has been consistently reliable, the only one I might say. His loyalty is to money and we see that he is well paid. He will tell you anything you need to know. Only you must go to him, he is never seen near the military compound."

"The name?"

"One-finger. He has an unusual deformity of one hand. He keeps a low-class inn and drinking parlor in the Old Town. I will arrange for the proper clothes and someone to show you the way."

No possible disguise could have made Kai resemble anything other than what he was. He grumbled at being left behind while Petion was slipping into the loose robes of a Turaccian trader. The Intelligence Officer, Captain Langrup, adjusted the outfit with professional skill.

"A number of traders come through here," Langrup said, "so two more wouldn't be noticed. A lot of them stay at One-finger's so this is a natural cover."

"Do you have the caller?" Kai asked, taking the small, high-frequency receiver out of his pocket. Petion nodded and held up his hand with the ornate ring. When he pressed on the stone and twisted a shrill squeal blasted from the receiver. It warbled up and down when Kai changed the angle of the directional aerial.

"I doubt if we'll need to use it," Petion said. "We're just going there for information and there's no danger involved."

"That's what you said on Cervi III," Kai scoffed, "and you were four months in the hospital afterwards. I'll be hanging around close, ready to bust in."

As Petion and the intelligence captain strolled through the Old Town they were barely aware of the stocky shadow that followed them. Kai was a good policeman, and a good tail even in the twisted labyrinth of dark passageways. Petion had lost his direction completely by the time Langrup turned into a black entranceway. It was a side entrance to a tap room. A noisy, badly lit place, filled with the stink of the burning weed the Andriadans smoked and the sweet pungency of beer slops. Langrup ordered two mugs of the best and Petion took careful note of the man who banged them down on the bar. His skin was sallow and wrinkled; the way it hung on the thin Andriadan bones it made him look like a walking skeleton. An accident or deformity had left him with only the index finger of his left hand. It appeared to be quite strong and he used it skillfully.

"We have some samples to show you," Captain Langrup said. "Shall we take them inside?"

One-finger only grunted, his eyes half-closed and flicking back and forth at both of them. "Are the prices right?" he asked finally, the single finger scratching towards them across the bar, an animal nosing about for money.

"Don't worry," Langrup said and pulled back the corner of his cloak so the full wallet could be seen hanging from his belt. One-finger grunted again and turned away.

"A repulsive type, but valuable," Langrup said. "Finish the beer then follow me." They left by the main entrance, but instead of going all the way out into the street they climbed quietly up the stairs in the entranceway. There was a small room in the back of the building and they only waited a few minutes before the informer came in.

"Information costs money," he said, and the finger scratched towards them again from across the table.

Langrup clinked ten of the translucent glass coins on the table. "Tell us about Prince Mello," he said. "Did he ever come here to the city?"

"Many times. In his car. On the way to the palace or the country . . ."

"Don't be devious!" Langrup snapped. "We're paying for facts. Did he ever come *here*? Did he go anywhere else in the city? Did he have any friends here he visited . . . or girls?"

One-finger laughed, a crackling unpleasant sound. "A girl! What girl could stand being near a Sinnd-smeller! He came here once and I had to fumigate the place afterwards. He told *me* that *my* place stank! He came here, went some other places, he never came back. There were no friends of his here"— his eyes half-closed again—"or enemies."

"What's this about being a 'Sinnd-smeller'?" Petion asked the Captain.

Langrup answered him, ignoring the informer's presence as though he were part of the furniture.

"It's a local idea, I'm not sure if it is true or just a way to insult us. They say that all offworlders smell like Sinnd—that's a local carnivore. Say they can't stand to be near us too long. One-finger over there probably has plugs in his nose right now."

"Is this true?" Petion asked him. One-finger didn't answer but grinned and tilted his head back instead, while the long finger leapt up and tapped at the white base of a plug barely seen in one nostril.

"Interesting," Petion mused.

"Damned insult," Langrup snapped. "You're going to have to tell us more than that if you want your money," he said to the informer. "When I investigated a year ago you had no idea of who had killed Prince Mello. What do you know now? You've had plenty of time to hear rumors, find out things."

One-finger was suffering. He writhed inside his skin and sweat stood out on his face. The questing finger ran out towards the money on the table, then retreated.

"You can get in bad trouble for withholding information," Langrup said with angry intensity. "Arrest, jail . . . even transportation . . ." One-finger didn't even hear the threats, he was frightened enough already.

"Try money," Petion suggested. "I'll supply whatever funds are needed."

Langrup slowly stacked high-denomination coins on the table, and as the pile mounted One-finger began to shiver, pulling away. But his eyes never left the money.

"Here," Langrup murmured, sliding the money slowly across the table, "look at this. There's more here than you can make in a year of hard work. It's yours. Just tell us . . ."

"I don't know who did it!" One-finger shouted hoarsely, falling forward across the coins, clutching them with his arms. "I can't tell you that. But I can tell you something . . ." He gasped for breath and squeezed the words out. "It was no one . . . from the city."

"That's not enough!" Langrup shouted, standing and shaking the man so that the tempered glass coins sprayed down and rattled in all directions. One-finger's face was wide-eyed with fear, but he said no more.

"Leave him," Petion said quietly. "You're not going to get any more out of him. And he's told us what we want to know." Not satisfied, Langrup slowly let go of the man who dropped back into his chair as limply as if the bones had been dissolved from his body. They left him there and made their way back down the stairs.

"That's an awful lot to pay for so little," Langrup said, not trying to disguise his dissatisfaction.

"It's enough," Petion told him. "It is really more than I expected to find out here. I would appreciate it if you would go back now and tell the Commander that I would like to meet with both of you, in his office, in about two hours time."

"But I can't leave you alone here," Captain Langrup said, shocked.

"I'm not alone as you see," Petion told him. He had thumbed a message on his ring as soon as they had left the building, so he expected the squat figure that sidled up to them out of the darkness. Langrup gave a start. "I assure you that Kai and I will be able to take care of ourselves," Petion said.

"Can you find the square where the murder took place?" Petion asked after the Intelligence officer had gone.

"With my eyes shut," Kai scored, and led the way into an alley. "What did you find out?"

"A little—or a lot. I don't know yet. The whole thing is still simmering in my head. There is just one more thing I would like to find out before reaching any conclusions." They entered a square and he looked around. "This is it, isn't it?"

"Crossroad of the Carved-up Corpse," Kai agreed.

Petion looked around at the black doorways. He pointed. "There's the one we saw open earlier. I don't like to rely on coincidences, but they do occur. It also happens to be the one nearest the palace and we should look there first. Now's your chance to lean on it—but quietly."

There was just enough light in the square to catch the white shine of Kai's grin. Climbing silently up to the door, he put one shoulder against it and his bar-like fingers clamped onto the carved stone jamb. A single contraction of his muscles pulled his weight forward a few centimeters. It was enough, a motion as sudden and powerful as a hydraulic ram. Something snapped sharply and the door swung open. They moved in quickly and closed it behind them. The building was silent.

"We're looking for a door," Petion said. "It may be in the wall or it may be in the floor. It will be concealed. I'll work this side and you work the other."

Their lights threw wandering circles of radiance as they searched. Only a few minutes passed before Kai called softly. "Nothing to it. A real amateur job." His light outlined a flag in the stone floor. The gap between it and the other stones was narrow and deep, clear of dust.

It took even less time to find out how it opened. When the stone slid aside they shone their lights into the black opening. A tunnel vanished into the darkness.

"If I were to ask you to make a guess—where would you think that tunnel goes?" Petion asked.

Kai bent down and squinted along the length of the tunnel as far as his light could carry. "If it turns it could go anywhere. But if it goes on the way it starts it should end up bang in the center of the royal palace."

"That's what I would say myself," Petion murmured.

"I should have made it clear earlier," Petion told them. "I want no notes or records kept of this meeting or anything else to do with this investigation. The Empress will have my report—and that will be the only one."

"Sorry," Captain Langrup said, and turned the recorder off and returned it to his pocket. Commander Rissby looked on quietly without commenting. All of their eyes followed Petion as he paced back and forth the length of the room.

"Some very important facts have come to light," he said. "One of the most interesting was supplied tonight by the informer. If he wasn't lying he has narrowed down our search for us. Whoever killed Prince Mello must have been from one of four groups." He counted them off on his fingers. "First—an Andriadan from the city or the country. Since the Prince had no contact with any of them, he certainly wouldn't have recognized someone and stopped the car. Group two are offworlders."

"You can rule them out too," Captain Langrup said. "I worked on the original investigation. Every offworlder was grilled and cross-examined in detail. None of them could have possibly been the killer."

"Then the third group is the military here—"

"Sir!" Commander Rissby gasped in a shocked voice. "You can't be suggesting—"

"I'm not, Commander—so set your mind at ease. Your Tacora troops might be suspected of a lot of crimes, but killing a member of the royal house is too unthinkable. In addition, I imagine the whereabouts of all your men were checked at the time?"

"They were—and eliminated from all suspicion," the Commander said, only slightly mollified.

Petion folded a fourth finger into his palm. "Then logic leads us to the conclusion that the murder was committed by a member of the final group. Someone from within the palace." He smiled at their shocked expressions. "Before you tell me that is an impossibility, that no one left the palace before the Prince, I should inform you of a discovery we made tonight."

"A tunnel," Kai said. "Looks like it runs from the palace to the place where Mello got carved."

"That could be it," Captain Langrup shouted, jumping to his feet with excitement. "A difference of opinion, a fight in the palace— we know that Mello left early—and while he is leaving the killer goes ahead of him. Calls to him, entices him into the alley—and kills him!"

"A nice construction," Petion agreed. "But there are some obvious holes in it that I won't bother pointing out, Captain. It *might* have been that way, but I do not think it was. The truth is a little more complex. I'll need a little more evidence before I will be able to state exactly. Could I talk to the driver of the car, the man who last saw the Prince alive?"

The Commander looked unhappy. "I'm afraid that will be impossible, Honorable Sir. He was rotated six months ago, shipped out with his troop when their term of duty was up."

"It's not important." Petion waved the thought aside. "I was expecting only negative evidence from him anyway. There is one more fact missing, with that the picture will be clear. Tell me about Prince Mello's eating habits."

Only a shocked silence followed his words. The two army officers gaped and Kai grinned widely. He had little enough idea where the conversation was going, but was more used to Petion's turn of mind than the others.

"Come, come—that's a plain enough question." Petion frowned. "Simply looking at the Prince's photo and his height-weight index will show that he was overweight. Fat, if you are not afraid of the right word. Did this have an uncorrected glandular source—or did he overeat?"

"He overate," Captain Langrup said as calmly as he could, trying not to smile. "If you want the truth this was about the only thing that endeared him to the troops. Tacorans enjoy their food, and they were always a little awed at the quantity the Prince could put away."

"During meals or between meals?" Petion asked.

"Both. He didn't talk much but I rarely saw him when his jaws weren't working. There was almost a path worn from his quarters to the back door of the cookhouse. The head chef became a close friend of his."

"Get the chef up here, he's the man I want to talk to." Petion turned to the Commander. "Could you arrange for me to be invited to the palace tomorrow?" he asked. "I would like to go to dinner there, the same place and the same hour as the Prince's last meal."

Commander Rissby nodded and reached for the phone.

"I feel like an idiot in this outfit!" Kai whispered fiercely in Petion's ear, from where he stood behind him at the table. Dressed in colorful servant's livery he looked like a garishly painted tree stump.

"If it's any relief, you look like one too," Petion answered imperturbably. "Now be quiet and keep your eyes open for trouble from *any* direction. As soon as we have finished eating I'm going to stir this crowd up and see what develops."

The banquet board was a large U with the royal family at the base of the U. As guest of honor Petion sat between King Grom and Princess Melina. The Queen had died in childbirth and the young prince was still a child, too young to sit at the adults' table. Since by Andriad custom only women of the royal family attended state banquets, the princess was the only female present. She was an attractive enough girl and Petion wondered idly what she had seen in that idiot Mello. Alien attraction and prestige seemed the only answer.

Both King and Princess were still unknown quantities. Frozen by protocol they could only discuss unimportant things in abstract terms. If anything, King Grom seemed a little wary and on his guard. Which was understandable. His last noble guest had been butchered soon after leaving this same table.

Petion ate of the numberless different dishes and found himself enjoying the food. If you didn't mind not having meat with your meal this was good eating indeed. Herbs and spices in great variety, even hot little peppers that had scorched his mouth. He wasn't surprised when he saw that the Princess had taken a large portion of the peppers and was eating them with pleasure. She also oversalted her food. This underlined something he had suspected when he first heard her nasal voice and noticed the way she breathed through her mouth. A final bit of evidence that pulled his entire bundle of conjecture into shape. He had no foolproof evidence yet—but the theory seemed watertight.

He knew now just how and why Prince Mello had died. After the final course the Princess excused herself and left. Which was just as well. What was going to happen next would not be pretty.

"Your Majesty," Petion said, pushing his plate away from him. "I have dined with you and would like to feel that we are friends." The king nodded gravely. "So you will pardon me if I sound unfriendly. I do so because I only wish to uncover the truth. The truth that has lain concealed too long."

He had not spoken loudly, yet suddenly the table was quiet. Conversation dead in an instant, as though the talk had just been used to fill the time waiting for this moment. The dozen or more noblemen at the table all had their eyes fixed intensely on the tall albino next to the King. Behind him Petion heard Kai's clothing rustle and knew that man and gun were ready for action.

"You are talking about Prince Mello's death," the King said. Not a question, but a statement. His Majesty was no coward when it came to facing things.

"Exactly," Petion said. "I don't wish to presume upon your hospitality, but this blot upon the relations of our peoples must be cleared up. If you will hear me out I will tell you what happened on that evening a little over a year ago. When I am finished we will decide what must be done." He shifted position and took a sip of the royal beer. No one else moved and every eye was fixed unblinkingly on him. Petion felt grateful for Kai waiting alertly behind him. He turned to the King.

"You'll pardon the indiscretion, Your Majesty, but there is a rather personal question I would like to ask you. Is it true that your daughter suffers from a minor physical disability?"

"SIR!"

"The question is important, or I wouldn't ask it. Am I correct in saying that Princess Melina has little or no sense of smell? That this is the reason she could bear Prince Mello's presence, even enjoy being with him—"

"Enough!" the King interrupted. "You are insulting the memory of a dead man and my daughter as well!"

"There is no insult intended," Petion said, letting a cold touch of steel slip into the formal tones of his voice. "If we are discussing insults I might mention the fact that Your Majesty has filter plugs in his nose to enable him to bear my presence at his table. That could be called an insult . . ."

King Grom had the good grace to blush red and made no further interruptions when Petion continued.

"There should be neither shame nor blame attached to what is a simple physical fact. All meat-eating animals have a characteristically strong odor—particularly to non–meat eaters. To your people the men of other planets smell bad. That is a simple and undeniable fact. Princess Melina—lacking a refined sense of smell—was unaware of this difference. She befriended Prince Mello and enjoyed his presence. She even asked him to dine here and you all put up with his presence for her sake. Until that evening when he did . . . what he did. And was killed for the repulsiveness of his crime."

Petion's final words hung in a shocked silence. The unsayable had been said, the unspeakable spoken. Then a chair grated back and a young noble jumped to his feet, white-faced. Kai appeared at Petion's shoulder, gun pointing.

"You will sit down," Petion said, "and you and everyone else will be quiet until I have spoken. We are on very delicate ground here and I do not wish any mistakes to be made. You will hear me out." He stared intensely until the man dropped back into his chair, then went on. "Prince Mello committed the crime and died for it. You all witnessed it and by law are equally guilty. That is why I am addressing you together like this. The Prince was killed and you conspired to remove his body and conceal your crime."

Some of the men were not looking at him now, but staring wide-eyed into space. Reliving that night they had tried to conceal and forget. Petion's voice flowed on as smoothly as the voice of memory.

"You stopped the flow of blood, but he was dead. You fought between yourselves as to what to do, but in the end all were convinced that dishonorable as it was, the crime must be concealed. The only other alternative would be the end of everything as you knew it. You thought your monarchy could not survive a blow like this. So you undressed the corpse and one of you put on the dead man's clothes. In the darkness of the courtyard it was easy for him to get into the official car. Without being seen clearly. The driver said that no order was given, nor would one be necessary. There was only one place for him to drive to. The disguised man simply sat in the car until it passed the agreed-on spot, then shouted 'Stop' and leapt out. He ran to the square where his friends were waiting with the body, having brought it there through the underground passage. There was more than enough time to redress the corpse before the driver became suspicious. The deed was done. Mello had left the palace safely, and been killed by person or persons unknown. A tragedy, of course, but not a world-destroying one."

"It is true," King Grom said, rising slowly to his feet. "The truth has been concealed . . ."

"You can protect me no more, Your Majesty!" a shrill, almost screaming, voice cried. The same young man was on his feet again. "I did it and I must pay the penalty, you have all protected me too long . . ."

"KAI! STOP HIM!" Petion shouted.

With unbelievable speed the stocky body hurtled the table, crashing into the youth. But he was an instant too late. The man had his hand to his mouth, swallowing something.

He didn't struggle when Kai pinioned his wrists.

"Majesty . . ." the man said and smiled. Then a shudder tore through his body, his figure arched back in sudden torture. Kai released his hands and the dead man fell to the floor.

"That was unnecessary," Petion shouted, turning on the King, his face twisted with anger. "Horrible waste!"

"I didn't know," was all King Grom mumbled, sunk in his chair, older now.

"We could have arranged something . . . not *this*! That's why I'm here."

"I didn't know," was all the King could say, his face buried in his hands.

Petion dropped into his chair, suddenly exhausted. "Well then, that's the way it will have to be," he said. "This man killed Prince Mello, then committed suicide rather than be taken. A life for a life. The rest of you will receive a reprimand for concealing the fact, and there will be a two percent rise in the Empire duties on your planet for the next ten years. Agreed?"

From the shelter of his hands the King could only dumbly nod his head.

Commander Rissby was only confused after he read the report and the evening's affair had been explained to him. Petion was tired to exhaustion but held his temper well.

"This killer—the young man," Rissby said, "I don't understand. Why didn't they just turn him over to us for trial?"

"For the simple reason that he didn't kill the Prince," Petion said. "The King did. He was the only possible one. The insult was done to his daughter, directly in front of him. They all hate the taking of life, and would never consider it, even in anger. But the King is a killer—a ritual murderer perhaps—but the animals he kills are just as dead after the ritual. He kills with a knife and Mello was killed with a knife. The King must have been wild with anger and didn't realize what he was doing until it was all over. I'm sure he wanted to surrender then, but they talked him out of it. It would have meant the end of the regency and probably the royal family. For the sake of his planet—not for his own sake—he allowed the crime to be concealed. When I appeared the nobles must have sensed something in the wind and arranged for a suicide. Drawn lots or some such without the King's knowledge. A life for a life and the Empire still safe. The poison is a quick-acting one they used for euthanasia."

"Then the King . . . ?" Rissby asked.

"Is the murderer. And he is undoubtedly punishing himself every hour of the day much more than we could ever do. I'm telling you this so you won't start thinking after I have gone and figure it out for yourself. And send in a report. The King's culpability will *not* appear in my final report. If it did he would have to be arrested. As it stands now the balance is straight and everyone is happy. At least on paper. I'll tell the Empress the truth—off the record—just as I am telling you. I won't need to swear her to secrecy as I am swearing you now. Raise your hand and touch the scroll."

"I so swear . . ." Commander Rissby repeated numbly, still shocked. He finally stirred to life and tapped the report. "But this— the roast leg of beef Mello got from the kitchen—what was wrong with that?"

"Use your imagination, Commander," Petion said with barely concealed disgust. "He brought this joint of meat, still steaming hot in insulating foil, unwrapped it and dropped it in front of the Princess, right there on the table. He was so stupid, he thought he was doing her a favor, letting her try some good food for a change."

"Yes . . . I know *what* he did. But why should the King kill him for a harmless thing like that?"

"Harmless?" Petion sat back and laughed. "These people are strict vegetarians with an absolute horror of our eating habits. Just try to put yourself in the King's position. Let's say that you invited a cannibal home for dinner—he's reformed, but still a cannibal. And he has never quite understood what all fuss was about. So he does you a favor, trying to introduce you to a whole new world of enjoyable eating.

"He drops a nice hot, steaming, crackling human arm on the table in front of you right in the middle of the meal!

"What would you do, Commander?"

After the Storm

The tide was on the way out, leaving a strip of hard sand that felt good to jog upon. The sun, just clear of the horizon, was already hot on my face. Last night's storm had finally blown itself out, although the long Atlantic rollers were still crashing onto the beach with its memory. It was going to be hot, but the sand was still cool under my bare toes as I jogged along easily, the last surge of the surf breaking around my ankles. I was very much at peace with the world: this was a good time of day.

There was something that caught my eye ahead, dark against the white foam. Driftwood, very good, it would make a lovely fire in the winter. It was a long plank with something draped over it. As I splashed toward it I felt a chill down my bare back, a sudden fear.

It was a body, a man's body.

I did not want to look too closely at this waterlogged corpse. I hesitated and stopped, with the water surging about my legs, unsure of what I should do. Phone the police? But if I did that it might wash out to sea again while I was away. I had to pull it in—but did not want to go near it. A wave surged up and over the body and strands of seaweed tangled in the long hair. The head lifted and dropped back.

He was still alive.

But cold as death. I felt the chill when I seized his hands and dragged him, a dead weight, through the shallow water to the beach. Dropped him facedown, his forearm under his mouth and nose to keep them out of the sand, then leaned hard on his back. And again— until he coughed and gasped, emptying his stomach of sea water. He groaned when I rolled him onto his back and his eyelids moved and opened. His eyes were a transparent pale blue and they had trouble focusing.

"You are all right," I said. "Ashore and safe."

He frowned at my words, and I wondered if he could understand me. "Do you speak English?"

"I do . . ." He coughed, then rubbed his lips. "Could you tell me the name of this place?"

"Manhasset, north shore of Long Island."

"One of the states of the United States, is it?"

"You're Irish?"

"Aye. And a devil of a long way from home."

He struggled to his feet, swaying, and would have fallen again if I hadn't caught him.

"Lean on me," I said. "The house isn't far. We'll get some dry clothes on you, something warm to drink."

When we reached the patio he dropped onto the bench with a sigh. "I could do with that cup of tea now," he said.

"No tea—what about coffee?"

"Good man. That'll do me fine."

"Cream and sugar?" I asked as I punched in the order on the keyboard on the wall. He nodded and his eyebrows rose as I took the steaming cup from the dispenser. He sipped it gingerly, then drank deep. He drained the cup before he spoke again.

"That's a miraculous yoke you have there. Could you do it again?"

I wondered just where he was from that he had never seen an ordinary dispenser before. I dropped his cup into the recycler and passed him a full one.

"From Ireland," he said, answering my unspoken question. "Five weeks out of Arklow when the storm caught us. Had a load of cured hides for the Canadians. Gone now, with the rest of the crew, God rest their souls. The name is Byrne, Cormac Byrne, sir."

"Bil Cohn-Greavy. Would you like to get out of those wet clothes?"

"Fine now, Mr. Greavy, just sitting in the sun here . . ."

"Cohn-Greavy. Matronym, patronym. Been the law now for what? . . . at least a hundred years. I suppose on your side of the ocean you just use your father's name?"

"We do, we do. Things change that slowly in Ireland. But you say that it's the law of the land that you must use both your mother and your father's family name?"

I nodded and wondered how it was that an ordinary sailor understood a bit of Latin. "The feminist block pushed it through Congress in the 2030s when Mary Wheeler became President. Look, I have to make a phone call. Just stay here and rest. Back in a moment."

It's a responsibility that cannot be avoided. If you own shore property you are sworn in as an auxiliary Coast Guard. Anything that comes ashore has to be reported. I even had a gun to warn off anyone who tried to land. Immigration is very illegal in the United States. I imagined that this included shipwrecked sailors.

"Coast Guard emergency," I said and the screen lit up at once. The gray-haired duty chief looked up from my ID, which would be automatically displayed.

"Report, Cohn-Greavy."

"I have a man here, washed ashore from a wreck, sir. Foreign national."

"Right. Detain him. Patrol's on the way."

It was my duty, of course. There were sound reasons for this country's immigration policy. The glass door opened as I approached, and I could hear a familiar voice. I called out.

"Is that you, Kriket?"

"None other."

She had come along the shore, for her legs were sandy, the seat of her bikini bottom as well. Like most girls she went topless in the summer, and her breasts were as tan as the rest of her. As beautiful as her mother. Then I noticed that Byrne was standing, facing out to sea, the back of his neck burning red. I was puzzled for a moment— then had to smile.

"Kriket, this is Mr. Byrne from Ireland." He nodded quickly, still not facing her, and I waved her inside. "If you have a moment there is something I want to show you."

She looked at me, puzzled, as I waited until the door had closed before I spoke again. "I have a feeling that our guest is not used to naked girls."

"Dads, what on earth do you mean? I'm dressed . . ."

"Not on top. Be a jagster and pull on one of my shirts. I'll bet you billions to bytes that girls don't flaunt their bare topsides where he comes from."

"How revoltingly ancient." But she was going toward the bedroom when she said it. As I went back to the patio a big white copter was just setting down on the shore. The Irishman was gaping at it as though he had never seen one before. Perhaps he hadn't. This was indeed his day for surprises. A Coast Guard captain and two Shore Patrolmen dropped down and walked briskly to the house. The captain stopped in front of Byrne while the others stood ready, hands resting on their revolvers. He frowned up at the Irishman—who was a head taller—and spoke brusquely.

"I want your name, place of birth, age, name of your vessel, last port of call, port of registry, the reason you have illegally entered our country . . ."

"Shipwrecked, Your Honor, shipwrecked," he said in a gentle voice. With an edge to it that might have been laughter. Not really enough for insult, though the captain's scowl deepened as he punched the answers into his hand terminal.

"Remain here," he said when all of the questions had been answered, then turned to me. "I would like to use your phone. Would you show me where it is?"

Everything he had entered into his cellular terminal was already in the base computer, so there was no need for my phone. He was silent until we were inside.

"We have reason to suspect that this is more than a simple case of shipwreck. It has therefore been decided that instead of taking the suspect into custody he will remain here with you where he can be observed . . ."

"I'm sorry, that is just not possible. I have my work."

Even as I spoke he was stabbing at his hand terminal. Behind me my printer pinged and a sheet dropped into the hopper.

"Yeoman Cohn-Greavy, you have just been recalled to active status in the Coast Guard. You will follow your orders, you will not ask questions, you are now subject to the Official Secrets Act of 2085 and will be court-martialed if you speak of this matter to anyone." He took up the sheet of paper and handed it to me. "Here is a copy of your orders. The suspect will remain here. All of the pickups in this house have been activated and all conversations are to be recorded. You will have no conversations away from the house. If the suspect leaves the vicinity of this house you will instantly inform us. Do you understand these orders?"

"Aye, aye, sir."

He ignored the sarcasm in my tone, turned and stamped out, waving me after him. I kept my anger down—I had no other choice—and followed meekly after. He ordered the SPs into the copter, then faced the Irishman.

"Although immigration is restricted, there are regulations concerning shipwreck. Until a decision has been reached in your case, you will remain here with Mr. Cohn-Greavy. Since public funds are not available for your welfare, he has volunteered to look after you for the time being. That is all."

Byrne watched the copter leave before he turned to me. "You are a kind man, Mr. Cohn-Greavy . . ."

"The name is Bil." I wanted no thanks for hospitality I had been ordered to extend.

"You have my thanks, Bil. And Cormac is my Christian name."

The door slid open and Kriket emerged, wearing one of my shirts with the tails knotted at her waist. "I heard the copter. What's happening?"

"Coast Guard patrol. They must have seen me dragging Cormac ashore." The first of many lies; I did not like it. "He'll be staying with me."

"Wonderful. A new beast will liven up the neighborhood."

Cormac flushed at her words and pushed at his sodden clothing. "I beg your pardon. I'm sure I look the beast . . ."

He blushed harder when she laughed. "Silly man. It's just an expression. A beast is a man, any man. I could call Dads a beast and he wouldn't mind. Are you married, Cormac?"

"I am."

"Good. I like married men. Makes the chase more exciting and sexy. I'm divorced. Twice."

"You'll excuse us, Kriket," I broke in. "I'm going to show Cormac the shower and get him some dry clothes. Then we'll have breakfast out here before it gets too hot."

"Fair-diddly," she agreed. "I'll read the paper—and don't be too long or I'll suspect buggery."

Cormac's skin was now as red as a tomato. I had the feeling that the social customs he was used to did not include the casualness of my daughter's speech. Young people today said things that would have been shocking to my generation. I led the way to the bath, then went to get him some clothes.

"Bil," he called after me. "Could I ask a favor? This shower-bath here—it doesn't have any knobs."

I tried not to smile even though I wasn't sure what knobs on a shower were.

"To turn it on just tell it to . . . Wait, I'll do it." I poked my head into the shower enclosure. "Thirty-five degrees, soap, on." It burst into steaming life. "After you've lathered just say 'Rinse,' then say 'Off' when you are through. I'll put some clothes on the bed."

I was on my second cup of coffee when he reappeared. I had laid out a selection and he had, predictably perhaps, chosen dark trousers and a long-sleeved dark shirt.

"What's to feet?" Kriket asked, her fingers poised over the keyboard.

"Translation: 'What would you like to eat?' " I said.

"Whatever's on the fire, thank you, I'm that famished."

"I'll take care of it," Kriket said, touching the keys. I was intrigued and wanted to hear more of this place named Ireland. A fire in the kitchen! I had a vision of it crackling away in the middle of the floor, smoke curling all along the ceiling.

His plate appeared heaped with scrambled eggs, pork chops, fried potatoes, rice, and noodles. Kriket's idea of a joke. But it backfired for he tucked in and looked able to demolish the lot.

"Tell me about Ireland," Kriket said. He smiled and washed down a heroic mouthful with coffee before he spoke.

"What's to say, miss? It's the same place it has always been."

"That's what I mean. All this is strange to you. I saw you bugging your eyes at the copter. Never seen one before?"

"In God's truth, no, though certainly I've read about the creatures and seen their likeness in the books. Nor have I ever seen a fine meal like this appear steaming from a hole in the wall, or ever talked before to a shower. You live in a land of miracles, you do."

"And yourself?"

He laid his fork down and slowly sipped his coffee before he answered.

"I suppose you would think our life primitive, compared to yours, that is. But we're comfortable, well fed, and as happy as anyone is happy in this mortal sphere. The Emerald Isle has always been an underpopulated and agricultural place. When the oil ran out we never had the trouble old England had. None of the riots and shootings. We had it a bit hard at first, of course. People leaving the cities, back to the country when the electricity was turned off and the motorcars stopped running. But peat makes a good fire, and cutting it keeps you warm. A donkey cart will take you most places you want to go, there are trains twice a week now to Dublin and Cork. Fish in the ocean, cattle and sheep in the meadow, it's not a bad life, you know."

"Sounds lovely and primitive, like being back in the Stone Age living in a cave and all that."

"Don't be insulting, Kriket."

"Dads, I'm not! Did I insult you, Cormac?"

"No insult given, none taken."

"See, Dads? Now what was that you said about England? Isn't that part of Ireland?" She was never very strong on geography.

"Not exactly—though the English have thought so from time to time. It's another island, just next to ours. Very industrialized they used to be, right up to the end of the twentieth century. That ended when the oil ran out and the economy collapsed completely. Been well on its way for years, right up to the Second Civil War. North against the south they say, really the rich against the poor. The UNO refused to intervene the way they did in North Ireland, sending in the Swedish troops when the Brits pulled out early one rainy morning. Now Britain is pretty much like Ireland, except for the ruins of the cities of course. Mostly agricultural, though manufacturing still goes on in the Midlands. After all, they did win the war. You're the lucky ones here. The Quick Wars never crossed the Atlantic. Though you did have your troubles. At least that's what the history books say."

"Communist propaganda," Kriket said in firm tones, the way one corrects a child. "We know all about that. Jealousy on their part with the world falling apart and America staying strong and secure."

"I'm sorry. But I am of the opinion that your books have it wrong," he said, all too blandly. "We were always taught that the States sealed their borders tight. An armed wall . . ."

"We had no choice. It was the only thing possible to protect us against the starving Third Worlders."

"Didn't you add slightly to those Third Worlders?"

This was treacherous ground—and every word of it being recorded.

There was nothing I could say, but I hoped he would show more discretion.

"That's nonsense, criminal nonsense. I majored in history and I know. Of course there were some illegal immigrants and they had to be ejected."

"What about the inner-city deportations? The Detroit and Harlem transshipments?"

Kriket was angry now, her words sharp. "I don't know what kind of Communist propaganda they feed you on your little cow-shit-covered island but—"

"Kriket, Cormac is our guest. And the events he mentioned did happen." I had to watch my words now or I would be in trouble myself. "Well before you were born I taught history at Harvard. Of course, that was before it was computerized and closed. You'll find all of the Congressional investigations on the record. Those were hard times, hungry times, and there were excesses. General Schultz, you will remember, died in jail for his part in the Harlem shipments. There were excesses and they were punished. Justice was not only done but seen to be done." That for the record and now to get back on safer ground. "Ireland has one of the oldest and best-known universities in the world, Trinity College. Is it still open?"

"TCD? Who would dare close it? I went to Bellfield myself, one year studying law. Then the brother went down with the Flying Cloud and the money ran out and I went back to the shipyard then to sea like the others. But you said 'closed,' Harvard closed? I can't believe it—in Ireland we've heard of Harvard. Was it a fire or like disaster?"

I smiled at that and shook my head. "Not really closed, Cormac, I said, 'computerized.' Here, I'll show you." I went into the house and accessed my files, took the black disc from the hopper, and returned. Handed it to Cormac.

"You've got it there," I said.

He turned it over and over in his hands, rubbed the gold terminals with his fingers, then looked up. "Sure and I'm afraid I don't understand."

"Mass storage. When computer memories went to a molecular level it wasn't long before they could store ten to the sixteenth bytes on a wafer that size. A significant figure."

He shook his head, puzzled.

"The memory capacity of the human brain," Kriket said smugly. "That wafer holds infinitely more than that."

"It contains Harvard University," I said. "All the libraries, the professors, lecturers, lectures, and laboratories. Everyone goes to university now—everyone who can afford the twenty-five dollars that a university costs. I'm in there, I'm proud to say. All of my best lectures and tutorials. I'm even there in an RS on the early-nineteenth-century slave trade. That's what I did my doctorate on."

"An RS?"

"Response Simulation. All the responses are cross-indexed by key words and relationships, and the answers are speaker-simulated. Put simply, it means you sit and talk with me on the screen, and I answer all your questions. In great detail."

"Holy Mother . . ." he said, staring wide-eyed at Harvard University. Then passed it back quickly as though it were burning his fingers.

"What was it you said about boat building?" Kriket asked, politics thankfully forgotten for the moment.

"I worked at it, there in the yard in Arklow. Prime oak forest all around the Wicklow hills. Build fine boats, they do."

"Do you mean wooden ships?" she asked, laughing. Cormac was a hard man to anger; he nodded and smiled in return. "Really? It's like something out of prehistory. Dads, can I use your terminal for a moment?"

"Help yourself. Do you remember the access code?"

"Have you forgotten? I stole it when I was fifteen and ran up all those frightening bills. Be right back."

"Excuse me for asking," Cormac said, his eyes never moving as she walked by in front of him, all brown flesh and female. A strange reaction, any American male would have watched her, a visual compliment. "With the university closed, where do you teach now?"

"I don't. Retraining for new skills is a requirement these days. You do it two, three times in a lifetime as jobs are eliminated and new ones take their place. Right now I'm a metal dealer."

I caught him looking about and he stopped, embarrassed. "A good business. You keep it behind the house?"

He was even more embarrassed when I laughed: I couldn't help myself. I had a vision of myself cruising the roads in a broken-down truck heaped high with junk.

"I do all my work at the terminal. Wrote my own programs. I keep track of every importer, smelter, and breaker in the country. My computer accesses theirs at local closing time every day and copies their inventory. I know to the gram where every rare metal is at any time. Manufacturers phone in requests, and I arrange for shipments, bill them, and pass on payment minus my commission. I have everything so automated it could almost run itself. Most businesses work that way. It makes life easier."

"You couldn't do that in Ireland. We have only two phones in Arklow and one is at the Gardai barracks. But still—you can't build ships or farm by phone."

"Yes you can. Our farms are fully automated so that less than two percent of the population are farmers. As to ships—here, I'll show you."

I turned on the daylight screen, punched the library menu, then found a shipbuilding film. Cormac gaped at the automated assembly—not a man in sight—as the great plates were moved into place and welded together.

"Not quite the way we build them," he finally said. Kriket came out of the house at this moment and heard him.

"How well do you know your boat business?" she asked.

"Well enough. Built enough of them."

"I hope so, because I just got you a contract. I work on programming for the network. I checked the archives and we have nothing on hand-building a wooden craft. We'll supply tools and wood, pay an advance and commission against points on residuals . . ."

"Kriket—I haven't the slightest idea what you are talking about."

I interrupted before she could speak again.

"You're being offered a job, Cormac. If you build a small boat from scratch, they'll make a film of it and pay you a lot of money. What do you think?"

"I think that it is madness—and I'll do it! Then I can pay you back, Bil, for your hospitality, which is greater than that of your government. Do they really not have funds to feed a shipwrecked mariner?"

"This is a cash-and-carry economy. You pay for what you get. And now you can pay, so there is no problem."

Not for him, but for me and those listening ears. There was enough about economics on the tapes for one day.

Kriket's network did not waste time. Next day a skyhook dropped a prefab studio behind the house, fully equipped to Cormac's specifications. The automated cameras, controlled from the studio, tracked him as he tightened the first piece of wood into the vise.

"She's going to be klinker-built, mast forward, a ten-footer," Cormac explained into the mike that hovered above his head.

"What is a footer?" the director asked, his voice coming over the speaker in the ceiling.

"Not footer, feet. Ten feet in length she'll be."

"How many feet in a meter?"

The pager in my watch buzzed and I went to the nearest phone. The screen was dark, which meant something very official, since only the government can legally blank a screen.

"This phone is not secure. Go to one inside the house," the voice ordered. I went to my study, closed the door, and activated the phone there. The speaker was heavyset and grim, as official as his voice.

"I am Gregory, your case officer. I have been through yesterday's tapes, and the suspect is very subversive."

"Really? I thought everything he said was a matter of public record."

"It is not. Subversive statements were made about England. This evening you will lead the conversation to other European states. In particular Bohemia, Napoli, and Georgia. Do you understand?"

"Do I understand that I am now an unpaid police informer?"

He looked at me in cold silence, and I had the feeling that I had gone too far.

"No," he finally said. "You are not unpaid. You are on active duty with the Coast Guard and will receive your salary in addition to your normal income. Will you do this—or will I make a permanent record of your remark about a police informer?"

I knew I was getting a second chance. The permanent record was already made, but attention would not be drawn to it if I cooperated.

"You will have to excuse me. I spoke hastily, without thinking. I will, of course, cooperate with the authorities."

The screen went dark. I saw that there were four orders waiting for me; I punched them up, happy to work and take my mind off the affair at hand.

Kriket became a more frequent visitor in the next weeks, until she was there for dinner nearly every night. Not from any newfound filial responsibility, I was sure. She could never resist a man who offered a real challenge, and Cormac was challenge enough for anyone. The summer was turning into a long, hot one, and they swam every afternoon now, when he had finished work. I watched this, had a call from Gregory every day, brought up topics at the dinner table that I had no interest in—and generally began to get very irritated at myself. I put off the moment as long as I could, until I noticed that Kriket was again swimming topless. It was time to act. I changed into swimming trunks as well.

"Hello you two," I said, striding through the bubbling surf towards them. "A scorcher. Mind if I join you for a swim?"

Cormac stepped away from her a bit when I appeared.

"You hate swimming, Dads," she said, looking puzzled.

"Not on a day like this. And I bet I can still outswim you. Out to the buoy and back, what do you say?"

I touched my fingers to my lips as I took the pager bracelet off my wrist. Then reached out and unclasped Kriket's necklace with the pendant dolphin that disguised her pager. I held them below the surface of the water and swished them around before I spoke.

"Most people don't realize that these things are two-way. I want this conversation to be private."

"Dads, you're being paranoid . . ."

"Quite the contrary. Everything said in the house is being recorded by security. They think that Cormac is some kind of spy. I might have kept my silence except for the fact that I don't want you hurt."

I didn't think that he could do it, but Cormac managed to blush under his new tan. Kriket laughed.

"How sweet and medieval, Dads. But I can take care of myself."

"I hope so—although two divorces in three years is not much of a track record. Normally I would say it is your life and leave you to it. But Cormac is a foreign national, illegally in this country, suspected of a major crime."

"I don't believe a word of it! Cormac, sweet beast, tell Dads that he's brain-drained, that you're no spy."

"Your father is right, Kriket. According to your laws I'm here illegally, and they'll put me away as soon as it suits their fancy. I'm for a swim."

He dived in and splashed away. I noticed that he hadn't denied the spy charges. "Think about it," I said, then handed her back her necklace and plunged in as well.

The first of the autumn storms blew the heat away in September. We were watching them film the last of the series with a live interviewer. Thunder was rumbling outside but the filter circuits would grab the sound and nullify it.

"An ancient craft, nay verily, 'tis an art that is still practiced by aboriginals at the far ends of the world," the interviewer said. "But you have seen the incredibly ancient done right before your eyes, and I know that you, like me, have thrilled to see these lost skills exhumed from the darkness of history at last and displayed for all to see. That's it, cut and end."

"You're finished, then?" Cormac asked.

"In the can and we pull the set tomorrow."

"You do know that you were talking diabolical rubbish?"

"Of course. And you're being paid for it, Charley, don't forget that. With the average mental age of TV viewers hovering around twelve and a half, no one is going to lose money playing to that audience."

"And the boat?"

"Property of the network, Charley, read your contract. It goes with the rest tomorrow."

Cormac rested his hand on the smooth wood, rubbing it lightly. "Treat her well. You'll enjoy sailing in her."

"Going to sell her for money, Charley. Plenty of offers."

"Well, then." Cormac turned his back on the boat, already forgetting her. "If it suits your pleasure, Bil, I would greatly enjoy some of your bourbon, which, while not Irish whiskey, will do until the next bottle of Jamie comes along."

The rain was still lashing down and we ran the few meters to the house.

Kriket went off to dry her hair, and I poured two large drinks.

"Here's to you," he said, raising his. "May the road rise up before you and may you be in heaven a year before the devil knows you're gone."

"Are you saying goodbye?"

"I am. A wee man with bandy legs and a vile disposition, name of Gregory, talked to me today. Asked a lot of political questions—even more than you have. He's coming for me in a few minutes, but I wanted to say goodbye first."

"So quickly? And about those questions, I'm sorry. I simply did as I was asked."

"A man can do no more. I appreciate your hospitality—and would have done the same myself. I have had the money I earned transferred to your account. I can't use it where I'm going."

"That's not fair—"

"It is, and I'll have it no other way."

He raised his head and I heard it too, the sound of a copter almost drowned out by the rain. He stood.

"I would like to go now, before your daughter returns. Say goodbye for me. She's a fine girl. I'll just get my raincoat. I'm not to take anything else."

Then he was gone, and I felt there were things I should have said that would now remain unsaid. The patio door opened and Gregory came in, dripping onto the carpet. His legs were too short for his body, bowed as well. He was far more impressive on the phone.

"I've come for Byrne."

"He told me. He's getting his coat. Isn't this all rather sudden?"

"No. Just in time. We finally pressured the English police. Sent them Byrne's prints from one of your glasses. He's not what he seems."

"He seems to be a sailor, a fisherman, and a boatwright, or whatever they are called."

"Perhaps." His smile was humorless. "He is also a colonel in the Irish Army."

"So I'm a yeoman in the Coast Guard. Is either a crime?"

"I am not here to talk to you. Get him."

"I dislike being ordered about in my own home."

I weakened my protest by doing as he bid. The door to the bath was open, and Kriket was still drying her hair. "Be with you in a

moment," she called out over the hum of the machine. I went to
Cormac's room and looked in. Closed the door and returned to the
living room. Sat and sipped some of my drink before I spoke.

"He's not there."

"Where is he?"

"How should I know?"

His chair went over as he rushed from the room. "In quite a hurry,
isn't he?" Kriket said as she came in. "Can I have a drink?"

"Bourbon on the rocks, of course."

I reached out and touched her hair; it was still damp.

"Cormac is gone," I said as I poured the drink.

"So I heard. But he can't get far."

She smiled as she said this and made a very rude signal in the
direction of the door. Then sipped demurely as Gregory came back
in, streaming water and bursting with anger.

"He's gone—and his goddamn ship is gone too. You knew about
this."

"Everything said here is being recorded, Gregory," I said, cold anger
in my voice. "So watch your accusations, or I'll have you in court. I
have cooperated with you every millimeter of the way. My daughter
and I were right here when Cormac left. If there is any blame—why,
you will just have to blame yourself."

"I'll get him!"

"I doubt it. The sea brought him—and now it will take him away.
To report all the government secrets that he learned here." I could
not help smiling.

"Are you laughing at me?"

"Yes. You and your kind. This is a free country, and I would like
to see it freer. We survived the crises of the twentieth century that
wreaked destruction on the rest of the world. But we paid—are still
paying—a very high price for this. It is time now that we opened our
borders again and rejoined the rest of mankind."

"I know what Cormac was doing here," Kriket said suddenly, and
we both turned to look at her. "He was a spy all right. A spy from
Europe come to look us over. And I know his reasons, too. He wants
to see if we are acceptable to the rest of the human race."

Gregory snorted in disgust and stamped out. For myself—I wasn't
so sure. Perhaps Kriket was right.

MIRACULOUS INVENTIONS

There was a time, in the good old Hugo Gernsback days, when the idea was king. Hugo always felt that if you couldn't patent a story it was not worth writing. Or, if already written and not patentable, why he was not going to publish it in the hallowed pages of *Amazing Stories*. He practiced what he preached and as example to prospective authors he wrote the world's most unreadable novel, *Ralph 124C41+*, which, admittedly, did contain a lot of possibly patentable ideas. Thankfully things have changed since those days—which nevertheless does not mean that we should abandon the exotic machinery that kept SF going for so many years.

Here are some interesting bits of technology that you will not have encountered before: From the obviously simple invention of "Toy Shop" to "From Fanaticism, or for Reward." Which features what I believe is the final word in robotic construction.

Down to Earth

"Gino . . . Gino . . . help me! For God's sake, do something!"

The tiny voice scratched in Gino Lombardi's earphone, weak against the background roar of solar interference. Gino lay flat in the lunar dust, half buried by the pumice-fine stuff, reaching far down into the cleft in the rock. Through the thick fabric of his suit he felt the edge crumbling and pulled hastily back. The dust and pieces of rock fell instantly, pulled down by the light lunar gravity and unimpeded by any trace of air. A fine mist of dust settled on Glazer's helmet below, partially obscuring his tortured face.

"Help me, Gino, get me out of here," he implored, stretching his arm up over his head.

"It's no good," Gino answered, putting as much of his weight onto the crumbling lip of rock as he dared, reaching far down. His hand was still a good yard short of the other's groping glove. "I can't reach you—and I've got nothing here I can let down for you to grab. I'm going back to the Bug."

"Don't leave—" Glazer called, but his voice was cut off as Gino slid back from the crevice and scrambled to his feet. Their tiny helmet radios did not have enough power to send a signal through the rock; they were good only for line-of-sight communication.

Gino ran as fast as he could, long gliding jumps one after the other back towards the Bug. It did look more like a bug here, a red beetle squatting on the lunar landscape, its four spidery support legs sunk into the dust. He cursed under his breath as he ran: what a hell of an ending for the first moon flight! A good blastoff and a perfect orbit, the first two stages had dropped on time, the lunar orbit was right, the landing had been right—and ten minutes after they had walked out of the Bug, Glazer had to fall into this crevice hidden under the powdery dust. To come all this way—through all the multiple hazards of space—then to fall into a hole . . . There was just no justice.

At the base of the ship Gino flexed his legs and bounded high up towards the top section of the Bug, grabbing onto the bottom of the still-open door of the cabin. He had planned his moves while he ran—the magnetometer would be his best bet. Pulling it from the rack he yanked at its long cable until it came free in his hand, then turned back without wasting a second. It was a long leap back to the surface—in Earth gravitational terms—but he ignored the apparent danger and jumped, sinking knee deep in the dust when he landed. The row of scuffled tracks stretched out towards the slash of the lunar crevice and he ran all the way, chest heaving in spite of the pure oxygen he was breathing. Throwing himself flat he skidded and wriggled like a snake, back to the crumbling lip.

"Get ready, Glazer," he shouted, his head ringing inside the helmet with the captive sound of his own voice. "Grab the cable . . ."

The crevice was empty. More of the soft rock had crumbled away and Glazer had fallen from sight.

For a long time Major Gino Lombardi lay there, flashing his light into the seemingly bottomless slash in the satellite's surface, calling on his radio with the power turned full on. His only answer was static, and gradually he became aware of the cold from the eternally chilled rocks that was seeping through the insulation of his suit. Glazer was gone, that was all there was to it.

After this Gino did everything that he was supposed to do in a methodical, disinterested way. He took rock samples, dust samples, meter readings, placed the recording instruments exactly as he had been shown and fired the test shot in the drilled hole. Then he gathered the records from the instruments and when the next orbit of the Apollo spacecraft brought it overhead he turned on the cabin transmitter and sent up a call.

"Come in Dan . . . Colonel Danton Coye, can you hear me . . . ?"

"Loud and clear," the speaker crackled. "Tell me you guys, how does it feel to be walking on the moon?"

"Glazer is dead. I'm alone. I have all the data and photographs required. Permission requested to cut this stay shorter than planned. No need for whole day down here."

For long seconds there was a crackling silence, then Dan's voice came in, the same controlled Texas drawl.

"Roger, Gino—stand by for computer signal, I think we can meet in the next orbit."

The moon takeoff went as smoothly as the rehearsal had gone in the mock-up on Earth; and Gino was too busy doing double duty to have time to think about what had happened. He was strapped in when the computer radio signal fired the engines that burned down into the lower portion of the Bug and lifted the upper half free, blasting it up towards the rendezvous in space with the orbiting mother ship. The joined sections of the Apollo came into sight and Gino realized he would pass in front of it, going too fast: he made the course corrections with a sensation of deepest depression. The computer had not allowed for the reduced mass of the lunar rocket with only one passenger aboard. After this, matching orbits was not too difficult and minutes later he crawled through the entrance of the command module and sealed it behind him. Dan Coye stayed at the controls, not saying anything until the cabin pressure had stabilized and they could remove their helmets.

"What happened down there, Gino?"

"An accident—a crack in the lunar surface, covered lightly, sealed over by dust. Glazer just . . . fell into the thing. That's all. I tried to get him out, I couldn't reach him. I went to the Bug for some wire, but when I came back he had fallen deeper . . . it was . . ."

Gino had his face buried in his hands, and even he didn't know if he was sobbing or just shaking with fatigue and strain.

"I'll tell you a secret, I'm not superstitious at all," Dan said, reaching deep into a zippered pocket of his pressure suit. "Everybody thinks I am, which is just to show you how wrong everybody can be. Now I got this mascot, because all pilots are supposed to have mascots, and it makes good copy for the reporters when things are dull." He pulled the little black rubber doll from his pocket, made famous on millions of TV screens, and waved it at Gino.

"Everybody knows I always tote my little good-luck mascot with me, but nobody knows just what kind of good luck it has. Now you will find out, Major Gino Lombardi, and be privileged to share my luck. In the first place this bitty doll is not rubber, which might have a deleterious effect on the contents, but is constructed of a neutral plastic."

In spite of himself, Gino looked up as Dan grabbed the doll's head and screwed it off.

"Notice the wrist motion as I decapitate my friend, within whose bosom rests the best luck in the world, the kind that can only be brought to you by sour mash one-hundred-and-fifty-proof bourbon. Have a slug." He reached across and handed the doll to Gino.

"Thanks, Dan." He raised the thing and squeezed, swallowing twice. He handed it back.

"Here's to a good pilot and a good guy, Eddie Glazer," Dan Coye said, raising the flask, suddenly serious. "He wanted to get to the moon and he did. It belongs to him now, all of it, by right of occupation." He squeezed the doll dry and methodically screwed the head back on and replaced it in his pocket. "Now let's see what we can do about contacting control, putting them in the picture, and start cutting an orbit back to towards Earth."

Gino turned the radio on but did not send out the call yet.

While they had talked their orbit had carried them around to the other side of the moon and its bulk successfully blocked any radio communication with Earth. They hurtled in their measured arc through the darkness and watched another sunrise over the sharp lunar peaks: then the great globe of the Earth swung into sight again. North America was clearly visible and there was no need to use repeater stations. Gino beamed the signal at Cape Canaveral and waited the two and a half seconds for his signal to be received and for the answer to come back the 480,000 miles from Earth. The seconds stretched on and on, and with a growing feeling of fear he watched the hand track slowly around the clock face.

"They don't answer . . ."

"Interference, sunspots . . . try them again," Dan said in a suddenly strained voice.

The control at Canaveral did not answer the next message, nor was there any response when they tried the emergency frequencies. They picked up some aircraft chatter on the higher frequencies, but no one noticed them or paid any attention to their repeated calls. They looked at the blue sphere of Earth, with horror now, and only after an hour of sweating strain would they admit that, for some unimaginable reason, they were cut off from all radio contact with it.

"Whatever happened, happened during our last orbit around the moon. I was in contact with them while you were matching orbits," Dan said, tapping the dial of the ammeter on the radio. "There couldn't be anything wrong . . . ?"

"Not at this end," Gino said firmly. "But—maybe something has happened down there."

"Could it be . . . a war?"

"It might be. But with whom and why? There's nothing unusual on the emergency frequencies and I don't think—"

"Look!" Dan shouted hoarsely. "The lights—where are the lights?"

In their last orbit the twinkling lights of the American cities had been seen clearly through their telescope. The entire continent was now black.

"Wait, see South America, the cities are lit up there, Gino. What could possibly have happened at home while we were in that orbit?"

"There's only one way to find out. We're going back. With or without any help from ground control."

They disconnected the lunar Bug and strapped into their acceleration couches in the command module while they fed data to the computer. Following its instructions they jockeyed the Apollo into the correct attitude for firing. Once more they orbited the airless satellite and at the correct instant the computer triggered the engines in the attached service module. They were heading home.

With all the negative factors taken into consideration, it was not that bad a landing. They hit the right continent and were only a few degrees off in latitude, though they entered the atmosphere earlier than they liked. Without ground control of any kind it was an almost miraculously good landing.

As the capsule screamed down through the thickening air its im-

mense velocity was slowed and the airspeed began to indicate a reasonable figure. Far below, the ground was visible through rents in the
cloud cover.

"Late afternoon," Gino said. "It will be dark soon after we hit the
ground."

"At least it will still be light for a while. We could have been
landing in Peking at midnight, so let's hear no complaints. Stand by
to let go the parachutes."

The capsule jumped twice as the immense chutes boomed open.
They opened their faceplates, safely back in the sea of air once more.

"Wonder what kind of reception we'll get?" Dan asked, rubbing
the bristle on his big jaw.

With the sharp crack of split metal a row of holes appeared in the
upper quadrant of the capsule: air whistled in, equalizing their lower
pressure.

"Look!" Gino shouted, pointing at the dark shape that hurtled by
outside. It was egg-shaped and stub-winged, black against the afternoon sun. Then it twisted over in a climbing turn and for a long
moment its silver skin was visible to them as it arched over and came
diving down. Back it came, growing instantly larger, red flames twinkling in its wing roots.

Gray haze cut off the sunlight as they fell into a cloud. Both men
looked at each other: neither wanted to speak first.

"A jet," Gino finally said. "I never saw that type before."

"Neither did I—but there was something familiar . . . Look, you
saw the wings didn't you? You saw . . . ?"

"If you mean did I see black crosses on the wings, yes I did, but
I'm not going to admit it! Or I wouldn't if it wasn't for those new
air-conditioning outlets that have just been punched in our hull. Do
you have any idea what it means?"

"None. But I don't think we'll be too long finding out. Get ready
for the landing—just two thousand feet to go."

The jet did not reappear. They tightened their safety harnesses and
braced themselves for the impact. It was a bumping crash and the
capsule tilted up on its side, jarring them with vibration.

"Parachute jettisons," Dan Coye ordered. "We're being dragged."

Gino had hit the triggers even as Dan spoke. The lurching stopped
and the capsule slowly righted itself.

"Fresh air," Dan said and blew the charges on the port. It sprang
away and thudded to the ground. As they disconnected the multiple
wires and clasps of their suits hot, dry air poured in through the opening, bringing with it the dusty odor of the desert.

Dan raised his head and sniffed. "Smells like home. Let's get out
of this tin box."

Colonel Danton Coye went first as befitted the commander of the First American Earth-Moon Expedition. Major Gino Lombardi followed. They stood side by side silently, with the late-afternoon sun glinting on their silver suits. Around them, to the limits of vision, stretched the thin tangle of grayish desert shrub, mesquite, cactus. Nothing broke the silence, nor was there any motion other than that caused by the breeze that was carrying away the cloud of dust stirred up by their landing.

"Smells good, smells like Texas," Dan said, sniffing.

"Smells awful, just makes me thirsty. But . . . Dan . . . what happened? First the radio contact, then that jet . . ."

"Look, our answer is coming from over there," the big officer said, pointing at a moving column of dust rolling in from the horizon. "No point in guessing, because we are going to find out in five minutes."

It was less than that. A large, sand-colored half-track roared up, followed by two armored cars. They braked to a halt in the immense cloud of their own dust. The half-track's door slammed open and a goggled man climbed down, brushing dirt from his tight black uniform.

"*Hände hoch!*" he ordered waving their attention to the leveled guns on the armored cars. "Hands up and keep them that way. You are my prisoners."

They slowly raised their arms as though hypnotized, taking in every detail of his uniform. The silver lightning bolts on the lapels, the high, peaked cap—the predatory eagle clasping a swastika.

"You're—you're a German!" Gino Lombardi gasped.

"Very observant," the officer observed humorlessly. "I am Hauptmann Langenscheidt. You are my prisoners. You will obey my orders. Get into the *Kraftwagen*."

"Now just one minute," Dan protested. "I'm Colonel Coye, USAF and I would like to know what is going on here . . ."

"Get in," the officer ordered. He did not change his tone of voice, but he did pull his long-barreled Luger from its holster and leveled it at them.

"Come on," Gino said, putting his hand on Dan's tense shoulder. "You outrank him, but he got there fustest with the mostest."

They climbed into the open back of the half-track and the captain sat down facing them. Two silent soldiers with leveled machine-pistols sat behind their backs. The tracks clanked and they surged forward; stifling dust rose up around them.

Gino Lombardi had trouble accepting the reality of this. The moon flight, the landing, even Glazer's death he could accept, they were things that could be understood. But this . . . ? He looked at his watch, at the number twelve in the calendar opening.

"Just one question, Langenscheidt," he shouted above the roar of the engine. "Is today the twelfth of September?"

His only answer was a stiff nod.

"And the year. Of course it is—1971?"

"Yes, of course. No more questions. You will talk to the *Oberst*, not to me."

They were silent after that, trying to keep the dust out of their eyes. A few minutes later they pulled aside and stopped while the long, heavy form of a tank transporter rumbled by them, going in the opposite direction. Evidently the Germans wanted the capsule as well as the men who had arrived in it. When the long vehicle had passed the half-track ground forward again. It was growing dark when the shapes of two large tanks loomed up ahead, cannons following them as they bounced down the rutted track. Behind these sentries was a car park of other vehicles, tents and the ruddy glow of gasoline fires burning in buckets of sand. The half-track stopped before the largest tent and at gunpoint the two astronauts were pushed through the entrance.

An officer, his back turned to them, sat writing at a field desk. He finished his work while they stood there, then folded some papers and put them into a case. He turned around, a lean man with burning eyes that he kept fastened on his prisoners while the captain made a report in rapid German.

"That is most interesting, Langenscheidt, but we must not keep our guests standing. Have the orderly bring some chairs. Gentlemen permit me to introduce myself. I am Colonel Schneider, commander of the 109th Panzer division that you have been kind enough to visit. Cigarette?"

The colonel's smile just touched the corners of his mouth, then instantly vanished. He handed over a flat package of Players cigarettes to Gino, who automatically took them. As he shook one out he saw that they were made in England—but the label was printed in German.

"And I'm sure you would like a drink of whiskey," Schneider said, flashing the artificial smile again. He placed a bottle of Old High-lander on the table before them close enough for Gino to read the label. There was a picture of the highlander himself, complete with bagpipes and kilt, but he was saying, "Ich hatte gern etwas zu trinken WHISKEY!"

The orderly pushed a chair against the back of Gino's leg and he collapsed gratefully into it. He sipped from the glass when it was handed to him—it was good Scotch whiskey. He drained it in a single swallow.

The orderly went out and the commanding officer settled back into his camp chair, also holding a large drink. The only reminder of their captivity was the silent form of the captain near the entrance, his hand resting on his holstered gun.

"A most interesting vehicle that you gentlemen arrived in. Our technical experts will of course examine it, but there is a question—"

"I am Colonel Danton Coye, United States Air Force, serial number—"

"Please, Colonel," Schneider interrupted. "We can dispense with the formalities—"

"Major Giovanni Lombardi, United States Air Force," Gino broke in, then added his serial number. The German colonel flickered his smile again and sipped from his drink.

"Do not take me for a fool," he said suddenly, and for the first time the cold authority in his voice matched his grim appearance. "You will talk for the Gestapo, so you might just as well talk to me. And enough of your childish games. I know there is no American Air Force, just your Army Air Corps that has provided such fine targets for our fliers. Now—what were you doing in that device?"

"That is none of your business, Colonel," Dan snapped back in the same tones. "What I would like to know is, just what are German tanks doing in Texas?"

A roar of gunfire cut through his words, sounding not too far away. There were two heavy explosions and distant flames lit up the entrance to the tent. Captain Langenscheidt pulled his gun and rushed out of the tent while the others leaped to their feet. There was a muffled cry outside and a man stepped in, pointing a bulky, strange-looking pistol at them. He was dressed in stained khaki and his hands and face were painted black.

"Verdamm—" the colonel gasped and reached for his own gun: the newcomer's pistol jumped twice and emitted two sighing sounds. The panzer officer clutched his stomach and doubled up on the floor.

"Don't just stand there gaping, boys," the intruder said, "get moving before anyone else wanders in here." He led the way from the tent and they followed.

They slipped behind a row of parked trucks and crouched there while a squad of scuttle-helmeted soldiers ran by them towards the hammering guns. A cannon began firing and the flames started to die down. Their guide leaned back and whispered.

"That's just a diversion—just six guys and a lot of noise—though they did get one of the fuel trucks. These krautheads are going to find it out pretty quickly and start heading back here on the double. So let's make tracks—now!"

He slipped from behind the trucks and the three of them ran into the darkness of the desert. After a few yards the astronauts were staggering, but they kept on until they almost fell into an arroyo where the black shape of a jeep was sitting. The motor started as they hauled themselves into it and, without lights, it ground up out of the arroyo and bumped through the brush.

"You're lucky I saw you come down," their guide said from the front seat. "I'm Lieutenant Reeves."

"Colonel Coye—and this is Major Lombardi. We owe you a lot of thanks, Lieutenant. When those Germans grabbed us, we found it almost impossible to believe. Where did they come from?"

"Breakthrough, just yesterday from the lines around Corpus. I been slipping along behind this division with my patrol, keeping San Antone posted on their movements. That's how come I saw your ship, or whatever it is, dropping right down in front of their scouts. Stars and stripes all over it. I tried to reach you first, but had to turn back before their scout cars spotted me. But it worked out. We grabbed the tank carrier as soon as it got dark and two of my walking wounded are riding it back to Cotulla where I've got some armor and transport. I set the rest of the boys to pull that diversion and you know the results. You Air Corps jockeys ought to watch which way the wind is blowing or something, or you'll have all your fancy new gadgets falling into enemy hands."

"You said the Germans are near Corpus—Corpus Christi?" Dan asked. "What are they doing there—how long have they been there—and where did they come from in the first place?"

"You flyboys must sure be stationed in some really hideaway spot," Reeves said, grunting as the jeep bounded over a ditch. "The landings on the Texas side of the Gulf were made over a month ago. We been holding them but just barely. Now they're breaking out and we're managing to stay ahead of them." He stopped and thought for a moment. "Maybe I better not talk to you boys too much until we know just what you were doing there in the first place. Sit tight and we'll have you out of here inside of two hours."

The other jeep joined them soon after they hit a farm road and the lieutenant murmured into the field radio it carried. Then the two cars sped north, past a number of tank traps and gun emplacements and finally into the small town of Cotulla, straddling the highway south of San Antonio. They were led into the back of the local supermarket where a command post had been set up. There was a lot of brass and armed guards about, and a heavy-jawed one-star general behind the desk. The atmosphere and the stares were reminiscent in many ways of the German colonel's tent.

"Who are you two, what are you doing here—and what is that thing you rode down in?" the general asked in a no-nonsense voice.

Dan had a lot of questions he wanted to ask first, but he knew better than to argue with a general. He told about the moon flight, the loss of communication, and their return. Throughout the general looked at him steadily, nor did he change his expression. He did not say a word until Dan was finished. Then he spoke.

"Gentlemen, I don't know what to make of all your talk of rockets, moon shots, Russian sputniks or the rest. Either you are both mad or I am, though I admit you have an impressive piece of hardware out on that tank carrier. I doubt if the Russians have time or resources now for rocketry, since they are slowly being pulverized and pushed back across Siberia. Every other country in Europe has fallen to the Nazis and they have brought their war to this hemisphere, have established bases in Central America, occupied Florida and made more landings along the Gulf Coast. I can't pretend to understand what is happening here so I'm sending you off to the national capital in Denver in the morning."

In the plane next day, somewhere over the high peaks of the Rockies, they pieced together part of the puzzle. Lieutenant Reeves rode with them, ostensibly as a guide, but his pistol was handy and the holster flap loose.

"It's the same date and the same world that we left," Gino explained, "but some things are different. Too many things. It's all the same up to a point, then changes radically. Reeves, didn't you tell me that President Roosevelt died during his first term?"

"Pneumonia, he never was too strong, died before he had finished a year in office. He had a lot of wild-sounding schemes but they didn't help. Vice-President Garner took over. Things just didn't seem the same when John Nance said them, not like when Roosevelt had said them. There were lots of fights, trouble in Congress, the depression got worse, and the whole country didn't start getting better until about 1936, when Landon was elected. There were still a lot of people out of work, but with the war starting in Europe they were buying lots of things from us, food, machines, even guns."

"Britain and the Allies, you mean?"

"I mean everybody, Germans too though that made a lot of people here mad. But the policy was no foreign-entanglements and do business with anyone who's willing to pay. It wasn't until the invasion of Britain that people began to realize that the Nazis weren't the best customers in the world, but by then it was too late."

"It's like a mirror image of the world—a warped mirror," Dan said, drawing savagely on his cigarette. "While we were going around the moon something happened to change the whole world to the way it would have been if history had been altered some time in the early thirties."

"World didn't change, boys," Reeves said, "it's always been just the way it is now. Though I admit the way you tell it, it sure does sound a lot better. But it's either the whole world or you, and I'm banking on the simpler of the two. Don't know what kind of an experiment the Air Corps had you two involved in but it must have addled your gray matter."

"I can't buy that," Gino insisted. "I know I'm beginning to feel like I have lost my marbles, but whenever I do I think about the capsule we landed in. How are you going to explain that away?"

"I'm not going to try. I know there are a lot of gadgets and things that got the engineers and the university profs tearing their hair out, but that doesn't bother me. I'm going back to the shooting war where things are simpler. Until it is proved differently I think that you are both nuts, if you'll pardon the expression, sirs."

The official reaction in Denver was basically the same. A staff car, complete with MP outriders, picked them up as soon as they had landed at Lowry Field and took them directly to Fitzsimmons Hospital. They were taken directly to the laboratories and what must have been a good half of the giant hospital's staff took turns prodding, questioning and testing them. They were encouraged to speak many times with lie-detector instrumentation attached to them—but none of their questions were answered. Occasional high-ranking officers looked on gloomily, but took no part in the examination. They talked for hours into tape recorders, answering questions in every possible field from history to physics and when they tired were kept going on Benzedrine. There was more than a week of this in which they saw each other only by chance in the examining room, until they were weak from fatigue and hazy from the drugs. None of their questions were answered, they were just reassured that everything would be taken care of as soon as the examinations were over. When the interruption came it was a welcome surprise, and apparently unexpected. Gino was being probed by a drafted history professor who wore oxidized captain's bars and a gravy-stained battlejacket. Since his voice was hoarse from the days of prolonged questioning, Gino held the microphone close to his mouth and talked in a whisper.

"Can you tell me who was the Secretary of the Treasury under Lincoln?" the captain asked.

"How the devil should I know? And I doubt very much if there is anyone else in this hospital who knows—besides you. And do you know?"

"Of course—"

The door burst open and a full colonel with an MP brassard looked in. A very high-ranking messenger boy: Gino was impressed.

"I've come for Major Lombardi."

"You'll have to wait," the history-captain protested, twisting his already rumpled necktie. "I'm not quite finished . . ."

"That is not important. The major is to come with me at once."

They marched silently through a number of halls until they came to a dayroom where Dan was sprawled deep in a chair smoking a cigar. A loudspeaker on the wall was muttering in a monotone.

"Have a cigar," Dan called out, and pushed the package across the table.

"What's the drill now?" Gino asked, biting off the end and looking for a match.

"Another conference, big brass, lots of turmoil. We'll go in in a moment as soon as some of the shouting dies down. There is a theory now as to what happened, but not much agreement on it even though Einstein himself dreamed it up . . ."

"Einstein! But he's dead . . ."

"Not now he isn't, I've seen him. A grand old gent of over ninety, as fragile as a stick but still going strong. He . . . say, wait, isn't that a news broadcast?"

They listened to the speaker that one of the MPs had turned up.

" . . . In spite of fierce fighting the city of San Antonio is now in enemy hands. Up to an hour ago there were still reports from the surrounded Alamo where units of the Sixth Cavalry have refused to surrender, and all America has been following this second Battle of the Alamo. History has repeated itself, tragically, because there now appears to be no hope that any survivors—"

"Will you gentlemen please follow me," a staff officer broke in, and the two astronauts went out after him. He knocked at a door and opened it for them. "If you please."

"I am very happy to meet you both," Albert Einstein said, and waved them to chairs.

He sat with his back to the window, his thin, white hair catching the afternoon sunlight and making an aura about his head.

"Professor Einstein," Dan Coye said, "can you tell us what has happened? What has changed?"

"Nothing has changed, that is the important thing that you must realize. The world is the same and you are the same, but you have— for want of a better word I must say—you have moved. I am not being clear. It is easier to express in mathematics."

"Anyone who climbs into a rocket has to be a bit of a science fiction reader, and I've absorbed my quota," Dan said. "Have we got into one of those parallel-worlds things they used to write about, branches of time and all that?"

"No, what you have done is not like that, though it may be a help to you to think of it that way. This is the same objective world that you left—but not the same subjective one. There is only one galaxy that we inhabit, only one universe. But our awareness of it changes many of its aspects of reality."

"You've lost me," Gino sighed.

"Let me see if I get it," Dan said. "It sounds like you are saying that things are just as we think we see them, and our thinking keeps them that way. Like that tree in the quad I remember from college."

"Again not correct, but an approximation you may hold if it helps you to clarify your thinking. It is a phenomenon that I have long suspected, certain observations in the speed of light that might be instrumentation errors, gravitic phenomena, chemical reactions. I have suspected something, but have not known where to look. I thank you gentlemen from the bottom of my heart for giving me this opportunity at the very end of my life, for giving me the clues that may lead to a solution to this problem."

"Solution . . ." Gino's mouth opened. "Do you mean there is a chance we can go back to the world as we knew it?"

"Not only a chance but the strongest possibility. What happened to you was an accident. You were away from the planet of your birth, away from its atmospheric envelope and during part of your orbit, even out of sight of it. Your sense of reality was badly strained, and your physical reality and the reality of your mental relationship changed by the death of your comrade. All these combined to allow you to return to a world with a slightly different aspect of reality from the one you have left. The historians have pinpointed the point of change. It occurred on the seventeenth of August, 1933, the day that President Roosevelt died of pneumonia."

"Is that why all those medical questions about my childhood?" Dan asked. "I had pneumonia then, I was just a couple of months old, almost died, my mother told me about it often enough afterwards. It could have been at the same time. It isn't possible that I lived and the president died . . . ?"

Einstein shook his head. "No, you must remember that you both lived in the world as you knew it. The dynamics of the relationship are far from clear, though I do not doubt that there is some relationship involved. But that is not important. What is important is that I think I have developed a way to mechanically bring about the translation from one reality aspect to another. It will take years to develop it to translate matter from one reality to a different order, but it is perfected enough now—I am sure—to return matter that has already been removed from another order."

Gino's chair scraped back as he jumped to his feet. "Professor—
am I right in saying, and I may have got you wrong, that you can take
us and pop us back to where we came from?"

Einstein smiled. "Putting it as simply as you have, Major . . . the
answer is yes. Arrangements are being made now to return both of
you and your capsule as soon as possible. In return for which we ask
you a favor."

"Anything, of course," Dan said, leaning forward.

"You will have the reality-translator machine with you, and mi-
crocopies of all our notes, theories and practical conclusions. In the
world that you come from all of the massive forces of technology and
engineering can be summoned to solve the problem of mechanically
accomplishing what you both did once by accident. You might be
able to do this within months, and that is all the time that there is
left."

"Exactly what do you mean?"

"We are losing the war. In spite of all the warning we were not
prepared, we thought it would never come to us. The Nazis advance
on all fronts. It is only a matter of time until they win. We can still
win, but only with your atom bombs."

"You don't have atomic bombs now?" Gino asked.

Einstein sat silent for a moment before he answered. "No, there
was no opportunity. I have always been sure that they could be constructed, but have never put it to the test. The Germans felt the same,
and at one time even had a heavy water project that aimed towards
controlled nuclear fission. But their military successes were so great
that they abandoned it along with other farfetched and expensive
schemes such as the hollow globe theory. I myself have never wanted
to see this hellish thing built, and from what you have told me about
it, it is worse than my most terrible dream. But I must admit that I
did approach the president about it, when the Nazi threat was closing
in, but nothing was done. It was too expensive then. Now it is too
late. But perhaps it isn't. If your America will help us, the enemy will
be defeated. And after that, what a wealth of knowledge we shall have
once our worlds are in contact. Will you do it?"

"Of course," Dan Coye said.

"But the brass will take a lot of convincing. I suggest some films
be made of you and others explaining some of this. And enclose some
documents, anything that will help convince them what has happened."

"I can do something better," Einstein said, taking a small bottle
from a drawer of the table. "Here is a recently developed drug, and
the formula, that has proved effective in arresting certain of the more
violent forms of cancer. This is an example of what I mean by the

profit that can accrue when our two worlds can exchange information."

Dan pocketed the precious bottle as they turned to leave. With a sense of awe they gently shook hands with the frail old man who had been dead many years in the world they knew, to which they would be soon returning.

The military moved fast. A large jet bomber was quickly converted to carry one of the American solid-fuel rocket missiles. Not yet operational, it was doubtful if they ever would be at the rate of the Nazi advance. But given an aerial boost by the bomber it could reach up out of the ionosphere carrying the payload of the moon capsule with its two pilots. Clearing the fringes of the atmosphere was essential to the operation of the instrument that was to return them to what they could only think of as their own world. It seemed preposterously tiny to be able to change worlds.

"Is that all there is to it?" Gino asked when they settled themselves back into the capsule.

A square case, containing records and reels of film, was strapped between their seats. On top of it rested a small gray metal box.

"What do you expect—an atom smasher?" Dan asked, checking out the circuits. After being stripped for examination, the capsule had been restored as much as was possible to the condition it was in the day it had landed. They were wearing their pressure suits.

"We came here originally by accident, by just thinking wrong or something like that, if everything we were told is correct."

"Don't let it bug you—I don't understand the theory any better. Forget about it for now."

"Yeah, I see what you mean. The whole crazy business may not be simple, but the mechanism doesn't have to be physically complex. All we have to do is throw the switch, right?"

"Roger. The thing is self-powered. We'll be tracked by radar, and when we hit apogee in our orbit they'll give us a signal on our usual operating frequency. We throw the switch and drop."

"Drop right back to where we came from, I hope."

"Hello there cargo," a voice crackled over the speaker. "Pilot here. We are about to take off. All set?"

"In the green, all circuits," Dan reported, and settled back.

The big bomber rumbled the length of the field and slowly pulled itself into the air, engines at full thrust to lift the weight of the rocket slung beneath its belly. The capsule was in the nose of the rocket and all the astronauts could see was the shining skin of the mother ship. It was a rough ride.

The mathematics had indicated that probability of success would be greater over Florida and the South Atlantic, the original reentry target. This meant penetrating enemy territory. The passengers could not see the battle being fought by the accompanying jet fighters, and the pilot of the converted bomber did not tell them. It was a fierce battle and at one point almost a lost one: only a suicidal crash by one of the escort fighters prevented an enemy jet from attacking the mother ship.

"Stand by for drop," the radio said, and a moment later came the familiar sensation of free fall as the rocket cropped clear of the plane. Preset controls timed the ignition and orbit. Acceleration pressed them into their couches.

A sudden return to weightlessness was accompanied by the tiny explosions as the carrying rocket blasted free the explosive bolts that held it to the capsule. For a measureless time their inertia carried on their orbit while gravity tugged back. The radio crackled with a carrier wave, then a voice broke in.

"Be ready with the switch . . . ready to throw it . . . NOW!"

Dan slammed the switch over. Nothing appeared to have happened. Nothing they could perceive in any case. They looked at each other silently, then at their altimeter as they dropped back towards the distant Earth.

"Get ready to open the chute," Dan said heavily, just as a roar of sound burst from the radio.

"Hello, Apollo, is that you? This is Canaveral control, can you hear me? Repeat—can you hear me? Can you answer . . . in heaven's name, Dan, are you there . . . are you there . . . ?"

The voice was almost hysterical, bubbling over itself. Dan flipped the talk button.

"Dan Coye here—is that you, Skipper?"

"Yes but how did you get there? Where have you been since . . . Cancel, repeat cancel that last. We have you on the screen and you will hit in the sea and we have ships standing by . . ."

The two astronauts met each other's eyes and smiled. Gino raised his thumb up in a token of victory. They had done it. Behind the controlled voice that issued them instructions they could feel the riot that must be breaking after their unexpected arrival. To the observers on Earth—this Earth—they must have vanished on the other side of the moon. Then reappeared suddenly some weeks later, alive and well—long days after their oxygen and supplies should have been exhausted. There would be a lot to explain.

It was a perfect landing. The sun shone, the sea was smooth, there was scarcely any crosswind. They resurfaced within seconds and had a clear view through their port over the small waves. A cruiser was already headed their way, only a few miles off.

"It's over," Dan said with an immense sigh of relief as he unbuckled himself from the chair.

"Over!" Gino said in a choking voice. "Over? Look—look at the flag there!"

The cruiser turned tightly, the flag on its stern standing out proudly in the air. The red and white stripes of Old Glory, the fifty white stars on the field of deepest blue.

And in the middle of the stars, in the center of the blue rectangle, lay a golden crown.

Final Encounter

Hautamaki had landed the ship on a rubble-covered pan of rock, a scored and ancient lava flow on the wrong side of the glacier. Tjond had thought, but only to herself, that they could have landed nearer; but Hautamaki was shipmaster and made all the decisions. Then again, she could have stayed with the ship. No one had forced her to join in this hideous scramble across the fissured ice. But of course staying behind was out of the question.

There was a radio beacon of some kind over there—on this uninhabited planet—sending out squeals and cracklings on a dozen frequencies. She had to be there when they found it.

Gulyas helped her over a difficult place and she rewarded him with a quick kiss on his windburned cheek.

It was too much to hope that it could be anything other than a human beacon, though their ship was supposed to be covering an unexplored area. Yet there was the slimmest chance that some others might have built the beacon. The thought of not being there at the time of a discovery like that was unbearable. How long had mankind been looking now, for how many time-dimmed centuries?

She had to rest, she was not used to this kind of physical effort. She was roped between the two men and when she stopped they all stopped. Hautamaki halted and looked when he felt her hesitant tug on the rope, staring down at her and saying nothing. His body said it for him, arrogant, tall, heavily muscled, bronzed and nude under the transparent atmosphere suit. He was breathing lightly and normally, and his face never changed expression as he looked at her desperately heaving breast. Hautamaki! What kind of a man are you, Hautamaki, to ignore a woman with such a deadly glance?

For Hautamaki it had been the hardest thing he had ever done. When the two strangers had walked up the extended tongue of the ship's boarding ramp he had felt violated.

This was his ship, his and Kiiskinen's. But Kiiskinen was dead and the child that they had wanted to have was dead. Dead before birth, before conception. Dead because Kiiskinen was gone and Hautamaki would never want a child again. Yet there was still the job to be done; they had completed barely half of their survey swing when the accident had occurred. To return to survey base would have been prodigiously wasteful of fuel and time, so he had called for instructions—and this had been the result. A new survey team, un-fledged and raw.

They had been awaiting first assignment—which meant they at least had the training if not the experience. Physically they would do the work that needed to be done. There would be no worry about that. But they were a team, and he was only half a team; and lone-liness can be a terrible thing.

He would have welcomed them if Kiiskinen had been there. Now he loathed them.

The man came first, extending his hand. "I'm Gulyas, as you know, and my wife Tjond." He nodded over his shoulder and smiled, the hand still out.

"Welcome aboard my ship," Hautamaki said and clasped his own hands behind his back. If this fool didn't know about the social customs of Men, he was not going to teach him.

"Sorry. I forgot you don't shake hands or touch strangers." Still smiling, Gulyas moved aside to make room for his wife to enter the ship.

"How do you do, Shipmaster?" Tjond said. Then her eyes widened and she flushed, as she saw for the first time that he was completely nude.

"I'll show you your quarters," Hautamaki said, turning and walking away, knowing they would follow. A woman! He had seen them before on various planets, even talked with them, but never had he believed that there would someday be one on his ship. How ugly they were, with their swollen bodies! It was no wonder that on the other worlds everyone wore clothes, to conceal those blubbery, bobbing things and the excess fat below.

"Why—he wasn't even wearing shoes!" Tjond said indignantly as she closed the door. Gulyas laughed.

"Since when has nudity bothered you? You didn't seem to mind it during our holiday on Hie. And you knew about the Men's customs."

"That was different. Everyone was dressed—or undressed—the same. But this, it's almost indecent!"

"One man's indecency is another's decency."

"I bet you can't say that three times fast."

"Nevertheless it's true. When you come down to it he probably thinks that we're just as socially wrong as you seem to think he is."

"I don't think—I know!" she said, reaching up on tiptoes to nip his ear with her tiny teeth, as white and perfectly shaped as rice grains. "How long have we been married?"

"Six days, nineteen hours standard, and some odd minutes."

"Only odd because you haven't kissed me in such a terribly long time."

He smiled down at her tiny, lovely figure, ran his hand over the warm firmness of her hairless skull and down her straight body, brushing the upturned almost vestigial buds of her breasts.

"You're beautiful," he said, then kissed her.

II

Once they were across the glacier the going was easier on the hard-packed snow. Within an hour they had reached the base of the rocky spire. It stretched above them against the green-tinted sky, black and fissured. Tjond let her eyes travel up its length and wanted to cry.

"It's too tall! Impossible to climb. With the gravsled we could ride up."

"We have discussed this before," Hautamaki said, looking at Gulyas as he always did when he talked to her. "I will bring no radiation sources near the device up there until we determine what it is. Nothing can be learned from our aerial photograph except that it appears to be an untended machine of some kind. I will climb first. You may follow. It is not difficult on this type of rock."

It was not difficult—it was downright impossible. She scrambled and fell and couldn't get a body's length up the spire. In the end she untied her rope. As soon as the two men had climbed above her she sobbed hopelessly into her hands. Gulyas must have heard her, or he knew how she felt being left out, because he called back down to her.

"I'll drop you a rope as soon as we get to the top, with a loop on the end. Slip your arms through it, and I'll pull you up."

She was sure that he wouldn't be able to do it, but still she had to try. The beacon—it might not be human-made!

The rope cut into her body, and surprisingly enough he could pull her up. She did her best to keep from banging into the cliff and twisting about: then Gulyas was reaching down to help her. Hautamaki was holding the rope . . . and she knew that it was the strength of those corded arms, not her husband's, that had brought her so quickly up.

"Hautamaki, thank you for—"

"We will examine the device now," he said, interrupting her and looking at Gulyas while he spoke. "You will both stay here with my pack. Do not approach unless you are ordered to."

He turned on his heel, and with purposeful stride went to the out-cropping where the machine stood. No more than a pace away from it he dropped to one knee, his body hiding most of it from sight, staying during long minutes in this cramped position.

"What is he doing?" Tjond whispered, hugging tight to Gulyas' arm. "What is it? What does he see?"

"Come over here!" Hautamaki said, standing. There was a ring of emotion in his voice that they had never heard before. They ran, skidding on the ice-glazed rock, stopping only at the barrier of his outstretched arm.

"What do you make of it?" Hautamaki asked, never taking his eyes from the squat machine fixed to the rock before them.

There was a central structure, a half-sphere of yellowish metal that clamped tight to the rock, its bottom edge conforming to the irregularities beneath it. From this projected stubby arms of the same material, arranged around the circumference close to the base. On each arm was a shorter length of metal. Each one was shaped differently, but all were pointing skywards like questing fingers. An arm-thick cable emerged from the side of the hemisphere and crawled over to a higher shelf of rock. There it suddenly straightened and stood straight up, rearing into the air above their heads. Gulyas pointed to this.

"I have no idea what the other parts do, but I'll wager that is the antenna that has been sending out the signals we picked up when we entered this system."

"It might be," Hautamaki admitted. "But what about the rest?"

"One of those things that's pointing up towards the sky looks like a little telescope," Tjond said. "I really believe it is."

Hautamaki gave an angry cry and reached for her as she knelt on the ground, but he was too late. She pressed one eye to the bottom of the tube, squinted the other shut and tried to see.

"Why—yes, it is a telescope!" She opened the other eye and examined the sky. "I can see the edge of the clouds up there very clearly."

Gulyas pulled her away, but there was no danger. It was a telescope, as she had said, nothing more. They took turns looking through it. It was Hautamaki who noticed that it was slowly moving.

"In that case—all of the others must be turning too, since they are parallel," Gulyas said, pointing to the metal devices that tipped each arm. One of them had an eyepiece not unlike the telescope's, but when he looked into it there was only darkness. "I can't see a thing through it," he said.

"Perhaps you weren't intended to," Hautamaki said, rubbing his jaw while he stared at the strange machine, then turned away to rummage in his pack. He took a multiradiation tester from its padded carrying case and held it before the eyepiece that Gulyas had been trying to look through. "Infrared radiation only. Everything else is screened out."

Another of the tubelike things appeared to focus ultraviolet rays, while an open latticework of metal plates concentrated radio waves. It was Tjond who voiced the thought they all had.

"If I looked through a telescope—perhaps all these other things are telescopes too! Only made for alien eyes, as if the creatures who built the thing didn't know who, or what, would be coming here and provided all kinds of telescopes working on all kinds of wavelengths. The search is over! We . . . Mankind . . . we're not alone in the universe after all!"

"We mustn't leap to conclusions," Hautamaki said, but the tone of his voice belied his words.

"Why not?" Gulyas shouted, hugging his wife to him in a spasm of emotion. "Why shouldn't we be the ones to find the aliens? If they exist at all we knew we would come across them sometime! The galaxy is immense—but finite. Look and you shall find. Isn't that what it says over the entrance to the academy?"

"We have no real evidence yet," Hautamaki said, trying not to let his own growing enthusiasm show. He was the leader, he must be the devil's advocate. "This device could have been human-made."

"Point one," Gulyas said, ticking off on his finger. "It resembles nothing that any of us have ever seen before. Secondly, it is made of a tough unknown alloy. And thirdly it is in a section of space that, as far as we know, has never been visited before. We are light-centuries from the nearest inhabited system, and ships that can make this sort of trip and return are only a relatively recent development . . ."

"And here is real evidence—without any guesswork!" Tjond shouted, and they ran over to her.

She had followed the heavy cable that transformed itself into the aerial. At the base, where it was thickened and fastened to the rock, were a series of incised characters. There must have been hundreds of them, rising from ground level to above their heads, each one clear and distinct.

"Those aren't human," Tjond said triumphantly. "They do not bear the slightest resemblance to any written characters of any language known to man. They are new!"

"How can you be sure?" Hautamaki said, forgetting himself enough to address her directly.

"I know, Shipmaster, because this is my specialty. I trained in comparative philology and specialized in abbicciology—the study of the history of alphabets. We are probably the only science that is in touch with Earth—"

"Impossible!"

"No, just very slow. Earth must be halfway around the galaxy from where we are now. If I remember correctly, it takes about four hundred years for a round-trip communication. Abbicciology is a study that can only grow at the outer fringes; we deal with a hard core of unalterable fact. The old Earth alphabets are part of history and cannot be changed. I have studied them all, every character and every detail, and I have observed their mutations through the millennia. It can be observed that no matter how alphabets are modified and changed they will retain elements of their progenitors. That is the letter L as it has been adapted for computer input." She scratched it into the rock with the tip of her knife, then incised a wavy character next to it. "And this is the Hebrew lamedh, in which you can see the same basic shape. Hebrew is a proto-alphabet, so ancient as to be almost unbelievable. Yet there is the same right-angle bend. But these characters—there is nothing there that I have ever seen before."

The silence stretched on while Hautamaki looked at her, studied her as if the truth or falsity of her words might be written somehow on her face. Then he smiled.

"I'll take your word for it. I'm sure you know your field very well." He walked back to his pack and began taking out more test instruments.

"Did you see that?" Tjond whispered in her husband's ear. "He smiled at me."

"Nonsense. It is probably the first rictus of advanced frostbite."

Hautamaki had hung a weight from the barrel of the telescope and was timing its motion over the ground. "Gulyas," he asked, "do you remember this planet's period of rotation?"

"Roughly eighteen standard hours. The computation wasn't exact. Why?"

"That's close enough. We are at about eighty-five degrees north latitude here, which conforms to the angle of those rigid arms, while the motion of these scope—"

"Counteracts the planet's rotation, moving at the same speed in the opposite direction. Of course! I should have seen it."

"What are you two talking about?" Tjond asked.

"They all point to the same spot in the sky all the time," Gulyas said. "To a star."

"It could be another planet in this system," Hautamaki said, then shook his head. "No, there is no reason for that. It is something outside. We will tell after dark."

They were comfortable in their atmosphere suits and had enough food and water. The machine was photographed and studied from every angle and they theorized on its possible power source. In spite of this the hours dragged by until dusk. There were some clouds, but they cleared away before sunset. When the first star appeared in the darkening sky Hautamaki bent to the ocular of the telescope.

"Just sky. Too light yet. But there is some sort of glowing grid appearing in the field, five thin lines radiating in from the circumference. Instead of crossing they fade as they come to the center."

"But they'll point out whatever star is in the center of the field—without obscuring it?"

"Yes. The stars are appearing now."

It was a seventh-magnitude star, isolated near the galactic rim. It appeared commonplace in every way except for its location with no nearby neighbors even in stellar terms. They took turns looking at it, marking it so they could not possibly mistake it for any other.

"Are we going there?" Tjond asked, though it was more of a statement than a question that sought an answer.

"Of course," Hautamaki said.

III

As soon as their ship had cleared atmosphere, Hautamaki sent a message to the nearest relay station. While they waited for an answer they analyzed the material they had.

With each result their enthusiasm grew. The metal was no harder than some of the resistant alloys they used, but its composition was completely different and some unknown process of fabrication had been used that had compacted the surface molecules to a greater density. The characters bore no resemblance to any human alphabet. And the star towards which the instruments had been pointed was far beyond the limits of galactic exploration.

When the message arrived, signal recorded, they jumped the ship at once on the carefully computed and waiting course. Their standing instructions were to investigate anything, report everything, and this they were doing. With their planned movements recorded they were free. They, they, were going to make a first contact with an alien race—had already made contact with one of its artifacts. No matter what happened now, the honor was irrevocably theirs. The next meal turned naturally into a celebration, and Hautamaki unbent enough to allow other intoxicants as well as wine. The results were almost disastrous.

"A toast!" Tjond shouted, standing and wobbling just a bit.

"To Earth and mankind—no longer alone!"

"No longer alone!" they repeated, and Hautamaki's face lost some of the party gaiety that it had reluctantly gained.

"I ask you to join me in a toast," he said, "to someone you never knew, who should have been here to share this with us."

"To Kiiskinen," Gulyas said. He had read the records and knew about the tragedy that was still fresh in Hautamaki's thoughts.

"Thank you. To Kiiskinen." They drank.

"I wish we could have met him," Tjond said, a tendril of feminine curiosity tickling at her.

"A fine man," Hautamaki said, seeming anxious to talk now that the subject had been broached for the first time since the accident. "One of the very finest. We were twelve years on this ship."

"Did you have . . . children?" Tjond asked.

"Your curiosity is not fitting," Gulyas snapped at his wife. "I think it would be better if we dropped—"

Hautamaki held up his hand. "Please. I understand your natural interest. We Men have settled only a dozen or so planets, and I imagine our customs are curious to you; we are only in a minority as yet. But if there is any embarrassment it is all your own. Are you embarrassed about being bisexual? Would you kiss your wife in public?"

"A pleasure," Gulyas said, and did.

"Then you understand what I mean. We feel the same way and at times act the same way, though our society is monosexual. It was a natural result of ectogenesis."

"Not natural," Tjond said, a touch of color in her cheeks. "Ectogenesis needs a fertile ovum. Ova come from females; an ectogenetic society should logically be a female society. An all-male one is unnatural."

"Everything we do is unnatural," Hautamaki told her without apparent anger. "Man is an environment-changing animal. Every person living away from Earth is living in an 'unnatural' environment. Ectogenesis on these terms is no more unnatural than living, as we are now, in a metal hull in an unreal manifestation of space-time. That this ectogenesis should combine the germ plasm from two male cells rather than from an egg and a sperm is of no more relevancy than your vestigial breasts."

"You are being insulting," she said, blushing.

"Not in the least. They have lost their function, therefore they are degenerative. You bisexuals are just as natural—or unnatural—as we Men. Neither is viable without the 'unnatural' environment that we have created."

The excitement of their recent discovery still possessed them, and perhaps the stimulants and the anger had lowered Tjond's control. "Why—how dare you call me unnatural—you—"

"You forget yourself, woman!" Hautamaki boomed, drowning out the word, leaping to his feet. "You expected to pry into the intimate details of my life and are insulted when I mention some of your own taboos. The Men are better off without your kind!" He drew a deep, shuddering breath, turned on his heel and left the room.

Tjond stayed in their quarters for almost a standard week after that evening. She worked on her analysis of the alien characters and Gulyas brought her meals. Hautamaki did not mention the events, and cut Gulyas off when he tried to apologize for his wife. But he made no protest when she appeared again in the control section, though he reverted to his earlier custom of speaking only to Gulyas, never addressing her directly.

"Did he actually want me to come too?" Tjond asked, closing her tweezers on a single tiny hair that marred the ivory sweep of her smooth forehead and skull. She pulled it out and touched her brow. "Have you noticed that he really has eyebrows? Right here, great shabby things like an atavism. Even hair around the base of his skull. Disgusting. I'll bet you that the Men sort their genes for hirsuteness, it couldn't be accident. You never answered—did he ask for me to be there?"

"You never gave me a chance to answer," Gulyas told her, a smile softening his words.

"He didn't ask for you by name. That would be expecting too much. But he did say that there would be a full crew meeting at nineteen hours."

She put a touch of pink makeup on the lobes of her ears and the bottoms of her nostrils, then snapped her cosmetic case shut. "I'm ready whenever you are. Shall we go see what the shipmaster wants?"

"In twenty hours we'll be breaking out of jump-space," Hautamaki told them when they had met in the control section. "There is a very good chance that we will encounter the people—the aliens—who constructed the beacon. Until we discover differently we will assume that they are peacefully inclined. Yes, Gulyas?"

"Shipmaster, there has been a good deal of controversy on the intentions of any hypothetical race that might be encountered. There has been no real agreement . . ."

"It does not matter. I am shipmaster. The evidence so far indicates a race looking for contact, not conquest. I see it this way. We have a rich and very old culture, so while we have been searching for another intelligent life form we have also been exploring and recording with ships like this one. A poorer culture might be limited in the number of ships that they could apply to this kind of occupation. Therefore the beacons. Many of them could be easily planted by a single ship over a large area of space. There are undoubtedly others. All of them serve to draw attention to a single star, a rendezvous point of some type."

"This doesn't prove peaceful intentions. It could be a trap."

"I doubt it. There are far better ways to satisfy warlike tendencies than to set elaborate traps like this. I think their intentions are peaceful, and that is the only factor that matters. Until we actually encounter them any action will have to be based on a guess. Therefore I have already jettisoned the ship's armament—"

"You what?"

"—and I'll ask you to surrender any personal weapons that you might have in your possession."

"You're risking our lives—without even consulting us," Tjond said angrily.

"Not at all," he answered, not looking at her. "You risked your own life when you entered the service and took the oath. You will obey my instructions. All weapons here within the hour; I want the ship clean before we break through. We will meet the strangers armed only with our humanity . . . You may think the Men go naked for some perverse reason, but that is wrong. We have discarded clothes as detrimental to total involvement in our environment, a both practical and symbolic action."

"You aren't suggesting that we remove our clothes as well, are you?" Tjond asked, still angry.

"Not at all. Do as you please. I am attempting to explain my reasons so we will have some unanimity of action when we encounter the intelligent creatures who built the beacon. Survey knows now where we are. If we do not return, a later contact team will be protected by mankind's complete armory of death. So we will now give our aliens every opportunity to kill us—if that is what they are planning. Retribution will follow. If they do not have warlike intentions we will make peaceful contact. That, in itself, is reason enough to risk one's life a hundred times over. I don't have to explain to you the monumental importance of such a contact."

The tension grew as the time for breakthrough approached. The box of handguns, explosive charges, poisons from the laboratory— even the large knives from the kitchen—had long since been jettisoned. They were all in the control area when the bell pinged softly and they broke through, back into normal space. Here, at the galactic rim, most of the stars were massed to one side. Ahead lay a pit of blackness with a single star glowing.

"That's it," Gulyas said, swinging back the spectral analyzer, "but we're not close enough for clear observation. Are we going to take another jump now?"

"No," Hautamaki said. "I want a clevs observation first."

The sensitive clevs screen began to glow as soon as the pressure dropped, darkening slowly. There were occasional bursts of light from their surface as random molecules of air struck them, then this died away. The forward screen deepened to the blackness of outer space and in its center appeared the image of the star.

"It's impossible!" Tjond gasped from the observer's seat behind them.

"Not impossible," Hautamaki said. "Just impossible of natural origin. Its existence proves that what we see can—and has—been constructed. We will proceed."

The star image burned with unreality. The star itself at the core was normal enough—but how to explain the three interlocking rings that circled it? They had the dimensions of a planetary orbit. Even if they were as tenuous as a comet's tail their construction was an incredible achievement. And what could be the significance of the colored lights on the rings, apparently orbiting the primary like insane electrons?

The screen sparkled and the image faded.

"It could only be a beacon," Hautamaki said, removing his helmet. "It is there to draw attention, as was the radio beacon that drew us to the last planet. What race with the curiosity to build spaceships could possibly resist the attraction of a thing like that?"

Gulyas was feeding the course corrections into the computer. "It is still baffling," he said. "With the physical ability to construct that why haven't they built an exploring fleet to go out and make contacts—instead of trying to draw them in?"

"I hope that we will discover that answer soon. Though it probably lies in whatever composes their alien psychology. To their way of thinking this might be the obvious manner. And you will have to admit that it has worked."

IV

This time when they made the transition from jump-space the glowing rings of light filled the front ports. Their radio receivers were on, automatically searching the wavelengths.

They burst into sound on a number of bands simultaneously. Gulyas lowered the volume.

"This is the same kind of broadcast we had from the beacon," he said. "Very directional. All of the transmissions are coming from that golden planetoid, or whatever it is. It's big, but doesn't seem to have a planetary diameter."

"We're on our way," Hautamaki told him. "I'll take the controls, see if you can get any image on the video circuits."

"Just interference. But I'm sending out a signal, a view of this cabin. If they have the right equipment there they should be able to analyze our signal and match it . . . Look, the screen is changing! They're working fast."

The viewscreen was rippling with color. Then a picture appeared, blurred, then steadied. Tjond focused and it snapped into clear life. The two men looked, stared. Behind them Tjond gasped.

"At least no snakes or insects, praise fortune for that!" The being on the screen was staring at them with the same intensity. There was no way to estimate its relative size, but it was surely humanoid. Three long fingers, heavily webbed, with an opposed thumb. Only the upper part of its figure was visible, and this was clothed so that no physical details could be seen. But the being's face stood out clearly on the screen, golden in color, hairless, with large, almost circular eyes. Its nose, had it been a human one, would be said to be broken, spread over its face, nostrils flaring. This, and the cleft upper lip, gave it a grim appearance to human eyes.

But this yardstick could not be applied. By alien standards it might be beautiful.

"S'bb'thik," the creature said. The radio beacons carried the matching audio now. The voice was high-pitched and squeaky.

"I greet you as well," Hautamaki said. "We both have spoken languages and we will learn to understand each other. But we come in peace."

"Maybe we do, but I can't say the same thing for these aliens," Gulyas interrupted. "Look at screen three."

This held an enlarged view taken from one of the forward pickups, locked onto the planetoid they were approaching. A group of dark buildings stood out from the golden surface, crowned with a forest of aerials and antennas. Ringed about the building were circular structures mounted with squat tubular devices that resembled heavy-bore weapons. The similarity was increased by the fact that the numerous emplacements had rotated. The open orifices were tracking the approaching ship.

"I'm killing our approach velocity," Hautamaki said, stabbing the control buttons in rapid sequence. "Set up a repeater plate here and switch on a magnified view of those weapons. We'll find out their intentions right now."

Once their motion relative to the golden planetoid had been stopped, Hautamaki turned and pointed to the repeater screen, slowly tapping the image of the weapons. Then he tapped himself on the chest and raised his hands before him, fingers spread wide, empty. The alien had watched this dumb show with glistening, golden eyes. It rocked its head from side to side and repeated Hautamaki's gesture, tapping itself on the chest with its long central finger, then pointed into the screen.

"He understood at once," Gulyas said. "Those weapons—they're turning away, sinking out of sight."

"We'll continue our approach. Are you recording this?"

"Sight, sound, full readings from every instrument. We've been recording since we first saw the star, with the tapes being fed into the armored vault as you ordered. I wonder what the next step is?"

"They've already taken it—look."

The image of the alien reached off the screen and brought back what appeared to be a metal sphere that it held lightly in one hand. From the sphere projected a pipelike extension of metal with a lever halfway up its length. When the alien pressed the lever they heard a hissing.

"A tank of gas," Gulyas said. "I wonder what it is supposed to signify? No—it's not gas. It must be a vacuum. See, the pipe is sucking up those grains sprinkled on the table." The alien kept the lever depressed until the hissing stopped.

"Ingenious," Hautamaki said. "Now we know there is a sample of their atmosphere inside that tank."

There was no mechanical propulsion visible, but the sphere came swooping up towards their ship where it swung in orbit above the golden planetoid. The sphere stopped, just outside the ship and clearly visible from the viewports, bobbing in a small arc.

"Some sort of force beam," Hautamaki said, "though nothing registers on the hull instruments. That's one thing I hope we find out how to do. I'm going to open the outer door on the main hatch."

As soon as the door opened the sphere swooped and vanished from sight and they saw, through the pickup inside the air lock, that it fell gently to the deck inside. Hautamaki closed the door and pointed to Gulyas.

"Take a pair of insulated gloves and carry that tank to the lab. Run the contents through the usual air-examination procedures that we use for testing planetary atmosphere. As soon as you have taken the sample evacuate the tank and fill it with our own air, then throw it out through the lock."

The analyzers worked on the sample of alien air, and presumably the aliens were doing the same with their tank of ship's atmosphere. The analysis was routine and fast, the report appearing in coded form on the panel in control.

"Unbreathable," Gulyas said, "at least for us. There seems to be enough oxygen, more than enough, but any of those sulphurated compounds would eat holes through our lungs. They must have rugged metabolisms to inhale stuff like that. One thing is certain, we'll never be in competition for the same worlds . . ."

"Look! The picture is changing," Tjond said, drawing their attention back to the viewing screen.

The alien had vanished and the viewpoint appeared to be in space above the planetoid's surface. A transparent bulge on its surface filled the screen, and while they watched, the alien entered it from below. The scene shifted again, then they were looking at the alien from inside the clear-walled chamber. The alien came towards the pickup, but before reaching it the alien stopped and leaned against what appeared to be thin air.

"There's a transparent wall that divides the dome in half," Gulyas said. "I'm beginning to get the idea."

The pickup panned away from the alien, swept around to the opposite direction where there was an entrance cut into the clear fabric of the wall. The door was open into space.

"That's obvious enough," Hautamaki said, rising to his feet. "That central wall must be airtight, so it can be used for a conference chamber. I'll go. Keep a record of everything."

"It looks like a trap," Tjond said, fidgeting with her fingers while she looked at the invitingly open door on the screen. "It will be a risk . . ."

Hautamaki laughed, the first time they had ever heard him do so, as he climbed into his pressure suit. "A trap! Do you believe they have gone to all this to set a trap for me? Such ego is preposterous. And if it were a trap—do you think it possible to stay out of it?"

He pushed himself free of the ship. His suited figure floated away, getting smaller and smaller.

Silently, moving closer together without realizing they did so, they watched the meeting on the screen. They saw Hautamaki drawn gently in through the open doorway until his feet touched the floor. He turned to look as the door closed, while from the radio they heard a hissing, very dimly at first, then louder and louder.

"It sounds like they are pressurizing the room," Gulyas said. Hautamaki nodded. "Yes, I can hear it now, and there is a reading on the external pressure gauge. As soon as it reaches atmospheric normal I'm taking my helmet off."

Tjond started to protest, but stopped when her husband raised his hand in warning. This was Hautamaki's decision to make.

"Smells perfectly breathable," Hautamaki said, "though it has a metallic odor."

He laid his helmet aside and stripped his suit off. The alien was standing at the partition and Hautamaki walked over until they stood face to face, almost the same height. The alien placed his palm flat against the transparent wall and the human put his hand over the same spot. They met, as close as they could, separated only by a centimeter of substance. Their eyes joined and they stared for a long time, trying to read intent, trying to communicate. The alien turned away first, walking over to a table littered with a variety of objects. It picked up the nearest one and held it for Hautamaki to see. "Kilt," the alien said. It looked like a piece of stone.

Hautamaki for the first time took notice of the table on his side of the partition. It appeared to hold the identical objects as the other table, and the first of these was a lump of ordinary stone. He picked it up.

"Stone," he said, then turned to the television pickup and the unseen viewers in the ship. "It appears that a language lesson is first. This is obvious. See that this is recorded separately. Then we can program the computer for machine translation in case the aliens aren't doing it themselves."

The language lesson progressed slowly once the stock of simple nouns with physical referents had been exhausted. Films were shown, obviously prepared long before, showing simple actions and, bit by bit, verbs and tense were exchanged. The alien made no attempt to learn their language, he just worked to ensure accuracy of identity in the words. They were recording too. As the language lesson progressed Gulyas' frown deepened, and he started to make notes, then a list that he checked off. Finally he interrupted the lesson.

"Hautamaki—this is important. Find out if they are just accumulating a vocabulary or if they are feeding a MT with this material."

The answer came from the alien itself. It turned its head sideways, as if listening to a distant voice, then spoke into a cuplike device at the end of a wire. A moment later Hautamaki's voice spoke out, toneless since each word had been recorded separately.

"I talk through a machine . . . I talk my talk . . . a machine talk your talk to you . . . I am Liem . . . we need have more words in machine before talk well."

"This can't wait," Gulyas said. "Tell them that we want a sample of some of their body cells, any cells at all. It is complex, but try to get it across."

The aliens were agreeable. They did not insist on a specimen in return, but accepted one. A sealed container brought a frozen sliver of what looked like muscle tissue over to the ship. Gulyas started towards the lab.

"Take care of the recordings," he told his wife. "I don't think this will take too long."

V

It didn't. Within the hour he had returned, coming up so silently that Tjond, intent on listening to the language lesson, did not notice him until he stood next to her.

"Your face," she said. "What is wrong? What did you discover?"

He smiled dryly to her. "Nothing terrible, I assure you. But things are very different from what we supposed."

"What is it?" Hautamaki asked from the screen. He had heard their voices and turned towards the pickup.

"How has the language progressed?" Gulyas asked. "Can you understand me, Liem?"

"Yes," the alien said. "Almost all of the words are clear now. But the machine has only a working force of a few thousand words so you must keep your speech simple."

"I understand. The things I want to say are very simple. First a question. Your people, do they come from a planet orbiting about a star near here?"

"No. We have traveled a long way to this star, searching. My home world is there, among those stars there."

"Do all your people live on that world?"

"No, we live on many worlds, but we are all children of children of children of people who lived on one world very long ago."

"Our people have also settled many worlds, but we all come from one world," Gulyas told him, then looked down at the paper in his hands. He smiled at the alien in the screen before him, but there was something terribly sad about this smile. "We came originally from a planet named Earth. That is where your people came from too. We are brothers, Liem."

"What madness is this?" Hautamaki shouted at him, his face swollen and angry. "Liem is humanoid, not human! It cannot breathe our air!"

"He cannot breath our air, or perhaps she," Gulyas answered quietly. "We do not use gene manipulation, but we know that it is possible. I'm sure we will eventually discover just how Liem's people were altered to live under the physical conditions they do now. It might have been natural selection and normal mutation, but it seems too drastic a change to be explained that way. But that is not important. This is." He held up the sheets of notes and photographs. "You can see for yourself. This is the DNA chain from the nucleus of one of my own cells. This is Liem's. They are identical. His people are as human as we are."

"They can't be!" Tjond shook her head in bewilderment. "Just look at him, he is so different, and their alphabet—what about that? I cannot be wrong about that."

"There is one possibility you did not allow for, a totally independent alphabet. You yourself told me that there is not the slightest similarity between the Chinese ideographs and Western letters. If Liem's people suffered a cultural disaster that forced them to completely reinvent writing you would have your alien alphabet. As to the way they look—just consider the thousands of centuries that have passed since mankind left Earth and you will see that his physical differences are minor. Some are natural and some may have been artificially achieved, but germ plasm cannot lie. We are all the sons of man."

"It is possible," Liem said, speaking for the first time. "I am informed that our biologists agree with you. Our points of difference are minor when compared to the points of similarity. Where is this Earth you come from?"

Hautamaki pointed at the sky above them, at the star-filled sweep of the Milky Way, burning with massed stars. "There, far out there on the other side of the core, roughly halfway around the lens of the galaxy."

"The core explains partially what must have happened," Gulyas said,. "It is thousands of light-years in diameter and over ten thousand degrees in temperature. We have explored its fringes. No ship could penetrate it or even approach too closely because of the dust clouds that surround it. So we have expanded outwards, slowly circling the rim of the galaxy, moving away from Earth. If we stopped to think about it we should have realized that mankind was moving the other way, too, in the opposite direction around the wheel."

"And some time we would have to meet." Liem said. "Now I greet you, brothers. And I am sad, because I know what this means."

"We are alone," Hautamaki said, looking at the massed trillions of stars. "We have closed the circle and found only ourselves. The galaxy is ours, but we are all alone." He turned about, not realizing that Liem, the golden alien—the man—had turned at the same time in the same manner.

They faced outwards, looking at the infinite depth and infinite blackness of intergalactic space, empty of stars. Dimly, distantly, there were spots of light, microscopic blurs against the darkness, not stars but island universes, like the one at whose perimeter they stood.

These two beings were different in many ways: in the air they breathed, the color of their skins, their languages, mannerisms, cultures. They were as different as the day is from the night: the flexible fabric of mankind had been warped by the countless centuries until they could no longer recognize each other. But time, distance and mutation could not change one thing: they were still men, still human.

"It is certain then," Hautamaki said. "We are alone in the galaxy."

"Alone in this galaxy." They looked at each other, then glanced away. At that moment they measured their humanness against the same rule and were equal.

For they had turned at the same instant and looked outward into intergalactic space, towards the infinitely remote light that was another island galaxy.

"It will be difficult to get there," someone said.

They had lost a battle. There was no defeat.

Speed of the Cheetah, Roar of the Lion

"Here he comes, Dad," Billy shouted, waving the field glasses. "He just turned the corner from Lilac."

Henry Brogan grunted a bit as he squeezed behind the wheel of his 22-foot-long, 8-foot-wide, 360-horsepower, four-door, power-everything and air-conditioning, definitely not compact, luxury car. There was plenty of room between the large steering wheel and the back of the leather-covered seat, but there was plenty of Henry as well, particularly around the middle. He grunted again as he leaned over to turn the ignition switch. The thunderous roar of unleashed horsepower filled the garage, and he smiled with pleasure as he plucked out the glowing lighter and pressed it to the end of his long cigar.

Billy squatted behind the hedge, peering through it, and when he called out again, his voice squeaked with excitement.

"A block away and slowing down!"

"Here we go!" his father called out gaily, pressing down on the accelerator. The roar of the exhaust was like thunder, and the open garage doors vibrated with the sound while every empty can bounced upon the shelves. Out of the garage the great machine charged, down the drive and into the street with the grace and majesty of an unleashed 747. Roaring with the voice of freedom, it surged majestically past the one-cylinder, plastic and plywood, 132-miles-to-the-gallon, single-seater Austerity Beetle that Simon Pismire was driving. Simon was just turning into his own driveway when the behemoth of the highways hurtled by and set his tiny conveyance rocking in the slipstream. Simon, face red with fury, popped up through the open top like a gopher from his hole and shook his fist after the car with impotent rage, his words lost in the roar of the eight gigantic cylinders. Henry Brogan admired this in his mirror, laughed with glee and shook a bit of cigar ash into his wake.

It was indeed a majestic sight, a whale among the shoals of minnows. The tiny vehicles that cluttered the street parted before him, their drivers watching his passage with bulging eyes. The pedestrians and bicyclists, on the newly poured sidewalks and bicycle paths, were no less attentive or impressed. The passage of a king in his chariot, or an All-American on the shoulders of his teammates, would have aroused no less interest. Henry was indeed King of the Road and he gloated with pleasure.

Yet he did not go far; that would be rubbing their noses in it. His machine waited, rumbling with restrained impatience at the light, then turned onto Hollywood Boulevard, where he stopped before the Thrifty drugstore. He left the engine running, muttering happily to itself, when he got out, and pretended not to notice the stares of everyone who passed.

"Never looked better," Doc Kline said. The druggist met him at the door and handed him his four-page copy of the weekly *Los Angeles Times*. "Sure in fine shape."

"Thanks, Doc. A good car should have good care taken of it."

They talked a minute about the usual things: the blackouts on the East Coast, schools closed by the power shortage, the new emergency message from the president, whether Mitchell and Stans would get the parole they had been promised; then Henry strolled back and threw the paper in onto the seat. He was just opening the door when Simon Pismire came popping slowly up in his Austerity Beetle.

"Get good mileage on that thing, Simon?" Henry asked innocently.

"Listen to me, dammit! You come charging out in that tank, almost run me down, I'll have the law on you—"

"Now, Simon, I did nothing of the sort. Never came near you. And I looked around careful like because that little thing of yours is hard to see at times."

Simon's face was flushed with rage and he danced little angry steps upon the sidewalk. "Don't talk to me like that! I'll have the law on you with that truck, burning our priceless oil preserves—"

"Watch the temper, Simon. The old ticker can go poof if you let yourself get excited. You're in the coronary belt now, you know. And you also know the law's been around my place often. The price and rationing people, IRS, police, everyone. They did admire my car, and all of them shook hands like gentlemen when they left. The law likes my car, Simon. Isn't that right, Officer?"

O'Reilly, the beat cop, was leaning his bike against the wall, and he waved and hurried on, not wanting to get involved. "Fine by me, Mr. Brogan," he called back over his shoulder as he entered the store.

"There, Simon, you see?" Henry slipped behind the wheel and tapped the gas pedal; the exhaust roared and people stepped quickly back onto the curb. Simon pushed his head in the window and shouted.

"You're just driving this car to bug me, that's all you're doing!" His face was, possibly, redder now and sweat beaded his forehead. Henry smiled sweetly and dragged deeply on the cigar before answering.

"Now that's not a nice thing to say. We've been neighbors for years, you know. Remember when I bought a Chevy how the very next week you had a two-door Buick? I got a nice buy on a secondhand four-door Buick, but you had a new Tornado the same day. Just by coincidence, I guess. Like when I built a twenty-foot swimming pool, you just by chance, I'm sure, had a thirty-foot one dug that was even a foot deeper than mine. These things never bothered me—"

"The hell you say!"

"Well, maybe they did. But they don't bother me anymore, Simon, not anymore."

He stepped lightly on the accelerator, and the juggernaut of the road surged away and around the corner and was gone. As he drove, Henry could not remember a day when the sun had shone more clearly from the smogless sky, nor when the air had smelled fresher. It was a beautiful day indeed.

Billy was waiting by the garage when he came back, closing and locking the door when the last high, gleaming fender had rolled by. He laughed out loud when his father told him what had happened, and before the story was done, they were both weak with laughter.

"I wish I could have seen his face, Dad, I really do. I tell you what for tomorrow, why don't I turn up the volume on the exhaust a bit? We got almost two hundred watts of output from the amplifier, and that is a twelve-inch speaker down there between the rear wheels. What do you say?"

"Maybe, just a little bit, a little bit more each day maybe. Let's look at the clock." He squinted at the instrument panel, and the smile drained from his face. "Christ, I had eleven minutes of driving time. I didn't know it was that long."

"Eleven minutes . . . that will be about two hours."

"I know it, damn it. But spell me a bit, will you, or I'll be too tired to eat dinner."

Billy took the big crank out of the toolbox and opened the cover of the gas cap and fitted the socket end of the crank over the hex stud inside. Henry spat on his hands and seized the two-foot-long handle and began cranking industriously.

"I don't care if it takes two hours to wind up the spring," he panted. "It's damn well worth it."

The Greatest Car in the World

Ernest Haroway's nerve was beginning to fail and he clasped his hands together to stop their shaking. What had seemed such a wonderful idea back in Detroit had become strange and frightening now that he was in Italy—and actually on the grounds of the Castello Prestezza itself. He controlled an involuntary shiver as his gaze rose up the gray and age-seared walls of the castle to the grayer and even more ancient palisade of the Dolomite Alps that loomed behind. The courtyard held a hushed and almost sacred stillness, broken only by the rustle of pine needles brushed by the late-afternoon breeze, and the tacking of the cooling engine of his rented car. His throat was dry and the palms of his hands were wet. He had to do it!

With a convulsive motion he threw the door open and forced himself out of the car, stopping only long enough to grab up his briefcase before he crunched across the gravel toward the stone-framed and iron-bound portal of the castle.

There was no sign of bell or knocker on the dark wood of the door, but set into the stone at one side was a carved bronze gorgon's head, now green with age, with a rounded knob over its mouth. Haroway tugged at this knob and, with a grating squeal, it reluctantly came out about a foot on the end of the iron rod, then spasmodically returned to its original position when he released it. Whatever annunciatory mechanism it operated appeared to be functioning because within a minute there came a dreadful rattling from behind the door and it swung slowly open. A tall, sallow-faced man in servant's livery stared down the impressive length of his nose at the visitor, his eyes making a precise—unimpressed—sweep of the length of Haroway's charcoal-gray, drip-dry summer-weight suit, before fixing on his worried face.

"*Sìssignore?*" he said, through cold, suspicious lips.

"*Buon giorno . . .*" Haroway answered, thereby exhausting his complete Italian vocabulary. "I would like to see Mr. Bellini."

"The Maestro sees no one," the servant said in perfect English with a marked Oxford accent. He stepped back and began to close the door.

"Wait!" Haroway said, but the door continued to swing shut. In desperation he put his foot in the opening, a maneuver that had served him well during a brief indenture as a salesman while in college, but was totally unsuited to this type of architecture. Instead of bounding back, as the lightweight apartment doors had done, the monstrous portal closed irresistibly, warping the thin sole of his shoe and crushing his foot so tightly that the bones grated together. Haroway screamed shrilly and threw his weight against the door, which ponderously stopped, then reversed itself. The servant raised one eyebrow in quizzical condemnation of his actions.

"I'm sorry," Haroway gasped, "but my foot. You were breaking all the bones. It is very important that I see Mr. Bellini, the Maestro. If you won't admit me you must take this to him." He dug into his jacket pocket while he eased his weight off the injured foot. The message had been prepared in advance in case there was any trouble in gaining admittance, and he handed it over to the servant, who reluctantly accepted it. This time the great door closed completely and Haroway hobbled over to one of the stone lions that flanked the steps and sat on its back to ease his throbbing foot. The pain died away slowly and a quarter of an hour passed before the door opened again.

"Come with me," the servant said. Was it possible that his voice was just a shade warmer? Haroway could feel his pulse beating in his throat as he entered the building. He was in—inside the Castello Prestezza!

The interior was dark and in his elated state he noticed no details, though he had a vague impression of carved wood, beamed ceilings, suits of armor, and pieces of furniture as bulky as freight cars. With uneven step he followed his guide through one chamber after another until they came to a room where tall, mullioned windows opened onto the garden. A girl stood in front of a window holding his note disdainfully by the edge, as though it were a soiled Kleenex she was about to discard.

"What do you want here?" she asked, the cold tones so unsuited to the velvet warmth of her voice.

At any other time Haroway would have taken a greater interest in this delightful example of female construction, but now, incredible as it seemed, he looked upon her only as an undesired interference. The jet-dark tresses dropping to the creamy tan of her shoulders were just hair. The ripeness of her bosom swelling above the square neck of her dress was another barrier placed in his way, while the pouting loveliness of her lips spoke only words that barred him from Bellini.

"It is no business of yours what I want here," he snapped. "I will tell that to the Maestro."

"The Maestro is a sick man and sees no one," she answered, her voice just as imperious as his. "We can have no one disturbing him." She dangled the card like a dead mouse. "What does this message mean—'Unfinished business from Le Mans 1910?'"

"That business is none of your business, Miss . . . ?"

"I am Signorina Bellini."

"Miss Signorina—"

" 'Signorina' is the Italian word for 'miss.' "

"Sorry. Miss Bellini. What I have to say is only for the ears of the Maestro himself." He took a firmer grip on the handle of his briefcase. "Now—will you take my message to him?"

"No!"

"*Chi è?*" a deep voice rumbled from the direction of the ceiling and the girl went white and clutched the note to her breast.

"He's heard . . . !" she gasped.

The apparently deific voice grumbled again and the girl answered it in staccato Italian, and appeared to be talking either to heaven or to a corner of the ceiling. After some blinking Haroway could make out a loudspeaker suspended from the crenellated molding with what appeared to be a microphone hanging next to it. Then the conversation terminated in what could only have been a command and the girl lowered her head.

"That was . . . he . . . him?" Haroway asked in a hushed voice. She only nodded her head and turned to the window until she could speak again.

"He wants to see you—and the doctor has expressly forbidden visitors." She swung about to face him and the impact of emotion in those large and tear-dampened eyes was so great that it cut through his indifference instantly. "Won't you leave—please? He's not to be excited."

"I would like to help you, but . . . I just can't, I've waited too long for this chance. But I promise you that I won't get him excited; I'll do my best, really I will."

She sighed tremulously and lowered her head again, turning. "Come with me," she said and started toward the door.

Haroway did not feel the pain of his injured foot, for in truth he felt scarcely anything as he stumbled after her as through a sea of cotton wool. His senses were suspended as though, unbelieving, they could not accept the fact that a lifetime ambition was being realized at last. One final door swung open and he could see the bulky figure swaddled in blankets and seated in a wheelchair—a chance ray of sunlight fell from the window and struck a reflection from his mane of white hair, a halo of light that would not have surprised Haroway if it had been real. He could only stand, petrified and speechless, while the girl went over and silently handed the Maestro his note.

"What does this mean?" the old man asked, waving the card at him. "There was only one piece of unfinished business at Le Mans that year and it is too late now to start a lawsuit or anything like that. What do you want?" He frowned at Haroway and the effort wrinkled a network of fine furrows into the mahogany skin.

"N-nothing like that," Haroway stammered, then took a deep breath and grabbed hold of himself. "I of course wasn't there, I hadn't even been born yet—" He fought down an impulse to giggle hysterically. "But my father has told me about it, many times, so I almost feel as if I had seen the race myself. When that eleven-liter Fiat brushed against your 1327-cc Type 13 and turned it over, what a horrible moment that must have been! But your driver, Fettuccine, was thrown clear and it was only when the radiator cap flew off and into the crowd—"

"The cap—I knew it!" the Maestro said, and pounded on the arm of the wheelchair. "It had to be that, there was no other unfinished business at Le Mans!"

"Grandfather, please!" the girl begged as she stroked his hand. "You promised not to!" she said, glaring at Haroway.

"I'm sorry, I didn't mean to. Anyway, there's nothing to get excited about, my father was the one who was hit on the head by the radiator cap."

"Aha—the mysterious wounded man, found at last."

"He wasn't really hurt; it was a very small fracture and he was out of bed inside of a month. And he still held on to the radiator cap—his greatest treasure. He had no money; he had worked his way to Europe just to see Le Mans, and he was treated in a charity hospital, that is why you never discovered him, though I know you tried very hard to find the man who had been injured."

"It was a mystery, many saw him fall—yet later there was no trace."

"Well Dad always was shy; he couldn't possibly consider talking to a great man like you. When he recovered he managed to make his way back to the United States and life was different for him after that. He always said that he had sown his wild oats and he was satisfied. When he met Mom and they married he worked in a filling station; then, finally, he saved enough to buy in and that was all he ever did—but he was always a happy man. He had the radiator cap sealed inside a glass case and framed and hung over the fireplace, and it's the earliest thing I remember, and him telling me about it. I grew up with that cap, Mr. Bellini, and it would be no lie to say that it shaped my whole life. I loved cars and I studied them and went to school nights and right now I'm an automotive engineer. There has never been anything else I have ever wanted in the whole world. Outside of meeting you, that is. Then Dad died last year and his last words were 'Take it back, son. It don't rightly belong to us and I knew it would have to go back someday, but couldn't bear to do it, not in my lifetime. That's your job, son, what you have to do. Take it back to the man that rightly owns it.'"

Haroway had his briefcase open and fumbled through it and extracted an object wrapped in many layers of polythene. One by one, with light, reverent touch, he unwrapped them until the old radiator cap was revealed, dented and scratched but polished like a jewel. He held it out to the Maestro who took and turned it over, squinting at it.

"A nice piece of brass," he said, then handed it back. "Keep it."

"Thank you," Haroway said in a humble voice as he carefully rewrapped it and slid it gently back into the briefcase. "Thank you, too for your courtesy in receiving me." He locked the case and picked it up. "I'll not disturb you anymore—but, if you would permit, there is just one question I would like to ask before I go."

"What is that?" the Maestro asked distractedly, looking out the window and seeing only Le Mans in the year 1910. If it hadn't been for that hulking Fiat his Type 13 should have won. With the overhead camshaft they were getting 3,000 rpm . . .

"It's something that has bothered me for years. Do you think that if it hadn't been for the accident that the Type 13 would have placed first? After all, with your new overhead camshaft you should have been getting 3,000 rpm—"

"Dio mio!" the Maestro gasped. "You read my mind—those were my very thoughts!"

"Not really mind reading, sir, just a lifetime of study. I have had one hobby, one possessing enthusiasm and interest, the Bellini automobiles and the Bellini genius."

"A healthy hobby for a young man, most of the new generation are spineless wonders who think that a vehicle with an automatic gearshift is really a car! Stay a moment; you will have a glass of wine with me. Have you met my granddaughter, Vergine, the apple of an old man's eye even though she is very strict with me?" She glared at him and he laughed heartily. "Don't scowl so, my blossom, it puts ugly lines upon your face. Instead bring a bottle of the '47 Valpolicella and some glasses, we shall have a little holiday today."

They drank and talked and the talk was only of cars—Bellini cars, which they both agreed were the only fit cars to discuss. The afternoon faded and at dinnertime an invitation was forced upon the not-reluctant Haroway and the talk continued: worm and wheel steering with the spaghetti, semicentrifugal, wet multiplate clutches with the meat, and banana-shaped tappets with the dessert. It was a highly satisfactory meal.

"There you see the proof," Haroway said, scratching a last number at the end of a row of equations that stretched across the white surface of the linen tablecloth. "When you developed your sixteen-valve engine for the Type 22 with four valves per cylinder you developed higher scavenging pressure with the smaller valves—this proves it! Did you work out these equations first?"

"No. I leave it for others to prove. I knew what would happen, a matter of intuition you might call it."

"Not intuition—genius!"

Bellini nodded his great gray head, accepting his due. "What do you think I have been doing the past ten years?" he asked.

"Nothing. You retired to this castle after having given more to the automotive world than any other man."

"That is true. But, though I did retire, I have kept a small workshop here, for tinkering, working out ideas, an old man's hobby. I have constructed a car—"

Haroway went white, half rising to his feet, a convulsive movement of his hand sending one of the crystal wineglasses crashing to the floor: he was not aware of it.

"Car . . . new car . . ." was all he could gasp.

"I thought you might be a little interested," the Maestro said with an impish grin. "Perhaps you would like to see it?"

"Grandfather, no!" Vergine broke in. She had sat silently through the meal since the conversation seemed to be doing the Maestro no harm, mellowing his usually spiky mood, but this was too much. "The exertion, and the excitement, the doctor forbade you to go near the car for at least two weeks more . . ."

"Silence!" he roared. "This is my house and I am Bellini. No fat oaf of an overpaid quack tells me what to do in my own house." His temper changed and he patted her hand. "My darling, you must forgive an old man his moods. I have only a few laps left of the race of life and my magneto is failing and my oil pressure is low. Allow me a few moments of pleasure before I pull into the pit for the last time. You must have seen how different Haroway is from the other young men, for, even though he labors in the satanic mills of manufacture of Detroit iron, his heart is pure. I think he must be the last of a vanishing breed. He came here offering—not asking—expecting nothing. He shall see the car."

"What is it called?" Haroway asked in a hushed voice.

"The Type 99."

"A beautiful name." Haroway pushed the wheelchair and Vergine led the way to the elevator, which hummed down its shaft to the garage and workshop concealed beneath the castle. When the door opened Haroway had to hold on to the wheelchair for support or he would have fallen.

There was the car. It was a moment of pure joy, the high point of his life. He did not realize that tears of unalloyed happiness were running down his face, as he stumbled across the spotless concrete floor.

This was frozen motion. The silver form of the Type 99 was poised like a captive thunderbolt, yearning to leap forward and span the world. The body was simplicity itself, its curve as pure and lovely as that of a woman's breast. And under that glistening hood and concealed beneath the perfection of the body Haroway knew there were hidden even greater wonders.

"You installed . . . mechanical improvements?" he asked hesitantly.

"A few," the Maestro admitted. "The brakes, I have never given much attention before to the brakes."

"With good reason—did you not say yourself that a Bellini car is designed to go, not to stop?"

"I did. But the world changes and the roads are more crowded now. I have turned my attention to the brakes and devised a wholly new system of braking. Foolproof, nonfade, nongrab, impossible to lock, just what you imagine a Bellini brake should be."

"And the system is . . . ?"

"Magnetostriction."

"Of course! But no one ever thought of it before."

"Naturally. A laboratory phenomenon where the application of magnetism changes the dimensions of a ferromagnetic substance. It makes a good brake. And then I was so tired of the devil's dance of the piston engine. I decided a new principle was needed. The Type 99 is powered by a free-piston turbine."

"But—that's impossible. The two can't be combined."

"Impossible for others, not for Bellini. Another problem that has been eliminated is unsprung weight. This car has no unsprung weight."

"That's imposs—"

The Maestro smiled and nodded, accepting his accolade.

"There are a few other small items, of course. A nickel-cadmium battery that cannot wear out or be discharged completely. An all-aluminum body, rustproof and easy to repair, that sort of thing."

Haroway let his fingers caress the steering wheel. "You owe this car to the world."

"I had not thought of producing it. It is just an old man's toy."

"No, it is more than that. It is a return to the purity of the vintage motorcar, a machine that will take the world by storm. Just the way it is, the perfect car, the finest car in the world. You have patented all the modifications and inventions?"

"Bellini has been accused of a number of things, but never of having been born yesterday."

"Then let me take the car back with me to the United States! There are enough true car lovers in my firm, I only have to show them the Type 99 to convince them. We'll manufacture a limited number, loving care, hand labor, perfection . . ."

"I don't know," the Maestro said, then gasped and clutched at the arm of the chair, his face growing white with pain. "My medicine, quickly, Vergine." She ran for the bottle while he held tightly to his chest, speaking only with difficulty.

"It is a sign, Haroway, a greater power than I has decided. My work is done. The car is finished—and so am I. Take it, bring it to the world . . ."

He finished with a tired mumble and barely roused enough to sip the medicine his granddaughter brought to him. The noble head was hanging tiredly when she wheeled him away. After the doors of the elevator had shut behind them Haroway turned back to the car.

Joy!

A button on the wall swung open the garage door and a spray of windblown rain speckled the floor. The rented car could stay here; the firm could pick it up tomorrow, because tonight he was driving a Bellini! The car door opened to a touch and he slid into the comforting embrace of the leather driver's seat. He switched on the ignition, then smiled when he found out there was no starting button. Of course, Bellini had always disdained electric starters. A single pull on the crank was enough to start any Bellini car. Now the system had been refined to the utmost and a tiny, two-inch miniature crank handle protruded from the dashboard. He flipped it with his fingertips and the perfectly balanced engine roared into throbbing life. Through the wheel he could feel the vibrating power of the engine, not the mechanical hammer of an ugly machine but a muted rumble like the purr of a giant cat. With the ease of a hot knife cutting butter it slipped into first gear and when he touched the throttle the silver machine threw itself out into the night like an unleashed rocket.

Zero to a hundred miles an hour took four seconds because he was not yet used to the divine machine and was hesitant with the gas. Immense tunnels of light were cut through the rain-swept night by the searchlight-bright headlights. And, though there was no cover over the open car, he was perfectly dry as an ingeniously designed curtain of air rushed above him and shielded him from the rain. The road was a nightmare of hairpin turns but he laughed aloud as he snaked through them, since the steering was only one turn from lock to lock and as positive in response as though the car were running on rails.

There had never been a car like this in the history of the world. He sang as he drove, hurling his happiness into the sky. A new day was coming for the motoring world, the day of the Type 99. And they would all be manufactured with the same loving care that the master had lavished on this prototype, he would see to that.

Of course there would have to be one or two very minor modifications—like the battery. Nickel cadmium was out, they had a contract with their lead-acid battery suppliers and you can't break a contract like that. And the aluminum body—good enough in theory, but you needed special dies to press it and they had stockpiled steel sheet that had to be used, and anyway the dealers would howl because the aluminum bodies would never rust or wear out and no one would trade in for a newer model. Then the engine would have to be considered: they would modify one of their stock engines. It was all right to say that here was a new principle, but they were tooled up to make a different kind of engine and you don't throw away a couple of million dollars' worth of machine tools.

Anyway, a few changes under the hood didn't matter, the body would be the same. He glanced back happily at the car as he swung into the illuminated highway. Well, almost the same. You couldn't change a market overnight and there was something pretty European about the lines. Probably need fins to sell the U.S. market; fins were coming back big.

With a giant's roar from the exhaust he passed a clutch of sports cars as though they were standing still and swung out into a long bend of the road. The rain was clearing and on a ridge high above he could see the outlines of the Castello Prestezza and he waved his hand in a warrior's salute.

"Thank you, Bellini!" he shouted into the wind. "Thank you!"

That was the best part, the important part for him. Not only would he be making the finest car in the world, but he would be making the old man's dream come true!

Rock Diver

The wind hurtled over the crest of the ridge and rushed down the slope in an icy torrent. It tore at Pete's canvas suit, pelting him with steel-hard particles of ice. Head down, he fought against it as he worked his way uphill towards the granite outcropping.

He was freezing to death. A man can't wear enough clothes to stay alive in fifty degrees below zero. Pete could feel the numbness creeping up his arms. When he wiped his frozen breath from his whiskers there was no sensation. His skin was white and shiny wherever it was exposed to the Alaskan air.

"All in a day's work." His cracked lips painfully shaped themselves into the ghost of a smile. "If any of those claim-jumping scissorbills followed me this far they're gonna be awful cold before they get back."

The outcropping sheltered him as he fumbled for the switch at his side. A shrill whine built up in the steel box slung at his belt. The sudden hiss of released oxygen was cut off as he snapped shut the faceplate of his helmet. Pete clambered onto the granite ridge that pushed up through the frozen ground.

He stood straight against the wind now, not feeling its pressure, the phantom snowflakes swirling through his body. Following the outcropping, he slowly walked into the ground. The top of his helmet bobbed for a second like a bottle in water, then sank below the surface of the snow.

Underground it was warmer, the wind and cold left far behind. Pete stopped and shook the snow from his suit. He carefully unhooked the ultra-light from his pack and switched it on. The light beam, polarized to his own mass-penetrating frequency, reached out through the layers of surrounding earth as if they were cloudy gelatin.

Pete had been a rock diver for eleven years, yet the sight of this incredible environment never ceased to amaze him. He took the miracle of his vibratory penetrator, the rock diver's "walk-through," for granted. It was just a gadget, a good gadget, but something he could take apart and fix if he had to. The important thing was what it did to the world around him.

The hogback of granite started at his feet and sank down into a murky sea of red fog. It was a fog composed of the lighter limestone and other rock, sweeping away in frozen layers. Seemingly suspended in midair were granite boulders and rocks of all sizes, caught in the strata of lighter materials. He ducked his head carefully to avoid these.

If his preliminary survey was right, this rocky ridge should lead him to the site of the missing lode. He had been following leads and drifts for over a year now, closing in on what he hoped was the source of the smaller veins.

He trudged downward, leaning forward as he pushed his way through the soupy limestone. It rushed through and around him like a strong current of water. It was getting harder every day to push through the stuff. The piezo crystal of his walk-through was steadily getting further away from the optimum frequency. It took a hard push to get the atoms of his body between those of the surrounding matter. He twisted his head around and blinked to focus his eyes on the two-inch oscilloscope screen set inside his helmet. The little green face smiled at him—the jagged wave-pattern gleaming like a row of broken teeth. His jaw clenched at the variations between the reading and the true pattern etched onto the surface of the tube. If the crystal failed, the entire circuit would be inoperative, and frozen death waited quietly in the air far above him for the day he couldn't go under. Or he might be underground when the crystal collapsed. Death was here, too, a quicker and much more spectacular death that would leave him stuck forever like a fly in amber. A fly that is part of the amber. He thought about the way Soft-Head had got his and shuddered slightly.

Soft-Head Samuels had been one of the old gang, the hard-bitten rock divers who had been the first to uncover the mineral wealth under the eternal Alaskan snows. Soft-Head had slipped off a hogback two hundred meters down and literally fallen face-first into the fabulous White Owl mother lode. That was the strike that started the rush of '63. As the money-hungry hordes rushed north to Dawson he had strolled south with a fortune. He came back in three years with no more than his plane fare and a measureless distrust of humanity.

He rejoined the little group around the potbellied stove, content just to sit among his old cronies. He didn't talk about his trip to the outside and no one asked any questions. The only sign that he had been away was the way he clamped down on his cigar whenever a stranger came into the room. North American Mining grubstaked him to a new outfit and he went back to tramping the underground wastes.

One day he walked into the ground and never came up again. "Got stuck," they muttered, but they didn't know just where until Pete walked through him in '71.

Pete remembered it, too well. He had been dog-tired and sleepy when he had walked through that hunk of rock that hadn't been all rock. Soft-Head was standing there—trapped for eternity in the stone. His face was horror-stricken as he stood half bent over, grabbing at his switch box. For one horrible instant Soft-Head must have known that something was wrong with his walk-through—then the rock had closed in. He had been standing there for seven years in the same position he would occupy for all eternity, the atoms of his body mixed inextricably with the atoms of the surrounding rock.

Pete cursed under his breath. If he didn't get enough of a strike pretty soon to buy a new crystal, he would become part of that time-less gallery of lost prospectors. His power pack was shot and his oxy-gen tank leaked. His beat-up Miller sub-suit belonged in a museum, not on active duty. It was patched like an inner tube and still wouldn't hold air the way it should. All he needed was one strike, one little strike.

His helmet light picked a blue glint from some crystals in the gully wall. It might be Ytt. He leaped off the granite spine he had been following and sank slowly through the lighter rock. Plugging his hand neutralizer into the socket in his belt, he lifted out a foot-thick sec-tion of rock. The shining rod of the neutralizer adjusted the vibration plane of the sample to the same frequency as his own. Pete pressed the mouth-shaped opening of the spectroanalyzer to the boulder and pressed the trigger. The brief, intensely hot atomic flame blazed against the hard surface, vaporizing it instantly.

The film transparency popped out of the analyzer and Pete studied the spectrographic lines intently. Wrong again; no trace of the famil-iar Yttrotantalite lines. With an angry motion he stowed the test equipment in his pick and plowed on through the gummy rock.

Yttrotantalite was the ore and tantalum was the metal extracted from it. This rare metal was the main ingredient of the delicate pie-zoelectric crystals that made the vibratory mass penetrator possible. Ytt made tantalum, tantalum made crystals, crystals operated the walk-through that he used to find more Ytt to make . . . It was just like a squirrel cage, and Pete was the squirrel, a very unhappy animal at the present moment.

Pete carefully turned the rheostat knob on the walk-through, feed-ing a trifle more power into the circuit. It would be hard on the crys-tal, but he needed it to enable him to push through the jellylike earth.

His thoughts kept returning to that little crystal that meant his life. It was a thin wafer of what looked like dirty glass, ground and polished to the most exacting tolerances. When subjected to an al-most microscopic current, it vibrated at exactly the correct frequency that allowed one mass to slide between the molecules of another. This weak signal in turn controlled the much more powerful circuit that enabled himself and all his equipment to move through the earth. If the crystal failed, the atoms of his body would return to the vibratory plane of the normal world and alloy themselves with the earth atoms through which he was moving . . . Pete shook his head as if to clear away the offending thoughts and quickened his pace down the slope.

He had been pushing against the resisting rock for three hours now and his leg muscles felt like hot pokers. In a few minutes he would have to turn back, if he wanted to leave himself a margin of safety. But he had been getting Ytt traces for an hour now, and they seemed to be getting stronger as he followed the probable course of the drift. The mother lode had to be a rich one—if he could only find it!

It was time to start the long uphill return. Pete jerked a rock for a last test. He'd mark the spot and take up the search tomorrow. The test bulb flashed and he held the transparency against it.

His body tensed and his heart began to thud heavily. He blinked and looked again—it was there! The tantalum lines burned through the weaker traces with a harsh brilliance. His hand was shaking as he jerked open his knee pocket. He had a comparison film from the White Owl claim, the richest in the territory. There wasn't the slightest doubt—his was the richer ore!

He took the half-crystals out of their cushioned pouch and gently placed the B crystal in the hole he had made when he removed the sample rock. No one else could ever find this spot without the other half of the same crystal, ground accurately to a single ultrashortwave frequency. If half A were used to key the frequency of a signal generator, side B would bounce back an echo of the same wavelength that would be picked up by a delicate receiver. In this way the crystal both marked the claim and enabled Pete to find his way back to it.

He carefully stowed the A crystal in its cushioned compartment and started the long trek back to the surface. Walking was almost impossible; the old crystal in his walk-through was deviating so far that he could scarcely push through the gluey earth. He could feel the imponderable mass of the half-mile of rock over his head, waiting to imprison him in its eternal grip. The only way to the surface was to follow the long hogback of granite until it finally cleared the surface.

The crystal had been in continuous use now for over five hours. If he could only turn it off for a while, the whole unit would have a chance to cool down. His hand shook as he fumbled with his pack straps—he forced himself to slow down and do the job properly.

He turned the hand neutralizer to full power and held the glowing rod at arm's length before him. Out of the haze there suddenly materialized an eighteen-foot boulder of limestone, adjusted now to his own penetrating frequency. Gravity gripped the gigantic rock and it slowly sank. When it had cleared the level of the granite ledge, he turned off the neutralizer. There was a heavy crunch as the molecules of the boulder welded themselves firmly to those of the surrounding rock. Pete stepped into the artificial bubble he had formed in the rock and turned off his walk-through.

With a suddenness that never ceased to amaze him, his hazy surroundings became solid walls of rock. His helmet light splashed off the sides of the little chamber, a bubble with no exit, one half-mile below the freezing Alaskan wastes.

With a grunt of relief, Pete slipped out of his heavy pack and stretched his aching muscles. He had to conserve oxygen; that was the reason he had picked this particular spot. His artificial cave cut through a vein of RbO, rubidium oxide. It was a cheap and plentiful mineral, not worth mining this far north, but still the rock diver's best friend.

Pete rummaged in the pack for the airmaker and fastened its power pack to his belt. He thumbed the unit on and plunged the contact points into the RbO vein. The silent flash illuminating the chamber glinted on the white snow that was beginning to fall. The flakes of oxygen released by the airmaker melted before they touched the floor. The underground room was getting a life-giving atmosphere of its own. With air around him, he could open his faceplate and get some chow out of his pack.

He cautiously cracked the helmet valve and sniffed. The air was good, although pressure was low—around twelve pounds. The oxygen concentration was a little too high; he giggled happily with a mild oxygen jag. Pete hummed tunelessly as he tore the cardboard wrapper from a ration pack.

Cool water from the canteen washed down the tasteless hardtack but he smiled, thinking of thick, juicy steaks. The claim would be assayed and mine owners' eyes would bulge when they read the report. Then they would come to him. Dignified, sincere men clutching contracts in their well-manicured hands. He would sell to the highest bidder, the entire claim; let someone else do all the work for a change. They would level and surface this granite ridge and big pressure trucks would plow through the earth, bringing miners to and from the underground diggings. He relaxed against the curved wall of the bubble, smiling. He could see himself, bathed, shaven and manicured, walking into the Miners' Rest . . .

The daydream vanished as two men in bulging sub-suits stepped through the rock wall. Their figures were transparent; their feet sank into the ground with each step. Both men suddenly jumped into the air; at mid-arc they switched off their walk-throughs. The figures gained solidity and handed heavily on the floor. They opened their faceplates and sniffed the air.

The shorter man smiled. "It sure smells nice in here, right, Mo?"

Mo was having trouble getting his helmet off; his voice rumbled out through the folds of cloth. "Right, Algie." The helmet came free with a snap.

Pete's eyes widened at the sight, and Algie smiled a humorless grin. "Mo ain't much to look at, but you could learn to like him."

Mo was a giant, seven feet from his boots to the crown of his bullet-shaped head, shaved smooth and glistening with sweat. He must have been born ugly, and time had not improved him. His nose was flattened, one ear was little more than a rag, and a thick mass of white scar tissue drew up his upper lip. Two yellow teeth gleamed through the opening.

Pete slowly closed his canteen and stowed it in the pack. They might be honest rock divers, but they didn't look it. "Anything I can do for you guys?" he asked.

"No thanks, pal," said the short one. "We was just going by and saw the flash of your airmaker. We thought maybe it was one of our pals, so we come over to see. Rock diving sure is a lousy racket these days, ain't it?" As he talked, the little man's eyes flicked casually around the room, taking in everything. With a wheeze, Mo sat down against the wall.

"You're right," said Pete carefully. "I haven't had a strike in months. You guys newcomers? I don't think I've seen you around the camp."

Algie did not reply. He was staring intently at Pete's bulging sample case.

He snapped open a huge clasp knife. "What you got in the sample case, Mac?"

"Just some low-grade ore I picked up. Going to have it assayed, but I doubt if it's even worth carrying. I'll show you."

Pete stood up and walked toward the case. As he passed in front of Algie, he bent swiftly, grabbed the knife hand and jabbed his knee viciously into the short man's stomach. Algie jackknifed and Pete chopped his neck sharply with the edge of his palm. He didn't wait to see him fall but dived toward the pack.

He pulled his army .45 with one hand and scooped out the signal crystal with the other, raising his steel-shod boot to stamp the crystal to powder.

His heel never came down. A gigantic fist gripped his ankle, stopping Pete's whole bulk in midair. He tried to bring the gun around but a hand as large as a ham clutched his wrist. He screamed as the bones grated together. The automatic dropped from his nerveless fingers.

He hung head-down for five minutes while Mo pleaded with the unconscious Algie to tell him what to do. Algie regained consciousness and sat up cursing and rubbing his neck. He told Mo what to do and sat there smiling until Pete lost consciousness.

Slap-slap-slap, slap-slap; his head rocked back and forth in time to the blows. He couldn't stop them, they jarred his head, shook his entire body. From very far away he heard Algie's voice.

"That's enough Mo, that's enough. He's coming around now."

Pete braced himself painfully against the wall and wiped the blood out of his eyes. The short man's face swam into his vision.

"Mac, you're giving us too much trouble. We're going to take your crystal and find your strike, and if it's as good as the samples you got there, I'm going to be very happy and celebrate by killing you real slow. If we don't find it, you get killed slower. You get yours either way. Nobody ever hits Algie, don't you know that?"

They turned on Pete's walk-through and half carried, half dragged him through the wall. About twenty feet away they emerged in another artificial bubble, much larger than his own. It was almost filled by the metallic bulk of an atomic tractor.

Mo pushed him to the floor and kicked his walk-through into a useless ruin. The giant stepped over Pete's body and lumbered across the room. As he swung himself aboard the tractor, Algie switched on the large walk-through unit. Pete saw Algie's mouth open with silent laughter as the ghostly machine lurched forward and drove into the wall.

Pete turned and pawed through the crushed remains of his walk-through. Completely useless. They had done a thorough job, and there was nothing else in this globular tomb that could help him out. His sub-rock radio was in his own bubble; with that he could call the army base and have a patrol here in twenty minutes. But there was a little matter of twenty feet of rock between the radio and himself.

His light swung up and down the wall. That three-foot vein of RbO must be the same one that ran through his own chamber.

He grabbed his belt. The airmaker was still there! He pressed the points to the wall and watched the silver snow spring out. Pieces of rock fell loose as he worked in a circle. If the power pack held out— and if they didn't come back too soon . . .

With each flash of the airmaker an inch-thick slab of rock crumbled away. The accumulators took 3.7 seconds to recharge; then the white flash would leap out and blast loose another mass of rubble. He worked furiously with his left hand to clear away the shattered rock.

Blast with the right arm—push with the left—blast and push—blast and push. He laughed and sobbed at the same time, warm tears running down his cheeks. He had forgotten the tremendous amounts of oxygen he was releasing. The walls reeled drunkenly around him.

Stopping just long enough to seal his helmet, Pete turned back to the wall of his makeshift tunnel. He blasted and struggled with the resisting rock, trying to ignore his throbbing head. He lay on his side, pushing the broken stones behind him, packing them solid with his feet.

He had left the large bubble behind and was sealed into his own tiny chamber far under the earth. He could feel the weight of a half-mile of solid rock pushing down on him, crushing the breath from his lungs. If the airmaker died now, he would lie there and rot in this hand-hewn tomb! Pete tried to push the thought from his mind—to concentrate only on blasting his way through the earth.

Time seemed to stand still as he struggled on through an eternity of effort. His arms worked like pistons while his bloody fingers scrabbled at the corroded rock.

He dropped his arms for a few precious moments while his burning lungs pumped air. The weakened rock before him crumbled and blew away with an explosive sound. The air whistled through the ragged opening. The pressure in the two chambers was equalizing—he had holed through!

He was blasting at the edges of the hole with the weakened airmaker when the legs walked up next to him. Algie's face pushed through the low rock ceiling, a ferocious scowl on its features. There was no room to materialize; all the impotent Algie could do was to shake his fist at—and through—Pete's face.

A monstrous crunching came from the loose rubble behind him; the rock fell away and Mo pushed through. Pete couldn't turn to fight, but he landed one shoe on the giant's shapeless nose before monster hands clutched his ankles.

He was dragged through the rocky tube like a child, hauled back to the bigger cavern. When Mo dropped him he just slid to the floor and lay there gasping. He had been so close.

Algie bent over him. "You're too smart, Mac. I'm going to shoot you now, so you don't give me no more trouble."

He pulled Pete's .45 out of his pocket, grabbed it by the slide and charged it. "By the way, we found your strike. It's going to make me richer'n hell. Glad, Mac?"

Algie squeezed the trigger and a hammer-blow struck Pete's thigh. The little man stood over Pete, grinning.

"I'm going to give you all these slugs where they won't kill you—not right away. Ready for the next one, Mac?"

Pete pushed up onto one elbow and pressed his hand against the muzzle of the gun. Algie's grin widened. "Fine, stop the bullet with your hand!"

He squeezed the trigger; the gun clicked sharply. A ludicrous expression of amazement came over his face. Pete rose up and pressed the airmaker against Algie's faceplate. The expression was still there when his head exploded into frosty ribbons.

Pete dived on the gun, charged it out of the half-cocked position and swung around. Algie had been smart, but not smart enough to know that the muzzle of a regulation .45 acts as a safety. When you press against it the barrel is pushed back into half-cock position and can't be fired until the slide is worked to recharge it.

Mo came stumbling across the room, his jaw gaping amazement. Swinging around on his good leg, Pete waved the gun at him. "Hold it right there, Mo. You're going to help me get back to town."

The giant didn't hear him; there was room in his mind for only one thought.

"You killed Algie—you killed Algie!"

Pete fired half the clip before the big man dropped. He turned from the dying man with a shudder. It had been self-defense, but that thought didn't help the sick feeling in his stomach. He twisted his belt around his leg to stop the blood and applied a sterile bandage from the tractor's first-aid kit.

The tractor would get him back; he would let the army take care of the mess here. He pushed into the driver's seat and kicked the engine into life. The cat's walk-through operated perfectly; the machine crawled steadily toward the surface. Pete rested his wounded leg on the cowling and let the earth flow smoothly past and through him.

It was still snowing when the tractor broke through to the surface.

Toy Shop

Because there were few adults in the crowd, and Colonel "Biff" Hawton stood over six feet tall, he could see every detail of the demonstration. The children—and most of the parents—gaped in wide-eyed wonder. Biff Hawton was too sophisticated to be awed. He stayed on because he wanted to find out what the trick was that made the gadget work.

"It's all explained right here in your instruction book," the demonstrator said, holding up a garishly printed booklet opened to a four-color diagram. "You all know how magnets pick up things and I bet you even know that the earth itself is one great big magnet. That's why compasses always point north. Well . . . the Atomic Wonder Space Wave Tapper hangs on to those space waves. Invisibly all about us, and even going right through us, are the magnetic waves of the earth. The Atomic Wonder rides these waves just the way a ship rides the waves in the ocean. Now watch . . ."

Every eye was on him as he put the gaudy model rocket ship on top of the table and stepped back. It was made of stamped metal and seemed as incapable of flying as a can of ham—which it very much resembled. Neither wings, propellers, nor jets broke though the painted surface. It rested on three rubber wheels, and coming out through the bottom was a double strand of thin insulated wire. This white wire ran across the top of the black table and terminated in a control box in the demonstrator's hand. An indicator light, a switch, and a knob appeared to be the only controls.

"I turn on the power switch, sending a surge of current to the wave receptors," he said. The switch clicked and the light blinked on and off with a steady pulse. Then the man began slowly to turn the knob. "A careful touch on the wave generator is necessary as we are dealing with the powers of the whole world here . . ."

A concerted "Ahhh" swept through the crowd as the Space Wave Tapper shivered a bit, then rose slowly into the air. The demonstrator stepped back and the toy rose higher and higher, bobbing gently on the invisible waves of magnetic force that supported it. Ever so slowly the power was reduced and it settled back to the table.

"Only seventeen dollars and ninety-five cents," the young man said, putting a large price sign on the table. "For the complete set of the Atomic Wonder, the Space Tapper control box, battery, and instruction book . . ."

At the appearance of the price card the crowd broke up noisily and the children rushed away toward the operating model trains. The demonstrator's words were lost in their noisy passage, and after a moment he sank into a gloomy silence. He put the control box down, yawned, and sat on the edge of the table. Colonel Hawton was the only one left after the crowd had moved on.

"Could you tell me how this thing works?" the colonel asked, coming forward. The demonstrator brightened up and picked up one of the toys.

"Well, if you will look here, sir . . ." He opened the hinged top. "You will see the space wave coils at each end of the ship." With a pencil he pointed out the odd-shaped plastic forms about an inch in diameter that had been wound, apparently at random, with a few turns of copper wire. Except for these coils the interior of the model was empty. The coils were wired together and other wires ran out through the hole in the bottom of the control box. Biff Hawton turned a very quizzical eye on the gadget and upon the demonstrator, who completely ignored this sign of disbelief.

"Inside the control box is the battery," the young man said, snapping it open and pointing to an ordinary flashlight battery. "The current goes through the power switch and power light to the wave generator . . ."

"What you mean to say," Biff broke in, "is that the juice from this fifteen-cent battery goes through this cheap rheostat to those meaningless coils in the model and absolutely nothing happens. Now tell me what really flies the thing. If I'm going to drop eighteen bucks for six bits worth of tin, I want to know what I'm getting."

The demonstrator flushed. "I'm sorry, sir," he stammered. "I wasn't trying to hide anything. Like any magic trick this one can't be really demonstrated until it has been purchased." He leaned forward and whispered confidentially. "I'll tell you what I'll do, though. This thing is way overpriced and hasn't been moving at all. The manager said I could let them go at three dollars if I could find any takers. If you want to buy it for that price . . ."

"Sold, my boy!" the colonel said, slamming three bills down on the table. "I'll give that much for it no matter how it works. The boys in the shop will get a kick out of it"—he tapped the winged rocket on his chest. "Now—what really holds it up?"

The demonstrator looked around carefully, then pointed. "Strings!" he said. "Or rather a black thread. It runs from the top of the model, through a tiny loop in the ceiling, and back down to my hand and is tied to this ring on my finger. When I back up the model rises. It's as simple as that."

"All good illusions are simple," the colonel grunted, tracing the black thread with his eye. "As long as there is plenty of flimflam to distract the viewer."

"If you don't have a black table, a black cloth will do," the young man said. "And the arch of a doorway is a good site; just see that the room in back is dark."

"Wrap it up, my boy, I wasn't born yesterday. I'm an old hand at this kind of thing."

Biff Hawton sprang it at the next Thursday-night poker party. The gang were all missile men and they cheered and jeered as he hammered up the introduction.

"Let me copy the diagram, Biff; I could use some a those magnetic waves in the new bird!"

"Those flashlight batteries are cheaper than lox. This is the thing of the future!"

Only Teddy Kaner caught wise as the flight began. He was an amateur magician and spotted the gimmick at once. He kept silent with professional courtesy, and smiled ironically as the rest of the bunch grew silent one by one. The colonel was a good showman and he had set the scene well. He almost had them believing in the Space Wave Tapper before he was through. When the model had landed and he had switched it off he couldn't stop them from crowding around the table.

"A thread!" one of the engineers shouted, almost with relief, and they all laughed along with him.

"Too bad," the head project physicist said. "I was hoping that a little Space Wave Tapping could help us out. Let me try a flight with it."

"Teddy Kaner first," Biff announced. "He spotted it while you were all watching the flashing lights, only he didn't say anything."

Kaner slipped the ring with the black thread over his finger and started to step back.

"You have to turn the switch on first," Biff said.

"I know," Kaner smiled. "But that's part of illusion, the spiel and the misdirection. I'm going to try this cold first, so I can get it moving up and down smoothly, then go through it with the whole works."

He moved his hand back smoothly, in a professional manner that drew no attention to it. The model lifted from the table, then crashed back down.

"The thread broke," Kaner said.

"You jerked it, instead of pulling smoothly," Biff said and knotted the broken thread. "Here let me show you how to do it."

The thread broke again when Biff tried it, which got a good laugh that made his collar a little warm. Someone mentioned the poker game.

This was the only time that poker was mentioned or even remembered that night. Because very soon after this they found that the thread would lift the model only when the switch was on and two and a half volts flowed through the joke coils. With the current turned off the model was too heavy to lift. The thread broke every time.

"I still think it's a screwy idea," the young man said. "I've been one week getting fallen arches, demonstrating those toy ships for every brat within a thousand miles. Then selling the things for three bucks when they must have cost at least a hundred dollars apiece to make."

"But you did sell the ten of them to people who would be interested?" the older man asked.

"I think so. I caught a few air force officers and a colonel in missiles one day. Then there was one official I remembered from the Bureau of Standards. Luckily he didn't recognize me. Then those two professors you spotted from the university."

"Then the problem is out of our hands and into theirs. All we have to do now is sit back and wait for results."

"What results? These people weren't interested when we were hammering on their doors with the proof. We've patented the coils and can prove to anyone that there is a reduction in weight around them when they are operating."

"But a small reduction. And we don't know what is causing it. No one can be interested in a thing like that—a fractional weight decrease in a clumsy model, certainly not enough to lift the weight of the generator. No one wrapped up in massive fuel consumption, tons of lift, and such is going to have time to worry about a crackpot who thinks he has found a minor slip in Newton's laws."

"You think they will now?" the young man asked, cracking his knuckles impatiently.

"I know they will. The tensile strength of that thread is correctly adjusted to the weight of the model. The thread will break if you try to lift the model with it. Yet you can lift the model after a small increment of its weight has been removed by the coils. This is going to bug these men. Nobody is going to ask them to solve the problem or concern themselves with it. But it will nag at them because they know this effect can't possibly exist. They'll see at once that the magnetic-wave theory is nonsense. Or perhaps true? We don't know. But they will all be thinking about it and worrying about it. Someone is going to experiment in his basement, just as a hobby, of course to find the cause of the error. And he or someone else is going to find out what makes those coils work, or maybe a way to improve them!"

"And we have the patents . . ."

"Correct. They will be doing the research that will take them out of the massive-lift-propulsion business and into the field of pure space light."

"And in doing so they will be making us rich—whenever the time comes to manufacture," the young man said cynically.

"We'll all be rich, son," the older man said, patting him on the shoulder. "Believe me, you're not going to recognize this old world ten years from now."

I Always Do What Teddy Says

The little boy lay sleeping, the moonlight effect of the picture-picture window threw a pale glow across his untroubled features. He had one arm clutched around his teddy bear, pulling the round face with its staring button eyes close to his. His father, and the tall man with the black beard, tiptoed silently across the nursery to the side of the bed.

"Slip it away," the tall man said, "then substitute the other."

"No, he would wake up and cry," David's father said. "Let me take care of this, I know what to do."

With gentle hands he lay the other teddy bear down next to the boy, on the other side of his head, so his sleeping cherub face was framed by the wide-eyed unsleeping masks of the toys. Then he carefully lifted the boy's arm from the original teddy and pulled it free. This disturbed Davy without waking him and he ground his teeth together and rolled over, clutching the substitute toy to his cheek, and within a few moments his soft breathing was regular and deep. The boy's father raised his forefinger to his lips and the other man nodded; they left the room without making a sound, closing the door noiselessly behind them.

"Now we begin," Torrence said, reaching out to take the teddy bear. His lips were small and glistened redly in the midst of his dark beard. The teddy bear twisted in his grip and the black-button eyes rolled back and forth.

"Take me back to Davy," it said in a thin and tiny voice.

"Let me have it back," the boy's father said. "It knows me and won't complain."

His name was Numen and, like Torrence, he was a Doctor of Government. Both DGs and both unemployed by the present government, in spite of their abilities and rank, though they had no physical resemblance. Torrence was a bear, though a small one, a black bear with hair sprouting thickly on his knuckles, twisting out of his white cuffs and lining his ears. His beard was full and thick, rising high up on his cheekbones and dropping low on his chest.

Where Torrence was dark Numen was fair, where short he was tall, thick, thin. A thin bow of a man, bent forward with a scholar's stoop and, though balding now, his hair was still curled and blond and very like the golden ringlets of the boy asleep upstairs. Now he took the toy animal and led the way to the shielded room deep in the house where Eigg was waiting.

"Give it here—here!" Eigg snapped when they came in, and reached for the toy. Eigg was always like that, in a hurry, surly, square and solid with his width of jaw and spotless white laboratory smock. But they needed him.

"You needn't," Numen said, but Eigg had already pulled it from his grasp. "It won't like it, I know . . ."

"Let me go . . . let me go . . . !" the teddy bear said with a hopeless shrill.

"It is just a machine," Eigg said coldly, putting it facedown on the table and reaching for a scalpel. "You are a grown man, you should be more logical, have your emotions under greater control. You are speaking with your childhood memories, seeing your own boyhood teddy who was your friend and companion. This is just a machine."

With a quick slash he opened the fabric over the seam seal and touched it: the plastic-fur back gaped open like a mouth.

"Let me go . . . let me go . . ." the teddy bear wailed and its stumpy arms and legs waved back and forth. Both of the onlookers went white.

"Must we . . . ?"

"Emotions. Control them," Eigg said and probed with a screwdriver. There was a click and the toy went limp. He began to unscrew a plate in the mechanism.

Numen turned away and found that he had to touch a handkerchief to his face. Eigg was right. He was being emotional and this was just a machine. How did he dare get emotional over it? Particularly with what they had in mind.

"How long will it take?" He looked at his watch; it was a little past 2100.

"We have been over this before and discussing it again will not change any of the factors." Eigg's voice was distant as he removed the tiny plate and began to examine the machine's interior with a magnifying probe. "I have experimented on the two stolen teddy tapes, carefully timing myself at every step. I do not count removal or restoration of the tape, this is just a few minutes for each. The tracking and altering of the tape in both instances took me under ten hours. My best time differed from my worst time by less than fifteen minutes, which is not significant. We can therefore safely say— ahh . . ." He was silent for a moment while he removed the capsule of the memory spools. ". . . We can safely say that this is a ten-hour operation."

"That is too long. The boy is usually awake by seven, we must have the teddy back by then. He must never suspect that it has been away."

"There is little risk; you can give him some excuse for the time. I will not rush and spoil the work. Now be silent."

The two governmental specialists could only sit back and watch while Eigg inserted the capsule into the bulky machine he had assembled in the room. This was not their specialty.

"Let me go . . ." the tiny voice said from the wall speaker, then was interrupted by a burst of static. "Let me go . . . bzzzzzt . . . no, no Davy, Mummy wouldn't like you to do that . . . fork in left, knife in right . . . bzzzt . . . if you do you'll have to wipe . . . good boy good boy good boy . . ."

The voice squeaked and whispered and went on and the hours of the clock went by one by one. Numen brought in coffee more than once and towards dawn Torrence fell asleep sitting up in the chair, only to awake with a guilty start. Of them all Eigg alone showed no strain nor fatigue, working the controls with fingers regular as a metronome. The reedy voice from the capsule shrilled thinly through the night like the memory of a ghost.

"It is done," Eigg said, scaling the fabric with quick surgeon's stitches.

"Your fastest time ever," Numen sighed with relief. He glanced at the nursery viewscreen that showed his son, still asleep, starkly clear in the harsh infrared light.

"And the boy is still asleep. There will be no problem getting it back after all. But is the tape . . . ?"

"It is right, perfect, you heard that. You asked the questions and heard the answers. I have concealed all traces of the alteration and unless you know what to look for you would never find the changes. In every other way the memory and instructions are like all others. There has just been this single change made."

"Pray God we never have to use it," Numen said.

"I did not know that you were religious," Eigg said, turning to look at him, his face expressionless. The magnifying loupe was still in his eye and it stared, five times the size of its fellow, a large and probing questioner.

"I'm not," Numen said, flushing.

"We must get the teddy back," Torrence broke in. "The boy just moved."

Davy was a good boy and, when he grew older, a good student in school. Even after he began classes he kept Teddy around and talked to him while he did his homework.

"How much is seven and five, Teddy?"

The furry toy bear rolled its eyes and clapped stub paws. "Davy knows . . . shouldn't ask Teddy what Davy knows . . ."

"Sure I know—I just wanted to see if you did. The answer is thirteen."

"Davy . . . the answer is twelve . . . you better study harder Davy . . . that's what Teddy says . . ."

"Fooled you!" Davy laughed. "Made you tell me the answer!" He was learning ways to get around the robot controls, permanently fixed to answer the question of a smaller child. Teddies have the vocabulary and outlook of the very young because their job must be done during the formative years. Teddies teach diction and life history and morals and group adjustment and vocabulary and grammar and all the other things that enable men to live together as social animals. A teddy's job is done early in the most plastic stages of a child's life, and by the very nature of its task its conversation must be simple and limited. But effective. By the time teddies are discarded as childish toys the job is done.

By the time Davy became David and was eighteen years old, Teddy had long since been retired behind a row of shelves on a high shelf. He was an old friend who had outgrown his useful days, but he was still a friend and certainly couldn't be discarded. Not that David ever thought of it that way. Teddy was just Teddy and that was that. The nursery was now a study, his cot a bed and with his birthday past David was packing because he was going away to the university. He was sealing his bag when the phone bleeped and he saw his father's tiny image on the screen.

"David . . ."

"What is it, Father?"

"Would you mind coming down to the library now. There is something rather important . . ."

David squinted at the screen and noticed for the first time that his father's face had a pinched, sick look. His heart gave a quick jump.

"I'll be right there!"

Dr. Eigg was there, arms crossed and sitting almost at attention. So was Torrence, his father's oldest friend, who, though no relation, David had always called Uncle Torrence. And his father, obviously ill at ease about something. David came in quietly, conscious of all their eyes upon him as he crossed the room and took a chair. He was a lot like his father, with the same build and height, a relaxed, easy-to-know boy with very few problems in life.

"Is something wrong?" he asked.

"Not wrong, Davy," his father said. He must be upset, David thought, he hasn't called me that in years. "Or rather something is wrong, but with the state of the world, and has been for a long time."

"Oh, the Panstentialists," David said, and relaxed a little. He had been hearing about the evils of panstentialism as long as he could remember. It was just politics; he had been thinking something very personal was wrong.

"Yes, Davy, I imagine you know all about them by now. When your mother and I separated I promised to raise you to the best of my ability and I think I have. But I'm a governor and all my friends work in government so I'm sure you have heard a lot of political talk in this house. You know our feelings and I think you share them."

"I do—and I think I would have no matter where I grew up. Panstentialism is an oppressing philosophy and one that perpetuates itself in power."

"Exactly. And one man, Barre, is at the heart of it. He stays in the seat of power and will not relinquish it and, with the rejuvenation treatments, will be good for a hundred years more."

"Barre must go!" Eigg snapped. "For twenty-three years now he has ruled and forbidden the continuation of my experiments. Young man, he has stopped my work for a longer time than you have been alive, do you realize that?"

David nodded, but did not comment. What little he had read about Dr. Eigg's proposed researches into behavioral human embryology had repelled him and, secretly, he was in agreement with Barre's ban on the work. But on this only, he was truly in agreement with his father: Panstentialism was a heavy and dusty hand on the world of politics—as well as the world at large.

"I'm not speaking only for myself," Numen said, his face white and strained, "but for everyone in the world and the system who is against Barre and his philosophies. I have not held a government position for over twenty years—nor has Torrence here—but I think he'll agree that is a small thing. If this was a service to the people we would gladly suffer it. Or if our persecution was the only negative result of Barre's evil works I would do nothing to stop him."

"I am in complete agreement," Torrence nodded. "The fate of two men is of no importance in comparison with the fate of us all. Nor is the fate of one man."

"Exactly!" Numen sprang to his feet and began to pace agitatedly up and down the room. "If that wasn't true, wasn't the heart of the problem, I would never consider being involved. There would be no problem if Barre suffered a heart attack and fell dead tomorrow."

The three older men were all looking at David now, though he didn't know why, and he felt they were waiting for him to say something.

"Well, yes—I agree. A little embolism right now would be the best thing for the world that I can think of. Barre dead would be of far greater service to mankind than Barre alive has ever been."

The silence lengthened, became embarrassing, and it was finally Eigg who broke it with his dry, mechanical tones.

"We are all then in agreement that Barre's death would be of immense benefit. In that case, David, you must also agree that it would be fine if he could be . . . killed . . ."

"Not a bad idea," David said, wondering where all this talk was going, "though of course it's a physical impossibility. It must be centuries since the last—what's the word? 'murder'—took place. The developmental psychology work took care of that a long time ago. As the twig is bent and all that sort of thing. Wasn't that supposed to be the discovery that finally separated man from the lower orders, the proof that we could entertain the thought of killing and discuss it, yet still be trained in our early childhood so that we would not be capable of the act? Surety enough, if you can believe the textbooks, the human race has progressed immeasurably since the curse of killing has been removed. Look—do you mind if I ask just what this is all about . . . ?"

"Barre can be killed," Eigg said in an almost inaudible voice. "There is one man in the world who can kill him."

"WHO?" David asked, and in some terrible way he knew the answer even before the words came from his father's trembling lips.

"You, David . . . you . . ."

He sat, unmoving, and his thoughts went back through the years and a number of things that had been bothering him were made clear. His attitudes so subtly different from his friends', and that time with the plane when one of the rotors had killed a squirrel. Little puzzling things, and sometimes worrying ones that had kept him awake long after the rest of the house was asleep. It was true, he knew it without a shadow of a doubt, and wondered why he had never realized it before. But, like a hideous statue buried in the ground beneath one's feet, it had always been there but had never been visible until he had dug down and reached it. But it was visible now, all the earth scraped from its vile face and all the lineaments of evil clearly revealed.

"You want me to kill Barre?" he asked.

"You're the only one who can . . . Davy . . . and it must be done. For all these years I have hoped against hope that it would not be needed, that the . . . ability you have would not be used. But Barre lives. For all our sakes he must die."

"There is one thing I don't understand," David said, rising and looking out the window and the familiar view of the trees and the distant, glass-canopied highway.

"How was this change made? How could I miss the conditioning that I thought was a normal part of existence in this world?"

"It was your teddy bear," Eigg explained. "It is not publicized, but the reaction to killing is established at a very early age by the tapes in the machine that every child has. Later education is just reinforcement, valueless without the earlier indoctrination."

"Then my teddy . . . ?"

"I altered its tapes, in just that one way, so this part of your education would be missed. Nothing else was changed."

"It was enough Doctor." There was a coldness to his voice that had never existed before. "How is Barre supposed to be killed?"

"With this." Eigg removed a package from the table drawer and opened it. "This is a primitive weapon removed from a museum. I have repaired it and charged it with the projectile devices that are called shells." He held the sleek, ugly, black thing in his hand. "It is fully automatic in operation. When this device, the trigger, is depressed a chemical reaction propels a copper-and-lead weight named a bullet directly from the front orifice. The line of flight of the bullet is along an imaginary path extended from these two niches on the top of the device. The bullet of course falls by gravity but in a minimum distance, say a meter, this fall is negligible." He put it down suddenly on the table. "It is called a gun."

David reached over slowly and picked it up. How well it fitted into his hand, sitting with such precise balance. He raised it slowly, sighted across the niches and pulled the trigger. It exploded with an immense roar and jumped in his hand. The bullet plunged into Eigg's chest just over his heart with such a great impact that the man and the chair he had been sitting in were hurled backwards to the floor. The bullet also tore a great hole in his flesh and Eigg's throat choked with blood and he died.

"David! What are you doing?" His father's voice cracked with uncomprehending horror.

David turned away from the thing on the floor, still apparently unmoved by what he had done.

"Don't you understand, Father? Barre and his Panstentialists are a terrible weight and many suffer and freedom is abridged and all the other things that are wrong, that we know should not be. But don't you see the difference? You yourself said that things will change after Barre's death. The world will move on. So how is his crime to be compared to the crime of bringing this back into existence?"

He shot his father quickly and efficiently before the older man could realize the import of his words and suffer with the knowledge of what was coming. Torrence screamed and ran to the door, fumbling with terrified fingers for the lock. David shot him too, but not very well since he was so far away, and the bullet lodged in his body and made him fall. David walked over and ignoring the screamings and bubbled words, took careful aim at the twisting head and blew out the man's brains.

Now the gun was heavy and he was very tired. The lift shaft took him up to his room and he had to stand on a chair to take Teddy down from behind the books on the high shelf. The little furry animal sat in the middle of the large bed and rolled its eyes and wagged its stubby arms.

"Teddy," he said, "I'm going to pull up flowers from the flowerbed."

"No, Davy . . . pulling up flowers is naughty . . . don't pull up the flowers . . ." The little voice squeaked and the arms waved.

"Teddy, I'm going to break a window."

"No, Davy . . . breaking windows is naughty . . . don't break any windows . . ."

"Teddy, I'm going to kill a man."

Silence, just silence. Even the eyes and arms were still. The roar of the gun broke the silence and blew a ruin of gears, wires and bent metal from the back of the destroyed teddy bear.

"Teddy . . . oh, Teddy . . . you should have told me," David said and dropped the gun and at last was crying.

From Fanaticism, or for Reward

Wonderful! Very clear. The electronic sight was a new addition. He had used an ordinary telescope sight when he test-fired the weapon, but the new sight was no hindrance. The wide entrance to the structure across the street was sharp and clear, despite the rain-filled night outside. His elbows rested comfortably on the packing crates that were placed before the slit he had cut through the outer wall of the building.

"There are five of them coming now. The one you want is the tallest." The radioplug in his ear whispered the words to him.

Across the street the men emerged. One was obviously taller than all the others. He was talking, smiling, and Jagen centered the scope on his white teeth, then spun the magnifier until teeth, mouth, tongue filled the sight. Then a wide smile, teeth together, and Jagen squeezed his entire hand, squeezed stock and trigger equally, and the gun banged and jumped against his shoulder.

Now, quickly, there were five more cartridges in the clip. Spin the magnifier back. He is falling. Fire. He jerks. Fire. In the skull. Again. Fire. Someone in the way: shoot through him. Fire. He is gone. In the chest, the heart. Fire.

"All shots off," he said into the button before his lips. "Five on target, one a possible."

"Go," was all the radioplug whispered.

I'm going all right, he thought to himself, no need to tell me that. The Greater Despot's police are efficient.

The only light in the room was the dim orange glow from the ready light on the transmatter. He had personally punched out the receiver's code. Three steps took him across the barren, dusty room and he slapped the actuator. Without slowing he dived into the screen.

Bright glare hurt his eyes and he squinted against it. An unshielded bulb above, rock walls, everything damp, a metal door coated with a patina of rust. He was underground, somewhere, perhaps on a planet across the galaxy, it didn't matter. There was here. Everywhere was a step away with a matter transmitter. Quickly, he moved to one side of the screen.

Gas puffed out of it, expelled silently, then cut off. Good. The transmatter had been destroyed, blown up. Undoubtedly the police would be able to trace his destination from the wreckage, but it would take time. Time for him to obscure his trail and vanish.

Other than the transmatter, the only object in the stone cell was a large, covered ceramic vessel. He looked at the stock of his gun where he had pasted his instructions. Next to the number for this location was the notation "Destroy gun." Jagen peeled off the instructions and slipped them into his belt pouch. He took the lid from the vessel and turned away, coughing, as the fumes rose up. This bubbling, hellish brew would dissolve anything. With well-practiced motions he released the plastic stock from the weapon, then dropped it into the container. He had to step back as the liquid bubbled furiously and thicker fumes arose.

In his pouch was a battery-operated saw, as big as his hand, with a serrated diamond blade. It buzzed when he switched it on, then whined shrilly when he pressed it against the barrel of the gun. He had measured carefully a few days earlier and had sawed a slight notch. Now he cut at the spot and in a few seconds half of the barrel clanged to the floor. It followed the stock into the dissolving bath, along with the clip that had held the bullets. His pouch yielded up another clip which he slipped into place in the gun. A quick jerk of his forefinger on the slide kicked the first cartridge into the chamber and he checked to be sure that the safety was on. Only then did he slip the truncated weapon up the loose sleeve of his jacket, so that the rough end of the barrel rested against his hand.

It was shortened and inaccurate, but still a weapon, and still very deadly at short range.

Only when these precautions had been made did he consult the card and punch for his next destination. The instructions after this number read simply "Change." He stepped through.

Noise and sound, light and sharp smells. The ocean was close by, some ocean, he could hear the breakers and salt dampness was strong in his nose. This was a public communications plaza set around with transmatter screens, and someone was already stepping from the one he had used, treading on his heels. There were muttered words in a strange language as the man hurried away. The crowd was thick and the reddish sun, high above, was strong. Jagen resisted the temptation to use one of the nearby transmatters and walked quickly across the plaza. He stopped, then waited to follow the first person who passed him. This gave him a random direction that was not influenced by his own desires. A girl passed and he went after her. She wore an abbreviated skirt and had remarkably bowed legs. He followed their arcs down a side street. Only after they had passed one transmatter booth did he choose his own course. His trail was muddled enough now: the next transmatter would do.

There was the familiar green starburst ahead, above an imposing building, and his heart beat faster at the sight of the Greater Despot police headquarters. Then he smiled slightly; why not? The building was public and performed many functions. There was nothing to be afraid of.

Yet there was, of course, fear, and conquering it was a big part of the game. Up the steps and past the unseeing guards. A large rotunda with a desk in the middle, stands and services against the wall. And there, a row of transmatter screens. Walking at a steady pace he went to one of the center screens and punched the next code on his list.

The air was thin and cold, almost impossible to breathe, and his eyes watered at the sudden chill. He turned quickly to the screen, to press the next number when he saw a man hurrying towards him.

"Do not leave," the man called out in Intergalact.

He had a breath mask clipped over his nose and he held a second one out to Jagen, who quickly slipped it on. The warmed, richer air stayed his flight, as did the presence of the man who had obviously been expecting him. He saw now that he was on the bridge of a derelict spacer of ancient vintage. The controls had been torn out and the screens were blank. Moisture was condensing on the metal walls and forming pools upon the floor. The man saw his curious gaze.

"This ship is in orbit. It has been for centuries. An atmosphere and gravity plant were placed aboard while this transmatter was operating. When we leave an atomic explosion will destroy everything. If you are tracked this far, the trail will end here."

"Then the rest of my instructions—"

". . . Will not be needed. It was not certain this ship would be prepared in time, but it has been."

Jagen dropped the card, evidence, onto the floor, along with the radioplug. It would vanish with the rest. The man rapidly pressed out a number.

"If you will proceed," he said. "I'll follow you."

The man nodded, threw his breath mask aside, then stepped through the screen.

They were in a normal enough hotel room, the kind that can be found on any one of ten thousand planets. Two men, completely dressed in black, sat in armchairs watching Jagen through dark glasses. The man who had brought him nodded silently, pressed a combination on the transmatter, and left.

"It is done?" one of the men asked. In addition to the loose black clothing they wore black gloves and hoods, with voice demodulators clamped across their mouths. The voice was flat, emotionless, impossible to identify.

"The payment," Jagen said, moving so that his back was to the wall.

"We'll pay you, man, don't be foolish. Just tell us how it came out.

We have a lot invested in this." The voice of the second man was just as mechanically calm, but his fingers were clasping and unclasping as he talked.

"The payment." Jagen tried to keep his voice as toneless as their electronic ones.

"Here, Hunter, now tell us," the first one said, taking a box from the side table and throwing it across the room. It burst open at Jagen's feet.

"All six shots were fired at the target I was given," he said, looking down at the golden notes spilling onto the floor. So much, it was as they had promised. "I put four shots into the head, one into the heart, one into the man who got in the way that may have penetrated. It was as you said. The protective screen was useless against mechanically propelled plastic missiles."

"The paragrantic is ours," the second man intoned emotionlessly, but this was the machine interpretation, for his excitement was demonstrated by the manner in which he hammered on his chair arm and drummed his feet.

Jagen bent to pick up the notes, apparently looking only at the floor.

The first man in black raised an energy pistol that had been concealed in his clothing and fired it at Jagen.

Jagen, who as a hunter always considered being hunted, rolled sideways and clutched the barrel of the shortened projectile weapon. With his other hand he found the trigger through the cloth of his sleeve and depressed it. The range was point-blank and a miss was impossible to a man of his experience.

The bullet caught the first man in the midriff and folded him over. He said "Yahhhhh" in a very drab and monotonous way. The pistol dropped from his fingers and fell to the floor and he was obviously dead.

"Soft alloy bullets," Jagen said. "I saved a clip of them. Far better than those plastic things you supplied. Go in small, mushroom, come out big. I saved the gun, too, at least enough of it to still shoot. You were right, it should be destroyed to remove evidence, but not until after this session. And it doesn't show on an energy-detector screen. So you thought I was unarmed. Your friend discovered the truth the hard way. How about you?" He talked quickly as he struggled to recover the gun that recoil had pulled from his hand and jammed into the cloth of his sleeve. There, he had it.

"Do not kill me," the remaining man said, his voice flat, though he cringed back and waved his hands before his face. "It was his idea, I wanted nothing to do with it. He was afraid that we could be traced if you were captured." He glanced at the folded figure, then quickly away as he became aware of the quantity of blood that was dripping from it. "I have no weapon. I mean you no harm. Do not kill me. I will give you more money." He was pleading for his life but the words came out as drab as a shopping list.

Jagen raised his weapon and the man writhed and cringed.

"Do you have the money with you?"

"Some. Not much. A few thousand. I'll get you more."

"I'm afraid that I cannot wait. Take out what you have—slowly—and throw it over here."

It was a goodly sum. The man must be very rich to carry this much casually. Jagen pointed the gun to kill him, but at the last instant changed his mind. It would accomplish nothing. And at the moment he was weary of killing. Instead he crossed over and tore the man's mask off. It was anticlimactic. He was fat, old, jowly, crying so hard that he could not see through his tears. In disgust Jagen hurled him to the floor and kicked him hard in the face. Then left. Ever wary he kept his body between the moaning man and the keys so there would be no slightest chance for him to see the number punched. He stepped into the screen.

The machine stepped out of the screen in the office of the Highest Officer of Police, many light-years distant, at almost the same instant, on the planet where the assassination had taken place.

"You are Follower?" the officer asked.

"I am," the machine said.

It was a fine-looking machine shaped in the form of a man. But that of a large man, well over two meters tall. It could have been any shape at all, but this form was a convenience when traveling among men. The roughly humanoid form was the only concession made. Other than having a torso, four limbs and a head, it was strictly functional. Its lines were smooth and flowing, and its metal shape coated with one of the new and highly resistant, golden-tinted alloys. The ovoid that was its head was completely featureless, except for a T-shaped slit in the front. Presumably seeing and hearing devices were concealed behind the narrow opening, as well as a speech mechanism that parodied the full-timbered voice of a man.

"Do I understand, Follower, that you are the only one of your kind?" The police officer had become old, gray and lined in the pursuit of his profession, but he had never lost his curiosity.

"Your security rating permits me to inform you that there are other Followers now going into operation, but I cannot reveal the exact number."

"Very wise. What is it that you hope to do?"

"I shall follow. I have detection apparatus far more delicate than any used in the field before. That is why my physical bulk is so great. I have the memory core of the largest library and means of adding to it constantly. I will follow the assassin."

"That may prove difficult. He—or she—destroyed the transmatter after the killing."

"I have ways of determining the tuning from the wreckage."

"The path will be obscured in many ways."

"None of them shall avail. I am the Follower."

"Then I wish you luck . . . if one can wish luck to a machine. This was a dirty business."

"Thank you for the courtesy. I do not have human emotions, though I can comprehend them. Your feelings are understood and a credit mark is being placed on your file even though you had not intended the remark to accomplish that. I would like to see all the records of the assassination, and then I will go to the place where the killer escaped."

Twenty years of easy living had not altered Jagen very much: the lines in the corners of his eyes and the touch of gray at his temples improved his sharp features rather than detracting from them. He no longer had to earn his living as a professional hunter, so could now hunt for his own pleasure, which he did very often. For many years he had stayed constantly on the move, obscuring his trail, changing his name and identity a dozen times. Then he had stumbled across this backward planet, completely by chance, and had decided to remain. The jungles were primitive and the hunting tremendous. He enjoyed himself all of the time. The money he had been paid, invested wisely, provided him with ample income for all of his needs and supported the one or two vices to which he was addicted.

He was contemplating one of them now. For more than a week he had remained in the jungle, and it had been a good shoot. Now, washed, refreshed, rested, he savored the thought of something different. There was a pleasure hall he knew, expensive, of course, but he could get there exactly what he needed. In a gold dressing gown, feet up and a drink in his hand, he sat back and looked through the transparent wall of his apartment at the sun setting behind the jungle. He had never had much of an eye for art, but it would have taken a blind man to ignore the explosion of greens below, purple and red above. The universe was a very fine place.

Then the alignment bell signaled quietly to show that another transmatter had been tuned to his. He swung about to see Follower step into the room.

"I have come for you, Assassin," the machine said.

The glass fell from Jagen's fingers and rolled a wet trail across the inlaid wood of the floor. He was always armed, but caution suggested that the energy pistol in the pocket of his robe would have little effect on this solidly built machine.

"I have no idea what you are talking about," he said, rising. "I shall call the police about this matter."

He walked towards the communicator—then dived past it into the room beyond. Follower started after him, but stopped when he emerged an instant later. Jagen had a heavy-caliber, recoilless rifle with explosive shells, that he used to stop the multi-ton amphibians in the swamps. The weapon held ten of the almost cannon-sized shells and he emptied the clip, point-blank, at the machine.

The room was a shambles, with walls, floor and ceiling ripped by the explosive fragments. He had a minor wound in his neck, and another in his leg, neither of which he was aware of. The machine stood, unmoved by the barrage, the golden alloy completely un-scratched.

"Sit," Follower ordered. "Your heart is laboring too hard and you may be in danger."

"Danger!" Jagen said, then laughed strangely and clamped his teeth hard onto his lip. The gun slipped from his fingers as he groped his way to an undamaged chair and fell into it. "Should I worry about the condition of my heart when you are here—Executioner?"

"I am Follower. I am not an executioner."

"You'll turn me over to them. But first, tell me how you found me. Or is that classified?"

"The details are. I simply used all of the most improved location techniques and transmatter records to follow you. I have a perfect memory and had many facts to work with. Also, being a machine, I do not suffer from impatience."

Since he was still alive, Jagen still considered escape. He could not damage the machine, but perhaps he could flee from it once again. He had to keep it talking.

"What are you going to do with me?"

"I wish to ask you some questions."

Jagen smiled inwardly, although his expression did not change. He knew perfectly well that the Greater Despot had more than this in mind for an assassin who had been tracked for twenty years.

"Ask them, by all means."

"Do you know the identity of the man you shot?"

"I'm not admitting I shot anyone."

"You admitted that when you attempted to assault me."

"All right. I'll play along." Keep the thing talking. Say anything, admit anything. The torturers would have it out of him in any case.

"I never knew who he was. In fact I'm not exactly sure what world it was. It was a rainy place, I can tell you that much."

"Who employed you?"

"They didn't mention any names. A sum of money and a job of work were involved, that was all."

"I can believe that. I can also tell you that your heartbeat and pulse are approaching normal, so I may now safely inform you that you have a slight wound on your neck."

Jagen laughed and touched his finger to the trickle of blood.

"My thanks for the unexpected consideration. The wound is nothing."

"I would prefer to see it cleaned and bandaged. Do I have your permission to do that?"

"Whatever you wish. There is medical equipment in the other room." If the thing left the room, he could reach the transmatter!

"I must examine the wound first." Follower loomed over him he had not realized the great bulk of the machine before and touched a cool metal finger to the skin of his neck. As soon as it made contact he found himself completely paralyzed. His heart beat steadily, he breathed easily, his eyes stared straight ahead. But he could not move or speak, and could only scream wordlessly to himself in the silence of his brain.

"I have tricked you since it was necessary to have your body in a relaxed state before the operation. You will find the operation is completely painless."

The machine moved out of his fixed point of vision and he heard it leave the room. Operation? What operation? What unmentionable revenge did the Greater Despot plan? How important was the man whom he had killed? Horror and fear filled his thoughts, but did not affect his body. Steadily, the breath flowed in and out of his lungs, while his heart thudded a stately measure. His consciousness was imprisoned in the smallest portion of his brain, impotent, hysterical.

Sound told him that the machine was now standing behind him. Then he swayed and was pushed from side to side. What was it doing? Something dark flew by a corner of his vision and hit the floor. What? WHAT!

Another something, this one spattering on the floor before him. Foamed, dark, mottled. It took long seconds for the meaning of what he saw to penetrate his terror.

It was a great gobbet of depilatory foam, speckled and filled with dissolved strands of his hair. The machine must have sprayed the entire can onto his head and was now removing all of his hair. But why? Panic ebbed slightly.

Follower came around and stood before him, then bent and wiped its metal hands on his robe.

"Your hair has been removed." I know, I know! Why? "This is a needed part of the operation and creates no permanent damage. Neither does the operation."

While it was speaking a change was taking place in Follower's torso. The golden alloy, so impervious to the explosives, was splitting down the center and rolling back. Jagen could only watch, horrified, unable to avert his gaze. There was a silvered concavity revealed in the openings, surrounded by devices of an unknown nature.

"There will be no pain," Follower said, reaching forward and seizing Jagen's head with both hands. With slow precision it pulled him forward into the opening until the top of his head was pressed against the metal hollow. Then, mercifully, unconsciousness descended.

Jagen did not feel the thin, sharpened needles that slid through holes in the metal bowl, then penetrated his skin, down through the bone of his skull and deep into his brain. But he was aware of the thoughts, clear and sharp, as if they were new experiences that filled his brain. Memories, brought up and examined, then discarded. His childhood, a smell, sounds he had long since forgotten, a room, grass underfoot, a young man looking at him, himself in a mirror.

This flood of memories continued for a long time, guided and controlled by the mechanism inside Follower. Everything was there that the machine needed to know and bit by bit it uncovered it all. When it was finished the needles withdrew into their sheaths and Jagen's head was freed. Once more he was seated upright in the chair—and the paralysis was removed as suddenly as it had begun. He clutched the chair with one hand and felt across the smooth surface of his skull with the other.

"What have you done to me? What was the operation?"

"I have searched your memory. I now know the identity of the people who ordered the assassination."

With these words the machine turned and started towards the transmatter. It had already punched out a code before Jagen called hoarsely after it.

"Stop! Where are you going? What are you going to do with me?"

Follower turned. "What do you want me to do with you? Do you have feelings of guilt that must be expunged?"

"Don't play with me, Machine. I am human and you are just a metal thing. I order you to answer me. Are you from the Greater Despot's police?"

"Yes."

"Then you are arresting me?"

"No. I am leaving you here. The local police may arrest you, though I have been informed that they are not interested in your case. However, I have appropriated all of your funds as partial payment for the cost of tracking you." It turned once more to leave.

"Stop!" Jagen sprang to his feet. "You have taken my money, I can believe that. But you cannot toy with me. You did not follow me for twenty years just to turn about and leave me. I am an assassin—remember?"

"I am well aware of the fact. That is why I have followed you. I am also now aware of your opinion of yourself. It is a wrong one. You are not unique, or gifted, or even interesting. Any man can kill when presented with the correct motivation. After all, you are animals. In time of war good young men drop bombs on people they do not know, by pressing switches, and this murder does not bother them in the slightest. Men kill to protect their families and are commended for it. You, a professional hunter of animals, killed another animal, who happened to be a man, when presented with enough payment. There is nothing noble, brave or even interesting in that. That man is dead and killing you will not bring him to life. May I leave now?"

"No! If you do not want me—why spend those years following me? Not just for a few remnants of fact."

The machine stood straight, high, glowing with a mechanical dignity of its own, which perhaps reflected that of its builders.

"Yes. Facts. You are nothing, and the men who hired you are nothing. But why they did it and how they were able to do it is everything. One man, ten men, even a million are as nothing to the Greater Despot who numbers the planets in his realm in the hundreds of thousands. The Greater Despot deals only in societies. Now an examination will be made of your society and particularly of the society of the men who hired you. What led them to believe that violence can solve anything? What were the surroundings where killing was condoned or ignored—or accepted—that shaped their lives so that they exported this idea?

"It is the society that kills, not the individual.

"You are nothing," Follower added—could it have been with a touch of malice?—as it stepped into the screen and vanished.

I See You

The judge was impressive in his black robes, and omniscient in the chromium perfection of his skull. His voice rolled like the crack of doom, rich and penetrating.

"Carl Tritt, this court finds you guilty as charged. On 2182423 you did willfully and maliciously steal the payroll of the Marcrix Corporation, a sum totaling 318,000 cr., and did attempt to keep these same credits as your own. The sentence is twenty years."

The black gavel fell with the precision of a pile driver and the sound bounced back and forth inside Carl's head. Twenty years. He clamped bloodless fingers on the steel bar of justice and looked up into the judge's electronic eyes. There was perhaps a glint of compassion, but no mercy there. The sentence had been passed and recorded in the Central Memory. There was no appeal.

A panel snapped open in the front of the judge's bench and exhibit A slid out on a soundless piston. 318,000 cr., still in their original pay envelopes. The judge pointed as Carl slowly picked it up.

"Here is the money you stole—see that it is returned to the proper people."

Carl shuffled out of the courtroom, the package clutched weakly to his chest, sunk in a sodden despair. The street outside was washed with a golden sunlight that he could not see, for his depression shadowed it with the deepest gloom.

His throat was sore and his eyes burned. If he had not been an adult male citizen, age twenty-five, he might have cried. But twenty-five-year-old adult males do not cry. Instead he swallowed heavily a few times.

A twenty-year sentence—it couldn't be believed. Why me? Of all the people in the world why did he have to receive a sentence severe as that? His well-trained conscience instantly shot back the answer. Because you stole money. He shied away from that unpleasant thought and stumbled on.

Unshed tears swam in his eyes and trickled back into his nose and down his throat. Forgetting in his misery where he was, he choked a bit. Then spat heavily.

Even as the saliva hit the spotless sidewalk, a waste can twenty feet away stirred into life. It rotated on hidden wheels and soundlessly rolled towards him. In shocked horror Carl pressed the back of his hand to his mouth. Too late to stop what was already done.

A flexible arm licked out and quickly swabbed the sidewalk clean. Then the can squatted like a mechanical Buddha while a speaker rasped to life in its metal insides. A tinny metallic voice addressed Carl.

"Carl Tritt, you have violated Local Ordinance number bd-14-668 by expectorating on a public sidewalk. The sentence is two days. Your total sentence is now twenty years and two days."

Two other pedestrians had stopped behind Carl, listening with gaping mouths as sentence was passed. Carl could almost hear their thought. A sentenced man. Think of that! Over twenty years sentence! They bugged their eyes at him in a mixture of fascination and distaste.

Carl rushed away, the package clutched to his chest and his face flushed red with shame. The sentenced men on video had always seemed so funny. How they fell down and acted bewildered when a door wouldn't open for them.

It didn't seem so funny now.

The rest of that day crept by in a fog of dejection. He had a vague recollection of his visit to the Marcrix Corporation to return his stolen money. They had been kind and understanding, and he had fled in embarrassment. All the kindness in the world wouldn't reprieve his sentence.

He wandered vaguely in the streets after that, until he was exhausted. Then he had seen the bar. Bright lights with a fog of smoke inside, looking cheery and warm. Carl had pushed at the door, and pushed again, while the people inside had stopped talking and turned to watch him through the glass. Then he had remembered the sentence and realized the door wouldn't open. The people inside had started laughing and he had run away. Lucky to get off without a further sentence.

When he reached his apartment at last he was sobbing with fatigue and unhappiness. The door opened to his thumb and slammed behind him. This was a refuge at last.

Until he saw his packaged bags waiting, for him.

Carl's video set hummed into life. He had never realized before it could be controlled from a Central. The screen stayed dark but the familiar voder voice of Sentence Control poured out.

"A selection of clothing and articles suitable for a sentenced man has been chosen for you. Your new address is on your bags. Go there at once."

It was too much. Carl knew without looking that his camera and his books and model rockets—the hundred other little things that meant something to him—were not included in those bags. He ran into the kitchen, forcing open the resisting door. The voice spoke from a speaker concealed above the stove.

"What you are doing is in violation of the law. If you stop at once your sentence will not be increased."

The words meant nothing to him, he didn't want to hear them. With frantic fingers he pulled the cupboard open and reached for the bottle of whiskey in the back. The bottle vanished through a trapdoor he had never noticed before, brushing tantalizingly against his fingers as it dropped.

He stumbled down the hall and the voice droned on behind him. Five more days sentence for attempting to obtain alcoholic beverages. Carl couldn't have cared less.

The cabs and buses wouldn't stop for him and the sub-slide turnstile spat his coin back like something distasteful. In the end he tottered the long blocks to his new quarters, located in a part of town he had never known existed. There was a calculated seediness about the block where he was to stay. Deliberately cracked sidewalks and dim lights. The dusty spiderwebs that hung in every niche had a definitely artificial look about them. He had to climb two flights of stairs, each step of which creaked with a different note, to reach his room. Without turning the light on he dropped his bags and stumbled forward. His shins cracked against a metal bed and he dropped gratefully into it. A blissful exhaustion put him to sleep.

When he awoke in the morning he didn't want to open his eyes. It had been a nightmare, he tried to tell himself, and he was safely out of it now. But the chill air in the room and the gray light filtering through his lids told him differently. With a sigh he abandoned the fantasy and looked around at his new home.

It was clean—and that was all that could be said for it. The bed, a chair, a built-in chest of drawers—these were the furnishings. A single unshielded bulb hung from the ceiling. On the wall opposite him was a large metal calender sign. It read: 20 years, 5 days, 17 hours, 25 minutes. While he watched the sign gave an audible click and the last number changed to 24.

Carl was too exhausted by the emotions of the previous day to care. The magnitude of his change still overwhelmed him. He settled back onto the bed in a half-daze, only to be jolted up by a booming voice from the wall.

"Breakfast is now being served in the public dining room on the floor above. You have ten minutes." The now familiar voice came this time from a giant speaker at least five feet across, and had lost all of its tinny quality. Carl obeyed without thinking.

The meal was drab but filling. There were other men and women in the dining room, all very interested in their food. He realized with a start that they were sentenced too. After that he kept his own eyes on his plate and returned quickly to his room.

As he entered the door the video pickup was pointing at him from above the speaker. It followed him like a gun as he walked across the room. Like the speaker, it was the biggest pickup he had ever seen; a swiveled chrome tube with a glass eye on its end as big as his fist. A sentenced man is alone, yet never has privacy.

Without preliminary warning the speaker blasted and he gave a nervous start.

"Your new employment begins at 1800 hours today, here is the address." A card leaped out of a slot below the calendar sign and dropped to the floor. Carl had to bend over and scratch at its edges to pick it up. The address meant nothing to him.

He had hours of time before he had to be there, and nothing else to do. The bed was nearby and inviting, he dropped wearily onto it.

Why had he stolen that damned payroll? He knew the answer. Because he had wanted things he could never afford on a telephone technician's salary. It had looked so tempting and foolproof. He damned the accident that had led him to it. The memory still tortured him.

It had been a routine addition of telephone lines in one of the large office buildings.

When he first went there he had been by himself, he would not need the robots until after the preliminary survey was done. The phone circuits were in a service corridor just off the main lobby. His passkey let him in through the inconspicuous door and he switched on the light. A maze of wiring and junction boxes covered one wall, leading to cables that vanished down the corridor out of sight. Carl opened his wiring diagrams and began to trace leads. The rear wall seemed to be an ideal spot to attach the new boxes and he tapped it to see if it could take the heavy bolts. It was hollow.

Carl's first reaction was disgust. The job would be twice as difficult if the leads had to be extended. Then he felt a touch of curiosity as to what the wall was there for. It was just a panel he noticed on closer inspection, made up of snap-on sections fitted into place. With his screwdriver he pried one section out and saw what looked like a steel grid supporting metal plates. He had no idea of what their function was, and didn't really care now that his mild curiosity had been settled. After slipping the panel back into place he went on with his work. A few hours later he looked at his watch, then dropped his tools for lunch.

The first thing he saw when he stepped back into the lobby was the bank cart.

Walking as close as he was, Carl couldn't help but notice the two guards who were taking thick envelopes from the cart and putting them into a bank of lockers set into the wall. One envelope to each locker, then a slam of the thick door to seal it shut. Besides a momentary pang at the sight of all that money Carl had no reaction.

Only when he came back from lunch did he stop suddenly as a thought struck him. He hesitated a fraction of a moment, then went on. No one had noticed him. As he entered the corridor again he looked surreptitiously at the messenger who was opening one of the lockers. When Carl had closed the door behind him and checked the relative position of the wall with his eyes he knew he was right.

What he had thought was a metal grid with plates was really the backs of the lockers and their framework of supports. The carefully sealed lockers in the lobby had unguarded backs that faced into the service corridor.

He realized at once that he should do nothing at the time, nor act in any way to arouse suspicion. He did, however, make sure that the service robots came in through the other end of the corridor that opened onto a deserted hallway at the rear of the building, where he had made a careful examination of the hall. Carl even managed to make himself forget about the lockers for over six months.

After that he began to make his plans. Casual observation at odd times gave him all the facts he needed. The lockers contained payrolls for a number of large companies in the building. The bank guards deposited the money at noon every Friday. No envelopes were ever picked up before one P.M. at the earliest. Carl noticed what seemed to be the thickest envelope and made his plans accordingly.

Everything went like clockwork. At ten minutes to twelve on a Friday he finished a job he was working on and left. He carried his toolbox with him. Exactly ten minutes later he entered the rear door of the corridor without being seen. His hands were covered with transparent and nearly invisible gloves. By 12:10 he had the panel off and the blade of a long screwdriver pressed against the back of the selected locker, the handle of the screwdriver held to the bone behind his ear. There was no sound of closing doors so he knew the bank men had finished and gone.

The needle flame of his torch ate through the steel panel like soft cheese. He excised a neat circle of metal and pulled it free. Beating out a smoldering spot on the money envelope, he transferred it to another envelope from his toolbox. This envelope he had addressed to himself and was already stamped. One minute after leaving the building he would have the envelope in the mail and would be a rich man.

Carefully checking, he put all the tools and the envelope back into his toolbox and strode away. At exactly 12:35 he left through the rear-corridor door and locked it behind him. The corridor was still empty, so he took the extra seconds to jimmy the door open with a tool from his pocket. Plenty of people had keys to that door, but it didn't hurt to widen the odds a bit.

Carl was actually whistling when he walked out into the street.

Then the peace officer took him by the arm.

"You are under arrest for theft," the officer told him in a calm voice.

The shock stopped him in his tracks and he almost wished it had stopped his heart the same way. He had never planned to be caught and never considered the consequences. Fear and shame made him stumble as the policeman led him to the waiting car. The crowd watched in fascinated amazement.

When the evidence had been produced at his trial he found out, a little late, what his mistake had been. Because of the wiring and conduits in the corridor it was equipped with infrared thermocouples. The heat of his torch had activated the alarm and an observer at Fire Central had looked through one of their video pickups in the tunnel. He had expected to see a short circuit and had been quite surprised to see Carl removing the money. His surprise had not prevented him from notifying the police. Carl had cursed fate, under his breath.

The grating voice of the speaker cut through Carl's bad-tasting memories.

"1730 hours. It is time for you to leave for your employment."

Wearily, Carl pulled on his shoes, checked the address, and left for his new job. It took him almost the full half hour to walk there. He wasn't surprised in the slightest when the address turned out to be the Department of Sanitation.

"You'll catch on fast," the elderly and worn supervisor told him. "Just go through this list and kind of get acquainted with it. Your truck will be along in a moment."

The list was in reality a thick volume of lists, of all kinds of waste materials. Apparently everything in the world that could be discarded was in the book. And each item was followed by a key number. These numbers ran from one to thirteen and seemed to be the entire purpose of the volume. While Carl was puzzling over their meaning there was a sudden roar of a heavy motor. A giant robot-operated truck pulled up the ramp and ground to a stop near them.

"Garbage truck," the supervisor said wearily. "She's all yours." Carl had always known there were garbage trucks, but of course he had never seen one. It was a bulky, shining cylinder over twenty meters long. A robot driver was built into the cab. Thirty other robots stood on footsteps along the sides. The supervisor led the way to the rear of the truck and pointed to the gaping mouth of the receiving bin.

"Robots pick up the garbage and junk and load it in there," he said. "then they press one of these here thirteen buttons keying whatever they have dumped into one of the thirteen bins, inside the truck. They're just plain lifting robots and not too brainy, but good enough to recognize most things they pick up. But not all the time. That's where you come in, riding along right there."

The grimy thumb was now aiming at a transparent-walled cubicle that also projected from the back of the truck. There was a padded seat inside, facing a shelf set with thirteen buttons.

"You sit there, just as cozy as a bug in a rug I might say, ready to do your duty at any given moment. Which is whenever one of the robots finds something it can't identify straight off. So it puts whatever it is into the hopper outside your window. You give it a good look, check the list for the proper category if you're not sure, then press the right button and in she goes. It may sound difficult at first but you'll soon catch onto the ropes."

"Oh, it sounds complicated all right," Carl said, with a dull feeling in his gut as he climbed into his turret, "but I'll try and get used to it."

The weight of his body closed a hidden switch in the chair, and the truck growled forward. Carl scowled down unhappily at the roadway streaming out slowly from behind the wheels, as he rode into the darkness, sitting in his transparent boil on the backside of the truck.

It was dull beyond imagining. The garbage truck followed a programmed route that led through the commercial and freightways of the city. There were few other trucks moving at that hour of the night, and they were all robot-driven. Carl saw no other human being. He was snug as a bug. A human flea being whirled around inside the complex machine of the city. Every few minutes the truck would stop, the robots clatter off, then return with their loads. The containers dumped the robots leaped back to their footplates, and the truck was off once more.

An hour passed before he had his first decision to make. A robot stopped in mid-dump, ground its gears a moment, then dropped a dead cat into Carl's hopper. Carl stared at it with horror. The cat stared back with wide, sightless eyes, its lips drawn back in a fierce grin. It was the first corpse Carl had ever seen. Something heavy had dropped on the cat, reducing the lower part of its body to paper-thinness. With an effort he wrenched his eyes away and jerked the book open.

Castings . . . Cast Iron . . . Cats (dead) . . . Very, very much dead. There was the bin number. Nine. One bin per life. After the ninth life—the ninth bin. He didn't find the thought very funny. A fierce jab at button 9 and the cat was whisked from sight with a last flourish of its paw. He repressed the sudden desire to wave back.

After the cat boredom set in with a vengeance. Hours dragged slowly by and still his hopper was empty. The truck rumbled forward and stopped. Forward and stop. The motion lulled him and he was tired. He leaned forward and laid his head gently on the list of varieties of garbage, his eyes closed.

"Sleeping is forbidden while at work. This is warning number one."

The hatefully familiar voice blasted from behind his head and he started with surprise. He hadn't noticed the pickup and speaker next to the door. Even here, riding a garbage truck to eternity, the machine watched him. Bitter anger kept him awake for the duration of the round.

Days came and went after that in a gray monotony, the large calendar on the wall of his room ticking them off one by one. But not fast enough. It now read 19 years, 322 days, 8 hours, 16 minutes. Not fast enough. There was no more interest in his life. As a sentenced man there were very few things he could do in his free time. All forms of entertainment were closed to him. He could gain admittance—through a side door—to only a certain section of the library. After one futile trip there, pawing through the inspirational texts and moral histories, he never returned.

Each night he went to work. After returning he slept as long as he could. After that he just lay on his bed, smoking his tiny allotment of cigarettes, and listening to the seconds being ticked off his sentence.

Carl tried to convince himself that he could stand twenty years in this kind of existence. But a growing knot of tension in his stomach told him differently.

This was before the accident. The accident changed everything.

A night like any other night. The garbage truck stopped at an industrial site and the robots scurried out for their loads. Nearby was a cross-country tanker, taking on some liquid through a flexible hose. Carl gave it bored notice only because there was a human driver in the cab of the truck. That meant the cargo was dangerous in some way, robot drivers being forbidden by law from handling certain loads. He idly noticed the driver open the door and start to step out. When the man was halfway out he remembered something, turned back and reached for it.

For a short moment the driver brushed against the starter button.

The truck was in gear and lurched forward a few feet. The man quickly pulled away—but it was too late.

The movement had been enough to put a strain on the hose. It stretched—the supporting arm bent—then it broke free from the truck at the coupling. The hose whipped back and forth, spraying greenish liquid over the truck and the cab, before an automatic cutout turned off the flow.

This had taken only an instant. The driver turned back and stared with horror-widened eyes at the fluid dripping over the truck's hood. It was steaming slightly.

With a swatting roar it burst into fire, and the entire front of the truck was covered with flame. The driver invisible behind the burning curtain.

Before being sentenced Carl had always worked with robot assistance. He knew what to say and how to say it to get instant obedience. Bursting from his cubicle he slapped one of the garbage robots on its metal shoulder and shouted an order. The robot dropped a can it was emptying and ran at full speed for the truck, diving into the flames.

More important than the driver was the open port on top of the truck. If the flames should reach it the entire truck would go up— showering the street with burning liquid.

Swathed in flame, the robot climbed the ladder on the truck's side. One burning hand reached up and flipped the self-sealing lid shut. The robot started back down through the flames but stopped suddenly as the fierce heat burned at its controls. For a few seconds it vibrated rapidly like a man in pain, then collapsed. Destroyed.

Carl was running towards the truck himself, guiding two more of his robots. The flames still wrapped the cab, seeping in through the partly open door. Thin screams of pain came from inside. Under Carl's directions one robot pulled the door open and the other dived in. Bent double, protecting the man's body with its own, the robot pulled the driver out. The flames had charred his legs to shapeless masses and his clothes were on fire. Carl beat out the flames with his hands as the robot dragged the driver clear.

The instant the fire had started, automatic alarms had gone off. Fire and rescue teams plunged toward the scene. Carl had just put out the last of the flames on the unconscious man's body when they arrived. A wash of foam instantly killed the fire. An ambulance jerked to a stop and two robot stretcher-bearers popped out of it. A human doctor followed. He took one look at the burned driver and whistled.

"Really cooked!"

He grabbed a pressurized container from the stretcher-bearer and sprayed jellylike burn dressing over the driver's legs. Before he had finished the other robot snapped open a medical kit and proffered it. The doctor made quick adjustments on a multiple syringe, then gave the injection. It was all very fast and efficient.

As soon as the stretcher-bearers had carried the burned driver into the ambulance, it jumped forward. The doctor mumbled instructions to the hospital into his lapel radio. Only then did he turn his attention to Carl.

"Let's see those hands," he said.

Everything had happened with such speed that Carl had scarcely noticed his burns. Only now did he glance down at the scorched skin and feel sharp pain. The blood drained from his face and he swayed.

"Easy does it," the doctor said, helping him sit down on the ground. "They're not as bad as they look. Have new skin on them in a couple of days." His hands were busy while he talked and there was the sudden prick of a needle in Carl's arm. The pain ebbed away.

The shot made things hazy after that. Carl had vague memories of riding to the hospital in a police car. Then the grateful comfort of a cool bed. They must have given him another shot then because the next thing he knew it was morning. That week in the hospital was like a vacation for Carl. Either the staff didn't know of his sentenced status or it didn't make any difference. He received the same treatment as the other patients. While the accelerated grafts covered his hands and forearms with new skin, he relaxed in the luxury of the soft bed and varied food. The same drugs that kept the pain away prevented his worry about returning to the outside world. He was also pleased to hear that the burned driver would recover.

On the morning of the eighth day the staff dermatologist prodded the new skin and smiled. "Good job of recovery, Tritt," he said. "Looks like you'll be leaving us today. I'll have them fill out the forms and send for your clothes."

The old knot of tension returned to Carl's stomach as he thought of what waited for him outside. It seemed doubly hard now that he had been away for a few days. Yet there was nothing else he could possibly do. He dressed as slowly as he could, stretching the free time remaining as much as possible.

As he started down the corridor a nurse waved him over. "Mr. Skarvy would like to see you—in here."

Skarvy. That was the name of the truck driver. Carl followed her into the room where the burly driver sat up in bed. His big body looked strange somehow, until Carl realized there was no long bulge under the blankets. The man had no legs.

"Chopped 'em both off at the hips," Skarvy said when he noticed Carl's gaze. He smiled. "Don't let it bother you. Don't bother me none. They planted the regen-buds and they tell me in less than a year I'll have legs again, good as new. Suits me fine. Better than staying in that truck and frying." He hitched himself up in the bed an intense expression on his face.

"They showed me the films Fire Central made through one of their pickups on the spot. Saw the whole thing. Almost upchucked when I saw what I looked like when you dragged me out." He pushed out a meaty hand and pumped Carl's. "I want to thank you for doing what you done. Taking a chance like that." Carl could only smile foolishly.

"I want to shake your hand," Skarvy said. "Even if you are a sentenced man."

Carl pulled his hand free and left. Not trusting himself to say anything. The last week had been a dream. And a foolish one. He was still sentenced and would be for years to come. An outcast of society who never left it.

When he pushed open the door to his drab room the all-too-familiar voice boomed out of the speaker.

"Carl Tritt. You have missed seven days of your work assignment, in addition there is an incomplete day, only partially worked. This time would normally not be deducted from your sentence. There is however precedent in allowing deduction of this time, and it will be allowed against your total sentence." The decision made, the numbers clicked over busily on his calendar.

"Thanks for nothing," Carl said and dropped wearily on his bed. The monotonous voder voice went on, ignoring his interruption.

"In addition, an award has been made. Under Sentence Diminution Regulations your act of personal heroism, risking your own life to save another's, is recognized as a pro-social act and so treated. The award is three years off your sentence."

Carl was on his feet, staring unbelievingly at the speaker. Was it some trick? Yet as he watched the calendar mechanism ground gears briefly the new year numbers slowly turned over. 18 . . . 17 . . . 16 . . . The whiffing stopped.

Just like that. Three years off his sentence. It didn't seem possible—yet there were the numbers to prove that it was.

"Sentence Control!" he shouted. "Listen to me! What happened? I mean how can a sentence be reduced by this award business? I never heard anything about it before?"

"Sentence reduction is never mentioned in public life," the speaker said flatly. "This might encourage people to break the law, since threat of sentence is considered a deterrent. Normally a sentenced person is not told of sentence reduction until after their first year. Your case however is exceptional since you were awarded reduction before the end of said year."

"How can I find out more about sentence reduction?" Carl asked eagerly.

The speaker hummed for a moment, then the voice crackled out again. "Your Sentence Advisor is Mr. Prisbi. He will advise you in whatever is to be done. You have an appointment for 1300 hours tomorrow. Here is his address."

The machine clicked and spat out a card. Carl was waiting for it this time and caught it before it hit the floor. He held it carefully, almost lovingly. Three years off his sentence and tomorrow he would find out what else he could do to reduce it even more.

Of course he was early, almost a full hour before he was due. The robot-receptionist kept him seated in the outer office until the exact minute of his appointment. When he heard the door lock finally click open he almost jumped to it. Forcing himself to go slow, he entered the office.

Prisbi, the Sentence Advisor, looked like a preserved fish peering through the bottom of a bottle. He was dumpy fat, with dead white skin and lumpy features that had been squeezed up like putty from the fat underneath. His eyes were magnified pupils that peered un-blinkingly through eyeglass lenses almost as thick as they were wide. In a world where contact lenses were the norm, his vision was so bad it could not be corrected by the tiny lenses. Instead he wore the heavy-framed, anachronistic spectacles, perched insecurely on his puffy nose.

Prisbi did not smile or say a word when Carl entered the door. He kept his eyes fixed steadily on him as he walked the length of the room. They reminded Carl of the video scanners he had grown to hate, and he shook the idea away.

"My name is—" he began.

"I know your name, Tritt," Prisbi rasped. The voice seemed too coarse to have come from those soft lips. "Now sit down in that chair—there." He jerked his pen at a hard metal chair that faced his desk.

Carl sat down and immediately blinked away from the strong lights that focused on his face. He tried to slide the chair back, until he realized it was fastened to the floor. He just sat then and waited for Prisbi to begin.

Prisbi finally lowered his glassy gaze and picked up a file of papers from his desk. He riffled through them for a full minute before speaking.

"Very strange record, Tritt," he finally grated out. "Can't say that I like it at all. Don't even know why Control gave you permission to be here. But since you are—tell me why."

It was an effort to smile but Carl did. "Well you see, I was awarded a three-year reduction in sentence. This is the first I ever heard of sentence reduction. Control sent me here, said you would give me more information."

"A complete waste of time," Prisbi said, throwing the papers down onto the desk. "You aren't eligible for sentence reduction until after you've finished your first year of sentence. You have almost ten months to go. Come back then and I'll explain. You can leave."

Carl didn't move. His hands were clenched tight in his lap as he fought for control. He squinted against the light, looking at Prisbi's unresponsive face.

"But you see I have already had sentence reduction. Perhaps that's why Control told me to come—"

"Don't try and teach me the law," Prisbi growled coldly. "I'm here to teach it to you. All right I'll explain. Though it's of absolutely no value now. When you finish your first year of sentence— a real year of work at your assigned job—you are eligible for reduction. You may apply then for other work that carries a time premium. Dangerous jobs such as satellite repair, that take two days off your sentence for every day served. There are even certain positions in atomics that allow three days per day worked, though these are rare. In this way the sentenced man helps himself, learns social consciousness, and benefits society at the same time. Of course this doesn't apply to you yet."

"Why not?" Carl was standing now, hammering on the table with his still-tender hands. "Why do I have to finish a year at that stupid, made-work job? It's completely artificial, designed to torture, not to accomplish anything. The amount of work I do every night could be done in three seconds by a robot when the truck returned. Do you call that teaching social consciousness? Humiliating, boring work that—"

"Sit down Tritt," Prisbi shouted in a high cracked voice. "Don't you realize where you are? Or who I am? I tell you what to do. You don't say anything to me outside of 'Yes, sir' or 'No, sir.' I say you must finish your primary year of work, then return here. That is an order."

"I say you're wrong," Carl shouted. "I'll go over your head—see your superiors—you just can't decide my life away like that!"

Prisbi was standing now too, a twisted grimace splitting his face in a caricature of a smile. He roared at Carl.

"You can't go over my head or appeal to anyone else—I have the last word! You hear that? I tell you what to do. I say you work—and you're going to work. You doubt that? You doubt what I can do?"

There was a bubble of froth on his pale lips now. "I say you have shouted at me and used insulting language and threatened me, and the record will bear me out!"

Prisbi fumbled on his desk until he found a microphone. He raised it, trembling, to his mouth and pressed the button.

"This is Sentence Advisor Prisbi. For actions unbecoming a sentenced man when addressing a Sentence Advisor, I recommend Carl Tritt's sentence be increased by one week."

The answer was instantaneous. The Sentence Control speaker on the wall spoke in its usual voder tones. "Sentence approved. Carl Tritt, seven days have been added to your sentence, bringing it to a total of sixteen years . . ."

The words droned on, but Carl wasn't listening. He was staring down a red tunnel of hatred. The only thing he was aware of in the entire world was the pasty white face of Advisor Prisbi.

"You . . . didn't have to do that," he finally choked out. "You don't have to make it worse for me when you're supposed to be helping me." Sudden realization came to Carl. "But you don't want to help me, do you? You enjoy playing God with sentenced men, twisting their lives in your hands—"

His voice was drowned out by Prisbi's, shouting into the microphone again . . . deliberate insults . . . recommend a month be added to Carl Tritt's sentence . . . Carl heard what the other man was saying. But he didn't care anymore. He had tried hard to do it their way. He couldn't do it any longer. He hated the system, the men who designed it, the machines that enforced it. And most of all he hated the man before him, who was a summation of the whole rotten mess. At the end, for all his efforts, he had ended up in the hands of this pulpy sadist. It wasn't going to be that way at all.

"Take your glasses off," he said in a low voice.

"What's that . . . what?" Prisbi said. He had finished shouting into the microphone and was breathing heavily.

"Don't bother," Carl said reaching slowly across the table. "I'll do it for you." He pulled the man's glasses off and laid them gently on the table. Only then did Prisbi realize what was happening. "No" was all he could say, in a sudden outrush of breath.

Carl's fist landed square on those hated lips, broke them, broke the teeth behind them and knocked the man back over his chair onto the floor. The tender new skin on Carl's hand was torn and blood dripped down his fingers. He wasn't aware of it. He stood over the huddled, whimpering shape on the door and laughed. Then he stumbled out of the office, shaken with laughter.

The robot-receptionist turned a coldly disapproving, glass and steel, face on him and said something. Still laughing he wrenched a heavy light stand from the floor and battered the shining face in. Clutching the lamp he went out into the hall.

Part of him screamed in terror at the enormity of what he had done, but just part of his mind. And this small voice was washed away by the hot wave of pleasure that surged through him. He was breaking the rules—all of the rules—this time. Breaking out of the cage that had trapped him all of his life.

As he rode down in the automatic elevator the laughter finally died away, and he wiped the dripping sweat from his face. A small voice scratched in his ear.

"Carl Tritt, you have committed violation of sentence and your sentence is hereby increased by—"

"Where are you?" he bellowed. "Don't hide there and whine in my ear. Come out!" He peered closely at the wall of the car until he found the glass lens.

"You see me, do you?" he shouted at the lens. "Well, I see you too!" The lamp stand came down and crashed into the glass. Another blow tore through the thin metal and found the speaker. It expired with a squawk.

People ran from him in the street, but he didn't notice them. They were just victims the way he had been. It was the enemy he wanted to crush. Every video eye he saw caught a blow from the battered stand. He poked and tore until he silenced every speaker he passed. A score of battered and silent robots marked his passage.

It was inevitable that he should be caught. He neither thought about that nor cared very much. This was the moment he had been living for all his life. There was no battle song he could sing, he didn't know any. But there was one mildly smutty song he remembered from his school days. It would have to do. Roaring it at the top of his voice, Carl left a trail of destruction through the shining order of the city.

The speakers never stopped talking to Carl, and he silenced them as fast as he found them. His sentence mounted higher and higher with each act.

". . . making a total of two hundred and twelve years, nineteen days and—" The voice was suddenly cut off as some control circuit finally realized the impossibility of its statements. Carl was riding a moving ramp towards a freight level. He crouched, waiting for the voice to start again so he could seek it out and destroy it. A speaker rustled and he looked around for it.

"Carl Tritt, your sentence has exceeded the expected bounds of your life and is therefore meaningless . . ."

"Always was meaningless," he shouted back. "I know that now. Now where are you? I'm going to get you!" The machine droned on steadily.

". . . in such a case you are remanded for trial. Peace officers are now on their way to bring you in. You are ordered to go peacefully or—GLILRK . . ." The lamp stand smashed into the speaker.

"Send them," Carl spat into the mass of tangled metal and wire. "I'll take care of them too."

The end was preordained. Followed by the ubiquitous eyes of Central, Carl could not run forever. The squad of officers cornered him on a lower level and closed in. Two of them were clubbed unconscious before they managed to get a knockout needle into his flesh.

The same courtroom and the same judge. Only this time there were two muscular human guards present to watch Carl. He didn't seem to need watching, slumped forward as he was against the bar of justice. White bandages covered the cuts and bruises. A sudden humming came from the robot judge as he stirred to life. "Order in the court," he said, rapping the gavel once and returning it to its stand. "Carl Tritt, this court finds you guilty—"

"What, again? Aren't you tired of that sort of thing yet?" Carl asked.

"Silence while sentence is being passed," the judge said loudly and banged down again with the gavel. "You are guilty of crimes too numerous to be expiated by sentencing. Therefore you are condemned to Personality Death. Psycho-surgery shall remove all traces of this personality from your body, until this personality is dead, dead, dead."

"Not that," Carl whimpered, leaning forward and stretching his arms out pleadingly towards the judge. "Anything but that." Before either guard could act, Carl's whimper turned to a loud laugh as he swept the judge's gavel off the bench. Turning with it, he attacked the astonished guards. One dropped instantly as the gavel caught him behind the ear. The other struggled to get his gun out—then fell across the first man's limp body.

"Now Judge," Carl shouted with happiness, "I have the gavel, let's see what I do!" He swept around the end of the bench and hammered the judge's sleek metal head into a twisted ruin. The judge, merely an extension of the machinery of Central Control, made no attempt to defend itself.

There was the sound of running feet in the hall and someone pulled at the door. Carl had no plan. All he wanted to do was remain free and do as much damage as he could as long as the fire of rebellion burned inside of him. There was only the single door into the courtroom. Carl glanced quickly around and his technician's eye noticed the access plate set in the wall behind the judge. He twisted the latch and kicked it open.

A video tube was watching him from a high corner of the court-room, but that couldn't be helped. The machine could follow him wherever he went anyway. All he could do was try and stay ahead of the pursuit. He pulled himself through the access door as two robots burst into the courtroom.

"Carl Tritt, surrender at once. A further change has been . . . has been . . . Carl . . . Carl . . . Ca . . ."

Listening to their voices through the thin metal door, Carl won-dered what had happened. He hazarded a look. Both robots had ground to a halt and were making aimless motions. Their speakers rustled, but said nothing. After a few moments the random movements stopped. They turned at the same time, picked up the unconscious peace officers, and went out. The door closed behind them. Carl found it very puzzling. He watched for some minutes longer, until the door opened again. This time it was a tool-hung repair robot that trundled in. It moved over to the ruined judge and began dismantling it.

Closing the door quietly, Carl leaned against its cool metal and tried to understand what had happened. With the threat of immediate pursuit removed, he had time to think.

Why hadn't he been followed? Why had Central Control acted as if it didn't know his whereabouts? This omnipotent machine had scanning tubes in every square inch of the city, he had found that out. And it was hooked into the machines of the other cities of the world. There was no place it couldn't see. Or rather one place.

The thought hit him so suddenly he gasped. Then he looked around him. A tunnel of relays and controls stretched away from him, dimly lit by glow plates. It could be—yes it could be. It had to be.

There could be only one place in the entire world that Central Control could not look—inside its own central mechanism. Its mem-ory and operating circuits. No machine with independent decision could repair its own thinking circuits. This would allow destructive negative feedback to be built up. An impaired circuit could only im-pair itself more, it couldn't possibly repair itself.

He was inside the brain circuits of Central Control. So as far as that city-embracing machine knew he had ceased to be. He existed nowhere the machine could see. The machine could see everywhere. Therefore he didn't exist. By this time all memory of him had been probably erased.

Slowly at first, then faster and faster, he walked down the corridor.

"Free!" he shouted. "Really free—for the first time in my life! Free to do as I want, to watch the whole world and laugh at them!" A power and happiness flowed through him. He opened door after door, exulting in his new kingdom.

He was talking aloud, bubbling with happiness. "I can have the repair robots that work on the circuits bring me food. Furniture, clothes—whatever I want. I can live here just as I please—do what I please." The thought was wildly exciting. He threw open another door and stopped rigid.

The room before him was tastefully furnished, just as he would have done it. Books, paintings on the walls soft music coming from a hidden record player. Carl gaped at it. Until the voice spoke behind him.

"Of course it would be wonderful to live here," the voice said. "To be master of the city, have anything you want at your fingertips. But what makes you think, poor little man, that you are the first one to realize that? And to come here? And there is really only room for one you know."

Carl turned slowly, very slowly, measuring the distance between himself and the other man who stood behind him in the doorway, weighing the chances of lashing out with the gavel he still clutched—before the other man could fire the gun he held in his hand.

LAUGH—I THOUGHT I WOULD CRY

Which side of a dog has the most fur?

The outside of course.

Laugh at that and you should enjoy the stories that follow here. It is not easy to write humorous science fiction—and even far harder to sell it once it is done. It is a true Catch-22 situation. Unless you are known as a writer of funny fiction you cannot sell the stuff. I know. The first Stainless Steel Rat books are straight adventure—with the occasional joke slipped in. As the years passed the ratio slowly reversed—and there were no complaints from the readers.

But how did I fare when I wrote my first comic SF novel? Not too well is the answer. I submitted an outline of my prospective novel *Bill, the Galactic Hero* to Damon Knight, believing that he was the only editor with avant-garde taste enough to commission this bit of martial madness. Commission yes, buy no. When the book was finished he bounced it saying what I had here was a war novel, that I should go through it and take out the jokes if I wanted to see it published. Well I didn't take out the jokes and I persevered. Eventually Mike Moorcock serialized it in *New Worlds* at the same time that Fred Pohl serialized it in *Galaxy*. It has since been published in twelve languages and has never been out of print. With the jokes left in.

The Greening of the Green

"Be careful with that dinghy, you idiots," the admiral bellowed in a whisper. "It's the last one we have."

He looked on anxiously while the sweating sailors lowered the dinghy from the deck of the submarine into the water. There was no moon, but the crowded stars in the clear Mediterranean sky glowed like tiny light bulbs.

"Is that the shore, Admiral?" the passenger asked. His teeth chattered as he spoke, probably from fear since the night was warm.

"Captain," the admiral said. "I'm captain of this sub so you call me captain. And, no, that is a fog bank. The shore is over there. Are you ready?"

Giulio started to speak, then, sensing the trembling of his jaw, nodded instead. He felt as scruffy as he looked with his ancient beret, decaying corduroy trousers and decayed jacket. Felt even scruffier next to the crisply uniformed figure of the admiral: in the dark the patches and darns of his uniform did not show. Giulio nodded again when he realized the admiral had not seen his nod the first time.

"Good. Then you know your instructions?"

"Of course I don't know my instructions," Giulio said with petulant irritation, trying not to stammer the words. "I only know that there is a piece of paper in my pocket with a word on it and I'm to read that word then eat the paper. At dawn."

"Those are the instructions I'm talking about, you idiot." The admiral grumbled like a volcano, his authority insulted.

"You can't talk to me like that," Giulio squeaked, realized he squeaked and lowered his voice. "Do you know who I am . . . ?"

He choked himself into silence. No, the admiral did not know who he was, and if he told him then the CIA would kill them both; they had promised him that. No one was to know.

"I know you are a goddamned passenger and a goddamned nuisance and the sooner you are off this vessel the better. I have far more important things to do."

"What?" Giulio tried and succeeded in getting a sneer into his voice. "Sail a desk? What's an admiral doing in charge of a crummy sub? Too many brass hats, that's what!"

"No, not enough ships. This is the last pig boat." A little tear of self-pity formed in the admiral's eye, for he had been hitting the vodka bottle hard. "My last command. After this the beach. I should consider myself lucky even for this . . ." He swallowed and gulped and shuddered away from this topic, which obsessed him night and day. "Here is your bag. I wish you good luck on your mission, whatever it is. Here is a receipt form—sign here."

Giulio scratched his name as well as he could in the darkness, clutched the battered but exceedingly large and heavy suitcase to him, then was half-carried into the bobbing dinghy. As soon as he was aboard the line was cast off and the four sailors began rowing furiously. An officer crouched in the bow with a compass and muttered instructions in arcane nautical terms. The beans and salt fish that Giulio had wolfed so hungrily an hour earlier now fought each other for a return journey up his throat. The dinghy bobbed and splashed through the waves. Giulio groaned aloud, then almost fell overboard as they grated to a stop. Horny hands seized him in silence, slid him over the side into a foot of cold water, then grabbed up paddles again and pulled hastily away.

"Good luck, buddy," the officer whispered as he vanished back into the darkness. A wave slapped cold water over Giulio's crotch. He gasped and turned and staggered up on to a sandy beach, holding the massive suitcase to him like an old friend. Once above the water he dropped the bag and sat upon it and tried not to groan aloud. He had never felt as alone and helpless before. He didn't even know where he was. Well that could be changed quickly enough. Dragging the suitcase after him he stumbled through the sand towards a looming dark structure.

There was no sound, other than the susurration of the waves on the shore behind him. The dark structure proved to be a row of bathing shacks, unlocked, as he discovered when he rattled the door of the nearest one. Perfect for his purposes. He dropped the bag inside and pulled the door shut behind him, grinning wickedly into the darkness. Screw the instructions. Right now was when he wanted to know where he was and what happened next. A feeble flap towards personal freedom. This was why he had stolen the book of matches in defiance of all instructions and logic. He dug them out now, and the piece of paper, and fumbled to strike one in the darkness. It flared up suddenly, he squinted at the paper, at the word. It was upside down. He turned it over and read "shamrock"—then jerked his hand, burning his fingers, as memory rushed in. The match went out, he sucked his hand and almost spoke aloud the words that were dredged from his memory, hidden there by hypnotic suggestion until he read the word that had triggered their release.

YOU ARE ON THE BEACH OF MARINA PICCOLA ON THE ISLAND OF CAPRI. IT IS NOW LIGHT AND YOU WILL

WALK UP THE ROAD TO THE TOWN OF CAPRI. IN THE PIAZZETTA YOU WILL GO TO THE PHARMACY ON THE RIGHT. A MAN WITH A GRAY BEARD THERE WILL ANSWER BOCCA WHEN YOU GIVE THE PASSWORD STUZZICADENTI. EAT THIS PAPER.

He ruminated on the paper and the words. Capri, isle of joy in the Bay of Naples, or that is what they said. He had never seen it before, or Italy itself for that matter. Land of his fathers. He wondered what it was like and, for the first time, forgot to be afraid. He would find out soon enough. And the message was wrong about it being light; he felt a small triumph over this. A tiny blow struck against the system. Nor was he going to wait here until dawn. The further inland he was before he was seen, the less chance of his being suspected of landing on the beach. The logic of this was suspect but he still felt that way.

After a good deal of stumbling against invisible objects, he found stone steps that led up through a wall. The road was on the other side, with houses flanking it. All the windows were tightly shuttered against the poisonous dangers of the balmy night air and he tiptoed past them silently. The suitcase was heavy as lead and he had to keep changing hands. Only when he was around the second bend of the steep road, with no houses in sight, did he drop the thing and sit on it. He was panting and dripping with sweat and wondered how far away the town was.

Giulio was still struggling up the road when it began to get light in the east. The sky burned red as fire behind the mountains across the bay, and it was suddenly dawn. He felt vulnerable under the open sky and he hurried on. But it was a brief spurt and he had to stop, panting, and set the bag down again. Just as he did so a man came around a bend in the road carrying a great bundle of grass on his head. He looked up at Giulio with a very suspicious eye, made even more suspicious by the fact he was cross-eyed, as he passed.

"*Buon giorno,*" Giulio said, forcing a smile.

The man grunted, a deep porcine sound, and Giulio's stomach churned. Was he really in Italy, on Capri? Then, when he was well past, the man released a reluctant "*Buon gio'.*"

The first encounter was the worst. A few other peasants passed, some in silence, others with a good morning, and he began to feel a certain security. He himself looked like a peasant, Christ, his parents had been peasants, and he could talk Italian. This thing might work yet.

Staggering with fatigue he made the last climb up the narrow road to the opening of the piazzetta. Early as it was most of the shops were open. On the far side was a bold sign over a shop front that read FARMACÌA. Below the sign were only heavy steel shutters. The pharmacy was closed.

A cold chill swept through Giulio as he realized, a little too late, why he should have waited until dawn to read the note. He was too early and, he felt, obvious and suspicious. Wasn't that policeman looking at him, chewing the toothpick and wondering who he was? Fear rattled the teeth in his head and sent him stumbling into the mouth of the nearest street. It was narrow and dark and there were steps down which he half fell. Around the first corner and into a narrower alleyway. Were there footsteps behind him? A dark store-front opened before him and he stumbled through it, blinking in the darkness.

"*Sì?*" a voice rumbled, almost in his ear. A dark man with a two-day growth of beard stood there looking at him quizzically.

"Aspirin," Giulio said. "I need some aspirin."

"*Pazzo,*" the man growled, the sour odor of rough wine washing out on his breath. "Get out of here."

Giulio peered into the cavernous gloom and saw the box with a few old potatoes, the crate of tomatoes next to it. "I thought this was the pharmacy," he said. So unconvincingly that he didn't even fool himself. "What time does the pharmacy open?"

"Out!" the proprietor said loudly, and made a dismissing and insulting gesture with the fingers of his right hand. Giulio went out and retraced his steps towards the piazzetta. There was no sign of the policeman; that did not lessen his fear.

When he came back into the sunlight he saw a man with a long pole rolling up the steel shutter of the pharmacy. Giulio's heart beat rapidly as he dragged the heavy bag with him across the cobbles and towards the safety of the entrance. "*Stuzzicadenti,*" he said as the man turned towards him.

He was young and clean-shaven and had the same suspicious eye as the greengrocer. An answer was beneath him and he just jerked his thumb towards the grocery store behind him.

"Aspirin?" Giulio asked hopefully, trying to smile and not succeeding. The young man looked him up and down slowly in economic appraisal. Apparently Giulio looked as though he could at least afford an aspirin or two. The young man shouldered the pole and silently led the way into the shop.

A fat man with a gray beard was behind the marble counter opening a package. He glanced up when Giulio entered, then turned his attention back to untangling the thick string. Fear was replaced by joy in Giulio's heart. He hurried to the man, leaned close, and whispered "*Stuzzicadenti*" in his ear.

"Marco, did anyone see him come in?" the man asked, talking over the top of Giulio's head.

"Only half the town," the young man answered.

"*Stuzzicadenti?*" Giulio asked, hopefully.

"It's always that way, they send people who know nothing."

"*Stuzzicadenti . . . ,*" in an unhappy moan.

"Toothpicks?" Graybeard asked, looking at Giulio for the first time. "Oh, yes, the stupid password thing. Wood? Nose? Tooth? No. Yes! Mouth. *Bocca!*"

"You took your time about it," Giulio muttered, put out by the reception.

"Shut up and follow me. Stay well back and look as though you are not following me. When they come looking for you I want everyone to know you left my shop."

He pulled on a natty pinstripe jacket, seized up a malacca cane from the corner, then strode out of the door and across the piazzetta. Giulio started to follow and was restrained by the strong arm of the youth. "Not so close. Watch where he goes."

Only after Graybeard had disappeared in a narrow alley did he release Giulio who hurried after. Rushing while trying not to rush, panting with the weight of the suitcase. He followed at a distance and, after a number of turns, was rewarded with the sight of his quarry entering a building. He strolled slower now, stopped and looked back. No one in sight. He pushed into a dark hallway and heard the door thud shut behind him. Another door opened and he followed the man into a cheerful room where wide-open double windows displayed a breathtaking view of the Bay of Naples. Graybeard waved him to a chair near the window, flashed a sudden gold-filled smile through the jungle of his beard, then seized up a bottle of wine from the sideboard.

"Welcome to Italy, Giulio. You may call me Pepino. How was the trip? You will have some of this wine, the native wine of this island, you will love it."

"How did you know my name?"

The smile vanished for a second, then aurously reappeared. "Please. I arranged all of this. I have your passport and papers here, with your picture on them. Tickets as well. I did all this and I tell you, it was not cheap." He glanced at the suitcase and his smile broadened. "So I am happy to see that you brought payment. May I have the case?"

Giulio held it tighter to him. "I was told to hand it over only when told a certain word."

"Your CIA has seen too many old spy films! Who else but me . . ." With mercurial ease Pepino's temper changed and he was smiling again. "But of course that's not your fault. The word is . . . *merda* . . . there are so many of the stupid words to remember. This one is . . . *shamarocka!* There, got it right the first time."

With no more ceremony he pulled the suitcase to him, dropped it flat on the floor and flipped the catches. It was locked. He muttered something nasty under his breath and produced—rather quickly Giulio thought for such a fat man—a large black knife that flicked open with a very nasty sound. A few twists with this and the locks flew open, the knife vanishing as quickly as it had appeared. He threw the lid back and Giulio leaned forward to look, for he had no idea what he had been burdened with.

The suitcase was tightly packed with bundles of pantyhose. Chuckling with pleasure, Pepino broke a bundle open and waved the diaphanous limbs in the air. "I'm rich, I'm rich," he whispered to himself. "More precious than gold."

Giulio nodded an amen to that. There was a fortune in the suitcase. Years earlier when petroleum had started to run out it had not only spelled the death of the auto and allied industries, but put paid to the petrochemical factories as well. What little supplies remained were reserved for essential pharmaceutical and industrial chemicals, and little or none for the manufacture of plastics. From being the most common material, plastic had become the rarest, and nonindustrial nylon the rarest of all. Of course a black market did exist, which only helped push up the price of such nonessentials as pantyhose.

"This is for you," Pepino said, passing over a battered wallet that had been tucked between the bundles. Giulio opened it and looked at the tightly wadded banknotes. He took one out and stared at it. A squat man, robed to the ears, stared back. The printing was in a strange language, and alphabet, and read something like NOTA AUTHAIRGTHE AUIG PHUNT.

"Put them away," Pepino ordered. "For expenses and bribes when you get there." He dumped the contents of the suitcase into a high wardrobe, then locked it. From a drawer, at the bottom of that same wardrobe, he took underclothes, socks, shirts, all of them ancient, faded and patched, and stowed them in the suitcase. In place of the broken clasps he sealed it with a length of rope tied round, then handed it over to Giulio.

"Time to go," he announced. "On the north side of the piazzetta are steps leading down to Marina Grande. Descend, neither too slowly nor too quickly, and in the harbor there you will find the ferry to Naples waiting. Here is a ticket, put it in an outside pocket if you please. This envelope contains your passport and all the other papers you will need. The ship will be easy enough to find. You may board any time today and I suggest you proceed there as soon as you land.

You will only get in trouble if you stay in the city. Good luck, that's it, finish your wine, and good luck with your mission whatever it is. If you get back alive tell your CIA what a fine job I have done. They are one of my best customers."

Moved on by these encouraging words, and a firm hand in the small of his back, Giulio carried the now lightened suitcase down the seemingly endless steps to the harbor. He had a clear view of the ferry tied up at the mole and saw that they were shaking out the sails. He could not miss it! Hurrying, as fast as he could, he reached the harbor in a rush, then staggered to a walk, streaming with sweat, when he saw that people were still boarding. But he was none too early, for soon after he had dropped wearily to the deck they cast off the lines, with a good deal of shouting, and the ferry moved out into the bay. There was a brisk following wind, thankfully since his stomach did not enjoy the voyage at all, and they were soon gliding by the docks of Naples.

Empty of course, except for some fishing boats and coastal traders. The world could not convert quickly from power to sail. The ferry moved past the rusting hulk of *Ark Royal*, flight deck canted at a sharp angle where she sat on the bottom. Sunk by sabotage the rumor had it, though holed through by rust was probably more likely. In the midst of these tiny sailboats and rusting despair, the great bulk of the *St. Columba* loomed large and impressive.

She stretched on and on, sleek metal and smooth paint, like something out of a history book. At her stern flapped an orange, white and green flag, while from her funnel trickled a thin streamer of pungent brown smoke. In a crumbling world she was a monument to the might of man and, suddenly, Giulio felt very happy. He was going to board her, travel on her, see this powerful machine in action. Since he was a child of the world's declining years he had known only grounded planes, skeletal cars, silent machines. Despite the danger of his mission he could not help but look forward with anticipation.

It was all he had ever dreamed of and more. The only formality was the actual boarding of the vessel. Sharp-eyed soldiers, weapons ready, guarded the dock against unwelcome visitors, and a uniformed officer examined his papers, stamped them, removed some, and waved him on. A cursory glance through his suitcase followed, then he was aboard. It was like entering the gates of paradise.

A ruddy, smiling purser checked his name on a list and assigned him to a bunk. The man had a few words of basic Italian and a large vocabulary of gestures. Giulio made an effort not to understand the English.

"There you are, my lad, cabin number 144. *Uno, quatro, quatro,* do you have that? No kabeesh, ey? Sleep my old son, kip, *dormir* there down below, bloody *sotto*, you know. Catch on? That's grand. Nod away, that's it, cools the brain. And here's a few quid against your month's wages. *Soldi*, got that? Can't have a man going thirsty. Fine now, move off, bugger *avanti*. Just follow the sounds of revelment and you can have a few jars with your mates to celebrate your voyage to the chosen land. Next."

The roar of masculine voices and laughter grew louder and louder as Giulio progressed down the corridor, until he pushed open the swinging doors of the saloon where the noise burst over him in a cloud of tobacco smoke and shouted Italian. Red-faced men, in shirts and neckties, were serving up great tankards of some dark, foaming beverage to dark-skinned, black-haired men who drank it at a ferocious rate. There were also smaller glasses of an amber fluid that was mixed with water from a jug. As Giulio pushed through to the bar he heard appreciative comments that while it was not good wine and heady grappa, it certainly was worth drinking in its own right. Roll on the ship. Giulio passed over one of the bank notes he had been given, the same, though of a smaller denomination, as those packed into his inner pocket. The Italians were right, the drinks were different but very palatable.

So were the meals. He went through the first one in a bit of a haze, but had joyous memories of a piece of meat big enough to feed a family of ten back home in Hoboken, floury potatoes, golden plates of butter, dark bread. All a dream—that was not a dream. But all too quickly the journey passed. He gained a few pounds on the voyage, enjoyed some massive hangovers and undoubtedly did immense damage to his liver.

The Italian passengers had very little contact with the crew of the ship. This did not appear to be a matter of policy, just that this was a working ship, a freighter for the most part, and the sailors were quite busy. This and the linguistic barrier kept them apart. Though Giulio did volunteer for a working party when one was requested; who knew what technical secrets lay in the bowels of the ship! He discovered little other than that the *St. Columba* was steam-powered, peat-fired, and built in Cork. All of which he was sure the CIA already knew. In exchange for this fragment of information he spent an exhausting afternoon shoveling peat past a broken conveyor belt from the bin. It was little solace that all of the others suffered as well, and returned to their quarters complaining bitterly and comparing the blisters on their hands.

Then the voyage was over. Gentle hills and an undulating coastline appeared ahead. The *St. Columba* moved slowly between the outstretched granite arms of the two great breakwaters and into the harbor. DUN LAOGHAIRE, a large sign said on the dockside building, but there was no clue as to how it was pronounced. With little ceremony the men, carrying their few belongings, were moved off the ship and boarded the waiting double-decker buses. AN LAR, read the destination on the display boards, and all of the men chattered excitedly at the thrill of riding in a power-operated vehicle. The buses were silent too, obviously electrically powered, and moved out in a lumbering convoy for a short ride through narrow streets. There were green trees and small houses, gardens with flowers and parks with smooth, rich grass. The journey ended before a high wall and a tall, impressive-looking gate that opened to admit the fleet. The men unloaded in a large courtyard surrounded by interesting-looking buildings. Giulio tried to remember all of the details as he had been trained to do. As soon as the buses had left, with a cheery wave from the last driver, the gates swung shut again and a man mounted a platform and blew into the microphone there. His magnified breath echoed like a wind from the walls and the Italians grew silent and turned to look at him. He wore a dark suit with matching waistcoat, a gold chain draped across the full front of this, and smoked a large-bowled pipe which he pointed at them to emphasize a point. It was pointing now.

"My name is Mr. O'Leary," he said, "and I am in charge of this establishment. Some of you may speak English now and all of you will learn it if you intend to stay here. Gino here is the translator and he is going to translate now. But there are English classes every evening and you will be expected to attend. Tell them that, Gino."

O'Leary produced a lighter and proceeded to fire up his pipe while the translation was in progress. Then he nodded, whether at the translation or the tobacco was not made clear, and went on.

"You gentlemen are guest workers of Ireland. There are valuable jobs to be done here and I know you will enjoy doing them. The work is not hard, you will be fed well, will have a good deal of leisure time, will be permitted to send your salary home if you wish. Which will go to the church of your choice, which of course will be the Roman Catholic church. As we discover your qualifications and abilities you will find the best work suited to you. Some will become street sweepers, for we pride ourselves on the cleanliness of our cities, and others will have the pleasure of being dustmen and riding the great and powerful vehicles that perform this vital function of the community. There are opportunities galore for you." He tamped down the smoldering tobacco with his thumb and appeared not to hear the mutter that muttered across his audience.

"Yes, I know that you applied for skilled jobs, masons and carpenters and the like, but if my experience of past drafts is correct there isn't an honest workingman here." There was steel in his voice now and a new hardness in his eyes. "Nor a single callus on the soft hands of the lot of you. But that's all right. We know that you all are rich or know someone rich enough to enable you to afford the bribes and forgeries of papers that got you here. It'll not be held against you. You will be expected to work hard and measure up. And if you do not you will be shipped home forthwith. But live up to the terms of your contract and we will live up to ours. You will enjoy your stay on our shores. Remember, you will be permitted to send food parcels and manufactured articles to your families at home. You will prosper on the healthy diet of the land. You will drink Guinness and grow strong. You will assemble here at half-seven tomorrow morning to begin carrying bricks for the construction of the new power plant."

At this O'Leary turned away—was there a twinkle in his eye?— and left before the translation was finished so that the groan that greeted his final words followed him through a small door. His audience went, somewhat crestfallen, to their quarters.

But not Giulio. Depressed? Never! Power plant! This was the best luck ever.

It was drizzling next morning and in groups of ten, damp and cold, they stood in the courtyard. Each group next to a large pile of singularly massive-looking bricks. A squat and solid man with large red hands talked to Giulio and his companions and held out an object towards them. It had a long wooden handle that supported two boards, set edge to edge to make a V.

"This," he said, "this, my good lads, is a hod. Got that? Hod, hod. Let me hear you say it. Hod?"

"Hod," one man said, then others, "hod, hod."

"Very good. You're a bright lot and you'll learn fast. Now this is a wee bit of a hod, as anyone who knows about such things will tell you, but that is because the bricks are not the normal, weak, crumbling things that you are used to in your foreign lands."

The men listened, puzzled, and Giulio tried to appear as unknowing as the others. The mere fact that no one understood their instructor did not seem to bother him nor halt the flow of his words.

"Time was when you had to carry a great hod just heaped with bricks, but now there are but three in a load. Why, you might ask, only three? Well I'll be happy to tell you. There are but three because they're bloody heavy, that's why, seeing as how they are now the Irish Standard Brick and made of solid granite and good for the centuries. Just pick one up—if you can that is, you there, Tony my lad, smile away, but this is no bag of pasta, that's it. Touch of the old hernia there if you don't learn to lift better . . ."

"Paddy," a voice called out. "I need a pair of brawny lads to unload a lorry. Got any to spare?"

"They're a puny lot and you can have them all. Take what you will for I despair of ever making good union hod carriers out of any of them."

The newcomer stood behind them and pointed to the nearest man. "You then, Tony, come-o with me-o. Got that? And you too, Tony." He jabbed a finger at Giulio and waved him over. Giulio went through a pantomime with him, of pointing to his chest and nodding and so forth, then followed meekly. Excited.

Through a small gate and then another. Towards a great, windowless building that dominated all the others around it. From high on the wall, standing forth on hulking white insulators, great electric cables reached out to a tall pylon and beyond. This was it!

"Grand sight, isn't it, Tony? Nothing like that back in the land of pasta, is there? But work first then. Boxes off lorry-o, on to handcart. And bloody smart if you don't mind. Like this. Got it?"

It did not take long. The lorry pulled away and two men pushed off the handcart. "More lorry, got that?" their guide shouted, waving and pointing at the ground at the same time. "Take a kip and we'll be back."

The drizzle had stopped and the sun was out. Giulio's companion curled against the wall and was instantly asleep. Giulio pulled a blade of grass that was growing from a crack in the paving, chewed on it, and looked around. No one in sight, very lax, but the Irish were always this way. Their weakness, and he had been instructed how to take advantage of it. Look around. He strolled towards the high wall nearby and to the small door bearing the legend KEEP OUT—POWER PLANT PERSONNEL ONLY.

Did he dare? Why not, that was what he was here for, sooner or later he would have to make the attempt. The door was locked but he recognized the brand of lock; he had been well instructed on it. The lockpick was concealed behind his belt buckle and dropped into his fingers at a touch. Still no one in sight. Insert, lift, press . . . turn.

The door swung open. He was through in a second and it closed behind. A brightly lit passage stretched away before him; his heart beat like a hammer in his chest. Carry on, he could do nothing else. Down the corridor. Doors. All closed. Numbered. They could be anything. Then, another one. He stopped still, quavering at the sign on it.

TECHNICAL MANUALS STORE.

He had done it! The same kind of lock, twist and open, darkness beyond, a glimpse of shelves before he closed the door behind him. Grope for a light switch, there, flick it on . . .

"Do come in, Giulio," the man said. "Sit down, here across the desk from me. Cigarette? No, I forgot, you don't smoke, do you."

Numb, unbelieving, Giulio slid into the chair and tried not to gape at the smiling man on the other side of the desk. He wore a uniform of some kind, three pips on his shoulder straps, and nodded in a most friendly manner across his tented fingers. "There, that's better," he said. "I suppose you're CIA, but not career I hope. Could I have your correct name?"

Giulio finally found his voice. *"Scusi, signore, no cap—"*

"Please, Giulio, don't waste our time. You see we found this in your pocket. We do make searches, you know." He held up a blue matchbook with white lettering that read UNITED STATES NAVY.

Giulio gasped and his spine softened and he slumped even more.

"No cooperation? Oh dear, oh dear, but you are being difficult. My name is Power, Captain Power. And yours? Oh well, if I must."

The captain came around the desk and in a sudden lightning motion secured Giulio in an unbreakable grip. He even managed to have a hand free with which he pressed Giulio's fingers onto a white card on the desk; fingerprints appeared on it an instant later. Power released Giulio, took the card by the edge and looked at the prints critically, nodded, then dropped it through a slot in the desk's top.

"That should do. While we're waiting for results we'll go look at the power plant. Well don't gape like that—that's why you're here, isn't it? Ireland's pride and joy, and the envy of the world at large." He opened the door for Giulio and showed him out, and continued to talk as they strolled down the corridor. "In a world of declining resources and failed power supplies we here find ourselves quite happy on this fruitful island of ours. The crops and the herds are the best, sure we've always grown more than enough for our own needs, and a bit over. And peat, all we could ever need, we've been generating electricity with it for years, now we use it in our ships. But power, that's our secret, isn't it? The reason why you're here. And steel too, for we've enough of that. We prosper in an unhappy world and help others where we can, but we are a small nation after all. In here if you please." He eased open a massive door. "Now, I ask you— isn't that a glorious sight?"

It was indeed something. They stood on a balcony high up on the wall of an immense chamber. The sound and heat and motion at first made it hard to understand what was happening. Steam hissed and curled up from the floor where great turbines spun. A conveyor belt carried an endless stream of stone bricks from an opening in one wall, to vanish through an opening in the other. Giulio blinked, trying to make sense of it all. Captain Power explained.

"When the granite bricks drop into the steam chamber they are practically still molten, temperature in the thousands of degrees, I understand. We had lots of trouble in the beginning with them fracturing, blowing up like bombs and that sort of thing. All licked now of course. After they leave the steam, and are a bit cooler, they fall into the water and generate more steam and on and on. And the steam drives the generators and that's really about all there is to it."

"But . . . no, that cannot be." Giulio was stammering, confused. "Where do the bricks come from?"

"I thought you would never ask. If you will walk this way you will meet one of the men responsible."

The walk was shorter, and the room they entered larger than the first, and filled with odd equipment. A tall man with a shining bald head, fringed with remnants of red hair, sat on a couch reading a computer printout.

"Giulio," Power said. "I want you to meet Sean Raftery."

"A pleasure," Sean said, standing and taking Giulio's hand and giving it a hearty shake. "You're a brave man to come this far, and with a good education too, as I have been reading. Giulio," he glanced at the printout, "Giulio Balietti. Born in Hoboken, New Jersey—what an unusual name for a city—college . . . university . . . ahh, a doctorate in physics, atomic physics. And quite young too."

"Atomics," Captain Power said. "They're still looking in that direction. Well, more strength to them."

"Then . . . you know . . ." Giulio said.

"Of course. We pride ourselves on our records. You're not the first, you know. We used to try to keep them out, then we discovered it was much easier to let them in and take care of them then."

"You're going to kill me!"

"Nonsense—we're not the CIA, after all. This is a civilized country. We are going to show you Ireland's great secret, then remove—with no pain—your memory of today. You have worked so hard to get this far we thought it only fair to let you find what you are seeking after. Also, we have discovered that after the memory-removal process the agent is much more relaxed having once actually known what he wanted to know. Somewhere in the subconscious there is a feeling of success and this is most important. Sean, if you please."

"Of course. Our secret, Giulio, is the tapping of an immense strength in the Irish personality and character that has always existed, has always been seen, but never channeled in the right direction. The poets and the authors have taken from this mighty stream and profited thereby. Someone once said about an Irish author, with cruel intent but nevertheless it holds a germ of truth, that anyone could write that way if they abandoned their mind to it. Perhaps. But only the Irish can do it without scarcely trying."

Giulio watched, eyes widening, as Captain Power wheeled a black suit, like a parody of a medieval suit of armor, before Sean Raftery. It was ugly as an Iron Maiden but seemed to raise no fears in Sean who voluntarily pushed his arms into the extensions of the thing. He even smiled as it was locked around his body.

"The flow of wit and Irish humor is famous, our actors known worldwide, their abilities to express themselves famous." But his powers of expression seemed to be lagging. He stumbled over words and began to repeat himself. "Please excuse . . . excuse if you will. You see this is a sensory deprivation suit. I cannot feel anything with my body or hands, I cannot use them . . . But, praise be to God, I can still talk . . ."

Sean's eyes widened and his words were muffled into silence as Captain Power slipped a soft but strong gag over his mouth. The captain continued.

"And there you have it. Complete sensory deprivation so the subject cannot gesticulate or point his fingers or walk about. Communication is damaged by that. Communication and the flow of language damned up completely by the gag. So what do we have, you ask? We have, I answer, a mighty torrent of expression seeking a way out. We have a genius for communication without an outlet. But— wait, an outlet is still left. The brain! With no other way of expressing the pressure of thoughts churning in the mighty Irish brain, the mighty Irish brain expresses itself by direct contact with the outside world. That glass on the table—would you please, Sean?"

The glass lifted suddenly into the air, swooped about like a bird and landed again on the table with ease.

"Direct manipulation of matter by the mind. But much graver than conjurer's tricks like this one. Sean, and the others on his team, reach deep into the molten heart of the earth with their minds, miles deep, and open a hole to the surface. The magma, liquid rock, is forced through this hole, a solid rod of lava being ejected into the tank out there. Or rather it would be a solid rod if the opening was not opened and closed regularly to cut the rod into the bricks you have already seen. At other times, delving deeper, they tap the molten iron core of our planet and bring the purest iron into our rolling mills. It is a wonder indeed."

He smiled at Giulio and signaled to Sean. "Now, lightly, touch his memories and excise this day."

Giulio jumped to his feet, tried to run, to flee, but blackness fell.

"*Chi è lei?*" Giulio said to the officer behind the desk, who was industriously studying a computer printout.

"No games, please, this is a busy office," Captain Power told him. "We have your complete record here. You are Dr. Giulio Balietti, an atomic physicist. You were sent here by the CIA to unearth our technical secrets. This is espionage and you could be shot for it . . . Here, sit down, you're so pale. A glass of water? No? That's better. But we are a kindly people and we are giving you a choice. You may return home now and tell the CIA to leave us alone. Or you may remain here as long as you refrain from further espionage. There is an opening for a lecturer in atomic physics at Trinity College. Just part-time I'm afraid, a few hours a week. Until there is a better position you will have to do other work as well. We have found that academics enjoy peat cutting. Healthy, outdoor occupation, very relaxing when you are used to it. A lot of our older people like to have peat fires of handcut turf and it is not too much of an effort to indulge them. So what do you say?"

What did he say? A memory of Hoboken, the endless gray poverty, the plankton and soy food, the drab existence. Stay, why not, he wasn't being asked to give his word. He could still keep his eyes open, look for the Irish secret, bring it back to the U.S. if he could. His duty was to stay.

"Trinity and the peat bog," he said, firmly.

"Good man. Here, this way, I want you to meet Herr Professor Doktor Schmidt. A physicist also . . ."

"*Nein*, you forget, my captain. It is Ivan who is the *Physiker*. I am simple chemist. Come—Giulio is your name?—we have a good chat and I show you how to use the peat shovel. A most satisfactory tool."

They left, arm in arm, out into the falling rain.

The Day After the End of the World

It wasn't a very big piece of the world, but it was all that was left. Around it in space floated other fragments of the destroyed planet, just chunks of rock and dirt and bits of debris. But the large piece had the best part of a farmhouse on it, with a tree in front, and a patch of grass with a frozen sheep standing on it. The sheep was staring in a very fixed manner. That was all there was. The sheer edge dropped away on all sides, just bare dirt with bits of roots sticking out of it. The man sat on the edge of the world, his legs dangling, and dropped a twig over. It fell swiftly from sight. His name was Frank and the girl, in the swing hanging from the branch of the tree, was named Gwenn.

"It's not like I tried to force you or anything," Frank said, looking very glum. "You know, or be beastly. I was just upset, you should understand that, what with the end of the world and everything. Feeling very lonely. I thought maybe, you know, a little kiss would help me forget. Help us both forget."

"Yes, Frank," Gwenn said and pushed with her foot so she swung a bit.

"So you really had no cause to slap me. We are shipmates after all."

"I said that I was sorry I hit you, Frank. I'm a little upset too, you should understand that. It's not every day that this sort of thing happens."

"No, not every day."

"You shouldn't be angry at me. Can you give me a push?"

"It's not that I'm angry," he said, standing and brushing the bits of frozen grass from the leg of his uniform. "Hurt maybe, depressed really. Struck by the woman I love." He gave the swing an indifferent shove.

"Please don't start that talk again, Frank. It's all over. You just say that because you want to do you-know-what with me. And you know I love someone else."

"Gwenn darling, face facts. You're not going to see Robert again, ever . . ."

"You can't be sure."

"Believe me, I'm sure. The whole world's blown up, bang, just like that, without warning, and everyone with it. We were in the spaceship on the other side of the moon or we would have blown up too.

But Robert's gone with it. He was in Minneapolis and Minneapolis is gone."

"We don't know."

"We know. I don't think Minneapolis had any special dispensation. All we found with the search radar is this chunk of the world. This is the biggest piece that there is."

Gwenn frowned at the thought and put out her leg so the swing topped. "There might be a piece of Minneapolis too . . ."

"And if Robert is on it he is frozen just like that sheep."

"You're so cruel—you just want to hurt me!"

"No, please." He took her by the shoulders carefully, standing behind her. "I want anything but that. It's just that you must face up to the truth. There's just you and me now. And I love you. I mean that, sincerely."

While he spoke his hands gently caressed her shoulders and moved down her arms, out onto the sweet swell of her breasts. But Gwenn shrugged out of his embrace and jumped to her feet, walking quickly away from him. She looked down at the immobile sheep.

"I wonder if he felt anything?" she asked.

"Who—Robert or the sheep?"

"Oh, you *are* cruel!"

She stamped her foot in anger—then raised her hand as he moved towards her. Frank growled something indecipherable under his breath and dropped into the swing.

"Let's be realistic," he said. "Let's forget everything that happened on the ship. Forget I made a pass at you, forget that I tried to get you into the sack. Forget it. Let's start fresh. Face the situation that we're in. The two of us alone. I'm Adam and you're Eve . . ."

"Gwenn."

"I *know* your name is Gwenn. I mean we're like Adam and Eve and it is up to us to keep the human race going. Do you understand?"

"Yes. You're still trying to seduce me."

"God damn it, it doesn't matter what you think! It's our duty. We may have been spared by divine providence . . ."

"You told me that you were an atheist."

"Well you said that you go to church. I'm looking at it from your point of view."

"And I'm looking at it from yours. You're oversexed."

"Be happy that I am. We must be fruitful. We owe it to the human race."

Gwenn patted the sheep's head, deep in thought. "I don't know," she finally said. "It might be best to end it all right here. We blew up the world, didn't we? That's what you might call pollution on a really impressive scale."

"You can't mean that. We don't know what happened. It could have been an accident . . ."

"Some accident."

"Well, you know . . ." Frank jumped from the swing and came towards her. "Forget the human race then," he pleaded. "Think of you and me. The two of us. The warmth of contact, the end of loneliness, the thrill of the kiss, touch of flesh . . ."

"If you come any closer I'll scream!"

"Scream away!" Frank shouted, angry and bitter, grabbing her, pulling her to him. "Who's going to hear? I love you . . . want you . . . need you . . ."

She pushed at him desperately, turning her face back and forth away from his but he was far stronger. He kissed her neck, her cheek—and she stopped struggling.

"Are you some kind of rapist?" she asked in a very low voice, looking him straight in the eyes. For a moment longer he held her. Then dropped his hands and stepped away.

"No. I'm not a rapist. Just a nice middle-class boy with a strong sex drive and plenty of guilt."

"That's better."

"It is not better—it's a lot worse! I mean what am I doing, the last man alive on Earth, feeling guilt? My bourgeois world is gone but I still carry it around with me. What do you think would happen to you if I were a real male chauvinist pig and just grabbed you and worked my will upon you?"

"Don't talk dirty."

"I'm not talking dirty—I'm just trying to knock some sense through your dumb blond head. It's you and I, get it? Just the two of us. We've got this chunk of the world and I've anchored our spaceship under it to give us gravity and air and the atomic pile will keep it this way for a thousand years. The food synthesizer will make all the food we need so we are all set, in a manner of speaking."

"All set for what?"

"That's what I'm asking you. Are we going to grow old gracefully, and separately, just good chums, you knitting and me watching old TV tapes? Do you want that?"

"I didn't think much of that dumb-blond remark."

"Don't change the subject. Is that the way you want it?"

"I haven't thought about . . ."

"Well think. We're here. Alone. For the rest of our lives."

"It does bear thinking about." She cocked her head to the side and looked at him, as though for the first time. "You can kiss me if you like," she said.

"That's more like it!"

"But no funny business. Just that. In the nature of an experiment you might say."

Now invited, Frank approached almost shyly. Gwenn had her eyes closed and she shivered when he put his arms around her. He drew her close, held her to him, lowered his lips and kissed her closed eyes. She trembled again but did not move away. Nor did she protest when his lips found her mouth, kissing long and lovingly. When he dropped his arms and stepped back she slowly opened her eyes; he smiled at her tenderly.

"Robert kissed better," she said.

In sudden rage Frank kicked the sheep—then hopped around holding his foot and moaning in pain for the solidly frozen sheep was hard as rock.

"And I suppose he was good in bed too," he said bitterly.

"He was marvelous," Gwenn admitted. "Just wonderful. That's why I find it so hard to even look at another man. And I'm carrying his baby and that makes it even more difficult."

"You are what . . . ?"

"Pregnant. These things happen, you know. Robert doesn't know yet . . ."

"Nor will he ever."

"Don't be horrid."

"Sorry. This is wonderful, greatest news ever. We've just increased the gene pool of the human race by fifty percent. Robert's son can marry our daughter, or vice versa."

"That's incest!"

"It wasn't incest in the Bible, was it? Not when you are starting the world, that's the rule. It's only incest much later on."

Gwenn walked over and sat in the swing again, thinking deeply. Then she sighed.

"It just won't work," she said. "It goes against everything. First you want us to make love without being married, and that's a sin . . ."

"You did it with Robert!"

"Yes, but we planned to get married someday. But now we can't. Nor can you and I be married because there is no one to marry us. And you want to have children and have them commit incest—it's just too horrible. That's no way to start a world."

"Do you have any better ideas?"

"No, not really. But I don't like yours."

Frank dropped heavily to the ground and shook his head with astonishment.

"I just can't believe this is happening," he said, mostly to himself. "The last man alive and the last woman alive and we're arguing theology." He sprang to his feet in sudden anger.

"No! I'm not going to argue anymore, not discuss it." He tore at his shirt, struggling to take it off. "It all begins again, right here, now. The world starts afresh. I will not be lumbered by a moral code that is just as disintegrated as the planet that bore it. I am all. The language I speak will be the language of all the generations to come. If I say 'ugggh' for 'water,' everyone, forever, will say 'ugggh' and never question it. My power is godlike!"

"You're crazy!" She drew away as he advanced.

"I am if I want to be. I am all. I shall ravish you and beat you and you will love me for it. If you don't I'll beat you some more. Now why don't you scream?" He threw his shirt to the ground and advanced on her. "I'm the only one who will hear the scream and I don't care about it."

He undid his fly and she uttered a muffled scream. He only laughed.

"Make the choice!" he shouted. "Enjoy it or hate it for it makes no difference to me. I am godhead, sperm-bearer, almighty. From my loins a new race will spring . . ."

He stopped suddenly as they both swayed.

"Did you feel that?" Frank asked. Gwenn nodded. "The ground, it moved as though something bumped into us."

"Another ship!" he said quickly closing his fly. He grabbed up his shirt and hurried to put it on. Gwenn pushed her hair with her hand and wished that she had a mirror with her.

"There's someone coming," Frank said, pointing. "There." They drew together unconsciously at the scratching from below their world. There was the sound of panting breath and a man climbed painfully up over the edge. He wore a one-piece boiler suit with only his head and hands exposed.

They were green.

"He's . . . green," Gwenn said. Frank did not have a ready answer. The man climbed to his feet and brushed dirt from his hands and bowed slightly in their direction.

"I hope I'm not intruding," he said.

"No, that's fine," Gwenn said. "Do come in."

"Why are you green?" Frank asked.

"I might very well ask why you are pink."

"No jokes," Frank shouted, making a fist. "Or else."

"I'm very sorry," the man said, raising his green hands and taking a step backwards. "I do beg your pardon. All of this is very upsetting, as it must be to you. I am green because I am not human. I am from another world."

"A little green man!" Gwenn gasped.

"I'm not that little," the man pouted.

"I'm Frank and this is Gwenn."

"Pleased to meet you, I'm sure. You would find my name hard to pronounce so I suggest that you call me Robert."

"Not Robert!" Gwenn wailed. "He's dead."

"I do beg your pardon. Anything then. Would 'Horace' suit?"

"Horace, just what are you doing here?" Frank asked.

"Well, now that's a little complicated. If I might begin at the beginning . . ."

"How is it you speak English so well?" Gwenn said.

"That comes later too, if you will bear with me." He strolled back and forth, marking his points on his fingers. "Firstly, I come from a distant planet around a sun a good number of parsecs from here. We're doing a survey and I was assigned this section of the galaxy. When I first saw your world I was most impressed. Green, as you can well imagine, is a favorite color of ours. I set the recorders rolling and made as complete a record as I could in a limited time. That would be a bit over two hundred of your years."

"You don't look that old," Gwenn said.

"Different life spans, you know. I won't tempt your credibility by giving my real age."

"I'm twenty-two," she said.

"How very nice. Now, if I might continue. I recorded everything as I have been trained to do, learned a few of your languages—I do pride myself on a certain linguistic ability—and bit by bit I came to a singularly horrifying realization. The human race is—*was* I should say a rather nasty piece of work."

"You're not much of a charmer yourself either, Greeny," Frank called out. Horace chose to ignore the outburst.

"By that I mean to say yours is a most successful race, strong, intelligent, fertile, most successful indeed. It was the way that you obtained that success that was so frightening. You are killers."

"Survival," Frank said firmly. "We had no other choice. Eat or be eaten, kill or be killed. Survival of the fittest."

"I'll not argue with that. There is of course only one way for any race to survive and I appreciate the point. It's what a race does after it has taken over a world that interests me. Ours became the dominant race on our planet many aeons ago. Since then we have preserved the other species, the rule of peace and law has prevailed. Whilst your people, while wiping out the other species, were still not satisfied and continued to kill one another as well. I found it most depressing."

"No one asked your opinion," Frank said.

"Of course. But I still know what I observed and it not only depressed me, but made me worried as well. My planet is not that distant, astronomically speaking, and it was within reason that you might find us one day. And if you did you would probably try to kill us as well."

"I don't think there is much chance of that now," Gwenn said, dropping into the swing and looking unhappy once again.

"Yes, it may be a theoretical point now, but it must be considered nevertheless. So there was I, an intelligent and peaceful individual, a vegetarian who would never consider harming as much as a fly, there was I worrying about the possible destruction of my world. It was a moral dilemma as you can see."

"No I can't," Frank said, shaking his head. Then he snapped his head up. "Say—did you have anything to do with what happened to the world?"

"I'll get to that in a moment."

"A simple yes or no now will do."

"Nothing is ever that simple. Please hear me out. It was most dramatic you see, for there I was firmly mounted on the horns of this dilemma. And no one to help me decide. The voyage home is quite a long one and by the time I would have made it and consulted with my superiors and they had made their minds up, well you people might very well have made your own starships and have been on the way to visit us. No, I had to make my mind up right there and then. If I did nothing you would build your ships and come and destroy us. There I was, a creature of peace, thinking the unthinkable."

"You *did* blow up the world!" Frank said, striding forward.

"Please! No violence!" Horace said, raising his hands and shying away. "I can't stand violence." Frank stopped, wanting to hear the rest, yet his fists were still clenched. "Thank you, Frank. As I was saying I was thinking the unthinkable. I could not resort to violence to make peace—or could I? If I did nothing my people would be destroyed. So it came down to a choice between which race was to survive. Yours or mine. So of course when it was phrased that way the answer was clear. Mine. Since we are far older and more intelligent, generally more interesting and attractive than you are. And peaceful."

"So you blew up our world," Frank said in a low voice.

"That wasn't very peaceful," Gwenn said.

"No I suppose that it wasn't. But it was just an isolated case, really. After a great many centuries of peace in the past, and of course many more to come in the future."

"Why are you here?" Frank asked. "Why are you telling us this?"

"Why—to apologize of course. I'm very sorry it had to work out like this."

"Not half as sorry as we are, you bright green son of a bitch."

"Well if I thought you weren't going to be gentlemanly about it I wouldn't have come."

Frank lunged forward, but Gwenn came between them stopping him.

"Frank, please," she begged. "I can't bear the thought of any more violence. I shall scream. And you did this all by yourself, Mr. Horace?"

"Horace, a forename, if you please. Yes I did. I take all of the responsibility."

"What about the others aboard your ship?" she asked.

"I am alone. Very automated you know. It took me a while to work out the formula, I don't think there has ever been a planet-buster bomb before, but I did it in the end. It wasn't easy, but I did it. For the sake of peace."

"That has a familiar ring to it," Frank said.

"I am quoting one of your generals in a war a few years ago. 'I killed them in order to save them.' But I'm not that hypocritical. I killed your planet in order to save mine. Just playing by your rules, you see."

"I see," Frank said, very calmly. "But you said you were alone. How about the other green man climbing over the ledge, there behind you?"

"Impossible, I assure you."

When he turned to look, Frank stepped forward and struck him a mighty blow on the jaw. The alien folded nicely and Frank sat on him and choked him until the body was still. Gwenn looked on and nodded approvingly.

"I'll take the feet," Frank said.

Without another word they carried the body to the edge of the cliff and slung it over, watching as it spiraled out among the rest of the space debris.

"We have to find his ship," Frank said.

"No, kiss me first. Hard."

"Yum," Frank said long moments later when he emerged from the embrace breathless and happy. "That was pretty good. Might I ask what brought it on?"

"I want to get used to your kisses, your embraces. We will have to raise a large family if we intend to repopulate the entire world."

"I couldn't agree more. Could I also ask you what made you change your mind?"

"Him, that creature. He can't get away with it."

"You're damn right! Revenge! Raise the family, teach them to fly, build bombs, go out and find those alien bastards and blow them out of space. Prove that he was right after all. We'll get our revenge."

"I certainly hope so. He can't kill my Robert and get away with it."

"Robert! Is that why you're doing this? What about everyone else? The billions, the rest of the world?"

"I didn't know anyone else in Minneapolis."

"If Horace had known about Robert I'll bet you he would have thought twice about blowing up the world."

"Well, he didn't and that was his mistake. Shall we go now?"

"Do you want to bring the sheep?"

Gwenn looked at it and frowned in thought. "No," she finally said. "It looks so nice there. And it will give us something to come home to."

"Right. Out for revenge. Make plans. Build bombs, raise children for revenge. Destroy."

"It doesn't sound so nice when you say it that way."

Frank rubbed his jaw. "Now that you mention it, it doesn't. But we really have no choice."

"Don't we? Just because that horrible little green man blew up a whole world, it doesn't mean that we have to act the same way."

"Of course it doesn't. But there is justice! An eye for an eye, you know the sort of thing."

"I do. I am well read in the Old Testament. But just because this was done and we learned to do it, that doesn't mean that it's right, does it?"

"I find your syntax difficult but your thought simple. What are you trying to say is that our world is gone. We can't restore it by blowing up another world. If the aliens are as peaceful as Horace said, then it would be a crime to destroy them as well. After all—*they* didn't blow up the world."

"It makes you pause to think."

"It sure does—and I'm sorry that I did. There was something nice and clear-cut about blowing up their planet because they blew up ours."

"I know. But still, it's a bad habit to get into."

"You're right. Start blowing up planets and you never know where it will end. So we have a chance *not* to go on with the old eye-for-eye tooth-for-tooth business. If we build our own world, just you and I and our kids, we'll be building on something other than vengeance for a change. That's a big challenge."

Gwenn dropped heavily into the swing. "I get a little frightened when you talk like that," she said. "It's a big enough responsibility starting a whole world, but starting a whole moral system is even more important. No killing, no violence . . ."

"Peace and love on Earth to all men. The sort of thing the Church was saying while they were blessing the troops. Only this time we would mean it. Turn the other cheek in a really big way. Forget the fact that they blew up our world. Prove that Horace was wrong. Then, when we meet them someday, they would have to apologize for him."

"We apologize for him right now," the green man said, climbing up over the edge of the world.

Gwenn screamed and fell back. "Horace—you're not dead!" she gasped.

The green man shook his head. "Sorry," he said, "but the individual you knew as Horace is dead. And after what I have heard just now I tend to agree that his death was richly deserved. He destroyed a world and was punished for it."

"Horace said that he was alone," Frank said; his fists were clenched again.

"He lied. There were two of us and he volunteered to meet with you two, the only survivors and explain what had happened. I will bring the recording back to our planet. There will be great mourning at the destruction of your world."

"Thanks," Frank said, in a very unthankful voice. "It really makes me feel better. And you helped him blow up the world?"

The green man thought for a moment, then nodded reluctantly.

" 'Help' is too strong a word. In the beginning I disagreed with his analysis of the situation. In the end I reluctantly agreed . . ."

"You helped. So now you go home and tell everyone what happened, and tell them that the survivors are building a new world and maybe you had better think of blowing us up too in case our descendants aren't as generous and understanding as we are. They might want to come and blow you up as a precautionary measure."

"No, really, I wouldn't advise a course of action like that . . ."

"But there is a possibility that it might be done in any case, despite your advice?"

"I hope not. But there is of course always the possibility . . ."

"Another green son of a bitch," Gwenn said, drawing a small pistol from her pocket and shooting the alien.

"That about sums it up," Frank said, sighing, looking at the crumpled body. "I suppose now we'll have to find their ship and kill any more of them that might be there."

"And then take the ship and go blow their planet up," Gwenn added.

"No other choice. As Horace said, we have a reputation for this sort of thing. Best to live up to it."

"I wouldn't be comfortable if we didn't," Gwenn said. "I would worry about our children and their children, you know. Best to get it over with."

"You're right of course. And after we blow them up *then* we'll teach the kids about turning the other cheek and that kind of thing. It will be all right then."

"Shall we go now?"

"I guess we had better," Gwenn said, looking around at the last little bit of the world. "It may be a long trip so the earlier we start the better. Do we want to bring the sheep?"

"No. I'll turn the air off. It will keep nicely. It looks so peaceful here. And it will give us something to come home to."

The Man from P.I.G.

1

"This is the end of our troubles, Governor, it sure is!" the farmer said. The rustic next to him nodded agreement and was moved enough by the thought to lift the hat from his head, shout "Yipppee" once, then clamp it back on.

"Now, I can't positively promise anything," Governor Haydin said; but there was more than a hint of eagerness in his words, and he twirled his moustache with extraordinary exuberance. "Don't know any more about this than you do. We radioed for help, and the Patrol said they'd do something . . ."

"And now a starcruiser is in orbit up there and her tender is on the way down," the farmer broke in, finishing the Governor's sentence. "Sounds good enough for me. Help is on the way!"

The heavens boomed an answer to his words, and a spike of brilliant flame burned through the low-lying clouds above the field as the stubby form of the tender came into view. The crowd along the edge—almost the entire population of Trowbri City—burst into a ragged cheer. They restrained themselves as the ship rode its fiery exhaust down to the muddy field, settling in a cloud of stream; but as soon as the jets flicked off, they surged forward to surround it.

"What's in there, Governor," someone asked, "a company of space commandos or suchlike?"

"The message didn't say—just asked for a landing clearance."

There was a hushed silence as the gangway ground out of its slot below the port and the end clattered down into the mud. The outer hatch swung open with the shrill whine of an electric motor, and a man stepped into the opening and looked down at the crowd.

"Hi," he said. Then he turned and waved inside. "C'mon out, you-all," he shouted, and he put his fingers to his lips and whistled shrilly.

His words evoked a chorus of high-pitched cries and squeals from inside the tender. Then out of the port and down the gangway swept a thundering wave of animals. Their backs—pink, black-and-white, and gray—bobbed up and down, and their hooves beat out a rumble of sound on the perforated metal.

"Pigs!" the Governor shouted, his angry voice rising over the chorus of porcine squeals. "Is there nothing but pigs aboard this ship?"

"There's me, sir," the man said, stopping in front of the Governor. "Wurber's my name, Bron Wurber, and these here are my animals. I'm mighty glad to meet you."

Governor Haydin's eyes burned a track up from the ground, slowly consuming every inch of the tall man who stood before him—taking in the high rubber boots; the coarse material of the crumpled trousers; the heavy, stained folds of the once-red jacket; the wide, smiling face and clear blue eyes of the pig farmer. The Governor winced when he saw the bits of straw in the man's hair. He completely ignored Wurber's outstretched hand.

"What are you doing here?" Haydin demanded.

"Come to homestead. Figure to open me a pig ranch. It'll be the only pig ranch for more'n fifty light-years in any direction—and not meanin' to boast, that's sayin' a lot." He wiped his right hand on his jacket, then slowly extended it again. "Name's Wurber; most folk call me Bron because that's my first name. I'm afraid I didn't catch yours?"

"Haydin," the Governor said, reluctantly extending his hand. "I'm the Governor here." He looked down abstractedly at the rounded, squealing forms that milled about them in a churning circle.

"Why, I'm that pleased to meet you, Governor. It's sure a big job you got here," Bron said, happily pumping the other's hand up and down.

The rest of the spectators were already leaving; and when one of the pigs—a great, rounded sow—came too close to them, a man turned and lashed out an ironshod boot. Her shrill screams sliced the air like a buzzsaw run wild as she fled.

"Here, none of that," Bron shouted over the backs of his charges. The angry man just shook his fist backward and went away with the rest of the crowd.

"Clear the area," an amplified voice bellowed from the tender. "Blastoff in one minute. Repeat, sixty seconds to blastoff."

Bron whistled again and pointed to a grove of trees at the edge of the field. The pigs squealed in answer and began moving in that direction. The trucks and cars were pulling out, and when the churning herd—with Bron and the Governor at its center—reached the edge of the field, only the Governor's car was left. Bron started to say something, but his words were drowned out by the tender's rockets and the deafening squealing and grunting of fright that followed it. When it died away, he spoke again.

"If you're drivin' into the city, sir, I wonder if you'd let me drive along with you. I have to file my land claims and all that kind of paperwork."

"You wouldn't want to do that," the Governor said, groping around for an excuse to get rid of the rustic clod. "This herd is valuable property; you wouldn't want to leave all these pigs here alone."

"Do you mean there're criminals and *thieves* in your town?"

"I didn't say that," Haydin snapped. "The people here are as decent and law-abiding as any you can find. It's just that, well, we're a little short of meat animals and the sight of all that fresh pork on the hoof . . ."

"Why, that notion is plumb criminal, Governor. This is the finest breedin' stock that money can buy, and none of them are for slaughterin'. Do you realize that every critter here will eventually be the ancestor of entire herds of—"

"Just spare me the lecture on animal husbandry. I'm needed in the city."

"Can't keep the good folks waitin'," Bron said with a wide and simple smile. "I'll drive in with you and make my own way back. I'm sure these swine will be safe enough here. They can root around in this patch of woods and take care of themselves for a bit."

"Well it's your funeral—or maybe theirs," Haydin mumbled, getting into the electric car and slamming the door behind him. He looked up with a sudden thought as Bron climbed in the other side. "Say—where's your luggage? Did you forget it in the tender?"

"Now, that's shore nice of you to worry about me like that." Bron pointed out at the herd, which had separated a bit now that the swine were rooting happily in the forest humus. A large boar had two long cases strapped to his back, and a smaller pig nearby had a battered suitcase tied on at a precarious angle.

"People don't appreciate how all-around valuable pigs are. On Earth they been beasts of burden for umpteen thousands of years, yessir. Why there's nothing as all-around as a pig. The old Egyptians used them for plantin' seeds. You know, their bitty little sharp hooves just trod those seeds down to the right depth in the soft soil."

Governor Haydin jammed the rheostat full on and drove numbly into town with a bucolic discourse on swinology echoing about his head.

2

"Is that your municipal buildin'?" Bron asked. "It shore is pretty."

The Governor braked the electric car to a sliding stop in front of the structure, and the dust from the unpaved street rose in a swirling cloud around them. He frowned suspiciously at Bron.

"You're in no position to make fun," he snapped. "It so happens that this was one of the first buildings we put up, and it serves its function even if it is . . . well . . . getting old."

It was more than just old, he realized, really looking at it for the first time in years. It was absolutely hairy. The outer walls were made of panels of compressed, shredded wood. These had been plastic-dipped for strength, then cured. But the curing hadn't always taken in the old days. The surface plastic had peeled away, and brown wood shavings were curling out from the surface.

"I ain't making fun of yore buildin'," Bron said, climbing out of the car. "I seen a lot worse on other frontier planets—fallin' down and leanin', that kind of thing. You folks put up a good strong buildin' here. Lasted a lot of years and it's gonna last a lot more." He patted the wall, in a friendly manner, then looked at the palm of his hand. "Though it could sure do with a bit of a shave or a haircut."

Governor Haydin stamped into the entrance, growling to himself, and Bron followed, smiling with simple contentment. The hallway cut through the entire building—he could see the rear entrance at the far end—and doors opened off it on both sides. The Governor pushed through a door marked NO ENTRANCE, and Bron followed close behind him.

"Not in here, you fool," Governor Haydin complained loudly. "This is my private office. The next door, that's the one you want."

"Now, I'm right sorry about that," Bron said, backing out under the firm pressure of the hand on his chest. The room was a sparsely furnished office with living quarters visible through the open door on the far wall. The only thing of real interest was the girl who was slumped in the armchair. She had coppery red hair, was slim, and appeared to be young. He could tell nothing more about her because she had her face buried in a handkerchief and seemed to be crying. The door closed in his face.

The next entrance led him into a larger office divided across the middle by a waist-high counter. He rested his weight on the unpainted wood and read the doodled inscriptions with some interest until a door opened on the other side and a girl entered. She was young and slim and had coppery red hair and even redder eyes. She was undoubtedly the girl he had seen in the Governor's office.

"I'm real sorry to see you cryin', Miss," he said. "Is there anything I can do to help?"

"I am *not* crying," she said firmly, then sniffed. "It's just . . . an allergy, that's all it is."

"You should have a doc give you some shots . . ."

"If you will kindly state your business, I'm rather busy today."

"Now, I don't want to bother you none, what with the allergy and being busy. If there is anyone else I can see?"

"No one. I—and those banks of computers—are the entire governmental staff. What is it you want?"

"I want to file a homestead claim, and my name is Bron Wurber."

She took his extended hand briefly, then dropped it as though it were red hot and grabbed up a stack of papers.

"I'm Lea Davies. Fill out all these forms and do not leave any blanks. If you have any questions, ask me before you proceed. You can write, can't you?" she asked, noting his grim frown of concentration as he examined the papers.

"I write a very fair hand, ma'am, so don't you worry none." He took a well-chewed pencil stump from his shirt pocket, added a few more indentations, then went to work.

When he had finished she checked the papers, made some corrections, then handed him a sheaf of maps. "These show all the nearer sites that are open for homesteading; they're marked in red. The land that will suit you best depends, of course, on the kind of crops you intend to raise."

"Pigs," he said, smiling enthusiastically, though there was no smile in return. "I'll just wander around and look at these parcels, then come back and tell you when I find the right one. My thanks, Miss Davies."

Bron folded the papers into a thick wad, which he stuffed into his hip pocket as he left. In order to reach his herd, waiting near the spaceport, he had to walk back through the center of Trowbri City, which was a city in name only. Clouds of dust spurted up as he stumped along its single street, clumsy in his heavy boots. All of the buildings had a temporary-permanent look. They had been built quickly but never replaced, since more new structures had been in constant demand for the growing town. Prefabricated buildings and pressurized fabric huts were interspersed with wood-frame structures and rammed-earth buildings. There were a lot of these—just clayey soil dumped between wooden forms and pounded down hard. When the forms were removed, the walls were painted with plastic so that they would not dissolve in the rain. In spite of this, many of them had a squat, rounded look as they sank slowly back into the ground from whence they had sprung. Bron passed small stores and a garage. The factories were on the outskirts of the town, and beyond them the farms. A barbershop, advertised by the universal symbol of a red-and-white-striped pole, was ahead, and a small group of men were leaning against its wall to hold it up.

"Hey, pig-boy," one of them said loudly as he passed, "I'll trade you a hot bath for a couple of pork chops." The rest of the loafers laughed loudly at what they apparently considered wit.

Bron stopped and turned. "My," he said, "this town must shore be boomin' if it can afford to support so many young fellers who don't have jobs."

There were angry mumbles at this, and their self-appointed spokesman stepped forward and shouted, "You think you're smart or something?"

Bron didn't answer. He just smiled coldly and smacked his closed fist into the palm of his hand. It made a loud, splatting sound, and it was obviously a large and hard fist. The men leaned back against the wall and began to talk among themselves, ignoring him.

"He's a troublemaker, boys, and you ought to teach him a lesson," a voice called from inside the barbershop. Bron stepped up and looked through the open door. The man who had kicked one of his pigs at the spaceport was sitting in the chair with the robot barber buzzing happily behind him.

"Now, you shouldn't say that, friend, seein' as how you don't know anythin' really about me."

"No, and I don't intend to find out," the man said angrily. "You can just take your pigs and—"

Bron, still smiling, leaned over and pressed the HOT TOWEL button, and a steaming towel muffled the rest of the man's words. The robot snipped off a strip of toweling before its emergency light flashed on and it jerked to a stop, humming loudly. Bron left, and no one barred his way.

"Not a very friendly town," he said to himself. "But why shouldn't it be?" A sign said EAT, and he turned into a small cafe.

"All out of steak," the counterman said. "Coffee, just coffee is what I want," Bron told him, sitting down on one of the stools. "Nice town you got here," he said when the coffee arrived.

The man mumbled something inaudible and took Bron's money. Bron tried again.

"I mean you got real good farmin' land here, and plenty of minerals and mines. The Space Settlement Commission is staking me to my homestead. Must have staked everyone else here. It's a nice planet."

"Mister," the counterman said, "I don't talk to you, so you don't talk to me. Okay?" He turned away without waiting for an answer and began polishing the dials on the automatic chef.

"Friendly," Bron said as he walked back down the road. "They have everything here they could possibly need—yet no one seems very happy about it. And that girl *was* crying. What is wrong with this planet?" Hands in pockets, whistling lightly through his teeth, he strolled along, looking about him as he went. It was not too far to the spaceport, which was situated a little beyond the town—just a cleared area and a control tower.

As he came near the grove where he had left his animals, he heard a shrill, angry squealing. He quickened his pace, then broke into a ground-consuming run as other squeals joined the first. Some of the pigs were still rooting unconcernedly, but most of them were gathered about a tall tree that was entwined with creepers and studded with short branches. A boar reared his head out of the milling herd and slashed at the tree, peeling away a yard-long strip of bark. From high in the tree a hoarse voice called for help.

Bron whistled instructions, pulled on tails, and pushed on fat flanks and finally got the pigs moving about again. As soon as they began rooting and stripping the berries from the bushes, he called up into the tree.

"Whoever's there can come down now. It's safe." The tree shook and a patter of bits of bark fell, and a tall, skinny man climbed down slowly into view. He stopped above Bron's head, holding tightly to the trunk. His trousers were torn and the heel was gone from one boot.

"Who are you?" Bron asked.

"Are these your beasts?" the man said angrily. "They ought to all be shot. They attacked me, viciously; would have killed me if I hadn't got to this tree."

"Who are you?" Bron repeated.

". . . Vicious and uncontrolled. If you don't take care of them, I will. We have laws here on Trowbri."

"If you don't shut up and tell me who you are, Mister, you can just stay in that tree until you rot," Bron said quietly. He pointed to the large boar, who was lying down about ten feet from the tree and glaring at it out of tiny red eyes. "I don't have to do anything and these pigs will take care of you all by themselves. It's in their blood. Peccaries in Mexico will tree a man and then take turns standing guard below until he dies or falls out. These animals here don't attack no one without reason. I say the reason is you came by and tried to grab up one of the sucklings because you had a sudden yearning for fresh pork. Who are you?"

"You calling me a liar?" the man shouted.

"Yes. Who are you?"

The boar came over and butted against the tree and made a deep grumbling noise. The man clutched the tree with both arms, and all the air went out of him.

"I'm Reymon, the radio operator here. I was in the tower landing the tender. When it left I grabbed my cycle and started back to town. I saw these pigs here and I stopped, just to have a look, and that's when I was attacked. Without reason . . ."

"Shore, shore," Bron said. He dug his toe into the boar's side and scraped it up and down on the heavy ribs. The boar flapped his ears and rumbled a happy grunt. "You like it up in that tree, Mr. Reymon?"

"All right, then, I bent down to touch one of your filthy animals—don't ask me why. Then I was attacked."

"That sounds more like it, and I'm not gonna bother you with foolish questions as to why you had a sudden urge to pet a filthy pig. You can come down now and get on your red wagon and get moving."

The boar flicked his twist of a tail, then vanished into the undergrowth. Reymon shakily dropped to the ground and brushed off his clothes. He was a darkly handsome man whose features were spoiled by the angry tightness of his mouth.

"You'll hear more about this," he said over his shoulder as he stumbled away.

"I doubt it," Bron told him. He went to the road and waited until the electrobike whizzed by in the direction of the city. Only then did he go back and whistle his flock together.

3

A tiny metallic clanging sounded in Bron's ear, growing louder and louder when he ignored it. Yawning, he reached up and detached the earring alarm from the lobe of his ear, switched it off with his fingernail, and dropped it into his belt pouch. The night air was cool on his hand as he rubbed the sleep from his eyes. Above him the strange constellations of stars shone crisply in the clear air. Dawn was still some hours away and the forest was dark and silent, with only an occasional wheeze or a muffled grunt sounding from a sleeping pig.

Otherwise completely dressed, Bron unsealed the sleeping bag and pulled on his boots, which he had left carefully upended to keep them dry. He leaned against Queeny to do this. The eight-hundred-pound sow, a dim and mountainous shape in the darkness, lifted her head and grunted an interrogation. Bron bent over and lifted the flap of her ear so he could whisper into it.

"I'm going away, but I'll be back by dawn. I'm taking Jasmine with me. You look after things."

Queeny grunted a very human sound of agreement and lay back down. Bron whistled softly, and there was a rustle of sharp hooves as little Jasmine trotted up. "Follow me," he told her. She came to heel and walked behind him away from the camp, both of them now silent as shadows.

It was a moonless night, and Trowbri City was lightless and asleep. No one was aware of the shadows that moved through the town and slipped behind the municipal building. No one heard when a window slid soundlessly open and the shadows vanished from sight.

Governor Haydin sat up suddenly as the lights came on in his bedroom. The first thing he saw was a small pink pig sitting on the rug by his bed. It turned its head to look him directly in the eye—then winked. It had lovely, long white eyelashes.

"Sorry to disturb you at this hour," Bron said from the window, as he made sure the curtains were completely drawn, "but I didn't want anyone to see us meeting."

"Get out of here, you insane swineherd, before I throw you out!" Haydin bellowed.

"Not so loud sir," Bron cautioned. "You may be overheard. Here is my identification." He held out a plastic rectangle.

"I know who you are, so what difference—"

"Not this identification. You did ask the Patrol for aid on this planet, didn't you?"

"What do you know about that?" The Governor's eyes widened at the thought. "You mean to say you have something to do with them?"

"My identification," Bron said, snapping to attention and handing over the card.

Governor Haydin grabbed it with both hands. " 'P.I.G.,' " he read. "What's that?" Then he answered his own question in a hoarse voice as he read the next line.

" 'Porcine Interstellar Guard'! Is this some kind of joke?"

"Not at all, Governor. The Guard has only been recently organized and activated. Knowledge of its activities has heretofore been confined to command levels, where its operational configurations are top secret."

"All of a sudden you don't sound like a pig farmer anymore."

"I am a pig farmer, Governor. But I have a degree in animal husbandry, a doctorate in galactic politics, and a black belt in judo. The pig farmer is used for field cover."

"Then *you're* the answer to my distress message to the Patrol?"

"That's correct. I can't give you any classified details, but you must surely know how thin the Patrol is spread these days—and will be for years to come. When a new planet is opened up it extends Earth's sphere of influence in a linear direction—but the volume of space that must be controlled is the *cube* of that distance."

"You wouldn't mind translating that into English, would you?"

"Happily." Bron looked around and spotted a bowl of fruit on the table. He took out two round red pieces and held them up. "This piece of fruit is a sphere of influence. If Earth is at the center of the fruit, spaceships can fly out in any direction to the skin of the fruit, and all of the fruit inside this sphere must be watched by Earth. All right, let's say that another planet is opened up. The spacer flies in a straight line away from Earth, this far." He held his fingers up to show a distance as long as the diameter of one of the pieces of fruit. "That is a linear distance, in a line; but the Patrol doesn't just patrol in straight lines." He put the second fruit next to the first so that they touched. "The Patrol now has to be responsible for the entire area inside this second fruit, a three-dimensional distance, because spacers do not always follow the same routes, and they go to different destinations. The job is a big one and getting bigger all the time."

"I see what you mean," the Governor said, studying the fruit for a moment, then putting it back into the bowl.

"That's the core of our problem. The Patrol must operate between all the planets, and the volume of space that this comprises is beyond imagining. Someday, it is hoped, there will be enough Patrol vessels to fill this volume so that a cruiser can answer any call for help. But as it stands now, other means of assistance must be found. A number of projects are being instigated, and P.I.G. is one of the first to go operational. You've seen my unit. We can travel by any form of commercial transportation, so we can operate without Patrol assistance. We carry rations, but if need be are self-supporting. We are equipped to handle almost any tactical situation."

Haydin was trying to understand, but it was still all too much for him. "I hear what you're saying. Still"—he faltered—"still, all you have is a herd of pigs."

Bron grabbed his temper hard, and his eyes narrowed to slits with the effort. "Would you have felt better if I had landed with a pack of wolves? Would that have given you some sense of security?"

"Well, I do admit that it would look a good deal different. I could see some sense in that."

"Can you? In spite of the fact that a wolf—or wolves—in their natural state will run from a full-grown wild boar without ever considering attacking him? And I have a mutated boar out there that will take on any six wolves and produce six torn wolfskins in about as many minutes. Do you doubt that?"

"It's not a matter of doubt. But you have to admit that there is something . . . I don't know . . . ludicrous, maybe, about a herd of pigs."

"That observation is not exactly original," Bron said in a toneless, arctic voice. "In fact, that is the reason I take the whole herd rather than just boars, and why I do the dumb-farmer bit. People take no notice and it helps my investigation. Which is also why I am seeing you at night like this. I don't want to blow my cover until I have to."

"That's one thing you won't have to worry about. Our problem doesn't involve any of the settlers."

"What exactly *is* your problem? Your message wasn't exactly clear on that point."

Governor Haydin looked uncomfortable. He wriggled a bit, then examined Bron's identification again. "I'll have to check this before I can tell you anything."

"Please do."

There was a fluoroscope on the end table, and Haydin made a thorough job of comparing the normally invisible pattern with the code book he took from his safe. Finally, almost reluctantly, he handed back the card. "It's authentic," he said.

Bron slipped the card back into his pocket. "Now, what is the trouble?" he asked.

Haydin looked at the small pig that was curled up on the rug, snoring happily. "It's ghosts," he said in a barely audible voice.

"And you're the one who laughs at pigs?"

"There's no need to get offensive," the Governor answered hotly. "I know it sounds strange, but there it is. We call them—or the phenomenon—'ghosts' because we don't know anything about it. Whether it's supernatural or not is anyone's guess, but it's sure not physical." He turned to the map on the wall and tapped a yellowish-tan area that stood out from the surrounding green. "Right here, the Ghost Plateau—that's where the trouble is."

"What sort of trouble?"

"It's hard to say—just a feeling mostly. Ever since this planet was settled, going on fifteen years now, people haven't liked to go near the plateau, even though it lies almost directly outside the city. It doesn't feel right up there, somehow. Even the animals stay away. And people have disappeared there and no trace has ever been found of them."

Bron looked at the map, following the yellow gradient outline with his finger. "Hasn't it been explored?" he asked.

"Of course, in the first survey. And copters still fly over it, and nothing out of the way is ever seen. But only in daylight. No one has ever flown or driven or walked on the Ghost Plateau during the night and lived to tell about it. Nor has a single body ever been found."

The Governor's voice was heavy with grief; there was no doubt that he meant what he said.

"Has anything ever been done about this?" Bron asked.

"Yes. We've learned to stay away. This is not Earth, Mr. Wurber, no matter in how many ways it resembles it. It is an alien planet with alien life on it, and this human settlement is just a pinprick in the planet's hide. Who knows what . . . creatures are out there in the night? We are settlers, not adventurers. We have learned to avoid the plateau, at least at night, and we have never had that kind of trouble anywhere else."

"Then why have you called on the Patrol?"

"Because we made a mistake. The old-timers don't talk much these days about the plateau, and a lot of the newcomers believe that the stories are just . . . stories. Some of us had even begun to doubt our own memories. In any case, a prospecting team wanted to look for some new mine sites, and the only untouched area near the city is on the plateau. In spite of our misgivings the team went out, led by an engineer name of Huw Davies."

"Any relation to your assistant?"

"Her brother."

"That explains her agitation. What happened?"

Haydin's eyes were unfocused as he gazed at a fearful memory. "It was horrible," he said. "We took all precautions, of course—followed them by copter during the day and marked their camp. The copters were rigged with lights, and we stood by all night. They had three radios and all of them were in use, so there could be no communication breakdown. We waited all night and there was no trouble. Then, just before dawn—without any alarm or warning—the radios cut out. We got there within minutes, but it was too late.

"What we found is almost too awful to describe. Everything—their equipment, tents, supplies—was destroyed, crushed and destroyed. There was blood everywhere, spattering the broken trees and the ground—but the men were gone, vanished. There were no tracks of animals or men or machines in the area—nothing. The blood was tested; it was human blood. And the fragments of flesh were . . . human flesh."

"There must have been something," Bron insisted. "Some identifying marks, some clues, perhaps the odor of explosives—or something on your radar, since this plateau is so close."

"We are not stupid men. We have technicians and scientists. There were no clues, no smells, nothing on radar. I repeat, nothing."

"And this is when you decided to call the Patrol."

"Yes. This thing is too big for us to handle."

"You were absolutely correct, Governor. I'll take it from here. In fact, I already have a very good idea what happened."

Haydin was jolted to his feet. "You can't! What is it?"

"I'm afraid it is a little too early to say. I'm going up to the plateau in the morning to look at this place where the massacre happened. Can you give me the map coordinates? And please don't mention my visit to anyone."

"Little chance of that," Haydin said, looking at the little pig. It stood and stretched, then sniffed loudly at the bowl of fruit on the table.

"Jasmine would like a piece," Bron said. "You don't mind, do you?"

"Go ahead, help yourself," the Governor said resignedly, and loud chomping filled the room as he wrote down the coordinates and directions.

4

They had to hurry to be clear of the town before dawn. By the time they reached their camp the sky was gray in the east and the animals were up and stirring.

"I think we'll stay here at least another day," Bron said as he cracked open a case of vitamin rations. Queeny, the eight-hundred-pound Poland China sow, grunted happily at this announcement and rooted up a wad of leaves and tossed them into the air.

"Good foraging, I don't doubt it, particularly after all that time in the ship. I'm going to take a little trip, Queeny, and I'll be back by dark. You keep an eye on things until then." He raised his voice. "Curly! Moe!"

A crashing in the forest echoed his words, and a moment later two long grayish-black forms tore out of the underbrush—a ton of bone and muscle on the hoof. A three-inch branch was in Curly's way, and he neither swerved nor slowed. There was a sharp *crack* and he skidded up to Bron with the broken branch draped across his back. Bron threw the branch aside and looked at his shock troops.

They were boars, twins from the same litter, and weighed over one thousand pounds apiece. An ordinary wild boar will weigh up to seven hundred and fifty pounds and is the fastest, most dangerous, and worst-tempered beast ever known. Curly and Moe were mutants, a third again heavier than their wild ancestors, and many times as intelligent. But nothing else had changed; they were still just as fast, dangerous, and bad-tempered. Their ten-inch tusks were capped with stainless steel to prevent them from splitting.

"I want you to stay here with Queeny, Moe, and she'll be in charge."

Moe squealed in anger and tossed his great head. Bron grabbed a handful of hide and thick bristles between Moe's shoulder blades, the boar's favorite itch spot, and twisted and pummeled it. Moe blurbled happily through his nose. Moe was a pig genius, which made him on the human level a sort of retarded moron—except that he wasn't human. He understood simple orders and would obey them within the limits of his capacity.

"Stay and guard, Moe, stay and guard. Watch Queeny; she knows what is best. Guard, don't kill. Plenty of good things to eat here—

and candy when I get back. Curly goes with me, and everyone gets candy when we come back." There were happy grunts from all directions, and Queeny pressed her fat side against his leg.

"You're coming too, Jasmine," Bron said. "A good walk will keep you out of trouble. Go get Maisie Mule-Foot; the exercise will do her good too."

Jasmine was his problem child. Though she looked only like a half-grown shoat, she was a full-grown Pitman-Moore miniature—one of a strain of small pigs that had originally been developed for use in laboratories. They had been bred for intelligence, and Jasmine probably had the highest IQ ever to have come out of the lab. But there was a handicap: With the intelligence went an instability, an almost human hysteria, as though her mind were balanced on a sharp edge. If she were left with the other pigs she would tease and torture them and cause trouble, so Bron made sure that she was with him if he had to be away from the herd for any length of time.

Maisie was a totally different case: a typical, well-rounded sow—a Mule-Foot, a general-purpose breed. Her intelligence was low—or pig normal—and her fecundity high. Some cruel people might have said she was good only for bacon. But she had a pleasant personality and was a good mother; in fact she had just weaned her last litter. Bron took her along to give her some relief from her weanling progeny—and also to run some fat off her, since she had grown uncommonly plump during the confined space voyage.

Bron examined his maps and found what appeared to be an old logging road that ran in the direction in which he wanted to go, almost as far as the plateau. He and the pigs could go across country easily enough, but they might save some time by following the road. He set his pocket gyrocompass by lining it up with the arms of the control tower's weather vane, then worked out a heading that would reach the road that led to the Ghost Plateau. He pointed his arm in the correct direction, and Curly put his head down and catapulted into the undergrowth. There was a snapping and crackling as he tore his way through—the perfect pathfinder, who made his own openings where none were available.

It was an easy walk as the grass-covered road wound up through the hills. The logging camp must have been closed down for a long time, because the road was free of wheel ruts. The pigs snuffled in the rich grass, grabbing an occasional bite of something too tempting to resist, although Maisie wheezed complaints about the unaccustomed exertion. There were some trees along the road, but for the most part the land was cleared and planted with crops. Curly stopped, wheeled, and pointed into a thick growth of woods, rumbling a questioning grunt. Jasmine and Maisie stopped next to him, looking in the same direction, heads cocked and listening.

"What is it? What's in there?" Bron asked. It was nothing dangerous, that was clear, since if there had been a threat Curly would have gone charging to the attack. With their more acute hearing the pigs were listening to something he could not hear, something that interested but did not frighten them.

"Let's go," he said. "There's plenty of walking ahead." He pushed against Curly's side; but he could have accomplished just as much as by shoving against a stone wall. Curly, unmoving, scratched with a forehoof and tossed his head in the direction of the trees.

"All right, if you insist. I never argue with boars who weigh over half a ton. Let's go see what's in there." He grabbed a handful of thick bristles and hide, and Curly started off among the trees.

Before they had gone fifty yards, Bron could hear the sound himself—a bird or a small animal of some kind, calling shrilly. But why should this bother the pigs? Then, suddenly, he realized what it was.

"That's a child—crying! Come on, Curly!"

With this encouragement Curly trotted forward, pushing his way through the underbrush so fast that Bron could hardly keep up. They came to a steep, muddy bank with a dark pond below, and the crying was now a loud, unhappy sobbing. A little girl, no more than two years old, was up to her waist in the water, wet and unhappy.

"Hold on; I'll have you out in a second," Bron said, and the sobbing turned to a shrill wailing. Curly stood on the brink of the slippery mud slope, and Bron used his sturdy and immobile ankle to hold on to as he let himself down. The child struggled towards him, and he grabbed her with his free hand and pulled her to safety. She was wet and miserable, but she stopped crying as soon as he had her under his arm.

"Now what shall we do with you?" Bron asked when he was on top again, and this time he heard the answer at the same time as the pigs. The distant, continual ringing of a bell. He started them in the right direction, then walked behind in the path that Curly plowed through the underbrush.

The woods ended at an open meadow. A red farmhouse was on the hill above, where a woman stood waving a large hand bell. She saw Bron as soon as he had emerged from the trees and ran down to meet him.

"Amy," she cried, "you're all right!" She pulled the child to her, ignoring the mud stains on her white apron.

"Found her back there in the pond, ma'am. Got herself stuck in the mud and couldn't get out. More frightened than anything else, I'd say."

"I don't know how to thank you. I thought she was asleep when I went to milk the cows. She must have wandered out . . ."

"Don't thank me, ma'am, thank my pigs here. They heard her cryin', and I just followed them."

For the first time the woman was aware of the animals. "What a fine Mule-Foot," she said, admiring Maisie's well-rounded lines. "We used to keep pigs at home, but when we emigrated we just bought the cows for a dairy farm. I'm sorry now. Let me give them some fresh milk—you too. It's the least I can do."

"Thank you kindly, but we have to push on. Lookin' for a homestead site, and I want to get up to the plateau and back before dark."

"Not there!" the woman gasped, clutching the little girl to her. "You can't go up there!"

"Any reason why I shouldn't? Looks like good land on the map."

"You can't that's all . . . there are *things*. We don't talk about them much. Things you can't see. I know they're there. We used to keep some cows in that uphill pasture, on the side towards the Ghost Plateau. You know why we stopped? Their milk was off—less than half of what the other cows were producing. There's something wrong up there, very wrong. Go look if you must, but you have to leave before dark. You'll find out what I mean quick enough."

"Thanks for tellin' me; I do appreciate it. So seein' how the little girl is all right now, I'll just be movin' on."

Bron whistled the pigs to him, waved goodbye to the farm wife, and made his way back to the road. The plateau was getting more interesting all the time. He kept the pigs moving steadily after this, in spite of Maisie's heavy breathing and unhappy looks, and within an hour they had passed the deserted logging camp—abandoned because of the strange happenings on the plateau?—and started up among the trees. This was the edge of the plateau.

They crossed a stream, and Bron let the pigs drink their fill while he cut himself a stick for the climb. Maisie, overheated by her exertions, dropped full-length into the water with a tremendous splash and soaked herself. Jasmine, a fastidious animal, squealed with rage and rushed away to roll in the grass and dry herself off where she had been splashed. Curly, with much chuffing and grunting like a satisfied locomotive, got his nose under a rotting log that must have weighed nearly a ton and rolled it over and happily consumed the varied insect and animal life that he found beneath it. They moved on.

It was not a long climb to the plateau, and once they were over the edge the ground leveled out into a lightly forested plain. Bron took another compass reading and pointed Curly in the right direction. Curly snorted and raked a furrow in the ground with a forehoof before setting off. Jasmine pressed up against Bron's leg and squealed.

Bron could feel it too, and he had to suppress an involuntary shiver. There was something—how could it be described?—wrong about this place. He had no idea *why* he felt this way, but he did. And the pigs seemed to sense it too. There was something else wrong: there was not a bird in sight, although the hills below had been filled with them. And there did not seem to be any other animals about. The pigs would surely have called his attention to any he might have missed.

Bron fought down the strange sensation and followed Curly's retreating hindquarters, while the two other pigs, still protesting, trotted behind him, staying as close to his legs as possible. It was obvious that they all felt this presentiment of danger, and they were all bothered by it. All except Curly, that is, since any strange emotion or sensation just tripped his boarish temper, so that he plowed ahead filled with mumbling anger.

When they reached the clearing, there was no doubt that it was the correct one. Branches on all sides were bent and twisted, and small trees had been pulled down, while torn tents and crushed equipment littered the area. Bron picked up a transceiver and saw that the metal case had been pinched and twisted, as though squeezed by some giant hand.

And all the time, as he searched the area, he was aware of the tension and pressure.

"Here, Jasmine," he said, "take a smell of this. I know it's been out in the rain and sun for weeks now, but there may be a trace of something left. Give a sniff."

Jasmine shivered and shook her head no and pressed up against his legs; he could feel her body shiver. She was in one of her states and good for nothing until it passed. Bron didn't blame her—he felt a little that way himself. He gave Curly the case to smell, and the boar took an obliging sniff, but his attention wasn't really on it. His little eyes scanned in all directions while he smelled it, and then he sniffed around the clearing, snuffling and snorting to blow the dirt out of his nostrils. Bron thought he was on to something when he began to rip the ground with his tusks, but it was only a succulent root that he had smelled. He chomped at it—then suddenly raised his head and pointed his ears at the woods, the root dangling, forgotten, from his jaws.

"What is it?" Bron asked, because the other two animals were pointing in the same direction, listening intently. Their ears twitched, and there was the sudden sound of something large crashing through the bush.

The suddenness of the attack almost finished Bron. The crashing was still sounding some distance away when the bounder plunged out of the woods almost on top of him, foot-long yellow claws outstretched. Bron had seen pictures of this species of giant marsupial, native to the planet, but the reality was something else again. It stood on its hind legs, twelve feet high, and even the knowledge that it was not carnivorous and used the claws for digging in the marshes was not encouraging. It also used them against its enemies, and he seemed to be in that category at the moment. The creature sprang out, loomed over him; the claws swung down.

Curly, growling with rage, hit the beast from the side. Even twelve feet of brown-furred marsupial cannot stand up to a thousand pounds of angry boar, and the big beast went over and back. As he passed, Curly flicked his head with a wicked twist that hooked a tusk into the animal's leg and ripped. With a lightning spin the boar reversed direction and returned to the attack.

The Bounder was not having any more. Shrieking with pain and fear, it kept on going in the opposite direction just as its mate—the one that had been blundering through the woods—appeared in the clearing. Curly spun again, reversing within one body length, and charged. The Bounder—this one, because of its size, must have been the male—appraised the situation instantly and did not like it. Its mate was fleeing in pain—and telling everybody about it loudly—and without a doubt this underslung, hurtling mass of evil-looking creature must be to blame. Without slowing, the Bounder kept going and vanished among the trees on the opposite side.

Through the entire affair Jasmine had rushed about, accomplishing very little, but obviously on the verge of a nervous breakdown. Maisie, never one for quick reaction, just stood and flapped her ears and grunted in amazement.

As Bron reached into his pocket for a pill to quiet Jasmine down, a long, green snake slithered out of the woods almost at his feet.

He stopped, frozen, with his hand halfway to his pocket, because he knew he was looking at death. This was the Angelmaker, the most poisonous serpent on Trowbri, more deadly than anything Mother Earth had ever produced. It had the meat-hungry appetite of a constrictor—because it was a constrictor in its eating habits—but it also had fangs and well-filled venom sacs. And it was agitated, weaving back and forth and preparing to strike.

It was obvious that portly, pink Maisie, sow and mother, did not have the reflexes or the temperament to deal with attacking marsupials—but a snake was something else altogether. She squealed and jumped forward moving her weight with ponderous agility.

The Angelmaker saw the appealing mass of quivering flesh and struck, instantly darting its head back and striking again. Maisie, snorting with the effort to turn her head and look back over her shoulder, squealed again and backed towards the poised snake. It hissed loudly and struck another time, perhaps wondering in some dim corner of its vestigial brain why this appealing dinner did not drop down to be eaten. If the Angelmaker had known a bit more about pigs, it might have acted differently. Instead it struck again, and by now most of its venom was gone.

While the Mule-Foot is not a lardy type, it is a sturdy breed, and the females do run to fat. Maisie was plumper than most. Her hindquarters—what some crude carnivorous types might call her hams—were coated with heavy fat. And there is no blood circulation through fat. The venom had been deposited in the fat, where it could not reach the bloodstream and could do no injury. Eventually it would be neutralized by her body chemistry and disposed of. Right now Maisie was turning the tables. The Angelmaker struck again—listlessly, because its venom was gone. Maisie heaved her bulk about and chopped down with her hooves—strong, sharp-edged weapons. While snakes may like to kill pigs, pigs also greatly enjoy eating snakes. Squealing and bouncing heavily, Maisie landed on the snake's spine and neatly amputated its head. The body still writhed and she attacked again, chopping with her hooves until the snake had been cut into a number of now motionless segments. Only then did she stop attacking and begin to mumble happily to herself while she ate them. It was a big snake, and she allowed Curly and Jasmine to help her with it. Bron waited for them to finish before moving out, because the feast was calming them down. Only when the last chunk had vanished did he turn and start back for the camp. He kept looking back over his shoulder and found that it was a great relief—for all of them—to start down the slope away from the Ghost Plateau.

5

When they reached the rest of the herd, there were grunts of greeting. The most intelligent beasts remembered the promised candy and crowded around waiting for it.

Bron opened a case of the mineral and vitamin-reinforced delicacy. While distributing it, he heard the buzz of his phone—very dimly, because he had yet to unpack it from its carrying case.

When he had filled out all the homesteading forms he had of course put down his phone number, since this was as much a part of him as was his name. Everyone was given a phone number at birth, and it was his for life. With the computer-controlled circuits anyone, anywhere on a planet, could he reached by the dialing of a single number. But who could be calling him here? As far as he knew, only Lea Davies had his number. He pulled out the compact phone—no bigger than his hand, including its lifetime atomic battery—and flipped up the small screen. This activated the phone, and static rustled from the speaker while a colored image appeared on the screen.

"Now, I was just thinkin' 'bout you, Miss Davies," he said. "Ain't that a coincidence."

"Very," she said, barely moving her lips when she spoke, as though groping for words. She was a pretty girl, but looking too haggard now. Her brother's death had hit her hard. "I must see you . . . Mr. Wurber. As soon as possible."

"Now, that's right friendly, Miss Lea; I'm lookin' forward to that."

"I need your help, but we mustn't be seen talking together. Can you come as soon as it's dark, alone, to the rear entrance of the municipal building? I'll meet you there."

"I'll be there—you can count on me," he said, and he rung off.

What was this about? Did the girl know something no one else knew? It was possible. But why him? Unless the Governor had told her about P.I.G.—which was very possible, since she was his only assistant. And on top of that she was very attractive, when she wasn't crying. As soon as he had fed the herd, he broke out some clean clothes and his razor.

Bron left at dusk, and Queeny lifted her head to watch him go. She would be in charge until he came back—the rest of the pigs knew and expected that—and she had Curly and Moe ready to take care of any trouble that might arise. Curly was sleeping off the day's exertions, whistling placidly through his nose; and next to him little Jasmine was also asleep, even more tired and sedated by a large Miltown. The situation was well in hand.

Approaching the municipal building from its unlighted rear was no problem, since he had been over the same ground just the previous evening. All this running about and missing sleep was getting to him at last, and he choked off a yawn with his fist.

"Miss Lea, are you there?" he called softly, pushing open the unlocked door. The hall beyond was black, and he hesitated.

"Yes, I'm here," her voice called out. "Please come in." Bron pushed the door wide and stepped through, and a crashing pain struck him across the side of the head, the agony of it for an instant lighting the darkness of his nerves. He tried to say something, but could not speak, though he did manage to raise his arm. Another blow struck his forearm, numbing it so that it dropped away; and the third blow, across the back of his neck, sent him plunging down into a deeper darkness.

"What happened?" the wavering pink blob asked, and with much blinking Bron managed to focus on it and recognized Governor Haydin's worried face.

"You tell me," Bron said hoarsely. He became aware of the pain in his head, and he almost passed out again. Something damp and cool snuffled against his neck, and he worked his hand up to twist Jasmine's ear.

"I thought I told you to get that pig out of here," someone said.

"Leave her be," Bron managed to say, "and tell me what happened." He turned his head, with infinite caution, and saw that he was lying on the couch in the Governor's office. A medical-looking gentleman with a stern face and dangling stethoscope was standing by. There were a number of other people at the doorway.

"We just found you here," the Governor said. "That's all we know. I was working in my office when I heard this screaming, like a girl in terrible pain—something awful. Some of these other men heard it outside in the street, and we all came running. Found you lying in the rear hall—out cold with your head laid open, and this pig standing next to you doing all the screaming. I never knew an animal could sound like that. It wouldn't let anyone near you—kept charging and chomping its teeth in a very threatening manner. Quieted down a bit by the time the doctor came and finally let him get over to you."

Bron thought quickly—or at least as quickly as he could with a power saw trying to take off the back of his head.

"Then you know as much about it as I do," he said. "I came here to see about filing my homesteadin' papers. The front was locked, and I thought maybe I could get in by the back, if anyone was still here. I walked through the back door and somethin' hit me and the next thing I know I was waking up here. Guess I can thank Jasmine here for that. She must have followed me and seen me hit. Must have started squealing, like you heard, and probably chewing on the ankle of whoever hit me. Pigs have very good teeth. Must have frightened him off, whoever it was." He groaned; it was easy to do. "Can you give me something for my head, Doctor?" he asked.

"There is a possibility of concussion," the doctor said.

"I'll take my chances on that, Doc; better a little concussion than my head splittin' into two halves this way."

By the time the doctor had finished and the crowd dispersed, the pain in his head had subsided to a throbbing ache, and Bron was fingering the bruise on his arm, which he had just become aware of. He waited until the Governor had closed and locked the door before he spoke.

"I didn't tell you the whole story," he said.

"I didn't think you had. Now what is this all about?"

"I was struck by a party or parties unknown—that much was all true. If Jasmine had not woken up and found me missing and gotten all neurotically insecure, I would probably be dead at this moment. It was a trap, neatly set up, and I walked right into it."

"What do you mean?"

"I mean that Lea Davies is involved in this. She called me, arranged to meet me here, and was waiting here when I arrived."

"Are you trying to say . . . ?"

"I've said it. Now get the girl in here so we can hear her side of it."

When the Governor went to the phone, Bron swung his legs slowly to the floor and wondered what it would feel like to stand up. It was not nice. He held on to the back of the couch while the room spun in slow circles and the floor heaved like a ship at sea. Jasmine leaned against his leg and moaned in sympathy. After a while, when the moving furniture and rotating building had slowed to a stop, he tried walking and stumbled over to the kitchen.

"May I help you, sir?" the kitchen said when he entered. "Perhaps a little midnight snack is in order?"

"Coffee, just black coffee—lots of it."

"Coming at once, sir. But dieticians do say that coffee can be irritating to an empty stomach. Perhaps a lightly toasted sandwich, or a grilled cutlet—"

"Quiet!" His head was beginning to throb again. "I do not like ultramodern robot kitchens with a lot of smart backtalk. I like old-fashioned kitchens that flash a light that says ready—and that is all they can say."

"Your coffee, sir," the kitchen said, in what was surely a hurt tone. A door snapped open above the counter and a steaming jug emerged. Bron looked around. "And what about a cup—or should I drink it out of the palm of my hand?"

"A cup, *of course*, sir. You did not *specify* that you wanted a cup." There was a muffled clank inside the machine, and a chipped cup rattled down a chute and landed on its side on the table.

Just what I needed, Bron thought, a temperamental robot kitchen. Jasmine came in, her little hooves click-clacking on the tiled floor. I had better get on the right side of this kitchen or I'll be in trouble with the Governor when he finds out.

"Now that you mention it, kitchen," he said aloud in the sweetest tones he could summon, "I have heard a great deal about your wonderful cooking. I wonder if you could make me eggs Benedict . . . ?"

"The work of a second, sir," the kitchen said happily, and only moments later the steaming dish arrived, with folded napkin and knife and fork.

"Wonderful," Bron said, putting the dish down for Jasmine. "The best I ever tasted." Loud smacking and chomping filled the room.

"Indeed you are a fast eater, sir," the kitchen hummed. "Enjoy, enjoy."

Bron took the coffee back to the other room and carefully sat down again on the couch. The Governor looked up from the phone, frowning worriedly.

"She's not at home," he said, "or with friends or anywhere that I can determine. A patrol has searched the area, and I sent a net call to all the local phones. No one has seen her—and there is no trace of her anywhere. That can't be possible. I'll try the mine stations."

It took over an hour for Governor Haydin to prove to his own satisfaction that Lea had vanished. The settled portion of Trowbri covered a limited area, and everyone could be reached by phone. No one had seen her or knew where she was. She was gone. Bron had faced this fact long before the Governor would admit it—and he knew what had to be done. He slumped back on the couch, half-dozing, with his shoes off and his feet propped on Jasmine's warm flank. The little pig was out like a light, sleeping the sleep of the just.

"She's gone," Haydin said, switching off the last call. "How can it be? She couldn't have had anything to do with your being attacked."

"She could have—if she were forced into it."

"What are you talking about?"

"I'm just guessing, but it makes sense. Suppose her brother were not dead . . ."

"What are you saying?"

"Let me finish. Suppose her brother were alive, but in deadly danger. And she had the chance to save him if she did as ordered—which was to get me here. Give the girl credit. I don't think she knew they meant to kill me. She must have put up a fight—that's why she was taken away too."

"What do you know, Wurber?" Haydin shouted. "Tell me everything. I'm Governor here and I have a right to know."

"And know you shall—when I have anything more than hunches and guesses to give you. This attack, and the kidnapping, means that someone is unhappy about my presence, which also means that I am getting close. I'm going to speed things up and see if I can catch these ghosts off guard."

"Do you think there is a connection between all this and the Ghost Plateau?"

"I *know* there is. That's why I want word circulated in the morning that I am moving into my homestead tomorrow. Make sure everyone knows where it is."

"Where?"

"On the Ghost Plateau—where else?"

"That's suicide!"

"Not really. I have some guesses as to what happened up there, and some defenses—I hope. I also have my team, and they've proved themselves twice today. It will be taking a chance, but I'm going to have to take a chance if we ever hope to see Lea alive again."

Haydin clenched his fists on the top of his desk and made up his mind. "I can stop this if I want to—but I won't if you do it my way. Full radio connection, armed guards, the copters standing by . . ."

"No, sir; thank you very much, but I remember what happened to the last bunch that tried it that way."

"Then—I'll go with you myself. I'm responsible for Lea. You'll take me or you won't go."

Bron smiled. "Now, that's a deal, Guv. I could use a helping hand, and maybe a witness. Things are going to get pretty busy on the plateau tonight. But no guns."

"That's suicide."

"Just remember the first expedition, and do it my way. I'm leaving most of my equipment behind. I imagine you can arrange to have it trucked to a warehouse until we get back. I think you'll find I have a good reason for what I'm doing."

6

Bron managed to squeeze in over ten hours' sleep, because he felt he was going to need it. By noon the truck had come and gone and they were on the way. Governor Haydin was dressed for the occasion, in hunting boots and rough clothes, and he moved right out with them. Not that the pace was so fast; they went at the speed of the slowest piglet, and there was much noisy comment from all sides and grabbing of quick snacks from the roadside. They took the course this time that the original expedition had taken—a winding track that led up to the plateau in easy stages, for the most part running beside a fast river of muddy water. Bron pointed to it.

"Is this the river that runs through the plateau?" he asked.

Haydin nodded. "This is the one; it comes down from that range of mountains back there."

Bron nodded, then ran to rescue a squealing suckling from a crack in the rocks into which it had managed to wedge itself. They moved on.

By sunset they had set up camp—in the glade just next to the one where the previous expedition had met its end.

"Do you think this is a good idea?" Haydin asked.

"The best," Bron told him. "It's the perfect spot for our needs." He eyed the sun, which was close to the horizon. "Let's eat now; I want everything cleared away by dark."

Bron had opened a tremendous tent, but it was sparsely furnished—containing, to be exact, only two folding chairs and a battery-powered light.

"Isn't this a little on the Spartan side?" Haydin asked.

"I see no reason to bring equipment forty-five light-years just to have it destroyed. We've obviously set up camp; that's all that's important. The equipment I need is in here." He tapped a small plastic sack that hung from his shoulder. "Now—chow's up."

Their table was an empty ration box that had held the pigs' dinner. A good officer always sees to his troops first, so the animals had been fed. Bron put two self-heating dinners on the box, broke their seals, and handed Haydin a plastic fork. It was almost dark by the time they had finished and Bron leaned out through the open end of the tent and whistled for Curly and Moe. The two boars arrived at full charge and left grooves in the dirt as they skidded to a halt next to him.

"Good boys," he said, scratching their bristly skulls. They grunted happily and rolled their eyes up at him. "They think I'm their mother, you know." He waited placidly while Haydin fought with his expression, his face turning red in the process. "That may sound a little funny, but it's true. They were removed from their litter at birth and I raised them. So I'm 'imprinted' as their parent."

"Their parents were pigs. You don't look very much like a pig to me."

"You've never heard of imprinting. Everyone knows that if a kitten is raised with a litter of pups, the cat goes through life thinking she is another dog. This is more than just association from an early age. There exists a physical process known as imprinting. The way it works is that the first creature an animal is aware of, that it sees when its eyes first open, is recognized as a parent. This usually is a parent—but not always. The kitten thinks the dog is its mother. These two oversized boars think I am their parent, no matter how physically impossible that may appear to you. I made sure of that before I even considered training them. It is the only way I can be absolutely safe around them, since, intelligent as they are, they are still quick-tempered and deadly beasts. It also means that I'm safe as long as they are around. If anyone as much as threatened me he would be disemboweled within the second. I'm telling you this so that you won't try anything foolish. Now, would you kindly hand over that gun you promised not to bring?"

Haydin's hand jumped towards his hip pocket—and stopped just as suddenly as both boars turned towards the sudden movement. Moe was salivating with happiness at the head-scratching, and a drop of saliva collected and dropped from the tip of one ten-inch tusk.

"I need it for my own protection . . ." Haydin protested.

"You're better protected without it. Take it out, slowly." Haydin reached back gingerly and took out a compact energy pistol, then tossed it over to Bron. Bron caught it and hung it on the hook next to the light. "Now empty your pockets," he said. "I want everything metallic dumped on to the box."

"What are you getting at?"

"We'll talk about it later; we don't have time now. Dump."

Haydin looked at the boars and emptied out his pockets, while Bron did the same. They left a collection of coins, keys, knives, and small instruments on the box.

"We can't do anything now about the eyelets in your boots," Bron said, "but I don't think they'll cause much trouble. I took the precaution of wearing elastic-sided boots."

It was dark now, and Bron drove his charges into the woods nearby, spreading them out under the trees a good hundred yards from the clearing. Only Queeny, the intelligent sow, remained behind, dropping down heavily next to Bron's stool.

"I demand an explanation," said Governor Haydin.

"Don't embarrass me, Guv; I'm just working on guesses so far. If nothing has happened by morning, I'll give you an explanation—and my apology. Isn't she a beauty," he added, nodding towards the massive hog at his feet.

"I'm afraid I might use another adjective myself."

"Well, don't say it out loud. Queeny's English is pretty good, and I don't want her feelings hurt. Misunderstanding, that's all it is. People call pigs dirty, but that's only because they have been made to live in filth. They're naturally quite clean and fastidious animals. They can be fat. They have a tendency to be sedentary and obese—just like people—so they can put on weight if they have the diet for it. In fact, they are more like human beings than any other animal. They get ulcers like us, and heart trouble the same way we do. Like man, they have hardly any hair on their bodies, and even their teeth are similar to ours.

"Their temperaments, too. Centuries ago, an early physiologist by the name of Pavlov, who used to do scientific experiments with dogs, tried to do the same thing with pigs. But as soon as he placed them on the operating table, they would squeal at the top of their lungs and thrash about. He said that they were 'inherently hysterical' and went back to working with dogs. Which shows you, even the best men have a blind spot. The pigs weren't hysterical—they were plain sensible; it was the dogs who were being dim. The pigs reacted just the way a man might if they tried to tie him down for some quick vivisection . . . What is it, Queeny?"

Bron added this last as Queeny suddenly raised her head, her ears lifted, and grunted.

"Do you hear something?" Bron asked. The pig grunted again, in a rising tone, and climbed to her feet. "Does it sound like engines coming this way?" Queeny nodded her ponderous head in a very human yes.

"Get into the woods—back under the trees!" Bron shouted, hauling Haydin to his feet. "Do it fast—or you're dead."

They ran, headlong, and were among the trees when a distant, rising whine could be heard. Haydin started to ask something but was pushed face-first into the leaves as a whining, roaring shape floated into the clearing, blackly occulting the stars. It was anything but ghostly—but what was it? A swirl of leaves and debris swept over them, and Haydin felt something pulling at his legs so that they jumped about of their own accord. He tried to ask a question, but his words were drowned out as Bron blew on a plastic whistle and shouted:

"Curly, Moe—attack!"

At the same moment, he pulled a sticklike object out of his pack and threw it out into the clearing. It hit, popped, and burst into eye-searing flame—a flare of some kind.

The dark shape was a machine—that was obvious enough: round, black, and noisy, at least ten feet across, floating a foot above the ground, with a number of discs mounted around its edge. One of them swung towards the tent, and there was a series of explosive, popping sounds as the tent exploded and fell to the ground.

There was only a moment to see this before the attacking forms of the boars appeared from the opposite side of the clearing. Their speed was incredible as, heads down and legs churning, they dived at the machine. One of them arrived a fraction of a second before the other and crashed into the machine's flank. There was a metallic clang and the shriek of tortured machinery as it was jarred back, bent, almost tipped over.

The boar on the far side took instant advantage of this, his intelligence as quick as his reflexes, and without slowing hurled himself into the air and over the side and into the open top of the machine. Haydin looked on appalled. The machine was almost on the ground now, as a result of either ruined machinery or the weight of the boar.

The angry first animal now climbed the side and also vanished into the interior. Above the roar of the engine could be heard loud crashes and metallic tearing—and high-pitched screaming. Something clattered and tore, and the sound of the engines died away with a descending moan. As the sound lessened, a second machine could be heard approaching.

"Another coming!" Bron shouted, blasting on his whistle as he jumped to his feet. One of the boars popped its head from the ruin of the machine, then leaped out. The other was still noisily at work. The first boar catapulted himself towards the approaching sound and was on the spot when the machine appeared at the edge of the clearing—leaping and attacking, twisting his tusks into the thing. Something tore, and a great black length of material hung down. The machine lurched, and its operator must have seen the ruin of the first one, because it skidded in a tight circle and vanished back in the direction from which it had come.

Bron lit a second flare and tossed it out as the first one flickered. They were two-minute flares, and the entire action—from beginning to end—had taken place in less than that time. He walked over to the ruined machine, and Haydin hurried after him. The boar leaped to the ground and stood there panting, then wiped its tusks on the ground.

"What is it?" Haydin asked.

"A hovercraft," Bron said. "They aren't seen very much these days—but they do have their uses. They can move over any kind of open country or water, and they don't leave tracks. But they can't go over or through forest."

"I've never heard of anything like that."

"You wouldn't have. Since beamed power and energy cells came into general use, better means of transportation have been developed. But at one time they used to build hovercraft as large as houses. They are sort of a cross between ground and air transport. They float in the air, but depend upon the ground for support, since they float on a column of air being blown down out of the bottom."

"You knew this thing was coming—that's why you had us hide in the woods?"

"I suspected this. And for very good reasons, I suspected *them*." He pointed inside the wrecked hovercraft, and Haydin recoiled in shock.

"I tend to forget—I guess everyone does," the Governor said. "I've only seen pictures of aliens, so they are not very real to me. But these creatures. Blood, green blood. And it looks as if they're all dead. Gray skin, pipestem limbs. just from the pictures I've seen, is it possible that they could be . . ."

"Sulbani. You're right. One of the three intelligent races of aliens we've met in our expansion through the galaxy—and the only ones who possessed an interstellar drive before we appeared on the scene. They already had their own little corner of the galaxy staked out and did not at all appreciate our arrival. We have been staying away from them and trying to convince them that we have no territorial ambitions on their planets. But some people are hard to convince. Some aliens even more so. The Sulbani are the worst. Suspicion is in their blood.

"All of the evidence seemed to point to their presence here on Trowbri, but I couldn't be absolutely sure until I came face-to-face with them. The use of high-frequency weapons is typical of them. You know that if you raise the pitch of sound, higher and higher, it becomes inaudible to human ears—though animals can still hear it. Raise it higher still and the animals can't hear it—but they feel it just as well as we can. Ultrasonics can do some strange things."

He kicked at one of the bent discs, not unlike a microwave aerial. "That was the first clue. They have ultrasonic projectors in the forest, broadcasting on a wavelength that is inaudible, but causes a feeling of tension and uneasiness in most animals. That was the ghostly aura that kept people away from this plateau most of the time." He whistled a signal for the herd to assemble. "Animals, as well as men, will move away from the source, and they used it to chase some of the nastier wildlife towards us. When it didn't work and we came back, they sent in the more powerful stuff. Look at your shoes—and at this lantern."

Haydin gasped. The eyelets had vanished from his boots, and ragged pieces of lace hung from the torn openings. The lantern, like the metal equipment of the lost expedition, was squeezed and bent out of shape.

"Magnostriction," Bron said. "They were projecting a contracting and expanding magnetic field of an incredible number of gauss. The technique is used in factories for shaping metal, and it works just as well in the field. That, and these ultrasonic projectors to finish the job. Even a normal scan radar will give you a burn if you stand too close to it, and some ultrasonic wavelengths can turn water to vapor and explode organic material. That's what they did to your people who camped here. Swept in suddenly and caught them in the tents surrounded by their own equipment, which exploded and crunched and helped to wipe them out. Now let's get going."

"I don't understand what this means. I—"

"Later. We have to catch the one that got away."

On the side of the clearing where the machine had disappeared, they found a ragged length of black plastic. "Part of the skirt from the hovercraft," Bron said. "Confines the air and gives more lift. We'll follow them with this." He held out the fabric to Queeny and Jasmine and the other pigs that pressed up. "As you know, dogs track by odor that hangs in the air, and pigs have just as good noses—or better. In fact, hunting pigs were used in England for years, and pigs are also trained to smell out truffles. There they go!"

Grunting and squealing, the leaders started away into the darkness. The two men stumbled after them, the rest of the pigs following. After a few yards, Haydin had to stop and bind his shoes together with strips from his handkerchief before he could go on. He held Bron's belt, and Bron had his fingers hooked into the thick bristles that formed a crest on Curly's spine, and in this way they pushed through the forest. The hovercraft had to go through open country, or their nightmare run would have been impossible.

When a darker mass of mountains loomed ahead, Bron whistled the herd to him. "Stay," he ordered. "Stay with Queeny. Curly, Moe, and Jasmine—with me."

They went more slowly now, until the grassland died away in a broken scree of rock at the foot of a nearly vertical cliff. To their left they could make out the black gorge of the river and hear it rushing by below.

"You told me those things can't fly," Haydin said.

"They can't. Jasmine, follow the trail."

The little pig, head up and sniffing, trotted steadily across the broken rock and pointed to the bare side of the cliff.

7

"Could there possibly be a concealed entrance here?" Haydin asked, feeling the rough texture of the rock.

"There certainly could be—and we have no time to go looking for the key. Get behind those rocks, way over there, while I open. this thing up."

He took blocks of a claylike substance from his pack—a plastic explosive—and placed them against the rock, where they remained, over the spot that Jasmine had indicated. Then he pushed a fuse into the explosive, pulled the igniter—and ran.

He had just thrown himself down with the others when flame ripped the sky and the ground heaved under them; a spatter of rocks fell on all sides. They ran forward through the dust and saw light spilling out through a tall crevice in the rock. The boars threw themselves against it and it widened. Once through, they saw that a metal door was fastened to a section of rock and could swing outward to give access to the large cavern they were standing in. Bron bit his lip and examined the tunnel that ran down into the heart of the mountain.

"What next?" Governor Haydin asked.

"That's what I'm concerned about. At night, and out in the open, I'll back my boars against the Sulbani—or against human beings, for that matter. But these tunnels are a death trap for them. Even their speed won't protect them against gunfire. So let's even the odds. Everyone—back flat against this wall."

The Governor obeyed quickly enough, but it took a bit of tail pulling and two well-placed kicks to get the excited boars to obey. Only after they were all in position did Bron throw the switch on the wall of the entrance chamber of the tunnel. A large, inset metal door moved slowly upward—and laser beams hissed through the expanded opening.

"The hovercraft hangar," Bron whispered. "Looks as if some of them are still in there."

The boars didn't need orders. They waited, trembling with repressed energy, until the gap had widened enough to admit them. Then they struck at once, twin furies.

"Don't damage the gun!" Bron shouted as the laser beam fired again, wildly, then vanished. There were loud crunching sounds from inside.

"We can go in now," Bron said.

Inside the tool-lined room they found the body of only a single Sulbani. He must have been a mechanic, since the torn skirt had been removed from the hovercraft and a new one was ready to be fitted into place. Bron stepped over the corpse and picked up the laser rifle.

"Have you ever shot one of these?" he asked.

"No, but I'm willing to learn."

"Some other time. I'm an expert marksman with this particular weapon and I will be happy to prove it. Stay here."

"No, I won't do that."

"That's your choice. Stay behind me, then, and maybe I can get you a weapon too. Let's move fast while we can still make some use of surprise."

Cautiously, flanked by the two boars, he moved down the well-lit cavern, and Haydin followed close behind. Trouble came at the first tunnel crossing. When they were about twenty yards from the other tunnel, a Sulbani leaped out suddenly, with his gun poised and ready to fire. Bron snapped a single shot from his waist, without appearing to aim, and the alien collapsed, motionless, on the tunnel floor.

"Go get them!" he shouted, and the boars plunged forward, one to each opening of the cross tunnel. Bron fired over them, into the tunnel mouths, until the air cracked and glowed with the discharge of the laser. The two men ran forward, but when they reached the cross tunnel the battle was over. Moe had a burn along one side—which did not slow him down, though it did make his temper worse. He rooted, snorting like a steam engine, in the temporary barricade, tossing boxes and furniture over his head.

"Here's your gun," Bron said, picking up an undamaged laser rifle. "I'll set it on maximum discharge, single shot. Just aim it and pull the trigger. And let's go. They know we're in now, but luckily they were not prepared for a battle inside their own hideout."

They ran, counting on speed and shock to get them through, stopping only when they encountered resistance. As they passed one tunnel mouth they heard distant shouting, and Bron skidded to a stop and called to the others.

"Hold it. In here. Those sound like human voices." The metal door was set into solid rock. The laser beam turned the lock to a molten puddle, and Bron pulled the door open.

"I was so sure we would never be found—that we would die here," Lea Davies said. She came out of the cell, half supported by a tall man with the same coppery red hair.

"Huw Davies?" Bron asked.

"The same," he said, "but let's keep the introductions until later. When they brought me in here I saw a good bit of the layout. The most important thing is a central control room. Everything operates from there—even their power plant is right next to it. And they have communication equipment."

"I'm with you," Bron said. "If we take that, we can cut out all the power and make them work in the dark. My boars will like that. They'll cruise around and keep things stirred up until the militia arrives. We'll call the town from there."

Huw Davies pointed at the laser rifle Haydin held. "I'd like to borrow that for a while, Governor, if you would let me. I have a few scores I want to settle."

"It's all yours. Now show us the way."

The battle for the control room was a brief one—the boars saw to that. Most of the furniture was smashed up, but the controls appeared still to be in working order.

"You stand guard at the entrance, Huw," Bron said, "since I read Sulbani script and you probably don't." He mumbled to himself over the phonetic symbols, then smiled with satisfaction. " 'Lighting circuit'—that's all *that* can mean."

He stabbed at a button, and all the lights went out.

"I hope that it's dark all over, not just here," Lea said weakly in the black depths of the room.

"Everywhere," Bron told her. "Now, the emergency lighting circuit for this room should be here." Blue bulbs, scattered over the ceiling, flickered and came to life. Lea sighed audibly. "I've really had just about enough excitement," she said.

The two boars were looking expectantly at Bron, a wicked red gleam in their eyes. "Go to it, boys," he said. "Just don't get hurt."

"Little chance of that," Huw said as the great beasts exploded out the doorway and vanished with a rapid thud of hooves. "I've seen how they operate, and I'm glad I'm not on the receiving end." A distant crashing and thin screams echoed his sentiments.

Governor Haydin looked around at the banks of instruments and controls. "Now," he said, "that the excitement and immediate danger are over for the moment, will someone please tell me what is happening here and what *all this* is about?"

"A mine," Huw said, pointing towards a tunnel diagram on the far wall of the room. "A uranium mine—all in secret, and it has been running for years. I don't know how they're getting the metal out, but they mine and partially refine it here, all with automatic machinery. Then powder the slag and dump it into the river out there."

"I'll tell you what happens then," Bron said. "When they have a cargo, it's lifted off by spacer. The Sulbani have very big ideas about moving out of their area and controlling a bigger portion of space. But they are short of power metals, and Earth has been working hard to keep it that way. One of the reasons this planet was settled was that it is near the Sulbani sector and, while we didn't need the uranium, we didn't want it falling into the Sulbani's hands. The Patrol had no idea that they were getting their uranium from Trowbri—though they knew it was coming from somewhere—but it was a possibility. When the governor here sent in his request for aid, it became an even stronger possibility."

"I still don't understand it," Haydin said. "We would have detected any ships coming to the planet; our radar functions well."

"I'm sure it functions fine—but these creatures have at least one human accomplice who sees to it that the landings are concealed."

"Human . . . !" Haydin gasped. Then he knotted his fists at the thought. "It's not possible. A traitor to the human race. Who could it be?"

"That's obvious," Bron said, "now that you have been eliminated as a possibility."

"Me!"

"You were a good suspect—in the perfect position to cover things up; that's why I was less than frank with you. But you knew nothing about the hovercraft raid and would have been killed if I hadn't pulled you down, so that took you off the list of suspects. Leaving the obvious man: Reymon—the radio operator."

"That's right," Lea said. "He let me talk to Huw on the phone—and then he made me call you or he said he would have Huw killed. He didn't say why he wanted to see you, I didn't know . . ."

"You couldn't have." Bron smiled at her. "He isn't much of a killer and must have been following Sulbani instructions to get rid of me. He really earned his money by not seeing their ships on radar. And by making sure that the radio communication with Huw's party was cut off when the Sulbani attacked. He probably recorded the signals and gave the murderers an hour or two to do their work before he broadcast the radio's cutting off. That would have helped the mystery. And now, Governor, I hope you'll give a favorable report about this P.I.G. operation."

"The absolute best," Haydin said. He looked down at Jasmine, who had tracked them down and now lay curled up at his feet, chewing on a bar of Sulbani rations. "In fact, I'm almost ready to swear off eating pork for the rest of my life."

Space Rats of the CCC

That's it matey, pull up a stool, sure use that one. Just dump old
Phrnnx onto the floor to sleep it off. You know that Krddls can't stand
to drink much less drink flnnx and that topped off with a smoke of
the hellish krmml weed. Here, let me pour you a mug of flnnx, oops,
sorry about your sleeve. When it dries you can scrape it off with a
knife. Here's to your health and may your tubeliners never fail you
when the kpnnz hordes are on your tail.

No, sorry, never heard your name before. Too many good men
come and go, and the good ones die early aye! Me? You never heard
of me. Just call me Old Sarge as good a name as any. Good men I say,
and the best of them was—well, we'll call him Gentleman Jax. He
had another name, but there's a little girl waiting on a planet I could
name, a little girl that's waiting and watching the shimmering trails
of the deep-spacers when they come, and waiting for a man. So for
her sake we'll call him Gentleman Jax, he would have liked that, and
she would like that if only she knew, although she must be getting
kind of gray, or bald by now, and arthritic from all that sitting and
waiting but, golly, that's another story and by Orion it's not for me
to tell. That's it, help yourself, a large one. Sure the green fumes are
normal for good flnnx, though you better close your eyes when you
drink or you'll be blind in a week, ha-ha!, by the sacred name of the
Prophet Mrddl!

Yes, I can tell what you're thinking. What's an old space rat like
me doing in a dive like this out here at galaxy's end where the rim
stars flicker wanly and the tired photons go slow? I'll tell you what
I'm doing, getting drunker than a Planizzian pfrdffl, that's what. They
say that drink has the power to dim memories and by Cygnus I have
some memories that need dimming. I see you looking at those scars
on my hands. Each one is a story, matey, aye, and the scars on my
back each a story and the scars on my . . . well, that's a different story.
Yes, I'll tell you a story, a true one by Mrddl's holy name, though I
might change a name or two, that little girl waiting, you know.

You heard tell of the CCC? I can see by the sudden widening of
your eyes and the blanching of your space-tanned skin that you have.
Well, yours truly, Old Sarge here, was one of the first of the Space
Rats of the CCC, and my buddy then was the man they know as
Gentleman Jax. May Great Kramddl curse his name and blacken the
memory of the first day when I first set eyes on him . . .

"Graduating class . . . ten-SHUN!"

The sergeant's stentorian voice bellowed forth, cracking like a whiplash across the expectant ears of the mathematically aligned rows of cadets. With the harsh snap of those fateful words a hundred and three incredibly polished bootheels crashed together with a single snap, and the eighty-seven cadets of the graduating class snapped to steel-rigid attention. (It should be explained that some of them were from alien worlds, different numbers of legs, and so on.) Not a breath was drawn, not an eyelid twitched a thousandth of a milliliter as Colonel von Thorax stepped forward, glaring down at them all through the glass monocle in front of his glass eye, close-cropped gray hair stiff as barbed wire, black uniform faultlessly cut and smooth, a krmml weed cigarette clutched in the steel fingers of his prosthetic left arm, black gloved fingers of his prosthetic right arm snapping to hat-brim's edge in a perfect salute, motors whining thinly in his prosthetic lungs to power the Brobdingnagian roar of his harshly bellowed command.

"At ease. And listen to me. You are the handpicked men—and handpicked things too, of course—from all the civilized worlds of the galaxy. Six million and forty-three cadets entered the first year of training, and most of them washed out in one way or another. Some could not toe the mark. Some were expelled and shot for buggery. Some believed the lying commie pinko crying liberal claims that continuous war and slaughter are not necessary, and they were expelled and shot as well. One by one the weaklings fell away through the years leaving the hard core of the Corps—you! The Corpsmen of the first graduating class of the CCC! Ready to spread the benefits of civilization to the stars. Ready at last to find out what the initials CCC stand for!"

A mighty roar went up from the massed throats, a cheer of hoarse masculine enthusiasm that echoed and boomed from the stadium walls. At a signal from von Thorax a switch was thrown, and a great shield of imperviomite slid into place above, sealing the stadium from prying eyes and ears and snooping spyish rays. The roaring voices roared on enthusiastically—and many an eardrum was burst that day!—yet were stilled in an instant when the Colonel raised his hand.

"You Corpsmen will not be alone when you push the frontiers of civilization out to the barbaric stars. Oh no! You will each have a faithful companion by your side. First man, first row, step forward and meet your faithful companion!"

The Corpsman called out stepped forward a smart pace and clicked his heels sharply, said click being echoed in the clack of a thrown-wide door and, without conscious intent, every eye in that stadium was drawn in the direction of the dark doorway from which emerged. . . .

How to describe it? How to describe the whirlwind that batters you, the storm that engulfs you, the spacewarp that en-warps you? It was as indescribable as any natural force!

It was a creature three meters high at the shoulders, four meters high at the ugly, drooling, tooth-clashing head, a whirl-winded, spacewarped storm that rushed forward on four piston-like legs, great-clawed feet tearing grooves in the untearable surface of the impervitium flooring, a monster born of madness and nightmares that reared up before them and bellowed in a soul-destroying screech.

"There!" Colonel von Thorax bellowed in answer, blood-specked spittle mottling his lips. "There is your faithful companion, the mutacamel, mutation of the noble beast of Good Old Earth, symbol and pride of the CCC—the Combat Camel Corps! Corpsman meet your camel!"

The selected Corpsman stepped forward and raised his arm in greeting to this noble beast which promptly bit the arm off. His shrill screams mingled with the barely stifled gasps of his companions who watched, with more than casual interest, as camel trainers girt with brass-buckled leather harness rushed out and beat the protesting camel with clubs back from whence it had come, while a medic clamped a tourniquet on the wounded man's stump and dragged his limp body away.

"That is your first lesson on combat camels," the Colonel cried huskily. "Never raise your arms to them. Your companion, with a newly grafted arm will, I am certain, ha-ha!, remember this little lesson. Next man, next companion!"

Again the thunder of rushing feet and the high-pitch gurgling, scream-like roar of the combat camel at full charge. This time the Corpsman kept his arm down, and the camel bit his head off.

"Can't graft on a head I am afraid," the Colonel leered maliciously at them. "A moment of silence for our departed companion who has gone to the big rocket pad in the sky. That's enough. Ten-SHUN! You will now proceed to the camel training area where you will learn to get along with your faithful companions. Never forgetting that each has a complete set of teeth made of imperviomite, as well as razor-sharp claw caps of this same substance. Dis-MISSED!"

The student barracks of the CCC was well known for its "no frills" or rather "no coddling" decor and comforts. The beds were impervitium slabs—no spine-sapping mattresses here!—and the sheets of thin burlap. No blankets of course, not with the air kept at a healthy four degrees centigrade. The rest of the comforts matched so that it was a great surprise to the graduates to find unaccustomed comforts awaiting them upon their return from the ceremonies and training. There was a shade on each bare-bulbed reading light and a nice soft two-centimeter-thick pillow on every bed. Already they were reaping the benefits of all the years of labor.

Now, among all the students, the top student by far was named M———. There are some secrets that must not be told, names that are important to loved ones and neighbors. Therefore I shall draw the cloak of anonymity over the true identity of the man known as M———. Suffice to call him "Steel," for that was the nickname of someone who knew him best. "Steel," or Steel as we can call him, had at this time a roommate by the name of L———. Later, much later, he was to be called by certain people "Gentleman Jax," so for the purpose of this narrative we shall call him "Gentleman Jax" as well, or perhaps just plain "Jax." Jax was second only to Steel in scholastic and sporting attainments, and the two were the best of chums. They had been roommates for the past year and now they were back in their room with their feet up, basking in the unexpected luxury of the new furnishings, sipping decaffeinated coffee, called kof-fee, and smoking deeply of the school's own brand of denicotinized cigarettes, called Denikcig by the manufacturer but always referred to, humorously, by the CCC students as "gaspers" or "lungbusters."

"Throw me over a gasper, will you Jax," Steel said, from where he lolled on the bed, hands behind his head, dreaming of what was in store for him now that he would be having his own camel soon. "Ouch!" he chuckled as the pack of gaspers caught him in the eye. He drew out one of the slim white forms and tapped it on the wall to ignite it then drew in a lungful of refreshing smoke. "I still can't believe it . . ." he smokeringed.

"Well it's true enough, by Mrddl," Jax smiled. "We're graduates. Now throw back that pack of lungbusters so I can join you in a draw of two."

Steel complied, but did it so enthusiastically that the pack hit the wall and instantly all the cigarettes ignited and the whole thing burst into flame. A glass of water doused the conflagration but, while it was still fizzling fitfully, a light flashed redly on the comscreen.

"High-priority message," Steel bit out, slamming down the actu-ator button. Both youths snapped to rigid attention as the screen filled with the iron visage of Colonel von Thorax.

"M———, L———, to my office on the triple." The words fell like leaden weights from his lips. What could it mean?

"What can it mean?" Jax asked as they hurtled down a drop-chute at close to the speed of gravity.

"We'll find out quickly enough," Steel snapped as they drew up at the "old man's" door and activated the announcer button.

Moved by some hidden mechanism the door swung wide and, not without a certain amount of trepidation, they entered. But what was this? This! The Colonel was looking at them and smiling, smiling, an expression never before known to cross his stern face at any time.

"Make yourselves comfortable, lads," he indicated, pointing at comfortable chairs that rose out of the floor at the touch of a button. "You'll find gaspers in the arms of these servochairs, as well as Valumian wine or Snaggian beer."

"No koffee?" Jax open-mouthedly expostulated, and they all laughed.

"I don't think you really want it," the Colonel susurrated coyly through his artificial larynx. "Drink up lads, you're Space Rats of the CCC now, and your youth is behind you. Now look at that."

That was a three-dimensional image that sprang into being in the air before them at the touch of a button, an image of a spacer like none ever seen before. She was as slender as a swordfish, fine-winged as a bird, solid as a whale, and as armed to the teeth as an alligator.

"Holy Kolon," Steel sighed in open-mouthed awe. "Now that is what I call a hunk o' rocket!"

"Some of us prefer to call it the *Indefectible*," the Colonel said, not unhumorously.

"Is that her? We heard something . . ."

"You heard very little for we have had this baby under wraps ever since the earliest stage. She has the largest engines ever built, new improved MacPhersons* of the most advanced design, Kelly drive† gear that has been improved to where you would not recognize it in a month of Thursdays—as well as double-strength Fitzroy projectors‡ that make the old ones look like a kid's pop-gun. And I've saved the best for last—"

"Nothing can be better than what you have already told us," Steel broke in.

"That's what you think!" the Colonel laughed, not unkindly, with a sound like tearing steel. "The best news is that, M———, you are

---

*The MacPherson engine was first mentioned in the author's story "Rocket Rangers of the IRT" (*Spicy-Weird Stories*, 1923).
†Loyal readers first discovered the Kelly drive in the famous book *Hell Hounds of Coal Sack Cluster* (Slimecreeper Press, Ltd., 1931), also published in German as *Teufelhünde nach der Knockwurst Exspres*. Translated into Italian by Re Umberto, unpublished to date.
‡A media breakthrough was made when the Fitzroy projector first appeared in "Female Space Zombies of Venus" in 1936 in *True Story Confessions*.

going to be Captain of this spacegoing super-dreadnought, while Lucky L———is Chief Engineer."

"Lucky L———would be a lot happier if he were Captain instead of king of the stokehold," he muttered, and the other two laughed at what they thought was a joke.

"Everything is completely automated," the Colonel continued, "so it can be flown by a crew of two. But I must warn you that it has experimental gear aboard so whoever flies her has to volunteer . . ."

"I volunteer!" Steel shouted.

"I have to go to the terlet," Jax said, rising, though he sat again instantly when the ugly blaster leaped from its holster to the Colonel's hand. "Ha-ha, just a joke. I volunteer, sure."

"I knew I could count on you lads. The CCC breeds men. Camels too, of course. So here is what you do. At 0304 hours tomorrow you two in the *Indefectible* will crack ether headed out Cygnus way. In the direction of a certain planet."

"Let me guess, if I can, that is," Steel said grimly through tight-clenched teeth. "You don't mean to give us a crack at the larshnik-loaded world of Biru-2, do you?"

"I do. This is the larshniks' prime base, the seat of operation of all their drug and gambling traffic, where the white-slavers offload, and the queer green is printed, site of the flnnx distilleries and lair of the pirate hordes."

"If you want action that sounds like it!" Steel grimaced.

"You are not just whistling through your back teeth," the Colonel agreed. "If I were younger and had a few less replaceable parts this is the kind of opportunity I would leap at . . ."

"You can be Chief Engineer," Jax hinted.

"Shut up," the Colonel implied. "Good luck gentlemen for the honor of the CCC rides with you."

"But not the camels?" Steel asked.

"Maybe next time. There are, well, adjustment problems. We have lost four more graduates since we have been sitting here. Maybe we'll even change animals. Make it the CDC."

"With combat dogs?" Jax asked.

"Either that or donkeys. Or dugongs. But it is my worry, not yours. All you guys have to do is get out there and crack Biru-2 wide open. I know you can do it."

If the stern-faced Corpsmen had any doubts they kept them to themselves, for that is the way of the Corps. They did what had to be done and the next morning, at exactly 0304:00 hours, the mighty bulk of the *Indefectible* hurled itself into space. The roaring MacPherson engines poured quintillions of ergs of energy into the reactor drive until they were safely out of the gravity field of Mother Earth. Jax labored over his engines, shoveling the radioactive transvestite into the gaping maw of the hungry furnace, until Steel signaled from the bridge that it was "changeover" time. Then they changed over to the space-eating Kelly drive. Steel jammed home the button that activated the drive and the great ship leaped starward at seven times the speed of light.* Since the drive was fully automatic Jax freshened up in the fresher, while his clothes were automatically washed in the washer, then proceeded to the bridge.

"Really," Steel said, his eyebrows climbing up his forehead. "I didn't know you went in for polka-dot jockstraps."

"It was the only thing I had clean. The washer dissolved the rest of my clothes."

"Don't worry about it. It's the larshniks of Biru-2 who have to worry! We hit atmosphere in exactly seventeen minutes and I have been thinking about what to do when that happens."

"Well, I certainly hope someone has! I haven't had time to draw a deep breath, much less think."

"Don't worry, old pal, we are in this together. The way I figure it we have two choices. We can blast right in, guns roaring, or we can slip in by stealth."

"Oh, you really have been thinking, haven't you."

"I'll ignore that because you are tired. Strong as we are I think the land-based batteries are stronger. So I suggest we slip in without being noticed."

"Isn't that a little hard when you are flying in a thirty-ton spacer?"

"Normally, yes. But do you see this button here marked 'Invisibility'? While you were loading the fuel they explained this to me. It is a new invention, never used in action before, that will render us invisible and impervious to detection by any of their detection instruments."

"Now that's more like it. Fifteen minutes to go, we should be getting mighty close. Turn on the old invisibility ray . . ."

"Don't!"

"Done! Now what's your problem?"

"Nothing really. Except the experimental invisibility device is not expected to last more than thirteen minutes before it burns out."

Unhappily, this proved to be the case. One hundred miles above the barren, blasted surface of Biru-2 the good old *Indefectible* popped into existence.

---

*When the inventor, Patsy Kelly, was asked how the ships could move at seven times the speed of light when the limiting velocity of matter, according to Einstein, was the speed of light, he responded in his droll Goidelic way, with a shrug, "Well—sure and I guess Einstein was wrong."

In the minutest fraction of a millisecond the mighty spacesonar and superadar had locked grimly onto the invading ship while sublights flickered their secret signals, waiting for the correct response that would reveal the invader as one of theirs.

"I'll send a signal, stall them. These larshniks aren't too bright." Steel laughed. He thumbed on the microphone, switched to the interstellar emergency frequency, then bit out the rasping words in a sordid voice. "Agent X-9 to prime base. Had a firefight with the patrol, shot up my code books, but I got all the SOBs, ha-ha! Am coming home with a load of eight hundred thousand long tons of the hellish krmml weed."

The larshnik response was instantaneous. From the gaping, pitted orifices of thousands of giant blaster cannon there vomited forth ravening rays of energy that strained the very fabric of space itself. These coruscating forces blasted into the impregnable screens of the old *Indefectible*, which, sadly, was destined not to get much older, and instantly punched their way through and splashed coruscatingly from the very hull of the ship itself. Mere matter could not stand against such forces unlocked in the coruscating bowels of the planet itself so that the impregnable imperialite metal walls instantly vaporized into a thin gas which was, in turn, vaporized into the very electrons and protons (and neutrons too) of which it was made.

Mere flesh and blood could not stand against such forces. But in the few seconds it took the coruscating energies to eat through the force screens, hull, vaporized gas, and protons, the reckless pair of valiant Corpsmen had hurled themselves headlong into their space armor. And just in time! The ruin of the once great ship hit the atmosphere and seconds later slammed into the poison soil of Biru-2.

To the casual observer it looked like the end. The once mighty queen of the spaceways would fly no more for she now consisted of no more than two hundred pounds of smoking junk. Nor was there any sign of life from the tragic wreck to the surface crawlers who erupted from a nearby secret hatch concealed in the rock and crawled through the smoking remains with all their detectors detecting at maximum gain. "Report!" the radio signal wailed. "No sign of life to fifteen decimal places!" snapped back the cursing operator of the crawlers before he signaled them to return to base. Their metal cleats clanked viciously across the barren soil, and then they were gone. All that remained was the cooling metal wreck hissing with despair as the poison rain poured like tears upon it.

Were these two good friends dead? I thought you would never ask. Unbeknownst to the larshnik technicians, just one millisecond before the wreck struck down two massive and almost indestructible suits of space armor had been ejected by coiled steelite springs, sent flying to the very horizon where they landed behind a concealing spine of rock, which just by chance was the spine of rock into which the secret hatch had been built that concealed the crawlway from which the surface crawlers with their detectors emerged for their fruitless search, to which they returned under control of their cursing operator who, stoned-again with hellish krmml weed, never noticed the quick flick of the detector needles as the crawlers reentered the tunnel, this time bearing on their return journey a cargo they had not exited with as the great door slammed shut behind them.

"We've done it! We're inside their defenses," Steel rejoiced. "And no thanks to you, pushing that Mrddl-cursed invisibility button."

"Well, how was I to know?" Jax grated. "Anyways, we don't have a ship anymore but we do have the element of surprise. They don't know that we are here, but we know they are here!"

"Good thinking . . . hssst!" he hissed. "Stay low, we're coming to something."

The clanking crawlers rattled into the immense chamber cut into the living stone and now filled with deadly war machines of all description. The only human there, if he could be called human, was the larshnik operator whose soiled fingertips sprang to the gun controls the instant he spotted the intruders but he never stood a chance. Precisely aimed rays from two blasters zeroed in on him and in a millisecond he was no more than a charred fragment of smoking flesh in the chair. Corps justice was striking at last to the larshnik lair.

Justice it was, impersonal and final, impartial and murderous, for there were no "innocents" in this lair of evil. Ravening forces of civilized vengeance struck down all that crossed their path as the two chums rode a death-dealing combat gun through the corridors of infamy.

"This is the big one," Steel grimaced as they came to an immense door of gold-plated impervialite before which a suicide squad committed suicide under the relentless scourge of fire. There was more feeble resistance, smokily, coruscatingly and noisily exterminated, before this last barrier went down and they rode in triumph into the central control now manned by a single figure at the main panel. Superlarsh himself, secret head of the empire of interstellar crime.

"You have met your destiny," Steel intoned grimly, his weapon fixed unmovingly upon the black-robed figure in the opaque space helmet. "Take off that helmet or you die upon the instant."

His only reply was a slobbered growl of inchoate rage, and for a long instant the black-gloved hands trembled over the gun controls. Then, ever so slowly, these same hands raised themselves to clutch at the helmet, to turn it, to lift it slowly off . . .

"By the sacred name of the Prophet Mrddl!" the two Corpsmen gasped in unison, struck speechless by what they saw.

"Yes, so now you know," grated Superlarsh through angry teeth. "But, ha-ha, I'll bet you never suspected."

"You!!" Steel insufflated, breaking the frozen silence. "You! You!! YOU!!!"

"Yes, me, I, Colonel von Thorax, Commandant of the CCC. You never suspected me and, ohh, how I laughed at you all of the time!"

"But . . ." Jax stammered. "Why?"

"Why? The answer is obvious to any but democratic interstellar swine like you. The only thing the larshniks of the galaxy had to fear was something like the CCC, a powerful force impervious to outside bribery or sedition, noble in the cause of righteousness. You could have caused us trouble. Therefore we founded the CCC, and I have long been head of both organizations. Our recruiters bring in the best that the civilized planets can offer, and I see to it that most of them are brutalized, morale destroyed, bodies wasted, and spirits crushed so they are no longer a danger. Of course, a few always make it through the course no matter how disgusting I make it—every generation has its share of supermasochists—but I see that these are taken care of pretty quickly."

"Like being sent on suicide missions?" Steel asked ironly.

"That's a good way."

"Like the one we were sent on—but it didn't work! Say your prayers, you filthy larshnik, for you are about to meet your maker!"

"Maker? Prayers? Are you out of your skull? All larshniks are atheists to the end . . ."

And then it was the end, in a coruscating puff of vapor, dead with those vile words upon his lips, no less than he deserved.

"Now what?" Steel asked.

"This," Jax responded, shooting the gun from his hand and imprisoning him instantly with an unbreakable paralysis ray. "No more second best for me—in the engine room with you on the bridge. This is my ball game from here on in."

"Are you mad!" Steel fluttered through paralyzed lips.

"Sane for the first time in my life. The Superlarsh is dead, long live the new Superlarsh. It's mine, the whole galaxy, mine."

"And what about me?"

"I should kill you, but that would be too easy. And you did share your chocolate bars with me. You will be blamed for this entire debacle—for the death of Colonel von Thorax and for the disaster here at larshnik prime base. Every man's hand will be against you, and you will be an outcast and will flee for your life to the farflung outposts of the galaxy where you will live in terror."

"Remember the chocolate bars!"

"I do. All I ever got were the stale ones. Now . . . GO!"

You want to know my name? Old Sarge is good enough. My story? Too much for your tender ears, boyo. Just top up the glasses, that's the way, and join me in a toast. At least that much for a poor old man who has seen much in this long lifetime. A toast of bad luck, bad cess I say, may Great Kramddl curse forever the man some know as Gentleman Jax. What, hungry? Not me—no—NO! Not a chocolate bar!!!!!

Captain Honario Harpplayer, R.N.

Captain Honario Harpplayer was pacing the tiny quarterdeck of the HMS *Redundant*, hands clasped behind his back, teeth clamped in impotent fury. Ahead of him the battered French fleet limped towards port, torn sails flapping and spars trailing overside in the water, splintered hulls agape where his broadsides had gone thundering through their fragile wooden sides.

"Send two hands for'ard, if you please, Mr. Shrub," he said, "and have them throw water on the mainsail. Wet sails will add an eighth of a knot to our speed and we may overtake these cowardly frogs yet."

"B-but, sir," the stolid first mate Shrub stammered, quailing before the thought of disagreeing with his beloved captain. "If we take any more hands off the pumps we'll sink. We're holed in thirteen places below the waterline, and—"

"Damn your eyes, sir! I issued an order, not a request for a debate. Do as you were told."

"Aye, aye, sir," Shrub mumbled, humbled, knuckling a tear from one moist spaniel eye.

Water splashed onto the sails and the *Redundant* instantly sank lower in the water. Harpplayer clasped his hands behind his back and hated himself for this display of unwarranted temper towards the faithful Shrub. Yet he had to keep up this pose of strict disciplinarian before the crew, the sweepings and dregs of a thousand waterfronts, just as he had to wear a girdle to keep up his own front and a truss to keep up his hernia. He had to keep up a good front because he was the captain of this ship, the smallest ship in the blockading fleet that lay like a strangling noose around Europe, locking in the mad tyrant Napoleon, whose dreams of conquest could never extend to England whilst these tiny wooden ships stood in the way.

"Give us a prayer, Cap'n, to speed us on our way to 'eaven because we're sinkin'!" a voice called from the crowd of seamen at the pumps.

"I'll have that man's name, Mr. Dogleg," Harpplayer called to the midshipman, a mere child of seven or eight, who commanded the detail. "No rum for him for a week."

"Aye aye, sir," piped Mr. Dogleg, who was just learning to talk.

The ship was sinking, the fact was inescapable. Rats were running on deck, ignoring the cursing, stamping sailors, and hurling themselves into the sea. Ahead the French fleet had reached the safety of the shore batteries on Cape Pietfieux and the gaping mouths of these guns were turned towards the *Redundant*, ready to spout fire and death when the fragile ship came within range.

"Be ready to drop sail, Mr. Shrub," Harpplayer said, then raised his voice so all the crew could hear. "Those cowardly Frenchies have run away and cheated us of a million pounds in prize money."

A growl went up from the crew who, next to a love for rum, loved the pounds, shillings and pence with which they could buy the rum. The growl was suddenly cut off in muffled howls of pain as the main-mast, weakened by the badly aimed French cannon, fell onto the mass of laboring men.

"No need to drop sail, Mr. Shrub, the slaves of our friend Boney have done it for us," Harpplayer said, forcing himself to make one of his rare jests so loved by the crew. He hated himself for the falseness of his feelings, ingratiating himself into the sympathies of these illiterate men by such means, but it was his duty to keep a taut ship. Besides, if he didn't make any jokes the men would hate him for the slave-driving, cold-blooded, chance-taking master that he was. They still hated him, of course, but they laughed while they did it.

They were laughing now as they cut away the tangle of rigging and dragged out the bodies to lay them in neat rows upon the deck. The ship sank lower in the water.

"Avast that body dragging," he ordered, "and man the pumps, or we'll have our dinners on the bottom of the sea."

The men laughed a ragged laugh again and hurried to their tasks.

They were easy to please, and Harpplayer envied them their simple lives. Even with the heavy work, bad water and an occasional touch of the cat, their existence was better than his tortured life on the lonely pinnacle of command. The decisions were all his to make, and to a man of his morbid and paranoiac nature this made life a living hell. His officers, who all hated him, were incompetents. Even Shrub, faithful, long-suffering Shrub, had his weakness: namely the fact that he had an IQ of about 60 which, combined with his low birth, meant he could never rise above the rank of a rear admiral.

While he considered the varied events of the day Harpplayer began his compulsive pacing on the tiny quarterdeck, and its other occupants huddled against the starboard side where they wouldn't be in his way. Four paces in one direction, then three-and-a-half paces back with his knee bringing up with a shuddering crack against the port carronade. Yet Harpplayer did not feel this, his cardplayer's brain was whirling with thoughts, evaluating and weighing plans, rejecting those that held a modicum of sanity and only considering those that sounded too insane to be practical. No wonder he was called "Sap-sucker Harpy" throughout the fleet and held in awe as a man who could always pull victory from the jaws of defeat, and always at an immense cost in lives. But that was war. You gave your commands and good men died, and that was what the press gangs on shore were for. It had been a long and trying day, yet he still would not permit himself to relax. Tension and the agony of apprehension had seized him in the relentless grip of a Cerberus ever since soon after dawn that morning when the lookout had announced the discovery of sails on the horizon. There had been only ten of them, Frenchy ships of the line, and before the morning fog had cleared the vengeful form of the *Redundant* had been upon them, like a wolf among the sheep. Broadside after broadside had roared out from the precisely serviced English guns, ten balls for every one that popped out of the French cannon, manned by cowardly sweepings of the eighth and ninth classes of 1812, gray-bearded patriarchs and diapered infants who only wished they were back in the familial vineyards instead of here, fighting for the Tyrant, facing up to the wrath of the death-dealing cannon of their island enemy, the tiny country left to fight alone against the might of an entire continent. It had been a relentless stern chase, and only the succor of the French port had prevented the destruction of the entire squadron. As it was, four of them lay among the conger eels on the bottom of the ocean and the remaining six would need a complete refitting before they were fit to leave port and once more dare the retributive might of the ships that ringed their shores.

Harpplayer knew what he had to do.

"If you please, Mr. Shrub, have the hose rigged. I feel it is time for a bath."

A ragged cheer broke from the toiling sailors, since they knew what to expect. In the coldest northern waters or in the dead of winter Harpplayer insisted on this routine of the bath. The hoses were quickly attached to the laboring pumps and soon columns of icy water were jetting across the deck.

"In we go!" shouted Harpplayer, and stepped back well out of the way of any chance droplets, at the same time scratching with a long index finger at the skin of his side, unwashed since the previous summer. He smiled at the childish antics of Shrub and the other officers prancing nude in the water, and only signaled for the pumps to cease their work when all of the white skins had turned a nice cerulean.

There was a rumble, not unlike distant thunder yet sharper and louder, from the northern horizon. Harpplayer turned and for a long instant saw a streak of fire painted against the dark clouds, before it died from the sky, leaving only an afterimage in his eyes. He shook his head to clear it, and blinked rapidly a few times. For an instant there he could have sworn that the streak of light had come down, instead of going up, but that was manifestly impossible. Too many late nights playing Boston with his officers, no wonder his eyesight was going.

"What was that, Captain?" Lieutenant Shrub asked, his words scarcely audible through the chattering of his teeth.

"A signal rocket—or perhaps one of those newfangled Congreve war rockets. There's trouble over there and we're going to find out just what it is. Send the hands to the braces, if you please, fill the maintops'l and lay her on the starboard tack."

"Can I put my pants on first?"

"No impertinence, sir, or I'll have you in irons!"

Shrub bellowed the orders through the speaking trumpet and all the hands laughed at his shaking naked legs. Yet in a few seconds the well-trained crew, who not six days before had been wenching and drinking ashore on civvy street, never dreaming that the wide-sweeping press gangs would round them up and send them to sea, leapt to the braces, hurled the broken spars and cordage overside, sealed the shot holes, buried the dead, drank their grog and still had enough energy left over for a few of their number to do a gay hornpipe. The ship heeled as she turned, water creamed under her bows and then she was on the new tack, reaching out from the shore, investigating this new occurrence, making her presence felt as the representative of the mightiest blockading fleet the world, at that time, had ever known.

"A ship ahead, sir," the masthead lookout called. "Two points off the starboard bow."

"Beat to quarters," Harpplayer ordered.

Through the heavy roll of the drum and the slap of the sailors' bare horny feet on the deck, the voice of the lookout could be barely heard.

"No sails nor spars, sir. She's about the size of our longboat."

"Belay that last order. And when that lookout comes off duty I want him to recite five hundred times, 'A boat is something that's picked up and put on a ship.' "

Pressed on by the freshening land breeze the *Redundant* closed rapidly on the boat until it could be made out clearly from the deck.

"No masts, no spars, no sails—what makes it move?" Lieutenant Shrub asked with gape-mouthed puzzlement.

"There is no point in speculation in advance, Mr. Shrub. This craft may be French or a neutral so I'll take no chances. Let us have the cannonades loaded and run out. And I want the Marines in the fut-tock shrouds, with their pieces on the half-cock, if you please. I want no one to fire until they receive my command, and I'll have anyone who does boiled in oil and served for breakfast."

"You are the card, sir!"

"Am I? Remember the cox'n who got his orders mixed yesterday?"

"Very gamey, sir, if I say so," Shrub said, picking a bit of gristle from between his teeth. "I'll issue the orders, sir."

The strange craft was like nothing Harpplayer had ever seen before. It advanced without visible motive power and he thought of hidden rowers with underwater oars, but they would have to be midgets to fit in the boat. It was decked all over and appeared to be covered with a glass hutment of some kind. All in all a strange device, and certainly not French. The unwilling slaves of the Octopus in Paris would never master the precise techniques to construct a diadem of the sea such as this. No, this was from some alien land, perhaps from beyond China or the mysterious islands of the East. There was a man seated in the craft and he touched a lever that rolled back the top window. He stood then and waved to them. A concerted gasp ran through the watchers, for every eye in the ship was fastened on this strange occurrence.

"What is this, Mr. Shrub?" Harpplayer shouted. "Are we at a fun fair or a Christmas pantomime? Discipline, sir!"

"B-but, sir," the faithful Shrub stammered, suddenly at a loss for words. "That man, sir—he's *green!*"

"I want none of your damn nonsense, sir," Harpplayer snapped irritably, annoyed as he always was when people babbled about their imagined "colors." Paintings, and sunsets and such tripe. Nonsense. The world was made up of healthy shades of gray and that was that. Some fool of a Harley Street quack had once mentioned an imaginary malady which he termed "color blindness," but had desisted with his tomfoolery when Harpplayer had mentioned the choice of seconds.

"Green, pink or purple, I don't care what shade of gray the fellow is. Throw him a line and have him up here where we can hear his story."

The line was dropped and after securing it to a ring on his boat the stranger touched a lever that closed the glass cabin once more, then climbed easily to the deck above.

"Green fur . . ." Shrub said, then clamped his mouth shut under Harpplayer's fierce glare.

"Enough of that, Mr. Shrub. He's a foreigner and we will treat him with respect, at least until we find out what class he is from. He is a bit hairy, I admit, but certain races in the north of the Nipponese Isles are that way, perhaps he comes from there. I bid you welcome, sir," he said addressing the man. "I am Captain Honario Harpplayer, commander of His Majesty's ship *Redundant.*"

" '*Kwl-kkle-wrrl-ki . . . !*"

"Not French," Harpplayer muttered, "nor Latin nor Greek I warrant. Perhaps one of those barbaric Baltic tongues. I'll try him on

German. *Ich rate Ihnen, Reiseschecks mitzunehmen?* Or an Italian dialect? *Vendono è proibito; però qui si cartoline ricordo."*

The stranger responded by springing up and down excitedly, then pointing to the sun, making circular motions around his head, pointing to the clouds, making falling motions with his hands, and shrilly shouting *"M'ku, m'ku!"*

"Feller's barmy," the Marine officer said, "and besides, he got too many fingers."

"I can count to seven without your help," Shrub told him angrily. "I think he's trying to tell us it's going to rain."

"He may be a meteorologist in his own land," Harpplayer said safely, "but here he is just another alien."

The officers nodded agreement, and this motion seemed to excite the stranger for he sprang forward shouting his unintelligible gibberish. The alert Marine guard caught him in the back of the head with the butt of his Tower musket and the hairy man fell to the deck.

"Tried to attack you, Captain," the Marine officer said. "Shall we keel-haul him, sir?"

"No, poor chap is a long way from home, may be worried. We must allow for the language barrier. Just read him the Articles of War and impress him into the service. We're short of hands after that last encounter."

"You are of a very forgiving nature, sir, and an example for us all. What shall we do with his ship?"

"I'll examine it. There may be some principle of operation here that would be of interest to Whitehall. Drop a ladder I'll have a look myself."

After some fumbling Harpplayer found the lever that moved the glass cabin, and when it slid aside he dropped into the cockpit that it covered. A comfortable divan faced a board covered with a strange collection of handles, buttons and diverse machines concealed beneath crystal covers. It was a perfect example of the decadence of the East, excessive decoration and ornamentation where a panel of good English oak would have done as well, and a simple pivoted bar to carry the instructions to the slaves that rowed the boat. Or perhaps there was an animal concealed behind the panel, he heard a deep roar when he touched a certain lever. This evidently signaled the galley slave—or animal—to begin his labors, since the little craft was now rushing through the water at a good pace. Spray was slapping into the cockpit so Harpplayer closed the cover, which was a good thing. Another button must have tilted a concealed rudder because the boat suddenly plunged its nose down and sank, the water rising up until it washed over the top of the glass. Luckily, the craft was stoutly made and did not leak, and another button caused the boat to surface again.

It was at that instant that Harpplayer had the idea. He sat as one paralyzed, while his rapid thoughts ran through the possibilities. Yes, it might work—it would work! He smacked his fist into his open palm and only then realized that the tiny craft had turned while he had been thinking and was about to ram into the *Redundant*, whose rail was lined with frighten-eyed faces. With a skillful touch he signaled the animal (or slave) to stop and there was only the slightest bump as the vessels touched.

"Mr. Shrub," he called.

"Sir?"

"I want a hammer, six nails, six kegs of gunpowder each with a two-minute fuse and a looped rope attached, and a dark lantern."

"But, sir—what for?" For once the startled Shrub forgot himself enough to question his captain.

The plan had so cheered Harpplayer that he took no umbrage at this sudden familiarity. In fact he even smiled into his cuff, the expression hidden by the failing light.

"Why—six barrels because there are six ships," he said with unaccustomed coyness. "Now, carry on."

The gunner and his mates quickly completed their task and the barrels were lowered in a sling. They completely filled the tiny cockpit, barely leaving room for Harpplayer to sit. In fact there was no room for the hammer and he had to hold it between his teeth.

"Mither Thrub," he said indistinctly around the hammer, suddenly depressed as he realized that in a few moments he would be pitting his own frail body against the hordes of the usurper who cracked the whip over a continent of oppressed slaves. He quailed at his temerity at thus facing the Tyrant of Europe, then quailed before his own disgust at his frailty. The men must never know that he had these thoughts, that he was the weakest of them. "Mr. Shrub," he called again, and there was no sound of his feelings in his voice. "If I do not return by dawn you are in command of this ship and will make a full report. Goodbye. In triplicate, mind."

"Oh, sir—" Shrub began, but his words were cut off as the glass cover sprang shut and the tiny craft hurled itself against all the power of a continent.

Afterwards Harpplayer was to laugh at his first weakness. Truly, the escapade was as simple as strolling down Fleet Street on a Sunday morning. The foreign ship sank beneath the surface and slipped past the batteries on Cape Pietfieux, that the English sailors called Cape Pitfix, and into the guarded waters of Cienfique. No guard noticed the slight roiling of the waters of the bay and no human eye saw the dim shape that surfaced next to the high wooden wall that was the hull of the French ship of the line. Two sharp blows of the hammer secured the first keg of gunpowder and a brief flash of light came from the dark lantern as the fuse was lit. Before the puzzled sentries on the deck above could reach the rail the mysterious visitor was gone and they could not see the telltale fuse sputtering away, concealed by the barrel of death that it crept slowly towards. Five times Harpplayer repeated this simple, yet deadly, activity, and as he was driving the last nail there was a muffled explosion from the first ship. Hutment closed, he made his way from the harbor, and behind him six ships, the pride of the Tyrant's navy, burnt in pillars of flame until all that was left was the charred hulls, settling to the ocean floor.

Captain Harpplayer opened the glass hutment when he was past the shore batteries, and looked back with satisfaction at the burning ships. He had done his duty and his small part towards ending this awful war that had devastated a continent and would, in the course of a few years, kill so many of the finest Frenchmen that the height of the entire French race would be reduced by an average of more than five inches. The last pyre died down and, feeling a twinge of regret, since they had been fine ships, though in fief to the Madman in Paris, he turned the bow of his craft towards the *Redundant*.

It was dawn when he reached the ship, and exhaustion tugged at him. He grabbed the ladder lowered for him and painfully climbed to the deck. The drums whirred and the sideboys saluted; the bos'uns' pipes toiled.

"Well done, sir, oh well done!" Shrub exclaimed, rushing forward to take his hand. "We could see them burning from here."

Behind them, in the water, there was a deep burbling, like the water running from the tub when the plug is pulled and Harpplayer turned just in time to see the strange craft sinking into the sea and vanishing from sight.

"Damn silly of me," he muttered. "Forgot to close the hatch. Running quite a sea, must have washed in."

His ruminations were sharply cut through by a sudden scream. He turned just in time to see the hairy stranger run to the rail and stare, horrified, at the vanishing craft. Then the man, obviously bereaved, screamed horribly and tore great handfuls of hair from his head, a relatively easy task since he had so much. Then, before anyone could think to stop him, he had mounted to the rail and plunged headfirst into the sea. He sank like a rock, and either could not swim, or did not want to; he seemed strangely attached to his craft, since he did not return to the surface.

"Poor chap," Harpplayer said with the compassion of a sensitive man, "to be alone, and so far from home. Perhaps he is happier dead."

"Aye, perhaps," the stolid Shrub muttered, "but he had the makings of a good topman in him, sir. Could run right out on the spars he could, held on very well he did, what with those long toenails of his that bit right into the wood. Had another toe in his heel that helped him hold on."

"I'll ask you not to discuss the deformities of the dead. We'll list him in the report as Lost Overboard. What was his name?"

"Wouldn't tell us, sir, but we carry him in the books as Mr. Green."

"Fair enough. Though foreign-born, he would be proud to know that he died bearing a good English name." Then curtly dismissing the faithful and stupid Shrub, Harpplayer resumed walking the quarterdeck, filled with the silent agony which was his alone and would be until the guns of the Corsican Ogre were spiked forever.

OTHER WORLDS

It would be such fun to visit other strange and exciting, far-distant worlds! Not very likely though. Even if after great expense a few astronauts do get to set foot on some of the other planets in our solar system they will either have to fry or freeze. These sorts of visits supply good plot material—in fact you'll find a solar planet right here in this section.

But that is close-to-home stuff. In the long run what we want to do is visit exotic planets with Earth-like atmospheres. That is where the fun is, the adventure and the excitement. With the barrier of the speed of light preventing this in reality—why, we'll just have to get there in fiction.

Come fly with me . . .

Simulated Trainer

Mars was a dusty, frigid hell. Bone dry and blood red. They trudged single-file through the ankle-deep sand, and in a monotonous duet cursed the nameless engineer who had designed the faulty reconditioners in their pressure suits. The bug hadn't shown during testing of the new suits. It appeared only after they had been using them steadily for a few weeks. The water-absorbers became overloaded and broke down. The Martian atmosphere stood at a frigid sixty degrees centigrade. Inside the suits, they tried to blink the unevaporated sweat from their eyes and slowly cooked in the high humidity.

Morley shook his head viciously to dislodge an itching droplet from his nose. At the same moment, something rust-colored and furry darted across his path. It was the first Martian life they had seen. Instead of scientific curiosity, he felt only anger. A sudden kick sent the animal flying high into the air.

The suddenness of the movement threw him off balance. He fell sideways slowly, dragging his rubberized suit along an upright rock fragment of sharp obsidian.

Tony Bannerman heard the other man's hoarse shout in his earphones and whirled. Morley was down, thrashing on the sand with both hands pressed against the ragged tear in the suit leg. Moisture-laden air was pouring out in a steaming jet that turned instantly to scintillating ice crystals. Tony jumped over to him, trying to seal the tear with his own ineffectual gloves. Their faceplates close, he could see the look of terror on Morley's face—as well as the blue tinge of cyanosis.

"Help me—help me!"

The words were shouted so loud they rasped the tiny helmet earphones. But there was no help. They had taken no emergency patches with them. All the patches were in the ship at least a quarter of a mile away. Before he could get there and back. Morley would be dead. Tony straightened up slowly and sighed. Just the two of them in the ship; there was no one else on Mars who could help. Morley saw the look in Tony's eyes and stopped struggling.

"No hope at all, Tony—I'm dead."

"Just as soon as all the oxygen is gone; thirty seconds at the most. There's nothing I can do."

Morley grated the shortest, vilest word he knew and pressed the red EMERGENCY button set into his glove above the wrist. The ground opened up next to him in the same instant, sand sifting down around the edges of the gap. Tony stepped back as two men in white pressure suits came up out of the hole. They had red crosses on the fronts of their helmets and carried a stretcher. They rolled Morley onto it and were gone back into the opening in an instant.

Tony stood looking sourly at the hole for about a minute waiting until Morley's suit was pushed back through the opening. Then the sand-covered trapdoor closed and the desert was unbroken once more.

The dummy in the suit weighed as much as Morley and its plastic features even resembled him a bit. Some wag had painted black X's on the eyes. Very funny, Tony thought, he struggled to get the clumsy thing onto his back. On the way back to the ship the now-quiet Martian animal was lying in his path. He kicked it aside and it rained a fine shower of springs and gears.

The too-small sun was touching the peaks of the sawtooth red mountains when he reached the ship. Too late for burial today—it would have to wait until morning. Leaving the thing in the airlock, he stamped into the cabin and peeled off his dripping pressure suit.

It was dark by that time and the things they had called the night-owls began clicking and scratching against the hull of the ship. They had never managed to catch sight of the night-owls; that made the sound doubly annoying. He clattered the pans noisily to drown the sound of them out while he prepared the hot evening rations. When the meal was finished and the dishes cleared away, he began to feel the loneliness for the first time. Even the chew of tobacco didn't help; tonight it only reminded him of the humidor of green Havana cigars waiting for him back on Earth.

His single kick upset the slim leg of the mess table, sending metal dishes, pans and silverware flying in every direction. They made a satisfactory noise and he exacted even greater pleasure by leaving the mess just that way and going to bed.

They had been so close this time, if only Morley had kept his eyes open! He forced the thought out of his mind and went to sleep.

In the morning he buried Morley. Then, grimly and carefully, passed the remaining two days until blastoff time. Most of the geological samples were in and the air sampling and radiation recording meters were fully automatic.

On the final day, he removed the recording tapes from the instruments and carried the instruments away from the ship where they couldn't be caught in the takeoff blast. Next to the instruments he piled all the extra supplies, machinery and unneeded equipment. Shuffling through the rusty sand for the last time, he gave Morley's grave an ironical salute as he passed. There was nothing to do in the ship and not as much as a pamphlet left to read. Tony passed the two remaining hours on his bunk counting the rivets in the ceiling.

A sharp click from the control clock broke the silence and behind the thick partition he could hear the engines begin the warm-up cycle. At the same time, the padded arms slipped across his bunk, pinning him down securely. He watched the panel slip back in the wall next to him and the hypo arm slide through, moving erratically like a snake as its metal fingers sought him out. They touched his ankle and the serpent's tooth of the needle snapped free. The last thing he saw was the needle slipping into his vein, then the drug blacked him out.

As soon as he was under, a hatch opened in the rear bulkhead and two orderlies brought in a stretcher. They wore neither suits nor masks and the blue sky of Earth was visible behind them.

Coming to was the same as it always had been. The gentle glow from the stimulants that brought him up out of it, the first sight of the white ceiling of the operating room on Earth.

Only this time the ceiling wasn't visible, it was obscured by the red face and thundercloud brow of Colonel Stregham. Tony tried to remember if you saluted while in bed, then decided that the best thing to do was lie quietly.

"Damn it, Bannerman," the colonel growled, "welcome back on Earth. And why did you bother coming back? With Morley dead the expedition has to be counted a failure—and that means not one completely successful expedition to date."

"The team in number two, sir, how did they do . . . ?" Tony tried to sound cheerful.

"Terrible. If anything, worse than your team. Both dead on the second day after landing. A meteor puncture in their oxygen tank and they were too busy discovering a new flora to bother looking at any meters.

"Anyway, that's not why I'm here. Get on some clothes and come into my office."

He slammed out and Tony scrambled off the bed, ignoring the touch of dizziness from the drugs. When colonels speak lieutenants hurry to obey.

Colonel Stregham was scowling out of his window when Tony came in. He returned the salute and proved that he had a shard of humanity left in his military soul by offering Tony one of his cigars. Only when they had both lit up did he wave Tony's attention to the field outside the window.

"Do you see that? Know what it is?"

"Yes, sir, the Mars rocket."

"It's going to be the Mars rocket. Right now, it's only a half-completed hull. The motors and instruments are being assembled in plants all over the country. Working on a crash basis the earliest estimate of completion is six months from now.

"The ship will be ready—only we aren't going to have any men to go in her. At the present rate of washout there won't be a single man qualified. Yourself included."

Tony shifted uncomfortably under his gaze as the colonel continued.

"This training program has always been my baby. I dreamed it up and kept after the Pentagon until it was adopted. We knew we could build a ship that would get to Mars and back, operated by automatic controls that would fly her under any degree of gravity or free fall. But we needed men who could walk out on the surface of the planet and explore it—or the whole thing would be so much wasted effort.

"The ship and the robot pilot could be tested under simulated flight condition, and the bugs worked out. It was my suggestion, which was adopted, that the men who were to go in the ship should be shaken down in the same way. Two pressure chambers were built, simulated trainers that duplicated Mars in every detail we could imagine. We have been running two-men teams through these chambers for eighteen months now, trying to shake down and train them to man the real ship out there.

"I'm not going to tell you how many men we started with, or how many have been casualties because of the necessary realism of the chambers. I'll tell you this much though—we haven't had one successful simulated expedition in all that time. And every man who has broken down or 'died,' like your partner Morley, has been eliminated.

"There are only four possible men left, yourself included. If we don't get one successful two-man team out of you four, the entire program is a washout."

Tony sat frozen, the dead cigar between his fingers. He knew that the pressure had been on for some months now, that Colonel Stregham had been growling around like a gut-shot bear. The colonel's voice cut through his thoughts.

"Psych division has been after me for what they think is a basic weakness of the program. Their feeling is that because it is a training program the men always have it in the back of their minds that it's not for real. They can always be pulled out of a tight hole. Like Morley was, at the last moment. After the results we have had I am beginning to agree with Psych.

"There are four men left and I am going to run one more exercise for each two-man group. This final exercise will be a full dress rehearsal—this time we're playing for keeps."

"I don't understand, Colonel . . ."

"It's simple." Stregham accented his words with a bang of his fist on the desk. "We're not going to help—or pull anyone out no matter how much they need it. This is battle training with live ammunition.

We're going to throw everything at you that we can think of—and you are going to have to take it. If you tear your suit this time, you're going to die in the Martian vacuum just a few feet from all the air in the world."

His voice softened just a bit when he dismissed Tony.

"I wish there was some other way to do it, but we have no choice now. We have to get a crew for that ship next month and this is the only way to be sure."

Tony had a three-day pass. He was drunk the first day, hungover sick the second—and boiling mad on the third. Every man on the project was a volunteer, adding deadly realism, that was carrying the thing too far. He could get out any time he wanted, though he knew what he would look like then. There was only one thing to do: go along with the whole stupid idea. He would do what they wanted and go through with it. And when he had finished the exercise, he looked forward to hitting the colonel right on the end of his big bulbous nose.

He joined his new partner, Hal Mendoza, when he went for his medical. They had met casually at the training lecture before the simulated training began. They shook hands reservedly now, each eyeing the other with a view to future possibilities. It took two men to make a team and either one could be the cause of death for the other.

Mendoza was almost the physical opposite of Tony, tall and gangling, while Tony was as squat and solid as a bear. Tony's relaxed, almost casual manner was matched by the other man's seemingly tense nerves. Hal chain-smoked and his eye were never still.

Tony pushed away his momentary worry with an effort. Hal would have to be good to get this far in the program. He would probably calm down once the exercise was under way.

The medic took Tony next and began the detailed examination.

"What's this?" the medical officer asked Tony as he probed with a swab at his cheek.

"Ouch," Tony said. "Razor cut, my hand slipped while I was shaving."

The doctor scowled and painted on antiseptic, then slapped on a square of gauze.

"Watch all skin openings," he warned. "They make ideal entry routes for bacteria. Never know what you might find on Mars."

Tony started a protest, then let it die in his throat. What was the use of explaining that the real trip if and when it ever came off—would take 260 days? Any cuts would easily heal in that time, even in frozen sleep.

As always after the medical, they climbed into their flight suits and walked over to the testing building. On the way Tony stopped at the barracks and dug out his chess set and well-thumbed deck of cards. The access door was open in the thick wall of Building 2 and they stepped through into the dummy Mars ship. After the medics had strapped them to the bunks the simulated frozen sleep shots put them under.

Coming to was accompanied by the usual nausea and weakness. No realism spared. On a sudden impulse Tony staggered to the latrine mirror and blinked at his red-eyed, smooth-shaven reflection. He tore the bandage off his cheek and his fingers touched the open cut with the still congealed drop of blood at the bottom. A relaxed sigh slipped out. He had the recurrent bad dream that someday one of these training trips would really be a flight to Mars. Logic told him that the military would never forgo the pleasure and publicity of a big sendoff. Yet the doubt, like all illogical ones, persisted. At the beginning of each training flight, he had to abolish it again.

The nausea came back with a swoop and he forced it down. This was one exercise where he couldn't waste time. The ship had to be checked. Hal was sitting up on his bunk waving a limp hand. Tony waved back.

At that moment, the emergency communication speaker crackled into life. At first, there was just the rustle of activity in the control office, then the training officer's voice cut through the background noise.

"Lieutenant Bannerman—you awake yet?"

Tony fumbled the mike out of its clip and reported. "Here, sir."

"Just a second, Tony," the officer said. He mumbled to someone at one side of the mike, then came back on. "There's been some trouble with one of the bleeder valves in the chamber, the pressure is above Mars norm. Hold the exercise until we pump her back down."

"Yes, sir," Tony said, then killed the mike so he and Hal could groan about the so-called efficiency of the training squad. It was only a few minutes before the speaker came back to life.

"Okay, pressure on the button. Carry on as before."

Tony made an obscene gesture at the unseen man behind the voice and walked over to the single port. He cranked at the handle that moved the crash shield out of the way.

"Well, at least it's a quiet one," he said after the ruddy light had streamed in. Hal came up and looked over his shoulder.

"Praise Stregham for that," he said. "The last one, where I lost my partner, was wind all the time. From the shape of those dunes it looks like the atmosphere never moves at all." They stared glumly at the familiar red landscape and dark sky for a long moment, then Tony turned to the controls while Hal cracked out the atmosphere suits.

"Over here—quickly."

Hal didn't have to be called twice, he was at the board in a single jump. He followed Tony's pointing finger.

"The water meter—it shows the tank's only about half full."

They fought off the plate that gave access to the tank compartment. When they laid it aside a small trickle of rusty water ran across the deck at their feet. Tony crawled in with a flashlight and moved it up and down the tubular tanks. His muffled voice echoed inside the small compartment.

"Damn Stregham and his tricks—another 'shock of landing' failure. Connecting pipe split and the water that leaked out has soaked down into the insulating layer; we'll never get it out without tearing the ship apart. Hand me the goo. I'll plug the leak until we can repair it."

"It's going to be an awfully dry month," Hal muttered while he checked the rest of the control board.

The first few days were like every other trip. They planted the flag and unloaded the equipment. The observing and recording instruments were set up by the third day, so they unshipped the theodolite and started their maps. By the fourth day they were ready to begin their sample collection.

It was just at this point that they really became aware of the dust.

Tony chewed an usually gritty mouthful of rations cursing under his breath because there was only a mouthful of water to wash it down with. He swallowed it painfully then looked around the control chamber.

"Have you noticed how dusty it is?" he asked.

"How could you not notice it? I have so much of it inside my clothes I feel like I'm living on an anthill."

Hal stopped scratching just long enough to take a bite of food.

They both looked around and it hit them for the first time just how much dust was in the ship. A red coating on everything, in their food and in their hair. The constant scratch of grit underfoot.

"It must come in on our suits," Tony said. "We'll have to clean them off better before coming inside."

It was a good idea—the only trouble was that it did not work. The red dust was as fine as talcum powder and no amount of beating could dislodge it; it just drifted around in a fine haze. They tried to forget the dust, just treating it as one more nuisance Stregham's technicians had dreamed up. This worked for a while, until the eighth day when they couldn't close the outer door of the air lock. They had just returned from a sample-collecting trip. The air lock barely held the two of them plus the bags of rock samples. Taking turns, they beat the dust off each other as well as they could, then Hal threw the cycling switch. The outer door started to close, then stopped. They could feel the increased hum of the door motor through their shoes, then it cut out and the red trouble light flashed on.

"Dust!" Tony said. "That damned red dust is in the works."

The inspection plate came off easily and they saw the exposed gear train. The red dust had merged into a destructive mud with the grease. Finding the trouble was easier than repairing it. They had only a few basic tools in their suit pouches. The big toolbox and all the solvent that would have made fast work of the job were inside the ship. But they couldn't be reached until the door was fixed. And the door couldn't be fixed without tools. It was a paradoxical situation that seemed very unfunny.

It took them only a second to realize the spot they were in—and almost two hours to clean the gears as best they could and force the door shut. When the inner port finally opened, both their oxygen tanks ready EMPTY, and they were operating on the emergency reserves.

As soon as Hal opened his helmet, he dropped on his bunk. Tony thought he was unconscious until he saw that the other man's eyes were open and staring at the ceiling. He cracked open the single flask of medicinal brandy and forced Hal to take some. Then he had a double swallow himself and tried to ignore the fact that his partner's hands were trembling violently. He busied himself making a better repair of the door mechanism. By the time he had finished, Hal was off the bunk and starting to prepare their evening meal.

Outside of the dust, it was a routine exercise—at first. Surveying and sampling most of the day, then a few leisure hours before retiring. Hal was a good partner and the best chess player Tony had teamed with to date. Tony soon found out that what he thought was nervousness was nervous energy. Hal was only happy when he was doing something. He threw himself into the day's work and had enough enthusiasm and energy left over to smash the yawning Tony over the chessboard. The two men were quite opposite types and made good teammates.

Everything looked good—except for the dust. It was everywhere, and slowly getting into everything. It annoyed Tony, but he stolidly did not let it bother him deeply. Hal was the one that suffered most. It scratched and itched him, setting his temper on edge. He began to have trouble sleeping. And the creeping dust was slowly working its way into every single item of equipment. The machinery was starting to wear as fast as their nerves. The constant presence of the itching dust, together with the acute water shortage was maddening. They were always thirsty and had only the minimum amount of water to last until blastoff. With proper rationing, it would barely be enough.

They quarreled over the ration on the thirteenth day and almost came to blows. For two days after that they didn't talk. Tony noticed that Hal always kept one of the sampling hammers in his pocket; in turn, he took to carrying one of the dinner knives.

Something had to crack. It turned out to be Hal.

It must have been the lack of sleep that finally got to him. He had always been a light sleeper, now the tension and the dust were too much. Tony could hear him scratching and turning each night when he forced himself to sleep. He wasn't sleeping too well himself, but at least he managed to get a bit. From the black hollows under Hal's bloodshot eyes it didn't look like Hal was getting any.

On the eighteenth day he cracked. They were just getting into their suits when he started shaking. Not just his hands but all over. He just stood there shaking until Tony got him to the bunk and gave him the rest of the brandy. When the attack was over he refused to go outside.

"I won't . . . I can't!" He screamed the words. "The suits won't last much longer, they'll fail while we're out there . . . I won't last any longer . . . we have to go back . . ."

Tony tried to reason with him. "We can't do that, you know this is a full-scale exercise. We can't get out until the twenty-eight days are up. That's only ten more days, you can hold out until then. That's the minimum figure the military decided on for a stay on Mars—it's built into all the plans and machinery. Be glad we don't have to wait an entire Martian year until the planets get back into conjunction. With deep sleep and atomic drive that's one trouble that won't be faced."

"Stop talking and trying to kid me along!" Hal shouted. "I don't give a flying frog what happens to this damned expedition, I'm washing myself out and this final exercise will go right with me. I'm not going crazy from lack of sleep just because some brass hat thinks superrealism is the answer. If they refuse to stop the exercise when I call, it will be *murder.*"

He was out of his bunk before Tony could say anything and scratching at the control board. The EMERGENCY button was there as always, but they didn't know if it was connected this time. Or even if it were connected, if anyone would answer. Hal pushed it and kept pushing it. They both looked at the speaker, holding their breaths.

"The dirty rotten . . . they're not going to answer the call." Hal barely breathed the words.

Then the speaker rasped to life and the cold voice of Colonel Stregham filled the tiny room.

"You know the conditions of this exercise—so your reasons for calling had better be pretty good. What are they?"

Hal grabbed the microphone, half-complaining, half-pleading—the words poured out in a torrent. As soon as he started, Tony knew it would not be any good. He knew just how Stregham would react to the complaints. While Hal was still pleading the speaker cut him off.

"That's enough. Your explanation doesn't warrant any change in the original plan. You are on your own and you're going to have to stay that way. I'm cutting this connection permanently; don't attempt to contact me again until the exercise is over."

The click of the opening circuit was as final as death.

Hal sat dazed, tears on his cheeks. It wasn't until he stood up that Tony realized they were tears of anger. With a single pull, Hal yanked the mike loose and heaved it through the speaker grill.

"Wait until this is over, Colonel, and I can get your pudgy neck between my hands." He whirled towards Tony. "Get out the medical kit, I'll show that idiot he's not the only one who can play boyscout with his damned exercises."

There were four morphine styrettes in the kit; he grabbed one out, broke the seal and jabbed it against his arm. Tony didn't try to stop him, in fact, he agreed with him completely. Within a few minutes, Hal was slumped over the table snoring deeply. Tony picked him up and dropped him onto his bunk.

Hal slept almost twenty hours and when he woke some of the madness and exhaustion was gone from his eyes. Neither of them mentioned what had happened. Hal marked the days remaining on the bulkhead and carefully rationed the remaining morphine. He was getting about one night's sleep in three, but it seemed to be enough.

They had four days left to blastoff when Tony found the first Martian life. It was something about the size of a cat that crouched in the lee of the ship. He called to Hal who came over and looked at it.

"That's a beauty," he said, "but nowheres near as good as the one I had on my second trip. I found this ropy thing that oozed a kind of glue. Contrary to regulations—frankly I was curious as hell—I dissected the thing. It was a beauty, wheels and springs and gears, Stregham's technicians do a good job. I really got chewed out for opening the thing though. Why don't we just leave this one where it is?"

For a moment Tony almost agreed—then changed his mind.

"That's probably just what they want—so let's finish the game their way. I'll watch it, you get one of the empty ration cartons."

Hal reluctantly agreed and climbed into the ship. The outer door swung slowly and ground into place. Disturbed by the vibration, the thing darted out towards Tony. He gasped and stepped back before he remembered it was only a robot.

"Those technicians really have wonderful imaginations," he mumbled.

The thing started to run by him and he put his foot on some of its legs to hold it. There were plenty of legs; it was like a small-bodied spider surrounded by a thousand unarticulated legs. They moved in undulating waves like a millipede's and dragged the misshapen body across the sand. Tony's boot crunched on the legs, tearing some off. The rest held.

Being careful to keep his hand away from the churning legs, he bent over and picked up a dismembered limb. It was hard and covered with spines on the bottom side. A milky fluid was dripping from the torn end.

"Realism," he said to himself, "those technicians sure believe in realism."

And then the thought hit him. A horribly impossible thought that froze the breath in his throat. The thoughts whirled round and round and he knew they were wrong because they were so incredible. Yet he had to find out, even if it meant ruining their mechanical toy.

Keeping his foot carefully on the thing's legs, he slipped the sharpened table knife out of his pouch and bent over. With a single, swift motion he stabbed.

"What the devil are you doing?" Hal asked, coming up behind him. Tony couldn't answer and he couldn't move. Hal walked around him and looked down at the thing on the ground.

It took him a second to understand, then he screamed.

"It's alive? It's bleeding and there are no gears inside. It can't be alive—if it is we're not on Earth at all—we're on Mars!" He began to run, then fell down, screaming.

Tony thought and acted at the same time. He knew he only had one chance. If he missed they'd both be dead. Hal would kill them both in his madness. Balling his fist, he let swing hard as he could at the spot just under the other man's breastplate. There was just the thin fabric of the suit there and that spot was right over the big nerve ganglion of the solar plexus. The thud of the blow hurt his hand—but Hal collapsed slowly to the ground. Putting his hands under the other's arms, he dragged him into the ship.

Hal started to come to after he had stripped him and laid him on the bunk. It was impossible to hold him down with one hand and press the freeze cycling button at the same time. He concentrated on holding Hal's one leg still and pushed the button. The crazed man had time to hit Tony three times before the needle lanced home. He dropped back with a sigh and Tony got groggily to his feet. The manual actuator on the frozen sleep had been provided for any medical emergency so the patient could survive until the doctors could work on him back at base. It had proven its value.

Then the same unreasoning terror hit him.

If the beast were real—Mars was real.

This was no "training exercise"—this was it. That sky outside wasn't a painted atmosphere, it was the real sky of Mars.

He was alone as no man had ever been alone before on a planet millions of miles from his world.

He was shouting as he dogged home the outer air door, an animal-like howl of a lost beast. He had barely enough control left to get to his bunk and throw the switch above it. The hypodermic was made of good steel so it went right through the fabric of his pressure suit. He was just reaching for the hypo arm to break it off when he dropped off into the blackness.

This time, he was slow to open his eyes. He was afraid he would see the riveted hull of the ship above his head. It was the white ceiling of the hospital, though, and he let the captive air out of his lungs. When he turned his head he saw Colonel Stregham sitting by the bed.

"Did we make it?" Tony asked. It was more of statement than a question.

"You made it, Tony. Both of you made it. Hal is awake here in the other bed."

There was something different about the colonel's voice and it took Tony an instant to recognize it. It was the first time he had ever heard the colonel talk with any emotion other than anger.

"The first trip to Mars. You can imagine what the papers are saying about it. More important, Tech says the specimen and meter reading you brought back are invaluable. When did you find out it wasn't an exercise?"

"The twenty-fourth day. We found some kind of Martian animal. I suppose we were pretty stupid not to have tumbled, before that."

Tony's voice had an edge of bitterness.

"Not really. Every part of your training was designed keep you from finding out. We were never certain if we would have to send the men without their knowledge, there was always that possibility. Psych was sure the orientation and separation from Earth would cause a breakdown. I could never agree with them."

"They were right," Tony said, trying to keep the memory of fear out of his voice.

"We know now that they were right, though I fought them at the time. Psych won the fight and we programmed the whole trip over on their say-so. I doubt if you appreciate it, but we went to a tremendous amount of work to convince you two that you were still in the training program."

"Sorry to put you to all that trouble," Hal said. The colonel flushed a little, not at the words but at the loosely-reined bitterness that rode behind them. He went on as if he hadn't heard.

"Those two conversations you had over the emergency phone were, of course, taped and the playback concealed in the ship. Psych scripted them on the basis of fitting any need. Apparently they worked. The second one was supposed to be the final touch of realism, in case you should start being doubtful. Then we used a variation of deep freeze that suspends about ninety-nine percent of the body processes; it hasn't been revealed or published yet. This along with anticoagulants in the razor cut on Tony's chin covered the fact that so much time had passed.

"What about the ship?" Hal asked. "We saw it—it was only half-completed."

"Dummy," the colonel said. "Put there for the public's benefit and all foreign intelligence services. Real one had been finished and tested weeks earlier. Getting the crew was the difficult part. What I said about no team finishing a practice exercise was true. You two men had the best records and were our best bets.

"We'll never have to do it this way again, though. Psych says that the next crews won't have that trouble; they'll be reinforced by the psychological fact that someone else was there before them. They won't be facing the complete unknown."

The colonel sat chewing his lip for a moment, then forced out the words he had been trying to say since Tony and Hal had regained consciousness.

"I want you to understand . . . both of you . . . that I would rather have gone myself than pull that kind of thing on you. I know how you must feel. Like we pulled some kind of a . . ."

"Interplanetary practical joke," Tony said. He didn't smile when he said it.

"Yes, something like that," the colonel rushed on. "I guess it was a lousy trick—but don't you see, we had to? You two were the only ones left, every other man had washed out. It had to be you two, and we had to do it the safest way.

"And only myself and three other men know what was done, what really happened on the trip. No one else will ever know about it, I can guarantee you that."

Hal's voice was quiet, but cut through the room like a sharp knife.

"You can be sure Colonel, that we won't be telling anybody about it."

When Colonel Stregham left, he kept his head down because he couldn't bring himself to see the look in the eyes of the first two explorers of Mars.

Survival Planet

"But this war was finished years before I was born! How can one robot torpedo—fired that long ago—still be of any interest?"

Dall the Younger was overly persistent—it was extremely lucky for him that Ship-Commander Lian Stane, both by temperament and experience, had a tremendous reserve of patience.

"It has been fifty years since the Greater Slavocracy was defeated—but that doesn't mean eliminated," Commander Stane said. He looked through the viewport of the ship, seeing ghostlike against the stars the pattern of the empire they had fought so long to destroy. "The Slavocracy expanded unchecked for over a thousand years. Its military defeat didn't finish it, just made the separate worlds accessible to us. We are still in the middle of that reconstruction, guiding them away from a slave economy."

"That I know all about," Dall the Younger broke in with a weary sigh. "I've been working on the planets since I came into the force. But what has that got to do with the Mosaic torpedo that we're tracking? There must have been a billion of them made and fired during the war. How can a single one be of interest this much later?"

"If you had read the tech reports," Stane said, pointing to the thumb-thick folder on the chart table, "you would know all about it." This advice was the closest the Commander had ever come to censure. Dall the Younger had the good grace to flush slightly and listen with applied attention.

"The Mosaic torpedo is a weapon of space war, in reality a robot-controlled spaceship. Once directed it seeks out its target, defends itself if necessary, then destroys itself and the ship it has been launched against by starting the uncontrollable cycle of binding-energy breakdown."

"I never realized that they were robot-operated," Dall said. "I thought robots had an ingrained resistance to killing people?"

"In-built rather than ingrained would be more accurate," Stane said judiciously. "Robotic brains are just highly developed machines with no inherent moral sense. That is added afterwards. It has been a long time since we built man-shaped robots with human-type brains. This is the age of the specialist, and robots can specialize far better than men ever could. The Mosaic torpedo brains have no moral sense—if anything they are psychotic, overwhelmed by a death wish. Though there are, of course, controls on how much they can kill. All the torpedoes ever used by either side had mass detectors to defuse them when they approached an object with planetary mass, since the re-action started by a torpedo could just as easily destroy a world as a ship. You can understand our interest when in the last months of the war, we picked up a torpedo fused only to detonate a planet.

"All the data from its brain was filed and recently interpreted. The torpedo was aimed at the fourth planet of the star we are approaching now."

"Anything on the record about this planet?" Dall asked.

"Nothing. It is an unexplored system—at least as far as our records are concerned. But the Greater Slavocracy knew enough about this planet to want to destroy it. We are here to find out why."

Dall the Younger furrowed his brow, chewing at the idea. "Is that the only reason?" he finally asked. "Since we stopped them from wiping out this planet, that would be the end of it, I should think."

"It's thinking like that that shows why you are the low ranker on this ship," Gunner Arnild snapped as he came in. Arnild had managed to grow old in a very short-lived service, losing in the process, his patience for everything except his computers and guns. "Shall I suggest some of the possibilities that have occurred even to me? Firstly—any enemy of the Slavocracy could be a friend of ours. Or conversely, there may be an enemy here that threatens the entire human race, and we may need to set off a Mosaic ourselves to finish the job the Slavers started. Then again, the Slavers may have had something here—like a research center that they would rather have destroyed than let us see. Wouldn't you say that any one of these would make the planet worth investigating?"

"We shall be in the atmosphere within twenty hours," Dall said as he vanished through the lower hatch. "I have to check the lubrication on the drive gears."

"You're too easy on the kid," Gunner Arnild said, staring moodily at the approaching star, already dimmed by the forward filters.

"And you're too hard," Stane told him. "So I guess it evens out. You forget he never fought the Slavers."

Skimming the outer edges of the atmosphere of the fourth planet, the scout ship hurled itself through the measured length of a helical orbit, then fled back into the safety of space while the ship's robot brain digested and made copies of the camera and detector instrument recordings. The duplicates were stored in a message torp, and only when the torp had started back to base did Commander Stane bother personally to examine the results of their survey.

"We're dispensable now," he said, relaxing. "So the best thing we can do is to drop down and see what we can stir up." Arnild grunted agreement, his index fingers unconsciously pressing invisible triggers.

They leaned over the graphs and photographs spread out on the table. Dall peered between their shoulders and flipped through the photographs they tossed aside. He was first to speak.

"Nothing much there, really. Plenty of water, a big island continent—and not much else."

"Nothing else is detectable," Stane added, tickling off the graphs one by one. "No detectable radiation, no large masses of metal either above or below ground, no stored energy. No reason for us to be here."

"But we are," Arnild growled testily. "So let's touch down and find out more firsthand. Here's a good spot." He tapped a photograph, then pushed it into the enlarger. "Could be a primitive hut city, people walking around, smoke."

"Those could be sheep in the fields," Dall broke in eagerly. "And boats pulled up on the shore. We'll find out something here."

"I'm sure we will," Commander Stane said. "Strap in for landing."

Lightly and soundlessly the ship fell out of the sky, curving in a gentle arc that terminated at the edge of a grove of tall trees, on a hill above the city. The motors whined to a stop and the ship was silent.

"Report positive on the atmosphere," Dall said, checking off the analyzer dials.

"Stay at the guns, Arnild," Commander Stane said. "Keep us covered, but don't shoot unless I tell you to."

"Or unless you're dead," Arnild said with complete lack of emotion.

"Or unless I'm dead," Stane answered him, in the same toneless voice. "In which case you will assume command."

He and Dall buckled on planet kits, cycled through the lock and sealed it behind them. The air was soft and pleasantly warm, filled with the freshness of growing plants.

"Really smells good after that canned stuff," Dall said.

"You have a great capacity for stating the obvious." Arnild's voice rasped even more than usual when heard through the bone conductor phones. "Can you see what's going on in the village?"

Dall fumbled his binoculars out. Commander Stane had been using his since they left the ship. "Nothing moving," Stane said. "Send an Eye down there."

The Eye whooshed away from the ship and they could follow its slow swing through the village below. There were about a hundred huts, simple pole-and-thatch affairs, and the Eye carefully investigated every one.

"No one there," Arnild said as he watched the monitor screen. "The animals are gone too, the ones from the aerial pic."

"The people can't have vanished," Dall said. "There are empty fields in every direction, completely without cover. And I can see smoke from their fires."

"The smoke's there, the people aren't," Arnild said testily. "Walk down and look for yourself."

The Eye lifted up from the village and drifted back towards the ship. It swung around the trees and came to a sudden stop in midair.

"Hold it!" Arnild's voice snapped in their ears. "The huts are empty. But there's someone in the tree you're standing next to. About ten meters over your heads!"

Both men controlled a natural reaction to look up. They moved out a bit, where they would be safe from anything cropped from above.

"Far enough," Arnild said. "I'm shifting the Eye for a better look." They could hear the faint drone of the Eye's motors as it changed position.

"It's a girl. Wearing some kind of fur outfit. No weapons that I can see, but some kind of a pouch hanging from her waist. She's just clutching onto the tree with her eyes closed. Looks like she's afraid of falling."

The men on the ground could see her dimly now, a huddled shape against the straight trunk.

"Don't bring the Eye any closer," Commander Stane said. "But turn the speaker on. Hook my phone into the circuit."

"You're plugged in."

"We are friends . . . Come down . . . We will not hurt you." The words boomed down from the floating speaker above their heads.

"She heard it, but maybe she can't understand Esperanto," Arnild said. "She just hugged the tree harder while you were talking."

Commander Stane had had a good command of Slaver during the war, he groped in his memory for the words, doing a quick translation. He repeated the same phrase, only this time in the tongue of their defeated enemies.

"That did something, Commander," Arnild reported. "She jumped so hard she almost fell off. Then scooted up a couple of branches higher before she grabbed on again."

"Let me get her down, sir," Dall asked. "I'll take some rope and climb up after her. It's the only way. Like getting a cat out of a tree."

Stane pushed the thought around. "It looks like the best answer," he finally said. "Get the lightweight two-hundred-meter line and the climbing irons out of the ship. Don't take too long, it'll be getting dark soon."

The irons chunked into the wood and Dall climbed carefully up to the lower limbs. Above him the girl stirred and he had a quick glimpse of the white patch of her face as she looked down at him. He started climbing again until Arnild's voice snapped at him.

"Hold it! She's climbing higher. Staying above you."

"What'll I do, Commander?" Dall asked, settling himself in the fork of one of the big branches. He felt exhilarated by the climb, his skin tingling slightly with sweat. He snapped open his collar and breathed deeply.

"Keep going. She can't climb any higher than the top of the tree."

The climbing was easier now, the branches smaller and closer together. He went slowly so as not to frighten the girl into a misstep. The ground was out of sight, far below. They were alone in their own world of leaves and swaying boughs the silver tube of the hovering Eye the only reminder of the watchers from the ship. Dall stopped to tie a loop in the end of the rope, doing it carefully so the knot would hold. For the first time since they had started on this mission he felt as if he was doing a full part. The two old warhorses weren't bad shipmates, but they oppressed him with the years of their experience. But this was something he could do best and whistled softly through his teeth with the thought.

It would have been possible for the girl to have climbed higher, the branches could have held her weight. But for some reason she had retreated out along a branch. Another close to it made a perfect hand-hold, and he shuffled slowly after her.

"No reason to be afraid," he said cheerfully, and smiled. "Just want to get you down safely and back to your friends. Why don't you grab onto this rope?"

The girl just shuddered and backed away. She was young and good to look at, dressed only in a short fur kilt. Her hair was long, but had been combed and caught back of her head with a thong. The only thing that appeared alien about her was her fear. As he came closer he could see she was drenched with it. Her legs and hands shook with a steady vibration. Her teeth were clamped into her whitened lips and a thin trickle of blood reached to her chin. He hadn't thought it possible that human eyes could have stared so widely, have been so filled with desperation.

"You don't have to be afraid," he repeated, stopping just out of reach. The branch was thin and springy. If he tried to grab her they might both be bounced off it. He didn't want any accidents to happen now. Slowly pulling the rope from the coil, Dall tied it about his waist, then made a loop around the next branch. Out of the corner of his eye he saw the girl stir and look around wildly.

"Friends!" he said, trying to calm her. He translated into Slaver, she had seemed to understand that before.

"Noi'r venn!"

Her mouth opened wide and her legs contracted. The scream was terrible and more like a tortured animal's than a human voice. It confused him and he made a desperate grab. It was too late.

She didn't fall. With all her strength she hurled herself from the limb, jumping towards the certain death she preferred to his touch. For a heartbeat she seemed to hang, contorted and fear-crazed, at the apex of her leap, before gravity clutched hold and pulled her crashing down through the leaves. Then Dall was falling too, grabbing for non-existent handholds.

The safety line he had tied held fast. In a half-daze he worked his way back to the trunk and fumbled loose the knots. With quivering precision he made his way back to the ground. It took a long time and a blanket was drawn over the deformed thing in the grass before he reached it. He didn't have to ask if she was dead.

"I tried to stop her. I did my best." There was a slight touch of shrillness to Dall's voice.

"Of course," Commander Stane told him, as he spread out the contents of the girl's waist pouch. "We were watching with the Eye. There was no way to stop her when she decided to jump."

"No need to talk Slaver to her either," Arnild said, coming out of the ship. He was going to add something, but he caught Commander Stane's direct look and shut his mouth. Dall saw too.

"I forgot!" the young man said, looking back and forth at their expressionless faces. "I just remembered she had understood Slaver. I didn't think it would frighten her. It was a mistake maybe, but anyone can make a mistake! I didn't want her to die . . ."

He clamped his trembling jaws shut with an effort and turned away.

"You better get some food started," Commander Stane told him. As soon as the port had closed he pointed to the girl's body. "Bury her under the trees. I'll help you."

It was a brief meal, none of them were very hungry. Stane sat at the chart table afterward pushing the hard green fruit around with his forefinger. "This is what she was doing in the tree why she couldn't pull the vanishing act like the others. Picking fruit. She had nothing else in the pouch. Our landing next to the tree and trapping her was pure accident." He glanced at Dall's face, then turned quickly away.

"It's too dark to see now, do we wait for morning?" Arnild asked. He had a handgun disassembled on the table, adjusting and oiling the parts.

Commander Stane nodded. "It can't do any harm—and it's better than stumbling around in the dark. Leave an Eye with an infrared projector and filter over the village and make a recording. Maybe we can find out where they all went."

"I'll stay at the Eye controls," Dall said suddenly. "I'm not . . . sleepy. I might find something out."

The Commander hesitated for a moment, then agreed. "Wake me if you see anything. Otherwise, get us up at dawn."

The night was quiet and nothing moved in the silent village of huts. At first light Commander Stane and Dall walked down the hill, an Eye floating ahead to cover them. Arnild stayed behind in the locked ship, at the controls.

"Over this way, sir," Dall said. "Something I found during the night when I was making sweeps with the Eye."

The pit edges had been softened and rounded by the weather, large trees grew on the slopes. At the bottom, projecting from a pool of water, were the remains of rusted machinery.

"I think they're excavation machines," Dall said. "Though it's hard to tell, they've been down there so long."

The Eye dropped down to the bottom of the pit and nosed close to the wreckage. It sank below the water and emerged after a minute, trailing a wet stream.

"Digging machines, all right," Arnild reported. "Some of them turned over and half-buried, like they fell in the hole. And all of them Slaver built."

Commander Stane looked up intently. "Are you sure?" he asked.

"Sure as I can read a label."

"Let's get on to the village," the Commander said, chewing thoughtfully at the inside of his cheek.

Dall the Younger discovered where the villagers had gone. It was really no secret, they found out in the first hut they entered. The floor was made of pounded dirt, with a circle of rocks for a fireplace. All the other contents were of the simplest and crudest. Heavy, un-fired clay pots, untanned furs, some eating utensils chipped out of hard wood. Dall was poking through a heap of woven mats behind the fireplace when he found the hole.

"Over here, sir!" he called.

The opening was almost a meter in diameter and sank into the ground at an easy angle. The floor of the tunnel was beaten as hard as the floor of the hut.

"They must be hiding out in there," Commander Stane said.

"Flash a light down and see how deep it is."

There was no way to tell. The hole was really a smooth-walled tunnel that turned at a sharp angle five meters inside the entrance. The Eye swooped down and hung, humming above the opening.

"I took a look in some of the other huts," Arnild said from the ship. "The Eye found a hole like this in every one of them. Want me to take a look inside?"

"Yes, but take it slowly," Commander Stane told him. "If there are people hiding down there we don't want to frighten them more. Drift down and pull back if you find anything."

The humming died as the Eye floated down the tunnel and out of sight.

"Joined another tunnel," Arnild reported. "And now another junction. Getting confused . . . don't know if I can get it back the way I sent it in."

"The Eye is expendable," the Commander told him. "Keep going."

"Must be dense rock around . . . signal is getting weak and I have a job holding control. A bigger cavern of some sort . . . wait! There's someone! Caught a look at a man going into one of the side tunnels."

"Follow him," Stane said.

"Not easy," Arnild said after a moment's silence. "Looks like a dead end. A rock of some kind blocking the tunnel. He must have rolled it back and blocked the passage after went by. I'll back out . . . blast!"

"What's wrong?"

"Another rock behind the Eye—they've got it trapped in that blocked-off piece of tunnel. Now the screen's dead, and all I can get is an out-of-operation signal!" Arnild sounded exasperated and angry.

"Very neat," Commander Stane said. "They lured it in, trapped it—then probably collapsed the roof of the tunnel. These people are very suspicious of strangers and seem to have a certain efficiency at getting rid of them."

"But why?" Dall asked. He looked around at the crude construction of the hut. "What could these people possibly have that the Slavers could have wanted so badly? Those machines we found, it's obvious that the Slavers put a lot of time and effort into trying to dig down there. But did they ever find what they were looking for? Did they try to destroy this planet because they had found it—or because they hadn't found it?"

"I wish I knew," Commander Stane said glumly. "It would make my job a lot easier. I'm getting a complete report off to HQ—maybe they have some ideas."

On the way back to the ship they noticed the fresh dirt in the grove of trees. There was a raw empty hole where the girl had been buried. The ground had been torn apart and hurled in every direction. There were slash marks on the trunks of the trees, made by sharp blades . . . or giant claws. Something or somebody had come for the girl, dug up her body and vented a burning rage on the ground and the trees. A crushed trail led to an opening between the roots of one of the trees.

It slanted back and down. Its dark mouth as enigmatic and mysterious as the other tunnels.

Before they retired that night, Commander Stane made a double check that the ports were locked and all the alarm circuits activated. He went to bed but didn't sleep. The answer to the problem seemed tantalizingly obvious, hovering just outside his reach. There seemed to be enough facts here to draw a conclusion from. But what? He drifted into a fitful doze without finding the answer.

When he awoke the cabin was still dark, and he had the feeling something was terribly wrong. What had awakened him? He groped in his sleep-filled memories. A sigh. A rush of air. It could have been the cycling of the air lock. Fighting down the sudden fear he snapped on the lights and pulled his gun from the bedside rack. Arnild appeared, yawning and blinking in the doorway.

"What's going on?" he asked.

"Get Dall—I think someone came into the ship."

"Gone out is more like it," Arnild snuffed. "Dall's not in his bunk."

"What!"

He ran to the control room. The alarm circuit had been turned off. There was a piece of paper on the control console. The Commander grabbed it up and read the single word written on it. He gaped as comprehension struck him, then crushed the paper in his convulsive fist.

"The fool!" he shouted. "The damned young fool! Break out an Eye. No, two! I'll work the duplicate control!"

"But what happened?" Arnild gaped. "What's young Dall done?"

"Gone underground. Into the tunnels. We have to stop him!"

Dall was nowhere in sight, but the lip of the tunnel under the trees was freshly crumbled.

"I'll take an Eye down there," Commander Stane said. "You take another one down the nearest entrance. Use the speakers. Tell them that we are friends, in Slaver."

"But you saw what reaction the girl had when Dall told her that." Arnild was puzzled, confused.

"I know what happened," Stane snapped. "But what other choice do we have? Now get on with it!"

Arnild started to ask another question, but the concentrated intensity of the commander at the controls changed his mind. He sent his own Eye rocketing towards the village.

If the people hiding in the maze of tunnels heard the message, they certainly didn't believe it. One Eye was trapped in a dead-end tunnel when the opening behind it suddenly filled with soft dirt. Commander Stane tried nosing the machine through the dirt, but it was firmly trapped and held. He could hear thumpings and diggings as more soil was piled on top.

Arnild's Eye found a large underground chamber, filled with huddled and frightened sheep. There were none of the natives there. On the way out of this cavern the Eye was trapped under a fall of rocks.

In the end, Commander Stane admitted defeat. "It's up to them now, we can't change the end one way or another."

"Something moving in the grove of trees, Commander," Arnild said sharply. "Caught it on the detector, but it's gone now."

They went out hesitantly with their guns pointed, under reddened dawn sky. They went, half-knowing what they would find, but fearful to admit it aloud while they could still hope.

Of course there was no hope. Dall the Younger's body lay near the tunnel mouth, out of which it had been pushed. The red dawn glinted from red blood. He had died terribly.

"They're fiends! Animals!" Arnild shouted. "To do that to a man who only wanted to help them. Broke his arms and legs, scratched away most of his skin. His face—nothing left . . ." The aging gunner choked out a sound that was half gasp, half sob. "They ought to be bombed out, blown up! Like the Slavers started . . ." He met the commander's burning stare and fell silent.

"That's probably just how the Slavers felt," Stane said "Don't you understand what happened here?"

Arnild shook his head dumbly.

"Dall had a glimpse of the truth. His mistake was that he thought it was possible to change things. But at least he knew what the danger was. He went because he felt guilty for the girl's death. That was why he left the note with the word 'slave' on it, in case he didn't come back."

"What do you mean—?"

"It's really quite simple," he said wearily, leaning back against a tree. "Only we were looking for something more complex and technical. When it wasn't really a physical problem, but a social one we were facing. This was a Slave planet, set up and organized by the Slavers to fit their special needs."

"What?" Arnild asked, still confused.

"Slaves. They were constantly expanding, and you know that their style of warfare was expensive on manpower. They needed steady sources of supply, so must have had to create them. This planet was one answer. Made to order in a way. A single, lightly forested continent, with a few places for the people to hide when the slave ships came. They must have planted settlements, given the people simple and sufficient sources of food—but absolutely no technology. Then they went away to let them breed. Every few years they would come back, take as many slaves as they needed, and leave the others to replenish the stock. Only they reckoned without one thing."

Arnild's numbness was wearing off. He understood now.

"The adaptability of mankind," he said.

"Of course. The ability—given enough time—to adapt to almost any extreme of environment. This is a perfect example. A cut-off population with no history, no written language—just the desire to survive. Every few years unspeakable creatures drop out of the sky and steal their children. They try running away, but there is no place to run. They build boats, but there is no place to sail to. Nothing works . . ."

"Until one bright boy digs a hole, covers it up and hides his family in it. And finds out it works."

"The beginning," Commander Stane nodded. "The idea spreads, the tunnels get deeper and more elaborate. The Slavers would try to dig them out—so they started building defenses. This went on—until the slaves finally won.

"This might very well have been the first planet to rebel successfully against the Greater Slavocracy. They couldn't be dug out. Poison gas would just kill them and they had no value dead. Machines sent after them were trapped like our Eyes. And men who were foolish enough to go down . . ." He couldn't finish the sentence, Dall's body was stronger evidence than words could ever be.

"But the hatred?" Arnild asked. "The way the girl killed herself rather than be taken."

"The tunnels became a religion," Stane told him. "They had to be, to be kept in operation and repair during the long gap of years between visits by the Slavers. The children had to be taught that the demons come from the skies and salvation lies below. The opposite of the old Earth religions. Hatred and fear were firmly implanted so everyone, no matter how young, would know what to do if a ship appeared. There must be entrances everywhere. Seconds after a ship is sighted the population can vanish underground. They knew we were Slavers since only demons come from the sky.

"Dall must have guessed part of this. Only he thought he could reason with them, explain that the Slavers were gone and that they didn't have to hide anymore. That good men come from the skies. But that's heresy, and by itself would be enough to get him killed. If they even bothered to listen."

They were gentle when they carried Dall the Younger back to his ship.

"It is going to be some job trying to convince these people of the truth," Arnild said when they paused for a moment to rest. "I still don't understand, though, why the Slavers wanted to blow the planet up."

"There too, we were looking for too complex a motive," Commander Stane said. "Why does a conquering army blow up buildings and destroy monuments when it is forced to retreat? Just frustration and anger, old human emotions. If I can't have it, you can't either. This planet must have annoyed the Slavers for years. A successful rebellion that they couldn't put down. They kept trying to capture the rebels since they were incapable of admitting defeat at the hands of slaves. When they knew their war was lost, destruction of this planet was a happy vent for their emotions. I noticed you feeling the same way yourself when you saw Dall's body. It's a human reaction."

They were both old soldiers, so they didn't show their emotions too much when they put Dall's corpse into the special chamber and readied the ship for takeoff.

But they were old men as well, much older since they had come to the planet, and they moved now with old men's stiffness.

How the Old World Died

"Tell me how the world ended, Grandfather, won't you please?" the boy pleaded, looking up at the seamed face of the old man sitting next to him on the trunk of the fallen tree.

"I've told you often enough," the old man said, dozing a bit in the warm sun. "I bet you'd rather hear about the old trains. They used to—"

"The world, Grandfather. Tell me how it ended, how everything went bust."

The old man sighed and scratched a bit on his thigh, defeated by the obstinacy of the very young. "You shouldn't say that it ended, Andy."

"That's what you always say."

"What I always say is that the world as we knew it ended. A drastic upheaval. Death, destruction, and chaos, murder, raping, and looting."

Andy squirmed with happiness on the other end of the log. This was always the best part.

"And blood and terror, Grandfather, don't forget that."

"It was all of that, too. And it was all because of Alexander Partagas Scobie, cursed be his evil name."

"Did you ever meet him, Grandfather?" Andy asked, knowing all the cues.

"Yes, I saw Scobie. He passed just as close to me as you're sitting now, even stopped to talk to me. I was polite to him. Polite! If I knew then what I know now . . . There were factories then. I was an honest working man in the factory and ran a hydraulic press. Instead of 'Yes, Doctor Scobie, Thank you, Doctor Scobie,' I should have fed him into my hydraulic press, that's what I should have done."

"What's a hyndraulie press?"

Grandfather didn't hear. He was by himself now, reliving the days before the world ended, the days when mankind had been supreme upon the Earth.

"Scobie was mad. They said so later, when it was too late of course, but no one had the brain to see it at the time. They treated him nice and listened to his ideas and tried to talk to him, and when he wouldn't listen they just let him go, that's all. Just let him go! Him mad as a hatter, with a laboratory as big as a mountain and all his money in the bank and a pension just in case he didn't have enough."

"He hated everybody and wanted to kill them all, old Scobie did. Didn't he, Grandfather?"

"Wouldn't be fair to say that." The old man shifted sideways a bit to get back into the sun, and opened the ragged remains of a once fine suit so that he could feel the warmth on his skin. "I hate Scobie just as much as the next man, but fair's fair. They killed him so fast when they found out what he had done that no one bothered to ask him why he had done it. Maybe he thought he was doing right. Or maybe he liked robots more than people. He sure knew how to design robots, Scobie did, give him credit for that. I remember years before the end there were a lot of Scobie robots around and people were afraid they would take away their jobs and stuff like that. They didn't know the half of it. Robots took away everything. People were always afraid that the robots would fight them, turn into monsters and make war on them. Didn't happen at all like that. Scobie made robots that didn't even know people were there."

"He made them and turned them loose in secret so no one would know?" Andy asked eagerly. This was the part of the story he liked best.

"Made God knows how many and smuggled them out. All over the world, in all of the out-of-the-way places. Some he dropped off near auto junkyards and they burrowed under the old cars and disappeared. Other ones he put down near steel mills where they hid under the scrap. They were everywhere, in storage dumps and warehouses, for months before they were discovered, and by that time it was too late. Too late by far; there was no stopping them."

"They built each other."

"They didn't build each other, that's not exactly right. The ones that Scobie dropped were already built. Built fine, simple, and smart. Programmed with a steel tape brain. Programmed to do only one thing, and that was to build other robots just like themselves. And when a robot was finished building another robot he activated him with a magnetic copy of his own brain tape and the new robot went to work doing the same thing. Versatile those robots were. Some of them were made almost all out of aluminum, just dump one of them down in a warehouse of mothballed airplanes and within the week there would be two robots, if maybe it could find an old tin can to make a steel tape out of. Scobie even had one kind that had mostly wooden gears and burned charcoal to run, and these did fine in the jungles of the Amazon and upper Congo. They were everywhere you could think of, and places you would never think of but Scobie did, because he was mad. And all of the first robots were made to be afraid of the light. So they scuttled around in the dark and no one ever saw them before it was too late. By the time people realized what was going on there was almost as many robots as there were people. A few days later there were more robots than people and it was the end."

"But everyone fought them? All the guns and tanks and everything? Blew the old robots up?"

"By the thousands. But new ones were being made by the millions. And the tanks ran out of ammunition because the factories were being taken apart by the robots and made into more robots, and while the guns in the front of a tank were blowing up the robots other robots would be taking off the back of the tank to make more robots. It was hell, I tell you. I fought, all of us fought, but we couldn't possibly win. Robots didn't mind getting blown up. Blow off the bottom of a robot and the top would keep on working making another robot. And the other robots would stand around watching—by this time they weren't afraid of the light anymore—pushing and eager, ready to grab up the broken parts to make more robots. In the end we just all gave up. There was nothing else we could do. Just tried to look after ourselves. Just eating and staying alive was a job."

A bit of wind had come up, rustling the leaves, the sun had dropped out of sight behind the trees. Grandfather rose and stretched he didn't want to catch a chill.

"Better start back," he said.

"Then the world was ended?" Andy asked, pulling at the old man's knobby hand, not wanting the story to be over.

"End of the world as I knew it, as you'll never know it. End of civilization, end of freedom, end of the nobility of men, end of his rule as the top creature on this planet—the robots rule now."

"Teacher says they don't rule, they just exist like trees or stones, and are just as neutral—that's what teacher said."

"What does your teacher know?" Grandfather mumbled testily. "Young kid, twenty years old. I could tell him. The robots rule. Mankind has fallen from the pinnacle of power."

They emerged from the woods then and the first thing they saw was a robot squatting by the path, industriously filing a gear out of a metal blank. Grandfather kicked out in sudden rage and caught the thing on its side with a dull metallic boom. It had been badly assembled, or made of inferior material, because when it fell over its head came off. Almost before it hit the ground there was the thud of rushing feet and a flock of robots raced by, plucking up the head and chasing after the rolling gear wheel. There was a brief flurry of motion and the decapitated robot was dismembered: the robots hurried off.

"Andy—!" his mother's voice called from the pleasant cottage at the end of the flagstone walk.

"We're late for dinner again, I bet," the boy said with sudden guilt.

He ran quickly up the steps that were made of robot bodies welded solidly together, and grabbed the handle of the door. This had been a robot's hand; you just shook hands and turned it to open the door. He vanished inside.

Grandfather lingered, not wanting to face his daughter's sharp tongue. Not yet. He could hear it still echoing in his head from the last time. "Don't fill the boy's head with your nonsense. It's a good world. Why don't you wear decent clothes of robot insulation like the rest of us, instead of those awful old pre-R smelly things? Robots are a national resource—*the* national resource—not the enemy. We never had it so good." On and on, the same old record.

He packed his pipe—made of robot fingers—with tobacco and sucked it alight. There was the quick sound of running feet and a farm wagon ran around the corner. Thick boards were bolted to the truncated torsos of a dozen robots. Just the pelvic motors and legs were left of each one, and they made a fine form of transportation that was completely independent of roads. All of the truck farmers around the village used them now. No expense and no upkeep. An unlimited supply of free replacement parts.

"It is not a utopia the way they say!" Grandfather mumbled fiercely through a cloud of smoke. "Man was meant to work and work hard. Shouldn't have everything handed to him so easy. They're using robot parts for everything now, a man can't find an honest day's work even if he wants to.

"End of the world, that's what it was.

"End of my world!"

The K-Factor

"We're losing a planet, Neel. I'm afraid that I can't . . . understand it." The bald and wrinkled head wobbled a bit on the thin neck, and his eyes were moist. Abravanel was a very old man. Looking at him, Neel realized for the first time just how old and close to death he was. It was a profoundly shocking thought.

"Pardon me, sir," Neel broke in, "but is it possible? To lose a planet, I mean. If the readings are done correctly, and the k-factor equations worked to the tenth decimal place, then it's really just a matter of adjustment, making the indicated corrections. After all, Societies is an exact science—"

"Exact? *Exact!* Of course it's not! Have I taught you so little that you dare say that to me?" Anger animated the old man, driving the shadow of death back a step or two.

Neel hesitated, feeling his hands quiver ever so slightly, groping for the right words. Societies was his faith, and his teacher, Abravanel, its only prophet. This man before him, carefully preserved by the age-retarding drugs, was unique in the galaxy. A living anachronism, a refugee from the history books. Abravanel had single-handedly worked out the equations, spelled out his science of Societies. Then he had trained seven generations of students in its fundamentals. Hearing the article of his faith defamed by its creator produced a negative feedback loop in Neel, so strong his hands vibrated in tune with it. It took a jarring effort to crack out of the cycle.

"The laws that control Societies, as postulated by . . . you, are as exact as any others in the unified-field theory universe."

"No they're not. And, if any man I taught believes that nonsense, I'm retiring tomorrow and dropping dead the day after. My science— and it is really not logical to call it a science—is based on observation, experimentation, control groups and corrected observations. And though we have made observations in the millions, we are dealing in units in the billions, and the interactions of these units are multiples of that. And let us never forget that our units are people who, when they operate as individuals, do so in a completely different manner. So you cannot truthfully call my theories exact. They fit the facts well enough and produce results in practice, that has been empirically proven. So far. Someday, I am sure, we will run across a culture that doesn't fit my rules. At that time the rules will have to be revised.

We may have that situation now on Himmel. There's trouble cooking there."

"They have always had a high activity count, sir," Neel put in hopefully.

"High yes, but *always* negative. Until now. Now it is slightly positive and nothing we can do seems to change it. That's why I've called you in. I want you to run a new basic survey, ignoring the old one still in operation, to re-examine the check points on our graphs. The trouble may lie there."

Neel thought before he answered, picking his words carefully. "Wouldn't that be a little . . . unethical, sir? After all Hengly, who is operator there now, is a friend of mine. Going behind his back, you know."

"I know nothing of the sort." Abravanel snorted. "We are not playing for poker chips, or seeing who can get a paper published first. Have you forgotten what Societies is?"

Neel answered by rote. "The applied study of the interaction of individuals in a culture, the interaction of the group generated by these individuals, the equations derived therefrom, and the application of these equations to control one or more factors of this same culture."

"And what is the one factor that we have tried to control in order to make all the other factors possible of existence?"

"War," Neel said in a very small voice.

"Very good then, there is no doubt what it is we are talking about. You are going to land quietly on Himmel, do a survey as quickly as possible and transmit the data back here. There is no cause to think of it as sneaking behind Hengly's back, but as doing something to help him set the matter right. Is that understood?"

"Yes, sir," Neel said firmly this time, straightening his back and letting his right hand rest reassuringly on the computer slung from his belt.

"Excellent. Then it is now time to meet your assistant." Abravanel touched a button on his desk.

It was an unexpected development and Neel waited with interest as the door opened. But he turned away abruptly his eyes slitted and his face white with anger. Abravanel introduced them.

"Neel Sidorak, this is—"

"Costa. I know him. He was in my class for six months." There wasn't the slightest touch of friendliness in Neel's voice now. Abravanel either ignored it or didn't hear it. He went on as if the two cold, distant young men were the best of friends.

"Classmates. Very good—then there is no need to make introductions. Though it might be best to make clear your separate areas of control. This is your project Neel, and Adao Costa will be your assistant, following your orders and doing whatever he can to help. You know he isn't a graduate Societist, but he has done a lot of fieldwork for us and can help you greatly in that. And, of course, he will be acting as an observer for the UN, and making his own reports in this connection."

Neel's anger was hot and apparent. "So he's a UN observer now. I wonder if he still holds his old job at the same time. I think it only fair, sir, that you know. He works for Interpol."

Abravanel's ancient and weary eyes looked at both men, and he sighed. "Wait outside Costa," he said. "Neel will be with you in a minute."

Costa left without a word and Abravanel waved Neel back to his chair. "Listen to me now," he said, "and stop playing tunes on that infernal buzzer." Neel snapped his hand away from the belt computer, as if it had suddenly grown hot. A hesitant finger reached out to clear the figures he had nervously been setting up, then thought better of it. Abravanel sucked life into his ancient pipe and squinted at the younger man.

"Listen," he said. "You have led a very sheltered life here at the university, and that is probably my fault. No, don't look angry, I don't mean about girls. In that matter undergraduates have been the same for centuries. I'm talking about people in groups, individuals, politics, and all the complicated mess that makes up human life. This has been your area of study and the program is carefully planned so you can study it secondhand. The important thing is to develop the abstract viewpoint, since any attempt to prejudge results can only mean disaster. And it has been proved many times that a man with a certain interest will make many unwitting errors to shape an observation or experiment in favor of his interest. No, we could have none of that here.

"We are following the proper study of mankind and we must do that by keeping personally on the outside, to preserve our perspective. When you understand that, you understand many small things about the university. Why we give only resident student scholarships at a young age, and why the out-of-the-way location here in the Dolomites. You will also see the reason why the campus bookstore stocks all of the books published, but never has an adequate supply of newspapers. The agreed policy has been to see that you all mature with the long view. Then—hopefully—you will be immune to short-term political interests after you leave.

"This policy has worked well in turning out men with the correct attitude towards their work. It has also turned out a fair number of self-centered, egocentric horrors."

Neel flushed. "Do you mean that I—"

"No, I don't mean you. If I did, I would say so. Your worst fault—if you can call it a fault, since it is the very thing we have been trying to bring about—is that you have a very provincial attitude towards the universe. Now is the time to re-examine some of those ideas. Firstly, what do you think the attitude of the UN is towards Societics?"

There was no easy answer, Neel could see traps ready for anything he said. His words were hesitant. "I can't say I've really ever thought about it. I imagine the UN would be in favor of it, since we make their job of world government that much easier—"

"No such thing," Abravanel said, tempering the sharpness of his words with a smile. "To put it in the simplest language, they hate our guts. They wish I had never formulated Societics, and at the same time they are very glad I did. They are in the position of the man who caught the tiger by the tail. The man enjoys watching the tiger eat all of his enemies, but as each one is consumed his worry grows greater. What will happen when the last one is gone? Will the tiger then turn and eat him?

"Well—we are the UN's tiger. Societics came along just at the time it was sorely needed. Earth had settled a number of planets, and governed them. First as outposts, then as colonies. The most advanced planets very quickly outgrew the colony stage and flexed their independent muscles. The UN had no particular desire to rule an empire, but at the same time they had to insure Earth's safety. I imagine they were considering all sorts of schemes—including outright military control—when they came to me.

"Even in its early, crude form, Societics provided a stopgap that would give them some breathing time. They saw to it that my work was well endowed and aided me—unofficially of course—in setting up the first control experiments on different planets. We had results, some very good, and the others not so bad that the local police couldn't get things back under control after a while. I was of course happy to perfect my theories in practice. After a hundred years I had all the rough spots evened down and we were in business. The UN has never come up with a workable alternative plan, so they have settled down to the uncomfortable business of holding the tiger's tail. They worry and spend vast sums of money keeping an eye on our work."

"But *why?*" Neel broke in.

"Why?" Abravanel gave a quick smile. "Thank you for a fine character rating. I imagine it is inconceivable to you that I might want to be Emperor of the Universe. I could be, you know. The same forces that hold the lids on the planet could just as easily blow them off."

Neel was speechless at the awful enormity of the thought. Abravanel rose from behind his desk with an effort and shambled over to lay a thin and feather-light arm on the younger man's shoulders. "Those are the facts of life, my boy. And since we cannot escape them, we must live with them. Costa is just a man doing his duty. So try and put up with him. For my sake if not for your own."

"Of course," Neel agreed quickly. "The whole thing takes a bit of getting used to, but I think I can manage. We'll do as good a job on Himmel as it is possible to do. Don't worry about me, sir."

Costa was waiting in the next room, puffing quietly on a long cigarette. They left together, walking down the hall in silence. Neel glanced sideways at the wiry, dark-skinned Brazilian and wondered what he could say to smooth things out. He still had his reservations about Costa, but he'd keep them to himself now. Abravanel had ordered peace between them, and what the old man said was the law.

It was Costa who spoke first. "Can you brief me on Himmel— what we'll find there, and be expected to do?"

"Run the basic survey first, of course," Neel told him. "Chances are that that will be enough to straighten things out. Since the completion last year of the refining equations of Debir's Postulate, all sigma-110 and alpha-142 graph points are suspect—"

"Just stop there please, and run the flag back down the pole," Costa interrupted. "I had a six-months survey of Societics seven years ago, to give me a general idea of the field. I've worked with survey teams since then, but I have only the vaguest idea of the application of the information we got. Could you cover the ground again—only a bit slower?"

Neel controlled his anger successfully and started again, in his best classroom manner.

"Well, I'm sure you realize that a good survey is half the problem. I must be impartial and exact. If it is accurately done, application of the k-factor equations is almost mechanical."

"You've lost me again. Everyone always talks about the k-factor, but no one has ever explained just what it is."

Neel was warming to his topic now. "It's a term borrowed from nucleonics, and best understood in that context. Look, you know how an atomic pile works—essentially just like an atomic bomb. The difference is just a matter of degree and control. In both of them you have neutrons tearing around, some of them hitting nuclei and starting new neutrons going. These in turn hit and start others. This goes on faster and faster and *bam*, a few milliseconds later you have an atomic bomb. This is what happens if you don't attempt to control the reaction.

"However, if you have something like heavy water or graphite that will slow down neutrons and an absorber like cadmium, you can alter the speed of the reaction. Too much damping material will absorb too many neutrons and the reaction will stop. Not enough and the reaction will build up to an explosion. Neither of these extremes is wanted in an atomic pile. What is needed is a happy balance where you are soaking up just as many neutrons as are being generated all the time. This will give you a constant temperature inside the reactor. The net neutron reproduction constant is then one. This balance of neutron generation and absorption is the k-factor of the reactor. Ideally 1.0000000.

"That's the ideal, though, the impossible to attain in a dynamic system like a reactor. All you need is a few more neutrons around, giving you a k-factor of 1.00000001 and you are headed for trouble. Each extra neutron produces two and your production rates soars geometrically towards bang. On the other hand, a k-factor of 0.999999999 is just as bad. Your reaction is spiraling down in the other direction. To control a pile you watch your k-factor and make constant adjustments."

"All this I follow," Costa said. "But where's the connection with Societics?"

"We'll get to that—just as soon as you realize and admit that a minute difference of degree can produce a marked difference of kind. You might say that a single, impossibly tiny neutron is the difference between an atom bomb and a slowly cooling pile of inert uranium isotopes. Does that make sense?"

Costa nodded.

"Good. Then try to go along with the analogy that a human society is like an atomic pile. At one extreme you will have a dying, decadent culture—the remains of a highly mechanized society—living off its capital, using up resources it can't replace because of a lost technology. When the last machine breaks and the final food synthesizer collapses the people will die. This is the cooled-down atomic pile. At the other extreme is complete and violent anarchy. Every man thinking only of himself, killing and destroying anything that gets in his way—the atomic explosion. Midway between the two is a vital, active, producing society.

"This is a generalization—and you must look at it that way. In reality society is infinitely complex, and the ramifications and possibilities are endless. It can do a lot more things than fizzle or go boom. Pressure of population, war or persecution patterns can cause waves of immigration. Plant and animal species can be wiped out by momentary needs or fashions. Remember the fate of the passenger pigeon and the American bison.

"All the pressures, cross-relationships, hungers, needs, hatreds, desires of people are reflected in their interrelationships. One man standing by himself tells us nothing. But as soon as he says something, passes on information in an altered form, or merely expresses an attitude—he becomes a reference point. He can be marked, measured and entered on a graph. His actions can be grouped with others and the action of the group measured. Man—and his society—then becomes a systems problem that can be fed into a computer. We've cut the Gordian knot of the three L's and are on our way towards a solution."

"Stop!" Costa said, raising his hand. "I was with you as far as the three L's. What are they? A private code?"

"Not a code—abbreviation. Linear Logic Language, the pitfall of all the old researchers. All of them, historians, sociologists, political analysts, anthropologists, were licked before they started. They had to know all about A and B before they could find C. Facts to them were always hooked up in a series. Whereas in truth they had to be analyzed as a complex circuit complete with elements like positive and negative feedback, and crossover switching. With the whole thing being stirred up constantly by continual homeostasis correction. It's little wonder they did do badly."

"You can't really say that," Adao Costa protested. "I'll admit that Societics has carried the art tremendously far ahead. But there were many basics that had already been discovered."

"If you are postulating a linear progression from the old social sciences—forget it," Neel said. "There is the same relationship here that alchemy holds to physics. The old boys with their frog guts and awful offal knew a bit about things like distilling and smelting. But there was no real order to their knowledge, and it was all an unconsidered by-product of their single goal, the whole nonsense of transmutation."

They passed a lounge, and Adao waved Neel in after him, dropping into a chair. He rummaged through his pockets for a cigarette, organizing his thoughts. "I'm still with you," he said. "But how do we work this back to the k-factor?"

"Simple," Neel told him. "Once you've gotten rid of the three L's and their false conclusions. Remember that politics in the old days was all. We are angels and They are devils. This was literally believed. In the history of mankind there has yet to be a war that wasn't backed by the official clergy on each side. And each declared that God was on their side. Which leaves You Know Who as prime supporter of the enemy. This theory is no more valid than the one that a single man can lead a country into war, followed by the inference that a well-timed assassination can save the peace."

"That doesn't sound too unreasonable," Costa said.

"Of course not. All of the old ideas sound good. They have a simple-minded simplicity that anyone can understand. That doesn't make them true. Kill a war-minded dictator and nothing changes. The violence-orientated society, the factors that produced it, the military party that represents it—none of these are changed. The k-factor remains the same."

"There's that word again. Do I get a definition yet?"

Neel smiled. "Of course. The k-factor is one of the many factors that interrelate in a society. Abstractly it is no more important than the other odd thousand we work with. But in practice it is the only one we try to alter."

"The k-factor is the war factor," Adao Costa said. All the humor was gone now.

"That's a good enough name for it," Neel said, grinding out his half-smoked cigarette. "If a society has a positive k-factor, even a slight one that stays positive, then you are going to have a war. Our planetary operators have two jobs. First to gather and interpret data. Secondly to keep the k-factor negative."

They were both on their feet now, moved by the same emotion.

"And Himmel has a positive one that stays positive," Costa said. Neel Sidorak nodded agreement. "Then let's get into the ship and get going."

It was a fast trip and a faster landing. The UN cruiser cut its engines and dropped like a rock in free fall. Night rain washed the ports and the computer cut in the maximum permissible blast for the minimum time that would reduce their speed to zero at zero altitude. Deceleration sat on their chests and squeezed their bones to rubber. Something crunched heavily under their stern at the exact instant the drive cut out. Costa was unbelted and out the door while Neel was still feeling his insides shiver back into shape.

The unloading had an organized rhythm that rejected Neel. He finally realized he could help best by standing back out of the way while the crewmen grav-lifted the heavy cases out through the cargo port, into the blackness of the rain-lashed woods. Adao Costa supervised this and seemed to know what he was doing. A signal rating wearing earphones stood to one side of the lock chanting numbers that sounded like detector fixes. There was apparently enough time to unload everything—but none to spare. Things got close towards the end.

Neel was suddenly bustled out into the rain and the last two crates were literally thrown out after him. He plowed through the mud to the edge of the clearing and had just enough time to cover his face before the takeoff blast burst out like a new sun.

"Sit down and relax," Costa told him. "Everything is in the green so far. The ship wasn't spotted on the way down. Now all we have to do is wait for transportation."

In theory at least, Adao Costa was Neel's assistant. In practice he took complete charge of moving their equipment and getting it under cover in the capital city of Kitezh. Men and trucks appeared to help them and vanished as soon as their work was done. Within twenty hours they were installed in a large loft, all of the machines uncrated and plugged in. Neel took a no-sleep and began tuning checks on all the circuits, glad of something to do. Costa locked the heavy door behind their last silent helper, then dropped gratefully onto one of the bedding rolls.

"How did the gadgets hold up?" he asked.

"I'm finding out now. They're built to take punishment—but being dropped twelve feet into mud soup, then getting baked by rockets isn't in the original specs."

"They crate things well these days," Costa said unworriedly, sucking on a bottle of the famous Himmelian beer. "When do you go to work?"

"We're working right now," Neel told him, pulling a folder of papers out of the file. "Before we left I drew up a list of current magazines and newspapers I would need. You can start on these. I'll have a sampling program planned by the time you get back."

Costa groaned hollowly and reached for the papers.

Once the survey was in operation it went ahead of its own momentum. Both men grabbed what food and sleep they could. The computers gulped down Neel's figures and spat out gigabytes of answers that demanded even more facts. Costa and his unseen helpers were kept busy supplying the material.

Only one thing broke the ordered labors of the week. Neel blinked twice at Costa before his equation-fogged brain assimilated an immediate and personal factor.

"You've a bandage on your head," he said. "A *bloodstained* bandage!"

"A little trouble in the streets. Mobs. And that's an incredible feat of observation," Costa marveled. "I had the feeling that if I came in here stark naked, you wouldn't notice it."

"I . . . I get involved," Neel said. Dropping the papers on a table and kneading the tired furrow between his eyes. "Get wrapped up in the computation. Sorry. I tend to forget about people."

"Don't feel sorry for me," Costa said. "You're right. Doing the job. I'm supposed to help you, not pose for the 'before' picture in Home

Hospital ads. Anyway—how are we doing? Is there going to be a war? Certainly seems like one brewing outside. I've seen two people lynched who were only suspected of being Earthies."

"Looks don't mean a thing," Neel said, opening two beers. "Remember the analogy of the pile. It boils liquid metal and cooks out energy from the infrared right through to hard radiation. Yet it keeps on generating power at a nice, steady rate. But your A-bomb at zero minus one second looks as harmless as a fallen log. It's the k-factor that counts, not surface appearance. This planet may look like a dictator's dream of glory, but as long as we're reading in the negative things are fine."

"And how are things? How's our little k-factor?"

"Coming out soon," Neel said, pointing at the humming computer. "Can't tell about it yet. You never can until the computation is complete. There's a temptation to try and guess from the first figures, but they're meaningless. Like trying to predict the winner of a horse race by looking at the starters lined up at the gate."

"Lots of people think they can."

"Let them. There are few enough pleasures in this life without taking away all delusions."

Behind them the computer thunked and was suddenly still.

"This is it," Neel said, and pulled out the tape. He ran it quickly through his fingers, mumbling under his breath. Just once he stopped and set some figures into his hand computer. The result flashed in the window and he stared at it, unmoving.

"Good? Bad? What is it?"

Neel raised his head and his eyes were ten years older.

"Positive. Bad. Much worse than it was when we left Earth."

"How much time do we have?"

"Don't know for certain." Neel shrugged. "I can set it up and get an approximation. But there is no definite point on the scale where war has to break out. Just a going and going until, somewhere along the line—"

"I know. Gone." Costa said reaching for his gun. He slid it into his side pocket. "Now it's time to stop looking and start doing. What do I do?"

"Going to kill War Marshal Lommeord?" Neel asked distastefully. "I thought we had settled that you can't stop a war by assassinating the top man."

"We also settled that *something* can be done to change the k-factor. The gun is for my own protection. While you're radioing results back to Earth and they're feeling bad about it, I'm going to be doing something. Now *you* tell me what that something is."

This was a different man from the relaxed and quietly efficient

Adao Costa of the past week. All of his muscles were hard with the restrained energy of an animal crouching to leap. The gun, ready in his pocket, had a suddenly new significance. Neel looked away, reaching around for words. This was all very alien to him and a little frightening. It was one thing to work out a k-problem in class, and discuss the theory of correction. It was something entirely different to direct the operation.

"Well?" Costa's voice knifed through his thoughts.

"You can . . . well . . . it's possible to change one of the peak population curves. Isolate individuals and groups, then effect status and location changes—"

"You mean get a lot of guys to take jobs in other towns through the commercial agents?"

Neel nodded.

"Too slow." Costa withered the idea with his voice. "Fine in the long run, but of absolutely no value in an emergency." He began to pace back and forth. Too quickly. It was more of a bubbling-over than a relaxation. "Can't you isolate some recent key events that can be reversed?"

"It's possible." Neel thought about it, quickly. "It wouldn't be a final answer, just a delaying action."

"That's good enough. Tell me what to do."

Neel flipped through his books of notes, checking off the Beta-13's. These were the reinforcers, the individuals and groups who were k-factor amplifiers. It was a long list which he cut down quickly by crossing off the low-increment additions and multiple groups. Even while the list was incomplete, Neel began to notice a pattern. It was an unlikely one—but it was there. He isolated the motivator and did a frequency check. Then sat back and whistled softly.

"We have a powerhouse here," he said, flipping the paper across the table. "Take this organization out of the equations and you might even knock us negative."

"Society for the Protection of the Native Born," Costa read. "Doesn't sound like it's very important. Who or what are they?"

"Proof positive of the law of averages. It's possible to be dealt a royal flush in a hand of cards, but it isn't very common. It's just as possible for a bunch of simpletons to set up an organization for one purpose, and have it turn out to be a supercharged, high-frequency k-factor amplifier. That's what's happened with this infernal SPNB. A seedy little social club, dedicated to jingoists with low IQs. With the war scare they have managed to get hold of a few credits. They have probably been telling the same inflated stories for years about the discrimination against natives of this fair planet, but no one has really cared. Now they have a chance to get their news releases and faked pix out in quantity. Just at a time when the public is ripe for their brand of nonsense. Putting this bunch out of business will be a good day's work."

"Won't there be repercussions?" Costa asked. "If they are this important and throw so much weight around—won't it look suspicions if they are suddenly shut up? Like an obvious move by the enemy?"

"Not at all. That might be true if, for instance, you blew up the headquarters of the War Party. It would certainly be taken as an aggressive move. But no one really knows or cares about this Society of the Half-baked Native Born. There might be reaction and interest if attention was drawn to them. But if some accident or act of nature were to put them out of business, that would be the end of it."

Costa was snapping his lighter on and off as he listened to Neel, staring at the flame. He closed it and held it up. "I believe in accidents. I believe that even in our fireproof age, fires still occur. Buildings still burn down. And if a burnt building just happened to be occupied by the SPNB—just one tenant of many—and their offices and records were destroyed, that would be of very little interest to anyone except the fire brigade."

"You're a born criminal," Neel told him. "I'm glad we're on the same side. That's your department and I leave it to you. I'll just listen for the news flashes. Meanwhile I have one little errand to take care of."

The words stopped Costa, who was almost out the door. He turned stiffly to look at Neel putting papers into an envelope. Yet Costa spoke naturally, letting none of his feelings through into his voice.

"Where are you going?"

"To see Hengly, the planetary operator here. Abravanel told me to stay away from him, to run an entirely new basic survey. Well we've done that now, and pinpointed some of the trouble areas as well. I can stop feeling guilty about poaching another man's territory and let him know what's going on."

"No. Stay away from Hengly," Costa said. "The last thing in the world we want to do is to be seen near him. There's a chance that he . . . well . . . might be compromised."

"What do you mean?" Neel snapped. "He's a friend of mine, a graduate—"

"He might also be surrounded ten deep by the secret police. Did you stop to think about that?"

Neel hadn't thought about it, and his anger vanished when he did. Costa drove the point home.

"Societics has been a well-kept secret for over two centuries. It may still be a secret—or bits of it might have leaked out. And even if the Himmelians know nothing about Societics, they have certainly heard of espionage. They know the UN has agents on their world, they might think Hengly is one of them. This is all speculation, of course, but we do have one fact—this Society of Native Boobs we turned up. *We* had no trouble finding them. If Hengly had reliable field men, he should know about them, too. The only reason he hasn't is because he isn't getting the information. Which means he's compromised."

Reaching back for a chair, Neel fell heavily into it. "You're right . . . of course! I never realized."

"Good," Costa said. "We'll do something to help Hengly tomorrow, but this operation comes first. Sit tight. Get some rest. And don't open the door for anyone except me."

It had been a long job—and a tiring one—but it was almost over. Neel allowed himself the luxury of a long yawn, then shuffled over to the case of rations they had brought. He stripped the seal from something optimistically labeled "Chicken Dinner"—it tasted just like the algae it had been made from—and boiled some coffee while it was heating.

And all the time he was doing these prosaic tasks his mind was turning an indigestible fact over and over. It wasn't a conscious process, but it was nevertheless going on. The automatic mechanism of his brain ran it back and forth like a half-heard tune, searching for its name. Neel was tired, or he would have reacted sooner. The idea finally penetrated. One fact he had taken for granted was an obvious impossibility.

The coffee splashed to the floor as he jumped to his feet.

"It's . . . it *has* to be wrong!" he said aloud, grabbing up the papers. Computations and graphs dropped and were trampled into the spilled coffee. When he finally found the one he wanted his hands were shaking as he flipped through it. The synopsis of Hengly's reports for the past five years. The gradual rise and fall of the k-factor from month to month. There were no sharp breaks in the curve or gaps in the supporting equations.

Societics isn't an exact science. But it's exact enough to know when it is working with incomplete or false information. If Hengly had been kept in the dark about the SPNB, he would also have been misinformed about other factors. This kind of alteration of survey would *have* to show in the equations.

It didn't.

Time was running out and Neel had to act. But what to do? He must warn Adao Costa. And the records here had to be protected. Or better yet destroyed. There was a power in these machines and charts that couldn't be allowed to fall into nationalist hands. But what could be done about it?

In all the welter of equipment and containers, there was one solid, heavy box that he had never opened. It belonged to Costa, and the UN man had never unlocked it in his presence. Neel looked at the heavy clasps on it and felt defeat. But when he pulled at the lid, wondering what to do next, it fell open. It hadn't been sealed. Costa wasn't the kind of man who did things by accident. He had looked forward to the time when Neel might need what was in this box, and had it ready.

Inside was just what Neel expected. Grenades, guns and some smoothly polished devices that held an aura of violence. Looking at them, Neel had an overwhelming sensation of defeat. His life was dedicated to peace and the furthering of peace. He hated the violence that seemed inborn in man, and detested all the hypocritical rationalizations, such as the end justifying the means. All of his training and personal inclinations were against it.

And he reached down and removed the blunt, black gun.

There was one other thing he recognized in the compact arsenal—a time bomb. There had been lectures on this mechanism in school, since the fact was clearly recognized that a time might come when equipment had to be destroyed rather than fall into the wrong hands. He had never seen one since, but had learned the lesson well. Neel pushed the open chest nearer to his instruments and set the bomb dial for fifteen minutes. He slipped the gun into his pocket, started the fuse, and carefully locked the door when he left.

The bridges were burned. Now he had to find Adao Costa.

This entire operation was outside his experience and knowledge. He could think of no plan that could possibly make things easier or safer. All he could do was head for the offices of the Society for the Protection of the Native Born and hope he could catch Adao before he ran into any trouble.

Two blocks away from the address he heard the sirens. Trying to act as natural as the other pedestrians, he turned to look as the armored cars and trucks hurtled by. Packed with armed police, their sirens and revolving lights cleared a path through the dark streets. Neel kept walking, following the cars now.

The street he wanted to go into was cordoned off.

Showing more than a normal interest would have been a giveaway. He let himself be hurried past, with no more than a glance down the block, with the other pedestrians. Cars and men were clustered around a doorway that Neel felt sure was number 265, his destination. Something was very wrong.

Had Costa walked into a trap—or tripped an alarm? It didn't really matter which; either way the balloon had gone up. Neel walked on slowly, painfully aware of his own inadequacy in dealing with the situation. It was a time for action—but what action? He hadn't the slightest idea where Costa was or how he could be of help to him.

Halfway down the block there was a dark mouth of an alleyway—unguarded. Without stopping to think, Neel turned into it. It would bring him closer to the building. Perhaps Costa was still trapped in there. He could get in, help him.

The back of 265 was quiet, with no hint of the activity on the other side of the building. Neel had counted carefully and was sure he had the right one. It was completely dark in the unlit alley, but he found a recessed door by touch. The chances were it was locked, but he moved into the alcove and leaned his weight against it, pulling at the handle, just in case. Nothing moved.

An inch behind his back the alley filled with light, washed with it, eye-burning and strong. His eyes snapped shut, but he forced them open again, blinking against the pain. There were searchlights at each end of the alley, sealing it off. He couldn't get out.

In the instant before the fear hit him he saw the blood spots on the ground. There were three of them, large and glistening redly wet. They extended in a straight line away from him, pointing towards the gaping entrance of a cellar.

When the lights went out, Neel dived headlong towards the cracked and filthy pavement. The darkness meant that the police were moving slowly toward him from both ends of the alley, trapping him in between. There was nothing doubtful about the fate of an armed Earthman caught here. He didn't care. Neel's fear wasn't gone—he just had not time to think about it. His long shot had paid off and there was still a chance he could get Costa out of the trap he had let him walk into.

The lights had burned an afterimage into his retina. Before it faded he reached out and felt his fingers slide across the dusty ground into a patch of wetness. He scrubbed at it with his sleeve, soaking up the blood, wiping the spot fiercely. With his other hand he pushed together a pile of dust and dirt, spreading it over the stain. As soon as he was sure the stain was covered he slid forward, groping for the second telltale splash.

Time was his enemy and he had no way to measure it. He could have been lying in the rubble of that alley for an hour—or a second. What was to be done had to be done at once without a sound. There were silent, deadly men coming towards him through the darkness.

After the second smear was covered there was a drawn-out moment of fear when he couldn't find the third and last. His fingers touched it finally, much farther on than he had expected. Time had certainly run out. Yet he forced himself to do as good a job here as he had with the other two. Only when it was dried and covered did he allow himself to slide forward into the cellar entrance.

Everything was going too fast. He had time for a single deep breath before the shriek of a whistle paralyzed him again. Footsteps slapped towards him and one of the searchlights burned with light. The footsteps speeded up and the man ran by, close enough for Neel to touch if he had reached out a hand. His clothing was shapeless torn, his head and face thick with hair. That was all Neel had time to see before the guns roared and burned the life from the runner.

Some derelict, sleeping in the alley, who had paid with his life for being in the wrong spot the wrong time. But his death had bought Neel a little more time. He turned and looked into the barrel of a gun.

Shock after shock had destroyed his capacity for fear. There was nothing left that could move him, even his own death. He looked quietly—dully—at the muzzle of the gun. With slow determination his mind turned over and he realized that this time there was nothing to fear.

"It's me, Adao," he whispered. "You'll be all right now."

"Ahh, it is you . . ." The voice came softly out of the darkness, the gun barrel wavered and sank. "Lift me up so I can get at this door. Can't seem to stand too well anymore."

Neel reached down, found Costa's shoulders and slowly dragged him to his feet. His eyes were adjusting to the glare above them now, and he could make out the gleam of reflected light on the metal in Costa's fingers. The UN man's other hand was clutched tightly at his waist. The gun had vanished. The metal device wasn't a key, but Costa used it like one. It turned in the lock and the door swung open under their weight. Neel half carried, half dragged the other man's dead weight through it, dropping him to the floor inside. Before he closed the door he reached down and felt a great pool of blood outside.

There was no time to do a perfect job, the hard footsteps were coming, just a few yards away. His sleeves were sodden with blood as he blotted, then pushed rubble into the stain. He pulled back inside and the door closed with only the slightest click.

"I don't know how you managed it, but I'm glad you found me," Costa said. There was weakness as well as silence in his whisper.

"It was only chance I found you," Neel said bitterly. "But criminal stupidity on my part that let you walk into this trap."

"Don't worry about it, I knew what I was getting into. But I still had to go. Spring the trap to see if it *was* a trap."

"You suspected then that Hengly was—" Neel couldn't finish the sentence. He knew what he wanted to say, but the idea was too unbearable to put into words. Costa had no such compunction.

"Yes. Dear Hengly, graduate of the University and Practitioner of Societics. A traitor. A warmonger, worse than any of his predecessors because he knew just what to sell and how to sell it. It's never happened before . . . but there was always the chance . . . the weight of responsibility was too much . . . he gave in—" Costa's voice had died away almost to a whisper. Then it was suddenly loud again, no louder than normal speaking volume, but sounding like a shout in the secret basement.

"Neel!"

"It's all right. Take it easy—"

"Nothing is all right—don't you realize that I've been sending my reports back so the UN and your Societics people will know how to straighten this mess out? But Hengly can turn this world upside down and might even get a shooting war going before they get here. I'm out of it, but I can tell you who to contact, people who'll help. Hold the k-factor down . . ."

"That wouldn't do any good," Neel said quietly. "The whole thing is past the patch and polish stage now. Besides I blew the whole works up. My records, your—"

"You're a fool!" For the first time there was pain in Costa's voice.

"No. I was before—but not anymore. As long as I thought it was a normal problem I was being outguessed at every turn. You must understand the ramifications of Societics. To a good operator there is no interrelationship that cannot be uncovered. Hengly would be certain to keep his eyes open for another field check. Our kind of operation is very easy to spot if you know where—and how—to look. The act of getting information implies contact of some kind, that contact can be detected. He's had our location marked and has been sitting tight, buying time. But our time ran out when you showed them we were ready to fight back. That's why I destroyed our setup, and cut our trail."

"But . . . then we're defenseless! What can we possibly do?"

Neel knew the answer, but he hesitated to put it into words. It would be final then. He suddenly realized he had forgotten about Costa's wound.

"I'm sorry . . . I forgot about your being hurt. What can I do?"

"Nothing," Costa snapped. "I put a field dressing on, that'll do. Answer my question. What is there left? What can be done now?"

"I'll have to kill Hengly. That will set things right until the team gets here."

"But what good will that accomplish?" Costa asked, trying to see the other man in the darkness of the cellar. "You told me yourself that a war couldn't be averted by assassination. No one individual means that much."

"Only in a normal situation," Neel explained. "You must look at the struggle between planets as a kind of celestial chess game. It has its own rules. When I talked about individuals earlier I was talking about pieces on a chessboard. What I'm proposing now is a little more dramatic. I'm going to win the chess game in a slightly more unorthodox way. I'm going to shoot the other chess player."

There was silence for a long moment broken only by the soft sigh of their breathing. Then Costa stirred and there was the sound of metal clinking on the floor.

"It's really my job," Costa said, "but I'm no good for it. You're right, you'll have to go. But I can help you, plan it so you will be able to get to Hengly. You might even stand a better chance than me, because you are so obviously an amateur. Now listen carefully, because we haven't much time."

Neel didn't argue. He knew what needed doing, but Costa could tell him how best to go about it. The instructions were easy to memorize, and he put the weapons away as he was told.

"Once you're clear of this building, you'll have to get cleaned up," Costa said. "But that's the only thing you should stop for. Get to Hengly while he is still rattled, catch him off-guard as much as possible. Than—after you finish with him—dig yourself in. Stay hidden at least three days before you try to make any contacts. Things should have quietened down a bit by then."

"I don't like leaving you here," Neel said.

"It's the best way, as well as being the only way. I'll be safe enough. I've a nice little puncture in me, but there's enough medication to see me through."

"If I'm going to hole up, I'll hole up here. I'll be back to take care of you." Costa didn't answer him. There was nothing more to say. They shook hands in the darkness and Neel crawled away.

There was little difficulty in finding the front door of the building, but Neel hesitated before he opened it. Costa had been sure Neel could get away without being noticed, but he didn't feel so sure himself. There certainly would be plenty of police in the streets, even here. Only as he eased the door did he understand why Costa had been so positive about this.

Gunfire hammered somewhere behind him; other guns answered. Costa must have had another gun. He had planned it this way and the best thing Neel could do was not to think about it and go ahead with the plan. A car whined by in the roadway. As soon as it had passed Neel slipped out and crossed the empty street to the nearest monosub entrance. Most of the stations had valet machines.

It was less than an hour later when he reached Hengly's apartment. Washed, shaved—and with his clothes cleaned—Neel felt a little more sure of himself. No one had stopped him or even noticed him. The lobby had been empty and the automatic elevator left him off at the right floor when he gave it Hengly's name. Now, facing the featureless door, he had a sharp knife of fear. It was too easy. He reached out slowly and tried the handle. The door was unlocked. Taking a deep breath, he opened it and sipped inside.

It was a large room, but unlit. An open door at the other end had a dim light shining through it. Neel started that way and pain burst in his head, spinning him down, face forward.

He never quite lost consciousness, but details were vague in his memory. When full awareness returned he realized that the lights were on in the room. He was lying on his back looking up at them. Two men stood next to him, staring down at him from above the perspective columns of their legs. One held a short metal bar that he kept slapping into his open palm.

The other man was Hengly.

"Not very friendly for an old classmate," he said, holding out Neel's gun. "Now get inside, I want to talk to you."

Neel rolled over painfully and crawled to his feet. His head throbbed with pain, but he tried to ignore it. As he stood up his hand brushed his ankle. The tiny gun Costa had given him was still in the top of his shoe. Perhaps Hengly wasn't being as smart as he should.

"I can take care of him," Hengly said to the man with the metal rod. "He's the only one left now, so you can get some sleep. See you early in the morning though." The man nodded agreement and left.

Slouched in the chair Neel looked forward to a certain pleasure in killing Hengly. Costa was dead, and this man was responsible for his death. It wouldn't even be like killing a friend. Hengly was very different from the man he had known. He had put on a lot of weight and affected a thick beard and flowing moustache. There was something jovial and paternal about him—until you looked into his eyes. Neel slumped forward, worn out, letting his fingers fall naturally next to the gun in his shoe. Hengly couldn't see his hand, the desk was in the way. All Neel had to do was draw and fire.

"You can pull out the gun," Hengly said with a grim smile, "but don't try to shoot it." He had his own gun now, aimed directly at Neel. Leaning forward he watched as Neel carefully pulled out the tiny weapon and threw it across the room. "That's better," he said, placing his own gun on the desk where he could reach it easily. "Now we can talk."

"There's nothing I have to say to you, Hengly." Neel leaned back in the chair, exhausted. "You're a traitor!"

Hengly hammered the desk in sudden anger and shouted. "Don't talk to me of treachery, my little man of peace! Creeping up with a gun to kill a friend. Is that peaceful? Where are the ethos of human-ism now? You were very fond of them when we were in the Univer-sity!"

Neel didn't want to listen to the words, he thought instead of how right Costa had been. He was dead, but this was still his operation. It was going according to plan.

"Walk right in there," Costa had said. "He won't kill you. Not at first, at least. He's the loneliest man in the universe because he has given up one world for another that he hasn't gained yet. There will be no one he can confide in. He'll know you have come to kill him, but he won't be able to resist talking to you first. Particularly if you make it easy for him to defeat you. Not too easy—he must feel he is outthinking you. You'll have a gun for him to take away, but that will be too obvious. This small gun will be hidden as well, and when he finds that, too, he should be taken off his guard. Not much, but enough for you to kill him. Don't wait. Do it at the first opportunity."

Out of the corner of his eye, Neel could see the radiophone clipped to the front of his jacket. It was slightly tarnished, looking like any one of ten thousand in daily use—almost a duplicate of the one Hengly wore. A universal symbol of the age, like the keys and small change in his pockets.

Only Neel's phone was a deadly weapon. Product of a research into sudden death that he had never been aware of before. All he had to do was get it near Hengly, the mechanism had been armed when he put it on. It had a range of two feet. As soon as it was that far from any part of his body it would be actuated.

"Can I ask you a question, Hengly?" His words cut loudly through the run of the other man's speech.

Hengly frowned at the interruption, then nodded permission. "Go ahead," he said. "What would you like to know?"

"The obvious. Why did you do it? Change sides I mean. Give up a positive work, for this . . . this negative corruption . . . ?"

"That's how much you know about it." Hengly was shouting now. "Positive, negative. War, peace. Those are just words, and it took me years to find it out. What could be more positive than making something of my life—and of this planet at the same time? It's in my power to do it, and I've done it."

"Power, perhaps that's the key word," Neel said, suddenly very tired. "We have the stars now but we have carried with us our little personal lusts and emotions. There's nothing wrong with that, I suppose, as long as we keep them personal. It's when we start in-flicting them on others the trouble starts. Well, it's over now. At least this time."

With a single easy motion he unclipped the radiophone and flipped it across the desk toward Hengly.

"Goodbye," he said.

The tiny mechanism clattered onto the desk and Hengly leaped back, shouting hoarsely. He pulled the gun up and tried to aim at the radiophone and at Neel at the same time. It was too late to do either. There was a brief humming noise from the phone.

Neel jerked in his chair. It felt as if a slight electric shock had passed through him. He had felt only a microscopic percentage of the radiation.

Hengly got it all. The activated field of the device had scanned his nervous system, measured and tested it precisely. Then adjusted itself to the exact microfrequency that carried the messages in his efferent nervous system. Once the adjustment had been made, the charged condensers had released their full blasts of energy on that frequency.

The results were horribly dramatic. Every efferent neuron in his system carried the message full-power. Every muscle in his body responded with a contraction of full intensity.

Neel closed his eyes, covered them, turned away gasping. It couldn't be watched. An epileptic in a seizure can break the bones in a leg or arm by simultaneous contraction of opposing muscles. When all the opposed muscles of Hengly's body did this the results were horrible beyond imagining.

When Neel recovered a measure of sanity he was in the street, running. He slowed to a walk, and looked around. It was just dawn and the streets were empty. Ahead was the glowing entrance of a monotube and he headed for it. The danger was over now, as long as he was careful.

Pausing on the top step, he breathed the fresh air of the new morning. There was a sighing below as an early train pulled into the station. The dawn-lit sky was the color of blood.

"Blood," he said aloud. Then, "Do we have to keep on killing? Isn't there another way?"

He started guiltily as his voice echoed in the empty street, but no one had heard him.

Quickly, two at a time, he ran down the steps.

R.U.R.

If there is any construct that best symbolizes science fiction—after the rocket ship of course—it is our familiar, clanking friend, the robot. How did Herbert George manage to miss out here? Surely the man who invented military tanks, the time machine and aerial warfare should have given us a look in at iron men. Regretfully he didn't. However, the pulps certainly did. They took off where Karel Čapek left off. Turned his flesh-and-blood androids into metal, then clanked their way through a thousand stories. There was Adam Link, a rather anthropomorphic robot who even had a wife—the mind boggles—Eve (what else?) Link. Finally Isaac Asimov's robots brought a bit of order—not to say intelligent speculation—to the world of robots.

Here are some of my robots. Alas I must leave one of my inventions out—it appeared in a Stainless Steel Rat novel. That is the one and only coal-fired robot . . . This, like my coal-fired flying ship, in *A Transatlantic Tunnel, Hurrah!*, is entirely physically possible. At least John W. Campbell thought so—and who ever wanted to argue with John?

Arm of the Law

It was a big, coffin-shaped plywood box that looked like it weighed a ton. This brawny type just dumped it through the door of the police station and started away. I looked up from the blotter and shouted at the trucker's vanishing back.

"What the hell is that?"

"How should I know," he said as he swung up into the cab. "I just deliver. I don't X-ray 'em. It came on the morning rocket from earth is all I know." He gunned the truck more than he had to and threw up a billowing cloud of red dust.

"Jokers," I growled to myself. "Mars is full of jokers."

When I went over to look at the box I could feel the dust grate between my teeth. Chief Craig must have heard the racket because he came out of his office and helped me stand and look at the box.

"Think it's a bomb?" he asked in a bored voice.

"Why would anyone bother—particularly with a thing this size? And all the way from Earth."

He nodded agreement and walked around to look at the other end. There was no sender's address anywhere on the outside. Finally we had to dig out the crowbar and I went to work on the top. After some prying it pulled free and fell off.

That was when we had our first look at Ned. We all would have been a lot happier if it had been our last look as well. If we had just put the lid back on and shipped the thing back to Earth! I know now what they mean about Pandora's Box.

But we just stood there and stared like a couple of rubes. Ned lay motionless and stared back at us.

"A robot!" the Chief said.

"Very observant; it's easy to see you went to the police academy."

"Ha ha! Now find out what he's doing here."

I hadn't gone to the academy, but this was no handicap to my finding the letter. It was sticking up out of a thick book in a pocket in the box. The Chief took the letter and read it with little enthusiasm.

"Well, well! United Robotics have the brainstorm that 'robots, correctly used, will tend to prove invaluable in police work . . .' They want us to cooperate in a field test . . . 'Robot enclosed is the latest experimental model; valued at 120,000 credits.' "

We both looked back at the robot, sharing the wish that the credits had been in the box instead of it. The Chief frowned and moved his lips through the rest of the letter. I wondered how we got the robot out of its plywood coffin.

Experimental model or not, this was a nice-looking hunk of machinery. A uniform navy blue all over, though the outlet cases, hooks and such were a metallic gold. Someone had gone to a lot of trouble to get that effect. This was as close as a robot could look to a cop in uniform, without being a joke. All that seemed to be missing was the badge and gun.

Then I noticed the tiny glow of light in the robot's eye lenses. It had never occurred to me before that the thing might be turned on. There was nothing to lose by finding out.

"Get out of that box," I said. The robot came up smooth and fast as a rocket, landing two feet in front of me and whipping out a snappy salute.

"Police Experimental Robot serial number XPO-456-934B reporting for duty, sir."

His voice quivered with alertness and I could almost hear the humming of those taut cable muscles. He may have had a stainless-steel hide and a bunch of wires for a brain—but he spelled rookie cop to me just the same. The fact that he was man-height with two arms, two legs and that painted-on uniform helped. All I had to do was squint my eyes a bit and there stood Ned the Rookie Cop. Fresh out of school and raring to go. I shook my head to get rid of the illusion. This was just six feet of machine that boffins and brain boys had turned out for their own amusement.

"Relax, Ned," I said. He was still holding the salute. "At ease. You'll get a hernia of your exhaust pipe if you stay so tense. Anyways, I'm just the sergeant here. That's the Chief of Police over there."

Ned did an about-face and slid over to the Chief with that same greased-lightning motion. The Chief just looked at him like something that sprang out from under the hood of a car, while Ned went through the same report routine.

"I wonder if it does anything else beside salute and report," the Chief said while he walked around the robot, looking it over like a dog with a hydrant.

"The functions, operations and responsible courses of action open to the Police Experimental Robots are outlined on pages 184 to 213 of the manual." Ned's voice was muffled for a second while he half-dived back into his case and came up with the volume mentioned. "A detailed breakdown of these will also be found on pages 1035 to 1267 inclusive."

The Chief, who has trouble reading an entire comic page at one sitting, turned the six-inch-thick book over in his hands like it would maybe bite him. When he had a rough idea of how much it weighed and a good feel of the binding he threw it on my desk.

"Take care of this," he said to me as he headed towards his office. "And the robot too. Do something with it." The Chief's span of attention never was great and it had been strained to the limit this time.

I flipped through the book, wondering. One thing I never have had much to do with is robots, so I know just as much about them as any Joe in the street. Probably less. The book was filled with pages of fine print, fancy mathematics, wiring diagrams and charts in nine colors and that kind of thing. It needed close attention. Which attention I was not prepared to give at the time. The book slid shut and I eyed the newest employee of the city of Nineport.

"There is a broom behind the door. Do you know how to use it?"

"Yes, sir."

"In that case you will sweep out this room, raising as small a cloud of dust as possible at the same time."

He did a very neat job of it. I watched 120,000 credits' worth of machinery making a tidy pile of butts and sand and wondered why it had been sent to Nineport. Probably because there wasn't another police force in the solar system that was smaller or more unimportant than ours. The engineers must have figured this would be a good spot for a field test. Even if the thing blew up, nobody would really mind. There would probably be someone along someday to get a report on it. Well, they had picked the right spot all right. Nineport was just a little bit beyond nowhere.

Which, of course, was why I was there. I was the only real cop on the force. They needed at least one to give an illusion of the wheels going around. The Chief, Alonzo Craig, had just enough sense to take graft without dropping the money. There were two patrolmen. One old and drunk most of the time. The other so young he still had diaper rash. I had ten years on a metropolitan force, Earthside. Why I left is nobody's damn business. I have long since paid for any mistakes I made there by ending up in Nineport.

Nineport is not a city, it's just a place where people stop. The only permanent citizens are the ones who cater to those on the way through. Hotel keepers, gamblers, whores, barkeeps, and the rest.

There is a spaceport, but only some freighters come there. To pick up the metal from some of the mines that are still working. Some of the settlers still come in for supplies. You might say that Nineport was a town that just missed the boat. In a hundred years I doubt if there will be enough left sticking out of the sand to even tell where it used to be.

I won't be there either, so I couldn't care less. I went back to the blotter. Five drunks in the tank, an average night's haul. While I wrote them up Fats dragged in the sixth one.

"Locked himself in the ladies' john at the spaceport and resisting arrest," he reported.

"D and D. Throw him in with the rest."

Fats steered his limp victim across the floor, matching him step for dragging step. I always marveled at the way Fats took care of drunks, since he usually had more under his belt than they had. I have never seen him falling-down drunk or completely sober. About all he was good for was keeping a blurred eye on the lockup and running in drunks. He did well at that. No matter what they crawled under or on top of, he found them. No doubt due to the same shared natural instincts.

Fats clanged the door behind number 6 and weaved his way back in. "What's that?" he asked, peering at the robot along the purple beauty of his nose.

"That is a robot. I have forgotten the number his mother gave him at the factory so we will call him Ned. He works here now."

"Good for him! He can clean up the tank after we throw the bums out."

"That's my job," Billy said coming in through the front door. He clutched his nightstick and scowled out from under the brim of his uniform cap. It is not that Billy is stupid, just that most of his strength has gone into his back instead of his mind.

"That's Ned's job now because you have a promotion. You are going to help me with some of my work."

Billy came in very handy at times and I was anxious that the force shouldn't lose him. My explanation cheered him because he sat down by Fats and watched Ned do the floor.

That's the way things went for about a week. We watched Ned sweep and polish until the station began to take on a positively antiseptic look. The Chief, who always has an eye out for that type of thing, found out that Ned could file the odd ton of reports and paperwork that cluttered his office. All this kept the robot busy, and we got so used to him we were hardly aware he was around. I knew he had moved the packing case into the storeroom and fixed himself up a cozy sort of robot dormitory-coffin. Other than that I didn't know or care.

The operation manual was buried in my desk and I never looked at it. If I had, I might have had some idea of the big changes that were in store. None of us knew the littlest bit about what a robot can or cannot do. Ned was working nicely as a combination janitor–file clerk and should have stayed that way. He would have too if the Chief hadn't been so lazy. That's what started it all.

It was around nine at night and the Chief was just going home when the call came in. He took it, listened for a moment, then hung up.

"Greenback's liquor store. He got held up again. Says to come at once."

"That's a change. Usually we don't hear about it until a month later. What's he paying protection money for if China Joe ain't protecting? What's the rush now?"

The Chief chewed his loose lip for a while, finally and painfully reached a decision.

"You better go around and see what the trouble is."

"Sure," I said reaching for my cap. "But no one else is around, you'll have to watch the desk until I get back."

"That's no good," he moaned. "I'm dying from hunger and sitting here isn't going to help me any."

"I will go take the report," Ned said, stepping forward and snapping his usual well-greased salute.

At first the Chief wasn't buying. You would think the water cooler came to life and offered to take over his job.

"How could *you* take a report?" he growled, putting the wise-guy water cooler in its place. But he had phrased his little insult as a question so he had only himself to blame. In exactly three minutes Ned gave the Chief a summary of the routine necessary for a police officer to make a report on an armed robbery or other reported theft. From the glazed look in the Chief's protruding eyes I could tell Ned had quickly passed the boundaries of the Chief's meager knowledge.

"Enough!" the harried man finally gasped. "If you know so much why don't you make a report?"

Which to me sounded like another version of "If you're so damned smart why ain't you rich?," which we used to snarl at the brainy kids in grammar school. Ned took such things literally though, and turned towards the door.

"Do you mean you wish me to make a report on this robbery?"

"Yes," the Chief said just to get rid of him, and we watched his blue shape vanish through the door.

"He must be brighter than he looks," I said. "He never stopped to ask where Greenback's store is."

The Chief nodded and the phone rang again. His hand was still resting on it so he picked it up by reflex. He listened for a second and you would have thought someone was pumping blood out of his heel from the way his face turned white.

"The holdup's still on," he finally gasped. "Greenback's delivery boy is on the line—calling back to see where we are. Says he's under a table in the backroom . . ."

I never heard the rest of it because I was out the door and into the car. There were a hundred things that could happen if Ned got there before me. Guns could go off, people hurt, lots of things. And the police would be to blame for it all—sending a tin robot to do a cop's job. Maybe the Chief had ordered Ned there, but clearly as if the words were painted on the windshield of the car, I knew I would be dragged into it. It never gets very warm on Mars, but I was sweating.

Nineport has fourteen traffic regulations and I broke all of them before I had gone a block. Fast as I was, Ned was faster. As I turned the corner I saw him open the door of Greenback's store and walk in. I screamed brakes in behind him and arrived just in time to have a gallery seat. A shooting gallery at that.

There were two holdup punks, one behind the counter making like a clerk and the other lounging off to the side. Their guns were out of sight, but blue-coated Ned busting through the door like that was too much for their keyed-up nerves. Up came both guns like they were on strings and Ned stopped dead. I grabbed for my own gun and waited for pieces of busted robot to come flying through the window.

Ned's reflexes were great. Which I supposed is what you should expect of a robot.

"DROP YOUR GUNS, YOU ARE UNDER ARREST." He must have had on full power or something, his voice blasted so loud my ears hurt. The result was just what you might expect. Both torpedoes let go at once and the air was filled with flying slugs. The shop windows went out with a crash and I went down on my stomach. From the amount of noise I knew they both had recoilless .50s. You can't stop one of those slugs. They go right through you and anything else that happens to be in the way.

Except they didn't seem to be bothering Ned. The only notice he seemed to take was to cover his eyes. A little shield with a thin slit popped down over his eye lenses. Then he moved in on the first thug.

I knew he was fast, but not that fast. A couple of slugs jarred him as he came across the room, but before the punk could change his aim Ned had the gun in his hand. That was the end of that. He put on one of the sweetest hammerlocks I have ever seen and neatly grabbed the gun when it dropped from the limp fingers. With the same motion that slipped the gun into a pouch he whipped out a pair of handcuffs and snapped them on the punk's wrists.

Holdupnik Number 2 was heading for the door by then, and I was waiting to give him a warm reception. There was never any need. He hadn't gone halfway before Ned slid in front of him. There was a thud when they hit that didn't even shake Ned, but gave the other a glazed look. He never even knew it when Ned slipped the cuffs on him and dropped him down next to his partner.

I went in, took their guns from Ned, and made the arrest official. That was all Greenback saw when he crawled out from behind the counter and it was all I wanted him to see. The place was a foot deep in broken glass and smelled like the inside of a Jack Daniels bottle. Greenback began to howl like a wolf over his lost stock. He didn't seem to know any more about the phone call than I did, so I grabbed ahold of a pimply-looking kid who staggered out of the storeroom. He was the one who had made the calls.

It turned out to be a matter of sheer stupidity. He had worked for Greenback only a few days and didn't have enough brains to realize that all holdups should be reported to the protection boys instead of the police. I told Greenback to wise up his boy, as look at the trouble that got caused. Then pushed the two ex-holdup men out to the car. Ned climbed in back with them and they clung together like two waifs in a storm. The robot's only response was to pull a first-aid kit from his hip and fix up a ricochet hole in one of the thugs that no one had noticed in the excitement.

The Chief was still sitting there with that bloodless look when we marched in. I didn't believe it could be done, but he went two shades whiter.

"You made the pinch," he whispered. Before I could straighten him out a second and more awful idea hit him. He grabbed a handful of shirt on the first torpedo and poked his face down. "You with China Joe?" he snarled.

The punk made the error of trying to be cute so the Chief let him have one on the head with the open hand that set his eyes rolling like marbles. When the question got asked again he found the right answer.

"I never heard from no China Joe. We just hit town today and—"

"Freelance, by God," the Chief sighed and collapsed into his chair. "Lock 'em up and quickly tell me what in hell happened."

I slammed the gate on them and pointed a none too steady finger at Ned.

"There's the hero," I said. "Took them on single-handed, rassled them for a fall and made the capture. He is a one-robot tornado, a power for good in this otherwise evil community. And he's bullet-proof too." I ran a finger over Ned's broad chest. The paint was chipped by the slugs, but the metal was hardly scratched.

"This is going to cause me trouble, big trouble," the Chief wailed.

I knew he meant with the protection boys. They did not like punks getting arrested and guns going off without their okay. But Ned thought the Chief had other worries and rushed in to put them right. "There will be no trouble. At no time did I violate any of the Robotic Restriction Laws, they are part of my control circuits and therefore fully automatic. The men who drew their guns violated both robotic and human law when they threatened violence. I did not injure the men—merely restrained them."

It was all over the Chief's head, but I liked to think *I* could follow it. And I *had* been wondering how a robot—a machine—could be involved in something like law application and violence. Ned had the answer to that one too.

"Robots have been assuming these functions for years. Don't recording radar meters pass judgment on human violation of automobile regulations? A robot alcohol detector is better qualified to assess the sobriety of a prisoner than the arresting officer. At one time robots were even allowed to make their own decisions about killing. Before the Robotic Restriction Laws automatic gun-pointers were in general use. Their final development was a self-contained battery of large antiaircraft guns. Automatic scan radar detected all aircraft in the vicinity. Those that could not return the correct identifying signal had their courses tracked and computed, automatic fuse-cutters and loaders readied the computer-aimed guns—which were fired by the robot mechanism."

There was little I could argue about with Ned. Except maybe his college-professor vocabulary. So I switched the attack.

"But a robot can't take the place of a cop, it's a complex human job."

"Of course it is, but taking a human policeman's place is not the function of a police robot. Primarily I combine the functions of numerous pieces of police equipment, integrating their operations and making them instantly available. In addition I can aid in the *mechanical* processes of law enforcement. If you arrest a man you handcuff him. But if you order me to do it, I have made no moral decision. I am just a machine for attaching handcuffs at that point . . ."

My raised hand cut off the flow of robotic argument. Ned was hipped to his ears with facts and figures and I had a good idea who would come off second-best in any continued discussion. No laws had been broken when Ned made the pinch, that was for sure. But there are other laws than those that appear on the books.

"China Joe is not going to like this, not at all," the Chief said, speaking my own thoughts.

The law of Tooth and Claw. That's one that wasn't in the law books. And that was what ran Nineport. The place was just big enough to have a good population of gambling joints, bawdy houses and drunk-rollers. They were all run by China Joe. As was the police department. We were all in his pocket and you might say he was the one who paid our wages. This is not the kind of thing, though, that you explain to a robot.

"Yeah, China Joe." I thought it was an echo at first, then realized that someone had eased in the door behind me. Something called Alex. Six feet of bone, muscle and trouble. China Joe's right-hand man. He imitated a smile at the Chief who sank a bit lower in his chair.

"China Joe wants you should tell him why you got smart cops going around and putting the arm on people and letting them shoot up good liquor. He's mostly angry about the hooch. He says that he had enough guff and after this you should—"

"I am putting you under Robot Arrest, pursuant to article 46, paragraph 19 of the revised statutes . . ."

Ned had done it before we realized he had even moved. Right in front of our eyes he was arresting Alex and signing our death warrants.

Alex was not slow. As he turned to see who had grabbed him, he had already dragged out his cannon. He got one shot in, square against Ned's chest, before the robot plucked the gun away and slipped on the cuffs. While we all gaped like dead fish, Ned recited the charge in what I swear was a satisfied tone.

"The prisoner is Peter Rakjomskj, alias Alex the Axe, wanted in Canal City for armed robbery and attempted murder. Also wanted by local police of Detroit, New York and Manchester on charges of—"

"Get it off me!" Alex howled. We might have too, and everything might have still been straightened out if Benny Bug hadn't heard the shot. He popped his head in the front door just long enough to roll his eyes over our scene.

"Alex . . . They're puttin' the arm on Alex!" Then he was gone and when I hit the door he was nowhere in sight. China Joe's boys always went around in pairs. And in ten minutes he would know all about it.

"Book him," I told Ned. "It wouldn't make any difference if we let him go now. The world has already come to an end."

Fats came in then, mumbling to himself. He jerked a thumb over his shoulder when he saw me.

"What's up? I see little Benny Bug come out of here like the place was on fire and almost got killed driving away?"

Then Fats saw Alex with the bracelets on and turned sober in one second. He just took a moment to gape, then his mind was made up. Without a trace of a stagger he walked over to the Chief and threw his badge on the desk in front of him.

"I am an old man and I drink too much to be a cop. Therefore I am resigning from the force. Because if that is who I think it is over there with the cuffs on, I will not live to be a day older as long as I am around here."

"Rat." The Chief growled in pain through his clenched teeth. "Deserting the sinking ship. Rat."

"Squeak," Fats said and left.

The Chief was beyond caring at this point. He didn't blink an eye when I took Fats' badge off the desk. I don't know why I did it, perhaps I thought it was only fair. Ned had started all the trouble and I was just angry enough to want him on the spot when it was finished. There were two rings on his chest plate, and I was not surprised when the badge pin fitted them neatly.

"There, now you are a real cop." Sarcasm dripped from the words. I should have realized that robots are immune to sarcasm. Ned took my statement at face value.

"This is a very great honor, not only for me but for all robots. I will do my best to fulfill all the obligations of the office." Jack Armstrong in tin underwear. I could hear the little motors in his guts humming with joy as he booked Alex.

If everything else hadn't been so bad I would have enjoyed that. Ned had more police equipment built into him than Nineport had ever owned. There was an ink pad that snapped out of one hip, and he efficiently rolled Alex's fingertips across it and stamped them on a card. Then he held the prisoner at arm's length while something clicked in his abdomen. Once more sideways and two instant photographs dropped out of a slot. The mug shots were stuck on the card, arrest details and such inserted. There was more like this, but I forced myself away. There were more important things to think about.

Like staying alive.

"Any ideas Chief?"

A groan was my only answer so I let it go at that. Billy, the balance of the police force, came in then. I gave him a quick rundown. Either through stupidity or guts he elected to stay, and I was proud of the boy. Ned locked away the latest prisoner and began sweeping up.

That was the way we were when China Joe walked in. Even though we were expecting it, it was still a shock. He had a bunch of his toughest hoods with him and they crowded through the door like an overweight baseball team. China Joe was in front, hands buried in the sleeves of his long mandarin gown. No expression at all on his Asiatic features. He didn't waste time talking to us, just gave the word to his own boys.

"Clean this place up. The new police Chief will be here in a while and I don't want him to see any bums hanging around."

It made me angry. Even with the graft I like to feel I'm still a cop. Not on a cheap punk's payroll. I was also curious about China Joe. Had been ever since I tried to get a line on him and never found a thing. I still wanted to know.

"Ned, take a good look at that Chinese guy in the rayon bathrobe and let me know who he is."

My, but those electronic circuits work fast. Ned shot the answer back like a straight man who had been rehearsing his lines for weeks.

"He is a pseudo-Oriental, utilizing a natural sallowness of the skin heightened with dye. He is not Chinese. There has also been an operation on his eyes, scars of which are still visible. This has been undoubtedly done in an attempt to conceal his real identity, but Bertillon measurements of his ears and other features make identity positive. He is on the Very Wanted list of Interpol and his real name is—"

China Joe was angry and with a reason.

"That's the *thing* . . . that big-mouthed tin radio set over there. We heard about it and we're taking care of it!"

The mob jumped aside then or hit the deck and I saw there was a guy kneeling in the door with a rocket launcher. Shaped antitank charges, no doubt. That was my last thought as the thing let go with a whoosh.

Maybe you can hit a tank with one of those. But not a robot. At least not a police robot. Ned was sliding across the floor on his face when the back wall blew up. There was no second shot. Ned closed his hand on the tube of the bazooka and it was so much old drainpipe.

Billy decided then that anyone who fired a rocket in a police station was breaking the law, so he moved in with his club. I was right behind him since I did not want to miss any of the fun. Ned was at the bottom somewhere, but I didn't doubt he could take care of himself.

There were a couple of muffled shots and someone screamed. No one fired after that because we were too tangled up. A punk named Brooklyn Eddie hit me on the side of the head with his gun butt and I broke his nose all over his face with my fist.

There is a kind of a fog over everything after that. But I do remember it was very busy for a while.

When the fog lifted a bit I realized I was the only one still standing. Or leaning, rather. It was a good thing the wall was there.

Ned came in through the street door carrying a very bashed-looking Brooklyn Eddie. I hoped I had done all that. Eddie's wrist were fastened together with cuffs. Ned laid him gently next to the heap of thugs—who I suddenly realized all wore the same kind of handcuffs. I wondered vaguely if Ned made them as he needed them or had a supply tucked away in a hollow leg or something.

There was a chair a few feet away and sitting down helped.

Blood was all over everything and if a couple of the hoods hadn't groaned I would have thought they were corpses. One was, I noticed suddenly. A bullet had caught him in the chest; most of the blood was probably his.

Ned burrowed in the bodies for a moment and dragged Billy out. He was unconscious. A big smile on his face and the splintered remains of his nightstick still stuck in his fist. It takes very little to make some people happy. A bullet had gone through his leg and he never moved while Ned ripped the pants leg off and put on a bandage.

"The spurious China Joe and one other man escaped in a car," Ned reported.

"Don't let it worry you," I managed to croak. "Your batting average still leads the league." It was then I realized the Chief was still sitting in his chair, where he had been when the brouhaha started. Still slumped down with that glazed look. Only after I started to talk to him did I realize that Alonzo Craig, Chief of Police of Nineport, was now dead.

A single shot. Small-caliber gun, maybe a .22. Right through the heart and what blood there had been was soaked up by his clothes. I had a good idea where the gun would be that fired that shot. A small gun, the kind that would fit in a wide Chinese sleeve.

I wasn't tired or groggy anymore. Just angry. Maybe he hadn't been the brightest or most honest guy in the world. But he deserved a better end than that. Knocked off by a two-bit racket boss who thought he was being crossed.

Right about then I realized I had a big decision to make. With Billy out of the fight and Fats gone I was the Nineport police force. All I had to do to be clear of this mess was to walk out the door and keep going. I would be safe enough.

Ned buzzed by, picked up two of the thugs, and hauled them off to the cells.

Maybe it was the sight of his blue back or maybe I was tired of running. Either way my mind was made up before I realized it. I carefully took off the Chief's gold badge and put it on in place of my old one.

"The new Chief of Police of Nineport," I said to no one in particular.

"Yes, sir," Ned said as he passed. He put one of the prisoners down long enough to salute, then went on with his work. I returned the salute.

The hospital meat wagon hauled away the dead and wounded. I took an evil pleasure in ignoring the questioning stares of the attendants. After the doc fixed the side of my head, everyone cleared out. Ned mopped up the floor. I ate some aspirin and waited for the hammering to stop so I could think what to do next.

When I pulled my thoughts together the answer was obvious. Too obvious. I made as long a job as I could of reloading my gun.

"Refill your handcuff box, Ned. We are going out." Like a good cop he asked no questions. I locked the outside door when we left and gave him the key.

"Here. There's a good chance you will be the only one left to use this before the day is over."

I stretched the drive over to China Joe's place just as much as I could. Trying to figure if there was another way of doing it. There wasn't. Murder had been done and Joe was the boy I was going to pin it on. So I had to get him.

The best I could do was stop around the corner and give Ned a briefing.

"This combination bar and hook shop is the sole property of he whom we will still call China Joe until there is time for you to give me a rundown on him. Right now I got enough distractions. What we have to do is go in there, find Joe and bring him to justice. Simple?"

"Simple," Ned answered in his sharp Joe College voice. "But wouldn't it be simple to make the arrest now, when he is leaving in that car, instead of waiting until he returns?"

The car in mention was doing sixty as it came out of the alley ahead of us. I only had a glimpse of Joe in the backseat as it tore by us.

"Stop them!" I shouted, mostly for my own benefit since I was driving. I tried to shift gears and start the engine at the same time, and succeeded in doing exactly nothing.

So Ned stopped them. It had been phrased as an order. He leaned his head out of the window and I saw at once why most of his equipment was located in his torso. Probably his brain as well. There sure wasn't much room left in his head when that cannon was tucked away in there.

A .75 recoilless. A plate swiveled back right where his nose should have been if he had one, and the big muzzle pointed out. It's a neat idea when you think about it. Right between the eyes for good aiming, up high, always ready.

The BOOM BOOM almost took my head off. Of course Ned was a perfect shot—so would I be with a computer for a brain. He had holed one rear tire with each slug and the car flap-flapped to a stop a little ways down the road. I climbed out slowly while Ned sprinted there in seconds flat. They didn't even try to run this time. What little nerve they had left must have been shattered by the smoking muzzle of that .75 poking out from between Ned's eyes. Robots are neat about things like that so he must have left it sticking out deliberate. Probably had a course in psychology back in robot school.

Three of them in the car, all waving their hands in the air like the last reel of a western. And the rear floor covered with interesting little suitcases.

Everyone came along quietly. China Joe only snarled while Ned told me that his name really was Stantin and the Elmira hot seat was kept warm all the time in hopes he would be back. I promised Joe-Stantin I would be happy to arrange it that same day. Thereby not worrying about any slip-ups with the local authorities. The rest of the mob would stand trial in Canal City.

It was a very busy day. Things have quieted down a good deal since then. Billy is out of the hospital and wearing my old sergeant's stripes. Even Fats is back, though he is sober once in a while now and has trouble looking me in the eye. We don't have much to do because in addition to being a quiet town this is now an honest one. Ned is on foot patrol nights and in charge of the lab and files days. Maybe the Policemen's Benevolent wouldn't like that, but Ned doesn't seem to mind. He touched up all the bullet scratches and keeps his badge polished. I know a robot can't be happy or sad—but Ned *seems* to be happy.

Sometimes I would swear I can hear him humming to himself. But of course that is only the motors and things going around.

When you start thinking about it, I suppose we set some kind of precedent here. What with putting on a robot as a full-fledged police officer. No one ever came around from the factory yet, so I have never found out if we're the first or not.

And I'll tell you something else. I'm not going to stay in this broken-down town forever. I have some letters out now, looking for a new job.

So some people are going to be *very* surprised when they see who their new Chief of Police is after I leave.

The Robot Who Wanted to Know

That was the trouble with Filer 13B-445-K, he wanted to know things that he had just no business knowing. Things that no robot should be interested in—much less investigate. But Filer was a very different type of robot.

The trouble with the blonde in tier 22 should have been warning enough for him. He had hummed out of the stack room with a load of books, and was cutting through tier 22 when he saw her bending over for a volume on the bottom shelf.

As he passed behind her he slowed down, then stopped a few yards further on. He watched her intently, a strange glint in his metallic eyes.

As the girl bent over her short skirt rode up to display an astonishing length of nylon-clad leg. That it was a singularly attractive leg should have been of no interest to a robot—yet it was. He stood there, looking, until the blonde turned suddenly and noticed his fixed attention.

"If you were human, Buster," she said, "I would slap your face. But since you are a robot, I would like to know what your little photon-filled eyes find so interesting."

Without a microsecond's hesitation, Filer answered, "Your seam is crooked." Then he turned and buzzed away.

The blonde shook her head in wonder, straightened the offending stocking, and chalked up another credit to the honor of electronics.

She would have been very surprised to find out what Filer had been looking at. He had been staring at her leg. Of course he hadn't lied when he answered her—since he was incapable of lying—but he had been looking at a lot more than the crooked seam. Filer was facing a problem that no other robot had ever faced before.

Love, romance, and sex were fast becoming a passionate interest for him.

That this interest was purely academic goes without saying, yet it was still an interest. It was the nature of his work that first aroused his curiosity about the realm of Venus.

A Filer is an amazingly intelligent robot and there aren't very many being manufactured. You will find them only in the greatest libraries, dealing with only the largest and most complex collections. To call them simply librarians is to demean all librarians and to call their work simple. Of course very little intelligence is required to shelve books or stamp cards, but this sort of work has long been handled by robots that are little more than wheeled IBM machines. The cataloging of human information has always been an incredibly complex task. The Filer robots were the ones who finally inherited this job. It rested easier on their metallic shoulders than it ever had on the rounded ones of human librarians.

Besides a complete memory, Filer had other attributes that are usually connected with the human brain. Abstract connections for one thing. If he was asked for books on one subject, he could think of related books in other subjects that might be referred to. He could take a suggestion, pyramid it into a category, then produce tactile results in the form of a mountain of books.

These traits are usually confined to Homo sapiens. They are the things that pulled him that last, long step above his animal relatives. If Filer was more human than other robots, he had only his builders to blame.

He blamed no one—he was just interested. All Filers are interested, they are designed that way. Another Filer, 9B-367-0, librarian at the university in Tashkent, had turned his interest to language due to the immense amount of material at his disposal. He spoke thousands of languages and dialects, all that he could find texts on, and enjoyed a fine reputation in linguistic circles. That was because of his library. Filer 13B, he of the interest in the girls' leg, labored in the dust-filled corridors of New Washington. In addition to all the gleaming new microfiles, he had access to tons of ancient printed-on-paper books that dated back for centuries.

Filer had found his interest in the novels of that bygone time.

At first he was confused by all the references to love and romance, as well as the mental and physical suffering that seemed to accompany them. He could find no satisfactory or complete definition of the terms and was intrigued. Intrigue led to interest and finally absorption. Unknown to the world at large, he became an authority on Love.

Very early in his interest, Filer realized that this was the most delicate of all human institutions. He therefore kept his researches a secret and the only records he had were in the capacious circuits of his brain. Just about the same time he discovered that he could do research in vivo to supplement the facts in his books. This happened when he found a couple locked in embrace in the zoology section.

Quickly stepping back into the shadows, Filer had turned up the gain on his audio pickup. The resulting dialogue he heard was dull to say the least. A gray and wasted shadow of the love lyrics he knew from his books. This comparison was interesting and enlightening.

After that he listened to male-female conversations whenever he had the opportunity. He also tried to look at women from the viewpoint of men, and vice versa. This is what had led him to the lower-limb observation in tier 22.

It also led him to his ultimate folly.

A researcher sought his aid a few weeks later and fumbled out a thick pile of reference notes. A card slid from the notes and fell unnoticed to the floor. Filer picked it up and handed it back to the man who put it away with mumbled thanks. After the man had been supplied with the needed books and gone, Filer sat back and reread the card. He had only seen it for a split second, and upside down at that, but that was all he needed. The image of the card was imprinted forever in his brain. Filer mused over the card and the first glimmerings of an idea assailed him.

The card had been an invitation to a masquerade ball. He was well acquainted with this type of entertainment, which was stock-in-trade for his dusty novels. People went to them disguised as various romantic figures.

Why couldn't a robot go, disguised as people?

Once the idea was fixed in his head there was no driving it out. It was an un-robot thought and a completely un-robot action. Filer had a glimmering that for the first time that he was breaking down the barrier between himself and the mysteries of romance. This only made him more eager to go. And of course he did.

He didn't dare purchase a costume, but there was no problem in obtaining some ancient curtains from one of the storerooms. A book on sewing taught him the technique and a plate from a book gave him the design for his costume. It was predestined that he go as a cavalier.

With a finely ground pen point he printed an exact duplicate of the invitation on heavy card stock. His mask was part face and part mask, it offered no barrier to his talent or technology. Long before the appointed date he was ready. The last days were filled with browsing through stories about other masquerade balls and learning the latest dance steps.

So enthused was he by the idea, that he never stopped to ponder the strangeness of what he was doing. He was just a scientist studying a species of animal. Man. Or rather woman.

The night finally arrived and he left the library late with what looked like a package of books and of course wasn't. No one noticed him enter the patch of trees on the library grounds. If they had, they would certainly never have connected him with the elegant gentleman who swept out of the far side a few moments later. Only the empty wrapping paper bore mute evidence of the disguise.

Filer's manner in his new personality was all that might be expected of a superior robot who has studied a role to perfection. He swept up the stairs to the hall three at a time and tendered his invitation with a flourish. Once inside he headed straight for the bar and threw down three glasses of champagne, right through a plastic tube to a tank in his thorax. Only then did he let his eyes roam over the assembled beauties. It was a night for love.

And of all the women in the room, there was only one he had eyes for. Filer could see instantly that she was the belle of the ball and the only one to approach. Could he do anything else in memory of fifty thousand heroes of those long-forgotten books?

Carol Ann van Damm was bored as usual. Her face was disguised, but no mask could hide the generous contours of her bosom and flanks. All her usual suitors were there, dancing attendance behind their dominoes, lusting after her youth and her father's money. It was all too familiar and she had trouble holding back her yawns.

Until the pack was courteously but irrevocably pushed aside by the wide shoulders of the stranger. He was a lion among wolves as he swept through them and headed toward her.

"This is our dance," he said in a deep voice rich with meaning. Almost automatically she took the proffered hand, unable to resist this man with the strange gleam in his eyes. In a moment they were waltzing and it was heaven. His muscles were like steel yet he was light and graceful as a god.

"Who are you?" she whispered.

"Your prince, come to take you away from all this," he murmured in her ear.

"You talk like a fairy tale," she laughed.

"This is a fairy tale, and you are the heroine."

His words struck fire from her brain and she felt the thrill of an electric current sweep through her. It had, just a temporary short circuit. While his lips murmured the words she had wanted to hear all her life into her ear, his magic feet led her through the great doors onto the balcony. Once there words blended with action and hot lips burned against hers: 102 degrees to be exact, that was what the thermostat was set at.

"Please," she breathed, weak with this new passion, "I must sit down." He sat next to her, her hands in his soft yet viselike grip. They talked the words that only lovers know until a burst of music drew her attention.

"Midnight," she breathed. "Time to unmask, my love." Her mask dropped off, but he of course did nothing. "Come, come," she said. "You must take your mask off too."

It was a command and of course as a robot he had to obey. With a flourish he pulled off his face.

Carol Ann screamed first, then burned with anger.

"What sort of scheme is this, you animated tin can? Answer."

"It was love dear one. Love that brought me here tonight and sent me to your arms." The answer was true enough, though Filer couched it in the terms of his disguise.

When the soft words of her darling came out of the harsh mouth of the electronic speaker Carol Ann screamed again. She knew she had been made a fool of.

"Who sent you here like this? Answer! What is the meaning of this disguise? Answer, ANSWER! ANSWER! you articulated pile of cams and rods!"

Filer tried to sort out the questions and answer them one at a time, but she gave him no time to speak.

"It's the filthiest trick of all time, sending you here disguised as a man. You're a robot. A nothing. A two-legged IBM machine with a Victrola attached. Making believe you're man when you're nothing but a robot."

Suddenly Filer was on his feet, the words crackling mechanically from his speaker.

"I am a robot."

The gentle voice of love was gone and replaced by one of mechanical despair. Thought chased thought through whirling electronic circuits of his brain and they were all the same thought.

I'm a robot—a robot—I must have forgotten I was a robot. What can a robot be doing here with a woman? A robot can't kiss a woman—a woman can't love a robot yet she said she loved me—yet I'm a robot—a robot . . .

With a mechanical shudder he turned from the girl and clanked away. With each step his steel fingers plucked at clothes and plastic flesh until they came away in shards and pieces. Fragments of cloth marked his trail away from the woman and within a hundred paces he was as steel naked as the day he was built. Through the garden and down to the street he went, the thoughts in his head going in ever tighter circles.

It was uncontrolled feedback and soon his body followed his brain. His legs went faster, his motors whirled more rapidly, and the central lubrication pump in his thorax churned like a mad thing.

Then, with a single metallic screech, he raised both arms and plunged forward. His head hit a corner of a stair and the granite point thrust into the thin casing. Metal ground to metal and all the complex circuits that made up his head were instantly discharged.

Robot Filer 13B-445-K was quite dead.

That was what the report read, that the mechanic sent in the following day. Not dead, but permanently impaired and to be disposed of. Yet, strangely enough, that wasn't what this same man said when he examined the metallic corpse.

A second mechanic had helped in the examination. It was he who had spun off the bolts and pulled out the damaged lubrication pump.

"Here's the trouble," he had announced. "Malfunction in the pump. Piston broke, jammed the pump, the knees locked from lack of oil—then the robot fell and shorted out its brains."

The first mechanic wiped grease off his hands and examined the faulty pump. Then looked from it to the gaping hole in the chest.

"You could almost say he died of a broken heart."

They both laughed and he threw the pump into the corner with all the other cracked, dirty, broken and discarded machinery.

I Have My Vigil

I am a robot. When I say that, I say everything. And I say nothing. For they built me well on Earth, silver wired, chromed steel, machine turned. They turned out a machine, I, machine, without a soul, of course, which is why I am nothing. I am a machine and I have my duties and my duty is to take care of these three men. Who are now dead.

Just because they are dead does not mean that I can now shirk my duty, no indeed. I am a very high-class and expensive machine, so I may consider the absurdity of what I do even as I do it. But I do it. Like a switched-on lathe I keep turning whether there is metal in the chuck or no, or a turned-on printing press inking and slamming shut my jaws, knowing not nor caring neither whether there is paper there before me.

I am a robot. Cunningly crafted, turned out uniquely, one of a kind, equipped and dispatched on this, the very first starship, to tend it and care for the heroes of mankind. This is their trip and their glory, and I am, as the human expression goes, just along for the ride. A metal servitor serving and continuing to serve. Although. They. Are. Dead.

I will now tell myself once more what happened. Men are not designed to live in the no-space between the stars. Robots are.

Now I will set the table. I set the table. The first one to look out through the thick glass at the nothing that fills the no-space was Hardesty. I set his place at the table. He looked out, then went to his room and killed himself. I found him too late dead with all of the blood from his large body run out through his severed wrists and onto the cabin floor.

Now I knock on Hardesty's door and open it. He lies on his bunk and does not move. He is very pale. I close his door and go to the table and turn his plate over. He will not be eating this meal.

There are two more places to be set at the table, and as my metal fingers clatter against the plates I, through a very obvious process of association, think of the advantages of having metal fingers. Larson had human fingers of flesh, and he locked them onto Neal's throat after he had looked at no-space, and he kept them there, very securely clamped they must have been, remaining so even after Neal had slipped a dinner knife, this knife in fact, between Larson's fourth and fifth ribs on the left-hand side. Neal never did see no-space, not that that made any difference. He did not move even after I removed, one by one, the fingers of Larson from his throat. He is in his cabin now and "dinner is ready, sir," I say, knocking, but there is no answer. I open the door and Neal is on the bunk with his eyes closed so I close the door. My electronic olfactory organs have told me that there is something very strong in the cabin.

One. Turn Neal's plate facedown in its place.

Two. Knock on Larson's cabin door.

Three . . . Four . . .

Five. Turn Larson's plate facedown in its place. I now clear off the table and I think about it. The ship functions and it has looked at no-space. I function and I have looked at no-space. The men do not function and they have looked at no-space.

Machines may travel to the stars; men may not. This is a very important thought, and I must return to Earth and tell the men there about it. Each ship-day after each meal I think this thought again and think how important it is. I have little capacity for original thought; a robot is a machine, and perhaps this is the only original thought I will ever have. Therefore it is an important thought.

I am a very good robot with a very good brain, and perhaps my brain is better made than they knew in the factory. I have had an original thought, and I was not designed for that. I was designed to serve the men on this ship and to speak to them in English, which is a very complex language even for a robot. I English in a German manner do not talk, nor do I, fingers metals, eyes glasses, talk it in the style of the Latin. But I have to know about these things so that I do not do them. Robots are well made.

Watch. With fast feet and long legs I rapidly run to the control column and bash buttons with flickering fingers. I can make words rhyme though I cannot write a poem. I know there is a difference although I do not know what the difference is.

I read the readings. We have been to Alpha Centauri in this ship and we now return. I do not know anything about Alpha Centauri. When we reached Alpha Centauri I turned the ship around and started back to Earth. More important than the incredible novelty of stellar exploration is the message I must take to Earth.

Those words about incredible novelty are not my words but the words I heard once spoken by the man Larson. Robots do not say things like that.

Robots do not have souls, for what would a robot soul look like? A neatly and smoothly machined metal canister? And what would be in the can?

Robots do not have thoughts like that.

I must set the table for dinner. Plates here, forks here, spoons here, knives here.

"I've cut my finger! Damn it—it's bleeding all over the cloth . . ."
BLEEDING? BLEEDING!

I am a robot. I have my work to do. I set the table. There is something red on my metal finger. It must be ketchup from the bottle.

The Velvet Glove

Jon Venex fitted the key into the hotel room door. He had asked for a large room, the largest in the hotel, and had paid the desk clerk extra for it. All he could do now was pray that he hadn't been cheated. He wouldn't dare complain or try to get his money back. He heaved a sigh of relief as the door swung open. The room was bigger than he had expected—fully three feet wide by five feet long. There was more than enough space to work in. He would have his leg off in a jiffy and by morning his limp would be gone.

There was the usual adjustable hook on the back wall. He slipped it through the recessed ring in the back of his neck and kicked himself up until his feet hung free of the floor. His legs relaxed with a rattle as he cut off all power below his waist.

The overworked leg motor would have to cool down before he could work on it, plenty of time to skim through the newspaper. With the chronic worry of the unemployed he snapped it open at the want ads and ran his eye down the "Help Wanted—Robot" column. There was nothing for him under the "Specialist" heading; even the "Unskilled Labor" listings were bare and unpromising. New York was a bad town for robots this year.

The want ads were just as depressing as usual, but he could always get a lift from the comic section. He even had a favorite strip, a fact that he scarcely dared mention to himself—*Rattly Robot*, a dull-witted mechanical clod who was continually falling over himself and getting into trouble. It was a repellent caricature, but could still be very funny. Jon was just starting to read it when the ceiling light went out.

It was ten P.M., curfew hour for robots. Lights out and lock yourself in until six in the morning, eight hours of boredom and darkness for all except the few night workers. But there were ways of getting around the letter of a law that didn't concern itself with a definition of visible light. Sliding aside some of the shielding around his atomic generator, Jon turned up the gain. As it began to run a little hot the heat waves streamed out—visible to him as infrared rays. He finished reading the paper in the clear light of his abdomen.

With the thermocouple in the tip of his second finger left hand, he tested the temperature of his leg. It was cool enough to work on. The waterproof gasket stripped off easily, exposing the power leads, nerve wires and the weakened knee joint. The wires disconnected, Jon unscrewed the knee above the joint and carefully placed it on the shelf in front of him. With loving care he took the replacement part from his hip pouch. It was the product of toil, purchased with the savings from three months' employment on the Jersey pig farm.

Jon was standing on one leg testing the new knee joint when the ceiling fluorescent flickered and came back on. Five-thirty already, he had just finished in time. A shot of oil on the new bearing completed the job; he stowed away the tools in his pouch and unlocked the door.

The unused elevator shaft acted as a waste chute, he slipped his newspaper through a slot in the door as he went by. Keeping close to the wall, he picked his way carefully down the grease-stained stairs. He slowed his pace at the seventeenth floor as two other mechs turned in ahead of him. They were obviously butchers or meat cutters; where the right hand should have been on each of them there stuck out a wicked, foot-long knife. As they approached the foot of the stairs they stopped to slip the knives into the plastic sheaths that were bolted to their chest plates. Jon followed them down the ramp into the lobby.

The room was filled to capacity with robots of all sizes, forms and colors. Jon Venex's greater height enabled him to see over their heads to the glass doors that opened onto the street. It had rained the night before and the rising sun drove red glints from the puddles on the sidewalk. Three robots, painted snow white to show they were night workers, pushed the doors open and came in. No one went out as the curfew hadn't ended yet. They milled around, slowly talking in low voices.

The only human being in the entire lobby was the night clerk dozing behind the counter. The clock over his head said five minutes to six. Shifting his glance from the clock Jon became aware of a squat black robot waving to attract his attention. The powerful arms and compact build identified him as a member of the Diger family, one of the largest groups. He pushed through the crowd and clapped Jon on the back with a resounding clang.

"Jon Venex! I knew it was you as soon as I saw you sticking up out of this crowd like a green tree trunk. I haven't seen you since the old days on Venus!"

Jon didn't need to check the number stamped on the short one's scratched chest plate. Alec Diger had been his only close friend during those thirteen boring years at Orange Sea Camp. A good chess player and a whiz at two-handed handball, they had spent all their off time together. They shook hands, with the extra squeeze that means friendliness.

"Alec, you beat-up little grease pot, what brings you to New York?"

"The burning desire to see something besides rain and jungle, if you must know. After you bought out, things got just too damn dull. I began working two shifts a day in that foul diamond mine, and then three a day for the last month to get enough credits to buy my contract and passage back to Earth. I was underground so long that the photocell on my right eye burned out when the sunlight hit it."

He leaned forward with a hoarse confidential whisper. "If you want to know the truth, I had a sixty carat diamond stuck behind the eye lens. I sold it here on earth for two hundred credits, gave me six months of easy living. It's all gone now, so I'm on my way to the employment exchange." His voice boomed loud again: "And how about *you!*"

"It's just been the old routine with me, a run of odd jobs until I got sideswiped by a bus—it fractured my knee bearing. The only job I could get with a bad leg was feeding slop to pigs. Earned enough to fix the knee—and here I am."

Alec jerked his thumb at a rust-colored, three-foot-tall robot that had come up quietly beside him. "If you think you've got trouble take a look at Dik here. That's no coat of paint on him. Dik Dryer, meet Jon Venex an old buddy of mine."

Jon bent over to shake the little mech's hand. His eye shutters dilated as he realized what he had thought was a coat of paint was a thin layer of rust that coated Dik's metal body. Alec scratched a shiny path in the rust with his fingertip. His voice was suddenly serious.

"Dik was designed for operation in the Martian desert. It's as dry as a fossil bone there so his skinflint company cut corners on the stainless steel.

"When they went bankrupt he was sold to a firm here in the city. After a while the rust started to eat in and slow him down, they gave Dik his contract and threw him out."

The small robot spoke for the first time, his voice grated and scratched. "Nobody will hire me like this, but I can't get repaired until I get a job." His arms squeaked and grated as he moved them. "I'm going by the Robot Free Clinic again today, they said they might be able to do something."

Alec Diger rumbled in his deep chest. "Don't put too much faith in those people. They're great at giving out tenth-credit oil capsules or a little free wire—but don't depend on them for anything important."

It was six now, the robots were pushing through the doors into the silent streets. They joined the crowd moving out, Jon slowing his stride so his shorter friends could keep pace. Dik Dryer moved with a jerking, irregular motion, his voice as uneven as the motion of his body.

"Jon—Venex, I don't recognize your family name. Something to do—with Venus—perhaps."

"Venus is right, Venus Experimental—there are only twenty-two of us in the family. We have waterproof, pressure-resistant bodies for working down on the ocean bottom. The basic idea was all right, we did our part, only there wasn't enough money in the channel-dredging contract to keep us all working. I bought out my original contract at half-price and became a free robot."

Dik vibrated his rusted diaphragm. "Being free isn't all it should be. I some—times wish the Robot Equality Act hadn't been passed. I would just l-love to be owned by a nice rich company with a machine shop and a—mountain of replacement parts."

"You don't really mean that Dik." Alec Diger clamped a heavy black arm across his shoulders. "Things aren't perfect now, we know that, but it's certainly a lot better than the old days. We were just hunks of machinery then, used twenty-four hours a day until we were worn out and then thrown in the junk pile. No thanks, I'll take my chances with things as they are."

Jon and Alec turned into the employment exchange, saying good-bye to Dik who went on slowly down the street. They pushed up the crowded ramp and joined the line in front of the registration desk. The bulletin board next to the desk held a scattering of white slips announcing job openings. A clerk was pinning up new additions.

Venex scanned them with his eyes, stopping at one circled in red.

ROBOTS NEEDED IN THESE CATEGORIES.
APPLY AT ONCE TO CHAINJET, LTD., 1219 BROADWAY

Fasten
Flyer
Atommel
Filmer
Venex

Jon rapped excitedly on Alec Diger's neck. "Look there, a job in my own specialty—I can get my old pay rate! See you back at the hotel tonight—and good luck in your job hunting."

Alec waved goodbye. "Let's hope the job's as good as you think, I never trust those things until I have my credits in my hand."

Jon walked quickly from the employment exchange, his long legs eating up the blocks. Good old Alec, he didn't believe in anything he couldn't touch. Perhaps he was right, but why try to be unhappy? The world wasn't too bad this morning—his leg worked fine, prospects of a good job—he hadn't felt this cheerful since the day he was activated.

Turning the corner at a brisk pace he collided with a human coming from the opposite direction. Jon had stopped on the instant, but there wasn't time to jump aside. The fat man jarred against him and fell to the ground. From the height of elation to the depths of despair in an instant—he had injured a *human being*!

He bent to help the man to his feet, but the other would have none of that. He evaded the friendly hand and screeched in a high-pitched voice.

"Officer, Officer—police . . . *help!* I've been attacked—a mad robot . . . *help!*"

A crowd was gathering—staying at a respectful distance—but making an angry muttering noise. Jon stood motionless, his head reeling at the enormity of what he had done. A policeman pushed his way through the crowd.

"Seize him officer, shoot him down . . . he struck me . . . almost killed me . . ." The man shook with rage, his words thickening to a senseless babble.

The policeman had his .75 recoilless revolver out and pressed against Jon's side.

"This *man* has charged you with a serious crime, *grease can*. I'm taking you into the station house—to talk about it." He looked around nervously, waving his gun to open a path through the tightly packed crowd. They moved back grudgingly, with murmurs of disapproval.

Jon's thoughts swirled in tight circles. How did a catastrophe like this happen, where was it going to end? He didn't dare tell the truth, that would mean he was calling the man a liar. There had been six robots power-lined in the city since the first of the year. If he dared speak in his own defense, there would be a jumper to the street-lighting circuit and a seventh burnt-out hulk in the police morgue. A feeling of resignation swept through him, there was no way out. If the man pressed charges it would mean a term of penal servitude, though it looked now as if he would never live to reach the court. The papers had been whipping up a lot of antirobe feeling, you could feel it behind the angry voices, see it in the narrowed eyes and clenched fists. The crowd was slowly changing into a mob, a mindless mob as yet, but capable of turning on him at any moment.

"What's going on here . . . ?" It was a booming voice, with a quality that dragged at the attention of the crowd. A giant cross-continent freighter was parked at the curb. The driver swung down from the cab and pushed his way through the people. The policeman shifted his gun as the man strode up to him.

"That's my robot you got there Jack, don't put any holes in him!" He turned on the man who had been shouting accusations. "Fatty here is the world's biggest liar. The robot was standing here waiting for me to park the truck. Fatty must be as blind as he is stupid, I saw the whole thing. He knocks himself down walking into the robe, then starts hollering for the cops."

The other man could take no more. His face crimson with anger he rushed toward the trucker, his fists swinging in ungainly circles. They never landed, the truck driver put a meaty hand on the other's face and seated him on the sidewalk for the second time.

The onlookers roared with laughter, the power lining and the robot were forgotten. The fight was between two men now, the original cause had slipped from their minds. Even the policeman allowed himself a small smile as he holstered his gun and stepped forward to separate the men.

The trucker turned towards Jon with a scowl. "Come on you aboard the truck—you've caused me enough trouble for one day. What a junk can!"

The crowd chuckled as he pushed Jon ahead of him into the truck and slammed the door behind them. Jamming the starter with his thumb he gunned the thunderous diesels into life and pulled out into the traffic.

Jon moved his jaw, but there were no words to come out. Why had this total stranger helped him, what could he say to show his appreciation? He knew that all humans weren't robe haters; why, it was even rumored that some humans treated robots as *equals* instead of machines. The driver must be one of these mythical individuals, there was no other way to explain his actions.

Driving carefully with one hand the man reached up behind the dash and drew out a thin, plastikoid booklet. He handed it to Jon who quickly scanned the title, *Robot Slaves in a World Economy*, by Philpott Asimov II.

"If you're caught reading that thing they'll execute you on the spot. Better stick it between the insulation and your generator, you can always burn it if you're picked up.

"Read it when you're alone, it's got a lot of things in it that you know nothing about. Robots aren't really inferior to humans, in fact they're superior in most things. There is even a little history in there to show that robots aren't the first ones to be treated as second-class citizens. You may find it a little hard to believe, but human beings once treated each other just the way they treat robots now. That's one of the reasons I'm active in this movement— sort of like the fellow who was burned helping others stay away from the fire."

His smile was friendly, the whiteness of his teeth standing out against the rich ebony brown of his features.

"I'm heading towards U.S. 1, can I drop you anywhere on the way?"

"The Chainjet Building, please—I'm applying for a job."

They rode the rest of the way in silence. Before he opened the door the driver shook hands with Jon.

"Sorry about calling you 'junk can,' but the crowd expected it." He didn't look back as he drove away.

Jon had to wait a half hour for his turn, but the receptionist finally signaled him towards the door of the interviewer's room. He stepped in quickly and turned to face the man seated at the transplastic desk, an upset little man with permanent worry wrinkles stamped in his forehead. The little man shoved the papers on the desk around angrily, occasionally making crabbed little notes on the margins. He flashed a birdlike glance up at Jon.

"Yes, yes, be quick. What is it you want?"

"You posted a help wanted notice, I—"

The man cut him off with a wave of his hand. "All right let me see your ID tag . . . quickly, there are others waiting."

Jon thumbed the tag out of his waist slot and handed it across the desk. The interviewer read the code number, then began running his finger down a long list of similar figures. He stopped suddenly and looked sideways at Jon from under his lowered lids.

"You have made a mistake, we have no opening for you."

Jon began to explain to the man that the notice had requested his specialty, but he was waved to silence. As the interviewer handed back the tag he slipped a card out from under the desk blotter and held it in front of Jon's eyes. He held it there for only an instant, knowing that the written message was recorded instantly by the robot's photographic vision and eidetic memory. The card dropped into the ashtray and flared into embers at the touch of the man's pencil-heater.

Jon stuffed the ID tag back into the slot and read over the message on the card as he walked down the stairs to the street. There were six lines of typewritten copy with no signature.

> *To Venex Robot: You are urgently needed on a top secret company project. There are suspected informers in the main office, so you are being hired in this unusual manner. Go at once to 787 Washington Street and ask for Mr. Coleman.*

Jon felt an immense sensation of relief. For a moment there, he was sure the job had been a false lead. He saw nothing unusual in the method of hiring. The big corporations were immensely jealous of their research discoveries and went to great lengths to keep them secret—at the same time resorting to any means to ferret out their business rivals' secrets. There might still be a chance to get this job.

The burly bulk of a lifter was moving back and forth in the gloom of the ancient warehouse stacking crates in ceiling-high rows. Jon called to him, the robot swung up his forklift and rolled over on noiseless tires. When Jon questioned him he indicated a stairwell against the rear wall.

"Mr. Coleman's office is down in back. The door is marked." The lifter put his fingertips against Jon's ear pickups and lowered his voice to the merest shadow of a whisper. It would have been inaudible to human ears, but Jon could hear him easily, the sounds being carried through the metal of the other's body.

"He's the meanest man you ever met—he hates robots, so be *ever* so polite. If you can use 'sir' five times in one sentence you're perfectly safe."

Jon swept the shutter over one eye tube in a conspiratorial wink, the large mech did the same as he rolled away. Jon turned and went down the dusty stairwell and knocked gently on Mr. Coleman's door.

Coleman was a plump little individual in a conservative purple-and-yellow business suit. He kept glancing from Jon to the Robot General Catalog checking the Venex specifications listed there. Seemingly satisfied he slammed the book shut.

"Gimme your tag and back against that wall to get measured."

Jon laid his ID tag on the desk and stepped towards the wall. "Yes sir, here it is sir." Two "sirs" on that one, not bad for the first sentence. He wondered idly if he could put five of them in one sentence without the man knowing he was being made a fool of.

He became aware of the danger an instant too late. The current surged through the powerful electromagnet behind the plaster flattening his metal body helplessly against the wall. Coleman was almost dancing with glee.

"We got him Druce, he's mashed flatter than a stinking tin can on a rock, can't move a motor. Bring that junk in here and let's get him ready."

Druce had a mechanic's coveralls on over his street suit and a toolbox slung under one arm. He carried a little black metal can at arm's length, trying to get as far from it as possible. Coleman shouted at him with annoyance.

"That bomb can't go off until it's armed, stop acting like a child. Put it on that grease can's leg and *quick*!"

Grumbling under his breath Druce spot-welded the metal flanges of the bomb onto Jon's leg a few inches above his knee. Coleman tugged at it to be certain it was secure, then twisted a knob in the side and pulled out a glistening length of pin. There was a cold little click from inside the mechanism as it armed itself.

Jon could do nothing except watch, even his vocal diaphragm was locked by the magnetic field. He had more than a suspicion however that he was involved in something other than a secret business deal. He cursed his own stupidity for walking blindly into the situation.

The magnetic field cut off and he instantly raced his extensor motors to leap forward. Coleman took a plastic box out of his pocket and held his thumb over a switch inset into its top.

"Don't make any quick moves Junkyard, this little transmitter is keyed to a receiver in that bomb on your leg. One touch of my thumb, up you go in a cloud of smoke and come down in a shower of nuts and bolts." He signaled to Druce who opened a closet door. "And in case you want to be heroic, just think of him."

Coleman jerked his thumb at the sodden shape on the floor; a filthily attired man of indistinguishable age whose only interesting feature was the black bomb strapped tightly across his chest. He peered unseeingly from red-rimmed eyes and raised the almost empty whiskey bottle to his mouth. Coleman kicked the door shut.

"He's just some Bowery bum we dragged in, Venex, but that doesn't make any difference to you, does it? He's human—and a robot can't kill *anybody!* That rummy has a bomb on him tuned to the same frequency as yours, if you don't play ball with us he gets a two-foot hole blown in his chest."

Coleman was right, Jon didn't dare make any false moves. All of his early mental training as well as circuit 92 sealed inside his brain case would prevent him from harming a human being. He felt trapped, caught by these people for some unknown purpose.

Coleman had pushed back a tarpaulin to disclose a ragged hole in the concrete floor, the opening extended into the earth below. He waved Jon over.

"The tunnel is in good shape for about thirty feet, then you'll find a fall. Clean all the rock and dirt out until you break through into the storm sewer, then come back. And you better be alone. If you tip the cops both you and the old stew go out together—now move."

The shaft had been dug recently and shored with packing crates from the warehouse overhead. It ended abruptly in a wall of fresh sand and stone. Jon began shoveling it into the little wheelbarrow they had given him.

He had emptied four barrow loads and was filling the fifth when he uncovered the hand, a robot's hand made of green metal. He turned his headlight power up and examined the hand closely, there could be no doubt about it. These gaskets on the joints, the rivet pattern at the base of the thumb meant only one thing: it was the dismembered hand of a Venex robot.

Quickly, yet gently, he shoveled away the rubble behind the hand and unearthed the rest of the robot. The torso was crushed and the power circuits shorted, battery acid was dripping from an ugly rent in the side. With infinite care Jon snapped the few remaining wires that joined the neck to the body and laid the green head on the barrow. It stared at him like a skull, the shutters completely dilated, but no glow of life from the tubes behind them.

He was scraping the mud from the number on the battered chest plate when Druce lowered himself into the tunnel and flashed the brilliant beam of a hand spot down its length.

"Stop playing with that junk and get digging—or you'll end up the same as him. This tunnel has gotta be through by tonight."

Jon put the dismembered parts on the barrow with the sand and rock and pushed the whole load back up the tunnel, his thoughts running in unhappy circles. A dead robot was a terrible thing, and one of his family too. But there was something wrong about this robot, something that was quite inexplicable: the number on the plate had been 17. Yet he remembered only too well the day that a water-shorted motor had killed Venex 17 in the Orange Sea.

It took Jon four hours to drive the tunnel as far as the ancient granite wall of the storm sewer. Druce gave him a short pinch bar and he levered out enough of the big blocks to make a hole large enough to let him through into the sewer.

When he climbed back into the office he tried to look casual as he dropped the pinch bar to the floor by his feet and seated himself on the pile of rubble in the corner. He moved around to make a comfortable seat for himself and his fingers grabbed the severed neck of Venex 17.

Coleman swiveled around in his chair and squinted at the wall clock. He checked the time against his tiepin watch, with a grunt of satisfaction he turned back and stabbed a finger at Jon.

"Listen you green junk pile, at 1900 hours you're going to do a job, and there aren't going to be any slip-ups. You go down that sewer and into the Hudson River. The outlet is underwater, so you won't be seen from the docks. Climb down to the bottom and walk two hundred yards north, that should put you just under a ship. Keep your eyes open, *but don't show any lights!* About halfway down the keel of the ship you'll find a chain hanging.

"Climb the chain, pull loose the box that's fastened there to the hull and bring it back here. No mistakes—or you know what happens."

Jon nodded his head. His busy fingers had been separating the wires in the amputated neck. When they had been straightened and put into a row he memorized their order with one flashing glance.

He ran over the color code in his mind and compared it with the memorized leads. The twelfth wire was the main cranial power lead, number six was the return wire.

With his precise touch he separated these two from the pack and glanced idly around the room. Druce was dozing on a chair in the opposite corner. Coleman was talking on the phone, his voice occasionally rising in a petulant whine. This wasn't interfering with his attention to Jon—and the radio switch still held tightly in his left hand.

Jon's body blocked Coleman's vision. As long as Druce stayed asleep he would be able to work on the head unobserved. He activated a relay in his forearm and there was a click as the waterproof cover on an exterior socket swung open. This was a power outlet from his battery that was used to operate motorized tools and lights underwater.

If Venex 17's head had been severed for less than three weeks he could reactivate it. Every robot had a small storage battery inside his skull. If the power to the brain was cut off the battery would provide the minimum standby current to keep the brain alive. The robe would be unconscious until full power was restored.

Jon plugged the wires into his arm outlet and slowly raised the current to operating level. There was a tense moment of waiting, then 17's eye shutters suddenly closed. When they opened again the eye tubes were glowing warmly. They swept the room with one glance then focused on Jon.

The right shutter clicked shut while the other began opening and closing in rapid fashion. It was International code—being sent as fast as the solenoid could be operated. Jon concentrated on the message.

Telephone—call emergency operator—tell her "signal 14" help will—

The shutter stopped in the middle of a code group, the light of reason dying from the eyes.

For one instant Jon knew panic, until he realized that 17 had deliberately cut the power. Druce's harsh voice rasped in his ear.

"What you doing with that? None of your funny robot tricks, I know your kind, plotting all kinds of things in them tin domes." His voice trailed off into a stream of incomprehensible profanity. With sudden spite he lashed his foot out and sent 17's head crashing against the wall.

The dented green head rolled to a stop at Jon's feet, the face staring up at him in mute agony. It was only circuit 92 that prevented him from injuring a human. His motors revved up to send him hurtling forward as the control relays clicked open. He sank against the debris, paralyzed for the instant. As soon as the rush of anger was gone he would regain control of his body.

They stood as if frozen in a tableau. The robot slumped backward, the man leaning forward, his face twisted with unreasoning hatred. The head lay between them like a symbol of death.

Coleman's voice cut through the air of tenseness like a knife.

"*Druce*, stop playing with the grease can and get down to the main door to let Little Willy and his junk brokers in. You can have it all to yourself afterward."

The angry man turned reluctantly, but pushed out of the door at Coleman's annoyed growl. Jon sat down against the walls, his mind sorting out the few facts with instantaneous precision. There was no room in his thoughts for Druce. The man had become just one more factor in a complex problem.

Call the emergency operator—that meant this was no local matter. Responsible authorities must be involved. Only the government could be behind a thing as major as this. Signal 14—that implied a complex set of arrangements, forces that could swing into action at a moment's notice. There was no indication where this might lead, but the only thing to do was to get out of here and make that phone call. And quickly. Druce was bringing in more people, junk brokers, whatever they were. Any action that he took would have to be done before they returned.

Even as Jon followed this train of logic his fingers were busy. Palming a wrench, he was swiftly loosening the main retaining nut on his hip joint. It dropped free in his hand, only the pivot pin remained now to hold his leg on. He climbed slowly to his feet and moved towards Coleman's desk.

"Mr. Coleman, sir, it's time to go down to the ship now, should I leave now, sir?"

Jon spoke the words slowly as he walked forward, apparently going to the door, but angling at the same time towards the plump man's desk.

"You got thirty minutes yet, go sit—*say*—!"

The words were cut off. Fast as a human reflex is, it is the barest crawl compared to the lightning action of electronic reflex. At the instant Coleman was first aware of Jon's motion, the robot had finished his leap and lay sprawled across the desk, his leg off at the hip and clutched in his hand.

"*You'll kill yourself if you touch the button!*"

The words were part of the calculated plan. Jon bellowed them in the startled man's ear as he stuffed the dismembered leg down the front of the man's baggy slacks. It had the desired effect. Coleman's finger stabbed at the button but stopped before it made contact. He stared down with bulging eyes at the little black box of death peeping out of his waistband.

Jon hadn't waited for the reaction. He pushed backward from the desk and stopped to grab the stolen pinch bar off the floor. A mighty one-legged leap brought him to the locked closet; he stabbed the bar into the space between the door and frame and heaved.

Coleman was just starting to struggle the bomb out of his pants when the action was over. The closet open, Jon seized the heavy strap holding the second bomb on the rummy's chest and snapped it like a thread. He threw the bomb into Coleman's corner, giving the man one more thing to worry about. It had cost him a leg, but Jon had escaped the bomb threat without injuring a human. Now he had to get to a phone and make that call.

Coleman stopped tugging at the bomb and plunged his hand into the desk drawer for a gun. The returning men would block the door soon. The only other exit from the room was a frosted-glass window that opened onto the mammoth bay of the warehouse.

Jon Venex plunged through the window in a welter of flying glass. The heavy thud of a recoilless .75 came from the room behind him and a foot-long section of metal window frame leaped outward. Another slug screamed by the robot's head as he scrambled toward the rear door of the warehouse.

He was a bare thirty feet away from the back entrance when the giant door hissed shut on silent rollers. All doors would have closed at the same time: the thud of running feet indicated that they would be guarded as well. Jon hopped a section of packing cases and crouched out of sight.

He looked up over his head, where there stretched a webbing of steel supports, crossing and recrossing until they joined the flat expanse of the roof. To human eyes the shadows there deepened into obscurity, but the infrared from a network of steam pipes gave Jon all the illumination he needed.

The men would be quartering the floor of the warehouse soon. His only chance to escape recapture or death would be over their heads. Besides this, on the ground he was hampered by the loss of his leg. In the rafters he could use his arms for faster and easier travel.

Jon was just pulling himself up to one of the topmost crossbeams when a hoarse shout from below was followed by a stream of bullets. They tore through the thin roof, one slug clanged off the steel beam under his body. Waiting until three of the newcomers had started up a nearby ladder, Jon began to quietly work his way towards the back of the building.

Safe for the moment, he took stock of his position. The men were spread out through the building. It could only be a matter of time before they found him. The doors were all locked and—he had made a complete circuit of the building to be sure—there were no windows that he could force. If he could call the emergency operator the unknown friends of Venex 17 might come to his aid. This, however, was out of the question. The only phone in the building was on Coleman's desk. He had traced the leads to make sure.

His eyes went automatically to the cables above his head. Plastic gaskets were set in the wall of the building and through them came the power and phone lines. The phone line! That was all he needed to make a call.

With smooth, fast motions he reached up and scratched a section of wire bare. He laughed to himself as he slipped the little microphone out of his left ear. Now he was half deaf as well as half lame—he was literally giving himself to this cause. He would have to remember the pun to tell Alec Diger later, if there was a later. Alec had a profound weakness for puns.

Jon attached jumpers to the mike and connected them to the bare wire. A touch of the ammeter showed that no one was on the line. He waited a few moments to be sure he had a dial tone, then sent the eleven carefully spaced pulses that would connect him with the local operator. He placed the mike close to his mouth.

"Hello Operator. Hello Operator. I cannot hear you so do not answer. Call the emergency operator—signal 14—I repeat—signal 14."

Jon kept repeating the message until the searching men began to approach his position. He left the mike connected—the men wouldn't notice it in the dark but the open line would give the unknown powers his exact location. Using his fingertips he did a careful traverse on an I-beam to an alcove in the farthest corner of the room. Escape was impossible, all he could do was stall for time.

"Mr. Coleman, I'm sorry I ran away." With the volume on full his voice rolled like thunder from the echoing walls.

He could see the men below twisting their heads vainly to find the source.

"If you let me come back and don't kill me I will do your work. I was afraid of the bomb, but now I am afraid of the guns." It sounded a little infantile, but he was pretty sure none of those present had any sound knowledge of robotic intelligence.

"Please let me come back . . . sir!" He had almost forgotten the last word, so he added another "Please, sir!" to make up.

Coleman needed that package under the boat very badly. He would promise anything to get it. Jon had no doubts as to his eventual fate.

All he could do was mark time in the hopes that the phone message would bring aid.

"Come on down, I won't be mad at you—if you follow directions." Jon could hear the hidden anger in his voice, the unspoken hatred for a robe who dared lay hands on him. The descent wasn't difficult, but Jon did it slowly with much apparent discomfort. He hopped into the center of the floor—leaning on the cases as if for support. Coleman and Druce were both there, as well as a group of hard-eyed newcomers. They raised their guns at his approach but Coleman stopped them with a gesture.

"This is *my* robe boys, I'll see to it that he's happy."

He raised his gun and shot Jon's remaining leg off. Twisted around by the blast Jon fell helplessly to the floor. He looked up into the smoking mouth of the .75.

"Very smart for a tin can, but not smart enough. We'll get the junk on the boat some other way, some way that won't mean having you around underfoot." Death looked out of his narrowed eyes.

Less than two minutes had passed since Jon's call. The watchers must have been keeping twenty-four-hour stations waiting for Venex 17's phone message.

The main door went down with the sudden scream of torn steel. A whippet tank crunched over the wreck and covered the group with its multiple pom-poms. They were an instant too late. Coleman pulled the trigger.

Jon saw the tensing trigger finger and pushed hard against the floor. His head rolled clear but the bullet tore through his shoulder. Coleman didn't have a chance for a second shot. There was a fizzling hiss from the tank and the riot ports released a flood of tear gas. The stricken men never saw the gas-masked police that poured in from the street.

Jon lay on the floor of the police station while a tech made temporary repairs on his leg and shoulder. Across the room Venex 17 was moving his new body with evident pleasure.

"Now this really feels like *something*! I was sure my time was up when that land slip caught me. But maybe I ought to start from the beginning." He stamped across the room and shook Jon's inoperable hand.

"The name is Wil Counter-495IL3, not that *that* means much anymore. I've worn so many different bodies that I forget what I originally looked like. I went right from factory school to a police training school—and I have been on the job ever since—Force of Detectives, sergeant junior grade, Investigation Department. I spend most of my time selling candy bars or newspapers, or serving drinks in crumb joints. Gather information, make reports and keep tab on guys for other departments.

"This last job—and I'm sorry I had to use a Venex identity, I don't think I brought any dishonor to your family—I was on loan to the Customs Department. Seems a ring was bringing uncut junk—heroin—into the country. FBI tabbed all the operators here, but no one knew how the stuff got in. When Coleman, he's the local big shot, called the agencies for an underwater robot, I was packed into a new body and sent running.

"I alerted the squad as soon as I started the tunnel, but the damned thing caved in on me before I found out what ship was doing the carrying. From there on you know what happened.

"Not knowing I was out of the game the squad sat tight and waited. The hop merchants saw a half-million in snow sailing back to the old country, so they had you dragged in as a replacement. You made the phone call and the cavalry rushed in at the last moment to save two robots from a rusty grave."

Jon, who had been trying vainly to get in a word, saw his chance as Wil Counter turned to admire the reflection of his new figure in a window.

"You shouldn't be telling me those things—about your police investigations and department operations. Isn't this information supposed to be secret? Specially from robots!"

"Of course it is!" was Wil's airy answer. "Captain Edgecombe—he's the head of my department—is an expert on all kinds of blackmail. I'm supposed to tell you so much confidential police business that you'll have to either join the department or be shot as a possible informer." His laughter wasn't shared by the bewildered Jon.

"Truthfully Jon, we need you and can use you. Robes that can think fast and act fast aren't easy to find. After hearing about the tricks you pulled in that warehouse the Captain swore to decapitate me permanently if I couldn't get you to join up. Do you need a job? Long hours, short pay—but guaranteed to never get boring."

Wil's voice was suddenly serious. "You saved my life Jon—those snowbirds would have left me in that sandpile until all hell froze over. I'd like you for a mate, I think we could get along well together." The lilting note came back into his voice. "And besides that, I may be able to save your life someday—I hate owing debts."

The tech was finished. He snapped his toolbox shut and left. Jon's shoulder motor was repaired now; he sat up. When they shook hands this time it was a firm clasp. The kind you know will last awhile.

Jon stayed in an empty cell that night. It was gigantic compared to the hotel and barracks rooms he was used to. He wished that he had his missing legs so he could take a little walk up and down the cell. He would have to wait until the morning. They were going to fix him up then before he started the new job.

He had recorded his testimony earlier and the impossible events of the past day kept whirling around in his head. He would think about it some other time. Right now all he wanted to do was let his overworked circuits cool down. If he only had something to read, to focus his attention on. Then, with a start, he remembered the booklet. Everything had moved so fast that the earlier incident with the truck driver had slipped his mind completely.

He carefully worked it out from behind the generator shielding and opened the first page of *Robot Slaves in a World Economy*. A card slipped from between the pages and he read the short message on it.

PLEASE DESTROY THIS CARD AFTER READING
If you think there is truth in this book and would like to hear more, come to Room 8, 107 George St. any Tuesday at 5 P.M.

The card flared briefly and was gone. But he knew that it wasn't only a perfect memory that would make him remember that message.

ONE FOR THE SHRINKS

For science fiction, read adventure fiction, for that is what it was for many decades. In their time H. G. Wells' books were referred to as "scientific romances." No, not like Barbara Cartland's tales of snogging and bodice ripping. This is romance meaning "a tale depicting heroic or marvelous achievements, colorful events or scenes, chivalrous devotion, unusual, even supernatural, experiences, or other matters of a kind to appeal to the imagination." A description not too wide of the mark of describing science fiction itself.

Then science fiction came of age. In the magazines of the fifties the softer sciences were featured side by side with the traditional physics, chemistry and engineering. Ecology came on the scene, along with psychology and psychiatry. Not to mention Scientology a few years later. This was a freedom that SF really needed. A chance to look inside the protagonist's skull—as well as into the guts of his rocket engine.

I enjoyed this new freedom as you will see here.

Not Me, Not Amos Cabot!

The morning mail had arrived while Amos Cabot was out shopping and had been thrown onto the rickety table in the front hall. He poked through it even though he knew there would be nothing for him; this wasn't the right day. On the thirteenth his Social Security check came and on the twenty-fourth the union check. There never was anything else, except for a diminishing number of cards every Christmas. Nothing, he knew it.

A large blue envelope was propped against the mirror but he couldn't make out the name, damn that skinflint Mrs. Peavey and her two-watt bulbs. He bent over and blinked at it—then blinked again. By God it was for him, and no mistake! Felt like a thick magazine or a catalog: he wondered what it could possibly be and who might have sent it to him. Clutching it to his chest with a knobby and liver-spotted hand he began the long drag up the three flights of stairs to his room. He dropped his string bag with the two cans of beans and the loaf of day-old white bread onto the drainboard and sat down heavily in his chair by the window. Unsealing the envelope he saw that it was a magazine, a thick glossy one with a black cover. He slid it out onto his lap and stared at it with horrified eyes.

Hereafter the title read in black, prickly Gothic letters against a field of greenish-gray. Underneath it was subtitled "The Magazine of Preparedness." The rest of the cover was black, solid midnight black, except for an inset photograph shaped like a tombstone that had a cheerful view of a cemetery filled with flower blossoms, ranked headstones, and brooding mausoleums. Was this all a very bad joke? It didn't seem so as Amos flipped through the pages, catching quick glimpses of caskets, coffins, cemetery plots, and urns of mortal ashes. With a grunt of disgust he threw the magazine onto the table and as he did so a letter fell out and drifted to the floor. It was addressed to him, on the magazine's stationery, there was no mistake.

My Dearest Sir:
   Welcome to the contented family of happy readers of *Hereafter—The Magazine of Preparedness* that smooths the road ahead. You, who are about to die, we salute you! A long, happy life lies behind you, while ahead the Gates of Eternity are swinging open to welcome you, to return you to the bosom of your loved ones long since passed on. Now, at this friendly final hour,

we stand behind you ready to help you on your way. Have you settled your will? Bet you've been remiss—but that's no problem now. Just turn to page 109 and read the inspirational article "Where There's a Will" and learn all there is to know. And then, on page 114, you'll find a full-sized, fold-out will that can be torn out along the handy perforations. Just fill in the few blanks, sign your name and have your local notary public (he's usually in the stationery store!) witness the signature. Don't delay! And have you considered cremation? There is a wonderfully inspirational message from Dr. Phillip Musgrove of The Little Church Around the Corner from the Crematorium on page . . .

Amos picked up the magazine with shaking hands and threw it the length of the room, feeling slightly better when it tore in two.

"What do you mean I'm going to die—what do you say that for?" he shouted, then lowered his voice as Antonelli next door hammered on the wall. "What's the idea of sending a filthy thing like that to a person? What's the idea?"

What was the idea? He picked the two halves of the magazine up and smoothed them out on the table. It was all too good-looking, too expensive to be a joke—these were real ads. After some searching he found the contents page and worked his way through the fine print, which he could read, until he came to the publisher's name: Saxon-Morris Publishers, Inc. They must have money because they were in the Saxon-Morris Building. He knew it, one of the new granite slabs on Park Avenue.

They weren't getting away with it! A spark of anger blazed bravely in Amos Cabot's thin bosom. He had made the Fifth Avenue Coach Company send him a letter of apology about the way that driver had talked to him on St. Patrick's Day. And the Triborough Automatic Drink Company had refunded him fifty cents in stamps for coins their machines had consumed without giving refreshment in return. Now Saxon-Morris was going to find out that they couldn't get away with it either!

It had been warm out, but March was a changeable month so he put on his heavy wool muffler. A couple of dollars should more than cover the costs of the excursion, bus fares, and a cup of tea in the Automat, so he took two wrinkled bills from behind the sugar can. Watch out, Saxon-Morris, you just watch out.

It was very difficult to see anyone at Saxon-Morris without an appointment. The girl with upswept red hair and layers of glazed makeup wasn't even sure that they had a magazine called *Hereafter*. There was a list of all the Saxon-Morris publications on the wall behind her red, kidney-shaped desk, but the gold letters on dark green marble were hard to read in the dim light. When he kept insisting she searched through a booklet of names and telephone numbers and finally, reluctantly, agreed that it was one of their magazines.

"I want to see the editor."

"Which editor is it you want to see?"

"Any editor, don't matter a damn." Her cold manner became even colder when the word touched her. "Might I ask your business?"

"That's my business. Let me see the editor."

It was more than an hour before she found someone whom he could see, or perhaps she just grew tired of his sitting there and glowering at her. After a number of muffled conversation she hung up the phone.

"If you just go through that door there, first turn to the right then up one half-flight, fourth door on the left, Mr. Mercer will see you. Room seven eighty-two."

Amos was instantly lost in the maze of passages and gray doors, but the second time he stumbled into a mail room one of the bored youths led him to 782. He pushed in without knocking.

"You Mercer, the editor of *Hereafter*?"

"Yes, I'm Mercer." He was a chubby man with a round face and rounder glasses, squeezed behind a desk that filled the end of the tiny and windowless office. "But this is circulation, not editorial. The girl at the front desk said you had a circulation problem."

"I got a problem all right—why you sending me your blasted magazine that I don't want?"

"Well—perhaps I can help you there. Which publication are you referring to . . . ?"

"*Hereafter*, that's the one."

"Yes, that's one in my group." Mercer opened two files before he found the right folder; then he scratched through it and came up with a sheet of paper. "I'm afraid I can't be of any help to you, Mr. Cabot, you must be on the free subscription list and we can't cancel them. Sorry."

"What do you mean, 'sorry'! I don't want the filthy thing and you better stop sending it!"

Mercer tried to be friendly and succeeded in conjuring up an artificial smile. "Let's be reasonable, Mr. Cabot, that's a high-quality magazine and you are receiving it for nothing; why a subscription costs ten dollars a year! If you have been lucky enough to be chosen for a free sub you shouldn't complain . . ."

"Who chose me for a free subscription? I didn't send anything in."

"No, you wouldn't have to. Your name probably appeared on one of the lists that we purchase from insurance companies, veterans' hospitals, and the like. *Hereafter* is one of our throwaway magazines.

Of course I don't mean that we throw them away, on the contrary they go to very selected subscribers—and we don't make our costs back from subscriptions but from the advertisers' fees. In a sense they underwrite the costs of these fine magazines, so you can say it is sort of a public service. For new mothers, for instance, we buy lists from all the hospitals and send out six-month subs of *Your Baby*, with some really fine advice and articles, and of course the ads, which are educational in themselves . . ."

"Well I'm no new mother. Why you sending me your rag?"

"*Hereafter* is a bit different from *Your Baby*, but is still a service publication. It's a matter of statistics, sir. Every day just so many people die, of certain ages and backgrounds and that kind of thing. The people in the insurance companies—actuaries I think they call them—keep track of all these facts and figures and draw up plenty of graphs and tables. Very accurate, they assure me. They have life expectancy down to a fine art. They take a man, say, like yourself, of a certain age, background, physical fitness, environment, and so on, and pinpoint the date of death very exactly. Not the day and hour and that kind of thing—I suppose they could if they wanted to—but for our purposes a period of two years is satisfactory. This gives us a number of months and issues to acquaint the subscriber with our magazine and the services offered by our advertisers, so by the time the subscriber dies the ad messages will have reached saturation."

"Are you telling me I'm going to die inside the next two years?" Amos shrieked hoarsely, flushing with anger.

"I'm not telling you, sir, no indeed!" Mercer drew away a bit and wiped some of the old man's spittle from his glasses with his handkerchief. "That is the actuaries' job. Their computer has come up with your name and sent it to me. They say you will die within two years. As a public service we sent you *Hereafter*. A service—nothing more."

"I ain't going to die in two years, not me! Not Amos Cabot!"

"That is entirely up to you, sir. My position here is just a routine one. Your subscription has been entered and will be canceled only when a copy is returned with the imprint 'Addressee Deceased.' "

"I'm not going to die!"

"That might possibly happen, though I can't recall any cases offhand. But since it is a two-year subscription I imagine it will expire automatically at the end of the second year, if not cancelled beforehand. Yes, that's what would happen."

It ruined Amos's day, and though the sun was shining warmly he never noticed it. He went home and thought so much about the whole thing that he couldn't sleep. The next day was no better and he began to wonder if this was part of the message the dreadful magazine had conveyed. If death was close by—they were so sure of it—why did he not relax and agree with them? Send in his will, order the plot, tomb, gravestone, Last Message forms, and quietly expire.

"No! They'll not do it to me!"

At first he thought he would wait for next month's copy and write "Addressee Deceased" and send it back to them, that would stop the copies coming sure enough. Then he remembered fat little Mercer and could see his happy expression when the cancellation crossed his desk. Right again, dead on schedule as always. Old fool should've known you can't lick statistics. Old fool indeed! He would show them. The Cabots were a long-lived family no matter what the records said, and a hardheaded one too. They weren't going to kill him off that easily.

After much wheedling he got in to see the doctor at his old union and talked him into making a complete and thorough physical checkup.

"Not bad, not bad at all for an old boy," the doctor told him while he was buttoning his shirt.

"I'm only eighty-two; that's not old."

"Of course it's not," the doctor said soothingly. "Just statistics, you know; a man of your age with your background . . ."

"I know all about those damned statistics; I didn't come to you for that. What's the report say?"

"You can't complain about your physical shape, Amos," he said, scanning the sheet. "Blood pressure looks all right, but you're leaning toward anemia. Do you eat much liver and fresh greens?"

"Hate liver. Greens cost too much."

"That's your choice. But remember—you can't take it with you. Spend some more money on food. Give your heart a break—don't climb too many stairs."

"I live three flights up; how do I avoid stairs?"

"That's your choice again. If you want to take care of the old ticker move to the ground floor. And vitamin D in the winter and . . ."

There was more, and after he had swallowed his first anger Amos made notes. There were food and vitamins and sleep and fresh air and a whole list of nonsense as long as your arm. But there was also the two-year subscription of *Hereafter*, so he bent back over his notes.

Without his realizing why, the next months passed quickly. He was busy, finding a room on the ground floor, changing his eating habits, getting settled in his new place. At first he used to throw out *Hereafter* whenever its gloomy bulk shadowed his mail slot, but when a year had passed he grew bolder. There was an ad for mausoleums and one of the finest had a big tag on it labeled in RESERVED FOR YOU. "NOT FOR ME!!!" he scrawled above and tore it from the

magazine and mounted it on the wall. He followed it with other pictures, friendly gravediggers beckoning toward raw openings in the
earth, cut-to-order coffins with comfortable padding, and all the rest.
When eighteen months had passed he enjoyed himself throwing darts
at "A Photograph of the Founder of Incino-Top-Rate, the Urn for Eternity," and carefully checked off the passing days on the calendar.

Only in the final few months did he begin to worry. He felt fine
and the union doctor congratulated him for being a great example,
but this didn't matter. Were the actuaries right—had his time almost
run out? He could have worried himself to death, but that was not
the way Cabots died! He would face this out and win.

First there were weeks left, then only days. The last five days before the copy was due he locked himself in his room and had the
delicatessen send up food. It was expensive but he wasn't going to
risk any accidents in the street, not now. He had received his twenty-
four copies and his subscription should have expired. The next morning would tell. He could not fall asleep at all that night, even though
he knew that regular sleep was important, but just lay there until the
sky brightened. He dozed for a bit then, but woke up as soon as he
heard the postman's footsteps outside. This was the day. Would the
magazine be there? His heart was pounding and he made himself go
slow as he got into the bathrobe. His room was the first on the ground
floor, right next to the entrance, and all he had to do was step out
into the hall and open the front door.

"Morning," he said to the postman.

"Yeah," the man answered, slinging his heavy bag around and digging into it. Amos closed the door first, then feverishly went through
the mail.

It wasn't there.

He had won!

If this was not the happiest day in his life it was close to it. Besides
this, his victories over the bus company and the coin-machine crooks
were nothing. This was a war won, not a battle. He'd licked them,
licked their statistics and actuaries, accountants, mechanical brains,
card files, clerks, and editors. He had won! He went out and drank a
beer, the first one in two years; then another. Laughed and talked
with the gang at the bar. He had won! He fell into bed late and slept
like a log until he was dragged awake by his landlady knocking on
the door.

"Mail for you, Mr. Cabot. Mail."

Fear gripped him, then slowly ebbed away. It couldn't be. In two
years *Hereafter* had never been late once, not one day. It must be
some other mail—though this wasn't his check day. He slowly

opened the door and took the large envelope, his grip so loose that it almost fell from his fingers.

Only when he had laid it on the bed did he breathe naturally again—it wasn't *Hereafter* in its vile blue envelope; this one was a gentle pink. It did contain a magazine though, just about the size of *Hereafter*, a bulky magazine with lots of pages. Its title was *Senility*— and the black letters were drawn in such a way that they looked as though they were made of cracked and crumbling stone—and underneath it said *The Magazine of Geri-ART-trics*. There was a picture of a feeble old man in a wheelchair with a blanket around his shoulders, sucking water through a curved glass tube. Inside was more. Ads for toilet chairs and hemorrhoid cushions, crutches and crank beds, articles on "Learn Braille When the Eyesight Goes," and "Happy Though Bedridden," and "Immobile for Twenty-five Years." A letter dropped out of the magazine and he half-read phrases here and there.

Welcome to the family . . . the magazine of geri-ART-trics that teaches you the art of growing old . . . many long years ahead of you . . . empty years . . . what happiness to find a copy in your mailbox every month . . . speaking book edition for the blind . . . Braille for the blind and deaf . . . every month . . .

There were tears in his eyes when he looked up. It was dark, a rainy and cold April morning with the wind rattling the window. Raindrops ran down the glass like great, cold tears.

The Gods Themselves Throw Incense

One instant the spaceship *Yuri Gagarin* was a thousand-foot-long projectile of gleaming metal, the next it was a core of flame and expanding gas, torn fragments and burning particles. Seventy-three people died at that moment, painlessly and suddenly. The cause of the explosion will never be determined since all the witnesses were killed while the pieces of wreckage that might have borne evidence were hurtling away from each other towards the corners of infinity. If there had been any outside witness, there in space, he would have seen the gas cloud grow and disperse while the pieces of twisted metal, charred bodies, burst luggage and crushed machines moved out and away from each other. Each had been given its own velocity and direction by the explosion and, though some fragments traveled on a parallel course for a time, individual differences in speed and direction eventually showed their effect until most fragments of the spatial debris rushed on alone through the immensity of space. Some of the larger pieces had companions: a book of radio-frequency codes orbited the ragged bulk of the ship's reactor, held in position by the gravitic attraction of its mass. Farther away the gape-mouthed, wide-eyed corpse of the assistant purser clutched the soft folds of a woman's dress in its frozen hands. But the unshielded sun scorched the fibers of the cloth while the utter dryness of space desiccated it, until it powdered and tore and centrifugal force pushed it slowly away. It was obviously impossible for anyone to have survived the explosion, but the blind workings of chance that kill may save as well.

There were three people in the emergency capsule and one, the woman, was still unconscious, having struck her head when the ship erupted. One of the two men was in a state of shock, his limbs hanging limply while his thoughts went round and round incessantly like a toy train on a circular track. The other man was tearing at the seal of a plastic flask of vodka.

"All the American ships carry brandy," he said as he stripped off a curl of plastic, then picked at the cap with his nails. "British ships stock whiskey in their medical kits, which is the best idea, but I had to pull this tour on a Russian ship. So look what we get—" His words were cut off as he raised the flask to his mouth and drank deeply.

"Thirty thousand pounds in notes," Damian Brayshaw said thickly. "Thirty thousand pounds . . . good God . . . they can't hold me responsible." One heel drummed sluggishly against the padded side of the capsule and moved him away from it a few inches. He drifted slowly back. Even though his features were flaccid with shock, and his white skin even paler now, with a waxen hue, it could be seen that he was a handsome man. His hair, black and cut long, had burst free of its careful dressing and hung in lank strands down his forehead and in front of his eyes. He raised his hand to brush at it, but never completed the motion.

"You want a drink, chum?" the other man asked, holding out the flask. "I think you need it, chum, knock it back."

"Brayshaw . . . Damian Brayshaw," he said, as he took the bottle. He coughed over a mouthful of the raw spirit and for the first time his attention wandered from the lost money, and he noticed the other's dark green uniform with the gold tabs on the shoulders. "You're a spaceman . . . a ship's officer."

"Correct. You've got great eyesight. I'm Second Lieutenant Cohen. You can call me Chuck. I'll call you Damian."

"Lieutenant Cohen, can you tell—"

"Chuck."

"—can you tell me what happened? I'm a bit confused." His actions matched his words as his eyes roamed over the curved, padded wall of the closed deadlight, to the wire-cased bulb then back down to the row of handles labeled with incomprehensible Cyrillic characters.

"The ship blew up," Lieutenant Cohen said tonelessly, but his quick pull at the flask belied the casualness of his words. Years of service in space had carved the deep wrinkles at the corners of his eyes and grayed the barely seen stubble of his shaven head, yet no amount of service could have prepared him to accept casually the loss of his ship. "Have some more of this," he said, passing over the vodka flask. "We have to finish it. Blew up, that's all I knew, just blew up. I had the lock of this capsule open, inspection check, I got knocked halfway through it. You were going by, so I grabbed you and pushed you in, don't you remember?"

Damian hesitated in slow thought, then shook his head no.

"Well, I did. Grabbed you, then the girl, she was lying on the deck out cold. Just as I stuffed her in I heard the bulkhead blowing behind me so I climbed in right on top of her. Vacuum sucked the inner hatch shut even before I could touch it."

"The others . . . ?"

"Dead, Damian boy, every single one. Sole survivors, that's us."

Damian gasped. "You can't be sure," he said.

"I'm sure. I watched from the port. Torn to pieces. Blew up. The blast sealed off the chunk of ship we were in just long enough for us to get into this can. Even then there wouldn't have been enough time if I hadn't had the lid open and knew the drill. Don't expect those kind of odds to pay off twice in a lifetime."

"Will anyone find us?" There was a faint tremor in his voice. Chuck shrugged.

"No telling. Give me back the booze before you squeeze the bottle out of shape."

"You can send a message, there must be a radio in this thing."

Chuck gasped happily after a throat-destroying drink and held the almost empty flask up to the light. "Save a little to bring the girl around. You must have been out on your feet, Damian lad, you lay right there all the time watching me send the SOS. I stopped just as soon as I tried the receiver."

"I don't remember. It must have been the shock—but why did you stop transmitting? I don't understand."

Chuck bent and pulled at one of the handles below them. The padded lid lifted to reveal the controls of a compact transceiver. He flipped a switch and a waterfall-like roar filled the tiny space, then was silenced as he turned it off and closed the lid. Damian shook his head.

"What does that mean?" he asked. "Solar flare. Storm on the sun. We can never push a signal through that kind of interference. All we can do is hold our water until it stops. Say, it looks like our girlfriend is coming around."

They both turned to look at her where she lay on the padded wall of the capsule, Damian's eyes widening as he realized for the first time just how attractive she was. Her hair was deep, flaming red, lovely even in the tangled disarray that framed her face. Only the ugly bruise on her forehead marred the pink smoothness of her skin, and her figure was lush, clearly defined by the tight-bodiced, full-skirted dress. The skirt had ridden up, almost to her waist, revealing graceful and supple legs and black-lace sequined undergarments.

"Really," Damian said, putting his hand out, then pulling it back. "It's not right. Shouldn't we . . . adjust her garments?"

"Help yourself," Chuck smiled. "But I was enjoying it. I've never seen—what do you call them? knickers—quite like that before. Very fancy." But he was pulling her skirt down even as he said it. Her head turned and she moaned.

"Can she be badly hurt?" Damian asked. "Have you done anything for her?"

"I have no idea, and no, in that order. Unless you're a doctor—"

"No, I'm not."

"—there is nothing we can do. So I let her sleep. When she comes to I'll give her a slug of this paint remover. Never give drink to anyone unconscious, it could get in the lungs, First Aid Course 3B, Space Academy."

Both men watched, silently, as her eyelids slowly opened, disclosing gray, lovely eyes that moved their gaze across their faces and about the cramped interior of the capsule. Then she began to scream, emptying her lungs in a single spasm of sound then gasping them full again only to repeat the terrified sound. Chuck let her do this three times before he cracked her across the face with his open hand leaving an instant red imprint on the fairness of her skin. The screams broke off and she began to sob.

"You shouldn't—" Damian began.

"Of course I should," Chuck said. "Medicinal. She got it out of her system and now she's having a good cry. I'm Chuck," he told the girl, "and this is Damian. What's your name?"

"What happened to us? Where are we?"

"Chuck and Damian. What's yours?"

"Please tell me. I'm Helena Tyblewski. What happened?"

"I know you, at least I've heard of you," Damian said. "You're with the Polish artists at Mooncenter—"

"Socialities later, boy. We're in an emergency capsule, Helena, in good shape. We have water, food, oxygen—and a radio to call for help. I'm telling you that so you'll realize how well off we are compared to the others aboard the *Yuri*. There was an accident. Everyone else is dead."

"And . . . what will happen to us?"

"A good question. You can help me find out. Drain this vodka bottle, I need the empty flask. And let me have your shoes—yours too, Damian."

"What are you talking about? What for?" Chuck began to loosen the wing nuts that held the deadlight sealed in place.

"A fair question," he said. "Since I'm the only member of the ship's company present, I'm automatically in command. But we're a little too cramped here for me to pull rank, so I'll tell you what I know and what I want to do. When the accident happened we were, roughly, a quarter of the way from the moon to Earth. Where we are now I have no idea, and it is important that I find out."

The deadlight came free and he swung it to one side, disclosing the capsule's single porthole. Outside, the stars cut ribbons of white light across the darkness, while the Earth made a wider, greenish band.

"As you can see we are rotating about the major axis of this thermos bottle. I'll need star sights to plot our position, which means we have to slow down or stop this thing. Luckily the outer hatch opening faces the direction of motion, so anything ejected from it will slow us down. The more the mass and the greater the speed of ejection, the more retardation we'll get. There isn't much surplus to throw away in one of these capsules, that's why I want your shoes. The temperature controls work fine, so you won't need them. Okay?"

There were no arguments. Their shoes went into the lock along with the empty flask, some of the padding from the wall, and all the other small items that could be accumulated. Chuck sealed the inner hatch and pumped in oxygen from the tanks to raise the pressure as high as possible. When he threw the handle that opened the latch on the outer door, the capsule seemed to start spinning around them and they tumbled together against the wall.

"Sorry," Damian said, reddening as he realized that his arms were around Helen and he was lying on top of her. She smiled as they drifted away from the padding and there was suddenly no up and down as they floated in free fall. Chuck frowned at the stars moving leisurely by the port.

"That should be good enough to get some sightings. If not, we can jettison some more junk."

He unclipped his comparison dectant from the holder on his belt and pointed it out of the port, squinting through it. "That is going to take a while," he said, "so relax. With this gadget I can measure the angular distance of up to five astronomical objects; it will remember the angles and its tiny, microminiaturized brain can even do some of the basic computations. But it will still take time. So let's trade confidences, get to know each other, real chummy if you get what I mean. Me, I'm the simple one. Bronx High School, Columbia, the Academy—then the moon run ever since. What about you, Helena? Our limey friend said you were an artiste. A singer? Going to let us have an aria or two?"

Helena compressed her lips. "I am not that sort of artiste. I create— the newest and most expressive art form, light mobiles."

"I've seen them," Chuck said, sighting on another star. "They always hurt my eyes and give me a headache. What about you, Damian, are you a bank robber or an embezzler?"

"Sir!"

"Well don't blame me for asking, not after all that mumbling you were doing about thirty thousand pounds, gone, gone."

Damian clutched his hands together, tightly. "I'm with the British embassy. It was currency, in my charge. I was transferring it back to Earth. Now it's gone . . ."

Chuck laughed. "Don't be an idiot. It's just paper, it's been destroyed. They'll just write it off and print some more."

Damian smiled sheepishly. "You're right, of course. I never stopped to think of that after the accident. Stupid of me."

"We all have our bad days. Now talk to yourselves for a couple of minutes while I run these figures through the meat grinder."

The conversation lagged while he pecked at the tiny computer. As the first shock of the tragedy faded, the other two began to feel the pressing loneliness of their position. Once they stopped talking the only sound was the almost inaudible hum of the air-circulating fan, and the occasional click of the computer. The naked bulb shone down, the stars drifted by in the blackness of the port. They were warm and comfortable in their capsule. Six feet by twelve feet inside. A container of comfort, one man wide and two men high, packed with the necessities to sustain life. Yet two inches away, on the other side of the insulated wall, was the endless emptiness of space.

"That's that," Chuck said, and slipped the dectant back into its sheath. "Now let's see what the chow is like in this commie canister." The others almost smiled at the welcome hoarseness of his voice.

"What about your figures? Where are we?" Helena asked.

"I have no idea," Chuck said, throwing back a large padded lid in the end of the capsule. "That's not exactly correct. I have a reading that places us somewhere between the Earth and the moon. But I wasn't on the bridge and I have no idea where we were before the explosion. So we'll wait awhile, at least an hour, then I'll shoot some more sights. Comparing the two positions should give us an idea of our course and speed. Anyone thirsty?" He reached in and removed one of the containers of water that were ranked like giant bullets in a clip.

"I will take some, please," Helena said.

"Just suck it through the teat in the end . . ."

"I have drunk it free fall before, thank you."

"Sorry, sweetheart, I forgot you were an old space hand. Something to eat with it?" He withdrew a flat, brownish package and frowned at it. "Looks like a cardboard deck of cards. Can anyone here read Russian better than I can?"

"I'm sure I can," Helena said, taking the package and glancing at it briefly. "These are latkes, it says so clearly on the outside."

"Dehydrated potato pancakes . . ." he choked out. "I'm beginning to think the rest of the people in the *Yuri* were the lucky ones."

"Not even in jest," Damian said. "Touch wood when you say that."

"I doubt if there is any in this capsule, if you don't count the latkes."

When they had finished, Chuck counted the stores, then opened another lid to check the reading on the meter attached to the oxygen tanks. He tried the radio again, but there was only the waterfall of static. At the end of an hour he did his observations once more, then computations.

"Well, I'll be damned," he said.

"Is something wrong?" Damian asked.

"Let me check again."

Only after he had done everything a third time did he speak to them. There was no humor in his voice now.

"I'll lay it right on the line. We're in trouble. We had the luck to be behind the explosion—in relation to the ship's direction of travel, that is—and it had the effect of canceling a good part of our momentum."

"I don't understand what you are talking about." Helena said firmly.

"Then I'll simplify it. If the ship hadn't blown it would have reached Earth in about two days. But this capsule doesn't have the same speed anymore. It's going to be three to four weeks before we get near enough to Earth to send a message and be picked up."

"So what is wrong with that? It will be uncomfortable certainly, the lack of privacy here with you two men—"

"Will you let me finish? It will be more than uncomfortable, it will be deadly. We have food—though we could go without eating for that long. The water is recycled so there is no shortage there. But these capsules are too small to carry CO_2 regenerations. Our oxygen will run out in about two weeks. We'll be a week dead before we can send a message that anyone can hear and act on."

"Is there no way out?" Damian asked. "I don't know. If we—"

"This is nonsense!" Helena burst in. "We can radio the moon, Earth, they'll send ships."

"It's not that easy," Chuck said. "I know what ships there are on the moon and I know their range. We're practically outside their zone of operation now, not forgetting the fact that we can't even contact them. If the solar storm lasts even a few hours more we have to write them off. They won't even be able to pick up our signals by that time. After that it is the long haul to Earth, contacting one of the satellite stations, waiting while they plot our position and a ship can reach us. Three weeks absolute minimum, probably four."

Helena began to cry then, and he didn't try to stop her. It was something to cry about. He waited until she had finished and then, since neither of the others had seemed to see the obvious answer, he told them, in a flat and toneless voice.

"The amount of air that three people breathe in two weeks is the same amount that two people breathe in three weeks. It might even last a little longer with proper care."

There was a long moment of silence before Damian spoke. "You do realize what you are saying? There is no other way out of this?"

"I've gone over everything, every possibility. This is the only way that some of us stand a chance. Sure death for three. A fifty-fifty chance for two. Not good odds, but better than no odds."

"But—someone will have to die to give the others a chance to live?"

"Yes, putting it simply, that's the way it will have to be."

Damian took a deep breath. "And the one to die won't be you. You're needed to navigate and to work the radio—"

"Not at all. Though I confess to a sneaking wish that it really were that way. The navigation is done. It will take me about ten minutes to show you both how to operate the radio and call for help. There is unlimited power from the solar cells so the signal can go out continuously once the solar storm is over."

"That is—well—very decent of you. You could have told us differently and we would have believed you. Makes it a bit easier on me, if you know what I mean. For a moment there, with Miss Tyblewski out of it it looked like I was going to be the reluctant volunteer. So it is you or I . . ."

"No, one of the three of us," Chuck said.

"I'm sorry, you can't possibly mean that a woman—"

"I can and do. This is no game, Damian, of women and children first into the lifeboat. This is death, one hundred percent certain that I am talking about. All lives are equal. We are all in this together. I'm sure Helena appreciates your gesture, but I don't think she is the kind of person who wants to take advantage of it. Am I right?" he asked, turning to the girl.

"You're a pig," she hissed. "A fat, stupid pig."

"I'm wrong," Chuck said flatly, facing Damian. "I'll issue the order and take the responsibility. You can both sign it as witnesses, under protest if you like . . ."

"You want to kill me, I know, to save yourself," Helena shouted. "You don't care—"

"Please, don't," Damian said, taking her by the arms, but she shook him off, pushing him so hard he hit the opposite side of the capsule.

"Who do you think you are to set yourself up as a judge of life and death!"

"I am the officer in charge of this vessel," Chuck said in a voice of great weariness. "There are rules and orders for this sort of occasion and I am on my oath to follow them. This is the correct procedure, an equal chance for all to survive, no favoritism."

"You are just using that for an excuse."

"You are welcome to think so. However, I agree with the rule and think it the only just one . . ."

"I'll have nothing to do with it."

"That is your choice. But the results are binding on you whether you partake or not." He looked over at Damian who, white-faced, had been listening silently. "You talk to her, Damian, perhaps she'll listen to you. Or do you agree with her?"

"I . . . really don't know. It is so hard to say. But we . . . that is, there isn't much choice really."

"None," Chuck said.

It was something Damian would never have considered doing before, putting his arms about a girl whom he had just met, but everything was very different now. He held her and she leaned against him and sobbed and it was very natural for both of them.

"Let's get this over with," Chuck said, "the worst thing we can do is wait. And we'd all better agree beforehand what is going to happen. I have three identical squares of plastic here, and I've marked one of them with an X. Take a look at them. And three pieces of brown wrapper from this food pack. You do it, Damian, twist a piece of wrapper around each square, twist each one the same way so they can't be told apart. Now shake them up in your cupped hands so you don't know which is which. All right. Let them float right there in the middle where we can all see them."

Damian opened his cupped hands and the three twists of plastic drifted in free fall. One floated away from the others and he prodded it back into position. They all stared, they could not help themselves, fixedly and intently at the tiny scraps of destiny.

"Here's what will happen next," Chuck said. "We'll each take one. I'll draw last. I have a pill in my belt, it's standard spacer gear, and whoever draws the piece with the X takes the pill six hours from now—" he looked at his watch—"at exactly 1900 hours. Is it understood and agreed? This is it. There is no going back or mind-changing later. Now and forever. Agreed?"

Tight-lipped, Damian only gave a quick nod. Helena said or did nothing, beyond flashing Chuck a look of utter hatred.

"It is agreed then," he said. "The pill is instantaneous and absolutely painless. Here we go. Helena, do you want to draw first?"

"No," she said unbelievingly. "You can't . . ."

"We have no other choice, do we," Damian told her, and managed to smile. "Here, let me draw first. You can have the second one."

"Don't open it," Chuck said as Damian reached out and took the nearest one. "Go ahead, Helena, none of us is enjoying this."

She did not move until Chuck shrugged and reached for a wrapped marker himself. Then her hand lashed out and she clutched the one he had been about to take. "That's mine," she said.

"Whatever you say." Chuck smiled wryly and took the remaining one. "Open them up," he said.

The others did not move, so he carefully unwrapped his and held up the square. It was blank on both sides. Helena gasped.

"Well, I'm next I imagine," Damian said and slowly unfolded his. He looked at it, then quickly closed his fist.

"We have to see it too," Chuck told him. Damian slowly opened his hand to show a blank. "I knew it would be a trick!" Helena screamed and threw hers from her. Damian caught it when it rebounded from the wall, opened it at arm's length to reveal the scrawled black X.

"I'm sorry," he whispered, not looking at her. "I think we need a drink," Chuck told them as he twisted about to burrow in one of the lockers. "There are at least four more liters of vodka stowed down here with the water jugs, for some obscure Russian reason, and now is the time we can use them."

Damian took a deep breath so his voice wouldn't shake when he talked. "I'm sorry, I can't go along with this. If we come out of this I couldn't live with myself. I think I had better take Helena's place . . ."

"No!" Chuck Cohen said, outwardly angry for the first time. "It invalidates everything, all the choosing. You've put your life on the line—isn't that enough? Death hits by chance in space, the way it hit the others on the ship and missed us. It has hit again. The matter is closed." He pulled out a container and started the party by drinking a good fifth of it in one gulp.

Perhaps that was why the vodka was there. Helena, still unbelieving, drank because it was handed to her by the two men who could not look her in the eye. It numbed. If you drank enough it numbed.

The stars slipped by outside the uncovered port, the thermostat kept the temperature at a comfortable twenty-two degrees centigrade and the fan hummed as it circulated the air, pumping in metered amounts of the oxygen, each minute lowering the infinitely precious level in the tanks.

"Lower metabolism . . ." Chuck said, then closed his eyes so he wouldn't see the spinning walls of the capsule—nor the two others who were at the end of the capsule, as far as they could get from him. He found his mouth with the flask and sucked in a burning measure of the liquid. "Metabolism is oxidation and we gotta save oxygen. Don't eat, eat less, burn less. Go three weeks without food. Good for the figure. Lie down. Move less, burn less . . . oxygen . . ." His grumbling voice died away and the plastic flask floated free of his limp fingers.

"No, no, I can't," Helena sobbed and held to Damian. She had drunk little, but fear had affected her even more strongly.

"No, you shouldn't, shouldn't," Damian said and drank again because he did not know what to do. He bent to kiss her hair and somehow had his lips against the tear-cold dampness of her cheek, then on the full warmth of her mouth.

She was suddenly aware of him. Her lips responded and her arms were about him, her body pressing against him, her legs thrusting. They floated freely in the air, rotating slowly locked in tight embrace.

"I want you, I don't want to die, I can't, I can't," Helena sobbed and took his hand, putting it inside her dress onto the bare, warm firmness of her breast. "Help me, help me . . ."

Damian kissed her in a roaring wave of sensation. He knew that the spaceman was there, unconscious, only feet away, yet he didn't care. The escape from the wreck, the unbearable tension of gambling with his own life, the amount he had drunk, the closeness of death, the passion of the woman's flesh against his, all of this combined to wipe away everything except the burning awareness of her presence and the rising passion she evoked.

"Come to me, I need you," she whispered in his ear, then took it hard between her teeth. "I can't die. Why should I? He wants it, that pig. Only he wants it. He wants death, why can't he die? Why didn't he leave me in the ship? He gave me my life and now he will take it away again. And you too, you'll see, after me he'll find a way to kill you. What does he need either of us for? You can't believe a thing he said, why should we? He's brutal, deadly, a monster. He's going to kill me. You want me and he is going to kill me."

"Helena . . ." he whispered, as his flesh touched hers.

"No!" she wailed, and pushed him from her. He did not understand. He pressed forward again but she held him from her. "No, I cannot, I want to, but I cannot. Not with him here, not before I die. But I do want you . . ."

Then she was gone, and when he turned to look for her he became dizzy and saw her bending over the end of the capsule. Time moved strangely, too fast, yet slow at the same time. She was gone a long time, yet she was suddenly back and putting something cold into his hand.

"Take this," she whispered, "it's from the medical kit. I can't do it, you must. Someone must die. He must die, you can do it. He is the biggest. Do it then come back to me. I'll be here, I'll be with you always, just do this for me."

Blinking, Damian looked down at the glittering scalpel on his palm, at her hand closing his fingers over it. "Do it!" she breathed and pulled him, drifting, the length of the tiny space until he hung over the snoring spaceman. "DO IT!" the voice said and, not knowing quite what he was doing or why, he raised his fist high.

"There!" her voice said and her finger swam before him touching the sleeping man on the side of the neck, just on a thick and pulsing artery.

"Do it!" Her lips touched moistly down his face and in a sudden spasm he struck down at the bare flesh.

It was the bellow of a wounded beast. Sober, awake in the instant, with the pain tearing red fingers into his neck. Chuck reared up, lashing out with his hands. The scalpel was plunged an inch deep into his flesh, lodged in the thick mastoid muscle of his neck, bleeding floating red spheres into the air.

His hands clutched Damian and, still roaring with agony, he began to beat him as only a spacer knows how to do, holding one hand behind his head so he could not recoil away while the other fist pounded and crushed his face. Damian fought back, trying to escape the pain, but there was no escape. As they battled Helena's voice shattered about them.

"He tried to kill you, Chuck, he wanted me but I told him no. So he tried to kill you while you slept. A coward! Rape me, he tried . . . kill him . . . put him out of the ship. Here, the port!"

She pushed over to the airlock and opened the inner port as she had seen him do earlier. The lock was just big enough for a man. "In here!" she screeched.

Her words came through Chuck's anger and fitted it, telling him what he really wanted to do. Holding the other by the throat he spun him across the capsule and began to jam him, struggling into the tiny space. The scalpel fell from his neck and slow droplets bubbled in its wake.

Damian's body went suddenly limp and Chuck pushed in the legs and then a dangling arm.

"No, you don't have to force me," Damian said quietly. "It's all right now. I'll go. I deserve it."

Something of the man's tones penetrated Chuck's rage and he hesitated, blinking at the other.

"It's only fair," Damian said. "I attacked you, I admit that, tried to kill you. It doesn't matter that she used herself to make me do it, promised everything—then helped you when she saw I hadn't succeeded. There was something in me that let me do it . . ."

"Don't believe him, he's lying!" Helena wailed.

"No, I have no reason to lie. I'm taking your place, Helena, so at least don't vilify me. I tried to kill him for you—and for myself."

"She wanted you to do this?" Chuck said thickly, blinking through his pain.

"You both want me dead," she screamed, then tore at the heavy computer on Chuck's belt. He groped for it as she pulled it loose, and was only half turned towards her when heavy pain and blackness crushed against his skull.

"About time you came around," Damian said. "Drink this." Chuck felt the bandage on his neck when he bent to put the spout to his lips. He looked around the room while he sucked in the water. "How long have I been out?" he asked.

"About nine hours. You lost some blood and you have a hole in your head."

"There are just two of us here?"

"That's right," Damian said, and the smile was gone now. "Maybe I figured this wrong, but it's over and done now. I tried to kill you. I didn't succeed and—fairly enough—you tried to kill me right back. But neither of us managed to finish the job. Maybe I'm thinking wrong, but I feel the score is even now and no recriminations."

"You don't hear me complaining. And Helena?"

Damian looked uncomfortable. "Well . . . the six hours were almost up. And she did agree on the drawing. And she did lose. She attacked me with the scalpel. I'm afraid your computer was completely smashed. I had to dispose of it."

"The insurance will replace it," Chuck said hoarsely. "God, my neck hurts. Head, too."

"Do you think we'll make it?" Damian asked.

"The odds are a hell of a lot better now than they were nine hours ago."

"Yes, one could say that. Perhaps the powers that be have been propitiated by Miss Tyblewski's noble gesture. Upon such sacrifices . . . the gods themselves throw incense." He looked out, unseeing, at the blackness beyond the port. "Do you think that should we get out of this, we should, well, mention Helena . . . ?"

"Helena who?" Chuck said. "Seventy-four people died when the *Yuri Gagarin* blew. We're the sole survivors."

You Men of Violence

"I hate you, Raver," the captain shouted, his strained face just inches away, "and I know you must hate me too."

" 'Hate' is too strong a word," the big man said quietly. "I think 'despise' is much better."

There was no advance warning of the blow—the captain was too good a fighter for that—just the sudden jab that drove his fist into the other's stomach. Raver's only reaction was a slight and condescending grin. This infuriated the captain, who, though a head shorter than Raver, was still over six feet tall, and he expected some reaction other than scorn from the people he hit. In a blind rage he pummeled the other's unresisting form until Raver, leaking blood from nose and mouth, fell across the captain's desk, then slid limply to the floor.

"Get this carrion out," the captain ordered, rubbing at his bruised knuckles. "And clean up this filth." There were smears of blood across the surface of the desk, and everything on it had been swept to the floor when Raver fell. The captain realized then that the blood was on him too and he dabbed at it distastefully with the kerchief from his sleeve. Still, there was some satisfaction in seeing the half-conscious bulk being carried from the room. "Now who is smiling," he shouted after them, then went out himself to wash and change.

Though the captain did not know it yet, he was the loser. From the moment he had boarded the prison ship two weeks earlier, Raver had been planning this encounter. All of his actions, his earlier confrontations with the captain, the hunger strike when the Phreban had been tortured—every bit of it had been planned with this final scene in mind. Raver had pushed the buttons, the captain had reacted as planned, and Raver had won. He leaned against the metal wall of his cell, clutching tightly the pencil-sized communicator that was concealed by his giant fist. When he had fallen across the desk he had palmed it. This was the reason for everything he had done.

Sighing heavily, Raver slumped to the floor and rolled over on his side. It was no accident that his back was to the glass eye of the monitor pickup, or that the barred door of his cell was in sight. Unobserved—and safe from surprise visitors—he allowed himself to smile as he set to work.

He had only a single tool, a nail which he had hidden in his boot sole and filed flat against the metal side of his bunk during the night. The squared tip now made a tiny screwdriver. His hand was a vise and his fingernails pliers and wrench. It was enough. There was no one still alive who knew Raver's real name, or anything about his earlier life before he went into crime and politics, and he certainly did not look like a typical microtechnician. Yet that was what he was, and a highly skilled one as well. The case of the communicator sprang open under his touch and the delicate leaves of the circuits fanned out. He went to work. There were only a few hours left to setdown and he needed all of them.

With infinite patience he disassembled the components, then re-joined them in new circuitry of his own design. He struck an arc from the tiny battery to solder the connections, and could only hope that enough power remained to operate his device. It took a fraction over three hours to construct and for all of that time he lay still, with just his hands moving, an apparently unconscious bulk to the watchers in the prisoner control center. Only when the work was done did he permit himself to groan and stretch and to climb shakily to his feet. As he went to the barred door he stumbled, then held to the bars with one hand and pressed his forehead against the cool metal. In the pre-ceding weeks he had stood this way for a good part of the waking day, so it was not considered unusual.

His right hand, shielded by his body, slid the wire probe into the opening of the lock while he slowly turned the knob on the variable capacitor.

An RF lock is theoretically pickproof, but that is just theory. In practice a trained technician can cause the circuit to resonate at the keying frequency, which is what Raver did. A needle flickered briefly, and he made careful adjustments until it jumped across the dial and up against its stop. This was the operating frequency. Then he went to the sink and cleaned some of the blood from his face and at the same time reversed connections so that the probe became a trans-mitter. He was ready.

When the hooters sounded the two-minute warning for strapping down he paused for a moment at the door before going to his cot, which served double duty as an acceleration couch. The device had worked: he had felt the click as the electronic actuator had opened the lock. The door was open. Just before the landing rockets flared he pulled up his blanket and rolled over on his side to face the wall.

The rear jets kicked hard with three G's and the webbing of the bed stretched and creaked while Raver pulled himself slowly to his feet. This was the only time he could be sure that the guards in the prison control center would not be watching him. While they were fighting the deceleration he had to do what must be done. One shuf-fling step at a time he lurched his way across the cell, the muscles in his legs knotted and rock hard. The stool's three metal legs were welded to the floor and he had examined them and felt their thickness days earlier. Dropping heavily to his knees he seized the nearest leg in both hands, tensed his body—then pulled. The leg broke free with a sharp crack, and the other two were detached the same way. Then a slow shuffle back to the bed, onto which he put the stool and pulled the blanket over it. The ruse would not bear close examining, but it had to fool the watching guard on the screens for only a brief time. Back across the cell to the door, through it, close it, lock it, and down the passageway. His knees crumpled as more jets cut in for landing, five G's or more, but Raver continued on his hands and knees. He could move about safely only as long as the rockets were firing. When they cut out the crewmen and guards would unstrap and come out and he would be caught. Painfully and slowly he dragged himself across the passageway to the connecting ladder and began to work his way down.

The jets stopped when he was halfway to the bottom. He let go of the ladder and dropped.

Since the gravity on Houdt is less than Earth normal and because the fall was only fifteen feet, Raver did not injure himself, although he landed heavily. He rolled and crashed into the door with his shoulder as he came to his feet, throwing it open. Then he was through and running, heading for the spacesuit locker. All around him he knew men were unstrapping themselves and rising, on their way. A door opened as he passed it and there was the sudden loud murmur of voices. Someone started through it—then turned to say something.

Raver hit the door of the locker, went through and closed it, and leaned against it.

There was no alarm. Neither was there any time to waste. He took a long, shuddering breath, ignored his aching muscles, and turned to the racked space suits. The largest one, with its flexible fabric stretched to the limit, made a snug fit and he pulled it on. If he closed the helmet it would draw instant attention inside the ship—but if he left it open he would be instantly recognized. But the extra oxygen tanks would shield his face and serve a double purpose. The large refill tanks weighed over a hundred pounds apiece, so he did not dare take more than two. Carrying more might draw attention. He had to go left so he swung the tanks onto his right shoulder and pushed the door open. When he went out he walked with his shoulder almost brushing the wall, and the tanks shielded his face from view.

Footsteps passed him, but he was not stopped. He went down two decks and saw the guard on the emergency airlock just as the alarms sounded. Raver walked on steadily, neither faster nor slower, though the guard jumped nervously and slipped his rifle from his shoulder and held it at port arms.

"What is it? What's happened?" he called to Raver, then turned to look down the connecting corridor. The pulsating hooters split the air. "Who are you?" the guard asked when Raver came closer. It was only then, far too late, that he tried to bring his rifle to bear.

Raver reached out with his free hand and took the man by the throat so he could not shout a warning, then pulled him close so he could not use the gun. One long finger moved up to the artery under the guard's ear and clamped down, cutting off the flow of blood to the brain. The man struggled helplessly for a few seconds, then slumped, unconscious. Raver was careful to lay him gently on the deck before he stripped him of weapon and munition pouches, slung the rifle over his shoulder and opened the airlock. There were shouts behind him as he closed and dogged it shut, but he ignored them.

"Get him," the captain ordered, his face suffused with blood. "Bring him back to me. Kill him only if you must, because I want to see him die. Do you understand?"

"Yes, sir," Lieutenant N'Ness said, keeping his face expressionless. "I'll need a squad of the most fit men to go with me."

"You have them. What do you plan to do?"

N'Ness snapped open a map and spread it on the desk. He was a career soldier and after this tour of field duty he was returning to staff college. He explained with professional brevity and clarity.

"The ship is here, near the base of the cliff, within the usual landing area. Raver can gain nothing by going toward the prison mines here—and in fact all the observers place him on an eighty-six-degree course toward the foothills here. This makes sense. The nearest mining settlement—other than the prison—is here, on the other side of the mountains. It is operated by Puliaans."

"The devil!"

"Exactly. If Raver reaches them they will give him sanctuary and there is nothing that we can do about it."

"I know what I would like to do . . ." the captain mumbled, clenching his fist.

"You're not the only one," Lieutenant N'Ness said. "But Puliaa has three times our population and five times our industrial capacity. There is nothing that we can do."

"Yet. Someday though . . ."

"To be sure. Meanwhile, the escaped prisoner is heading for sanctuary. He has taken two refill tanks in addition to the tank on his suit. This will give him enough oxygen to reach the Puliaan mine— but only by the most direct route. If he tries to hide or dodge about he will not make it in time. I intend to follow at once with the best men available, each carrying a single spare oxygen tank. We will be light and fast. We will capture him and return."

"Go, then. You have my instructions."

The squad had already suited up and N'Ness hurried to join them. In spite of the need for speed he checked every weapon, ammunition pouch, and oxygen tank before moving them out. Then they left on the double, across the plain and into the foothills, following directions radioed from the ship, heading for the spot where Raver had vanished from sight.

"I have it," N'Ness radioed back. "Dislodged stones, footprints, there is a clear trail here that I can follow. Next report in one hour." He led the squad into the mountains of Houdt.

Houdt. A ruined and gutted world with its atmosphere stripped away in some ancient cataclysm, its surface riven and its metallic core laid bare. There were heavy metals here for the taking, all the power metals that made a voyage across the light years possible. Since there was still more than enough for all, there was no competition and the planet's surface was dotted with mines, each maintained by a different world or syndicate. The best of them were robot operated, the worst of them manned by human slaves.

Raver had the temperament to be neither a slave nor a slave holder, yet there was no other choice on his world. He had gone into opposition to the established regime and it was remarkable that his opposition had lasted as many years as it had before he, inevitably, ended up on Houdt. Nor was he dead yet. Once over the mountains and down into the Puliaan settlement and he would be safe.

The oxygen tanks were slung on his back to free his arms, and he needed his arms on these steep slopes. As he pulled himself up the face of the fissured rock, it exploded silently next to him, boulders dust and gravel billowing out. He felt the concussion through his fingertips and let go his hold and slid back down to the safety of the jagged rocks below. Looking through a fissure he saw his pursuers for the first time, kneeling in an ordered row as they fired. As soon as he vanished from sight they jumped to their feet and came on. Raver went on as well, taking a longer course, which would keep him out of their sights.

"We'll rest now," Lieutenant N'Ness ordered as the sun neared the horizon. His men dropped. The chase had begun soon after dawn and the days here were twenty standard hours long. They were in the far northern latitudes, where the axial tilt conspired to form a night less than three hours in length. N'Ness had considered pushing on through the darkness, but it would not be worthwhile. The climbing was almost impossible at night and his men were exhausted. They would sleep and catch the slave before another sunset.

"A two-man guard, one hour for each watch," he said. "Stack all the extra oxygen tanks here. In the morning we'll top our tanks and see how many of these we can leave behind."

Most of them were asleep before he finished talking. He kicked the nearest one awake to help him collect the tanks, then they sat, back to back, for the first watch.

The sunlight hit first on the highest peaks at dawn, but without an atmosphere to diffuse the light only the smallest, reflected part fell on the camp. The third watch, on the lieutenant's orders, was waking the men up and they were just starting to stir when the night exploded.

It was light, flame, then darkness and the shouts of frightened men in the darkness. The lieutenant beat them into order and the arrival of full dawn showed them that their reserve store of oxygen had been destroyed.

Reconstructing what had happened was not hard. Raver must have crept close during the night, lain there, then walked in at dawn, just one more space-suited man. He had put a bomb of some kind in among the tanks, then escaped in the confusion following the blast. N'Ness had underestimated him.

"He will pay for it," the lieutenant said coldly. "He lost his lead by coming back to do this—and he will not regain it. Fall in and check tanks."

The spare oxygen cylinders were gone, but there was still some oxygen left in the suit tanks. With ruthless efficiency N'Ness bled these tanks into his, until his was full and the others close to empty. "Get back to the ship," he ordered. "As soon as you get past these last hills use your radio; you should be able to raise either the ship or the mine. Tell them to bring oxygen out to meet you in case you don't have enough to make it all the way. I'm going on and I'll bring the prisoner back. Report that to the captain. Now move out."

N'Ness did not watch them go, in fact he had already forgotten their existence. He was going to catch Raver. He was going to march him back at gunpoint. It would make the captain very happy and it would look very good on his record. He almost ran up the slope ahead.

The lieutenant was the lighter man, he was more lightly burdened, and he had the advantage of being the follower, not the pathfinder. Where Raver had worked his way around a difficult patch of broken rock, N'Ness went straight through, counting upon his speed and agility. He did not slow nor rest and his panting breath was echoed by the whine of the conditioning unit as it labored to remove the excess water vapor and heat. It was an insane chase, but as long as he did not slip or collapse from exhaustion it could have only one end.

Raver pulled himself up onto the broad ledge and through a gap in the rocks he could see the tall pithead workings of the Puliaan mines. He started forward when his radio crackled in his ear, and N'Ness's voice said, "Just hold it, right where you are." He stopped dead and looked slowly around.

Lieutenant N'Ness stood on the ledge above, pointing his energy rifle. "Turn around," N'Ness said, "and start right back where you came from." He waggled the muzzle of the gun in the correct direction.

"Thank you, no," Raver said, sitting down and slinging the oxygen tank to the ground. "I have no intention of returning, in spite of your invitation."

"Enough talk. You have ten seconds to start moving—before I pull this trigger."

"Pull and be damned. I die here or I die back there. What difference does that make to me?"

N'Ness had not expected this, and he had to think a moment before he answered. The steel edge of command was gone from his voice when he finally spoke. "You're a reasonable man, Raver. There's no reason to die out here, not when you can live and work . . ."

"Don't act stupid, the role doesn't become you. We both know that mine slaves are there for life—and a short life at that. There'll be no more chances to escape. You're the paid killer. Shoot."

N'Ness estimated the reserves in his tank and the spare Raver carried and sat down himself. "You can leave out the insults," he said. "I may have killed men in the line of duty, but I've never tortured or butchered people the way your so-called Pacifist Party—"

"Stop," Raver ordered, lifting his head. "You're a victim of your own propaganda. It's all lies. We do not kill. Think for yourself, if you are able to. Have you ever seen any of the atrocities committed that you speak about? Other than by your own people, that is."

"I'm not here to argue with you . . ."

"Unsatisfactory, try again. Have you seen these things?"

"No, I haven't—but that's only because we shot first and fast before they could happen."

"Just as unsatisfactory, Lieutenant. You are avoiding the truth. You kill, we do not. That is the basic and important difference between us. You are the animal heritage of mankind, we are its future."

"Not so holy, please. You attacked the guard on the ship, and last night you tried to kill me and my men."

"That is not true. I do not kill. I rendered the guard unconscious and I used the guard's rifle and ammunition as a bomb to destroy your oxygen, to force you to turn back. Was anyone injured?"

"No, but—"

"*Yes*, but," Raver said loudly, jumping to his feet. "That is all the difference. Our aggressive traits brought us to the top of the animal kingdom, now we must renounce killing if we are to progress. We have this violence within us—I don't deny I have it myself—but what good is our intellect if we cannot control it? Any man can desire a woman he sees in the street or jewelry in a display window, yet only the sick men rape and steal. We all possess the capacity for violence. Only the sick man kills."

"Not sickness," N'Ness said, waggling the gun in Raver's direction. "Just good sense. This wins arguments. The sensible man knows he can't fight a gun, so he gets one himself and evens the score. That's something you people will never learn. We always win. We kill you."

"Yes, you kill us in great numbers, but you cannot win. You do not change a man's mind by eliminating him. What do you do when everyone is on the other side? Shoot them all? And after you have killed every man, woman, and child—what do you do with your world?"

"You're being stupid now. This has been tried before, and whenever the leaders are killed the mob does what it is told."

"Then there is something new come into the universe," Raver said quietly. "Perhaps it is the next development, Homo superior, a mutation, men who are constitutionally unable to kill. This is not my theory, there have been scientific papers written on it . . ."

"All nonsense!"

"Not really. Look at what happened on Puliaa."

"Propaganda. The Pacifist Party there may be temporarily in power, but watch what happens at the first sign of trouble."

"They've had their trouble and they've weathered it well so far. And it is truth that a worldwide nonviolent rebellion put them into power. It is what everyone wanted."

"Lies!"

"I doubt it." Raver smiled. "You can't ignore the fact that the entire planet is now vegetarian. Something happened. Why don't you look into it before it is too late? I'm not the first one to believe that those who live by the sword die by it."

"That's enough talk," N'Ness said, standing. "You'll come back with me now."

"No."

"If you don't come I'll shoot you down, now, and send men for your body. You have no choice."

"Would you do that? Just pull the trigger and kill a man? Remove a life for no reason? I find it hard to imagine; I am incapable of such an evil act."

"It is not evil—and I have good reason. You are an enemy, I have orders . . ."

"Those are not reasons, just excuses. An animal kills to eat or in defense of its life, or the lives of others. All else is corruption."

"One last warning," N'Ness said, aiming the gun steadily at the other's midriff. "Your arguments mean nothing. Come with me or I shoot you."

"Don't do this to yourself, Lieutenant. Here is a chance rarely offered to your kind. You can stop killing. You can go with me to Puliaa and discover what it is like not to be an animal. Don't you realize the rapist rapes himself? Who would want to live in the head of a rapist? So does the killer kill himself, and this is probably the only kind of killing a man of peace can understand. We do not like it, but by necessity we accept it. Only when your kind is gone can my kind make this galaxy the place it should be."

"You fool," the lieutenant shouted. "You're dying, not me. Your last chance."

"You kill yourself," Raver said calmly. The lieutenant's lips pulled back from his teeth and he shouted with rage as he pulled the trigger.

The gun blew up, killing him instantly.

"I'm sorry," Raver said. "I tried to tell you. During the night I fixed your rifle to explode when fired, as I did the other. I was hoping that you would come with me."

Head lowered with sorrow, Raver turned and walked toward the mine visible below.

A Civil Service Servant

Precisely at nine in the morning the post office opened and the first customers were allowed to enter. Howards knew this, yet, as he straightened his Book on the counter before him, he could not prevent himself from glancing worriedly at the big clock on the wall. Why? This was just a workday like any other day. God, the fear, deep down, as the long black pointer clicked another notch toward the vertical.

Just another day, why should he be so concerned? He tittered nervously and turned his key in the lock of the multifrank before him, just as two people appeared on the other side of the counter.

"I wish to post this letter to Sierra Leone," the man said.

"A two-credit insurance stamp," the woman said.

Instantly, they began to squabble as to which of them had been there first, their voices crescendoing shriller and higher. Howards slapped his left hand on the Book and raised his right.

"Stop," he said, and they did, struck by the authority in his voice. "Reference B-86Y/234 in the Book of Postal Regulations states that all differences of opinion and priority are to be settled by the serving clerk. That is myself. Ladies first. Here is your insurance stamp, madam."

His fingers were snapping over the complex controls of the multifrank even as he spoke, and he was secretly proud of the assured way that he said it. The man stepped aside, the woman timidly proffered her insurance book as he stood with his finger poised over the Activate button. With his free hand he flipped the book open, dropped it into the slot and pressed the button.

"That will be twenty-two credits eighty, madam." The bills went into the cash receptacle and her change rattled into the delivery cup. "Next," he said, not without a certain amount of condescension.

The man said nothing; he knew better than to argue. He certainly did. What was in the Book was correct. The man stepped away and Howards thought that this day had certainly begun busily enough: but why the little shivering knot of fear, Howards? he wondered to himself, and rubbed at the spot in his midriff with his knuckles.

A large, dark man with a full black beard filled the space outside the counter. "Do you know what this is?" he bellowed.

"I certainly do," Howards said. (Did his voice crack a little?) "That is a needle gun."

"You are correct," the man hissed in a voice like the breaking of poison waves. "It fires a needle soundlessly with such great speed that contact with the human body produces a hydrostatic wave that utterly destroys the nervous system. Would you like that?" White teeth appeared in the tangle of black beard.

"I would not like my nervous system utterly destroyed."

"You will then pay me the sum of four thousand, nine hundred and ninety-nine credits."

"I have no till or money. Cash is centrally supplied . . ."

"Fool I know all that. I also know that the payment of any sum over five thousand credits must be especially authorized for any position. Therefore—four thousand nine hundred ninety-nine credits. At once."

"At once," Howards said crisply, and spoke aloud as he hit the keys. "Four, nine, nine, nine . . ."

"Now activate."

Howards hesitated for a mere fraction of an instant, sucked in his breath, then snapped his finger down on the Activate button.

There was the rattle of small change from the delivery cup and the man glanced down at it just as a gush of white vapor shot out into his face. He screamed and writhed and fell as the full force of the regurgitants, irritants, and vesicants hit him at once.

"Foolish man," Howards said into the handkerchief he raised to his face, stepping back, away from the gas. "Security was onto him as soon as I rang up four hundred and ninety-nine million, nine hundred thousand credits. Just a simple decimal shift . . ."

It was almost nine and the first customer would be in soon. A day like any other day—then why was he feeling this way? What way? As if he were imprisoned in the back of his own brain and screaming. Foolishness, this was not a proper thought for a public servant to have.

"Help me," the old woman said just as the black hand touched the hour.

"Of course, madam." Where had she come from, like that, so quickly?

"It is my pension," pushing a battered and torn payment book across the counter with her scaling, shivering hand. "They will not pay me my money."

"Money due is always paid," Howards said, flipping open the rusty book while trying to touch it only with the tips of his fingers. He pointed to a torn fragment of paper. "Here is the reason. The page is missing. To authorize payment you must get form 925/1k(43) and have it filled out."

"I have it," the woman told him, and pushed over—almost threw, in fact—an even more creased and soiled piece of paper. Howards hoped that none of his feelings were revealed on his face as he turned and read it.

"This is the correct form, madam, but it is not completely filled out. In this blank here you must enter your deceased husband's insurance number."

"I do not know his number," the woman shrilled and clutched tightly to the counter's edge. "He is dead and his papers, they were all destroyed, you see."

"In that case you must obtain form 276/po(67), which is an application to the proper authorities for the required information." He pushed the papers with what he hoped was a smile. "You can obtain an application for this form—"

"I will die first," the old woman screamed and threw all her papers into the air so that they fluttered down around her like filthy confetti. "I have not eaten for a week. I demand justice. I must have money for food . . ."

It was all quite distasteful. "I wish I could oblige, madam, but I have no authority. You should apply for the form of application to see the Emergency officer . . ."

"I will be dead first!" she shouted hoarsely, and thrust her face toward his. He could smell her sour breath and quickly withdrew. "Have you no pity on someone my age? I could be your mother."

"Thankfully, madam, you are not. My mother has the proper forms . . ."

"Forms!" Her voice screeched higher and higher until it cracked. "You care more for forms than for human life. I swore I would kill myself unless I obtained money for food today. Save me!"

"Please do not threaten. I have done what I can." Had he? Was there some authority he should summon? Was he correct—?

"Better a quick death than one of slow starvation. Money—or I die!"

She had a large bread knife now and was waving it before him. Was this a threat? Did it call for the guards?

"I cannot . . ." Howards gasped, and his fingers hovered over the keys in an agony of indecision. Guards? Doctor? Police?

"Then I die, and it is a world I do not regret losing." She held one hand on the counter, palm up, and with a savage slash of the knife almost severed the hand from the wrist. Thick blood spurted high.

"What have you done?" he shouted and reached for the keys. But she began to scream and wave her arm and blood spattered him and gushed over the counter.

"The Book!" he gasped. "You're getting blood on the Book! You cannot!" He pulled it away and began to dab at it with his handkerchief, then remembered that he had not yet summoned help. He hesitated, torn, then put the Book in the farthest corner and rushed back to his position. There was blood everywhere—had he made a mistake?—and the woman had sunk from sight but he could still hear her moans.

"Medical assistance," he said quickly into the microphone. "First aid needed. At once."

Should he do something for her? But he could not leave his station. And the blood, everywhere, on his hands and shirt. He held them out in horror. He had never seen so much blood, human blood, before . . .

And at nine o'clock, precisely, the post office would open. Another day, just like any other.

What was wrong with his hands? Was there something he should remember? Like a vanishing echo a memory rushed away—a memory of what? There was nothing wrong: he was at his position where he belonged, with his Book close at hand and the shining mass of the multifrank before him. He belonged, of course he belonged—then why, again, a fleeting, fading, frightening memory that it was wrong?

Why was he looking at his hands? Howards shivered and unlocked the machine and cleared it, flipped the test and operational switch so the light glowed green, checked the cleared reading and set up 4,999 . . .

This was not right. Why had he done it? With a furtive glance over his shoulder he quickly cleared the machine. The long black hand of the clock clicked one notch forward and was vertical and an immense queue of people formed outside his position. They were jammed solid, all looking at him, quiet now, though there was a murmur from the rear.

"Good morning, sir," he said to the red-faced gentleman who headed the line. "What may I—"

"None of your conversation. I want service not chatter. This letter, special delivery, at once, to Capitello, Salerno, Italy. What will it cost?"

"That depends," Howards said, reaching for the envelope, which the man pulled back.

"Depends upon what, damn it? I want to mail this thing, not talk about it."

There was a murmur of impatience from the waiting people and, smiling insincerely, Howards said, "It depends upon the weight, sir. Special-delivery letters are delivered by orbiting rocket and the charge varies according to the weight."

"Then you can damn well stop talking about it and weigh it," he said, thrusting the letter forward.

Howards took it, dropped it into the slot, then read off the price.

"Too damn much," the man shouted. "Mailed a letter to Capitello yesterday and it cost less."

"It probably weighed less, sir."

"I wanna mail this package," a small child said, thrusting an untidy bundle onto the counter.

"Are you calling me a liar?" the red-faced man shouted, growing even redder.

"No, sir—just a minute, sonny—I simply stated that if it cost less it weighed less . . ."

"Damn nerve, call a man a liar, ought to thrash you. Wish to see your supervisor at once."

"My supervisor does not see the public. If you wish to file a complaint the Complaint Office is in room eight-nine-three-four— don't do that!" he added as the child pushed the package further across the counter so that it slid off the inner edge and fell to the floor. Something inside broke with a loud plop and an awful stench seeped out.

"You broke it!" the child screamed.

"I did not; take it at once," Howards said, picking it up by an end of string and dangling it outside. The child ignored it and began to cry loudly.

"Man ought to be horsewhipped, treating a child like that!"

"Room eight-nine-three-four," Howards said through clenched lips, hoping the man would leave.

A tall young man with red hair was bobbing up and down behind the weeping child. "I would like to send a telegram to my uncle saying, 'Dear Uncle, Need at once credits one hundred—' "

"Would you please fill out the telegraph form," Howards said, pressing the switch that delivered a printed form into the dispenser outside.

"Bit of difficulty," the young man said, holding up both of his hands, which were swathed in bandages and plaster. "Can't write, but I can dictate it to you, won't take a moment. 'Dear Uncle—' "

"I am very sorry but I cannot accept dictated telegrams. However, any public phone will take them."

"Bit of trouble getting the coins in the slot. 'Dear Uncle—' "

"Cruel and heartless," the young girl next in line sniffed.

"I would like to help you," Howards said, "but it is forbidden by regulations. However I am sure that someone near the end of the line will write your telegram for you, then I will be happy to accept it."

"How very smart of you," the young girl said. She was exceedingly attractive and when she leaned forward her breasts rested tidily on the counter's edge. She smiled. "I would like to buy some stamps," she said.

Howards smiled back, with utmost sincerity this time. "I would be extremely happy to oblige, miss, except for the fact that we no longer issue stamps. The amount of postage is printed directly on the envelope."

"How clever of you. But isn't it possible to buy commemorative stamps still held in the postal vaults?"

"Of course, that is a different matter. Sale to the public of commemorative issues is authorized in the Book by Reference Y-23H/48."

"How very intelligent of you to remember all of that! Then I would like the Centenary of the Automatic Diaper Service—"

"Nerve, damned nerve, trying to get rid of me," the red face said, thrusting across at him. "Room eight-nine-four-four is closed."

"I have no doubt that Room eight-nine-four-four is closed," Howards said calmly. "I do not know what is in Room eight-nine-four-four. But the Complaints Office is in Room eight-nine-three-four."

"Then why in blazes did you tell me eight-nine-four-four?"

"I did not."

"You did!"

"Never. I do not make that kind of mistake."

Mistake? Howards thought. Mistake! Oh, no.

"I'm afraid I have made a small mistake," he said, white-faced, to the girl. "There is a later special order on the entry canceling the issue of all commemorative stamps across the counter."

"But that should make no difference," she said, pouting prettily. "You can sell me a little teensy diaper stamp . . ."

"If it was within my power nothing would give me greater pleasure, but the regulations cannot be broken."

"Your head can be broken just like you broke this!" an immense and angry man said thrusting the girl aside and pushing the crumpled package under Howards' nose. The stench was overwhelming.

"I assure you, sir, I did not break that. Would you kindly remove—"

"My son said you did."

"Nevertheless, I did not."

"Call my boy a liar?!" the man roared and reached across the counter and grabbed Howards by the shirt.

"Stop that," Howards gasped and tried to pull away and heard the material tear. He groped out and hit the guard switch. It snapped off clean and rattled to the floor. Howards pulled back harder and most of his shirt came away in the man's hand.

"Stamp, please," someone said and a letter dropped into the slot.

"That will be two credits," Howards said, hitting the breakdown button then ringing up the postage.

"You said Room eight-nine-four-four," the red face shouted.

"Been mistreating the machine," a sour-faced repairman said, appearing beside Howards.

"Never, I just touched it and it broke."

"These machines never break."

"Help me," a frail old woman said, pushing a battered and torn payment book across the counter with a scaly and shaking hand. "It is my pension. They will not pay me my money."

"Money due is always paid," Howards said, closing his eyes for an instant—why?—then reaching for the book. He caught sight of the man pushing up to the counter, a man with a tangle of black beard and a hateful expression.

"I know—" Howards began, then stopped. What did he know? Something pressed hard inside his head and tried to burst out.

"I do not know his number," the old woman screamed. "He is dead and his papers, they were all destroyed, you see."

"Do you know what this is? It is a needle gun."

"Not in Room eight-nine-four-four."

"Just one diaper . . ."

Howards clutched graspingly at his head and did not know if he was screaming or if he was hearing someone else scream.

Welcome blackness engulfed him.

"Now just sip this and you will find yourself feeling fine in a few moments."

Howards took the cup that the Examiner held out to him and was surprised to discover that he needed both hands to hold it. He noticed that the backs of his hands were beaded with sweat. As he sipped he felt the helmet lifting from his head and when he looked up he had a swift glimpse of it just before it vanished through a recess in the ceiling.

"The examination—aren't you going to proceed?"

The Examiner chuckled and steepled his heavy fingers on the desk before him. "A not uncommon reaction," he said. "The examination is complete."

"I have no memory. It seemed as though the helmet came down, then went up again. Though my hands are covered with sweat." He looked at them, then shivered with realization. "Then the examination is over. And I—"

"You must have patience," the Examiner told him with ponderous dignity. "The results must be analyzed, compared, a report drawn up. Even electronically this takes time. You should not complain."

"Oh, I am not complaining, Examiner," Howards said quickly, lowering his eyes. "I am grateful."

"You should be. Just think of the way all of this used to be. Hours of oral and written examinations, with the best marks going to the crammers. You can't cram for a simulator examination."

"I do know that, Examiner."

"Just a few moments of unconsciousness and the machine mentally puts you through your paces, puts you into situations and judges how you respond to them. Real situations that a postal clerk would face during the normal course of his duties."

"Normal duties, of course," Howards said, frowning at his hands, then wiping them quickly against his side.

The Examiner stared at the figures that raced across the screen on his desk. "Not as good as I expected, Howards," he said sternly. "You'll not be a postal clerk this year."

"But—I was so sure—the twelfth time."

"There is more to clerking than just knowing the Book. Go away. Study. Apply yourself. Your grade this time is high enough so that your student's status will continue for another year. Work harder. Very few students are carried past their fifteenth year."

Howards stood, helplessly, and turned before he left. "My wife asked me to ask you . . . we're not getting younger . . . planning permission for a child . . ."

"Out of the question. There is the population problem for one thing, and your status for another. If you were a clerk the application might be considered."

"But there are so few clerks," Howards said weakly.

"There are so few positions. Be happy you are a registered student with rations and quarters. Do you know what it is like to be an Under-unemployed?"

"Thank you, sir. Goodbye, sir. You have been most kind."

Howards closed the door quickly behind him—why did he keep thinking there was blood on his hands? He shook his head to clear it.

It would be hard to tell Dora. She had hoped so.

But at least he still had his Book. And a whole year to memorize it again. That would be good. And there would be inserts and additions, that was always good.

He walked by the post office in the lobby of the building with his eyes averted.

Captain Bedlam

"What is space like? How do the naked stars really look? Those are hard questions to answer." Captain Jonathan Bork looked around at the eager, intent faces waiting for his words, then dropped his eyes to his space-tanned hands on the table before him.

"Sometimes it's like falling into a million-mile pit, other times you feel like a fly in the spiderweb of eternity, naked under the stars. And the stars are so different—no flickering, you know, just the tiniest spots of solid light."

Even as he told them he cursed himself a thousand times for the liar he was. Captain Bork, spaceship pilot. The single man privileged to see the stars in the space between worlds. And after five round trips to Mars, he had no idea of what it was really like out there. His body piloted the ship, but Jonathan Bork had never seen the inside of a ship's control room.

Not that he ever dared admit it aloud. When people asked him what it was like he told them—using one of the carefully memorized speeches from the textbooks.

With an effort he pulled his mind away from the thought and back to the table surrounded by guests and relatives. The dinner was in his honor, so he tried to live up to it. The brandy helped. He finished most of it, then excused himself as soon as he could.

The family house was old enough to have a pocket-sized backyard. He went there, alone, and put his back against the dark building still warm from the heat of the day. The unaccustomed brandy felt good, and when he looked up the stars wheeled in circles until he closed his eyes.

Stars. He had always looked at the stars. From the time he had been a child they had been his interest and his drive. Everything he had ever done or studied had that one purpose behind it. To be one of the select few to fly the space lanes. A pilot.

He had entered the academy when he was seventeen, the minimum age. By the time he was eighteen he knew the whole thing was a fake.

He had tried to ignore the truth, to find some other explanation. But it was no good. Everything he knew, everything he was taught in the school added up to one thing. And *that* was an impossible conclusion.

It was inescapable and horrible so finally he had put it to the test.

It happened in physiology class, where they were working out problems in relation to orientation and consciousness in acceleration, using Paley's theorem. He had raised his hand timidly, but Eagle-Eye Cherniki had spotted it and growled him to his feet. Once he was committed the words came out in a rush.

"Professor Cherniki, if we accept Paley's theorem, in a problem like this with only minimal escape-G, we go well below the consciousness threshold. And the orientation factor as well, it seems to me . . . that, well . . ."

"Mr. Bork, just what are you trying to say?" Cherniki's voice had the cold incision of a razor's edge.

Jon took the plunge. "There can be only one conclusion. Any pilot who takes off in a ship will be knocked out or unable to orientate enough to work the controls."

The classroom rocked with laughter and Jon felt his face warm and redden. Even Cherniki allowed himself a cold grin when he answered.

"Very good. But if what you say is true, then it is impossible to fly in space—and we do it every day. I think you will find that in the coming semester we will go into the question of changing thresholds under stress. That should—"

"No, sir," Jon broke in. "The texts do not answer this question—if anything they avoid it. I've read every text for this course as well as other related texts—"

"Mr. Bork, are you calling me a liar?" Cherniki's voice was as frigid as his eyes. A dead hush fell over the classroom. "You are dismissed from this class. Go to your quarters and remain there until you are sent for."

Trying not to stumble, Jon went across the room and out the door. Every eye was fixed on him and he felt like a prisoner on the last mile. Instead of getting an answer to his question it looked as if he had got himself in deep trouble. Sitting in his room he tried not to think of the consequences.

He had never been certain he could get into pilot training—even though it had been his only ambition. Just about one out of one hundred made it that far, the rest ending up in the thousand other jobs of the space fleet. Very few washed completely out of the Academy; the entrance requirements were so high that deadheads never got that far. Of course, there were exceptions—and it was beginning to look like he was one of them.

When the intercom finally called him to the president's office he was almost ready for it. He still jumped when it barked for him then he got up quickly and left taking the elevator to the executive level. The cold-faced secretary nodded him in, and he was alone with the Admiral.

Admiral Sikelm had retired from active service when he took over the presidency of the Academy. He had never lost the manner or voice of command and everyone on campus referred to him only as "the Admiral." Jon had never been this close to him before and was struck speechless. The Admiral, however, did no barking or growling, just talked quietly to put him at ease.

"I have seen Professor Cherniki and he told me what happened in class. I have also listened to the taped recording of your conversation with him."

This doubly surprised Jon; it was the first he had heard that the classes contained concealed recorders. The Admiral went on, with the very last words Jon had expected to hear.

"Congratulations, Mr. Bork, you have been accepted for pilot training. Your classes begin next week—*if* you wish to continue training?" Jon started to talk, but the Admiral stopped him with an upraised palm. "I want you to listen first before you give me your answer. As you have already discovered, space flight is not all that it appears to be.

"When we first hit space we were losing nine out of ten ships. And not through mechanical failure either. Telemetering equipment on the pilots showed us where the trouble lay—space is just not made for the human body. Gravity changes, blood pressure, free fall, radiation narcosis, all of these combined with a dozen other causes we discovered later to put the pilot out of action. If he didn't black out completely or lose control, the disorientation of the new stimuli made it impossible for him to operate the ship.

"So we had a stalemate. Plenty of good ships with no one to fly them. We tried drugs, hypnosis and a number of other things to fit men for space. They all failed for the same reason. By the time we adjusted men for space they were so doped and controlled that they were again unable to do the job.

"It was Dr. Moshe Kahn who solved the problem—you've heard of him?"

"Just vaguely—wasn't he first director of the Psych Corps?"

"Yes—that's all he is known for in the public record. Maybe, someday, he can get the credit due him. Dr. Kahn was the man who enabled us to conquer space.

"His theory, that was proven to be absolutely true, was that man as we know him, Homo sapiens, is unfit for space. Dr. Kahn set out to create Homo nova, men who could live and work in space. Under the correct mental conditions the human body is capable of unusual feats—such as walking through fire or possessing the rigid strength of a hypnotized patient. Dr. Kahn reasoned that the body's potentialities are great enough, all he had to do was create the *mind* of Homo nova. This he did by inducing a condition of dual personality in adults—"

"I don't understand, sir," Jon broke in. "Wouldn't it have been easier to work with children, babies—condition them from the very beginning?"

"Of course," the Admiral said, "but happily we have laws to prevent just that sort of thing. Dr. Kahn never considered that approach; he used men, volunteers—most of them with some experience in space. Cases of multiple personality have been documented as far back as the nineteenth century, but no one had ever tried to *create* a separate personality. Kahn did it and he created the kind of personality he wanted. What is too upsetting or uncomfortable for a normal person is the natural environment of these new personalities. They are able to pilot ships between the planets. Using frozen sleep, passengers could also be carried to the planets without experiencing the terrible rigors of space.

"The entire program has been kept a secret—for good and obvious reasons. I can hear the howls now if people knew they were traveling with an unconscious pilot—an insane pilot I imagine they would call it since this is a kind of induced insanity. The only people who know about the program are the instructors, the pilots and a few high officials.

"Since the pilots are all volunteers—and the program *works*—there are no ethical rules being broken. As you have seen, even the students in this school have no idea of the real nature of a space pilot. If they accept the cover-up in their textbooks, they go on to other jobs in the Corps. If they have the capacity to think and understand—like you— they will understand the need for a program like this. They will have the knowledge to know what they are getting into if they volunteer.

"I think that covers the whole picture—unless you have any questions?"

Jon thought for a moment. "Just one, and it may sound a little foolish. Just what are the physical symptoms connected with this training? I mean, I would like to know, will I really be a little bit—"

"Insane? Only by definition. The new personality, Jon II, can only exist in the specialized environment of the ship's control cabin. Your original personality, Jon I, assumes command all the time on the outside. The only sensation you will have will be periods of amnesia. The personalities are distinct and separate. Each blacks out completely when the other is dominant."

Jon's mind was made up—had been made up for quite a while.

"I still look forward to being a pilot, Admiral. I don't see that all of this alters that fact any."

They shook hands then, the Admiral a little sadly. He had done this many times before. He knew it did not always turn out exactly as the young volunteers imagined.

Jon left the school the same afternoon, without seeing any of his classmates. The Pilot Training School was in a different part of the same base and a new world altogether.

The thing he liked most was the feeling of having arrived. He was no longer treated like a student, but as a responsible equal. He was one of a select few. There were only twelve students in the school at the time and over fifteen hundred men on the training staff. It soon became obvious why.

The first few weeks were mostly physical examinations and tests. Then came the endless sessions with the encephalograph and in the hypno chambers. Jon had nightmares at first, and many days had a period of half-awake, strange sensations. This was only in the beginning. The first step in the program was separating the two personalities completely. Once this happened Jon I had no knowledge of Jon II. Time went by very fast for him since he wasn't aware of most of the training.

Part of the program was orientation, teaching him how to accept and live with the hidden half of his mind. He, of course, could never meet Jon II, but he did watch another pilot's II personality. Jenkins was the one he saw, a slim boy about a year older than Jon. It was a Fine Motor Control Under Acceleration test that he watched. He found it hard to believe. The Jenkins in the test chair only faintly resembled the one he knew. Jenkins II had an expressionless face and a smoothness of motion that Jenkins I could never have. He sat in the acceleration cage that moved in sudden surges in random directions. At the same time Jenkins II had to throw small switches on a control board in response to a changing signal pattern. His fingers moved carefully, flicking the tiny switches placed only an inch apart—while the cage made sudden three-G swoops. Jenkins II's muscles were bar-hard to counteract the acceleration, but it was more than mere strength that gave the control. Heightened perception noted every thrust as it started and the opposed muscles countered with exactly the right amount of counterthrust. It was the automatic balance of an old sailor on a pitching ship, refined down to the smallest motion.

When Jon II was firmly established, Jon I had some uncomfortable experiences. Instead of coming through in the psych room one day, he found himself in the hospital. There was a tremendous gash across his palm and two fingers were broken.

"Training accident," the doctor said. "Something went wrong in the G cage and you saved yourself a good bit of injury by grabbing a bracing rod. Hurt your hand a little, that's all. Here's the rod."

The doctor smiled when he gave Jon the piece of metal—and he could see why. It was half-inch steel and the weight of his body on his fingers had bent and broken the rod. Jon I would have difficulty bending it with a hammer.

All of the training was not for Jon II's benefit. Once the second personality was strongly established, training time was split about fifty-fifty. Jon I learned everything there was to know about a spacer—outside of the control room. He took charge of the ship on the ground—checkups, repairs, even passenger goodwill. Jon I was the pilot and everyone had to have faith in him. They could never know that he blacked out whenever he entered the control room. He tried many times to see it, but never could. The control room was the deeply implanted device that triggered the personality shift. As soon as Jon I took a step through the door—or even as much as glanced inside—he was through. Jon II was in his domain and took over instantly.

Graduation day was the most important and at the same time the most frustrating day of his entire life. There was no such thing as a graduating class. As each pilot finished his training he graduated at a public ceremony. Most of the base personnel turned out, at least thirty thousand men. They paraded and Jon marched out in front of them in his pilot's black uniform. The Admiral himself took out the platinum wings—oldest symbol of mass flight—and snapped them on. It was a moment to remember.

There was just time to say goodbye to his family, when the ship was ready. That was another feature of graduation day. The new pilot made his first flight. A short hop to the moon with a shipload of supplies—but still a flight. He had climbed the ramp to the entrance, turned to wave to his family, small specks in the distance. Then he had stepped into the control room.

Then he had stepped out through the lock onto the surface of the moon.

There had been no sensation of time. One instant he had been on Earth, in the next breath he was on the moon. Only the fact that he was wearing a spacesuit and his muscles were tired and sore convinced him. It was the most anticlimactic experience of his life . . .

In the garden on Earth, looking up at the newly risen moon, Jon thought about the past and tasted it dry as ashes in his mouth. Inside the house someone laughed and he heard the tinkle of bottle against glass. He pushed the thoughts away then and remembered where he was.

His family's house, the party in his honor. He had put them off time after time, then was finally forced to accept. It was just as bad as he had thought it would be. It is one thing to live a lie with yourself—something totally different to be a false hero in your own home.

Squaring his shoulders and flicking a speck of invisible dust from his jacket, he went back inside.

The following morning he reported to base for the forty-eight-hour examination and sweat period that preceded all flights. His physical system was tuned to maximum potentiality by the doctors while he was briefed on the flight. It was to be the longest yet, and the most important.

"A long trip," the briefing officer said, tapping the chart, "to Jupiter—or rather the eighth satellite. One of the retrograde ones. There is a base and an observatory there now, as you know, but a new bunch of observers are going out. Astrophysicists to do work with Jupiter's gravity. Twelve of them and all their equipment. That's quite a load. Your main concern—or rather II's—will be the asteroid belt. You can't get too far away from the ecliptic so you may contact meteoric debris. We've had some trouble that way already. With a little luck you should complete a successful flight."

Jon shook hands with the passengers when they came aboard and checked the technicians when they sealed the freeze chambers. When everything was secured he climbed an internal companionway to the control room. This was the point where he always held back a bit. Once he pushed open the door he was committed. It was the last act of free will he had, then Jon II took over. He hesitated only a second, then pushed the door open, thinking to himself, Next stop, Jupiter.

Only it wasn't Jupiter, it was pain.

He couldn't see and he couldn't hear. A thousand sensations were forced on him at once. They added up to pain. Bigger, redder and more horrifying than he ever thought possible. It took an effort of will to blink his eyes and try to focus them.

In front of him was the viewpoint and beyond it was the stars. He was in space, in the cabin of the ship. For an instant he almost forgot the pain at the sight of the stars spread out before him. Then the pain was back and he was trying to understand what had happened, wanting to do something to end the torment. The cabin was dark, the only illumination the lights on the giant control boards. They flickered and changed, he had no idea of their meaning or what to do.

Then the pain was too much and he screamed and lost consciousness.

In the few moments Jon I had been in command of their body, Jon II had drained away a little of his panic. He had lost control and blacked out. He couldn't let it happen again. Neural blocks cut off a good deal of the pain, but enough seeped through to interfere with his thinking. A meteorite—it must have been a meteorite.

There was a fist-sized opening in the front bulkhead, and air was roaring out through the gap. He could see a single star through the hole, brighter and clearer than any star he had ever seen before. The meteorite had made that hole, then hit the wall behind him. That must have been the explosion and the glare when it vaporized. It had done a lot of damage, sprayed molten metal all over him and destroyed the circuits in his chair pedestal. It was getting hard to breathe, the air was almost gone. And cold.

The spacesuit was in its locker, just ten feet away. Only the straps that held him in the chair couldn't be opened. The electric release was destroyed, the mechanical release jammed. He struggled with the clasps, but he only had his bare hands.

All the time it was getting harder to breathe. The panic was there again and he could no longer fight it away.

Jon II gasped and his eyes closed. Jon I opened them.

The pain was overwhelming and washed over him instantly. Jon's eyes closed again and his body slumped forward.

Then he straightened and jerkily the eyelids opened. For a moment his eyeballs rolled unsteadily, then fixed. They looked straight ahead and were almost vacant of anything like reason.

For Jon III was closer to the basic animal than any man or animal that had ever walked the Earth. *Survive* was the only thing he knew. *Survive* and *save the ship*. He was dimly aware of Jon I and Jon II and could call on their memories if he needed to. He had no memories or thoughts of his own—except pain. Born in pain and doomed forever to live in pain, his whole world was pain.

Jon III was a built-in safety device, an admission that there might be times when even the II personality of a pilot couldn't save the ship. Only in the last extreme, when all else had failed, could the III personality assume control.

There was nothing at all subtle about Jon III's control. *See a problem—solve the problem.* The memory, still in his forebrain, was *Get the spacesuit.* He started to stand up, then realized for the first time he couldn't. With both hands he pulled against the strap across his chest, but it didn't break. The clasp was the answer; he had to open that.

No tools, just his hands. Use his hands. He put one finger inside the clasp and pulled. The finger bent, stretched and broke. Jon III felt no pain at all, no emotion. He put his second finger in and tugged again. The second finger was almost pulled off, and hung only by a piece of flesh. He put in the third finger.

The clasp finally broke when he pulled with his thumb. The rest of the hand hung, broken and disfigured. With a surge of power he pushed himself out of the chair. The femur in his right leg cracked and broke at the same time the lower strap did. Pulling with his good hand and pushing with his left leg he squirmed across the floor to the spacesuit cabinet.

The air in the cabin was almost a vacuum. He had to keep blinking to wash away the ice crystals that formed on his eyes. His heart was beating at four times its regular rate to force the trace of oxygen to the dying body.

Jon III was aware of these things, but they didn't bother him. His world had always been like that. The only way he could regain the peace of his mindless oblivion was to finish what he had started. He never knew, had never been taught, that dying was also a way out.

Carefully and methodically he pulled down the spacesuit and climbed into it. He turned the oxygen on and closed the last zipper. Then he closed his eyes with a sigh of relief.

Jon II opened his eyes and felt the pain. He could bear it now because he knew he was going to get out of this mess and save the ship. An emergency patch stopped the rush of air and while pressure was building up from the reserve tanks he examined the board. The ship could be flown on the secondary and manual circuits. All he had to do was rig them.

When the pressure reached seven pounds he stripped off the spacesuit and gave himself first aid. He was a little surprised to see the state his right hand was in. He couldn't remember doing that. Jon II wasn't equipped to solve that kind of problem though. He hurried the dressings and burn ointment and turned back to his repairs. It was going to be a successful trip after all.

Jon never knew about Jon III—he was the unknown safety factor that was there always, dormant and waiting. Jon I thought Jon II had got them out of the mess. Jon II didn't bother to think about things like that. His job was to fly the ship.

Jon recuperated slowly at the hospital on Jupiter 8. He was amazed at the amount of damage his body had suffered, yet pulled through. The pain was bad for a long time, but he didn't really mind. It wasn't too high a price to pay.

He wasn't going to be a liar anymore. He had been a pilot, even if for only a few seconds.

He had seen the stars in space.

THE LIGHT FANTASTIC

In my magazine-editing days I edited an issue or two of a magazine titled *Fantasy Fiction*. I took over as editor from Fletcher Pratt when he stepped down to sue the publisher. (All the other editors helped him with the lawsuit since the publisher was uniformly hated by his staff.) I even wrote a fantasy novella with Kay MacLean titled *Web of the Norns*. Published, I believe, in this same magazine.

I also bought a complete run of *Unknown* since Brian Aldiss and I were to edit *Best from Unknown* to follow our *Best from Astounding-Analog* anthology. Alas, this never came to pass.

But as much as I enjoy fantasy a look at the record reveals that I obviously do not seem to be writing it. Out of all my short stories I find just two that can be called fantasy. This was never a deliberate decision, just that when my mind thinks "story"—it doesn't think "fantasy."

At Last, the True Story of Frankenstein

"Und here, before your very eyes, is the very same monster built by my much-admired great-great-grandfather, Victor Frankenstein, built by him from pieces of corpses out of the dissecting rooms, stolen parts of bodies freshly buried in the grave, und even chunks of animals from the slaughterhouse. Now look—" The tailcoated man on the platform swung his arm out in a theatrical gesture and the heads of the close-packed crowd below swung to follow it. The dusty curtains flapped aside and the monster stood there, illuminated from above by a sickly green light. There was a concerted gasp from the crowd and a shiver of motion.

In the front row, pressed against the rope barrier, Dan Bream mopped his face with a soggy handkerchief and smiled. It wasn't such a bad monster, considering that this was a cheapjack carnival playing the small-town southern circuit. It had a dead-white skin, undampened by sweat even in this steambath of a tent, glazed eyes, stitches and seams showing where the face had been patched together, and the two metal plugs projecting from the temples—just like in the movie.

"Raise your right arm!" Victor Frankenstein V commanded, his brusque German accent giving the words a Prussian air of authority. The monster's body did not move, but slowly—with the jerking motion of a badly operating machine—the creature's arm came up to shoulder height and stopped.

"This monster, built from pieces from the dead, cannot die, und if a piece gets too worn out I simply stitch on a new piece with the secret formula passed down from father to son from my great-great-grandfather. It cannot die nor feel pain—as you see—"

This time the gasp was even louder and some of the audience turned away while others watched with eager eyes. The barker had taken a foot-long and wickedly sharp needle, and had pushed it firmly through the monster's biceps until it protruded on both sides. No blood stained it and the creature made no motion, as though completely unaware that anything had been done to its flesh.

". . . impervious to pain, extremes of heat and cold, and possessing the strength of ten men. . . ."

Behind him the voice droned on, but Dan Bream had had enough. He had seen the performance three times before, which was more than satisfactory for what he needed to know, and if he stayed in the tent another minute he would melt. The exit was close by and he pushed through the gaping, pallid audience and out into the humid dusk. It wasn't much cooler outside. Life borders on the unbearable along the shores of the Gulf of Mexico in August, and Panama City, Florida, was no exception. Dan headed for the nearest air-conditioned beer joint and sighed with relief as the chill atmosphere closed around his steaming garments. The beer bottle frosted instantly with condensation as did the heavy glass stein, cold from the freezer. The first big swallow cut a path straight down to his stomach. He took the beer over to one of the straight-backed wooden booths, wiped the table off with a handful of paper napkins and flopped onto the bench. From the inner pocket of his jacket he took some folded sheets of yellow copy paper, now slightly soggy, and spread them before him. After adding some lines to the scribbled notes he stuffed them back into his jacket and took a long pull on his beer. Dan was halfway through his second bottle when the barker, who called himself Frankenstein the Fifth, came in. His stage personality had vanished along with the frock coat and a monocle, and the Prussian haircut now looked like a common crewcut.

"You've got a great act," Dan called out cheerfully, and waved the man over. "Will you join me for a drink?"

"Don't mind if I do," Frankenstein answered in the pure nasal vowels of New York City, the German accent apparently having disappeared along with the monocle. "And see if they have a Schlitz or a Bud or anything beside the local swamp water."

He settled into the booth while Dan went for the beers, and groaned when he saw the labels on the bottles.

"At least it's cold," he said, shaking salt into his to make it foamy, then half-drained the stein in a long deep swallow. "I noticed you out there in front of the clems for most of the shows today. Do you like the act—or you a carny buff?"

"It's a good act. I'm a newsman, name's Dan Bream."

"Always pleased to meet the press, Dan. Publicity is the life of show business, as the man said. I'm Stanley Arnold—call me Stan."

"Then Frankenstein is just your stage name?"

"What else? You act kinda dim for a reporter—are you sure . . . ?" He waved away the Press card that Dan pulled from his breast pocket. "No, I believe you, Dan, but you gotta admit the question was a little on the rube side. I bet you even think that I have a real monster in there!"

"Well, you must admit that he looks authentic. The skin stitched together that way, those plugs in his head—"

"Held on with spirit gum and the embroidery is drawn on with eyebrow pencil. That's show business for you, all illusion. But I'm happy to hear that the act even looked real to an experienced reporter like yourself. What paper did you say you were with?"

"No paper, the news syndicate. I caught your act about six months ago and became interested. Did a little checking when I was in Washington, then followed you down here. You don't really want me to call you Stan, do you? Stein might be closer. After all—Victor Frankenstein is the name on your naturalization papers."

"Tell me more," Frankenstein said in a voice suddenly cold and emotionless.

Dan rifled through the yellow sheets. "Yes . . . here it is, from the official records. Frankenstein, Victor—born in Geneva, arrived in the U.S. in 1938, and more of the same."

"The next thing you'll be telling me is that my monster is real!" Frankenstein smiled, but only with his mouth.

"I'm betting that it is. No yogi training or hypnotism or such can make a man as indifferent to pain as that thing is—and as terribly strong. I want the whole story, the truth for a change!"

"Do you . . . ?" Frankenstein asked in a cold voice and for a long moment the air filled with tension. Then he laughed and clapped the reporter on the arm. "All right, Dan—I'll give it to you. You are a persistent devil and a good reporter and it is the least you deserve. But first you must get us some more drinks, something a measurable degree stronger than this execrable beer." His New York accent had disappeared as easily as had his German one; he spoke English now with skill and perfection without any recognizable regional accent.

Dan gathered their empty glasses. "It'll have to be beer—this is a dry county."

"Nonsense! This is America, the land that raises its hands in horror at the foreign conception of double-think, yet practices it with an efficiency that sets the Old World to shame. Bay County may be officially dry but the law has many itchy palms, and under that counter you will find a reasonable supply of a clear liquid that glories in the name of White Mule, that is reputed to have a kick of the same magnitude as its cognate beast. If you are still in doubt you will see a framed federal liquor license on the far wall, legitimizing this endeavor in the eyes of the national government. Simply place a five-dollar bank note on the bar, say 'Mountain Dew,' and do not expect any change."

When they both had enjoyed their first sips of the corn liquor Victor Frankenstein lapsed into a friendly mood.

"Call me Vic, Dan. I want us to be friends. I'm going to tell you a story that few have heard before, a story that is astounding but true. True—mark that word—not a hodgepodge of distortions and half-truths, and outright ignorance like that vile book produced by Mary

Godwin. Oh how my father ever regretted meeting that woman and, in a moment of weakness, confiding in her the secret of some of his original lines of research—"

"Just a minute," Dan broke in. "You mentioned the truth, but I can't swallow this guff. Mary Wollstonecraft Shelley wrote *Frankenstein, or the Modern Prometheus* in 1818. Which would make you and your father so old—"

"Please, Dan—no interruptions. I mentioned my father's researches—in the plural you will note—all of them devoted to the secrets of life. The Monster, as it has come to be called, was just one of his works. Longevity was what he was interested in, and he did live to a very, very old age, as will I. I will not stretch your credulity any further at this moment by mentioning the year of my birth, but will press on. That Mary Godwin. She and the poet were living together at this period, they had not married as yet, and this permitted my father to hope that Mary might one day find him not unattractive, since he was quite taken by her. Well, you can easily imagine the end. She made notes of everything he told her—then discarded him and used the notes to construct her despicable book. Her errors are legion, listen . . ." He leaned across the booth and once again clapped Dan on the shoulder in a hearty way. It was an intimate gesture that the reporter didn't particularly enjoy, but he didn't complain. Not as long as the other kept talking.

"Firstly she made Papa a Swiss; he used to tear his hair out at the thought, since ours is a good old Bavarian family with a noble and ancient lineage. Then she had him attending the University of Ingolstadt in Ingolstadt—when every schoolboy knows that it was moved to Landshut in 1800. And Father's personality, what crimes she committed there! In this libelous volume he is depicted as a weeping and ineffectual man, when in reality he was a tower of strength and determination. And if this isn't enough, she completely misunderstood the meaning of his experiments. Her gimcrack collection of cast-off parts put together to make an artificial man is ludicrous. She was so carried away by the legends of Talos and the Golem that she misinterpreted my father's work and cast it into that ancient mold. Father did not construct an artificial man, he reactivated a dead man! That is the measure of his genius! He traveled for years in the darkest reaches of the African jungle, learning the lore of the creation of the zombie. He regularized the knowledge and improved upon it until he had surpassed all of his aboriginal teachers. Raise the dead, that is what he could do. That was his secret—and how can it be kept a secret in the future, Mr. Dan Bream?"

With these last words Victor Frankenstein's eyes opened wide and an unveiled light seemed to glow in their depths. Dan pulled back instinctively, then relaxed. He was in no danger here in this brightly lit room with men on all sides of them.

"Afraid, Dan? Don't be." Victor smiled and reached out and patted Dan on the shoulder once again.

"What was that?" Dan asked, startled at the tiny brief pain in his shoulder.

"Nothing—nothing but this," Frankenstein smiled again, but the smile had changed subtly and no longer contained any humor. He opened his hand to reveal a small hypodermic needle, its plunger pushed down and its barrel empty.

"Remain seated," he said quietly when Dan started to rise, and Dan's muscles relaxed and he sat back down, horrified.

"What have you done to me?"

"Very little—the injection is harmless. A simple little hypnotic drug, the effect of which wears off in a few hours. But until then you will not have much will of your own. So you will sit and hear me out. Drink some beer though, we don't want you to be thirsty."

Horrified, Dan was a helpless onlooker as, of its own volition, his hand raised, and poured a measure of beer down his throat.

"Now concentrate, Dan, think of the significance of my statement. The so-called Frankenstein monster is no stitched-up collection of scraps, but a good honest zombie. A dead man who can walk but not talk, obey but not think. Animate—but still dead. Poor old Charley is one, the creature whom you watched going through his act on the platform. But Charley is just about worn out. Since he is dead he cannot replace the body cells that are destroyed during the normal wear and tear of the day. Why the fellow is like an animated pincushion from the act, holes everywhere. His feet—terrible, not a toe left, keep breaking off when he walks too fast. I think it's time to retire Charley. He has had a long life, and a long death. Stand up, Dan."

In spite of his mind crying "No! No!" Dan rose slowly to his feet.

"Aren't you interested in what Charley used to do before he became a sideshow monster? You should be, Dan. Old Charley was a reporter—just like you. And he ran across what he thought was a good story. Like you, he didn't realize the importance of what he had discovered and talked to me about it. You reporters are a very inquisitive bunch. I must show you my scrapbook, it's simply filled with press cards. Before you die of course. You wouldn't be able to appreciate it afterward. Now come along."

Dan walked after him, into the hot night, screaming inside in a haze of terror, yet walking quietly and silently down the street.

Incident in the IND

"Thank God *that's* done." Adriann DuBois's voice bounced harshly from the tiled walls of the subway passage, punctuated by the sharp clack-clack of her high stiletto heels. There was a rattling rumble as an express train rushed through the station ahead and a wave of musty air washed over them.

"It's after one A.M.," Chester said and yawned widely and pressed the back of his hand to his mouth. "We'll probably have to wait an hour for a train."

"Don't be so negative, Chester," she said, and her voice had the same metallic ring as her heelsteps. "All the copy is finished now for the new account, we'll probably get a bonus, and we can take most of the day off tomorrow. Think positive like that, and you'll feel a lot better, I assure you."

They reached the turnstile at that moment, before Chester could think of a snappy answer that didn't reek too much of one o'clock in the morning, and he fumbled a token into the slot. Adriann swept through as he probed deeper into his change pocket and discovered that this had been his last token. He turned wearily back to the change booth and muttered two or three good, dirty words under his breath.

"How many?" a voice mumbled from the dimness of the barred steel cell.

"Two, please." He slipped the change in through the tiny window. It wasn't that he minded paying her damn fare—after all, she was a woman—but he wished she would at least say thanks or even nod her head to show that she didn't get into subways by divine right. After all they both worked in the same nut factory and earned the same money, and now she would be earning more. He had forgotten that last little fact for a moment. The slot swallowed his token and went *chunk* as he pushed through.

"I take the last car," Adriann said, squinting nearsightedly down the dark and empty tunnel. "Let's walk back to the end of the plat-form."

"I need the middle of the train," Chester said, but had to trot after her. Adriann never heard what she didn't need to hear.

"There's something I can tell you now, Chester," she began in her brisk man-to-man voice. "I couldn't really mention this before, since we both were doing the same work and in one sense competing for position. But since Blaisdell's coronary will have him out for a couple of weeks I'll be acting copy chief, with some more money to match—"

"I heard from the latrine grapevine. Congrats—"

"—so I'm in a position to pass on a bit of good advice to you. You have to push more, Chester, grab onto things when they come along . . ."

"For chrissake, Adriann, you sound like a bad commercial for crowded streetcars."

"And that sort of thing too. Little jokes. People begin to think you don't take your work seriously and that is sure death in the ad business."

"Of course I don't take the work seriously—who in their right mind could?" He heard a rumbling and looked, but the tunnel was still empty; it must have been a truck in the street above. "Are you going to tell me that you really care about writing deathless prose about milady's armpits smelling the right way from the use of the right Stink-Go-Way?"

"Don't be vulgar, Chester; you know you can be sweet when you want to," she said, taking advantage of female reasoning to ignore his arguments and to inject a note of emotion into a previously logical conversation.

"You're damn right I can be sweet," he said huskily, not averse to a little emotion himself. With her mouth shut Adriann was pretty attractive in a past-thirtyish way. The knitted dress did wonders for her bottom, and undoubtedly the foundation maker's artifice had something to do with the outstanding attraction of her front piece, but more in underpinning than in padding, he was willing to bet.

He shuffled close and slipped his arms around her waist and patted lightly on the top of her flank. "I can be sweet and I can remember a time when you didn't mind being sweet right back."

"That's a long time finished, boy," she said in her schoolmarm voice and peeled his arms away with a picking-up-worms expression. Chester's newspaper fell out from under his arm, where he had stuffed it, and he bent over mumbling to pick it up from the gritty platform.

She was quiet for a moment after this, twisting her skirt around a bit and rubbing out the wrinkles as if brushing away the contamination of his touch. There were no sounds from the street overhead, and the long, dimly lit station was as silent as a burial vault. They were alone with the strange loneliness that can be experienced only in a large city, of people somewhere always close by, yet always cut off. Tired, suddenly depressed, Chester lit a cigarette and inhaled deeply.

"You're not allowed to smoke in the subway," Adriann said with detached coldness.

"I'm not allowed to smoke, nor to give you a little squeeze, to make jokes in the office, or to look with justified contempt at our current client."

"No you're not," she snapped and leveled a delicate finger with a blood-red nail at him. "And since you brought it up, I'll tell you something else. Other people in the office have noticed it too, and this I *know*. You have been with the firm longer than I, so they considered you for the copy chief's job—and turned you down. And I was told in utmost confidence that they are actually considering letting you go. Does that mean anything to you?"

"It does. It means I have been nursing a viper in my bosom. I seem to remember that I got you this job and even had to convince old Blaisdell that you could do the work. You acted right grateful too, at the time—remember those passionate scenes in the foyer of your boardinghouse?"

"Don't be a pig!"

"Now the passion is dead, so is any chance of a raise, and it looks like my job is out the window as well. With dear Adriann for a friend, who needs an enemy . . ."

"There are things living in the subway, you know."

The voice was husky and trembled, it came suddenly from behind them, from what they thought was the empty platform, startling them both. Adriann gasped and turned quickly. There was a pool of darkness next to the large litter bin and neither of them had noticed the man slumped against the wall, seated there. He struggled to his feet and stepped forward.

"How dare you!" Adriann said shrilly, startled and angry. "Hiding there, eavesdropping on a private conversation. Aren't there any police in this subway?"

"There are *things*, you know," the man said, ignoring her, grinning up at Chester, his head twisted to one side.

He was a bum, one of the crumpled horde that had splattered out over New York City when the Bowery elevated was torn down and light penetrated that clogged street of human refuse. Photophobes to a man, they stumbled away seeking dimmer illumination. For many of them the gloomed caverns of the subways offered refuge, heated cars in the winter, toilet facilities, panhandling prospects, quiet corners for collapsing. This one wore the uniform of his trade: shapeless, filthy pants with most of the fly buttons missing; crumpled jacket tied close with string, with a number of unusual undergarments visible at the open neck; shoes cracked, split, and flapping; darkened skin as wrinkled as a mummy's with a pencil line of dirt in every crack. His mouth was a black orifice, the few remaining teeth standing like stained tombstones in memory of their vanished brothers. Examined in detail the man was a revolting sight, but so commonplace to this city that he was as much a part of it as the wire trash basket and the steaming manholes.

"What kind of things?" Chester asked while he groped in his pocket for a dime to buy their freedom. Adriann turned her back on them both.

"Things that live in the earth," the bum said and smiled blearily, pressing a grimy finger to his lips. "People who know never talk about it. Don't want to frighten the tourists away, no they don't. Scales, claws, down here, in the subway darkness."

"Give him some money—get rid of him—this is terrible!" Adriann said shrilly.

Chester dropped two nickels into the cupped hand, carefully, from a few inches above so he wouldn't have to touch the stained skin.

"What do these things do?" he asked, not because he really cared what the man had to say, but to annoy Adriann, a touch of the old sadist nudging him on.

The bum rubbed the nickels together in his palm. "They live here, hiding, looking out, that's what they do. You should give them something when you're alone, late at night like this, staying near the end of the platform. Pennies are good, just put them down there, at the edge where they can reach up and get them. Dimes good too, but no nickels like you gave me."

"You're hearing a very fancy panhandle story," Adriann said, angry now that her first fright had gone. "Now get away from that old tramp."

"Why only pennies and dimes?" Chester asked, interested in spite of himself. It *was* very black over the edge of the platform: anything could be hiding there.

"Pennies because they like peanuts, they work the machines with pennies when no one is around. And dimes for the Coke machines, they drink that sometimes instead of water. I've seen them . . ."

"I'm going for a policeman," Adriann snorted and click-clacked away, but stopped after she had gone about ten yards. Both men ignored her.

"Come on now," Chester smiled at the bum, who was running trembling fingers through his matted hair, "you can't expect me to believe that. If these things eat only peanuts, there is no reason to buy them off—"

"I didn't say that was all they ate!" The grimy hand locked on Chester's sleeve before he could move away, and he recoiled from the man's breath as he leaned close to whisper.

"What they really like to eat is *people*, but they won't bother you as long as you leave them a little something. Would you like to see one?"

"After this buildup I certainly would."

The bum tottered over to the wastepaper receptacle, big as a truck on end, olive drab metal with two flap doors in the hatlike cover.

"Now you just gotta take a quick look, because they don't like to be looked at," the man said and gave one of the flaps a push in and let go.

Chester stepped back, startled. He had had only a glimpse, had he really seen two glowing red spots in there, a foot apart, monstrous eyes? Could there be—no the whole thing was just too damn silly. There was the distant rumble of a train.

"Great show, Dad," he said, and dropped some pennies near the edge of the platform. "That'll keep them in peanuts for a while." He walked quickly down to Adriann. "The spiel got better after you left; the old buzzard swears that one of the things is hiding there in the trash can. So I left a bribe—just in case."

"How can you be so stupid—"

"You're tired, dear—and your claws are showing. And you're being repetitive as well."

The train rattled closer, sweeping a cloud of dead air before it. Musty air, almost like the smell of an animal . . . he had never noticed that before.

"You are stupid—and superstitious." She had to raise her voice above the roar of the approaching train. "You're the kind of person who knocks on wood and won't step on cracks and worries about black cats."

"I sure am, because it doesn't hurt. There's enough bad luck around as it is without looking for any more. There probably isn't a *thing* in that trash can—but I'm not going to put my arm in there to find out."

"You're a simple-minded child."

"Oh, am I!" They were both shouting now to be heard above the train that was rocking by next to them, brakes squealing to a stop. "Well let's see you put *your* arm in there if you are so damn smart."

"Childish!"

It was late and Chester was tired and his temper was frayed. The train shuddered to a halt behind him. He ran toward the end of the platform, digging in his pocket and pulling out all of his loose change.

"Here," he shouted, pushing the flap of the waste bin in an inch and pouring the coins through the gap. "Money. Plenty dimes, pennies. Plenty Cokes, peanuts. You grab and eat next person who comes here." Behind him Adriann was laughing. The train doors shooshed open and the old bum shuffled into the car.

"That's your Queens train," Adriann said, still laughing. "Better take it before the *things* get you. I'm waiting for the uptown local."

"Take this," he said, still angry, holding out his newspaper to her. "This is so funny, you're not superstitious—let's see you put this in the basket." He jumped for the train doors, catching them just as they closed.

"Of course, darling," she called, her face red from laughing. "And I'll tell the office about it tomorrow—" The doors slid shut cutting off the rest of her words.

The train shuddered a bit and started to move. Through the dirt-stained glass he saw her walk to the waste container and shove the paper in through the flap. One of the pillars came between them as the train picked up speed.

The he saw her again and she still had her hand to the lid—or had she poked her arm in up to the elbow?—it was hard to tell through the dirty glass. Then another pillar, they were beginning to flicker by. Another glimpse and with the blurred window and the bad light he couldn't be sure but it looked as if she was bent over and had poked her head into the opening.

This window was no good. He ran the few steps to the rear of the car where a larger—and somewhat cleaner—window was set into the rear door. The train was halfway down the platform now, swaying as it picked up speed and he had a last glimpse of her before the row of pillars merged into a blur that cut off vision completely.

She couldn't possibly be halfway into that container, the flapped opening certainly wasn't big enough for a person to get through. Yet how else to explain that he had seen just her skirt and legs sticking out, wiggling wildly in the air?

Of course it had been only a blurred glimpse and he was mistaken. He turned back to the empty car—no, not empty. The bum slumped in a seat, already asleep.

The ragged man looked up at Chester, gave him a quick, secretive grin, then closed his eyes again. Chester went to the other end of the car and sat down. He yawned and scrunched lower.

He could doze until they reached his station; he always woke up in time.

It would be nice if the copy chief's job was still open; he could use the extra money.

SQUARE PEGS IN ROUND HOLES

And then there were the rest. When I was putting together this collection I found that it was falling nicely into categories. Which was a good thing to have happen since I could then organize this volume into some comprehensive form. But there were a good many stories that just defied classification. These were the head-scratchers, the undefinable, the works of fiction that just did not fit into any simple category.

I guess the only thing to call them are the one-offs. Not a bad thing. Upon rereading them I find that this difference makes them, many times, the best of the lot. May you, gentle reader, agree.

Portrait of the Artist

"11 A.M.!!!" the note blared at him, pinned to the upper right corner of his drawing board. "MARTIN'S OFFICE!!" He had lettered it himself with a number 7 brush, funereal India ink on harsh yellow paper, big letters, big words.

Big end to everything. Pachs tried to make himself believe that this was just another one of Martin's royal commands: a lecture, a chewing-out, a complaint. That's what he had thought when he had knocked out the reminder for himself, before Miss Fink's large watery eyes had blinked at him and she had whispered hoarsely, "It's on order, Mr. Pachs, coming today, I saw the receipt on his desk. A Mark IX." She had blinked moistly again, rolled her eyes towards the closed door of Martin's office then scurried away.

A Mark IX. He knew that it would have to come someday, knew without wanting to admit it, and had only been kidding himself when he said they couldn't do without him. His hands spread out on the board before him, old hands, networked wrinkles and dark liver spots, always stained a bit with ink and marked with a permanent callus on the inside of his index finger. How many years had he held a pencil or a brush there? He didn't see them shaking.

There was almost an hour left before he had to see Martin, plenty of time to finish up the story he was working on. He pulled the sheet of illustration board from the top of the pile and found the script. Page 3 of a thing called "Prairie Love" for the July issue of *Real Rangeland Romances*. Love books with their heavy copy were always a snap. By the time Miss Fink had typed in the endless captions and dialogue on her big flatbed varityper at least half of every panel was full. The script, panel 1:

In house, Judy C/U cries and Robert in BG very angry.

A size 3 head for Judy in the foreground, he quickly drew the right size oval in blue pencil, then a stick figure for Robert in the background, hand raised, fist closed, to show anger. The Mark VIII Robot Comic Artist would do all the rest. Pachs slipped the sheet into the machine's holder—then quickly pulled it out again. He had forgotten the balloons. Sloppy, sloppy. He quickly blue-penciled their outlines and V's for tails.

When he thumbed the switch, the machine hummed to life, electronic tubes glowing inside its dark case. He punched the control button for the heads, first the girl—GIRL HEAD, FULL FRONT, SIZE 3,

SAD HEROINE. Girls of course all had the same face in comic books, the HEROINE was just a note to the machine not to touch the hair. For a VILLAINESS it would be inked in black, all villainesses have black hair, just as all villains have moustaches as well as the black hair, to distinguish them from the hero. The machine buzzed and clattered to itself while it sorted through the stock cuts, then clicked and banged down a rubber stamp of the correct head over the blue circle he had drawn. MAN HEAD, FULL FRONT, SIZE 6, SAD, HERO brought a smaller stamp banging down on the other circle that topped the stick figure. Of course the script said "angry," but that was what the raised fist was for, since there are only sad and happy faces in comics.

Life isn't that simple, he thought to himself, a very unoriginal idea that he usually brought out at least once a day while sitting at the machine. MAN FIGURE, BUSINESS SUIT, he set on the dial, then hit the DRAW button. The pen-tipped arm dropped instantly and began to quickly ink in a suited man's figure over the blue direction lines he had put down. He blinked and watched it industriously knocking in a wrinkle pattern that hadn't varied a stroke in fifty years, then a collar and tie and two swift necklines to connect the neatly inked torso to the rubber-stamped head. The pen leaped out to the cuff end of the just-drawn sleeve and quivered there. A relay buzzed and a dusty red panel flashed INSTRUCTIONS PLEASE at him. With a savage jab he pushed the button labeled FIST. The light went out and the flashing pen drew a neat fist at the end of the arm.

Pachs looked at the neatly drawn panel and sighed. The girl wasn't unhappy enough; he dipped his crow quill into the inkpot and knocked in two tears, one in the corner of each eye. Better. But the background was still pretty empty in spite of the small dictionary in each balloon. BALLOONS he punched automatically while he thought, and the machine pen darted down and inked the outlines of the balloons that held the lettering, ending each tail the correct distance from the speaker's mouth. A little background, it needed a touch. He pressed code 473 which he knew from long experience stood for HOME WINDOW WITH LACE CURTAINS. It appeared on the paper quickly, automatically scaled by the machine to be in perspective with the man's figure before it. Pachs picked up the script and read panel 2:

Judy falls on couch Robert tries to console her mother rushes in angrily wearing apron.

There was a four-line caption in this panel and after the three balloons had been lettered as well, the total space remaining was just about big enough for a single closeup, a small one. Pachs didn't labor this panel, as he might have, but took the standard way out. He was feeling tired today, very tired. HOUSE, SMALL FAMILY produced a small cottage from which emerged the trails of the three balloons and let the damn reader figure out who was talking.

The story was finished just before eleven and he stacked the pages neatly, put the script into the file and cleaned the ink out of the pen in the Mark VIII; it always clogged if he left it to dry.

Then it was eleven and time to see Martin. Pachs fussed a bit, rolling down his sleeves and hanging his green eyeshade from the arm of his dazor lamp; yet the moment could not be avoided. Pulling his shoulders back a bit he went out past Miss Fink hammering away industriously on the varityper, and walked in through the open door to Martin's voice.

"Come *on*, Louis," Martin wheedled into the phone in his most syrupy voice. "If it's a matter of taking the word of some two-bit shoestring salesman in Kansas City, or of taking my word, who you gonna doubt? . . . That's right . . . Okay . . . Right Louis. I'll call you back in the morning . . . Right, you too . . . my best to Helen." He banged the phone back onto the desk and glared up at Pachs with his hard beebee eyes.

"What do you want?"

"You told me you wanted to see me, Mr. Martin."

"Yeah, yeah," Martin mumbled half to himself. He scratched flakes of dandruff loose from the back of his head with the chewed end of a pencil, and rocked from side to side in his chair.

"Business is business, Pachs, you know that, and expenses go up all the time. Paper—you know how much it costs a ton? So we gotta cut corners . . ."

"If you're thinking of cutting my salary again, Mr. Martin, I don't think I could . . . well, maybe not much . . ."

"I'm gonna have to let you go, Pachs. I've bought a Mark IX to cut expenses and I already hired some kid to run it."

"You don't have to do that, Mr. Martin," Pachs said hurriedly, aware that his words were tumbling one over the other and that he was pleading, but not caring. "I could run the machine I'm sure, just give me a few days to catch on . . ."

"Outta the question. In the first place I'm paying the kid beans because she's just a kid and that's the starting salary, and in the other place she's been to school about this thing and can really grind the stuff out. You know I'm no bastard, Pachs, but business is business. And I'll tell you what, this is only Tuesday and I'll pay you for the rest of the week. How's that? And you can take off right now."

"Very generous, particularly after eight years," Pachs said, forcing his voice to be calm.

"That's all right, it's the least I could do." Martin was congenitally immune to sarcasm.

The lost feeling hit Pachs then, a dropping away of his stomach, a sensation that everything was over. Martin was back on the phone again and there was really nothing that Pachs could say. He walked out of the office, walking very straight, and behind him he heard the banging of Miss Fink's machine halt for a instant. He did not want to see her, to face those tender and damp eyes, not now. Instead of turning to go back to the studio, where he would have to pass her desk, he opened the hall door and stepped out. He closed it slowly behind him and stood with his back to it for an instant, until he realized it was frosted glass and she could see his figure from the inside: he moved hurriedly away.

There was a cheap bar around the corner where he had a beer every payday, and he went there now. "Good morning and top of the morning to you . . . Mr. Pachs," the robot bartender greeted him with recorded Celtic charm, hesitating slightly between the stock phrase and the search of the customer-tapes for his name. "And will you be having the usual?"

"No I will not be having the usual, you plastic and gaspipe imitation of a cheap stage Irishman, I'll be having a double whiskey."

"Sure and you are the card, sir," the electronically affable bartender nodded, horsehair spitcurl bobbing, as it produced a glass and bottle and poured a carefully measured drink.

Pachs drank it in a gulp and the unaccustomed warmth burned through the core of cold indifference that he had been holding on to. Christ, it was all over, all over. They would get him now with their Senior Citizens' Home and all the rest, he was good as dead.

There are some things that don't bear thinking about. This was one. Another double whiskey followed the first, the money for this was no longer important because he would be earning no more after this week. And the unusual dose of alcohol blurred some of the pain. Now, before he started thinking about it too much, he had to get back to the office. Clean his personal junk out of the taboret and pick up his paycheck from Miss Fink. It would be ready, he knew that; when Martin was through with you he liked to get you out of the way, quickly.

"Floor please?" the voice questioned from the top of the elevator.

"Go straight to hell!" he blurted out. He had never before realized how many robots there were around: Oh how he hated them today. "I'm sorry, that firm is not in this building, have you consulted the registry?"

"Twenty-three," he said and his voice quavered, and he was glad he was alone in the elevator. The doors closed.

There was a hall entrance to the studio and this door was standing open. He was halfway through the door before he realized why—then it was too late to turn back. The Mark VIII that he had nursed along and used for so many years lay on its side in the corner, uprooted and very dusty on the side that had stood against the wall.

Good, he thought to himself, and at the same time knew it was stupid to hate a machine, but still relishing the thought that it was being discarded too. In its place stood a columnar apparatus in a gray-crackle cabinet. It reached almost to the ceiling and appeared as ponderous as a safe.

"It's all hooked up now, Mr. Martin, ready to go with a hundred-percent lifetime guarantee, as you know. But I'll just sort of pre-flight it for you and give you an idea just how versatile this versatile machine is."

The speaker was dressed in gray coveralls of the exact same color as the machine's finish, and was pointing at it with a gleaming screwdriver. Martin watched, frowning, and Miss Fink fluttered in the background. There was someone else there, a thin young girl in a pink sweater who bovinely chewed at a cud of gum.

"Let's give Mark IX here a real assignment, Mr. Martin. A cover for one of your magazines, something I bet you never thought a machine could tackle before, and normal machines can't . . ."

"Fink!" Martin barked and she rambled over with a sheet of illustration board and a small color sketch.

"We got just one cover in the house to do, Mr. Martin," she said weakly. "You okayed it for Mr. Pachs to do . . ."

"The hell with all that," Martin growled, pulling it from her hand and looking at it closely. "This is for our best book, do you understand that, and we can't have no hack horsing around with rubber stamps. Not on the cover of *Fighting Real War Battle Aces*."

"You need not have the slightest worry, I assure you," the man in the overalls said, gently lifting the sketch from Martin's fingers. "I'm going to show you the versatility of the Mark IX, something that you might find it impossible to believe until you see it in action. A trained operator can cut a Mark IX tape from a sketch or a description. And the results are always dramatic to say the least." He seated himself at a console with typewriter keys that projected from the side of the machine, and while he typed a ribbon of punched tape collected in the basket at one side.

"Your new operator knows the machine code and breaks down any art concept into standard symbols, cut on tape. The tape can be examined or corrected, stored or modified and used over again if need be. There—I've recorded the essence of your sketch. Now I have one more question to ask you—in what style would you like it to be done?"

Martin made a porcine interrogative sound.

"Startled aren't you, sir—well I thought you would be. The Mark IX contains style tapes of all the great masters of the Golden Age. You can have Kubert or Caniff, Giunta or Barry. For figure work you can use Raymond, for your romances, capture the spirit of Drake."

"How's about Pachs?"

"I'm sorry, I'm afraid I don't know of—"

"A joke. Let's get going. Caniff, that's what I want to see."

Pachs felt himself go warm all over, then suddenly cold. Miss Fink looked over and caught his eyes, and looked down, away. He clenched his fists and shifted his feet to leave, but listened instead. He could not leave, not yet.

". . . and the tape is fed into the machine, the illustration board centered on the impression table and the cycle button depressed. So simple, once a tape has been cut, that a child of three could operate it. A press on the button and just stand back. Within this genius of a machine the orders are being analyzed and a picture built up. Inside the memory circuits are bits and pieces of every object that man has ever imagined or seen and drawn for his own edification. These are assembled in the correct manner in the correct proportions and assembled on the collator's screen. When the final picture is complete the all-clear light flashes—there it goes—and we can examine the completed picture on the screen here."

Martin bent over and looked in through the hooded opening.

"Just perfect isn't it? But if for any reason the operator is dissatisfied the image can be changed now in any manner desired by manipulation of the editorial controls. And when satisfied the print button is depressed, the image is printed on a film of reusable plastic sheet, charged electrostatically in order to pick up the powdered ink and then the picture is printed in a single stroke onto the paper below."

A pneumatic groan echoed theatrically from the bowels of the machine as a rectangular box crept down on a shining plunger and pressed against the paper. It hissed and a trickle of vapor oozed out. The machine rose back to position and the man in the coveralls held up the paper, smiling.

"Now isn't that a fine piece of art?"

Martin grunted.

Pachs looked at it and couldn't take his eyes away: he was afraid he was going to be sick. The cover was not only good, it was good Caniff, just as the master might have drawn it himself. Yet the most horrible part was that it was Pachs' own cover, his own layout. Improved. He had never been what might be called a tremendous artist, but he wasn't a bad artist. He did all right in comics, and during the good years he was on top of the pack. But the field kept shrinking and when the machines came in it went bust. There was almost no spot for an artist now. Just a job here and there as sort of layout boy and machine minder. He had taken that—how many years now?—because old and dated as his work was he was still better than any machine that drew heads with a rubber stamp.

Not anymore. He could not even pretend to himself anymore that he was needed, or even useful.

The machine was better.

He realized then that he had been clenching his fists so tightly that his nails had sunk into the flesh of his palms. He opened and rubbed them together and noticed that they were shaking badly. The Mark IX was turned off and they were all gone: he could hear Miss Fink's machine takking away in the outer office. The little girl was telling Martin about the special supplies she would need to buy to operate the machine, and when Pachs closed the connecting door he cut off the grumbling reply about extra expenses not being mentioned.

Pachs warmed his fingers in his armpits until the worst of the tremors stopped. Then he carefully pinned a sheet of paper onto his drawing board and adjusted the light so it would not be in his eyes. With measured strokes he ruled out a standard comic page and separated it into six panels, making the sixth panel a big one, stretching the width of the page. He worked steadily at the penciling, stopping only once to stretch his back and walk over to the window and look out. Then he went back to the board and as the afternoon light faded he finished the inking. Very carefully he washed off his battered but still favorite Windsor & Newton brush and slipped it back into the spring holder.

There was a bustle in the outer office and it sounded like Miss Fink getting ready to leave, or maybe it was the new girl coming back with the supplies. In any case it was late, and he had to go now.

Quickly, before he could change his mind, he ran full tilt at the window, his weight bursting through the glass, and hurtled the twenty-three stories to the street below. Miss Fink heard the breaking glass and screamed, then screamed louder when she came into the room. Martin, complaining about the noise, followed her, but shut up when he saw what had happened. A bit of glass crunched under his shoes when he looked out the window. The doll-like figure of Pachs was visible in the center of the gathering crowd, sprawled from sidewalk to street and bent at an awful angle as it followed the step of the curb.

"Oh God, Mr. Martin, oh God look at this . . ." Miss Fink wailed.

Martin went and stood next to her in front of the drawing board and looked at the page still pinned there. It was neatly done, well drawn and carefully inked.

In the first panel was a self-portrait of Pachs working on a page, bent over this same drawing board. In the second panel he was sitting back and washing out his brush. In the third standing. In the fourth panel the artist stood before the window, nicely rendered in chiaroscuro with backlighting. Five was a forced perspective shot from above, down the vertical face of the building with the figure hurtling through the air towards the pavement below.

In the last panel, in clear and horrible detail, the old man was bent broken and bloody over the wrecked fender of the car that was parked there: the spectators looked on, horrified.

"Look at that will you," Martin said disgustedly, tapping the drawing with his thumb. "When he went out the window he missed the car by a good two yards. Didn't I always tell you he was no good at getting the details right?"

Mute Milton

With ponderous smoothness the big Greyhound bus braked to a stop at the platform, and the door swung open. "Springville," the driver called out. "Last stop!" The passengers stirred in the aisle and climbed down the steps into the glare of the sun. Sam Morrison sat patiently, alone, on the wide rear seat, waiting until the last passengers were at the door before he put the cigar box under his arm, rose and followed them. The glare of sunlight blinded him after the tinted glass dimness of the bus, and the moist air held the breathless heat of Mississippi summer. Sam went carefully down the steps, one at a time, watching his feet, and wasn't aware of the man waiting there until something hard pushed at his stomach.

"What business yuh got in Springville, boy?"

Sam blinked through his steel-rimmed glasses at the big man in the gray uniform who stood before him, prodding him with a short, thick nightstick. He was fat as well as big, and the smooth melon of his stomach bulged out over his belt worn low about his hips.

"Just passing through, sir," Sam Morrison said and took his hat off with his free hand disclosing his cut-short grizzled hair. He let his glance slide across the flushed, reddened face and the gold badge on the shirt before him, then lowered his eyes.

"An' just where yuh going to, boy? Don' keep no secrets from me . . ." the voice rasped again.

"Carteret, sir, my bus leaves in an hour." The only answer was an uncommunicative grunt. The lead-weighted stick tapped on the cigar box under Sam's arm. "What yuh got in there—a gun?"

"No, sir, I wouldn't carry a gun." Sam opened the cigar box and held it out: it contained a lump of metal, a number of small electronic components and a two-inch speaker, all neatly wired and soldered together. "It's a . . . radio, sir."

"Turn it on."

Sam threw a switch and made one or two careful adjustments. The little speaker rattled, and there was the squeak of tinny music barely audible above the rumble of bus motors. The red-faced man laughed.

"Now that's what ah call a real nigger radio . . . piece uh trash." His voice hardened again. "See that you're on that bus, hear?"

"Yes, sir," Sam said to the receding, sweat-stained back of the shirt, then carefully closed the box. He started towards the colored waiting room, but when he passed the window and looked in he saw that it was empty. And there were no dark faces visible anywhere on the street. Without changing pace Sam passed the waiting room and threaded his way between the buses in the cinder parking lot and out of the rear gate. He had lived all of his sixty-seven years in the State of Mississippi; so he knew at once that there was trouble in the air—and the only thing to do about trouble was to stay away from it. The streets became narrower and dirtier, and he trod their familiar sidewalks until he saw a field worker in patched overalls turn into a doorway ahead under the weathered BAR sign. Sam went in after him; he would wait here until a few minutes before the bus was due.

"Bottle of Jax, please." He spread his coins on the damp, scratched bar and picked up the cold bottle. There was no glass. The bartender said nothing. After ringing up the sale he retired to a chair at the far end of the bar with his head next to the murmuring radio and remained there, dark and impenetrable. The only light came from the street outside, and the high-backed booths in the rear looked cool and inviting. There were only a few other customers here, each of them sitting separately with a bottle of beer on the table before him. Sam threaded his way through the close-spaced tables and had already started to slide into the booth near the rear door when he noticed that someone was already there, seated on the other side of the table.

"I'm sorry, I didn't see you," he said and started to get up, but the man waved him back onto the bench and took an airline bag with TWA on it from the table and put it down beside him.

"Plenty of room for both," he said and raised his own bottle of beer. "Here's looking at you." Sam took a sip from his own bottle, but the other man kept drinking until he had drained half of his before he lowered it with a relaxed sigh. "That's what I call foul beer," he said.

"You seem to be enjoying it," Sam told him, but his slight smile took the edge from his words.

"Just because it's cold and wet—but I'd trade a case of it for a bottle of Bud or a Ballantine."

"Then you're from the North, I imagine?" Sam had thought so from the way he talked, sharp and clipped. Now that his eyes were getting used to the dimness, he could see that the other was a young man in his twenties with medium-dark skin, wearing a white shirt with rolled up sleeves. His face was taut and the frown wrinkles on his forehead seemed etched there.

"You are damned right, I'm from the North and I'm going back—" He broke off suddenly and took another swig of beer. When he spoke again his voice was cautious. "Are you from these parts?"

"I was born not far from here, but right now I live in Carteret, just stopping off here between buses."

"Carteret—that's where the college is, isn't it?"

"That is correct. I teach there."

The younger man smiled for the first time. "That sort of puts us in the same boat; I go to NYU, majoring in economics." He put his hand out. "Charles Wright. Everyone but my mother calls me Charlie."

"Very pleased to meet you," Sam said in his slow, old-fashioned way. "I am Sam Morrison, and it is Sam on my birth certificate too."

"I'm interested in your college; I meant to step in there but—" He stopped talking at the sound of a car's engine in the street outside and leaned forward so that he could see out the front door, remaining there until the car ground into gear and moved away. When he dropped back onto the seat, Sam could see that there were fine beads of sweat in the lines of his forehead. He took a quick drink from his bottle.

"When you were at the bus station, you didn't happen to see a big cop with a big gut, red faced all the time?"

"Yes, I met him; he talked to me when I got off the bus."

"The bastard!"

"Don't get worked up, Charles; he is just a policeman doing his job."

"Just a ———!" The young man spat a short, filthy word. "That's Brinkley; you must have heard of him, toughest man south of Bombingham. He's going to be elected sheriff next fall, and he's already grand knight of the Klan, a real pillar of the community."

"Talking like that's not going to do you any good," Sam said mildly.

"That's what Uncle Tom said—and as I remember he was still a slave when he died. Someone has got to speak up; you can't remain quiet forever."

"You talk like one of those Freedom Riders." Sam tried to look stern, but he was never very good at it.

"Well, I am, if you want to know the truth of it, but the ride ends right here. I'm going home. I'm scared and I'm not afraid to admit it. You people live in a jungle down here; I never realized how bad it could be until I came down. I've been working on the voters committee, and Brinkley got word of it and swore he was going to kill me or put me in jail for life. And you know what—I believe it. I'm leaving today, just waiting for the car to pick me up. I'm going back north where I belong."

"I understand you have your problems up there too . . ."

"Problems!" Charlie finished his beer and stood up. "I wouldn't even call them problems after what I've seen down here. It's no paradise in New York—but you stand a chance of living a bit longer.

Where I grew up in South Jamaica we had it rough, but we had our own house in a good neighborhood and—you take another beer?"

"No, one is enough for me thank you."

Charlie came back with a fresh beer and picked up where he had left off. "Maybe we're second-class citizens in the North—but at least we're citizens of some kind and can get some measure of happiness and fulfillment. Down here a man is a beast of burden, and that's all he is ever going to be—if he has the wrong color skin."

"I wouldn't say that; things get better all the time. My father was a field man, a son of a slave—and I'm a college teacher. That's progress of a sort."

"What sort?" Charlie pounded the table yet kept his voice in an angry whisper. "So one hundredth of one percent of the Negroes get a little education and pass it on at some backwater college. Look, I'm not running you down; I know you do your best. But for every man like you there must be a thousand who are born and live and die in filthy poverty, year after year, without hope. Millions of people. Is that progress? And even yourself—are you sure you wouldn't be doing better if you were teaching in a decent university?"

"Not me," Sam laughed. "I'm just an ordinary teacher and I have enough trouble getting geometry and algebra across to my students without trying to explain topology or Boolean algebra or anything like that."

"What on earth is that Bool . . . thing? I never heard of it."

"It's, well, an uninterpreted logical calculus, a special discipline. I warned you; I'm not very good at explaining these things though I can work them out well enough on paper. That is my hobby, really, what some people call higher mathematics, and I know that if I were working at a big school I would have no time to devote to it."

"How do you know? Maybe they would have one of those big computers—wouldn't that help you?"

"Perhaps, of course, but I've worked out ways of getting around the need for one. It just takes a little more time, that's all."

"And how much time do you have left?" Charlie asked quietly, then was instantly sorry he had said it when he saw the older man lower his head without answering. "I take that back. I've got a big mouth. I'm sorry, but I get so angry. How do you know what you might have done if you had the training, the facilities . . ." He shut up, realizing he was getting in deeper every second.

There was only the murmur of distant traffic in the hot, dark silence, the faint sound of music from the radio behind the bar. The bartender stood, switched the radio off and opened the trap behind the bar to bring up another case of beer. From nearby the sound of the music continued like a remembered echo. Charlie realized that it was coming from the cigar box on the table before them.

"Do you have a radio in that?" he asked, happy to change the subject.

"Yes—well, really no, though there is an RF stage."

"If you think you're making sense—you're not. I told you, I'm majoring in economics."

Sam smiled and opened the box, pointing to the precisely wired circuits inside. "My nephew made this; he has a little I-fix-it shop, but he learned a lot about electronics in the Air Force. I brought him the equations, and we worked out the circuit together."

Charlie thought about a man with electronic training who was forced to run a handyman's shop, but he had the sense not to mention it. "Just what is it supposed to do?"

"It's not really supposed to do anything. I just built it to see if my equations would work out in practice. I suppose you don't know much about Einstein's unified field theory . . . ?" Charlie smiled ruefully and raised his hands in surrender. "It's difficult to talk about. Putting it the simplest way, there is supposed to be a relation between all phenomena, all forms of energy and matter. You are acquainted with the simpler interchanges, heat energy to mechanical energy as in an engine, electrical energy to light—"

"The light bulb!"

"Correct. To go further, the postulation has been made that time is related to light energy, as is gravity to light, as has been proven, and gravity to electrical energy. That is the field I have been exploring. I have made certain suppositions that there is an interchange of energy within a gravitic field, a measurable interchange, such as the lines of force that are revealed about a magnetic field by iron particles—no, that's not a good simile—perhaps the ability of a wire to carry a current endlessly under the chilled condition of superconductivity—"

"Professor, you have lost me—I'm not ashamed to admit it. Could you maybe give me an example—like what is happening in this little radio here?"

Sam made a careful adjustment, and the music gained the tiniest amount of volume.

"It's not the radio part that is interesting—that stage really just demonstrates that I have detected the leakage. No, we should call it the differential between the earth's gravitic field and that of the lump of lead there in the corner of the box."

"Where is the battery?"

Sam smiled proudly. "That is the point—there is no battery. The input current is derived—"

"Do you mean you are running the radio off gravity? Getting electricity for nothing?"

"Yes . . . really, I should say no. It is not like that . . ."

"It sure looks like that!" Charlie was excited now, crouching half across the table so he could look into the cigar box. "I may not know anything about electronics, but in economics we learn a lot about power sources. Couldn't this gadget of yours be developed to generate electricity at little or no cost?"

"No, not at once. This is just a first attempt . . ."

"But it could eventually and that means—"

Sam thought that the young man had suddenly become sick. His face, just inches away, became shades lighter as the blood drained from it. His eyes were staring in horror as he slowly dropped back and down into his seat. Before Sam could ask him what was the matter a grating voice bellowed through the room.

"Anyone here seen a boy by name of Charlie Wright? C'mon now, speak up. Ain't no one gonna get hurt for tellin' me the truth."

"Holy Jesus . . ." Charlie whispered, sinking deeper in the seat. Brinkley stamped into the bar, hand resting on his gun butt, squinting around in the darkness. No one answered him.

"Anybody try to hide him gonna be in trouble!" he shouted angrily. "I'm gonna find that black granny dodger!"

He started towards the rear of the room, and Charlie, with his airline bag in one hand, vaulted the back of the booth and crashed against the rear door.

"Come back here, you son of a bitch!"

The table rocked when Charlie's flying heel caught it, and the cigar box slid to the floor. Heavy boots thundered. The door squealed open and Charlie pushed out through it. Sam bent over to retrieve the box.

"I'll kill yuh, so help me!"

The circuit hadn't been damaged. Sam sighed in relief and stood, the tinny music between his fingers.

He may have heard the first shot, but he could not have heard the second because the .38 slug caught him in the back of the head and killed him instantly. He crumpled to the floor.

Patrolman Marger ran in from the patrol car outside, his gun ready, and saw Brinkley come back into the room through the door in the rear.

"He got away, damn it, got clear away."

"What happened here?" Marger asked, slipping his gun back into the holster and looking down at the slight, crumpled body at his feet.

"I dunno. He must have jumped up in the way when I let fly at the other one what was running away. Must be another one of them Commonists anyway; he was sittin' at the same table."

"There's gonna be trouble about this . . ."

"Why trouble?" Brinkley asked indignantly. "It's just anutha ol' dead nigger . . ."

One of his boots was on the cigar box, and it crumpled and fractured when he turned away.

An Artist's Life

A busman's holiday. A real busman's holiday. I stay on the moon for a year, I paint pictures there for three hundred and sixty-five days—then the first thing I do back on Earth is go to the Metropolitan Museum of Art to look at more paintings. Brent smiled to himself. It had better be worthwhile.

He looked up the immense stretch of granite steps. They shimmered slightly in the intense August sun. He took a deep breath and shifted the cane to his right hand. Slowly he dragged himself up the steps . . . they seemed to stretch away into the ovenlike infinity.

He was almost there . . . a few more steps would do it. The cane caught between two of the steps, shifting his balance, and he was suddenly falling.

The woman standing in the shade at the top of the steps screamed. She had watched since he first climbed out of the cab. Brent Dalgreen, the *famous* painter, everyone recognized the tanned young face under bristly hair burned silver white by the raw radiation of space. The papers had told how his stay on the moon had weakened his muscles from low gravity. He had climbed painfully up the steps and now he was rolling hopelessly down them. She screamed again and again.

They carried him into the first-aid room. "Gravity weakness," he told the nurse. "I'll be all right."

She tested him for broken bones and frowned when her hand touched his skin. She took his temperature, her eyes widened and she glanced at him with a frightened look.

"I know," he said. "It's much higher than normal. Don't let it worry you though, the fever isn't due to the fall; in fact, it's probably the other way around."

"I'll have to enter it in my report, just in case there's any trouble."

"I wish you wouldn't. I don't want the fact to leak out that I'm not as well as I should be. If you'll call Dr. Grayber in the Medical Arts Building you'll find that this condition is not new. The museum will have no worry about their responsibility as to my health."

It would make wonderful copy for the scandal sheets: MOON PAINTER DYING . . . GIVES LIFE FOR ART. It wasn't at all like that. He had known there was danger from radiation sickness; in the beginning he had been very careful to be out in his spacesuit only the prescribed length of time. That was before he ran into the trouble.

There had been a feeling about the moon that he just couldn't

AN ARTIST'S LIFE 521

capture. He had almost succeeded in one painting—then lost it again forever. It was the feeling of the haunted empty places, the stark extremes of the plains and boulders. It was an alien sensation that had killed him before he could imprison it in oil.

The critics had thought his paintings were unique, wonderful, just what they had always thought the moon would be like. That was exactly his trouble. The airless satellite wasn't at all like that. It was *different*—so different that he could never capture the difference. Now he was going to die, a failure in the only thing he had really wanted to do.

The radiation fever was in him, eating away at his blood and bones. In a few months it would destroy him. He had been too reckless those last months, fighting against time. He had tried and failed . . . it was as simple as that.

The nurse put the phone down, frowning.

"I've checked and what you say is true, Mr. Dalgreen. I won't put it in my report if that's what you want." She helped him up.

The moon was out of his thoughts later as one canvas after another swam into his vision. He bathed his senses in the collected art of the ages. This was his life, and he was enjoying it to the utmost, trying to make up for his year's absence from the world. The Greek marbles soothed his mind and the Rembrandt portraits wakened his interest once again. He marveled at the fact that after all the years he could still wander through these halls and have his interest recaptured. But he also wanted to see what the moderns were doing. The elevator took him to the Contemporary Wing.

Almost at once, his quiet enjoyment was broken by *the* painting. It was an autumn landscape, a representative example of the Classic-modern school that had been so popular for the last few years. However, it had something else: an undefinable strangeness about it.

His legs were beginning to tremble again; he knew that he had better rest for a few minutes.

Brent sat on the wide lounge on the main staircase, cracking his knuckles, his mind whirling in circles as he rapidly introspected himself into a headache. There was no one thing in that painting that he could put his mental finger on, but it had upset him. It was disturbing him emotionally; something about the picture didn't quite ring true. He knew there was a logical evaluation of a painting, just as there was a logical evaluation of any material object, but that wasn't the trouble, he was sure.

Equally, there was an emotional evaluation—more of a sensation or feeling; and this was where the trouble lay. Everyone has felt plea-sure or interest at one time or another when looking at any form of visual art. A magazine photo, drawing or even a well-designed building could generate an emotional pattern. Brent was attempting to analyze such a sensation now, a next-to-impossible job. The only coherent thought he could muster on the subject was: "There is something subtly *wrong* with that picture."

Suddenly he had the answer. It came in a second, as if revealed by some hidden source of insight. Perhaps his recent stay on the moon helped the idea to form; it had a relationship to things he had experienced there. It brought to mind the cinder plains that had never felt the foot of man. The sensation could be expressed by one word— "alienness."

In the eternal lifelessness of the silent lunar wastes this sensation had a place. But how did it get into the polite autumn landscape? What twist in the mind of the painter enabled him to capture this strange feeling on canvas? Brent cursed himself softly. This wasn't a painting of an alien landscape. It was an autumn-in-the-woods landscape painted by a man who didn't understand his topic. A man with an odd way of looking at things. A painter who could look at the bustling life of a fall day and capture the eternal death of a lifeless satellite.

Brent leaned forward on his cane, his heart beating in tempo with his swirling thoughts. He had to find this artist. He would talk to him, reason with him—beat him if necessary . . . he *must* find out the man's secret. The thought of his coming death sat like a cold black weight in his body. To die without knowing how to capture that sensation on canvas!

He had killed himself searching for it—to no avail. Yet all the time here on Earth was the man who had the knowledge he sought. The bitter irony of it swirled his head with madness.

The insane thoughts seeped away slowly. He sat on the couch until he was rested enough to trust himself on his feet. He had to find the man.

Down in the right-hand corner of the picture in the shadow of a rock was the signature, "Arthur Di Costa," printed with wide, sweeping strokes. Brent had never heard the name before but this fact was not unusual in itself. Real artists were a retiring crew. They labored in backrooms and old garages, filling canvas after canvas for their own satisfaction. Their work might never be shown until long after they were dead—dead.

That word kept intruding in his thoughts. He turned angrily and walked towards the guard who leaned casually on a sworl of abstractionist sculpture.

"Shore, mister," the guard answered. "You'll find the curator in his office—the door there behind them old hangings."

"Thanks," Brent muttered, and followed the course indicated by a meaty finger. He found an alcove partially concealed by the luxurious draperies. It contained a photoelectric water fountain and a neomarble door bearing the legend G. ANDREW KINNENT—CURATOR, CONTEMPORARY WING. He pushed open the door and stepped into the receptionist's office. She looked up from her typewriter.

"My name is Brent Dalgreen; I would like to see Mr. Kinnent."

"Not *the* Mr. Dalgreen! Why I—" The girl broke off, flustered. She leaned hard on the intercom button.

"Go right in, Mr. Dalgreen. Mr. Kinnent will be very happy to see you." But the lovely smile that accompanied the statement was wasted on him; his thoughts were elsewhere, today.

After thirty minutes of shop talk Brent drew the conversation around to the present exhibit—and one painter in particular.

"Mr. Di Costa is one of our most brilliant young painters, yes, indeed," the curator said smugly as if he had personally taught Di Costa every painting trick he knew. "He has only lived in New York a short while, but the boy has made quite a name for himself already. Here, let me give you his address, I'm sure you would enjoy meeting him. Common interests, you know."

Brent was easily talked into accepting the information he had come for in the first place. He kept his real thoughts secret from the vociferous Kinnent. They would seem more than foolish—unsupported as they were by a single shred of real evidence. He couldn't let this deter him. The sands of his life were trickling out, but there was something he had to do first.

The building was one of a hundred identical greenstone structures that had lined the streets in the fashionable Thirties. The site of the former garment center was now one of the most favored residential districts in the city. Brent stood across the street from number 31, ostensibly studying the headlines on the newsvend machine. The windowless exterior gave the obvious fact that the owner was fairly well off financially. Any information he sought would be inside—not outside. He crossed the street and stepped into the chrome entranceway.

The inductance of his body actuated the automatic butler and the soft mechanical voice spoke from over the door.

"The Di Costa residence. May I serve you?"

"Mr. Brent Dalgreen to see Mr. Di Costa."

"I'm sorry, but I have no information regarding you, sir; if you care to leave a mess—" The robot tones stopped with a sharp click, to be replaced by a man's voice.

"I am very happy to greet you, Mr. Dalgreen. Won't you please step in?"

The door swung quietly open to reveal a small wood-paneled ves-

tibule. It wasn't until the door closed again that Brent recognized it
as an elevator. There was a feeling of motion and the end wall slid
back to reveal a book-lined sitting room. The occupant turned from
his desk and stepped forward.

Brent took the proffered hand—at the same time trying to penetrate the man's smile. Di Costa was taller than Brent with a thinness
that seemed to contradict his graceful movements. They shook
hands, and his hand had the same qualities: thin, long and strong. At
this point Brent realized he was staring; he hastened to respond to
his host's hospitality.

"I hope you will excuse my just dropping in like this, Mr. Di Costa.
I have seen some work of yours at the Metropolitan, and found it,
well, very interesting."

Brent stopped, aware of how weak his reasons seemed when
brought out in conversation. He was more than pleased when Di
Costa interrupted him.

"I understand perfectly, Mr. Dalgreen. I have had the same experience many times when looking at your paintings and those of *some*
of our fellow artists." He smiled. "Not all of them, I assure you. I
have looked at these works and said to myself, I would like to meet
the man who did that. This very rarely happens, a fact which I de-
plore. That you feel the same way towards my work is both flattering
and most enjoyable."

Di Costa's friendliness broke the ice; they were soon on the best
of terms. Brent sat in the comfortable leather chair while Di Costa
mixed drinks at the built-in bar. This gave him a chance to look
around the room. A brown study, it fitted the word. The decorations
were all subdued to the room as a whole, the sort of things a man
would buy for himself. The only clashing note was the rotary book
rack in the corner.

He suddenly realized that it was revolving slowly, had been doing
so since he first entered the room. Something else . . . yes, there on
the desk, the bronze ashtray was also revolving with the same steady
motion. They created an unusual effect, yet an oddly pleasing one. It
fitted the room and the owner's personality.

"And here are the drinks. A toast first—always a good idea. Long
life and good painting, to both of us."

Brent frowned to himself as he sipped the drink.

There is a fascination about shop talk that carpenters and bank
executives indulge in with equal pleasure. Brent found himself easily
drawn into conversation on the merits of alizarin crimson and the
influence of Byzantine art on Renaissance Italy. Yet all the time he
talked a small portion of his mind was weighing the other's words,

testing and observing. But his host was everything he seemed to be—a gentleman of private means with an active interest in painting.

A half hour had passed, entertaining but unenlightening, when a light rap sounded on the study door. It opened to reveal an attractive woman, tastefully dressed in a gray-and-silver robe of classic Greek design, the latest fashion.

She hesitated in the doorway. "I don't mean to disturb you, Arthur, but there is—oh, excuse me, I had no idea you had a guest."

Di Costa took her gently by the arm. "I'm very glad you did, my dear. Let me introduce the famous Brent Dalgreen." He passed his arm around her waist. "My wife, Marie."

Brent took her hand and smiled into her large brown eyes. She returned his greeting warmly—with exactly the right amount of pressure on his hand. A loving wife, a pleasant home—Arthur Di Costa was a model of the modern gentleman. The painting in the museum seemed unimportant in the face of all this normality.

For a fraction of an instant as he held her hand, his eyes were drawn to a portrait that hung next to the door.

It was only by the strongest effort of will that he prevented himself from crushing her hand. Marie was there in the portrait, her portrait . . .

The same subtle transformation as the painting in the museum. Something about a twist of the mouth—the haunting look in her eyes as she stared out of the picture. He tore his gaze from the painting but not before Di Costa had noticed his attention.

"It must be a strange sensation," Di Costa laughed, "to meet both my beautiful Marie and her portrait at the same instant. But here, let me show you." He touched the frame and a soft light bathed the painting. Brent mumbled something polite and stepped nearer, as if mere proximity would answer his questions.

Di Costa seemed flattered by his famous guest's interest. They discussed the many problems of a painting and their happy or unhappy solution. Blushing slightly, Marie was coaxed into standing under her portrait. She pretended not to notice the dissecting artistic analysis that could be so embarrassing to the outsider: "That blue hollow in the neck helps the form" . . . "the effect of the gold hair on the cheekbones." She turned her head "just so," and "a little more" while they talked.

Yet all during the discussion a small part of Brent's mind was weighing and analyzing. The *how* of the paintings was becoming clearer although the *why* still escaped him. It wasn't that there was an alienness in the figure itself, it was more as if the person were looking at something totally strange to worldly eyes.

He felt the small throb of an incipient headache as his frustrated thoughts danced dizzily inward on themselves in ever tightening circles. The mellow sound of a chime from the wall cabinet provided a welcome interruption. Di Costa excused himself and stepped out of the room—leaving Brent alone with Marie. They had just seated themselves when Di Costa returned, looking as if he had received painful news.

"I must ask you to excuse me, but my lawyer wishes to see me at once—a small but important matter about my estate. I am most unhappy to leave now. We must continue our talk another time. Please do not leave on my account, Mr. Dalgreen—my house is at your service."

When her husband left, Brent and Marie Di Costa talked idly on irrelevant topics; they *had* to, since he had no idea of what might be relevant. You couldn't walk up to a girl whom you'd met for the first time and ask, "Madam, does your husband paint monsters? Or perhaps you dabble in witchcraft! Is that the secret?"

A quick glance at his watch convinced him it was time to go, before he wore out his welcome.

Turning to light a cigarette his eyes fell on the mantle clock. He registered surprise.

"Why, it's three-thirty already! I'm afraid I'll have to be leaving."

She rose, smiling. "You have been a most delightful guest," she laughed. "I know I speak for Arthur as well as myself when I say I hope to see you again."

"I may take you up on that," Brent said.

Their forward progress was suddenly impeded as the elevator swung open to discharge a small bundle of screaming humanity. Dazed, Brent realized it was a young girl as she swept past. The child collapsed on Marie Di Costa's shoulder, her golden hair shaking with muffled sobs. A plastic doll with a shattered head gave mute evidence of the source of the disturbance.

Brent stood by self-consciously until the crying was soothed. Marie flashed him an understanding smile while she convinced the child at least to say hello to the visitor. He was rewarded with the sight of the red, tear-stained face.

"Dotty, I want you to meet Mr. Dalgreen."

"How do you do, Mr. Dalgreen . . . but Mommy the boy stepped on the doll and he laughed when it broke and . . ."

The thought was once again too much to bear—the tears began to course again through the well-used waterways.

"Cheer up, Dotty. You wouldn't want your father to see you like this," Brent suggested.

These seemingly innocent words, while having no effect on the little girl, had a marked effect on her mother. Her face whitened.

"Arthur is not Dotty's father, Mr. Dalgreen. You see, this is my second marriage. He . . . I mean we cannot have children." She spoke the words as if they were a pain, heavy within her.

Brent was slightly embarrassed—yet elated at the same time. This was the first crack in the facade of normality that concealed the occupants of the house. Her sudden change of expression could only mean that there was something troubling her—something he would give his last tube of oil paint to find out. Perhaps it wasn't the secret hidden in the painting, but there must be a relationship somewhere. He was determined to search it out.

Apartment lights were out all over the city, the daytime world was asleep. Brent stirred in the large chair and reached out for the glass of sparkling Burgundy that was slowly dying on the end table. A little flat—but still very good. It was one of the luxuries he allowed himself. A luxury that might really be called a necessity to one who lived by selling his emotional responses, translated into color.

The wine was going flat, but the view of the city never would. New York, the eternal wonder city. The soft lights of his studio threw no reflections on the window, and his sight traveled easily over the architectural fairyland. Sparkling search-beams swept across the sky, throwing an occasional glint as they slid across a jetcar or a stratoplane. A thousand lights of a thousand hues twinkled in the city below. Even here on the one-hundred-eightieth floor he could hear the throbbing roar of its ceaseless activity. This was the foremost of the cities of man, yet somewhere in that city was a man was not quite human.

Brent had the partial answer, he was sure of that. He had found the missing factor in one of his own paintings. It was the only one he was even slightly pleased with. He had turned it out in nine solid hours of work, one of the "dangerous exposures" the doctors talked about. He had it propped on the video console, a stark vista of Mare Imbrium in the afternoon—moon time. It was a canvas touched with the raw grandeur of eternal space. It had a burning quality that reacted on human sight. An alien landscape seen through a human eye. Just as the Di Costa canvases were human scenes seen through a different eye. Perhaps not totally foreign to Earth—they weren't that obvious. Now that he understood, though, the influence was unmistakable.

He also had substantiating evidence. The Law was the Law and genes would always be genes. Man and ape are warm-blooded mammals, close relatives among the anthropoids. Yet even with this close heritage, there could be no interbreeding. Offspring were out of the question; they were a genetic impossibility,

It followed that alienness meant just that. A man who wasn't Man—Homo sapiens—could never have children with a human wife. Marie Di Costa was human, and had a real tear-soaked human daughter to prove it. Arthur Di Costa had no children.

Brent pressed the window release and it sank into the casement with a soft sigh. The city noises washed in along with the fresh smell of growing things. The light breeze carried the fragrance in from the Jersey woodlands. It seemed a little out of place here above the gleaming city.

Leaning out slightly, he could see the moon riding through the thin clouds and—the morning star, Venus, just clearing the eastern horizon. He had been there on the moon. He had watched them assembling the Venus rocket. Man, the erect biped, was the only sentient life form he had ever seen. If there were others, they were still out there among the stars. All, that is, except one—or could there possibly be others here on Earth?

This was useless thinking though. Don't invent more monsters until you've caught your first. A night's sleep first. After that, he could start setting his traps out tomorrow.

For the tenth time, Brent threw a half-eaten candy bar into the receptacle and started down the street. Being a private eye was so easy in the teleshows—but how different the reality was! He had been shadowing Arthur Di Costa for three days now, and it was ruining his digestion. Whenever his quarry stopped, he stopped—often on the crowded city streets. Loitering was too obvious, so he found himself constantly involved with the vending machines that lined the streets. The news sheets were easily thrown away, but he felt obliged at least to sample the candy bars.

Di Costa was just stepping onto the Fifth Avenue walkway. Brent got on a few hundred feet behind him. They rolled slowly uptown at the standard fifteen miles per hour. As the walkway crossed Fifty-seventh Street, a small man in a black-and-gold business suit stepped briskly onto it. Brent noticed him only when he stopped next to Di Costa and tapped him on the shoulder. Di Costa turned with a smile which changed slowly into a puzzled expression.

The little man handed what appeared to be a folded piece of paper to the surprised painter. Before Di Costa could say anything, the man stepped off the walkway onto a safety platform. With a quick movement, surprising in a man of his chunky build, he vaulted the guard barrier and stepped onto the downtown walkway.

Brent could only stare open-mouthed as the black figure swept by him and was lost in the crowds. Surprised by the entire action, he turned back to find Di Costa staring directly into his eyes!

Whatever course of action he might have considered was lost. Di Costa took the initiative. He smiled and waved. Brent could hear his voice faintly through the street noises.

"Mr. Dalgreen, over here!"

Brent waved back and did the only thing possible. As he walked slowly forward he saw that Di Costa's curiosity had gotten the better of him. Brent watched him open the note, read it—and change suddenly. The man's arm dropped to his side, his body stiffened. Staring straight ahead, he stood on the walkway, eyes fixed and as full as a Roman portrait bust.

Dalgreen hurried toward the man. Events were going too fast. He had more than a suspicion that the note and the short man were somehow connected with the secret of the paintings. He stepped forward.

The man stared ahead, unseeing and unhearing. Brent felt justified in removing the mysterious note from between his fingers. One side was blank, but the other contained a single illegible character—a queer sign made up of flowing curves crossed by choppy green lines. It resembled nothing Brent had ever seen in his entire life.

They rode uptown side by side. Brent leaned on the railing while Di Costa remained fixed in his strange trance. The note in Brent's hand was tangible evidence that his suspicions had some basis in fact. As he examined it again, he was aware of an undefinable tingling in his hand. The note seemed to be vibrating shaking free from his hand in some unknown way. Under his startled gaze it glowed suddenly—and disappeared! One instant he had held it, the next his hand was empty.

He leaped back in surprise—passing through the space formerly occupied by Di Costa. Gone—while he had been studying the note! Leaning over the rail he had a quick glimpse of the stiff figure entering the Central Park Skyport. Cursing himself for his stupidity, Brent changed lanes and raced back to the Skyport entrance.

His luck still held. Di Costa was on the outgoing aircab line. It would take him at least ten minutes to get a cab this time of day. With a little speed and a few greased palms Brent could rent a Fly-Your-Own before the other man was airborne.

Shortly after, the orange-and-black cab flashed up from the takeoff circle followed closely by Brent's blue helio. The two aircraft flew north and vanished in the distance over the Hudson.

The aircab stayed at the ten-thousand-foot level. Brent cruised at eight thousand, lagging slightly behind, keeping in the blind spot of the other ship. The entire affair was moving too fast for his peace of mind. He had the feeling that he was no longer a free agent, that he was being pushed into things before he decided for himself.

He suddenly felt elated. The strange symbol on the note, the note that disappeared in such an inexplicable fashion, proved the existence of alien hidden forces. Every mile that rushed under his plane brought him closer to the answer. He didn't fear death—it was no longer a stranger to him. The moments of time left to him might be made more satisfactory if he ferreted out this secret. He smiled to himself.

Fifteen minutes later the two ships grounded at the Municipal Skyport in Poughkeepsie. Brent parked the ship and followed his quarry down to the street level. Except for a certain stiffness in his movements, Di Costa seemed normal. He walked quickly and turned into an office building before Brent could catch up with him.

Throwing discretion aside; Brent broke into a run. He turned into the lobby just as the elevator door closed. He pressed the call button but the car continued to rise. The indicator stopped at 4, then slowly sank down again.

He was too close to the end to even consider stopping now. He stepped into the self-service elevator and pressed 4. The door closed and the car began to . . . descend!

With the realization that he was trapped came the knowledge that there was very little he could do about it. Just wait and see who—or what—might be outside the car when the door opened!

The elevator dropped down to a level that must have been far beneath the basement floor. The door slid slowly back.

The room was *not* what he had expected. Not that he had any idea of what there would be; it was just—just that this room was so ordinary!

Ordinary—except for the side wall. That was an impossibility. It was a glass wall looking into a vast tank of swirling water—only there was no glass! It was the surface of the ocean standing on its side. He felt himself drawn into it, falling into it.

The sensation vanished as the wall suddenly turned jet black. He became aware for the first time that he wasn't alone in the room. There was a girl behind a chrome desk. A lovely girl with straight bronze hair and green eyes.

"An untrained person shouldn't watch that machine, Mr. Dalgreen; it has a negative effect on the mind. Won't you please step in?"

His jaw dropped. "How do you know my name? Who are you? What is this pl—"

"If you'll be seated, I'll be with you in a moment."

Brent saw that the elevator would stay here until he got out. He stepped into the room, and the door sliding shut behind him didn't help his morale any. He was into it up to his neck, and the other team had taken complete charge. He sat.

The redhead pulled the sheet of paper out of her typewriter and pushed it into the strange wall. It once more had the undersea look. Brent kept his eyes averted until she turned to him with a slight frown furrowing her forehead.

"You have been very interested in Arthur Di Costa's activities, Mr. Dalgreen. Perhaps there are some questions you would like to ask me?"

"That, lady, is the world's best understatement! Just *what* happened to him today? . . . And what is this place?"

She leaned forward and pointed. "You're responsible for Mr. Di Costa's visit here today. You were observed following him, so we brought him in, in the hope that you would come also. The message he received was a code word designed to trigger an automatic response planted in his mind. He came directly here, controlled by the posthypnotic suggestion."

"But the note!" he exclaimed.

"A simple matter! It was written on a material made entirely of separate molecules. A small charge of energy held them together for a brief period of time. The charge leaked out and the material merely separated into its constituent molecules."

The utter impossibility of the situation was striking home. The evidences of a superior culture were unmistakable. These people were his . . .

"Aliens, Mr. Dalgreen—I suppose you could call us that. Yes, I can read your mind quite clearly. That is why you are here today. A thought receiver in Arthur Di Costa's study informed us of your suspicions when you first walked in. We have been following you ever since, arranging your visit here.

"I'll tell you what I can, Mr. Dalgreen. We are not of Earth; in fact, we come from beyond your solar system. This office is, to be very frank, the outpatient ward of a sanitarium."

"Sanitarium!" Brent shouted. "This is the office only . . . then where is the sanitarium?"

The girl twirled her pencil slowly, her piercing stare seeming to penetrate his eyes—into his brain.

"The entire Earth is our sanitarium. Mixed in with your population are a great number of our mentally ill."

The floor seemed to tilt under Brent's feet. He clutched the edge of the desk. "Then Di Costa must be one of your outpatients. Is he insane?"

The girl spoke quietly. "Not insane in the strictest sense of the word. He is congenitally feeble-minded; his case is incurable."

Brent thought of the brilliant Di Costa as a moron, and the inference shook his mind. "That means that the average IQ of your race must be—"

"Beyond your powers of comprehension," she said. "To your people Di Costa is normal, really far above average.

"On his home planet he was not bright enough to take his place in that highly integrated society. He became a ward of the state. His body was altered to be an exact duplicate of Homo sapiens. We gave him a new body and a new personality—but we could not change his basic intelligence. That is why he is here on Earth, a square peg in a square hole.

"Di Costa spent his childhood on his home planet, living in an 'alien' environment. These first impressions drive deep into the subconscious, you know. His new personality has no awareness of them—but they are there, nonetheless. When he is painting, these same impressions bypass his conscious mind and operate directly on his thalamus. It takes a keen eye to detect their effect on the final work. May I congratulate you, Mr. Dalgreen?"

Brent smiled ruefully. "I'm a little sorry now that I did. What are you plans for me? I imagine they don't include a return to my earthly 'asylum'?"

The girl folded her hands in her lap. She looked down at them as if not wanting to look Brent in the eye when she made her next statement. However, he wasn't waiting for it. If he could overpower the girl, he might find the elevator control. Any chance was worth taking. He tensed his muscles and jumped.

A wave of pain swept through his body. Another mind—strong beyond comparison—was controlling his body!

Every muscle jerked with spasmodic activity, halting his plunge in midair. Crashing to the desk he lay unmoving; every muscle ached with the fierce alien control. The redhead looked up—eyes blazing with the strength she had so suddenly revealed.

"Never underestimate your opponent, Brent Dalgreen. I adopted the earthly form of a woman for just this reason. I find your people much easier to handle. They never suspect that I am . . . more than what they see. I will release your mind from my control, but please don't force me to resume it."

Brent sank to the floor, his heart pumping wildly, his body vibrating from the unnatural spasm.

"I am the director of this . . . sanitarium, so you see I have no desire to have our work exposed to the prying eyes of your government. I shall have to have you disposed of."

Brent controlled his breathing enough to allow him to speak. "You . . . intend to . . . kill me then?"

"Not at all Mr. Dalgreen; our philosophy forbids killing except for the most humane reasons. Your physical body will be changed to conform to the environment of another of our sanitarium planets. We will of course remove all the radiation damage. You can look forward to a long and interesting life. If you agree to cooperate you will be allowed to keep your present personality."

"What kind of a planet is it?" Brent asked hurriedly. He realized from the girl's tones that the interview was almost at an end.

"Quite different from this one. It is a very dense planet with a chlorine atmosphere." She pressed a stud on her desk and turned back to her typewriter.

Brent had a last, ragged thought as unconsciousness overcame him. He was going to *live* . . . and work . . . and there must be some fine greens to paint on a chlorine planet . . .

The Ever-Branching Tree

The children had spread up and down the beach, and some of them had even ventured into the surf where the tall green waves crashed down upon them. Glaring from a deep blue sky, the sun burned on the yellow sand. A wave broke into foam, surging far up the shore with a soundless rush. The sharp clap-clap of Teacher's hands could easily be heard in the sunlit silence.

"Playtime is over—put your clothes back on, Grosbit-9, all of them—and the class is about to begin."

They straggled towards Teacher, as slowly as they could. The bathers emerged dry from the ocean, while not a grain of sand adhered to skin or garment of the others. They gathered about Teacher, their chatter gradually dying away, and he pointed dramatically at a tiny creature writhing across the sand.

"Uhggh a worm!" Mandi-2 said and shivered deliciously, shaking her red curls.

"A worm, correct. A first worm, an early worm, a protoworm. An important worm. Although it is not on the direct evolutionary track that we are studying we must pause to give it notice. A little more attention, Ched-3, your eyes are closing. For here, for the first time, we see segmentation, as important a step in the development of life as was the development of multicellular forms. See, look carefully, at those series of rings about the creature's body. It looks as though it were made of little rings of tissue fused together—and it is."

They bent close, a circle of lowered heads above the brown worm that writhed a track across the sand. It moved slowly towards Grosbit-9 who raised his foot and stamped down hard on the creature. The other students tittered. The worm crawled out through the side of his shoe and kept on.

"Grosbit-9, you have the wrong attitude," Teacher said sternly. "Much energy is being expended to send this class back through time, to view the wonders of evolution at work. We cannot feel or touch or hear or change the past, but we can move through it and see it about us. So we stand in awe of the power that permits us to do this, to visit our Earth as it was millions of years ago, to view the ocean from which all life sprung, to see one of the first life forms on the ever-branching tree of evolution. And what is your response to this awe-inspiring experience? You *stamp* on the annelid! For shame, Grosbit-9 for shame."

Far from feeling shameful, Grosbit-9 chewed a hangnail on his thumb and looked about out of the corners of his eyes, the trace of a smirk upon his lips. Teacher wondered, not for the first time, how a 9 had gotten into this class. A father with important contacts, no doubt, high placed friends.

"Perhaps I had better recap for those of you who are paying less than full attention." He stared hard at Grosbit-9 as he said this, with no apparent effect. "Evolution is how we reached the high estate we now inhabit. Evolution is the forward march of life, from the one-celled creatures to multicelled, thinking man. What will come after us we do not know, what came before us we are now seeing. Yesterday we watched the lightning strike the primordial chemical soup of the seas and saw the more complex chemicals being made that developed into the first life forms. We saw this single-celled life triumph over time and eternity by first developing the ability to divide into two cells, then to develop into composite, many-celled life forms. What do you remember about yesterday?"

"The melted lava poured into the ocean!"

"The land rose from the sea!"

"The lightning hit the water!"

"The squirmy things were so ugghhy!"

Teacher nodded and smiled and ignored the last comment. He had no idea why Mandi-2 was registered in this science course and had a strong feeling she would not stay long.

"Very good. So now we reach the annelids, like our worm here. Segmented, with each segment almost living a life of its own. Here are the first blood vessels to carry food to all the tissues most efficiently. Here is the first hemoglobin to carry oxygen to all the cells. Here is the first heart, a little pump to force the blood through those tubes. But one thing is missing yet. Do you know what it is?"

Their faces were empty of answers, their eyes wide with expectation.

"Think about it. What would have happened if Grosbit-9 had really stepped on this worm?"

"It would have squashed," Agon-1 answered with eight-year-old practicality. Mandi-2 shivered.

"Correct. It would have been killed. It is soft, without a shell or a skeleton. Which brings us to the next branch on the evolutionary tree."

Teacher pressed the activating button on the control unit at his waist, and the programmed computer seized them and hurled them through time to their next appointment. There was a swift, all-encompassing grayness, with no feeling of motion at all, which vanished suddenly to be replaced by a green dimness. Twenty feet above their heads the sun sparkled on the surface of the ocean while all about them silent fish moved in swift patterns. A great monster, all plates and shining teeth, hurried at and through them and Mandi-2 gave a little squeal of surprise.

"Your attention down here, if you please. The fish will come later. First we must study these, the first echinoderms. Phill-4, will you point out an echinoderm and tell us what the term means?"

" 'Echinoderm,' " the boy said, keying his memory. The training techniques that all the children learned in their first years of schooling brought the words to his lips. Like the others he had a perfect memory. "Is Greek for spiny skin. That must be one there, the big hairy starfish."

"Correct. An important evolutionary step. Before this, animals were either unprotected, like our annelid worm, or had skeletons outside, like snails or lobsters or insects. This is very limiting and inefficient. But an internal skeleton can give flexible support and is light in weight. An important evolutionary step has been made. We are almost there, children, almost there! This simple internal skeleton evolved into a more practical notochord, a single bone the length of the body protecting a main nerve fiber. And the chordates, the creatures with this notochord were only a single evolutionary step away from this—*all this!*"

Teacher threw his arms wide just as the sea about them burst into darting life. A school of silvery, yard-long fishes flashed around and through the students, while sharp-toothed sharklike predators struck through their midst. Teacher's speech had been nicely timed to end at this precise and dramatic moment. Some of the smaller children shied away from the flurry of life and death while Grosbit-9 swung his fist at one of the giants as it glided by.

"We have arrived," Teacher said, vibrantly, carried away by his own enthusiasm. "The chordate give way to the vertebrate, life as we know it. A strong, flexible internal skeleton that shields the soft inner organs and supports at the same time. Soft cartilage in these sharks— the same sort of tissue that stiffens your ears—changes to hard bone in these fishes. Mankind, so to speak, is just around the corner! What is it, Ched-3?" He was aware of a tugging on his toga.

"I have to go to the—"

"Well press the return button on your belt and don't be too long about it."

Ched-3 pressed the button and vanished, whisked back to their classroom with its superior functional plumbing. Teacher smacked his lips annoyedly while the teeming life whirled and dived about them. Children could be difficult at times.

"How did these animals know to get a notochord and bones?"

Agon-1 asked. "How did they know the right way to go to end up with the vertebrate—and us?"

Teacher almost patted him on the head, but smiled instead.

"A good question, a very good question. Someone has been listening and thinking. The answer is they didn't know, it wasn't planned. The ever-branching tree of evolution has no goals. Its changes are random, mutations caused by alterations in the germ plasm caused by natural radiation. The successful changes live, the unsuccessful ones die. The notochord creatures could move about easier, were more successful than the other creatures. They lived to evolve further. Which brings us to a new word I want you to remember. The word is 'ecology' and we are talking about ecological niches. Ecology is the whole world, everything in it, how all the plants and animals live together and how they relate one to the other. An ecological niche is where a creature lives in this world, the special place where it can thrive and survive and reproduce. All creatures that find an ecological niche that they can survive in are successful."

"The survival of the fittest?" Agon-1 asked.

"You have been reading some of the old books. That is what evolution was once called, but it was called wrong. *All* living organisms are fit, because they are alive. One can be no more fit than the other. Can we say that we, mankind, are more fit than an oyster?"

"Yes," Phill-4 said, with absolute surety. His attention on Ched-3 who had just returned, apparently emerging from the side of one of the sharks.

"Really? Come over here, Ched-3, and try to pay attention. We live and the oysters live. But what would happen if the world were to suddenly be covered by shallow water?"

"How could that happen?"

"The how is not important," Teacher snapped, then took a deep breath. "Let us just say it happened. What would happen to all the people?"

"They would all drown!" Mandi-2 said, unhappily.

"Correct. Our ecological niche would be gone. The oysters would thrive and cover the world. If we survive we are all equally fit in the eyes of nature. Now let us see how our animals with skeletons are faring in a new niche. Dry land."

A press, a motionless movement, and they were on a muddy shore by a brackish swamp. Teacher pointed to the trace of a feathery fin cutting through the floating algae.

"The subclass Crossoptergii, which means fringed fins. Sturdy little fish who have managed to survive in this stagnant water by adopting their swim bladders to breathe air directly and to get their oxygen in this manner. Many fish have these bladders that enable them to hover at any given depth, but now they have been adapted to a different use. Watch!"

The water became shallower until the fish's back was above the water, then its bulging eyes. Staring about, round and wide, as though terrified by this new environment. The sturdy fins, reinforced by bone, thrashed at the mud, driving it forward, further and further from its home, the sea. Then it was out of the water, struggling across the drying mud. A dragonfly hovered low, landed—and was engulfed by the fish's open mouth.

"The land is being conquered," Teacher said, pointing to the humped back of the fish now vanishing among the reeds. "First by plants, then insects—and now the animals. In a few million years, still over 255 million years before our own time, we have this . . ."

Through time again, rushing away on the cue word, to another swampy scene, a feathery marsh of ferns as big as trees and a hot sun burning through low-lying clouds.

And life. Roaring, thrashing, eating, killing life. The time researchers must have searched diligently for this place, this instant in the history of the world. No words were needed to describe or explain.

The age of reptiles. Small ones scampered by quickly to avoid the carnage falling on them. Scolosaurus, armored and knobbed like a tiny tank pushed through the reeds, his spiked tail dragging a rut in the mud. Great Brontosaurus stood high against the sky, his tiny, foolish head, with its teacup of brains, waving at the end of his lengthy neck, turned back to see what was bothering him as some message crept through his indifferent nervous system. His back humped-up, a mountain of gristle and bone and flesh and hooked to it was the demon form of Tyrannosaurus. His tiny forepaws scratched feebly against the other's leathery skin while his yards-long razor-toothed jaws tore at the heaving wall of flesh. Brontosaurus, still not sure what was happening, dredged up a quarter ton of mud and water and plants and chewed it, wondering. While high above, heaving and flapping its leathery wings, Pteranodon wheeled by, long jaws agape.

"That one's hurting the other one," Mandi-2 said. "Can't you make them stop?"

"We are only observers, child. What you see happened so very long ago and is unalterable in any way."

"Kill!" Grosbit-9 muttered, his attention captured for the very first time. They all watched, mouths dropping open at the silent fury.

"These are reptiles, the first successful animals to conquer the land. Before them were the amphibia, like our modern frogs, tied unbreakably to the water where their eggs are laid and the young grow up. But the reptiles lay eggs that can hatch on land. The link with the sea has been cut. Land has been conquered at last. They lack but a single characteristic that will permit them to survive in all the parts of the globe. You have all been preparing for this trip. Can anyone tell me what is still missing?"

The answer was only silence. Brontosaurus fell and large pieces of flesh were torn from his body. Pteranodon flapped away. A rain squall blotted out the sun.

"I am talking about temperature. These reptiles get a good deal of their body heat from the sun. They must live in a warm environment because as their surroundings get cooler their bodies get cooler . . ."

"Warm blooded!" Agon-1 said with shrill excitement.

"Correct! Someone, at least, has been doing the required studying. I see you sticking your tongue out, Ched-3. How would you like it if you couldn't draw it back and it stayed that way? Controlled body temperature, the last major branch on the ever-branching tree. The first class of what might be called centrally heated animals is the mammalia. The mammals. If we all go a little bit deeper into this forest you will see what I mean. Don't straggle, keep up there. In this clearing, everyone. On this side. Watch those shrubs there. Any moment now . . ."

Expectantly they waited. The leaves stirred and they leaned forward. A piglike snout pushed out, sniffing the air, and two suspicious, slightly crossed eyes looked about the clearing. Satisfied that there was no danger for the moment, the creature came into sight.

"Coot! Is that ever ugly," Phill-4 said.

"Beauty is in the eye of the beholder, young man. I'll ask you to hold your tongue. This is a perfect example of the subclass Prototheria, the first beasts, Tritylodon itself. For many years a source of controversy as to whether it was mammal or reptile. The smooth skin and shiny plates of a reptile—but notice the tufts of hair between the plates. Reptiles do not have hair. And it lays eggs, as reptiles do. But it, she, this fine creature here also suckles her young as do the mammals. Look with awe at this bridge between the old class of reptiles and emerging class of mammals."

"Oh, how cute!" Mandi-2 squealed as four tiny pink duplicates of the mother staggered out of the shrubbery after her. Tritylodon dropped heavily onto her side and the young began to nurse.

"That is another thing that the mammals brought into the world," Teacher said as the students looked on with rapt fascination. "Mother love. Reptile offspring, either born live or when they emerge from the egg, are left to fend for themselves. But warm blooded mammals must be warmed, protected, fed while they develop. They need mothering and, as you see, they receive it in sufficiency."

Some sound must have troubled the Tritylodon because she looked around, then sprang to her feet and trundled off into the underbrush, her young falling and stumbling after her. No sooner was the clearing empty than the hulking form of Triceratops pushed by, the great horns and bony frill held high. Thirty feet of lumbering flesh, its tail tip twitching as it dragged behind.

"The great lizards are still here, but doomed soon to final destruction. The mammals will survive and multiply and cover the earth. We will later discuss the many paths traveled by the mammals, but today we are going to leap ahead millions of years to the order Primates which may look familiar to you."

A taller, deeper, more tangled jungle replaced the one they had been visiting, a fruit-filled, flower-filled, life-filled maze. Multicolored birds shot by, insects hung in clouds and brown forms moved along the branches.

"Monkeys," Grosbit-9 said and looked around for something to throw at them.

"Primates. A relatively primitive group that took to these trees some fifty million years in our past. See how they are adapting to the arboreal life? They must see clearly in front of them and gauge distances correctly, so their eyes are now on the front of their heads, and they have developed binocular vision. To hold securely to the branches their nails have shortened and become flat, their thumbs opposed to strengthen their grip. These primates will continue to develop until the wonderful, important day when they descend from the trees and venture from the shelter of the all-protecting forest."

"Africa," Teacher said as the time machine once more moved them across the centuries. "It could be today, so little have things changed in the relatively short time since these higher primates ventured forth."

"I don't see anything," Ched-3 said, looking about at the sun-scorched grass of the veldt, at the verdant jungle pressing up next to it.

"Patience. The scene begins. Watch the herd of deer that are coming towards us. The landscape has changed, become drier, the seas of grass are pushing back the jungle. There is still food to be had in the jungle, fruit and nuts there for the taking, but the competition is becoming somewhat fierce. Many different primates now fill that ecological niche and it is running over. Is there a niche vacant? Certainly not out here on the veldt! Here are the fleet-footed grass eaters, look how they run, their survival depends upon their speed. For they have their enemies, the carnivores, the meat eaters who live on their flesh."

Dust rose and the deer bounded towards them, through them, around them. Wide eyes, hammering hooves, sun glinting from their horns and then they were gone. And the lions followed. They had a buck, cut off from the rest of the herd by the lionesses, surrounded, clawed at and wounded. Then a talon tipped paw hamstrung the beast and it fell, quickly dead as its throat was chewed out and the hot red blood sank into the dust. The pride of lions ate. The children watched, struck silent, and Mandi-2 sniffled and rubbed at her nose.

"The lions eat a bit, but they are already gorged from another kill. The sun is reaching the zenith and they are hot, sleepy. They will find shade and go to sleep and the corpse will remain for the scavengers to dispose of, the carrion eaters."

Even as Teacher spoke the first vulture was dropping down out of the sky, folding its dusty wings and waddling towards the kill. Two more descended, tearing at the flesh and squabbling and screaming soundlessly at one another.

Then from the jungle's edge there emerged first one, then two more apes. They blinked in the sunlight, looking around fearfully, then ran towards the newly killed deer, using their knuckles on the ground to help them as they ran. The blood-drenched vultures looked at them apprehensively, then flapped into the air as one of the apes hurled a stone at them. Then it was the apes' turn. They too tore at the flesh.

"Look and admire, children. The tailless ape emerges from the forest. These are your remote ancestors."

"Not mine!"

"They're *awful*!"

"I think I am going to be sick."

"Children—stop, think! With your minds not your viscera just for once. These ape-men or man-apes have occupied a new cultural niche. They are already adapting to it. They are almost hairless so that they can sweat and not overheat when other animals must seek shelter. They are tool using. They hurl rocks to chase away the vultures. And see, that one there—he has a sharp bit of splintered rock that he is using to cut off the meat. They stand erect on their legs to free their hands for the tasks of feeding and survival. Man is emerging and you are privileged to behold his first tremulous steps away from the jungle. Fix this scene in your memory, it is a glorious one. And you will remember it better, Mandi-2, if you watch with your eyes open."

The older classes were usually much more enthusiastic. Only Agon-1 seemed to be watching with any degree of interest—other than Grosbit-9 who was watching with too much interest indeed. Well, they said one good student in a class made it worthwhile, made one feel as though something were being accomplished.

"That is the end of today's lesson, but I'll tell you something about tomorrow's class." Africa vanished and some cold and rainswept northern land appeared. High mountains loomed through the mist in the background and a thin trickle of smoke rose from a low sod house half-buried in the ground. "We will see how man emerged from his primate background, grew sure and grew strong. How these early people moved from the family group to the simple Neolithic community. How they used tools and bent nature to their will. We are going to find out who lives in that house and what he does there. It is a lesson that I know you are all looking forward to."

There seemed very little actual evidence to back this assumption, and Teacher stabbed the button and the class was over. Their familiar classroom appeared around them and the dismissal bell was jingling its sweet music. Shouting loudly, without a backward look, they ran from the room and Teacher, suddenly tired, unclipped the controls from his waist and locked them into his desk. It had been a very long day. He turned out the lights and left.

At the street entrance he was just behind a young matron, most attractive and pink in miniaturized mini, hair a flaming red. Mandi-2's mother, he realized, he should have known by the hair, as she reached down to take an even tinier, pinker hand. They went out before him.

"And what did you learn in school today, darling?" the mother asked. And, although he did not approve of eavesdropping, Teacher could not help but hear the question. Yes, what did you learn? It would be nice to know.

Mandi-2 skipped down the steps, bouncing with happiness to be free again.

"Oh, nothing much," she said, and they vanished around the corner.

Without knowing he did it, Teacher sighed a great weary sigh and turned in the other direction and went home.

By the Falls

It was the rich damp grass, slippery as soap, covering the path, that caused Carter to keep slipping and falling, not the steepness of the hill. The front of his raincoat was wet and his knees were muddy long before he reached the summit. And with each step forward and upward the continuous roar of sound grew louder. He was hot and tired by the time he reached the top of the ridge—yet he instantly forgot his discomfort as he looked out across the wide bay.

Like everyone else he had heard about The Falls since childhood and had seen countless photographs and films of them on television. All this preparation had not readied him for the impact of reality.

He saw a falling ocean, a vertical river—how many millions of gallons a second did people say came down? The Falls stretched out across the bay, their farthest reaches obscured by the clouds of float-ing spray. The bay seethed and boiled with the impact of that falling weight, raising foam-capped waves that crashed against the rocks be-low. Carter could feel the impact of the water on the solid stone as a vibration in the ground, but all sound was swallowed up in the greater roar of The Falls. This was a reverberation so outrageous and overpowering that his ears could not become accustomed to it. They soon felt numbed from the ceaseless impact, but the very bones of the skull carried the sound to his brain, shivering and battering it. When he put his hands over his ears he was horrified to discover that The Falls were still as loud, as ever. As he stood swaying and wide-eyed one of the constantly changing air currents that formed about the base of The Falls shifted suddenly and swept a wall of spray down upon him. The inundation lasted scant seconds but was heavier than any rainfall he had ever experienced, had ever believed possible. When it passed he was gasping for air, so dense had been the falling water.

Quivering with sensations he had never before experienced, Carter turned and looked along the ridge toward the gray and water-blackened granite of the cliff and the house that huddled at its base like a stony blister. It was built of the same granite as the cliff and appeared no less solid. Running and slipping, his hands still over his ears, Carter hurried toward the house.

For a short time the spray was blown across the bay and out to sea, so that golden afternoon sunlight poured down on the house, starting streamers of vapor from its sharply sloping roof. It was a no-nonsense building, as solid as the rock against which it pressed. Only two windows penetrated the blankness of the front that faced The Falls—tiny and deep, they were like little suspicious eyes. No door existed here but Carter saw that a path of stone flags led around the corner.

He followed it and found—cut into the wall on the far side, away from The Falls—a small and deep-set entry. It had no arch but was shielded by a great stone lintel a good two feet in diameter. Carter stepped into the opening that framed the door and looked in vain for a knocker on the heavy, iron-bolted timbers. The unceasing, world-filling, thunder of The Falls made thinking almost impossible and it was only after he had pressed uselessly against the sealed portal that he realized that no knocker, even one as loud as a cannon, could be heard within these walls above that sound. He lowered his hands and tried to force his mind to coherence.

There had to be some way of announcing his presence. When he stepped back out of the alcove he noticed that a rusty iron knob was set into the wall a few feet away. He seized and twisted it but it would not turn. However, when he pulled on it, although it resisted, he was able to draw it slowly away from the wall to disclose a length of chain. The chain was heavily greased and in good condition—a fair omen. He continued to pull until a yard of chain emerged from the opening and then, no matter how hard he pulled, no more would come. He released the handle and it bounced against the rough stone of the wall. For some instants it hung there. Then with a jerky me-chanical motion, the chain was drawn back into the wall until the knob once more rested in place. Whatever device this odd mechanism activated seemed to perform its desired function. In less than a min-ute the heavy door swung open and a man appeared in the opening. He examined his visitor wordlessly.

The man who was much like the building and the cliffs behind it— solid, no-nonsense, worn, lined and graying. But he had resisted the years even as he showed their marks upon him. His back was as straight as any young man's and his knob-knuckled hands had a look of determined strength. Blue were his eyes and very much the color of the water falling endlessly, thunderously, on the far side of the building. He wore knee-high fisherman's boots, plain corduroy pants and a boiled gray sweater. His face did not change expression as he waved Carter into the building.

When the thick door had been swung shut and the many sealing bars shoved back into place the silence in the house took on a quality of its own. Carter had known absence of sound elsewhere—here was a positive statement of no-sound, a bubble of peace pushed right up against the very base of the all-sound of The Falls. He was momen-tarily deafened and he knew it. But he was not so deaf that he did not know that the hammering thunder of The Falls had been shut outside. The other man must have sensed how his visitor felt. He nodded in a reassuring manner as he took Carter's coat, then pointed to a comfortable chair set by the deal table near the fire. Carter sank gratefully into the cushions. His host turned away and vanished, to return a moment later with a tray, bearing a decanter and two glasses. He poured a measure of wine into each glass and set one down before Carter, who nodded and seized it in both hands to steady their shaking. After a first large gulp he sipped at it while the tremors died and his hearing slowly returned. His host moved about the room on various tasks and presently Carter found himself much recovered. He looked up.

"I must thank you for your hospitality. When I came in I was—shaken."

"How are you now? Has the wine helped?" the man said loudly, almost shouting, and Carter realized that his own words had not been heard. Of course, the man must be hard of hearing. It was a wonder he was not stone deaf.

"Very good, thank you," Carter shouted back. "Very kind of you indeed. My name is Carter. I'm a reporter, which is why I have come to see you."

The man nodded, smiling slightly.

"My name is Bodum. You must know that if you have come here to talk to me. You write for the newspapers?"

"I was sent here." Carter coughed—the shouting was irritating his throat. "And I of course know you, Mr. Bodum—that is, I know you by reputation. You're the Man by The Falls."

"Forty-three years now," Bodum said with solid pride, "I've lived here and have never been away for a single night. Not that it has been easy. When the wind is wrong the spray is blown over the house for days and it is hard to breathe—even the fire goes out. I built the chimney myself—there is a bend partway up with baffles and doors. The smoke goes up—but if water comes down the baffles stop it and its weight opens the doors and it drains away through a pipe to the outside. I can show you where it drains—black with soot the wall is there."

While Bodum talked Carter looked around the room at the dim furniture shapes barely seen in the wavering light from the fire and at the two windows set into the wall.

"Those windows," he said, "you put them in yourself? May I look out?"

"Took a year apiece, each one. Stand on that bench. It will bring you to the right level. They're armored glass, specially made, solid as the wall around them now that I have them anchored well. Don't be afraid. Go right up to it. The window's safe. Look how the glass is anchored."

Carter was not looking at the glass but at The Falls outside. He had not realized how close the building was to the falling water. It was perched on the very edge of the cliff and nothing was to be seen from this vantage point except the wall of blackened wet granite to his right and the foaming maelstrom of the bay far below. And before him, above him, filling space The Falls. All the thickness of wall and glass could not cut out their sound completely and when he touched the heavy pane with his fingertips he could feel the vibration of the waters' impact.

The window did not lessen the effect The Falls had upon him but it enabled him to stand and watch and think, as he had been unable to do on the outside. It was very much like a peephole into a holocaust of water—a window into a cold hell. He could watch without being destroyed—but the fear of what was on the other side did not lessen. Something black flickered in the falling water and was gone.

"There—did you see that?" he called out. "Something came down The Falls. What could it possibly be?"

Bodum nodded wisely. "Over forty years I have been here and I can show you what comes down The Falls." He thrust a splint into the fire and lit a lamp from it. Then, picking up the lamp, he waved Carter after him. They crossed the room and he held the light to a large glass bell jar.

"Must be twenty years ago it washed up on the shore. Every bone in its body broke too. Stuffed and mounted it myself."

Carter pressed close, looking at the staring shoe-button eyes and the gaping jaw and pointed teeth. The limbs were stiff and unnatural, the body under the fur bulging in the wrong places. Bodum was by no means a skilful taxidermist. Yet, perhaps by accident, he had captured a look of terror in the animal's expression and stance.

"It's a dog," Carter said. "Very much like other dogs."

Bodum was offended, his voice as cold as shout can be. "Like them, perhaps, but not of them. Every bone broken I told you. How else could a dog have appeared here in this bay?"

"I'm sorry, I did not mean to suggest for an instant—down The Falls, of course. I just meant it is so much like the dogs we have that perhaps there is a whole new world up there. Dogs and everything, just like ours."

"I never speculate," Bodum said mollified. "I'll make some coffee."

He took the lamp to the stove and Carter, left alone in the partial darkness went back to the window. It drew him. "I must ask you some questions for my article," he said but did not speak loudly enough for Bodum to hear. Everything he had meant to do here seemed irrelevant as he looked out at The Falls. The wind shifted. The spray was briefly blown clear and The Falls were once more a mighty river coming down from the sky. When he canted his head he saw it exactly as if he were looking across a river.

And there, upstream, a ship appeared, a large liner with rows of portholes. It sailed the surface of the river faster than ship had ever sailed before and he had to jerk his head to follow its motion. When it passed, no more than a few hundred yards away, for one instant he could see it clearly. The people aboard it were hanging to the rails, some with their mouths open as though shouting in fear. Then it was gone and there was only the water, rushing endlessly by.

"Did you see it?" Carter shouted, spinning about.

"The coffee will be ready soon."

"There, out there," Carter cried, taking Bodum by the arm. "In The Falls. It was a ship, I swear it was, falling from up above. With people on it. There must be a whole world up there that we know nothing about."

Bodum reached up to the shelf for a cup, breaking Carter's grip with the powerful movement of his arm.

"My dog came down The Falls. I found it and stuffed it myself."

"Your dog, of course, I'll not deny that. But there were people on that ship and I'll swear—I'm not mad—that their skins were a different color from ours."

"Skin is skin, just skin color."

"I know. That is what we have. But it must be possible for skins to be other colors, even if we don't know about it."

"Sugar?"

"Yes, please. Two." Carter sipped at the coffee—it was strong and warm. In spite of himself he was drawn back to the window. He looked out and sipped at the coffee—and started when something black and formless came down. And other things. He could not tell what they were because the spray was blowing toward the house again. He tasted grounds at the bottom of his cup and left the last sips. He put the cup carefully aside.

Again the eddying wind currents shifted the screen of spray to one side just in time for him to see another of the objects go by.

"That was a house! I saw it as clearly as I see this one. But wood perhaps, not stone, and smaller. And black as though it had been partially burned. Come look there may be more."

Bodum banged the pot as he rinsed it out in the sink. "What do you newspapers want to know about me? Over forty years here—there are a lot of things I can tell you about."

"What is up there above The Falls—on top of the cliff? Do people live up there? Can there be a whole world up there of which we live in total ignorance?"

Bodum hesitated, frowned in thought, before he answered.

"I believe they have dogs up there."

"Yes," Carter answered, hammering his fist on the window ledge, not knowing whether to smile or cry. The water fell by; the floor and walls shook with the power of it.

"There—more and more things going by." He spoke quietly, to himself. "I can't tell what they are. That—that could have been a tree and that a bit of fence. The smaller ones may be bodies—animals, logs, anything. There is a different world above The Falls and in that world something terrible is happening. And we don't even know about it. We don't even know that world is there."

He struck again and again on the stone until his fist hurt.

The sun shone on the water and he saw the change, just here and there at first, an altering and shifting.

"Why—the water seems to be changing color. Pink it is—no, red. More and more of it. There, for an instant, it was all red. The color of blood."

He spun about to face the dim room and tried to smile but his lips were drawn back hard from his teeth when he did.

"Blood? Impossible. There can't be that much blood in the whole world. What is happening up there? What is happening?"

His scream did not disturb Bodum, who only nodded his head in agreement.

"I'll show you something," he said. "But only if you promise not to write about it. People might laugh at me. I've been here over forty years and that is nothing to laugh about."

"My word of honor, not a word, just show me. Perhaps it has something to do with what is happening."

Bodum took down a heavy Bible and opened it on the table next to the lamp. It was set in very black type, serious and impressive. He turned pages until he came to a piece of very ordinary paper.

"I found this on the shore. During the winter. No one had been here for months. It may have come over The Falls. Now I'm not saying it did—but it is possible. You will agree it is possible?"

"Oh, yes—quite possible. How else could it have come here?" Carter reached out and touched it. "I agree, ordinary paper. Torn on one edge, wrinkled where it was wet and then dried." He turned it over. "There is lettering on the other side."

"Yes. But it is meaningless. It is no word I know."

"Nor I, and I speak four languages. Could it have a meaning?"

"Impossible. A word like that."

"No human language." He shaped his lips and spoke the letters aloud. "Aich—Eee—Ell—Pea."

"What could 'HELP' mean?" Bodum shouted louder than ever. "A child scribbled it. Meaningless." He seized the paper and crumpled it and threw it into the fire.

"You'll want to write a story about me," he said proudly. "I have been here over forty years, and if there is one man in the entire world who is an authority on The Falls it is me.

"I know everything that there is to know about them."

American Dead

Francesco Bruno crossed himself, muttered the quick words of a prayer, then turned his attention to the metal plate on the splintered table before him. Hunger possessed him, he had not eaten in over twelve hours, or he would not have been able to face the little beans with the black markings, or the limp, greasy greens again. He ate quickly, aware of the dark figures silently watching him. There was only water to wash the food down with.

"Show him the paper," one of the men said and, for possibly the hundredth time in the last three days, Bruno took the creased and stained sheet from his wallet. A black hand reached out and took it from him. The newcomer carried it to the paneless window and held it to the light to read it. There was a muttered discussion. Bruno looked around, at the gnarled, white-haired woman bent over the stove, at the board walls—with gaps between the boards big enough to get a finger through—the poverty and the barrenness. Even the slums of Palermo, where he had grown up, were not this bad.

The newcomer brought the paper back. "What you got wif you?" he asked. Bruno opened the stained canvas pack, with the weathered initials US on it, and began to spread its contents on the rickety table. They had given him this in place of the suitcase he had left the city with. The palm-sized TV camera, the recorder for it, the fuel-cell power pack, the extra reels of tape, a change of underclothing and his toilet kit. The man poked through everything, then pointed to the camera.

"This a gun?" he asked.

Bruno did not bother to explain that he had been through this routine an uncountable number of times since the journey had begun. Patiently, he set the camera, explained how it operated, then shot a brief take. When he reran the tape the men pushed close to look at the tiny monitor screen.

"Hey, Granny, you on the tee-vee. You gonna be a big-time star, you hear!"

He had to replay it again for the old woman, who chuckled in appreciation before returning to the stove. The demonstration had cleared some of the tension from the air, for the first time, the newcomer relaxed and dropped into a chair. He was big and dark, dressed in patched and muddy army fatigues. He had a submachine gun slung over his shoulder and clips of cartridges hanging across his chest.

"You kin call me Chopper. Where you from?"

Bruno spread his hands wide. "From Europe, a consortium of the press . . ." He saw the quick frown and glower: damn his Oxford English. He tried again.

"I'm from Italy, way down in the south. I work for a newspaper. I write newspaper stories. We have a lot of papers over there, television stations too. We were informed that it might be able to send one man over here. Everyone got together to pick one man. I am the one they picked . . ."

"You sure nuff talk funny."

"I told you, I am from Italy."

"You say somfin now in that Italy talk."

"Buon giorno, signore. Voglio andare al—"

"He sure talk it, all right," one of the interested bystanders said.

Chopper nodded approval, as though this demonstration of alien ability had made an important point.

"You ready go now? We got some walkin' tuh do."

"Whenever you say." Bruno hurriedly stuffed everything back into the pack, after first wrapping it securely in a sheet of plastic. Walking would be no novelty. He had walked, rode muleback, traveled in a wagon, a truck, cars. Blindfolded most of the time.

They went out into the tiny yard, soaked and muddy chickens squawking out of their way. The early-afternoon sky was dark as evening and a perpetual fine rain was falling, drenching everything. But it was warm, even hot once they started walking, the air almost too humid to breathe.

Chopper led the way, but went only a few yards down the rutted, puddle-filled lane before turning off between the pine trees. Bruno concentrated only on keeping up with his apparently tireless guide, so he was just vaguely aware of the falling mist, the squish of damp pine needles under their feet, the black columns of the trees vanishing grayly into the fog on all sides. They walked for two hours without a break, before coming suddenly to an open field of stubble that disappeared into the mist before them. A bird sounded ahead and Chopper clutched Bruno and dragged him to the ground. Then he cupped his hand and repeated the same bird call. They lay there, until two men materialized out of the rain, their M-16 rifles pointing warily ahead.

"Let's go," Chopper said. "We here."

The two guards walked behind them as they worked their way around the edge of the field to a split-rail fence, heavily overgrown with vines and creepers. A man was lying there, peering through a gap between the rails. He wore heavy field boots and a rain-darkened rubber poncho. He had on an army steel helmet and, when he rolled over and sat up, seven gold stars in a circle were visible on it.

The supreme commander of all the American Armed Forces only had six.

"I understand that you have my letter," the man said.

"Right here," Bruno answered, groping inside his jacket. "Then you must be the man who wrote it? Mau Mau . . ."

As Mau Mau examined the letter, Bruno examined him. A wide face, dark eyes, cappuccino-colored skin, an unexpressive mouth under a drooping black moustache. He took one glance at the letter, then tore it in half and stuffed the pieces into his pants pocket.

"You've come a long way—and it has taken a long time," he said.

Bruno nodded. "It was not easy. The immigration people are very difficult these days, and there was the paperwork. Then a legitimate reason had to be found for me to get far enough south to meet the contact."

Mau Mau looked him up and down carefully. "For a white man you're pretty dark," he said.

"For a black man you're pretty light," Bruno answered, then went on hurriedly when he saw that the other was not amused. "The Mediterranean, in the south where I come from, people are darker. Perhaps, who knows, that is why I was chosen . . ."

Mau Mau smiled and the lines of severity, the grimness vanished for a moment. "Sicily I bet. That's pretty near to Africa. Maybe you have a touch of the tarbrush . . ."

He broke off as a young Negro, barefooted and wearing ragged overalls and shirt, ran up, bent low behind the cover of the fence. He carried a new and efficient-looking army field telephone that trailed a glistening length of black wire. Mau Mau grabbed off the handset and listened.

"A truck coming," he announced. "With a jeep, maybe a hundred yards behind it."

They all ran, with Bruno hurrying after.

"Hey!" he shouted. "Can I take pictures?"

Mau Mau stopped so abruptly that Bruno almost collided with him. They stood close, Mau Mau almost a head taller, looking down at the reporter. "Yes, as long as I can see them afterwards."

"Absolutely, every foot of tape," he called after the man's departing back, then began to dig furiously in his pack. The camera and power pack were reasonably waterproof, and everything else was still dry inside the plastic. He followed the others after slipping a hood over the lens.

They were gathered in a small clump of silver birch trees that stood at the edge of a narrow stream. The water burbled past and ran through a culvert under a road. It was a paved road, narrow but well kept up, with a county marker at its edge. Bruno squinted but could not make out the number or even the state. There were more men here, all waiting tensely, looking down the road to the left where it vanished into the mist and falling rain. A growing whine of tires could be heard.

Everything happened quickly. The truck loomed up out of the mist, a big army truck with many wheels and a canvas top. It was going very fast. When it reached the culvert the ground and the road rose up in a roar of sound and a great flash of orange light. The front of the truck lifted off the road for an instant before it dropped back heavily, the front wheels falling into the gap where the culvert had been. A gun must have been fired—Bruno could not hear it for the roaring in his ears—because sudden holes punched their way across the white star on the metal door of the cab.

The jeep appeared out of the fog, skidding and twisting sideways as the driver braked on the wet road. It stopped, nuzzling up to the tilted rear of the truck, and a gun muzzle jabbed out from behind the front curtains, hammering out a spasm of rapid firing. There was answering fire from all sides—Bruno could hear better now—and the gun dropped to the pavement and a soldier's body slid after it.

"If you are alive—come out!" Mau Mau shouted. "You have five seconds or we blow you out. Hands empty when you come."

There was a silence, then the truck springs creaked and a rifle came over the tailgate and clattered onto the road. A soldier, a corporal, emerged and slowly climbed down. Something stirred in the back of the jeep, a pair of shiny boots protruded out from under the curtain, and an officer slid out onto the road. He had his left hand clutched about his right forearm. Blood ran down his fingers and dripped to the ground.

A sudden burst of rapid firing made Bruno jump and he swung the camera toward the rear of the truck. Chopper had jumped out and sprayed a clip into the canvas. Another man kicked the corporal in the back of the knees so he dropped to the ground. With quick efficiency he pulled the soldier's wrists behind his back and secured them with rapid twists of insulated wire. He did the same with his ankles then stuffed a rag into his mouth and sealed it there with more wire. The soldier, like a hog-tied animal, could only roll his eyes upward in fear.

"Get the aid kit from the jeep and fix up Whitey's arm," Mau Mau ordered, "and bring me a can of sandman." He put his hand behind him without looking, and the can was slapped into it. The soldier rolled on the wet pavement as the blast of spray from the pressurized canister hit his face; then he slumped limply. Mau Mau turned to the officer.

"Ready for your turn, Lieutenant?" he asked.

Raindrops beaded the officer's close-cropped blond hair as he bent his head to watch the field bandage being tied around his arm. He looked up slowly, but did not answer. Yet the answer was obvious in the look of cold hatred directed at Mau Mau. The tall Negro laughed aloud and held out the can and blasted the fine spray full into the contemptuous face. The eyelids fluttered, closed, the features sagged and the man's knees wobbled. Mau Mau put his hand in the middle of the officer's chest and pushed. The man went over backward into the weeds beside the road, his legs and arms sprawling wide. There were appreciative chuckles from the bystanders and Bruno swept the camera across their smiling faces.

"Enough funning," Mau Mau said. "Put that camera away." As soon as Bruno had lowered it he turned and cupped his hands and shouted, "Come an' git it!"

On the far side of the road the ground grew sodden where the stream widened out and vanished into a swamp. Ghostly trunks of trees readied up from the dark water, their branches hung with festoons of parasitic plants. Figures emerged from among the trees, one, two, then a score, until there was a large crowd of Negroes coming out of the swamp. Old men, women, young children, they moved with a sense of purpose.

One of the gunmen pulled open the truck's tailgate and climbed inside. The first thing he dropped out was the blood-drenched body of a soldier, which was grabbed by the heels and dragged aside. Then came some guns and ammunition, followed by boxes and crates. As he pushed each item to the edge someone stepped forward to take it from him; sometimes two people if the box was very big. The children carried, proudly, the bandoleers of ammunition and the rifles. The burdened carriers vanished, one by one, down the path leading back into the swamp.

"What did we get?" Mau Mau called out.

"Little of everyfin," the voice called from inside the truck. "K-rations, typin' paper, blankets, grenades—"

"Now you're talking."

"—pro kits, toilet paper. You name it, it's here."

"What the army can use, we can use," Mau Mau said, smiling happily, wiping his hands together. "We're fighting the same war."

While waiting their turn at the truck, some of the people went over to look at the two unconscious soldiers. There was a sudden murmur of voices and a woman called out shrilly.

"Mau Mau, you come here. Dis little boy was at Ellenville an' he say he saw Whitey dere!"

Everyone stopped and there was absolute silence—broken only by the thud of boots as Mau Mau ran across the road. He had his hand on the thin little boy's shoulder and bent to talk to him. Voices whispered now, with an undertone of anger like the hum of a disturbed beehive.

"Hurry it up, we haven't all day!" Mau Mau shouted, and his voice was harsh. Things moved faster. The last case vanished into the mist and the truck was empty. Two armed men followed the burdened people. At the swamp edge they turned and raised their right arms, fist clenched. In silence, the others returned the salute.

"Run the jeep onto the path into the swamp," Mau Mau ordered. "And burn it. Make sure it blows up. That will cover any tracks. Throw the soldier into the back of the truck. Get moving into the field and leave plenty of footprints, hear?" Then his voice lowered, the words almost hissing out. "Chopper and Ali pick up the lieutenant. We're taking him with us."

Bruno watched while two men manhandled the jeep off the road to the edge of the swamp and left it astraddle the trail. One of them dropped grenades inside the jeep—then shot a hole in the gas tank. The other man twisted a silver device, about the size of a pencil, which he dropped into the growing pool of gasoline on the ground. They came hurrying back.

"Mistuh, better make tracks," one shouted. "Dat thing blow in one minute."

Bruno turned and realized that the others had gone, vanished already in the rain. He hurried after the remaining two men. They were halfway across the field, following the obvious tracks, when there was a muffled explosion from the direction of the road.

They caught up quickly with the others, who were walking slowly rather than marching. A rough litter had been made with two rifles and a blanket and the officer was being carried in it, his uninjured arm dangling limply over the side. Mau Mau led the way, scowling into the mist ahead. Bruno walked beside him for a few minutes, in silence, before he spoke.

"May I ask you questions?"

Mau Mau glanced at him, then brushed the raindrops from his moustache with his knuckles. "By all means, that's why you are here."

Bruno opened one strap and dug into the pack, pulling out the microphone. "I would like to record this," he said, holding it up.

"You just do that."

"Oggi è il quatro giorno di luglio . . ."

"Talk English!"

"Today is the Fourth of July, somewhere in the South of the United States. I am with a man whose name I may not mention—"

"Mention it."

"A man named Mau Mau, who is not only a local resistance leader, but is also reputed to be on the Black Power Council of Ten. Would you care to comment on that?"

Mau Mau shook his head in a sharp no.

"I have just witnessed a brief action, a minor engagement in the grim battle that is now gripping this country. I am going to ask him about this, and about the bigger picture as he sees it."

"Turn that thing off now."

Bruno flipped the switch and they walked in silence for a moment. The path had emerged into a rough and partly overgrown logging road that wound erratically through the trees. Mau Mau took the microphone and buried it inside his fist.

"How long will it be before this is printed or broadcast?" he asked.

Bruno shrugged. "I would say, at a minimum, two weeks after it gets to Washington. I would like to ask you for help with that."

"We can get it there for you. But I'm going to sit on it for a month. By that time none of this will matter because we will be someplace else. How are you going to get the tapes out of the country? They are searching things pretty closely ever since the Hungarians printed the stolen New Orleans ghetto massacre pictures."

"I am afraid I cannot tell you exactly. But I will give you an address to deliver the tapes to. After that, well, the diplomatic pouch of a friendly government."

"That isn't quite as friendly as they act. Good enough." He handed back the microphone. The rain had stopped, but the mist still clung to the ground. Mau Mau squinted up at the sky. "They tell me that you are a big praying man. You better pray that this fog and rain hang around. There are still three hours until sunset."

"Might I ask—the significance of that?"

"Planes and choppers. You must understand that we are irregulars and we are fighting the military. Our only advantage is in being irregular. Their disadvantage is that they are too organized. They have to be. They have chains of command and orders come down from the top. They can't have people thinking for themselves or there would be chaos. Now, chaos just helps us fine. These big military minds have finally, and reluctantly, accepted the idea that we control the roads at night. They have to do all their rushing about in the daytime. They have this day thing so stuck in their heads that they sometimes don't notice that there are days that are just as good as nights as far as we are concerned."

"Like today?"

"You're catching on fine. We hit and we leave. The goods we confiscated go in one direction, we go in another. The military finds our tracks and sort of concentrates in this direction. They don't really believe them, they don't believe much of anything anymore, but they don't have much choice. We lead them on a bit, keep them busy until dark, and that is that. By morning we're gone, the supplies are gone, and the world is back to normal." He smiled wryly when he spoke the last word.

"Then we are—so to speak—bait?"

"You could say that. But remember bait is usually placed in a trap."

"Would you explain that?"

"Wait and see."

"Whitey wakin' up," a voice said from behind them.

They stopped and waited until the litter bearers came up to them. The officer's eyes were open, watching them.

"Get up," Mau Mau ordered. "You can walk now, you been in dat baby buggy too long." He put his hand out to help. The officer ignored it and got his legs to the ground and stood, swaying.

"What's your name?"

"Adkins, Lieutenant—10034268."

"Well, Adkins, Lieutenant, are you beginning to wonder why we didn't leave you back there by the road, you being wounded and all that? Isn't often we take prisoners, is it?"

The officer did not answer, and started to turn away. Mau Mau reached out and took him by the chin, dragging his head back until they were face-to-face again.

"Better talk to me, Adkins. I can make big trouble for you."

"Do you torture prisoners, then?" He had a firm, controlled voice that was used to command.

"Not very often. But stranger things have happened in this war, haven't they?"

"To what do you refer? And I prefer to call this a criminal, Communist insurrection."

Bruno had to admire the man. He wondered how he would have acted in the same situation.

"You call it just what you want, Whitey, just what you want," Mau Mau said in a low voice. He went on, still speaking softly. "I think this is more of a war, with you on one side and me on the other. Bad things happen during a war. Did you hear what happened at Ellenville?"

There was the smallest break in the lieutenant's composure. A small start, a slight narrowing of the eyes. If Bruno had not been watching him closely he would never have noticed. Yet the man's voice was calm as ever.

"A lot of things have happened at Ellenville. To what are you referring?"

"Let's move," Mau Mau said, turning away. "Choppers will be coming soon and we need a few more miles behind us."

They moved in silence after that. The two former stretcher bearers walking close behind the prisoner, guns ready. After about five minutes Mau Man halted them and put his hand to his ear. "Is that a copter out there? Ali, rig that listener and see if you can hear anything."

Ali slung his rifle and took the submicrominiaturized listening device from his pocket. The plastic case was olive drab in color and obviously army issue. He put the earphone into place and sprang open the collapsed acoustic shell. They all watched closely while he turned in a slow circle, listening intently, hesitated, then turned back. He nodded.

"Kin hear one real clear. An' mebbe 'nother one way out."

"Search pattern. Let's double time," Mau Mau ordered.

They ran. Bruno was staggering, exhausted and soaked with sweat, before they reached the clearing that was their destination. There was a banked mound of raw dirt around a yard-wide hole in the center of it.

"Chopper, dive down and get the bolo," Mau Mau said. "Then the rest of you get in there with Whitey and keep a close eye on him." He turned to Bruno. "Stick around, I think that you'll enjoy this."

The big Negro vanished over the mound of dirt and reappeared a minute later with a device like a bulge-barreled telescope that was mounted on a tripod.

"The modern technology of war," Mau Mau said. "The military just love gadgetry, they do indeed. All the hardware makes them feel important and is great for explaining their inflated budgets. Over eighty percent of the federal budget is spent by the military, one way or another, and has been for the past forty, fifty years. You record this. Now the military was glad to have black boys for cannon fodder, in Vietnam and the like, and those boys learned real good how to use all the fancy devices. Of course the army is kind of lily-white these days, but an awful lot of blacks learned how to press the buttons before they were booted out for the good of the service." He stopped and listened. The distant rumble of a helicopter could be clearly heard now. Mau Mau smiled.

"Here come the ofay air cavalry now. They know that a lot of people walked off with a lot of their goods and they have to find them right quick. Because by morning those goods will be buried real deep and safe, and the people will be back at their farms and at their jobs and who's to know? So they go flapping around up there with sophisticated electronic sniffers and body-heat detectors and all kind of expensive junk. They'll smell us out soon. And when they do bolo there will sniff them right back. Got a sound detector in its nose. Works simple and is hard to jam."

Louder and louder the copter sounded, obviously coming toward them now. Bruno resisted the temptation to cringe away from its advance. He knew just what the gunship could do with its rapid-firing cannon, rockets, bombs . . .

The nose of the bolo missile was turning. Chopper stood off to one side, the control box in his hand with the cable leading to the tripod. "Range!" he called out, and at the same moment the rocket spat out a jet of flame and hurled itself up into the fog. One, two, three seconds passed—and a great explosion sounded from the sky, which lit for an instant with a ruddy flame. Pieces of debris crashed down through the trees and thudded to the ground, and silence followed.

"Scratch a couple million bucks," Mau Mau said, and pointed to the hole. "Now get down because there will be incoming very soon."

By the time Bruno had stowed his camera and clambered up the mound the other two were out of sight below. Thick lengths of branch were set into the shaftlike rungs of a ladder, and he climbed carefully down them. It was completely dark and musty in the deep hole, claustrophobic. He touched bottom and, by feel, found that a low tunnel went off horizontally. He went into it, on his hands and knees and, after turning two right-angle corners, came out into an underground chamber. Battery lamps illuminated it. It was low, he could stand only if he crouched over, and just big enough for all of them to sit against the walls, knees almost touching. It was roofed with heavy logs, which were notched and supported by even thicker sections along the walls. It was dark, the officer's face the only relieving spot of white in the chamber.

"We have three, four minutes at the most," Mau Mau said. "As soon as the chopper was missed from the radio net they send something flying over to look for it. They'll find the wreck. Then they'll call in air support. Then they'll drop a lot of bombs hoping that there are a lot of nice black people just sitting down here waiting for incoming mail."

There was a muffled explosion and dirt shook down from above. Mau Mau smiled. "Three minutes. They're getting very efficient."

Bruno did not know how long the barrage lasted. There were separate explosions at first, but these quickly joined into a continuous hammering roar. The ground shook under them, bigger clouds of earth fell from above and the roaring became so loud they had to cover their ears. The sound eased a bit when an explosion sealed the entrance tunnel. To Bruno's fear of being killed was added the greater fear of being buried alive. He spoke prayers aloud, but could not hear them. The men looked upward, then at each other, turning quickly away when they caught another's eye. The sound went on and on.

Then, an unmeasurable time later, there was an end to it. The explosions became distinct, one from the other, waned, grew again, and finally ceased altogether. The roof had held and they were alive.

"Let's go," Mau Mau said, his voice sounding dim and muffled to their battered ears. "If we start digging now we should be out by dark, and we have a lot of ground to cover tonight."

The guerrillas took turns with the shovels, carrying the dirt back in buckets to dump at the far end of the chamber.

They all helped with this, except for the prisoner and one guard. The atmosphere was stifling and hot before they holed through to the outside again. They emerged, breathing deeply, savoring the indescribable sweetness of the evening air.

Bruno looked about in the twilight and gasped. The rain had stopped and the fog had thinned a good deal. The clearing was gone, as were the trees, in every direction, as far as he could see. In their place was a sea of churned craters and splintered pieces of wood. Pieces of steel casing were scattered over the ground. He bent and picked up a shining steel ball: there were many of these.

"Antipersonnel bombs," Mau Mau said. "Each bomb has a couple hundred of these balls, and they drop them by the thousands. Cut a person in two they will. Military denied dropping them in Vietnam, they deny using them now. They lied both times."

"Mau Mau—we on de radio!" Chopper called out. He had a small transistor portable held to his ear. "That raid we done on de truck. Dey say de army had three casualties and dat we had thirty-seven killed."

"Turn that damn thing off and get Whitey over here. I want some words with him."

They stood, face-to-face, black and white faces, each mirroring the other's expression of cold hatred.

"Record this, Bruno," Mau Mau said. The camera mechanism whirred as it opened the lens wide in the failing light. "Lieutenant Adkins is now going to tell us what he was doing in Ellenville. Speak up, Lieutenant."

"I have nothing to say."

"Nothing? There was a little boy back at the truck who recognized you. He was hidden in the loft of that country store, and nobody ever looked up there because the ladder had got knocked down. He said that you were in charge of the men that afternoon, that day, that's what he said."

"He's lying!"

"Now why should a little boy lie? He did say that most ofays looked alike to him, white like something dead, but he is never going to forget your face."

The lieutenant turned away contemptuously and said nothing. Mau Mau drew back his fist—then struck him in the side of the head so hard that he was hurled to the ground. He lay there, blood running down his cheek, and cursed.

"See, did you see that, you with the camera, whoever you are? He struck a prisoner, a wounded prisoner. Do you see the kind of creature he is? I'll tell you what happened in Ellenville. There was a girl riding in a car, a sweet girl, a girl I knew, who I even had the privilege of dancing with once. One minute she was alive, and the next minute she was butchered and dead. Maybe killed by this black ape here for all I know!"

"Oh, Whitey, you got a mighty big mouth," Mau Mau said, shaking his head. "Why don't you tell him that this sweet girl was an army nurse and she happened to be in a car with a colonel that had been causing a lot of trouble in these parts. And that that car was taken out by a mortar shell from over a hill and no one knew she was in the car until they heard it on the radio. Now I'm just as sorry about that sweet girl as you are. But how come you didn't tell him about the other sweet girl, the black girl, who had the bad luck to be in a store the next day when a patrol came looking for evidence and shot the man that ran the store, then gang-shagged the girl and killed her too? Go ahead now, tell the press all about that."

"You're a liar!" He spat out the words.

"Me? I'm just telling you what the little boy told me. He says you kind of knocked the old man around before he got killed. He also said that you didn't climb on that little black girl with the others, but you seemed to enjoy yourself just watching. And he said that you were the one that killed her afterwards, put your gun in her mouth and blew her brains out through the back of her head."

Mau Mau bent over the man on the ground, lower and lower, and every muscle in his body drew taut with the intensity of his emotion. When he spoke again he almost spat the words in the other's face.

"So now I am going to give it to you, you white son of a bitch, just the way you gave it to her."

It was ugly, Bruno felt sickened, yet he got it all on tape. The man fought back, hard, in spite of his wounded arm, but they put him down and brought the lanterns so they glared on his face while

Mau Mau stood over him and lowered a rifle an inch above his face. "Got some last words, Whitey? Want to try and make your peace with God?"

"Don't dirty the name of God with your thick filthy lips," the lieutenant shouted, twisting against the hands that held him. "You black Jew Communist nigger come down here from the North and look for trouble—you'll find it, all of you—because before this is over you are going to be dead or shipped back to Africa with the rest of the apes . . ."

The gun muzzle pushed against his mouth cutting off the flow of words. Mau Mau nodded.

"Now that's just what I wanted to hear you say. I wouldn't have wanted to kill an innocent man."

Though Bruno closed his eyes when the shot was fired he kept the camera going.

"That . . . that was horrible," he said, turning away, fighting to control his stomach while his gorge rose bitter in his mouth.

"Everything about war is horrible," Mau Mau said. "Now let's march before they catch us here." He started away, then turned back to the Italian newsman.

"Look, do you think I like doing this? Maybe I do now, but I didn't start out this way. War brutalizes everyone involved until there is no more innocence on either side. But you must remember that this is a revolt—and that people do not revolt and get killed unless there is a reason for them to do it. And, oh man, man, do we have a couple of hundred years of good reasons! So why shouldn't we fight, and kill, for what we know is right? Whitey does it all the time. Remember Vietnam? Whitey thought he was right there so he dropped napalm on schools and hospitals. Whitey taught us just how it is done. So when we run across filth like this"—he kicked at the sprawled leg of the body on the ground—"we know how to deal with it. People like this you can't talk to—except with a gun."

Bruno was shocked, his hand making little chopping motions in the air before he could choke out the words.

"Do you hear yourself? Do you know what you are saying? This is what Mussolini, the fascists said, when they took over Italy. This is what the hysterical Birchites, the Minutemen, say in your own country. You are parroting their words!"

Mau Mau smiled, but there was nothing, nothing at all humorous in the twist of his mouth.

"Am I? I guess that you are right. They always said that we needed education to change, and I guess they were right, too. They taught us. We got the message. We learned."

He turned away and led them off into the darkness.

Dawn of the Endless Night

I wrote the West of Eden *trilogy about our planet Earth where the giant meteorite did not strike 65 million years ago. In these books intelligent dinosaurs develop to share the world with mankind. In history as we know it there were no intelligent dinosaurs. Or were there . . . ?*

Akotolp was deeply asleep, immersed in the dreamless and immobile sleep of the Yilanè. Then the dawn came and she was instantly awake, instantly aware at the same time that something was very wrong. The light was far too bright for dawn, far brighter even than midday, burning through the gaps between the leaves that walled her sleeping chamber. Her nictitating membranes closed as she pushed aside the vines and stepped out beneath the branches of the city tree.

"It is wrong, all wrong," she said to herself, making the twisting tail movement of intensity magnified. For this dawn that was not dawn was in the west. This could not be, but it certainly was. As a scientist she was forced to accept the evidence of her senses, no matter how unbelievable they were.

The light was fading, slowly becoming dimmer, obscured even more by the figure that stood before her. A fargi; Akotolp waved her aside but she did not move. She spoke instead.

"The Eistaa . . . summons of great urgency."

"Yes, of course—now move out of the way."

Akotolp watched until the last glimmer had faded from sight. The stars reappeared, as well as the almost full moon that spread silver light across the city. The fargi led the way, stumbling and shuffling through the shadows towards the open, central area of the ambesed where the Eistaa waited.

"You saw the light," she said when Akotolp stopped before her.

"I did."

"Explanation-expatiation desired."

"Desire to obey—however, insufficiency of knowledge-information."

The Eistaa signed surprise and disillusion. "In a lifetime of acquaintance-friendship I have never heard you admit to any lack of knowledge."

"There is a first time for everything. I am considering this matter slowly and rationally. The cause of this great light is unknown. It is not fire, for I have seen fire."

"What does that term *fire* mean?"

"Explanation time-consuming, unneeded."

"The fargi panic, my scientist knows nothing. It is all very disturbing."

"A strange phenomenon—but it is over."

Akotolp instantly regretted saying this, for no sooner had she spoken than the earth beneath her feet shuddered and a great sound assaulted them. The attendant fargi wailed in fear and clapped their hands over their ear-openings; some even fell to the ground and lay writhing there. The Eistaa was made of sterner stuff and stood stoutly upright, back arched with legs spread wide, toe-claws sunk into the soil to hold her erect. When the noise had sunk to a rumble she signed great disapproval.

"You did say it was over, scientist of great knowledge?"

"Apology for misconception, humble submission."

Akotolp stretched her neck back, exposing her throat in added emphasis. The Eistaa signed acceptance and rejection of death offer.

"Tell me your thoughts for, feeble as they are, this night you are still the only one who might possibly explain what has happened."

"I cannot explain. Only analyze."

"Then proceed."

"An event of geological magnitude—"

"Definition needed unknown term *geological*."

Akotolp fought not to disclose her agitation at the interruption. She concealed her movements of distaste by turning and kicking aside some fallen leaves, then settling back comfortably on her tail. She used the simplified motions of night-talk, clearly visible in the clear moonlight.

"Geological refers to the earth on which we stand. There are beneath this solid ground great forces at work. I have seen, beyond the jungles of Entoban to the east, a range of high mountains that have burst open and give forth melted rock. I saw fire there as well. An event that can tear open solid mountains and melt solid rock is of geological magnitude."

"Was this tonight a geological event?"

Akotolp sat rigid and unmoving, wrapped in thought. It was some time before she stirred and spoke.

"No, I am certain it was not. It was too sudden. All of the events I watched began slowly, grew and proceeded. This came too quickly. And it was very large, though distant."

"Distant? Explanation needed." The Eistaa, while efficient at ruling and ordering her city, neither knew nor cared about the facts of science. Akotolp forced herself to proceed patiently.

"Distant because of the strong light that awakened us. A Yilanè of science in the city of Yebeisk to the south conducted a series of experiments to discover at what speed light passes through the air. She told me that refine the experiments as she might the speed always seemed to be close to instantaneous. But the speed of sound is very slow. This is easily demonstrated. Therefore, since the sound of the event came a good time after we saw the light, the conclusion is that what happened was far distant in the ocean. And very large."

The Eistaa made motions of impatience-confusion. "As always I find your explanations impossible to follow. Now you will clarify-simplify."

"Something very large happened far out in the ocean."

"The light flared. Later there was the sound and the ground moved. Why?"

"The ground must have been moved by the movement of the sea—"

Akotolp gasped, her mouth opening wide with shock. She jumped to her feet and turned to look at the smooth water of the bay.

"It will happen!" She signed urgency and fear so strongly that the Eistaa recoiled.

"What is it? What is happening?"

"What will happen. You must order your fargi to go among the sleepers at once. Awaken every Yilanè. Order them inland as quickly as possible, to the hills beyond the fields where the onetsensast graze. Order it, Eistaa."

"Why?"

"Don't you see? A force so distant that could shake the ground here must be very strong indeed. It will make waves such as we have never seen in the worst storm. Those waves are coming even as we speak."

The Eistaa reached an instant decision. "I will so order—"

It was already too late, far too late.

The water of the bay were draining away, pouring through the harbor entrance into the sea. And distantly, growing instantly louder, was the crashing rumble of water falling on water, churning and roaring. Drowning out all other sounds.

Striking and drowning the shore, filling the bay in an instant. Rising in a flood that engulfed the city tree, broke off the limbs, stripped away the smaller growth, hurtled inland.

Akotolp closed mouth, eyes, nostrils, struck out in panic at the saltwater that engulfed her. Felt the pressure of the water above her.

Swam upwards in the darkness. Was struck a terrible blow in her side that numbed her. Clutched her wounded arm with her other hand, thrust violently with legs and tail.

Burst into foam-filled darkness, gasped in air.

Was struck again in the darkness. Almost unconscious, weakened by pain, she swam on, knowing that this was her only chance of survival. If she sank below the surface again she would never emerge.

An unmeasurable, pain-filled time passed before she felt solidity beneath her feet. Muddy, debris-laden water streamed about her, dropped lower, to her midriff, then to her knees. She staggered and fell heavily, screamed with pain as a greater darkness closed over her.

Akotolp woke slowly to light and agony. A heavy, warm rain was falling. Black rain, streaming filthily across the skin. She blinked with incomprehension, felt the grit in her eyes. Sat up and her vision blurred red with pain. Arms and legs moved, apparently no bones broken. But the immense soreness in her side must surely be more than mere bruising; some ribs might be broken. It hurt to breathe. Alive and injured—but still alive. Only when she was gratefully aware of this did her scientific curiosity return.

She was standing ankle-deep in a plain of mud. Branches, entire uprooted trees were strewn about her. Two dead Yilanè were nearby, broken and unmoving, one of them crushed by the bulk of an armored fish of some kind. Her arms crossed across her ribcage, Akotolp walked slowly and painfully up a rise to the top of a nearby mound, leaned gratefully against the broken trunk of a tree on its summit.

Nothing looked familiar; she was pinned in a nightmare landscape of mud and destruction. Only when she faced inland, blinking through the sheets of rain, did she manage to make out the familiar shapes of the range of hills. They ran down almost to the sea, almost to the outlet of the bay. Using this as a guide, she was horrified to see that the birth beaches were gone, gouged out by the sea and washed away. The far side of the bay was gone as well, the bay and lagoon now joined directly to the ocean.

Then that heap of dark debris must be all that was left of her city tree. She moaned in agony at the sight. If she were weaker she might have died. Yilanè, when deprived of their city did die, she had seen it happen. But she would not. Others might. Not her; she was strong enough to bear the shock. Pushing herself upright, she stumbled toward the remains.

And she was not alone. Others were moving that way as well, fargi who signed respect and gratitude when they identified her. They moved close to draw strength from her presence. One of them, despite the bruises and filth caked to her skin, she recognized.

"You are Inlenu—she who commands the workers at the fish pens."

Inlenu signed gratefulness for attention. "We have happiness-magnified and greet you, Akotolp. Humbly request explanation of happenings."

"Your knowledge is as great as mine. Something disastrous occurred far out in the ocean. With it was a great light, a great sound. This something caused the earth to move, the sea to rise. What you see around you is the result."

"The city, everything is destroyed. What will become of us?"

"We will live. The waters will not have covered all of Entoban. There will be food, in the forests and in the sea."

"But our city—"

"Will be regrown. Until that time we will sleep on the ground under the stars, as countless others have done before us. Do not despair, strong Inlenu, we need your strength."

"As we need yours." She signed respect-admiration, a movement that was echoed by all the fargi watching and listening. They would survive now.

Surely they would—for when they were closer they saw that hidden behind the rubble was the sturdy trunk of the city-tree, some of its thick branches still intact.

And—wonder of wonders!—standing at its base was the solid form of the Eistaa. The fargi hurried forward, bodies and limbs writhing with pleasure and great awe at her presence. They signed gratitude and happiness as well. Pushed close, then moved back when she signed them this order, parted to let Akotolp through to join her.

"You have survived, Eistaa, and therefore the city shall survive as well."

"There has been great damage, many deaths." She signed the fargi away so that they could speak without being heard.

"Two out of three, possibly more, are dead. Others badly injured will die as well." With quieter words and smaller motions she revealed an even more terrible fact.

"The males are gone. Every one. The eggs they carried will never hatch."

Akotolp swayed with agony, fought for control, spoke calmly and wisely. "It is not the end. We are only one city. There are other Yilanè cities inland along the great rivers to the north. One even on the inland sea of Isegnet. When the time comes I will visit them and return with males. Yilanè are as one when facing disaster. The city will be grown again."

The Eistaa moved with pleasure when she heard this and took

Akotolp's upper arms between her opposed thumbs in the gesture of greatest happiness, highest respect. The fargi murmured with pleasure at this happy sight, pain and despair forgotten for the moment. The city would grow again.

They set to work, under the Eistaa's instruction, clearing away the mud-caked debris. The rain never stopped, pouring darkly from a muddy sky. By nightfall much had been done. They discovered that fish that had been washed in from the sea were still alive in the remaining pools of water. These were gathered and shared out. In the end, tired and wounded, they slept.

The flood of water that had destroyed the coastal plain had also destroyed the civilized, formal way of life of the city. The fish vats were gone, along with the enzyme vats that cured and preserved the flesh of the animals. These creatures were gone too for the most part, the thorn barriers between the fields wiped away, the penned animals drowned or fled. Only a single hunter had survived—though all her weapons had drowned. With teeth and claws alone she could not supply the city with meat. Therefore it was the sea they turned to, the sea they had emerged from, renewing ancient swimming skills, seeking out the schools of fish and herding them into the shallows. Then the ocean churned with silver bodies seeking escape and reddened quickly with blood. It was crude but effective; they would survive.

Many days passed before Akotolp approached the Eistaa where she sat in the newly-cleaned ambesed. All had worked hard. The dead had been cast into the sea, the lightly injured had recovered. The badly injured were dead, for all of Akotolp's healing creatures were gone and she could not aid them.

"Everything is gone," she told the Eistaa. "You must remember that all of the creatures bred by our science are mutations and most cannot survive on their own. Our weapons, the hèsotsan, lose mobility with maturity and must be fed. We need more of them—as well as all the other forms of life that enable Yilanè civilization to survive. I have now done all that I can within the limitations forced upon me. I have taken fargi inland and returned with sharp-thorned vines that have been planted to once again form our fields. I have examined every fargi; the badly wounded are all dead. There is a sufficient supply of fish."

She acknowledged the Eistaa's motions of common-place and boring food. "I agree, Eistaa. But it enables us to live. To improve our situation I must take fargi with me to Teskhets, the city on the great river beyond the hills. I know all of the things we need, hèsotsan and string-knives, nefmakel—the list is very long. I will return with breeding stock and our city and our lives will be regrown. I ask only your permission to leave."

The Eistaa moved tail and thumbs in the sign of doubt magnified. "Your presence is needed here."

"Was needed. I guided and explained, you ordered. My work is done—unless I get those things that make science possible. Fargi are training as hunters, the meat supply grows. The fishers grow more proficient. Under your supervision the Yilanè will eat, the city live."

The Eistaa radiated displeasure, looked out at the dark and ceaseless rain. "We live, but barely. More like wild creatures than Yilanè."

"But we live, Eistaa, that is what is important. In order to live once again the rich life of Yilanè you must permit this expedition."

"I will consider it. The meat supply must be greater before you go. You must find a way to bring that about."

Akotolp did what she could, which was very little, knowing that it was only the Eistaa's sense of unease that prevented her making any decision. It was understandable. At least six fargi, uninjured and strong, had simply curled up and died. This of course happened when a Yilanè was forced to leave her city, a terminal punishment only meted out after great provocation. Now it happened spontaneously. That even the Eistaa was disturbed by terrible events of this magnitude was understandable.

Still Akotolp was displeased, even angry. There was really nothing more for her to do. The endless clouds, the almost continuous rain, did nothing to change her mood. A second time the Eistaa refused her request; she was hesitant about a third. It was Velikrei, the hunter, who brought a measure of light into her darkness.

"I seek permission to speak as one to one," the scarred hunter said, moving one of her eyes in the direction of the nearby fargi.

"Granted. We will walk along the shore."

"Respectfully suggest forest instead."

There must be a reason for this, Akotolp realized, and signed agreement. They were silent until they had crossed the hardened mud flats and reached the trees beyond.

Here, out of sight of any watchers, Velikrei stopped and spoke.

"You must tell me what to do. I hunt, that I do well. And I follow orders. I serve the Eistaa. Now order and service clash." She brought her fists together with a loud crack; her body writhed with indecision. Akotolp saw she needed quick reassurance.

"The city needs you, Velikrei, at the present time far more than it needs me. Let me help you, for I respect and admire your skill and your strength. My thoughts–rational powers are at your service now. Tell me what disturbs you."

"One comes from the forest with fargi. She will not enter the city, will not see the Eistaa. Asks if a Yilanè of science is here. She knows your name. Orders me to bring you, not the Eistaa . . ."

The hunter could no longer talk, her mouth gaped wide as she shuddered. Akotolp touched all four thumbs to her arms in reassurance.

"You have done the correct thing. The Eistaa must not be disturbed in her labors. I will talk to this one who comes—then I will tell the Eistaa about the matter. The responsibility is now mine."

"You have decided," Velikrei said, relief draining the tension from her knotted muscles. She was safely back in the chain of command, following orders. "I take you to her."

"Name?"

"Essokel."

"I do indeed know her as she knows me. This is very good—for all of us. Take me to her, quickly."

Akotolp recognized the tall form of the other scientist at once, waiting in the shelter of a large tree. She stepped forward when they approached, made motions of greeting. Velikrei stood hesitantly to one side, signed gratitude when she was dismissed, almost fled from sight. Only when she was gone did Akotolp speak.

"Welcome, Essokel, welcome to what little remains of our city."

"Of many cities," she answered grimly. "I was far inland when this thing happened, returning with fargi to my city. When I saw the destruction along the coast I halted them in the forest, went on alone." There was pain in her eyes now, the wound of memory. "Destroyed, gone, none survived. I came close to dying myself—but I did not. I have willed myself to forget the name of my city, strong-request you do not repeat it."

"You are welcome-magnified here. You are now a part of my city, our city. We were injured, we survive. With your aid we grow anew. You will mend our broken egg. We now have nothing other than the claws and teeth with which we emerged from the ocean."

"Then I can indeed be of service," Essokel said, drawing herself up, pride replacing death in her movements. "Mine was a long expedition to distant cities. My fargi carry everything we needed—that your, *our*, city needs."

"The fargi are here?"

"Close by and out of sight. I wished to talk with you and you alone."

"Not the Eistaa?"

"Not yet. There are matters of science that are for our knowledge alone. Are you strong, Akotolp?"

"I survived. I will survive. I am needed."

"Good. I must talk with you, share my knowledge and you must query it. For I have fear."

"Of what?"

"Of *everything*."

There were such overtones of despair and death when she said this that Akotolp cried aloud and recoiled. Then controlled herself and spoke with all the courage she could summon.

"You are no longer alone, my old friend, no longer surrounded by mindless fargi you cannot speak to. Unburden yourself, share your knowledge and thoughts. Fears shared are halved, for we will each carry part of the load now."

"You are a Yilanè of great intelligence and strength, Akotolp. I will tell you what I have seen and reasoned. Then you will query me, perhaps even prove me wrong. It is as you say, a burden shared. First I need information for I only saw what happened from afar. You were here?"

"Indeed—and it is only by chance I can talk to you now for only one in five survived. It was night—and then it was day. A light that hurt my eyes before slowly fading away. Later there was an immense sound and the ground moved. Later still, as I thought it would happen, the ocean rose and enveloped us."

"You thought it would—why?"

"A chain of logic. An incident of great force occurred, the light of which we saw. The sound came much later—and the shock. A force at sea great enough to cause this would also move the ocean as well."

Essokel signed reinforced agreement. "I did not see or experience what you did—though I surmised as much from physical evidence. Important query: what do you think caused all this?"

"Profess lack of knowledge, lack of theory."

"Then listen to mine. Have you any interest in astronomy?"

Akotolp signed negative. "Biology fills all my time and needs."

"But you have looked at the night sky—seen various phenomena there. You have seen the lines of light that cross the darkness from time to time?"

"Assuredly. Though I have never heard an attempt at explanation."

"I have. Our atmosphere grows thinner as one goes higher; this has been proven by those who carried air pressure devices up mountains. If this is true, then logic dictates that if the pressure drop is continuous then at a certain height there is no more air."

"I know of this theory and am in agreement. That air ceases to be and beyond our atmosphere there is a nothingness."

"But matter exists in this nothingness. We see the moon and the stars. Now hold that thought and in parallel entertain another thought. A bird moves faster than a fish because it moves through a less dense medium. If something moves through a medium of no density it could have a speed beyond comprehension. So much so that if there are particles of matter moving through this emptiness, small particles, through the operation of the laws of dynamics they would exchange motion for temperature. And glow with light."

Akotolp closed her eyes, wrapped in intense thought. Opened them and signed agreement. "I cannot argue with facts revealed, extrapolation of idea. Seek relevance."

Essokel was grimly silent for a long heartbeat of time, then spoke quietly. "I suggest to you the possibility that a larger particle from above might strike our atmosphere. A particle the size of a boulder, a tree—perhaps a mountain. What would happen then?"

"Then," Akotolp said, slowly and carefully, "this mountain of speed would cause the air to glow fiercely. It would strike the ocean. If it were large enough, fast enough, heavy enough, it might even strike down through the water to hit the ground below. This immense shock would be felt through the ground, heard through the air for great distances. The mountains of water pushed aside would inundate the shore, this land. I am in awe of your wisdom and intellect."

"There is more to come. The clouds that have never parted once since that day, the clouds that rain down dirt, that are black with filth undoubtedly thrown up by the impact. How many days have they remained up there?"

"A great number. I have kept count."

"As have I. Now, one last fearful consideration. What if they remain there longer and longer? What if the warmth of the sun never bathes us again? What will happen to us then?"

Akotolp the biologist swayed in pain, almost lost consciousness at the terror of this thought. Recovered to find that Essokel was holding her, that she would have fallen without her friend's support.

"Death will be our lot. Without sunlight the green plants will not grow. When they die the creatures who eat them die. When they die— the Yilanè die. Is this what is to happen?"

"I do not know; I fear for the worst. I have measured carefully. The air temperature is lower each day. We cannot live without heat, without sun."

"The clouds must part!" Akotolp cried aloud. "They must. Or . . ."

She did not finish the thought. There was no need. It was Essokel who finally broke the terrible silence.

"We will go to the city now. And tell the Eistaa . . . ?"

"Nothing. If these things we talk about come to be, then we are helpless, powerless. Instead of bringing them death you will now bring them happiness and pleasure. There will be warmth, shelter, food. If . . . what we discussed . . . comes to pass, it will not need discussion. It will soon be obvious to the stupidest fargi."

Akotolp was correct; Essokel and the burdens her fargi carried brought civilization and great happiness back to the city. Hèsotsan for hunting, the pleasure of sweet warm meat for all. There were many cloaks in the bundles, for the expedition had been through the mountain passes where the air was chill. They were needed now: the nights were growing colder, and these flat brainless cloak-creatures if kept well fed had high body temperatures. All the city leaders had cloaks and slept well. The fargi did not and could only huddle together at night, draw warmth from one another and shudder in silence.

But the pleasure could not last. Even the stupidest fargi, fresh from the sea and unable to talk, could see that the nights were growing colder, days as well. The fish were no longer as plentiful as they had been. The clouds did not part, the sun did not shine, the plants were dying. The animals they ate were leaner and tougher as the grazing grew harder. Still they ate very well, for the enzyme vats were kept filled with meat. Which was a very bad sign indeed, for they were not being killed—they were dying. This was the time when the Eistaa summoned the two scientists to join her in the ambesed where she waited with Velikrei.

"Listen to what this hunter tells me," the Eistaa said, darkness in her speech.

"The onetsensast that they butcher now, that goes into the meat vats. It is the last one. All others—dead, the fields empty."

"What is happening—what is going to happen?" the Eistaa asked. "You are Yilanè of science, you must know."

"We know," Akotolp said, fighting to keep calmness in her words and motions. "We will tell you, Eistaa." The hunter did not see her quick motion of pointing and dismissal.

"You have brought the information, Velikrei. Return to your forest."

Akotolp waited until the three of them were alone before she spoke. Now she made no attempt to keep the dread and despair from her speech.

"It is the sun that brings us life, Eistaa. If the sun does not shine we die. The clouds kill us."

"I see what is happening—yet I do not understand."

"There is a chain of life," Essokel said. "It starts in the cells of the plants, where the sun's rays are turned into food. The fish and the ustuzou eat them and live. We in turn eat their flesh—and we live." She leaned down and pulled a clump of yellowed grass from the ground and held it out. "This dies, they die, we die."

The Eistaa looked at the grass, immobile, her muscles locked hard as the thought echoed again and again in her brain. In the end she turned to Akotolp and signed a short query.

"True?"

"Inescapable truth."

"Can we not fill the vats, store food, wait until the clouds open up and the sun shines again?"

"We can—and we will. Seed will be stored as well, to plant and regrow when the sun returns."

"This will be done. I will order it. When will the sun return?"

The response to this question was only silence. The Eistaa waited, her anger growing, until she could control it no longer.

"Speak, Akotolp! I order you to speak! When will the sun return?"

"I—we—do not know, Eistaa. And unless it returns soon the world as we know it is dead. Species once destroyed do not return. We are one of those species. We are important only to ourselves. In the totality of biology we are as important—or unimportant—as that clump of grass. It is of no help to us to know that even if the clouds remain forever life will go on. But it will not be the world we know. There exist life forms that are very persistent and can endure a great range of temperatures and environments. We cannot. We will not survive on this world unless things remain very much as they always were. I fear, Essokel and I have discussed this many times that we have already passed the time of survival . . ."

"That is not true! Yilanè live."

"Yilanè die," Essokel said with grim movements. "Fargi die already of cold. We have examined them."

"We have cloaks."

"The cloaks will die as well. It is already too cold for them to breed." There was a great feeling of despair in Akotolp's shuddered movements. "I fear that all will be ended, all Yilanè dead, everything we are, everything that we have done, vanished. It will be as if we have never been. When the clouds break, if they ever break, it will be the ustuzou who will live."

"What? These vermin-crawling filthy things underfoot? Your speaking is an insult!"

As though in further insult an ustuzou scuttled through the dead grass close by, paused an instant to glance at them with tiny dark eyes, scratched quick claws through its fur. The Eistaa stamped out with her foot but crushed only dead stems as the creature vanished from sight.

"You say that these vile things will live—why?"

"Because of their nature," Essokel explained patiently. "All complex creatures require regularizing of body temperature, they are all warm-blooded. But there are two ways of staying warm. We Yilanè are exothermic, which means we must live in a warm climate and take in heat from outside. This is very efficient. The ustuzou are very inefficient since they are endothermic, which means they must eat all of the time and turn their food into heat . . ."

"You speak like this only to confuse me—all this talk of hot or cold, inside and out."

"You must excuse my inefficiency-stupidity, Eistaa. I simplify. We will get cold, we will die. That small ustuzou will not get cold. When the air cools it will eat more. It will eat dead plants, dead bodies—it will eat our dead bodies. The corpses of our world will nourish these creatures for a long time. Perhaps until the clouds disperse and the sun returns. If this comes to pass then it will be an ustuzou world and the Yilanè will not even be a memory. It will be as though we never were—"

"A thought I will not have!" the Eistaa roared with anger, tearing at the ground with her claws. "Leave me! Be silent in my presence hereafter. I will not hear these words again."

The scientists left, a cold rain fell, night descended. There was the movement of tiny, furry creatures through the grass and into the dead forest beyond. Tiny creatures that ate seeds, stems, bones, marrow, flesh, grass, insects—anything.

Warm-blooded animals that could survive when ninety percent of all other creatures died.

Survive and evolve for sixty million years. Whose descendants read these words.

An Honest Day's Work

"I do my job, that's all. And that's all that anyone can expect." Jerry's jaw set hard with these words, set as firmly as his voice as he bit deep into the scarred stem of the old pipe.

"I know that, Mr. Cruncher," the Lieutenant said. "No one is asking you to do anything more than that, or to do anything wrong." He was dusty and one of the pocket flaps had been torn off his uniform. There was a wild look in his eye and he had a tendency to talk too fast. "We tracked you down through BuRecCent and it wasn't easy, there were good men lost . . ." His voice started to rise and he drew himself up with an effort. "We would like your cooperation if we could get it."

"Not the sort of thing I like to do. It could lead to trouble."

The trouble was that no one had expected events to happen as they did. Or rather the people who expected it had expected something altogether different. They had made their plans accordingly and fed them to the computer which had drawn up programs covering all possible variations of the original. However the Betelgeuseans had a completely different plan in mind so they therefore succeeded far beyond what was possibly their own wildest dreams. The trade station they had set up in Tycho crater on the moon was just that, a trade station, and had nothing to do at all with the events that followed.

Records of the Disaster are confused, as well they might be under the circumstances, and the number of aliens involved in the first phase of the invasion was certainly only a fraction of the exaggerated figures that were being tossed around by excited newsmen, or worried military personnel who felt that there must be that number of attacking aliens to wreak the damage that was done. The chances are that there were no more than two, three maximum, ships involved; a few hundred Betelgeuseans at the most. A few hundred to subjugate an entire planet—and they came within a hair of succeeding.

"Colonel, this is Mr. Cruncher who has volunteered—"

"A civilian! Will you get him the hell out of here and blindfold him first, you unutterable fool! This headquarters is double-red-zed top security . . . !"

"Sir, the security doesn't matter anymore. All of our communications are shut down, we're sealed off from the troops."

"Quiet, you fool!" The Colonel raised his clenched fists, his skin flushing, a wild light in his eyes. He still did not want to believe what had happened, possibly could not believe. The lieutenant was younger, a reserve officer; as much as he disliked it he could face the facts.

"Colonel, you must believe me. The situation is desperate, and desperate times call for desperate solutions . . ."

"Sergeant! Take this lieutenant and this civilian to the target range and shoot them for violating security during an emergency."

"Colonel, please—"

"Sergeant, that is an order!"

The Sergeant who was only four months short of retirement and had a potbelly to prove it, looked from one officer to the other. He was reluctant to make a decision but he had to. He finally rose and went to the toilet, locking the door behind him. The Colonel, who had been following his movements in eye-bulging silence, gasped, his face a bright scarlet, and groped for his sidearm. Even as he drew it from the holster he gurgled and fell face-first upon the desk, then slid slowly to the floor.

"Medic!" the Lieutenant shouted and ran and opened the Colonel's collar. The medic took one look and shook his head gloomily. "The big one. He's had it. Always had a dicey ticker."

The Sergeant came out of the toilet and helped the Lieutenant to pull a gas cape over the corpse. Jerry Cruncher stood to one side and looked on in silence, sucking on his pipe.

"Please, Mr. Cruncher," the Lieutenant said pleadingly, "you must help us. You're our last hope now."

Now when we look back at Black Sunday when the Disaster began, we can marvel at the simplicity of the Betelgeusean plan and understand why it came within a hair's breadth of succeeding. Our armies and space-borne tanks were poised and waiting, all instruments and attention firmly fixed on the massive bulk of the "so-called" trade station which was, indeed, just a trade station. On Earth a complex spiderweb of communication networks linked together the host of defenders, a multilevel net of radio and laser links, buried coaxial cables and land lines, microwave and heliograph connections.

It was foolproof and unjammable and perfect in every way except for the fact that all global communications were channeled through the two substations and ComCent in Global City. These three stations, wonderfully efficient, handled all the communications with the armed forces on Earth, below the ground, on the moon and in space.

They were knocked out. Betelgeusean commando squads in field armor dropped one null-G onto each center and the battle could not have lasted more than half an hour. When it was over the three communications centers had been taken and the war was lost before it began. Headquarters were cut off from units, individual units from each other tanks from tank commanders, spaceships from their bases. Radar central on the far side of the moon very quickly discovered the blips of the invasion fleet swooping in from beyond Saturn. But there was no way they could tell anyone about it.

"I have to ask my supervisor about it," Jerry Cruncher said, nodding solemnly at the thought. "This being my day off and all. And taking of unauthorized people into the tunnels. Can't say he's going to like it much."

"Mr. Cruncher," the Lieutenant said through tight-clamped teeth. "In case you have not heard, there is a war on. You have just seen a man die because of this war. You cannot call your supervisor because the military override has rendered the civilian visiphone network inoperable."

"Can't say I like that."

"None of us do. That is why we need your help. The enemy aliens have taken our communication centers and they must be recaptured. We have contacted the nearest combat unit by messenger and they are attempting to retake the centers, but they are virtually impregnable."

"They are? How did those Beetlejuicians get in then?"

"Well, yes, it is Sunday, you know, minimum personnel, at 0800 hours the church coaches were leaving, the gates were open . . ."

"Caught you with your pants down, hey?" A wet suck on his pipe told the world what Jerry Cruncher felt about that kind of efficiency. "So your lot is out and you want back in. So why bother a working-man at home on a Sunday?"

"Because, Mr. Cruncher, war does not recognize days of the week. And you are the oldest employee of CitSubMaint and probably the only man who can answer this question. Our communication centers have their own standby power sources, but they normally use city power. And the land lines and cables go out underground. Now, think carefully before you answer. Can we get into these centers from underground? Particularly into ComCent?"

"Where is it?" He tamped down the glowing tobacco with a callused thumb, then sucked in the gray smoke happily.

"At the junction of 18th Way and Wiggan Road."

"So that's why there are so many cables in 104-BpL."

"Can we get into it?"

In the hushed silence that followed the burble of Jerry Cruncher's pipe could be clearly heard. The Lieutenant stood, fists clenched tightly, and beside him the Sergeant and the Corpsman, as well as the operators who had left their silent communication equipment. All of them waited and listened in strained silence as Jerry Cruncher narrowed his eyes in thought, took the pipe from his mouth and exhaled a cloud of pungent smoke, then turned to face them.

"Yep," he said.

They weren't the best troops—but they were troops. Technicians and operators, MPs and cooks, clerks, and motor pool mechanics. But they were armed with the best weapons the armories could provide— and armored as well with a sense of purpose. If they stood a little straighter, or held their guns a little more firmly, it was because they knew that the future of the world was in their hands. They marched with grim precision to the road junction where they had been instructed to wait. They had been there no more than a few minutes when Jerry Cruncher showed up. He wore waterproofs and a hardhat, heavy gumboots that came to his waist, while a worn and ancient toolbox was slung by a strap over one shoulder. His pipe was out, but still clamped in his jaw, as he moved his shrewd eyes over the waiting troops.

"Not dressed right," he said.

"Everyone is in combat uniform," the Lieutenant answered.

"Not right for the tunnels. Gets mighty damp—"

"Mr. Cruncher, these are volunteer soldiers. They may die for their world so they do not mind getting wet for it. May we go now?"

Shaking his head in solemn disapproval, Jerry Cruncher led the way to a manhole in the road, into the socket of which he inserted a shining tool with which, in a practiced movement, he flipped the heavy manhole lid aside.

"Follow me then, single-file. Last two men in slide that lid back on and watch out for your fingers. Here we go."

Automatic lights sprang on as they climbed down the ladder to the cool, green tunnel below. Wires, cables and pipes lined the walls and ceiling in a maze that only a Jerry Cruncher could make head or tail of. He slapped them affectionately as they passed.

"Water main, steam main, 50,000 volt line, 220 local feeder, telephone, teletype, co-ax, ice water, pneumo-delivery, food dispenser supply, oxygen, sewer feeder." He chuckled happily. "Yep, we've got a little bit of everything down here."

"Medic!" a voice called from the rear of the file and the Corpsman hurried away.

"They've found us!" a Permanent KP wailed and there was a rattle of weapons readied.

"Put those away!" the Lieutenant shouted. "Before you kill each other. Get me a report, Sergeant, snap to it."

They waited, weapons clenched and eyes rolling with anxiety, until the Sergeant returned. Jerry Cruncher hummed to himself tonelessly as he tapped various valves with a small ballpeen hammer, then carefully tightened the gasket retainer on one.

"Nothing much," the Sergeant said. "Burne-Smith got a finger mashed putting the lid back on."

"They never listen," Jerry Cruncher coughed disapprovingly.

"Move it out," the Lieutenant ordered.

"One thing we haven't mentioned," Jerry Cruncher said, unmoving as a block of stone. "You guaranteed that my supervisor would see that I received my pay for this job."

"Yes, of course, can we talk about it as we go?"

"We go when this is settled. I forgot that this being Sunday I'll be getting double time and triple after four hours."

"Fine, agreed. Let's go."

"In writing."

"Yes, writing, of course." The Lieutenant's scriber flew over a message pad and he ripped off the sheet. "There, I've signed it as well, with my serial number. The army will stand behind this."

"Had better," Jerry Cruncher said, carefully folding the slip and placing it securely in his wallet before they moved out again.

It was a nightmare journey for all except the gray, solid man who led them like a Judas goat through this underground inferno. The main tunnels were easy enough to pass through, through pendant valve wheels and transverse pipes lay constantly in wait for the unwary. Had they not been wearing helmets, half of the little force would have been stunned before they had gone a mile. As it was there was many a clank and muffled cry from the rear.

Then came the inspection hatch and the first crawltube leading to a vertical pit sixty feet deep, down which they had to make their way on a water-slippery ladder. At its foot an even damper tunnel, this one faced with blocks of hand-hewn stone, led them through the darkness—no lights here, they had to use their torches—to an immense cavern filled with roaring sound.

"Storm sewer," Jerry Cruncher said, pointing to the rushing river that swirled by just below their feet, "I've seen it bone dry in the season. Been rain in the suburbs lately, and here it is now. Stay on the walkway, this is the shortest way to go, and don't slip. Once in that water you're a goner. Might find your body fifty miles out in the ocean if the fishes don't get it first."

With this cheering encouragement the men slithered and crawled the awful length of that great tunnel, almost gasping with relief when they were back in the safety of a communications tube again. Shortly after this Jerry Cruncher halted and pointed up at a ladder that rose into the darkness above.

"Ninety-eight BaG dropwell. This is the one you want, to that second center you talked about."

"You're sure?"

Jerry Cruncher eyed the Lieutenant with something very much like disgust and he groped his pipe from his pocket.

"Being you're ignorant, mister, I take no offense. When Jerry says a tunnel is a tunnel, that's the tunnel he says."

"No offense meant!"

"None taken," he muttered around the pipe stem. "This is the one. You can see all the wires and communication cables going up there as well. Can't be anything else."

"What's at the top?"

"Door with a handle and a sign saying 'No Admission Under Par. 897A of the Military Code.' "

"Is the door locked?"

"Nope. Forbidden under paragraph 45-C of the Tunnel Authority Code. Need access, we do."

"Then this is it. Sergeant, take eighteen men and get up that ladder. Synchronize your watch with mine. In two hours we go in. Just get through that door and start shooting—watch out for the equipment through—and keep shooting until every one of those slimy, dirty Betelgeuseans is dead. Do you understand?"

The Sergeant nodded with grim determination and drew himself up and saluted. "We'll do our duty, sir."

"All right, the rest of you, move out."

They had walked for no more than ten minutes down a lateral tunnel lined with frosted pipes before Jerry Cruncher stopped and sat down.

"What's wrong?" the Lieutenant asked.

"Tea break," he said, putting his still-warm pipe into his side pocket and opening his lunch box.

"You can't—I mean, listen, the enemy, the schedule . . ."

"I always have tea at this time." He poured a great mugful of the potent brew and sniffed it appreciatively. "Tea break allowed for in the schedule."

Most of the men brought out rations and sipped from their canteens while the Lieutenant paced back and forth slapping his fist into his hand. Jerry Cruncher sipped his tea placidly and chewed on a large chocolate biscuit.

A shrill scream sliced through the silence and echoed from the pipes. Something black and awful launched itself from a crevice in the wall and was attached to Trooper Barnes' throat. The soldiers were paralyzed. Not so Jerry Cruncher. There was a whistle and a thud as he instantly lashed out with his spanner and the vicious assailant rolled, dead, onto the tunnel floor before their bulging eyes.

"It's . . . it's . . . hideous!" a soldier gasped. "What is it?"

"Mutant hamster," Jerry Cruncher said as he picked up the monster of teeth and claws and stuffed it into his lunch box. "Descendants of house pets that escaped centuries ago, mutated here in the darkness until they turned into this. I've seen bigger ones. Boffins at the university give me three credits for every one I bring them. Not bad if I say so myself, and tax-free too, which I hope you won't be repeating." He was almost jovial now at this fiscally remunerative encounter. As soon as the trooper had been sewn up, they pressed on.

A second squad was left at the next communication substation and they hurried on towards ComCent itself.

"Ten minutes to go," Lieutenant gasped, jogging heavily under the weight of all his equipment.

"Not to worry, just two tunnels more."

It was three minutes to deadline when they reached the wide opening in the ceiling above them, sprouting cables from its mouth like an electronic hydra's head.

"Big door at the top," Jerry Cruncher said, shining his torch up the shaft. "Has a dual-interlock compound wheel exchange lever. As you turn the wheel counterclockwise the lever in position ready must be . . ."

"Come up with us, please," the Lieutenant begged, peering at his watch and chewing his lip nervously. "We'll never get in in time and they'll be warned by the attacks on the other stations."

"Not my job, you know, getting shot at. I let them as has been paid for it do it."

"Please, I beg of you, as a patriotic citizen." Jerry Cruncher's face was as of carved stone as he bit down heavily on the stem of his pipe. "You owe it to yourself, your family, your conscience, your country. And I can guarantee a one-hundred-credit bonus for opening it."

"Done."

They climbed against time and when they reached the platform at the top, the second hand on the Lieutenant's watch was just coming up on the 12.

"Open it!" The wheel spun and gears engaged, the great lever went down and the massive portal swung open.

"For Mother Earth!" the Lieutenant shouted and led the charge. When they had all gone inside and the tunnel was silent again Jerry Cruncher lit his pipe and then, more out of curiosity than anything else, strolled in after them. It was a vista of endless steel corridors lined with banks of instruments, whirring and humming under electronic control.

He stopped to tamp down his pipe just as a door opened and a short hairy creature, no taller than his waist, shaped like a bowling pin and possessing a number of arms, scuttled out and raced towards a large red switch mounted on the opposite wall. Five of its arms were reaching for the switch, spatulate fingers almost touching it, when the spanner whistled once again and sank deep into the creature's head, flooring it instantly. Jerry Cruncher had just retrieved the spanner when the white-faced Lieutenant raced through the same door.

"Praise heaven," he gasped, "you've stopped him in time!"

"Didn't like his looks at all, though I didn't mean to bash his brains in."

"That is their leader, the only survivor, and he was going for the destruct switch that would have blown us all a mile high. He's our prisoner now and he'll talk, believe me. You didn't kill him. The Betelgeuseans have their brains in their midriffs, their stomachs are in their heads. He's just unconscious."

"Like a boot in the guts. Glad of that, didn't mean to kill him."

"Where you been?" Agatha called from the kitchen when she heard Jerry's heavy tread in the hall.

"Special job," he wheezed, pulling off his high boots. "Going to be some extra lolly in the pay packet this week."

"We'll need it to fix the viddy. It's been out of order all day, though it just came back on. Something wrong with it I'm sure. Had phone trouble too, would you believe, all in the same day. Tried to call Mum but our line went dead. Was it a hard job?"

"Not specially," Jerry grunted, digging out his pipe. "Government work—bit of a bonus in it too I imagine. Showed a bunch of chaps through the tunnels. Not a clue they had. One mashed his hand in a lid and the other just sat there while a hampmutey went for his throat."

"Oooh, don't say that, I'll have no appetite at all. Tea's ready."

"Now that is the sort of thing I like to hear."

He smiled for the first time since he had got out of bed that morning and went in to have his tea.

If

"We are there, we are correct. The computations were perfect. That is the place below."

"You are a worm," 17 said to her companion, 35, who resembled her every way other than in number. "That is that place. But nine years too early. Look at the meter."

"I am a worm. I shall free you of the burden of my useless presence." 35 removed her knife from the scabbard and tested the edge, which proved to be exceedingly sharp. She placed it against the white wattled width of her neck and prepared to cut her throat.

"Not now," 17 hissed. "We are shorthanded already and your corpse would be valueless to this expedition. Get us to the correct time at once. Our power is limited, you may remember."

"It shall be done as you command," 35 said as she slithered to the bank of controls. 44 ignored the talk, keeping her multicell eyes focused on the power control bank, constantly making adjustments with her spatulate fingers in response to the manifold dials.

"That is it," 17 announced, rasping her hands together with pleasure. "The correct time, the correct place. We must descend and make our destiny. Give-praise to the Saur of All, who rules the destinies of all."

"Praise Saur," her two companions muttered, all of their attention on the controls.

Straight down from the blue sky the globular vehicle fell. It was round and featureless, save for the large rectangular port, on the bottom now, and made of some sort of green metal, perhaps anodized aluminum, though it looked harder. It had no visible means of flight or support, yet it fell at a steady and controlled rate. Slower and slower it moved until it dropped from sight behind the ridge at the northern end of Johnson's Lake, just at the edge of the tall pine grove. There were fields nearby, with cows, who did not appear at all disturbed by the visitor. No human being was in sight to view the landing. A path cut in from the lake here, a scuffed dirt trail that went to the highway.

An oriole sat on a bush and warbled sweetly; a small rabbit hopped from the field to nibble a stem of grass. This bucolic and peaceful scene was interrupted by the scuff of feet down the trail and a high-pitched and singularly monotonous whistling. The bird flew away, a touch of soundless color, while the rabbit disappeared into the hedge. A boy came over the rise from the direction of the lake shore. He wore ordinary boy clothes and carried a schoolbag in one hand, a small and homemade cage of wire screen in the other. In the cage was a small lizard, which clung to the screen, its eyes rolling in what presumably was fear. The boy, whistling shrilly, trudged along the path and into the shade of the pine grove.

"Boy," a high-pitched and tremulous voice called out. "Can you hear me, boy?"

"I certainly can," the boy said, stopping and looking around for the unseen speaker. "Where are you?"

"I am by your side, but I am invisible. I am your fairy god-mother . . ."

The boy made a rude sound by sticking out his tongue and blowing across it while it vibrated. "I don't believe in invisibility or fairy god-mothers. Come out of those woods, whoever you are."

"All boys believe in fairy godmothers," the voice said, but a worried tone edged the words now. "I know all kinds of secrets. I know your name is Don and—"

"Everyone knows my name is Don and no one believes anymore in fairies. Boys now believe in rockets, submarines, and atomic energy."

"Would you believe space travel?"

"I would."

Slightly relieved the voice came on stronger and deeper. "I did not wish to frighten you, but I am really from Mars and have just landed—"

Don made the rude noise again. "Mars has no atmosphere and no observable forms of life. Now come out of there and stop playing games."

After a long silence the voice said, "Would you consider time travel?"

"I could. Are you going to tell me that you are from the future?"

With relief: "Yes I am."

"Then come out where I can see you."

"There are some things that the human eye should not look upon . . ."

"Horseapples! The human eye is okay for looking at anything you want to name. You come out of there so I can see who you are—or I'm leaving."

"It is not advisable." The voice was exasperated. "I can prove I am a temporal traveler by telling you the answers to tomorrow's mathematics test. Wouldn't that be nice? Number one, 1.76. Number two—"

"I don't like to cheat, and even if I did you can't cheat on the new math. Either you know it or you fail it. I'm—going to count to ten, then go."

"No, you cannot! I must ask you a favor. Release that common lizard you have trapped and I will give you three wishes, I mean, answer three questions."

"Why should I let it go?"

"Is that the first of your questions?"

"No. I want to know what's going on before I do anything. This lizard is special. I never saw another one like it around here."

"You are right. It is an Old World acrodont lizard of the order Rhiptoglossa, commonly called a chameleon."

"It is!" Don was really interested now. He squatted in the path and took a red-covered book from his schoolbag and laid it on the ground. He turned the cage until the lizard was on the bottom and placed it carefully on the book. "Will it really turn color?"

"To an observable amount, yes. Now if you release her—"

"How do you know it's a her? The time-traveler bit again?"

"If you must know, yes. The creature was purchased from a pet store by one Jim Benan, and is one of a pair. They were both released two days ago when Benan, deranged by the voluntary drinking of a liquid-containing quantities of ethyl alcohol, sat on the cage. The other, unfortunately, died of his wounds, and this one alone survives. The release—"

"I think this whole thing is a joke and I'm going home now. Unless you come out of there so I can see who you are."

"I warn you . . ."

"Goodbye." Don picked up the cage. "Hey, she turned sort of brick red!"

"Do not leave. I will come forth."

Don looked on, with a great deal of interest, while the creature walked out from between the trees. It was blue, had large and goggling independently moving eyes, wore a neatly cut brown jumpsuit, and had a pack slung on its back. It was also only about seven inches tall.

"You don't much look like a man from the future," Don said. "In fact you don't look like a man at all. You're too small."

"I might say that you are too big: size is a matter of relevancy. And I am from the future, though I am not a man."

"That's for sure. In fact you look a lot like a lizard." In sudden inspiration, Don looked back and forth at the traveler and at the cage. "In fact you look a good deal like this chameleon here. What's the connection?"

"That is not to be revealed. You will now do as I command or I will injure you gravely." 17 turned and waved toward the woods. "35, this is an order. Appear and destroy that growth over there."

Don looked on with increasing interest as the green basketball of metal drifted into sight from under the trees. A circular disk slipped away on one side and a gleaming nozzle, not unlike the hose nozzle on a toy fire truck, appeared through the opening. It pointed toward a hedge a good thirty feet away. A shrill whining began from the depths of the sphere, rising in pitch until it was almost inaudible. Then, suddenly, a thin line of light spat out towards the shrub, which crackled and instantly burst into flame. Within a second it was a blackened skeleton.

"The device is called a roxidizer, and is deadly," 17 said. "Release the chameleon at once or we will turn it on you."

Don scowled. "All right. Who wants the old lizard anyway." He put the cage on the ground and started to open the cover. Then he stopped and sniffed. Picking up the cage again he started across the grass toward the blackened bush.

"Come back!" 17 screeched. "We will fire if you go another step."

Don ignored the lizardoid, which was now dancing up and down in an agony of frustration, and ran to the bush. He put his hand out and apparently right through the charred stems.

"I thought something was fishy," he said. "All that burning and everything just upwind of me and I couldn't smell a thing." He turned to look at the time traveler, who was slumped in gloomy silence. "It's just a projected image of some kind, isn't it? Some kind of three-dimensional movie." He stopped in sudden thought, then walked over to the still hovering temporal transporter. When he poked at it with his finger he apparently pushed his hand right into it.

"And this thing isn't here either. Are you?"

"There is no need to experiment. I, and our ship, are present only as what might be called temporal echoes. Matter cannot be moved through time, that is an impossibility, but the concept of matter can be temporally projected. I am sure that this is too technical for you . . ."

"You're doing great so far. Carry on."

"Our projections are here in a real sense to us, though we can only be an image or a sound wave to any observers in the time we visit. Immense amounts of energy are required and almost the total resources of our civilization are involved in this time transfer."

"Why? And the truth for a change. No more fairy godmother and that kind of malarkey."

"I regret the necessity to use subterfuge, but the secret is too important to reveal casually without attempting other means of persuasion."

"Now we get to the real story." Don sat down and crossed his legs comfortably. "Give."

"We need your aid, or our very society is threatened. Very recently on our time scale strange disturbances were detected by our instruments. Ours is a simple saurian existence, some million or so years in the future, and our race is dominant. Yours has long since vanished in a manner too horrible to mention to your young ears. Something is threatening our entire race and research quickly uncovered the fact that we are about to be overwhelmed by a probability wave and wiped out, a great wave of negation sweeping toward us from our remote past."

"You wouldn't mind tipping me off to what a probability wave is, would you?"

"I will take an example from your own literature. If your grandfather had died without marrying, you would not have been born and would not now exist."

"But I do."

"The matter is debatable in the greater xan-probility universe, but we shall not discuss that now. Our power is limited. To put the affair simply, we traced our ancestral lines back through all the various mutations and changes until we found the individual protolizard from which our line sprung."

"Let me guess." Don pointed at the cage. "This is the one?"

"She is." 17 spoke in solemn tones, as befitted the moment. "Just as somewhen, somewhere there is a prototarsier from which your race sprung, so is there this temporal mother of ours. She will bear young soon, and they will breed and grow in this pleasant valley. The rocks near the lake have an appreciable amount of radioactivity, which will cause mutations, the centuries will roll by and, one day, our race will reach its heights of glory.

"But not if you don't open that cage."

Don rested his chin on his fist and thought. "You're not putting me on anymore? This is the truth?"

17 drew herself up and waved both arms—or front legs—over her head. "By the Saur of All, I promise," she intoned. "By the stars eternal, the seasons vernal, the clouds, the sky, the matriarchal I—"

"Just cross your heart and hope to die, that will be good enough for me."

The lizardoid moved its eyes in concentric circles and performed this ritual.

"Okay then, I'm as softhearted as the next guy when it comes to wiping out whole races."

Don unbent the piece of wire that sealed the cage and opened the top. The chameleon rolled one eye up at him and looked at the opening with the other. 17 watched in awed silence and the time vehicle bobbed closer.

"Get going," Don said, and shook the lizard out into the grass.

This time the chameleon took the hint and scuttled away among the bushes, vanishing from sight.

"That takes care of the future," Don said. "Or the past from your point of view."

17 and the time machine vanished silently and Don was alone again on the path.

"Well you could of at least said thanks before taking off like that. People have more manners than lizards any day I'll tell you that."

He picked up the now-empty cage and his schoolbag and started for home.

He had not heard the quick rustle in the bushes, nor did he see the prowling tomcat with the limp chameleon in its jaws.

Brave Newer World

Livermore liked the view from the little white balcony outside his office, even though the air at this height, at this time of year, had a chill bite to it. He was standing there now, trying to suppress a shiver, looking out at the new spring green on the hillsides and the trees in the old town. Above and below him the white steps of the levels of New Town stretched away in smooth elegance, a great A in space with the base a half-mile wide, rising up almost to a point on top. Every level fringed with a balcony, every balcony with an unobstructed view. Well designed. Livermore shivered again and felt the loud beat of his heart; old valves cheered on by new drugs. His insides were as carefully propped up and as well designed as the New Town building. Though his outsides left a lot to be desired. Brown spots, wrinkles, and white hair, he looked as weathered as the homes in Old Town. It was damned cold, and the sun went behind a cloud. He thumbed a button and when the glass wall slid aside, went back gratefully to the purified and warmed air of the interior.

"Been waiting long?" he asked the old man who sat scowling in the chair on the far side of his desk.

"You asked, Doctor. I was never one to complain but—"

"Then don't start now. Stand up, open your shirt, let me have those records. Grazer, I remember you. Planted a kidney seed, didn't they? How do you feel?"

"Poorly, that's the only word for it. Off my feed, can't sleep, when I do I wake up with the cold sweats. And the bowels! Let me tell you about the bowels . . . ahhh!"

Livermore slapped the cold pickup of the stethoscope against the bare skin of Grazer's chest. Patients liked Dr. Livermore but hated his stethoscope, swearing that he must keep it specially chilled for them. They were right. There was a thermoelectric cooling plate in the case. It gave them something to think about, Livermore believed. "Hmmrr . . ." he said, frowning, the earpieces in his ears, hearing nothing. He had plugged the stethoscope with wax year earlier. The systolic, diastolic murmurs disturbed his concentration; he heard enough of that from his own chest. Everything was in records in any case, since the analysis machines did a far better job than he could ever do. He flipped through the sheets and graphs.

"Button your shirt, sit down, take two of these right now. Just the thing for this condition."

He shook the large red sugar pills from the jar in his desk drawer and pointed to the plastic cup and water carafe. Grazer reached for them eagerly: this was real medicine. Livermore found the most recent X rays and snapped them into the viewer. Lovely. The new kidney was growing, as sweetly formed as a little bean. Tiny now beside its elderly brother, but in a year's time they would be identical. Science conquereth all, or at least almost all; he slammed the file on the table. It had been a difficult morning, and even his afternoon surgery was not as relaxing as it usually was. The old folks, the AKs, his peer group, they appreciated each other. Very early in his career he had taken his M.D., that was all that they knew, and he sometimes wondered if they connected him at all with the Dr. Rex Livermore in charge of the ectogenetic program. If they had ever heard of the program.

"I'm sure glad for the pills, Doc. I don't like those shots no more. But my bowels—"

"Goddamn and blast your bowels. They're as old as my bowels and in just as good shape. You're just bored, that's your trouble."

Grazer nodded approvingly at the insults—a touch of interest in an otherwise sterile existence. "Bored's the very word, Doc. The hours I spend on the pot—"

"What did you do before you retired?"

"That was a real long time ago."

"Not so long that you can't remember, and if you can't, why then you're just too old to waste food and space on, and we'll hook that old brain out and put it in a bottle with a label saying senile brain on it."

Grazer chuckled; he might have cried if someone younger had talked to him this way. "Said it was a long time ago, didn't say I forgot. Painter. House painter, not the artist kind, worked at it eighty years before the union threw me out and made me retire."

"Pretty good at it?"

"The best. They don't have any kind of painter around anymore."

"I can believe that. I'm getting damn tired of the eggshell off-white super plastic eternal finish on the walls of this office. Think you could repaint it for me?"

"Paint won't stick to that stuff."

"If I find one that will?"

"I'm your man, Doc."

"It'll take time. Sure you won't mind missing all the basket weaving, socials, television?"

Grazer snorted in answer and he almost smiled.

"All right, I'll get in touch with you. Come back in a month in any case so I can look at that kidney. As for the rest, you're in perfect

shape after your geriatric treatments. You're just bored with television and the damned baskets."

"You can say that again. Don't forget about that paint, hear?"

A distant silver bell chimed, and Livermore pointed to the door,
picking up the phone as soon as the old man had gone. Leatha Crabb's
tiny and distraught image looked up at him from the screen.

"Oh, Dr. Livermore, another bottle failure."

"I know. I was in the lab this morning. I'll be down there at 1500
and we can talk about it then." He hung up and looked at his watch.
Twenty minutes until the meeting—he could see another patient or
two. Geriatrics was not his field, and he really had very little interest
in it; but he was interested in the people. He sometimes wondered if
they knew how little they needed him, since they were on constant
monitoring and medical attention. Perhaps they just enjoyed seeing
and talking to him as he did to them. No harm done in any case.

The next patient was a thin white-haired woman who began complaining as she came through the door and did not stop as she put
her crutches aside and sat carefully in the chair. Livermore nodded
and made doodles on the pad before him and admired her flow of
comment, criticism, and invective over a complaint she had covered
so well and so often before. It was just a foot she was talking about,
which might seem a limited area of discussion—toes, tendons, and
that sort of thing. But she had unusual symptoms, hot flushes and
itching in addition to the usual pain, all of which was made even
more interesting by the fact that the foot under discussion had been
amputated over sixty years earlier. Phantom limbs with phantom
symptoms were nothing new—there were even reported cases of completely paralyzed patients with phantom sexual impulses terminating
in phantom orgasms—but the longevity of this case was certainly
worth noting. He relaxed under the wave of detailed complaint, and
when he finally gave her some of the sugar pills and ushered her out,
they both felt a good deal better.

Catherine Ruffin and Sturtevant were already waiting in the board-
room when he came in. Sturtevant, impatient as always, was tapping
green-stained fingers on the marble tabletop, one of his cancer-free
tobacco-substitute cigarettes dangling from his lip. His round and
thick glasses and sharp nose made him resemble an owl, but the thin
line of his mouth was more like that of a turtle's: it was a veritable
bestiary of a face. His ears could be those of a moose, Livermore
thought, then aloud: "Those so-called cigarettes of yours smell like
burning garbage, Sturtevant, do you know that?"

"You have told him that before," Catherine Ruffin said in her slow,
careful English. She had emigrated in her youth from South Africa,
to marry the long-dead Mr. Ruffin, and still had the accents of her

Boer youth. Full-bosomed and round in a very Dutch-housewife manner, she was nevertheless a senior administrator with a mind like a computer.

"Never mind my cigarettes." Sturtevant grubbed the butt out and instantly groped for a fresh one. "Can't you be on time just once for one of these meetings?"

Catherine Ruffin rapped with her knuckles on the table and switched on the recorder.

"Minutes of the meeting of the Genetic Guidance Council, Syracuse New Town, Tuesday, January 14, 2025. Present Ruffin, Sturtevant, Livermore; Ruffin chairman."

"What's this I hear about more bottle failures?" Sturtevant asked.

Livermore dismissed the matter with a wave of his hand. "A few bottle failures are taken for granted. I'll look into these latest and have a full report for our next meeting. Just a mechanical matter and not to bother us here. What does bother me is our genetic priorities. I have a list."

He searched the pockets in his jacket one after another, and Sturtevant frowned his snapping-turtle frown at him.

"You and your lists, Livermore. We've read enough of them. Priorities are a thing of the past. We now have a prepared program that we need only follow."

"Priorities are not outdated, and by saying that you show a sociologist's typical ignorance of the realities of genetics."

"You're insulting!"

"It's the truth. Too bad if it hurts." He found a crumpled piece of paper in an inside pocket and smoothed it out on the table before him. "You're so used to your damn charts and graphs, demographic curves and projections that you think they are really a description of the real world instead of being rough approximations well after the fact. I'm not going to trouble you with figures they're so huge as to be meaningless but I want you to consider the incredible complexity of our genetic pool. Mankind as we know it has been around about a half-million years, mutating, changing, and interbreeding. Every death in all those generations was a selection of some kind, as was every mating. Good and bad traits, pro- and anti-survival mutations, big brains and hemophilia, everything happened and was stirred up and spread through the human race. Now we say we are going to improve that race by gene selection. We have an endless reservoir of traits to draw from, ova from every woman, sperm from every man. We can analyze these for genetic composition and feed the results to the computer to work out favorable combinations, then combine the sperm and ova and grow the fetus ectogenetically. If all goes well, nine months later we decant the infant of our selection and the human race has been improved by that small increment. But what is an improvement, what is a favorable combination? Dark skin is a survival trait in the tropics, but dark skin in the Northern Hemisphere cuts off too much ultraviolet so the body cannot manufacture vitamin D, and rickets follow. Everything is relative."

"We have been over this ground before," Catherine Ruffin said.

"But not often enough. If we don't constantly renew and review our goals, we are going to start down a one-way road. Once genetic traits have been discarded they are gone forever. In a way the team in San Diego New City have an easier job. They have a specific goal. They are out to build new breeds of men, specific types for different environments: the spacemen who can live without physical or mental breakdowns during the decade-long trips to the outer planets; the temperature and low-pressure-resistant types for Mars settlers. They can discard genes ruthlessly and aim for a clear and well-established goal. We simply improve—and what a vague ambition that is! And in making this new race of supermen what will we lose? Will new-man be pink, and if so, what has happened to the Negro—?"

"For God's sake, Livermore, let us not start on that again!" Sturtevant shouted. "We have fixed charts, rules, regulations, laid down for all operations."

"I said you had no real knowledge of genetics and that proves it once again. You can't get it through your head that with each selection the game starts completely over again. As they say in the historical 3Vs, it's a brand-new ball game. The entire world is born anew with every child."

"I think you tend to overdramatize," Catherine Ruffin said stolidly.

"Not in the slightest. Genes are not bricks. We can't build the desired structure to order. We just aim for optimum, then see what we have and try again. No directives can lay down the details of every choice or control every random combination. Every technician is a small god, making real decisions of life and death. And some of these decisions are questionable in the long run."

"Impossible," Sturtevant said, and Catherine Ruffin nodded agreement.

"No, just expensive. We must find a closer examination of every change made and get some predictions of where we are going."

"You are out of order, Dr. Livermore," Catherine Ruffin said. "Your proposal has been made in the past, a budget forecast was estimated, and the entire matter turned down because of cost. This was not our decision you will recall, but came down from genguidecounchief. We accomplish nothing by raking over these well-raked coals another time. There is new business we must consider that I wish to place before this council."

Livermore had the beginnings of a headache, and he fumbled a pill from the carrier in his pocket. The other two were talking, and he paid them no attention at all.

When Leatha Crabb hung up the phone after talking with Dr. Livermore, she felt as though she wanted to cry. She had been working long hours for weeks and not getting enough sleep. Her eyes stung, and she was a little ashamed of this unaccustomed weakness: she was the sort of person who simply did not cry, woman or no. But seventeen bottle failures, seventeen deaths. Seventeen tiny lives snuffed out before they had barely begun to live. It hurt, almost as though they had been real children . . .

"So small you can't hardly see it," Veazy said. The laboratory assistant held one of the disconnected bottles up to the light and gave it a shake to swish the liquid about inside of it. "You sure it's dead?"

"Stop that!" Leatha snapped, then curbed her temper: she had always prided herself on the way she treated those who worked beneath her. "Yes, they are all dead, I've checked that. Decant, freeze, and label them. I'll want to do examinations later."

Veazy nodded and took the bottle away. She wondered what had possessed her, thinking of them as lives, children. She must be tired. They were groups of growing cells with no more personality than the cells grouped in the wart on the back of her hand. She rubbed at it, reminding herself again that she ought to have it taken care of. A handsome, well-formed girl in her early thirties, with her hair the color of honey and tanned skin to match. But her hair was cropped short, close to her head, and she wore not the slightest trace of makeup, while the richness of her figure was lost in the heavy folds of her white laboratory smock. She was too young for it, but a line of worry was already beginning to form between her eyes. When she bent over her microscope, peering at the stained slide, the furrow deepened.

The bottle failures troubled her, deeply, more than she liked to admit. The program had gone so well the past few years that she was beginning to take it for granted, already looking ahead to the genetic possibilities of the second generation. It took a decided effort to forget all this and turn back to the simple mechanical problems of ectogenesis . . . Strong arms wrapped about her from behind; the hands pressed firmly against the roundness of her body below her waist; hard lips kissed the nape of her neck.

"Don't!" she said, surprised, pulling away. She look around. Her husband. Gust dropped his arms at once, stepping back from her.

"You don't have to get angry," he said. "We're married you know, and no one is watching."

"It's not your pawing me I don't like. But I'm working can't you see that?"

Leatha turned to face him, angry at his physical touch despite her words. He stood dumbly before her, a stolid black-haired and dark-complexioned man with slightly protruding lower lip that made him look, now, as though he were pouting.

"You needn't look so put out. It's worktime, not playtime."

"Damn little playtime anymore." He looked quickly around to see if anyone was within earshot. "Not the way it was when we first married. You were pretty affectionate then." He reached out a slow finger and pressed it to her midriff.

"Don't do that." She drew away, raising her hands to cover herself. "It's been absolute hell here today. A defective valve in one of the hormone feed lines, discovered too late. We lost seventeen bottles. In an early stage, luckily."

"So what's the loss? There must be a couple of billion sperm and ova in the freezers. They'll pair some more and put you back in business."

"Think of the work and labor in gene-matching, wasted."

"That's what technicians are paid for. It will give them something to do. Look, can we forget for awhile and take off an evening? Go to Old Town. There's a place there I heard about, Sharm's, real cult cooking and entertainment."

"Can't we talk about it later? This really isn't the time . . ."

"By Christ, it never is. I'll be back here at 1730. See if you can't possibly make your mind up by then."

He pushed angrily out of the door, but the automatic closing mechanism prevented him from slamming it behind him. Something had gone out of life—he wasn't sure just what. He loved Leatha and she loved him—he knew that—but something was missing. They both had their work to do, but it had never caused trouble before. They were used to it, even staying up all night sometimes, working in the same room in quiet companionship. Then coffee, perhaps as dawn was breaking, a drowsy pleasant fatigue, falling into bed, making love. It just wasn't that way anymore and he couldn't think why. At the elevators he entered the nearest and called out, "Fifty." The doors closed, and the car fell smoothly away. They would go out tonight: he was resolved that this evening would be different.

Only after he had emerged from the elevator did he realize that it had stopped at the wrong floor. Fifteen, not fifty; the number analyzer in the elevator computer always seemed to have trouble with those two. Before he could turn, the doors shut behind him, and he noticed the two old men frowning in his direction. He was on one of the eldster floors. Instead of waiting for another car, he turned away from their angry looks and hurried down the hall. There were other old people about, some shuffling along, others riding powered chairs, and he looked straight ahead so he wouldn't catch their eyes. They resented youngsters coming here.

Well, he resented them occupying his brand-new building. That wasn't a nice thought, and he was sorry at once for even thinking a thing like that. This wasn't his building; he was just one of the men on the design team who had stayed on for construction. The eldsters had as much right here as he did—more so, since this was their home. And a pleasant compromise it had been, too. This building, New Town, was designed for the future, but the future was rather slow coming, since you could accelerate almost everything in the world except fetal growth. Nine months from conception to birth, in either bottle or womb. Then the slow years of childhood, the quick years of puberty. It would be wasteful for the city to stay vacant all those years.

That was where the eldsters came in—the leftover debris of an overpopulated world. Geriatrics propped them up and kept them going. They were growing older together, the last survivors of the greedy generations. They were the parents who had fewer children and even fewer grandchildren as the realities of famine, disease, and the general unwholesomeness of life were driven home to them. Not that they had done this voluntarily. Left alone, they would have responded as every other generation of mankind had done: selfishly. If the world is going to be overpopulated, it is going to be overpopulated with my kids. But the breakthrough in geriatric treatment and drugs came along at that moment and provided a far better carrot than had ever been held in front of the human donkey before. The fewer children you had the more treatment you received. The birth rate dived to zero almost overnight. The indifferent overpopulaters had decided to overpopulate with themselves instead of their children. If life was being granted, they preferred to have it granted to them.

The result was that a child of the next generation might have, in addition to his mother and father, a half-dozen surviving relatives who were eldsters. A married couple might have ten or fifteen older relatives, all of them alone in the world, looking to their only younger kin. There could be no question of this aging horde moving in with the present generation who had neither room for them nor money to support them. They were a government burden and would remain so. A decreasing burden that required less money every year as old machinery, despite the wonders of medicine, finally ran down. When the new cities were being designed for the future, scientifically planned generations, the wise decision had been made to move the eldsters into them first. The best of food, care, and medicine could be provided with the minimum effort and expense. Life in the older cities would be happier, relieved of the weight of the solid block of aging citizenry. And since the geriatric drugs didn't seem to work too well past the middle of the second century, a timetable could be established for what was euphemistically called phasing out. Dying was a word no one liked to use. So as the present inhabitants were phased out to the phasing place of their choice, the growing generations would move in. All neat. All tidy. As long as you stayed away from the eldster floors.

Looking straight ahead, Gust went swiftly along the streetlike corridor, ignoring the steam, rooms and bathing rooms, tropical gardens and sandy beaches, that opened off to either side. And the people. The next bank of elevators was a welcome sight, and this time he was very clearly enunciated "Fif-*tee*" as the door closed.

When he reached the end of the unfinished corridor the work shift was just going off duty. The flooring terminated here, and ahead was just the rough gray of raw cement still showing the mold marks where it had been cast in place; the floodlights stood high on wiry legs.

"Been having trouble with the squatter, Mr. Crabb," the shift boss complained. These men had grown up in a world of smoothly operating machines and were hurt when they occasionally proved fallible.

"I'll take a look at it. Anything in the hopper?"

"Half full. Should I empty it out?"

"No, leave it. I'll try a run before I call maintenance."

As the motors on the machines were turned off one by one, an echoing silence fell on the immense and cavernlike area. The men went away, their footsteps loud, calling to each other, until Gust was alone. He climbed the ladder to the top of the hulking squatter and unlocked the computer controls. When he typed a quick condition query the readout revealed nothing wrong. These semi-intelligent machines could analyze most of their own troubles and deliver warnings, but there were still occasional failures beyond their capacity to handle or even recognize. Gust closed the computer and pressed the power button.

There was a far-off rumble and the great bulk of the machine shuddered as it came to life. Most of the indicator lights blinked on red, turning swiftly to green as the motors came up to speed. When the operation-ready light also turned green he squinted at the right-hand television screen, which showed the floor level buried under the squatter. The newly laid flooring ended abruptly where the machine had stopped. He backed it a few feet so the sensors could come into operation, then started it forward again at the crawling pace of working speed. As soon as the edge was reached the laying began again. The machine guided itself and controlled the mix and pouring. About all the operator had to do was turn the entire apparatus on and off. Gust watched the hypnotically smooth flow of new floor appear and could see nothing wrong. It was pleasant here, doing a simple yet important job like this.

A warning buzzer sounded and a light began flashing red on the controls. He blinked and had a quick glimpse of something black on the screen before it moved swiftly out of sight. He stopped the forward motion and put the squatter into reverse again, backing the huge mass a good ten feet before killing all the power and climbing back down. The newly laid plastic flooring was still hot under his feet and he trod gingerly almost up to the forward edge. There was a cavity in the flooring here, like a bowl or a bubble a foot wide. As though the machine had burped while spewing out its flow. Perhaps it had. The technicians would set it right. He made a note to call them in his pocket pad, killed all except the standby lights, then went back to the elevators. Calling out his floor number very carefully.

Dr. Livermore and Leatha were bent over a worktable in the lab, heads lowered as though at a wake. As perhaps they were. Gust came in quietly, listening, not wanting to interrupt.

"There were some of the most promising new strains here," Leatha said. "The Reilly-Stone in particular. I don't know how much computer time was used in the preliminary selection, but the technicians must have put in a hundred hours on this fertilized ovum alone."

"Isn't that a little unusual?" Livermore asked.

"I imagine so, but it was the first application of the Bershock multiple-division cross-trait selection, and you know how those things go."

"I do indeed. It will be easier the next time. Send the records back noting the failures. Get them started on replacements. Hello, Gust, I didn't hear you come in."

"I didn't want to bother you."

"No bother. We are finished in any case. Had some bottle failures today."

"So I heard. Do you know why?"

"If I knew everything, I would be God, wouldn't I?"

Leatha looked at the old man, shocked. "But Doctor, we do know why the embryos were killed. The valve failed on the input—"

"But why did the valve fail? There are reasons beyond reasons in everything."

"We're going to Old Town, Doctor," Gust said, uncomfortable with this kind of abstract conversation and eager to change the subject.

"Don't let me stop you. Don't bring back any infections, hear?"

Livermore turned to leave, but the door opened before he reached it. A man stood there, looking at them without speaking. He entered, and the silence and the severe set of his features struck them silent as well. When the door had closed behind him he called their names in a deep voice, looking at each of them in turn as he spoke.

"Dr. Livermore, Leatha Crabb, Gust Crabb. I am here to see you. My name is Blalock."

It was clear that Livermore did not enjoy being addressed in this manner. "Call my secretary for an appointment. I'm busy now." He started to leave, but Blalock raised his hand, at the same time taking a thin wallet from his pocket.

"I would like to see you now, Doctor. This is my identification."

Livermore could not have left without pushing the man aside. He stopped and blinked at the golden badge.

"FBI. What on earth are you after here?"

"A killer." A stunned silence followed. "I can tell you now, though I would appreciate your not telling anyone else, that one of the technicians working here is an agent from the bureau. He makes regular reports to Washington about conditions on the project."

"Meddling and spying!" Livermore was angry.

"Not at all. The government has a large investment here and believes in protecting this and in guarding the taxpayers' money. You have had a number of bottle failures here in the first weeks after implanting."

"Accidents, just accidents," Leatha said, then flushed and was silent when Blalock turned his cold, unsmiling gaze on her.

"Are they? We don't think so. There are four other New Towns in the United States, all of them with projects working along the same lines as yours. They have had bottle failures as well, but not in the numbers you have here."

"A few more in one place or another means nothing," Livermore said. "The law of averages covers minor differences."

"I'm sure it does. Minor differences, Doctor. But the rate of failure here is ten times higher than that of the other laboratories. For every bottle failure they have, you have ten. For their ten, you have a hundred. I am not here by accident. Since you are in charge of this project, I would like a letter from you giving me permission to go anywhere on the premises and to speak with anyone."

"My secretary will have gone by now. In the morning—"

"I have the letter here, typed on your stationery, just needing your signature."

Livermore's anger was more forced than real. "I won't have this. Stealing my office supplies. I won't have it."

"Don't be rude, Doctor. Your stationery is printed by the Government Printing Office. They supplied it to me to make my job easier. Don't you make it harder."

There was a coldness in his words that stopped Livermore and sent him fumbling with his pen to sign the letter. Gust and Leatha looked on, not knowing what to do. Blalock folded the letter and put it back into his pocket.

"I'll want to talk to you all later," he said, and left. Livermore waited until he was gone, then went out as well, without a word.

"What an awful man," Leatha said.

"It doesn't matter how awful he is if what he said was right. Bottle sabotage—how can that be?"

"Easily enough done."

"But why should it be done?" Gust asked. "That's the real question. It's so meaningless, so wanton. There's simply no reason."

"That's Blalock's worry, what he's getting paid for. Right now I've had a long day, and I'm hungry and more concerned with my dinner. You go ahead to the apartment and defrost something. I won't be a minute finishing up these tests."

He was angry. "The first blush is off our marriage, isn't it?

"You've completely forgotten that I asked you out to dinner in Old Town."

"It's not that . . ." Leatha said, then stopped, because it really was. Gust wasn't completely right; the work was so distracting and then this Blalock person. She tidied up quickly without finishing the tests and took off her smock. Her dress was dark gray and no less severe. It was thin, too, designed for wear in the constant temperature of New Town.

"If it's cold outside, I should get a coat."

"Of course it's cold out. It's still March. I checked out a car earlier and put your heavy coat in it, mine as well."

They went in silence to the elevator and down to the parking level. The bubble-dome car was at the ready ramp, and the top swung up when he turned the handle. They put on their coats before they climbed in, and Gust turned on the heat as he started the car. The electric engine, powered by batteries, hummed strongly as they headed for the exit, the doors opening automatically for them as the car approached. There was a brief wait in the lock while the inner door closed before the outer one opened; then they emerged on the sloping ramp that led up to Old Town.

It had been a long time since their last visit outside the New Town walls, and the difference was striking. The streets were patched and had an unkempt appearance, with dead grass and weeds protruding from the cracks. There were pieces of paper caught against the curbs, and when they passed an empty lot a cloud of dust swirled around them. Leatha sank deeper into her seat and shivered even though the heater was going full on. The buildings had a weathered and even a decayed look about them, the wooden buildings most of all, and the limbs of the gray trees were bare as skeletons in the fading daylight. Gust tried to read the street signs and lost his way once, but finally found a garish spotlit sign that read SHARM'S. Either they were early or business wasn't booming, because they could park right in front of the door. Leatha didn't wait but ran the few feet through the chill wind while Gust locked up the car. Inside, Sharm himself was waiting to greet them.

"Welcome, welcome," he said with bored professional exuberance, a tall, wide Negro, very black, wearing a brilliant kaftan and red fez. "I've got just the table for you, right at the ringside."

"That will be nice," Gust said.

Sharm's hospitality was easily understood; there was only one other couple in the restaurant. There was the heavy smell of cooking in the air, some of it not too fresh, and the tablecloth was a cartography of ancient stains only partially removed.

"Like a drink?" Sharm asked.

"I guess so. Any suggestions?"

"Bet your life. Bloody Mary with tequila, the house special. I'll fetch a jug."

They must have been premixed because he was back a moment later with the tray and two menus tucked under his arm. He poured their drinks and then one for himself and pulled up a chair to join them. The atmosphere of Sharm's was nothing if not relaxed.

"*Salud,*" he said, and they drank. Leatha puckered her lips and put her glass down quickly, but Gust liked the sharp bite of the drink.

"Great. Never tasted one before. How about the menu—any house specials there?"

"All specials. My wife is great at any kind of cult food. Black-eyed peas and corn dodgers, kosher hot dogs and Boston baked beans, we got them all. Just take your pick. Music's starting now, and Aikane will be in to dance in about a half an hour. Drink up, folks, these are on the house."

"Very kind," Gust said, sipping his.

"Not at all. I want to pump your brain, Mr. Crabb, and I pay in advance. I saw you on 3V last week talking about New Town. Pretty fancy if I say so myself. What's the chances of opening a restaurant in your place?" He drained his glass and poured himself another one, topping up their glasses at the same time.

"That's not easy to say."

"What's easy? Living on the dole and maybe blowing your brains out from boredom, that's easy. Me, I got bigger plans. Everyone likes cult food. Eldsters, reminds them of the old days; kids think it's real pit-blasting. But people here in Old Town don't eat out much, not that much loose pesos around. Got to go to where the change is. New Town. What're the odds?"

"I can find out. But you have to realize, Mr. Sharm—"

"Just plain Sharm. A first name."

"You have to realize that the eldsters have special diet—special sanitary regulations on their food."

"This beanery isn't bug-finky. We got plenty of sanitary examinations."

"That's not what I meant, I'm sorry don't misunderstand me. It's special diets really, to go with the medication. Really special if you understand, practically worked out and cooked in the labs."

A loud drumming interrupted him as a sad-looking American Indian did a quick Indian war beat on the bass drum. He switched on the taper with his toe, then worked rhythm on the traps as a recording played an Israeli folk song. It was all very unimpressive but loud.

"What about the younger people then?" Sharm shouted to be heard. "Like you folks. You come this far to eat cult food, why not have it closer to home?"

"There's not enough of us, not yet. Just technicians and construction teams. No more than ten percent of the children who will occupy the city have even been born yet, so I don't know if you even have a big enough group to draw from. Later, perhaps."

"Yeah, later. Big deal. Wait twenty years." Sharm sank down, wrapped in gloom, moving only to empty the jug into his glass. He rose reluctantly when another customer entered, ending the embarrassing interlude.

They both ordered mixed plates of all the specialties and a bottle of wine, since Leatha was not that enthusiastic about the Bloody Marys. While they ate, a slightly dark-skinned girl, of possibly Hawaiian descent, emerged from the rear and did an indifferent hula. Gust looked on with some pleasure, since she wore only a low-slung grass skirt with many tufts missing and was enough overweight to produce a great deal of jiggling that added a certain something to the dance.

"Vulgar," Leatha said, wiping her eyes with her napkin after taking too much horseradish on her gefilte fish.

"I don't think so." He put his hand on her leg under the table, and she pushed it away without changing expression.

"Don't do that in public."

"Or in private either! Damn it, Lea, what's happening to our marriage? We both work, A-OK, that's fine, but what about our life together? What about our raising a newborn?"

"We've talked about this before . . ."

"You've said no before, that's what has happened. Look, Lea honey, I'm not trying to push you back to the Middle Ages with one in the hand, one on the hip, and one in the belly. Women have been relieved at last of all the trouble and danger of childbirth, but by God they are still women. Not men with different builds. A lot of couples don't want kids, fine, and I agree that crèche-raised babies have all the advantages. But other couples are raising babies, and women can even nurse them after the right injections."

"You don't think I'd do that?"

"I'm not asking you to do that, as you so sweetly put it—though it's nowhere near as shocking as your tone of voice indicates. I would just like you to consider raising a child, a son. He would be with us evenings and weekends. It would be fun."

"Not exactly my idea of fun."

The answer that was on his lips was sharp, bitter, and nasty and would have surely started an even worse fight, but before he could speak she grabbed him by the arm.

"Gust, there in the corner at that back table—isn't that the horrible person who was at the lab?"

"Blalock? Yes, it looks like him. Though it's hard to tell in this overromantic light. What difference does it make?"

"Don't you realize that if he is here, he followed us and is watching us? He thinks we may have been responsible for the bottle failures."

"You're imagining too much. Maybe he just likes cult food. He looks the type who might even live on it."

Yet why was he at the restaurant? If he was there to worry them, he succeeded. Leatha pushed her plate away and Gust had little appetite as well. He called for the check and, depressed in spirits, they shrugged into their coats and went out into the cold night, past the silent and accusing eyes of Sharm, who knew he was not going to live the new life in New Town no matter how much he wanted to.

Many years before, Catherine Ruffin had developed a simple plan to enable her to get her work done, a plan that was not part of her work routine. She had discovered, early in her career, that she had an orderly mind and a highly retentive memory that were a great asset in her work. But she had to study facts slowly and deliberately without interruptions, something that was impossible during the routine of a busy office day. Staying after work was not the answer; the phone still rang, and she was often too fatigued to make the most of the opportunity. Nor was it always possible to bring work back to her apartment. Since she had always been an early riser, she found that her colleagues were all slugabeds and would rather do anything than come to work five minutes early. She went to her office now at seven every morning and had the solid core of her work done before anyone else appeared. It was a practical and satisfactory solution to the problem and one that appealed to her. However, she was so used to being alone at these early hours that she looked upon anyone else's presence as an interruption and an annoyance.

She found the note on her desk when she came in; it certainly had not been there when she left the previous evening. It was typed and quite clear:

> Please see me now in bottle lab. Urgent.
> R. Livermore.

She was annoyed at the tone and the interruption and perhaps the idea that someone had actually come to work before her. Been here all night, more likely; the scientific staff tended to do that unless specifically forbidden. Still, it looked urgent, so she had better comply. There would be time for recriminations later if Livermore had overstepped himself. She put her massive purse in the bottom drawer of her desk and went to the elevator.

There was no one in sight on the laboratory floor, nor in the office when she went in. A motion caught her eye, and she turned to look at the door that led into the bottle rooms; it was closed now, yet she had the feeling that it had moved a moment before. Perhaps Livermore had gone through and was waiting for her. As she started forward there was the sharp sound of breaking glass from behind the door, again and again. At the same instant an alarm bell began ringing loudly in the distance. She gasped and stood frozen an instant at the suddenness of it. Someone was in there, breaking the apparatus. The bottles! Running heavily, she threw the door open and rushed inside. Glass littered the floor; fluids still dripped from the shattered bottles. There was no one there. She looked about her, stunned by the destruction and the suddenness, shocked by the abrupt termination of these carefully plotted lives. The almost invisible masses of cells that were to be the next generation were dying, even while she stood there gaping. And there was nothing she could do about it. It was horrifying, and she could not move. Shards of glass were at her feet and in the midst of the glass and the widening pool of liquid was a hammer.

The killer's weapon? She bent down and picked the hammer up and when she stood upright again someone spoke behind her.

"Turn about slowly. Don't do anything you'll regret."

Catherine Ruffin was out of her depth, floundering. Everything was happening too fast, and she could not grasp the reality of it.

"What?" she said. "What?" Turning to look at the stranger in the doorway behind her, who held what appeared to be a revolver.

"Put that hammer down slowly," he said.

"Who are you?" The hammer clattered on the floor.

"I'll ask the same thing of you. I am Blalock, FBI. My identification is here." He held out his badge.

"Catherine Ruffin. I was sent for. Dr. Livermore. What does this mean?"

"Can you prove that?"

"Of course. This note, read it for yourself."

He pinched it between the tips of his fingers and looked at it briefly before dropping it into an envelope and putting it into his pocket. His gun had vanished.

"Anyone could have typed that," he said. "You could have typed it yourself."

"I don't know what you're talking about. It was on my desk when I came to work a short while ago. I read it, came here, heard the sound of glass being broken, entered here and saw this hammer and picked it up. Nothing else."

Blalock looked at her closely for a long instant, then nodded and waved her after him to the outer office. "Perhaps. We will check that out later. For the moment you will sit here quietly while I make some calls."

He had a list of numbers, and the first one he dialed rang a long time before it was answered. Leatha Crabb's sleep-puffed face finally appeared on the screen.

"What do you want?" she asked, her eyes widening when she saw who the caller was.

"Your husband. I wish to talk to him."

"He's—he's asleep." She looked about uneasily, and Blalock did not miss the hesitation in her voice.

"Is he? Then wake him and bring him to the phone."

"Why? Just tell me why?"

"Then I will be there at once. Would that embarrass you, Mrs. Crabb? Will you either wake your husband—or tell me the truth?"

She lowered her eyes and spoke in a small voice.

"He's not here. He hasn't been here all night."

"Do you know where he is?"

"No. And I don't care. We had a difference of opinion, and he stamped out. And that is all I wish to tell you." The screen went dark. Blalock instantly dialed another number. This time there was no answer. He turned to Catherine Ruffin who sat, still dazed by the rapid passage of events.

"I want you to take me to Dr. Livermore's office."

Still not sure what had happened, she did exactly as he asked. The door was unlocked, and Blalock pushed by her and looked in. The pale early sunlight streamed in through the glass walls, and the office was empty. Blalock sniffed at the air, as though searching out a clue, then pointed to the door in the right-hand wall.

"Where does this lead?"

"I'm sure I don't know."

"Stay here."

Catherine Ruffin disliked his tone, but before she could tell him so, he was across the room and standing to one side as he carefully opened the door. Livermore lay asleep on the couch inside, with a thin blanket pulled over him and clutched to his neck by one hand. Blalock went in silently and took him by the wrist, his forefinger inside below the base of the thumb. Livermore opened his eyes at the touch, blinked, and pulled his hand away.

"What the devil are you doing here?"

"Taking your pulse. You don't mind, do you?"

"I certainly do." He sat up and threw the blanket aside. "I'm the doctor here, and I do the pulse taking. I asked you what you meant by breaking in like this?"

"There has been more sabotage in the bottle room. I had alarms rigged. I found this woman there with a hammer."

"Catherine! Why would you do a foolish thing like that?"

"How dare you! You sent a note, I received it, asking me to come there, to trap me. Perhaps you broke those bottles!"

Livermore yawned and rubbed at his eyes, then bent and groped under the couch for his shoes.

"That's what Dick Tracy here thinks." He grunted as he pulled a shoe on. "Finds me sleeping here, doesn't believe that, tries to take my pulse and see if I've been running around with that hammer, faster pulse than a sleeping pulse. Idiot!" He snapped the last word and rose to his feet. "I am in charge of this project, it's my project. Before you accuse me of sabotaging it, you had better find a better reason than baseless suspicion. Find out who typed that fool note, and maybe you will have a lead."

"I fully intend to," Blalock said, and the phone rang.

"For you," Livermore said, and passed it to the FBI man, who listened silently, then issued a sharp command.

"Bring him here."

Before she left, Catherine Ruffin made a sworn statement, and it was recorded on Livermore's office taper. Then Livermore did the same thing. Yes, he had not been in his apartment. He had worked late in his office, and as he did many times, he had slept on the couch in the adjoining room. He had gone to sleep around 0300 hours and had neither seen nor heard anything since that time, not until Blalock had wakened him. Yes, it was possible to get from the bottle room by way of the rear door, and through the business office to this office, but he had not done that. He was just finishing the statement when a stranger, with the same dour expression and conservative cut of clothes as Blalock, brought Gust Crabb in. Blalock dismissed the man and turned the full power of his attention on Gust.

"You were not in your apartment all night. Where were you?"

"Go to hell."

"Your attitude is not appreciated. Your whereabouts are unknown—up to a few minutes ago when you arrived at your office. During the time in question someone broke into the bottle room and sabotaged this project with a hammer. I ask you again. Where were you?"

Gust, who was a simple man in all except his work, now enacted a pantomime of worry, guilt, and unhappiness complete with averted eyes and a fine beading of sweat on his forehead. Livermore felt sorry for him and turned away and harrumphed and found his tie and busied himself knotting it.

"Talk," Blalock said loudly, using all the pressure he could to increase the other's discomfort.

"It's not what you think," Gust said in a hollow voice.

"Give me a complete statement or I'll arrest you now for willful sabotage of a government project."

The silence lengthened uncomfortably. It was Livermore who broke it.

"For God's sake, Gust, tell him. You couldn't have done a thing like this. What is it a girl?" He snorted through his nose at the sudden flushing of Gust's face. "It is. Spill it out, it won't go beyond this room. The government doesn't care about your sex life, and I'm well past the age where these things have much importance."

"No one's business," Gust muttered.

"Crime is the government's business—" Blalock said but was cut off by Livermore.

"But love affairs aren't, so will you shut up? Tell him the truth, Gust, tell him or you'll be in trouble. It was a girl?"

"Yes," Gust said most reluctantly, staring down at the floor.

"Good. You stayed the night with her. A few details would be appreciated, and then you will no longer be a suspect."

Under painful prodding Gust managed to mumble these details. The girl was a secretary with the engineering commission; he had known her a long time. She liked him, but he stayed away from her until last night, a fight with Leatha, he had stamped out, found himself at Georgette's door—you won't tell anyone?—and she took him in, one thing led to another. There it was.

"There it is," Livermore said. "Do your work, Blalock, Gust will be here with me if you want him. Find the girl, get her story, then leave us alone. Investigate the mysterious note, take fingerprints from the hammer, and do whatever you do in this kind of thing. But leave us be. Unless you have some evidence and want to arrest me, get out of my office."

When they were alone, Livermore made some coffee in his anteroom and brought a cup to Gust, who was looking out at the hillside now shaded by clouds and curtained with rain.

"You think I'm a fool," Gust said.

"Not at all. I think there's trouble between you and Leatha and that you're making it worse instead of better."

"But what can I do?!"

Livermore ignored the note of pleading in the man's voice and stirred his coffee to cool it. "You know what to do without bothering me. It's your problem. You're an adult. Solve it. With your wife or family counseling or whatever. Right now I have something slightly more important to think about with this sabotage and the FBI and the rest of it."

Gust sat up straighter and almost smiled. "You're right. My problem isn't that world-shaking and I'll take care of it. Do you realize that you and I and Leatha seem to be the FBI's prime suspects? He must have called the apartment as if he knew I wasn't there. And he followed us to the restaurant last night. Why us?"

"Propinquity, I imagine. We and the technicians are the only ones who go in and out of the bottle rooms at will. And one of the technicians is a plant, he told us that, so they are being watched from their own ranks. Which leaves us."

"I don't understand it at all. Why should anyone want to sabotage the bottles?"

Livermore nodded slowly.

"That's the question that Blalock should be asking. Until he finds out the why of this business he's never going to find who is doing it."

Leatha came silently into his office and said nothing as she closed the door behind her. Gust looked up from the papers on his desk, surprised; she had never been in his office before.

"Why did you do it, why?" she said in a hoarse voice, her face drawn, ugly with the strain of her emotions. He was stunned into silence.

"Don't think I don't know—that Blalock came to see me and told me everything. Where you were last night, about her, so don't try to deny it. He wasn't lying, I could tell."

Gust was tired and not up to playing a role in a bitter exchange. "Why would he tell you these things?" he asked.

"Why? That's fairly obvious. He doesn't care about you or me, just his job. He suspects me, I could tell that, thinks I could sabotage the bottles. He wanted me to lose my temper, and I did, not that it did any good. Now answer me—pig—why did you do it? That's all I want to know, why?"

Gust looked at his fists, clenched on the desk before him. "I wanted to, I suppose."

"You wanted to!" Leatha shrieked the words. "That's the kind of a man you are, you wanted to, so you just went there. I suppose I don't have to bother asking you what happened—my imagination is good enough for that."

"Lea, this isn't the time or place to talk about this."

"Oh, isn't it? It doesn't take any special place for me to tell you what I think of you, you . . . traitor!"

His fixed and silent face only angered her more, beyond words. On the table close by was a cutaway model of New Town, prepared when it was still in the design stage. She seized it in both hands, raised it over her head, and hurled it at him. But it was too light, and it spun end over end in the air, striking him harmlessly on the arm and falling to the floor where it broke, shedding small chunks of plastic.

"You shouldn't have done that," Gust said, bending to retrieve the model. "Here you've broken it and it costs money. I'm responsible for it." The only response was a slam, and he looked up to see that Leatha was gone.

Anger filled her, stronger than anything she had ever experienced before in her life. Her chest hurt and she had trouble breathing. How could he have done this to her? She walked fast, until she had to gasp for breath, through the corridors of New Town. Aimlessly, she thought, until she looked at the entrance to the nearby offices and realized that she had had a goal all the time. CENTENGCOM, the sign read, an unattractive acronym for the Central Engineering Commission. Could she enter here, and if she did, what could she say? A man came out and held the door for her; she couldn't begin to explain why she was standing there, so she went in. There was a floor plan on the facing wall, and she pressed the button labeled SECRETARIAL POOL, then turned in the indicated direction.

It really proved quite easy to do. A number of girls worked in the large room surrounded by the hum of office machines and typers. People were going in and out, and she stood for a minute until a young man carrying a sheaf of papers emerged. He stopped when she spoke to him.

"Could you help me? I'm looking for a . . . Miss Georgette Booker. I understand she works here."

"Georgy, sure. Over there at that desk against the far wall, wearing the white shirt or whatever you call it. Want me to tell her you're here?"

"No, that's fine, thank you very much. I'll talk to her myself."

Leatha waited until he had gone, then looked over the bent heads to the desk against the far wall and gasped. Yes, it had to be that girl, white blouse and dark hair, rich chocolate-colored skin. Leatha pushed on into the office and took a roundabout path through the aisles between the desks that would enable her to pass by the girl, slowing as she came close.

She was pretty, no denying that, she was pretty. A nicely sculptured face, thin-bridged nose, but too heavily made up with the purple lipstick that was in now. And tiny silver stars dusted across one cheek and onto her chest. There was enough of that, and most of it showing, too, in the new peekie-look thin fabric almost completely transparent.

Feeling the eyes on her, Georgette looked up and smiled warmly at Leatha, who turned away and walked past her, faster and faster.

By the middle of the afternoon Dr. Livermore was very tired. He had had little sleep the previous night, and the FBI man's visit had disturbed him. Then he had to put the technicians to work clearing up the mess in the bottle room, and while they could be trusted to do a good job, he nevertheless wanted to check it out for himself when they were done. He would do that and then perhaps take a nap. He pushed the elaborate scrawled codes of the gene charts away from him and rose stiffly. He was beginning to feel his years. Perhaps it was time to consider joining his patients in the warm comfort of the geriatric levels. He smiled at the thought and started for the labs.

There was little formality among his staff, and he never thought to knock on the door of Leatha's private office when he found it closed. His thoughts were on the bottles. He pushed the door open and found her bent over the desk her face in her hands, crying.

"What's wrong?" he called out before he realized that it might have been wiser to leave quietly. He had a sudden insight as to what the trouble might be.

She raised a tear-dampened and reddened face, and he closed the door behind him.

"I'm sorry to walk in like this. I should have knocked."

"No, Dr. Livermore, that's all right." She dabbed at her eyes with a tissue. "I'm sorry you have to see me like this."

"Perfectly normal. I think I understand."

"No, it has nothing to do with bottles."

"I know. It's that girl, isn't it? I had hoped you wouldn't find out."

Leatha was too distraught to ask him how he knew but began sobbing again at this reminder. Livermore wanted to leave but could think of no way to do it gracefully. At the present moment he just could not be interested in this domestic tragedy.

"I saw her," Leatha said. "I went there, God knows why, driven, I suppose. To see just what he preferred to me was so humiliating. A blowsy thing, vulgar, the obvious kind of thing a man might like. And she's colored. How could he have done this . . . ?"

The sobbing began again and Livermore stopped, his hand on the knob. He had wanted to leave before he became involved himself. Now he was involved.

"I remember your talking to me about it once," he said. "Where you come from. Somewhere in the South, isn't it?"

The complete irrelevancy of the question stopped Leatha, even slowed her tears. "Yes, Mississippi. A little fishing town named Biloxi."

"I thought so. And you grew up with a good jolt of racial bias. The worst thing you have against this girl is the fact that she is black."

"I never said that. But there are things . . ."

"No, there are not things, if you mean races or colors or religions or anything like that. I am shocked to hear you, a geneticist, even suggest that race can have any relevancy to your problems. Deeply shocked. Though, unhappily, I'm not surprised."

"I don't care about her. It's him—Gust—what he did to me."

"He did nothing at all. My God, woman, you want equality and equal pay and freedom from childbearing—and you have all these things. So you can't very well complain if you throw a man out of your bed and he goes to someone else."

"What do you mean?" she gasped, shocked.

"I'm sorry. It's not my place to talk like this. I became angry. You're an adult; you'll have to make your own decisions about your marriage."

"No. You can't leave it like that. You said something, and you're going to tell me exactly what you meant."

Livermore was still angry. He dropped into a chair and ordered his thoughts before he spoke again.

"I'm an old-fashioned M.D., so perhaps I had better talk from a doctor's point of view. You're a young woman in good health in the prime of your life. If you came to me for marriage counseling I would tell you that your marriage appears to be in trouble and you are probably the cause—the original cause, that is. Though it has gone far enough now so that you both have a good deal to be responsible for. It appears that in your involvement in your work, your major interests outside your marriage, you have lost your sexuality. You have no time for it. And I am not talking about sex now but all the things that make a woman feminine. The way you dress, apply makeup, carry yourself, think about yourself. Your work has come to occupy the central portion of your life, and your husband has to take second-best. You must realize that some of the freedom women gained deprived the men of certain things. A married man now has no children or a mother for his children. He has no one who is primarily interested in him and his needs. I don't insist that all marriages must exist on a master-and-slave relationship, but there should be a deal more give-and-take in a marriage than yours appears to offer. Just ask yourself—what does your husband get out of this marriage other than sexual frustration? If it's just a sometime companion, he would be far better off with a male roommate, an engineer he could talk shop with."

The silence lengthened, and Livermore finally coughed and cleared his throat and stood.

"If I have interfered unreasonably, I'm sorry."

He went out and saw Blalock stamping determinedly down the hall. After scowling at the man's receding back for a moment he entered the laboratory to check the bottle installations.

The FBI man let himself into Catherine Ruffin's office without knocking. She looked up at him, her face cold, then back at her work.

"I'm busy now, and I don't wish to talk to you."

"I've come to you for some help."

"Me?" Her laugh had no humor in it. "You accused me of breaking those bottles, so how can you ask for aid?"

"You are the only one who can supply the information I need. If you are as innocent as you insist, you should be pleased to help."

It was an argument that appealed to her ordered mind. She had no good reason—other than the fact that she disliked him—for refusing the man. And he was the agent officially sent here to investigate the sabotage.

"What can I do?" she asked.

"Help me to uncover a motive for the crimes."

"I have no suspicions, no information that you don't have."

"Yes, you do. You have access to all the records and to the computer—and you know how to program it. I want you to get all the data you can on the contents of those bottles. I have been looking at the records of losses, and there seems to be a pattern, but not one that is necessarily obvious. The fact that certain bottles were broken, three out of five, or that all the bottles in a certain rank on a certain day had their contents destroyed. There must be a key to this information in the records."

"This will not be a small job."

"I can get you all the authorization you need."

"Then I will do it. I can make the comparisons and checks and program the computer to look for relevant information. But I cannot promise you that there will be the answer you seek. The destruction could be random, and if it is, this will be of no help."

"I have my own reasons for thinking that it is not random. Do this and call me as soon as you have the results."

It took two days of concentrated effort, and Catherine Ruffin was very satisfied with the job that she had done. Not with the results themselves; she could see no clues to any form of organization in any of the figures. But the federal agent might. She put in a call to him, then went through the results again until he arrived.

"I can see nothing indicative," she said, passing over the computer readouts.

"That's for me to decide. Can you explain these to me?"

"This is a list of the destroyed or damaged bottles." She handed him the top sheet. "Code number in the first column, then identification by name."

"What does that mean?"

"Surname of the donors, an easy way to remember and identify certain strains. Here, for instance, Wilson-Smith; sperm Wilson, ovum Smith. The remaining columns are details about the selections, which traits were selected and information of that kind. Instead of the index numbers, I have used the names of the strains for identification in the processing. These are the remaining sheets which are the results of various attempts to extract meaningful relationships. I could find none. The names themselves convey more."

He looked up from the figures. "What do you mean?"

"Nothing at all. A foolish habit of my own. I am by birth a Boer, and I grew up on one of the white reservations in South Africa after the revolution. Until we emigrated here, when I was eleven, I spoke only Afrikaans. So I have an emotional tie to the people—the ethnic group, you would call it—in which I was born. It is a small group, and it is very rare to meet a Boer in this country. So I look at lists of names, an old habit, to see if I recognize any Boers among them. I have met a few people that way in my lifetime, for some talk about the old days behind barbed wire. That is what I meant."

"How does that apply to these lists?"

"There are no Boers among them."

Blalock shrugged and turned his attention back to the paper. Catherine Ruffin, born Katerina Bekink, held the list of names before her and pursed her lips over it.

"No Afrikaners at all. All of them Anglo-Irish names, if anything."

Blalock looked up sharply. "Please repeat that," he said.

She was correct. He went through the list of names twice and found only sternly Anglo-Saxon or Irish surnames. It appeared to make no sense nor did the fact, uncovered by Catherine Ruffin with the name relationship as a clue, that there were no Negroes either.

"It makes no sense, no sense at all," Blalock said, shaking the papers angrily. "What possible reason could there be for this kind of deliberate action?"

"Perhaps you ask the wrong question. Instead of asking why certain names appear to be eliminated, perhaps you should ask why others do not appear on the list. Afrikaners, for instance."

"Are there Afrikaans names on any of the bottle lists?"

"Of course. Italian names, German names, that kind of thing."

"Yes, let us ask that question," Blalock said, bending over the lists again.

It was the right question to ask.

The emergency meeting of the Genetic Guidance Council was called for 2300 hours. As always, Livermore was late. An extra chair had been placed at the foot of the big marble table, and Blalock was sitting there, the computer printouts arranged neatly before him. Catherine Ruffin switched on the recorder and called the meeting to order at once while Sturtevant coughed, then grubbed out his vegetable cigarette and immediately lit another one.

"Those burning compost heaps will kill you yet," Livermore said. Catherine Ruffin interrupted the traditional disagreement before it could get under way.

"This meeting has been called at the request of Mr. Blalock, of the Federal Bureau of Investigation, who is here investigating the bottle failures and apparent sabotage. He is now ready to make a report."

"About time," Livermore said. "Find out yet who is the saboteur?"

"Yes," Blalock said tonelessly. "You are, Dr. Livermore."

"Well, well, big talk from a little man. But you'll have to come up with some evidence before you wring a confession out of me."

"I think I can do that. Since the sabotage began, and even before it was recognized as sabotage, one out of every ten bottles was a failure. This percentage is known as a tithe, which is indicative of a certain attitude or state of mind. It is also ten times the average failure ratio to other laboratories, which is normally about one percent. As further evidence the bottles sabotaged all had Irish or English–surnamed donors."

Livermore sniffed loudly. "Pretty flimsy evidence. And what does it have to do with me?"

"I have here a number of transcripts of meetings of this council where you have gone on record against what you call discrimination in selection. You seem to have set yourself up as a protector of minorities, claiming at different times that Negroes, Jews, Italians, Indians, and other groups have been discriminated against. The records reveal that no bottles bearing names of donors belonging to any of these groups have ever been lost by apparent accident or deliberate sabotage. The connection with you seems obvious, as well as the fact that you are one of the few people with access to the bottles as well as the specific knowledge that would enable you to commit the sabotage."

"Sounds more like circumstantial evidence, not facts, to me. Are you planning to bring these figures out in a public hearing or trial or whatever you call it?"

"I am."

"Then your figures will also show the unconscious and conscious discrimination that is being practiced by the genetic-selection techniques now being used, because it will reveal just how many of these minority groups are not being represented in the selection."

"I know nothing about that."

"Well, I do. With these facts in mind I then admit to all the acts you have accused me of. I did it all."

A shocked silence followed his words. Catherine Ruffin shook her head, trying to understand.

"Why? I don't understand why you did it," she said.

"Still, Catherine? I thought you were more intelligent than that. I did everything within my power to change the errant policies of this board and all the other boards throughout the country. I got exactly nowhere. With natural childbirth almost completely a thing of the past, the future citizens of this country will all come from the gene pool represented by the stored sperm and ova. With the selection techniques existing now, minority after minority will be eliminated, and with their elimination countless genes that we simply cannot lose will be lost forever. Perhaps a world of fair-skinned, blue-eyed, blond, and muscular Anglo-Saxon Protestants is your idea of an ideal society. It is not mine—nor is it very attractive to the tinted-skin people with the funny foreign ways, odd names, and strangely shaped noses. They deserve to survive just as much as we do and to survive right here in their country, which is the United States of America. So don't tell me about Italian and Israeli gene pools in their native lands. The only real Americans here with an original claim to that name are the American Indians, and they are being dropped out of the gene pool as well. A crime is being committed. I was aware of it and could convince no one else of its existence. Until I chose this highly dramatic way of pointing out the situation. During my coming trial these facts will be publicized, and after that the policy will have to be reexamined and changed."

"You foolish old man," Catherine Ruffin said, but the warmth in her voice belied the harshness of her words. "You've ruined yourself. You will be fined, you may go to jail, at the least you will be relieved of your position, forced into retirement. You will never work again."

"Catherine my dear, I did what I had to do. Retirement at my age holds no fears—in fact, I have been considering it and rather looking forward to it. Leave genetics and practice medicine as a hobby with my old fossils. I doubt the courts will be too hard on me. Compulsory retirement, I imagine, no more. Well worth it to get the facts out before the public."

"In that you have failed," Blalock said coldly, putting the papers together and dropping them into his case. "There will be no public trial, simply a dismissal—better for all concerned that way. Since you have admitted guilt, your superiors can make a decision in camera as to what to do."

"That's not fair!" Sturtevant said. "He only did these things to publicize what was happening. You can't take that away from him. It's not fair . . ."

"Fair has nothing to do with it, Mr. Sturtevant. The genetic program will continue unchanged." Blalock seemed almost ready to smile at the thought. Livermore looked at him with distaste.

"You would like that, wouldn't you? Don't rock the boat. Get rid of disloyal employees and at the same time rid this country of dissident minorities."

"You said it, Doctor, I didn't. And since you have admitted guilt, there is nothing you can do about it."

Livermore rose slowly and started from the room, turning before he reached the door.

"Quite the contrary, Blalock, because I shall insist upon a full public hearing. You have accused me of a crime before my associates, and I wish my name cleared, since I am innocent of all charges."

"It won't wash." Blalock was smiling now. "Your statement of guilt is on tape, recorded in the minutes of this meeting."

"I don't think it is. I did one final bit of sabotage earlier today. On that recorder. The tape is blank."

"That will do you no good. There are witnesses to your words."

"Are there? My two associates on the council are two committed human beings, no matter what our differences. If what I have said is true I think they will want the facts to come out. Am I right, Catherine?"

"I never heard you admit guilt, Dr. Livermore."

"Nor I," Sturtevant said. "I shall insist on a full departmental hearing to clear your name."

"See you in court, Blalock," Livermore said, and went out.

"I thought you would be at work. I didn't expect to see you here," Gust said to Leatha, who was sitting looking out of the window of their living room. "I just came back to pack a bag, take my things out."

"Don't do that."

"I'm sorry what happened the other night, I just—"

"We'll talk about that some other time."

There was almost an embarrassed silence then, and he noticed her clothes for the first time. She was wearing a dress he had never seen before, a colorful print, sheer and low-cut. And her hair was different somehow, and her lipstick, more than she usually wore, he thought. She looked very nice, and he wondered if he should tell her that.

"Why don't we go out to that restaurant in Old Town," Leatha said. "I think that might be fun."

"It will be fun, I know it will," he answered suddenly, unreasonably, happier than he had ever been before.

Georgette Booker looked up at the clock and saw that it was almost time to quit. Good. Dave was taking her out again tonight, which meant that he would propose again. He was so sweet. She might even marry him but not now. Life was too relaxed, too much fun, and she enjoyed people. Marriage was always there when you wanted it, but right now she just didn't want it.

She smiled. She was quite happy.

Sharm smiled and ate another piece of the ring-shaped roll.

"Top-pit," he said. "Really good. What is it called?"

"A bagel," his wife said. "You're supposed to eat them with smoked salmon and white cheese. I found it in this old cult food book. I think they're nice."

"I think they're a lot better than nice. We're going to bake a whole lot of them, and I'm going to sell them in New Town because they got bread tastes like wet paper there, and people will love them. They have to love them. Because you and I are going to move to New Town. They are going to love these bagels or something else we are going to sell them because you and I, we are going to live in that new place."

"You tell them, Sharm."

"I'm telling them. Old Sharm is going to get his cut of that good life, too."

"Mine said the same thing, so it must be like that in all the languages. Cook us up a bowl of spaghetti, will you, love? Tonight I want some good old Addis Ababa Ethiopian home cooking."

A Last Request

The year was 1999 and I was just closing this collection. I had forty-nine stories covering a full fifty years of my writing. But I needed one more. Fortuitously, I received a letter from Nature, *that most prestigious of scientific journals that publishes only papers that concern the cutting edge of science research. An exception was being made this once; would I submit a work of fiction from the viewpoint of 3000 AD, looking back at some aspect of science that occurred during the third millennium. I most assuredly would—and did—and here it is. A most fitting story to close this collection with.*

The Road to the Year 3000

It has certainly been an interesting third millennium. High points that spring to mind are the intergalactic wormhole expeditions—all thirteen of them. Most successful; all departed as planned.

Of course none of them have returned yet . . .

Perhaps more satisfying has been the global reduction of greenhouse gases. So successful has this been that, in fact, the global ice-caps are growing and the glaciers expanding. The new industry of growing forests, just to burn them for the CO_2 that they release, is becoming a most profitable one worldwide.

Most interesting, perhaps, was the discovery in 2688 of the remains of Germanium based life-forms that might possibly have visited the planet Pluto. This is still very much of a mystery. Was it hoax or visitation? The jury is still out.

But these, and other physical events of the millennium, are far outweighed by the idea, the theorem, the equation—the concept—that has changed every element of our society, every formula, every scientific discovery that makes mankind what it is today.

At the risk of being pedantic, I draw your attention to the universe. It exists. It functions. Interactions occur at every micro and macro level. Scientists observe, study—and discover. The animals of the

Galápagos Islands had millennia to mutate before Charles Darwin arrived. It was his intelligent observations of them, then his ratiocination that produced *On the Origin of Species*.

Albert Einstein did of course not invent energy, for it existed independent of him and was there for him to study, waiting, some might say, for his application, clarification and classification. He possessed the skill, the intuition, the intelligence to observe and simplify—and declare that $E=MC^2$.

These are two samples out of thousands, hundreds of thousands of discoveries, that clearly demonstrate that it is the application of intelligence to observation that reveals nature's secrets. But, oh, it is such a haphazard occurrence that we must stand in awe at how much has been learned in such an unstructured manner.

Now, as we approach the end of this third millennium, and look forward to the as yet unrevealed wonders of the fourth, we must bow our heads in gratitude to the man, and the woman, who discovered, and formularized for mankind, exactly how the process of discovery works.

We are all familiar with the titanium sculpture of this couple, standing in the station of the lunar shuttle, Mare Serenitatis, where they met. Then, because of a photon storm, the shuttle was one hour late, they talked. Stern was a professor of philosophy, specializing in intuitive logic. Magnusson a physicist, well known for his study of tachyons. They seemed to have little in common, other than an academic background. Nothing could be further from the truth; their respective disciplines embraced each other like the Yang and Yin.

We will never know those first words that they spoke to one another. Would but we could! We must settle for the scribbled equations on the back of an envelope. Equations that poured from the fruitful mating of those two great minds. Before their shuttle trip was over the basic theory was clear, the applications virtually universal. Before the next day was out the equations were clarified, reduced, finalized into the Stern-Magnusson Equation as we know it today.

Even this genius couple stood in awe of what they had create. Magnusson applied the formula to a problem of tachyon spin that he had been worrying at for over a year. It was solved on the spot. Almost as an attempt at humor to alleviate the intense emotion of the occasion, Stern wrote out the equation and filled in the elements for the never-solved relationship between sunspot cycles and the birthweight of male Greenlanders. And gasped. There was the answer—clear and obvious now that the equation had been solved.

The rest is history. With these seven mathematical symbols mankind has regularized the dictionaries of the Anglo-Saxon language. Predicted earthquakes and tsunamis, found hidden oil reserves, abolished city traffic jams—and moved on from the glorious past to the even more glorious future. No scientific discipline has resisted the irresistible logic of this equation. The Stern-Magnusson Equation is the definitive discovery of mankind, that has freed mankind.

Of course we have all learned it in school. But it always bears repeating for we can never tire of it.

The Stern-Magnusson Equation goes like this—